GOLDEN

BOOK ONE OF THE GOLDEN TRILOGY

LOCKED

BOOK TWO OF THE GOLDEN TRILOGY

EDGE

BOOK THREE OF THE GOLDEN TRILOGY

FORGED

A GOLDEN TRILOGY PREQUEL NOVELLA

TEMPERED

A GOLDEN TRILOGY PREQUEL NOVELLA

K.M. ROBINSON

Published by Crescent Sea Publishing.
www.crescentseapublishing.com

Cover designed by Reading Transforms.
 Image copyright © K.M. Robinson Photography.
 Interior graphics by Alexis K. Johnson.

LETTER TO READERS

*The Golden Trilogy started as a book just for myself several years ago...a
way to explore the "real story" behind Goldilocks and the Three Bears.
It took years for some friends to convince me to release it to the world.
I queried for a while, turned down several offers, and decided it wasn't the
right time. Several years later, I found the perfect fit with Snowy Wings
Publishing and in the time since, it's be a wild ride.
Thank you for all of your love and support for Auluria and Dov. They are
my babies and I could not be more grateful for your adoration of them.*

*Goldilocks wasn't naive...
she was sent on a mission
and Dov Baer—and all of us—are her new mission.*

Time to see who is going to survive...

Stay inspired,
K. M. Robinson

GOLDEN

BOOK ONE OF THE GOLDEN TRILOGY

To those who make the right choices despite what has happened to them. You can't control what happens to you, but you do control your response to it. Well done for not turning your circumstances into excuses, but instead, choosing to make the best out of it.

THE CONDENSED VERSION OF MY STORY IS THIS:

The girl with the long golden hair, or Goldilocks, as they would eventually call me, was awakened by one of the three bears. She had no memory of how she got there. She sat on their furniture, ate their food and slept in their home. They found her, talked to her, and ultimately chased her away. That is the story they tell.

But there are things they didn't tell you. The stories never mention that I had been intentionally sent there to find the Baer family's weaknesses and use them to then destroy their group. No one ever said that I would fall for the youngest. Nobody talked about how he would try to save me, even when I couldn't be saved. And they never said my entire world would come crashing down around me as I tried to save him and betray the only family I had left.

I am Auluria, and this is my real story.

Chapter 1

THE FIRST THING I SMELLED WAS SWEET SPICES. A WAVE OF WARMTH washed over me, coaxing me out of my sleep.

Someone was breathing on me.

When I opened my eyes, all I saw was blue. Blue so deep and so intense I had to blink to bring it into focus. Dark fringe fell over the blue color as it sparked and flashed, awakening me fully. Those were eyes. The most brilliant blue eyes I'd ever seen.

Then it hit me…and I panicked.

"Who are you?" I snapped, sitting up so quickly I nearly collided with the boy next to me. No, not a boy; a man.

I clutched at my collar and backed away from the figure next to me. His face fell as I scrambled away. He reached for me, but not in time to save me from falling off the far side of the small bed and landing squarely on the ground. My flailing hand slammed into a small table near the cot and sent its contents crashing to the floor beside me.

"Auluria, stop," Blue Eyes said.

"How do you know my name?" I sputtered.

"You don't remember?" he asked, concerned. He stepped quickly around the bed and stood at the foot of it, unsure if I'd accept his help. He reached out his hand but pulled it back, looking disappointed as I recoiled.

"Are you all right?" he asked gently. He knelt to the floor submissively, trying to soothe my terror.

I looked around. I had made a mess, but I hadn't broken anything. Still, I was confused...I had no idea what was going on.

"Who are you?" I asked again, softer this time.

"I'm Dov." He placed his hand over his heart as he spoke. "You know me."

Breathing heavily, I tried to calm my gasping.

"Why am I here?"

"You came here. You came with me. You don't remember?"

"No." I didn't remember anything about him.

"We only just met yesterday. You've had quite an experience." He spoke softly to me as if trying to calm a child. "It's okay that you don't remember. You will."

He couldn't have been much older than me, maybe a year or two. The man was tall when he was standing, I could tell even from down on the floor. He had long, strong arms. Something about the way he brushed the hair back out of his eyes set me at ease.

I started to stand and he rose with me. He never took his eyes off me.

"And just how did we meet, Dov?"

"Come. Sit down and I'll tell you. Would you like something to drink? Water perhaps?"

I slowly made my way to the table at the far end of the room. I started to sink into one of the mismatched chairs.

"Actually, maybe not that one," Dov said, skirting around me and pulling out another chair. "This one is much more comfortable."

I obliged, though I didn't know why.

"Here," he said, handing me a glass of cool water. "Are you hungry? I can make you something."

Without waiting for me to respond, he walked over and started the stove. He reached for a pan and busied himself making food.

"So, why am I here?" I prompted after a few minutes of watching him cook. Once I was convinced he wasn't going to hurt me, I relaxed back into the seat and watched him work. It calmed my nerves to see him methodically creating breakfast.

"You are here, Auluria, for a great many reasons," he said dramatically, his grin making his eyes sparkle again. "One of which happens to be..."

The door flew open, interrupting him. I jumped as it crashed against the wall. Turning to look at the noise, I sent my hair cascading over the back of the chair and around to my shoulder where it hit me in the face before falling into my lap.

"Well, look who's up," a woman said, scoffing. "Sleeping Beauty."

"I can't believe you brought her back here, Dov. She's nothing but trouble," the man said. He was an older, darker version of Dov. He seemed to be plagued by something heavy. Even his steps were weighted as he moved about the room as if dragged down by some invisible chain.

"Are you hungry?" Dov asked ignoring their comments.

I watched as the woman glanced around the room. Her eyes fell on the bed. Its sheets were tangled from my fall. The man followed her gaze. They both cast Dov looks, raising their eyebrows at him. No one said anything. Suddenly, I was extremely self-conscious.

"Well, well, baby brother. Looks like you have a story to tell." The man howled with laughter. My cheeks burned and I ducked my head.

"Enough, Berwyn," the woman said quietly. She looked aside as he cast her a disparaging glance.

"Auluria doesn't remember us." Dov sounded annoyed.

"Oh, but we remember her," Berwyn said, making it sound like a bad thing.

I couldn't figure out what I had done to these people to make them so vicious toward me. Well, not all of them. But it was clear the man and woman were not pleased to find me there.

"I thought we told you to get rid of her," he said seriously, making my stomach jump into my throat. He slammed his fist against a table, and Dov ducked as though he had been hit.

"I won't and you know why. She won't hurt us; she's more likely to help us than anything else."

"Let her stay, Berwyn. I think it would be nice to have another girl around. And besides, Dov's been alone for so long, it's nice he has someone." I couldn't tell if she was being helpful or mocking.

"It is kind of a pain that he's always a third wheel, I guess," the big man relented.

"See? I knew it would work out," the woman said, her mid-length blonde curls bouncing as she strode toward him.

I opened my mouth to speak, but Dov caught my attention and signaled me to stay quiet with a quick shake of his head.

"Come on," the man finally said, leading the woman away.

I looked back to the stove where Dov was, but he was already at my side setting down a plate.

"That's my brother, Berwyn, and his wife, Eden," he said as a matter of fact.

"They're married?" I said, shocked. "He can't be more than twenty-five."

"Twenty-four, actually."

"How old is she?"

"Eden's twenty-three," he replied. "Do you want more water?"

"Dov, why am I here?" I asked again, trying to get him to focus. I needed answers.

"Do you remember being in the forest yesterday?" he asked me.

I shook my head.

"Well, I don't know why you were in the woods, but that's where I met you. You were running through the forest and you jumped over a small stream.

"I saw you flying through the air and thought, 'What must this crazy girl be doing to be running so quickly through such a dense part of the forest?' When you landed, you took three whole steps before you came face to face with me.

"I'd never seen a more panicked look in all my life. You clutched your skirts in your hand and whipped your head from side to side. I'd never seen such long hair on a girl; when it finally settled, it ran past your waist," he said as if I didn't know how long my hair was.

"And when you looked back to me, you whispered, 'Help.' I could see in your eyes that you were in trouble." He said this with grandeur, illustrating his story with his hands. "So I took you by the waist and spun you into the trees. We ducked behind some large rocks and hid among the vines. You were breathing so loudly I thought you were going to give us away."

I wondered how the story would sound if he dropped his dramatic tone. I assumed he was using it to try to keep me engaged.

"What was I running from?" I interrupted.

"Men. There were men chasing you. You refused to tell me why." He grinned as if it were all a game. I was in no mood for games.

"Once the first group of men chasing you was gone you started off again, barely throwing a 'thank you' over your shoulder. But I couldn't let you go alone, not after what I had seen, so I walked with you."

I hoped he would get to the point, but he had more to describe in detail.

"You only tolerated me for so long until you started throwing things at me. An apple. A tree branch. Some small pebbles. I admit, it hurt my feelings a bit."

He frowned playfully, but his eyes sparked to life from under his dark hair.

"But...persist I did, and I followed you for the better part of an hour, talking at you the whole time. That is, until I was attacked. In my blind disregard for my own safety"—he waved his hand to the side, as if I should be impressed—"I hadn't realized where we had wandered. I was taken completely by surprise when those guys jumped out of the trees and landed on top of me."

He laughed, his eyes lighting up. "But you, for as surprised as you were, ran right at us and tackled Jake to the ground. He hit the dirt so hard that it knocked the wind right out of him. I'm sure he couldn't ever believe a girl would ever consider dating him, much less throwing herself at him like you did."

I felt my eyes grow wide at his teasing words. He was only joking, a play on words, but still, I would never throw myself at a man in that context. It vexed me that he would insinuate that I might.

"Once I took out Marty, we found ourselves in the clear. That didn't stop us from trying to make a fast getaway though. We almost made it, too, but somehow Jake struggled to his feet and he went after you. Just as I subdued Marty and placed him on the ground, I lifted my head and saw Jake barreling toward you.

"I couldn't make it to you in time. The sound it made when he hit you...it was almost as if I could feel it from as far away as I was." He offered me a sad look, his eyes clouding.

"If it's any consolation, I slammed his face into a tree and messed him up pretty bad. You insisted that you were fine, but you could barely stand. I scooped you up and carried you.

"We talked all the way back here. Well, mostly I did." I refrained from rolling my eyes. Of course, he had been the talkative one. "You told me your name and then you asked a few questions before deciding to stay quiet. So as of right now, all I know is that your name is Auluria. You have long hair. You're running from something and you are being chased. And you're looking for a place to belong— though I added that last part on my own."

He counted his points off on his fingers for me as he summarized what had occurred yesterday.

"And what did you tell me about yourself?"

"Well, as you know, my name is Dov. Baer is my last name. You've met my brother and his wife yesterday briefly, and again today. As you can see, my brother doesn't trust you, but don't take offense, he doesn't trust anyone.

"You can't really blame him with all that's going on," he continued. "It's hard to trust anyone these days."

"I suppose."

I looked down to my dress, covered with dirt and mud at the bottom. There were a few small holes that I assumed occurred during my fall. That's when I remembered.

I had been running. I just couldn't remember why.

I remembered meeting him though. As the men gained on me, I leapt over a river, almost directly into Dov's arms. He hid me until the men passed. I never told him of the danger I must have surely been in and he was in for being with me.

"You remember." Dov's voice changed, snapping back to the conversation.

"I remember." I nodded. "Thank you for your help yesterday."

"Anything for a pretty lady." He half bowed to me from his seat next to mine.

"Now, tell me Auluria, why were you running from those men yesterday?" He grew serious again, wanting more information from me.

"They were chasing me," I said simply.

He chuckled. "But why?"

I swallowed hard. "I don't know."

"You don't remember?"

"It picks up from where I ran into you." His eyes narrowed intently, but soft enough to know he was concerned, not angry.

"Where do you belong, Auluria? We have to get you back to where it's safe." He took my hand in his own hands, the gesture so sudden that it shocked me into stillness. I let him hold my hand in his while his eyes searched me for answers.

"I...I don't belong anywhere." That was the truth. I never belonged there. "And do you really think going back is safe, since that's where I was coming from in the first place?"

Little flashes of memory floated through my mind. Not enough to blend together and form a picture, but pieces all the same.

"You will tell me eventually, Auluria," he said withdrawing his hand. He looked genuinely hurt that I wouldn't divulge any new information.

I didn't like that he thought I knew more than I was saying.

"You can stay here until you're ready," he added quietly, almost to himself.

I looked at him and it was as if he read my mind.

"You'll be safe here. They won't find you and Berwyn won't hurt you. I'll make sure of it."

That thought scared me. If this man was telling me I'd be safe from his brother, then what was so bad about his brother that made it potentially unsafe?

"Finished?" he interrupted my thoughts. Lifting my plate, he turned to the sink.

I watched as he washed the dishes, his shoulders rising and falling as he worked. His muscles looked stiff at times, seizing with pain. My gaze lingered on them as he worked. I watched his chest expand and shrink as he breathed.

When he turned, it startled me. Dov only raised an eyebrow and smirked. He nodded his head for me to join him in the makeshift living room, walking away from the kitchen.

Just as we started to sit, I blurted out, "What did you mean? 'Protect me from Berwyn'?"

"Oh. I see you don't remember all of yesterday after your rescue." He added apologetically, "Berwyn is just a lot to handle at times. Sometimes he gets a little too upset. At times, he says or does things without thinking. It's nothing to worry about. He won't hurt you, he's just…loud sometimes."

As if emphasizing his brother's point, at that very moment Berwyn crashed into the room and slammed the door behind him. He glared at us before stomping through the kitchen and marching out the door.

Eden appeared, rolling her eyes. She looked over to her young brother-in-law and gestured around the room.

"Baby, you need to get this taken care of." She turned on her heels and retreated the way she came.

I looked to Dov. "Baby?" I giggled.

"Oh, be quiet," he said, throwing a pillow at me as he stood, careful to avoid my face.

"Let me help you," I responded, rising to follow him, knowing that I owed him for his help the day before.

We started cleaning up the mess around the room. Bottles lay strewn about the floor. Unfolded laundry sat in a pile on a chair. It looked like there had been a celebration that someone forgot to clean up after.

"How's your head feeling?" he asked as we worked.

"It's okay," I said, feeling more secure about being alone with him. "What happened in here anyway?"

"Berwyn and Eden had a fight yesterday. It's best to get out of the house when that happens." He stooped to sweep up pieces of broken glass. "They never hurt each other, but they sure do know how to make it sound good."

"Was it about me?" I asked.

"It started out about you, but most of this is from after."

I helped him straighten the room. His eyes flitted over to me every so often, making sure I wasn't going to pass out from my injury the previous day.

The quiet that stretched between us was almost comforting. I've always liked the silence. It means that you are comfortable enough with a person that you don't feel the need to fill up the space with words. You can just exist together.

Berwyn and Eden didn't make another appearance until that evening. Dov had suggested I take a nap to help regain my strength, so after lunch, I lay on the couch under a light blanket. It really was too warm for a blanket, but I liked the protection it offered me.

I never truly drifted off to sleep. While I felt safe in that house, I knew I didn't really know these people very well and I didn't want to trust them too quickly.

"She's still here," Berwyn grumbled.

"I told you, we're not sending her back out there. She's being hunted and she can't remember by whom or why. We have to protect her."

"Stop it, Berwyn," Eden interrupted before he could say anything. "I don't like it either, but he's right. We're not sending her back out there until we have some answers. Your father started this whole thing to *help* people, so you need to *help* people. And start with *her*." I heard the edge in her voice when she talked about me. Maybe she *hadn't* been sincere about letting me stay.

"Fine," he huffed. "For now."

I kept my eyes closed, feigning sleep, and waited for them to leave. I heard their steps creak across the floorboards as they walked out of the room. A moment later I felt the couch arm dip slightly as someone leaned on it.

"You heard that, didn't you?" his gentle voice asked.

I opened my eyes. "Yeah," I acknowledged.

He took a deep breath and sighed. "At least he's letting you stay."

"For now," I added.

"For now," he said, worry slightly edging into his voice.

That probably wasn't their best choice.

Chapter 2

THE NEXT DAY I WOKE EARLY. DOV HAD GIVEN ME HIS COT AND HAD taken the couch for the evening. I heard him periodically check on me throughout the night. When he discovered I was still breathing, he would lay back down and wait an hour to check again.

"Dov?" I asked the next morning, getting his attention. "I'd like to help. What can I do?"

He gave me a curious look, unsure of what I meant.

"If I'm going to stay here, I need to help. So, give me something to do."

"Umm…" He glanced around the room, pushing his hair out of his eyes. "Well…you can help me cook. We cleaned up yesterday, so that's taken care of."

"I can cook," I assured him.

Walking into the kitchen, he led me where they kept everything. He showed me the food; clearly, they were running low.

"What if I help you get more food?" I suggested.

"You shouldn't go outside." He shook his head. "We still don't know who is looking for you."

"They have to be long gone by now. Really, who's going to find me out here? Come on, let's go."

"I really don't think..." He trailed off as I marched toward the door. "Auluria, please."

I didn't stop. I let the door go behind me. He caught it just before it slammed shut.

Dov stumbled as he pulled on his remaining shoe and hurried to catch up to me.

"You don't even know where you're going."

"So, show me," I said defiantly.

"Are you always this stubborn?" he asked.

"I wouldn't know." I grinned at him.

"Of course, you wouldn't." After a moment he grinned back. "You have an ever-convenient head injury. I bet you pull that card all the time to get your way."

"Yes, whenever I feel like someone won't do as I want, I'm sure to find a way to throw myself to the ground and get beaten up so I can use a head injury as an excuse to manipulate people. As you can see, I'm clearly a genius," I said sarcastically.

We marched through the woods, ducking under tree branches and hopping over fallen logs. The birds sang a path for us as we traveled further and further from the house. A few squirrels came out to greet us, stealing fallen nuts from their grassy beds.

"Where are we going, exactly?" I looked at my guide.

"To the storehouse. It's not much longer," he replied, glancing over at me.

The storehouse was hidden inside a cave. I wouldn't have even noticed it if Dov hadn't pointed it out to me. Inside, the cave dropped into a deep descent, pushing down into the earth.

It was cool and earthy, perfect for holding food. The walls were lit brightly, casting shadows from the crates of edible contents. People gathered around, collecting things to take with them.

"Who are all these people, Dov?"

I had never seen any place like it. Food was a scarcity in our society. There was barely enough for the people and the little they had was cause for great fighting.

The government had taken control of all food many years ago, to assuage a foreign nation. To avoid an attack, the officials took most of the society's food and resources and gave them to the enemy. The theory was to give them what they wanted and they'd leave us alone. Unfortunately, that didn't work. They came back for more. The threat became too great. Young men without high standing were sent to train for the military. Young women were encouraged to breed to get the population numbers up. Many girls disappeared—first those who wouldn't be noticed, then the rest, sent to breeding camps.

"Pick out what you like," Dov interrupted my thoughts, snapping me back to the present as he deftly evaded my question. I let the question of who all the people were rest between us, remaining unanswered. He handed me a basket and started browsing around.

"Where did all this come from?" I asked.

His eyes lit up like he was about to share a great secret, but he merely shrugged and tossed an apple into the basket.

"Here and there," he said. "Do you want some eggs?"

We filled several baskets full of food before he led me back toward the entrance.

"Good morning, Dov." A man about his age nodded to him.

"Good morning, Silas." He nodded back.

"Who's this?" the man asked curiously.

"A new friend." Dov smiled politely, refusing to tell him more.

"All right," he drawled. "But if she shows up again, you're going to have to start answering questions," he said with a chuckle.

"You picked a good one there, Missy," he added, ducking his head to me before moving on.

Missy.

Something flashed in my mind. That word. It was familiar.

A face darted before me and left just as quickly.

He had light hair and grey eyes. His eyes sparked as if he were angry.

"You okay?" Dov pulled me back.

"Yeah." I shook my head to clear it. "I saw a face. That's all."

"Do you know who?"

"No." I knew him though; just not how or who.

As we left the storehouse, we walked in silence. I could see the house in the distance before I spoke again.

"Dov, what was that place really? There's nowhere like that around here. And I've never seen that much food in my life. Tell me what's going on."

He sighed deeply. "Auluria, you don't need to know everything right now."

"But I don't know anything. I just want to understand what is going on," I said, frustrated.

"It's a storehouse. That's all you need to know."

"Is it stolen food? Who took it?"

"It's not stolen. It's reacquired."

"Reacquired?"

He didn't answer.

Eden was in the living room when we returned, arms crossed and ready for a fight.

"What were you thinking?" she scolded. "Taking her there—it could destroy us! No outsiders—remember that, Dov? Only the group is allowed in. We don't know her! We know nothing about her! She could be a spy; she could get us killed! You know what happens when people like us get caught! You know what happened to Griz!

"What is your problem?" her rant continued. "You haven't seen enough death for one lifetime? What are we supposed to do now, huh? Keep her locked up here forever? She can't go out—you knew that! Now we can't let her leave!"

"Eden, stop!" Dov exploded. "She is no threat. I've been watching her. She's a scared girl on the run. She's just trying to survive. She's not going to betray us."

"You don't know that!" Eden screeched.

"Yes, I do!" Dov shouted back.

"No, you don't!"

"Eden, she's fine—" His words were cut short as Eden lashed out her hand and slapped him hard across the face.

I gasped as he reeled back. Anger rippled through his blue eyes, but he didn't move toward her. Eden almost looked shocked as he turned back to face her, realizing she had hit him.

"You will not touch her," he said in a low, threatening, terrifying voice.

Eden backed up. She stood watching him for a moment before shifting her gaze to me. Looking back at him, she conceded and slowly turned to leave.

Once she had retreated, Dov turned to me, hand still on his face.

"Berwyn must never know."

I nodded quickly. These people were terrifying. Something told me this wasn't the first time Dov had been hit or threatened by his family.

"Ice," I whispered.

His face softened. "What?" he asked, unable to hear me.

"Ice," I said a bit louder, but my voice was still unsteady. "Do you want ice?"

Suddenly I found myself rushing to get ice. His face must be throbbing by now. A red handprint was forming under his fingers as he tried to rub the pain away.

I stumbled back to him as he lowered himself to the couch. He slouched in the corner and allowed the cushions to envelop him. I gently touched the ice to his cheek and he winced as it made contact.

"Are you all right?" I asked quietly, afraid to look him in the eye.

"I'm fine," he mumbled.

"This isn't the first time that's happened, is it?"

He looked me in the eye and I understood everything.

"You didn't have to do that for me."

"It's fine."

"No really, I don't want to cause any problems. I'll leave today," I offered, determined not to make the situation worse.

"You will not. Everything will be fine."

"But…"

"Auluria, you are staying. That is final. Besides, they're better behaved when you're around, so think of it like you are helping me," he tried to coax me into staying.

You are helping me.

"You are helping me," the blond man said. He had me by the shoulders and was looking deep into my eyes. "You have to do this. For me, for our family. You're the only one who can get in there," he said. I remembered nodding, agreeing, complying. I was on a mission of some kind. When I was caught. I was on a mission before I found Dov.

"You remembered something." He leaned away from me, taking the ice from my hand.

"I was on a mission when I found you. I was doing something for…someone. A man. A blond man. It had to do with…my family? I think. But I don't have a family, so how could that be?"

"No family?" he asked.

"No." I shook my head, thinking. "They…died. They died." I looked up at him. "They died. I have no parents."

"How?" he prompted softly.

"They…they…died."

"It's okay." He tapped my shoulder lightly. "You'll figure it out."

I hated not knowing. At least some of it was coming back to me. Slowly. I've always hated slowness.

Dov let me make lunch for him. As I worked, I tried to figure out why I was in the woods to begin with. *What sort of a mission was I on and who was the blond man?*

Dov wouldn't offer any further explanation for the storehouse. I didn't push him on it. The red mark slowly disappeared from his handsome face and the anger crept out of his eyes. He let me clear away his plate when he was finished, the only way I could think of to thank him for standing up for me.

"Dov?" I asked after I had cleaned up. "Why don't they like me?"

He looked at me, his usually sparkling blue eyes clouding.

"It's not you that they don't like. It's the situation. This has happened before and it didn't end well."

"What do you mean?" I pushed. I had to find out.

"We're very careful about who we let into our group. Sometimes people slip in, though, that shouldn't be here. There was a girl…"

He waited, trying to collect his thoughts.

"There was a girl, who joined us. She wanted to get away from a situation she was in, and she found us. We took her in. Some things happened and she was forced to turn against us."

"What happened?"

"She betrayed us, gave our secrets away. When the group found out, she was forced to leave."

"I understand how that would make the group nervous. I'm sure you must be wary of all new people. It would be awful if that happened to you all again."

He nodded, his dark hair falling around his eyes.

"I have another question, though," I added.

He gave a slight nod for me to go on.

"I understand why you won't let people in," I started slowly. "But… when Berwyn said to get rid of me, you said you wouldn't. You told him that he knew why. Dov…why?"

Dov moved closer to me and took my hands. Their warmth

reached all the way up my arms and tingled up to my neck and cheeks. Tipping his head, he looked straight into my eyes.

"Auluria, there are people out there who want to hurt us. They don't like what we stand for and they will find any way they can to hurt us.

"That girl, she went back to her group—not by choice—and they weren't happy. She had failed in her mission. They hurt her. Eventually, it got so bad she just gave out. They made sure we knew her death was our fault.

"And it's not just the other groups out there. It's the government. The Society wants information on us too. They're still mad about everything that happened in past years. They've been looking for us, and they won't hesitate to use you to find us.

"So, I'm not just going to let you back out there. You may be new, but you need protection. I won't send you away without it." He looked sad.

"That girl. You were close with her?"

"She was a friend."

I didn't believe that. He could tell I was skeptical.

"I wasn't with her, if that's what you want to know. She was a bit younger than me, and yes, Berwyn and Eden got it in their heads that she would be a good fit for me, so they kept her close, but I never wanted her like that."

"That explains why they were so angry. Betrayal is always bad, but betrayal by someone close is so much worse," I thought aloud.

He took his hands away from mine, leaving them suddenly cold and empty.

"Don't be nervous though. We'll protect you. You're not going to be kicked out, Auluria."

It was my turn to nod.

Deciding I needed to do something to reassure the Baers about me, I was planning a good meal for dinner to make peace with Berwyn and Eden later that night. For dessert, I wanted to have fresh fruit. Dov directed me to some berry bushes a few yards into the woods. He watched me from the window for a moment but turned away once I caught him staring.

I began to fill the bowl with raspberries and blueberries, humming to myself as I worked. I barely noticed the hand slip around my waist as a second hand clasped my mouth, preventing me from calling out. I silently hated myself for causing Dov to look away from his watch post.

I struggled against my captor as he pulled me further into the tree.

"Shh!" he hissed in my ear.

I pulled out of his grip, swinging around to confront him. As I was hit by his green eyes, it all came flooding back.

"Shadoe." I relaxed.

Shadoe was my handler. And my fiancé. My cousin—*my cousin, the blond man from my flashback*—had pushed Shadoe and me together. It was never a question, it just was.

I worked with my cousin, Lowell. He was part of a resistance movement that was working to bring down the corrupt government. When my parents had died, my aunt had taken me in. When she died, Lowell brought me into his group. I was trained and given missions for them.

I was on a mission now.

"Where have you been, Lur?" he asked, a mix of annoyance and concern.

"Shadoe," I said again. I shook my head to clear it. "After he found me, we got attacked. One of the guys hit me and knocked me out. I lost my memory. I *just* got it back when I saw you right now."

"You missed the first check in."

"Clearly." Now I was the one who was annoyed.

"What did you find?" he questioned.

"Not much yet. I didn't know why I was there so I didn't know I was supposed to be looking." I paused to think. "Well, we have a complication. Berwyn is married."

Suddenly I realized what that meant for the plan. My job had been to find a way into the Baer home and to get Berwyn to trust me. Lowell had sent me because I was Berwyn's type, or so he thought.

"That's not good." He looked worried. "What about the younger brother, Dov?"

"He's the one that rescued me. He's been protecting me this whole time."

"Good. He's the one then. Go after him. Get him to fall in love with you and use it to find the information."

I then realized just how awful this mission really would be. Manipulating Berwyn would have been one thing, but Dov had been nothing but kind. I didn't want to see him hurt in the fall out of my cousin's master plan.

"What else did you learn? Anything?" he cut me off.

"Umm…there's a storehouse. I don't know exactly where it is, but it exists and it's full of food."

"Find out. We need an exact location."

I nodded, creating a mental checklist for myself.

"We need exact information so we can pull this off," he continued.

I felt the lightness leave my shoulders as I slipped back into my old persona. A seriousness washed over me that I didn't know I was missing. I could feel my rib cage constrict around my lungs, forcing the air out and pulling me down.

"We'll meet in two days," Shadoe continued, drawing me out of my thoughts. "All right, Lur?"

"All right." I nodded, raising my hand to where my neck met my shoulder. I hoped it looked like I was working out a knot, but really, I was trying to calm my heart rate down.

"At the meeting place."

"Yes. I'll try to slip away."

He nodded, picking my hand up in his and giving a light squeeze before backing away.

"You can do this. Now that you're back, you'll be incredible," he said before turning, sounding far more like Lowell than himself.

"*Destructive* is more like it," I muttered as I turned to go back inside.

I snatched a few more berries along the way. When I walked back into the house Dov was standing in the kitchen moving some pans around.

"Find any?" he asked, barely looking up.

"Yep." I offered him a weak smile and held out the bowl even though he wasn't looking.

"Good," he said, tinkering with something. "So, who were you talking to out there?"

My heart slammed into my chest again. Apparently, it was a feeling I was going to have to get used to.

"What?" I asked, hoping my voice didn't betray my worry.

"Who were you talking to out there? You were gone an awfully long time." He laughed as if he were making a joke. Maybe he hadn't seen.

"Oh, just my…shadow," I tried to joke back.

I swept across the room with a lavish flourish and deposited the bowl of berries next to him on the table. I plucked one from the bowl and popped it into my mouth. "Mmm."

Dov looked at me and I swear he was amused.

For a moment, it flashed through my mind how easy it would be to get him to fall for me and tell me everything I needed to know. I instantly regretted that thought, ashamed that I would ever be okay with hurting someone as kind as Dov.

I reached for another berry just as he did. His hand covered mine for a brief second before I pulled away.

"Go ahead," I said, my hand still burning from where our skin touched. I felt the corners of my lips twitch up as I turned on my heels and moved further away.

Dipping down to the floor, I searched the cabinet for another bowl.

"I think I'll actually go pick some more," I added, desperate to be out of that house so I could think.

"I'll go with you," he said decidedly, scooping up yet another bowl. When he saw my hesitation, he added, "You take one side and I'll take the other."

"All right," I said softly, trying not to sound annoyed.

"Oh. I had Eden pick you up some new clothing. Now you won't have to borrow hers. They're over on the cot." He motioned to my temporary sleeping space.

"Thank you," I said, blushing. "That was so very kind of you."

Kind.

This boy was going to kill me. He was going to get us all killed.

We walked outside together and into the trees. True to his word, he stayed on his side and gave me space on mine. I deftly reached out and pulled the fruit from their bushes, listening to the birds singing, hoping for their advice.

I liked Dov. He was a good person. He didn't deserve to be hurt. I wanted to protect him. But Lowell was a good person too, and if he said this needed to be done, I had no reason to not believe him. No matter how hard I tried, I couldn't find a way to have Berwyn take the fall without involving Dov.

I couldn't.

My job was to find their weaknesses and use whatever it was against them. If I did my job right, *I* was supposed to be Dov's weakness.

But I couldn't.

My bowl was full by the time I finally settled on my only option. I had to play both sides. I would make sure Dov and I were friends but I wouldn't let him get close enough that it could hurt him. There would be no relationship, fake or otherwise. I'd get the information I could, but I'd do my best not to use Dov to get it. I'd report back to Shadoe and Lowell.

When the time came, I'd try to convince Dov to come with us. I'd tell him all about the mission and beg him to leave. Ultimately, though, my loyalty had to be to my only family, my cousin. I knew that. I had to believe that was right.

I'd keep Dov safe. I'd do whatever I could. If I was careful, I might be able to save Lowell *and* Dov. I had to try.

"You ready?" Dov asked, eyeing my full bowl.

"Yeah," I breathed. Some of the heaviness lifted from my shoulders. I could make this work.

"Wasn't that kind of her?" Dov prompted after dinner. The berries we had collected had been devoured quickly.

"Thanks," Berwyn grumbled as he stood. His gaze swept around the room, falling again to our sleeping arrangement. The clothes Eden had acquired for me sat alongside the cot, my only possessions in the world aside from what I had with me when I arrived.

"Did you get everything taken care of, little brother?" he asked, not commenting further on my temporary stay. I was grateful.

"Yes, everything is confirmed. We shouldn't have any problems." Dov nodded, walking away from the table. I rushed to clean up before Eden could start gathering dishes. I wanted to make myself useful so they wouldn't mind having me around as much.

She glared at me but allowed me to take care of them. I watched quietly as Berwyn directed Dov to the far side of the room, far enough away that I couldn't overhear. They both took turns nodding as Eden watched them from the table, fingers lightly tapping where her plate had once been. My eyes darted away as she glanced at me.

As she looked away, I studied the room from the far side of the kitchen. Light found its way in through the windows, an almost golden glow from the setting sun peeking in through the treetops outside. It danced along the floorboards, mesmerizing me for a moment. Each second they swayed a different way as the branches outside moved in the breeze. For a fleeting moment, I had the urge to run outside, far from the cabin. It was strange to be indoors again. It had been so long since I lived in a house of any kind.

Grounding myself, I forced my feet to stay in place, unmoving and unchanging. I longed to feel the air push back my hair. Instead, my hair blew away from my face as I exhaled sharply, my eyes catching Dov's from across the room. The corners of his eyes tweaked up as he flashed me a quick smile before turning back to his brother.

Quickly looking away, I turned to focus on the dishes in front of me, hoping Eden didn't notice. She did.

I could feel her watching me, her eyes on my every move. I hadn't even felt that scrutinized when Lowell watched my training. Eden scared me. If I didn't win her over, she could be my undoing. I had to find a way to connect with her. She had been the one to finalize the decision to allow me to stay, in a moment of apparently uncharacteristic kindness, but now it was as if she was searching my very soul, ready to attack at any moment.

The room tensed. I braved a glance at my hosts, immediately wishing I hadn't. Berwyn was watching me, a hungry look in his eyes. He was waiting for me to make a mistake; he was waiting for me to give myself away. The man was like a starving animal watching his prey. I could almost hear him growl when he caught my eye.

Dov looked up as I fumbled to catch the plate that I had nearly dropped. Glaring at his brother, he forced his attention back to their conversation. Eden smirked as she looked away from the scene. For someone that looked like she should be so soft, she had an incredibly rough edge. I imagined it had been why she had survived so well in our world.

Berwyn ended the conversation abruptly and nodded for Eden to follow. Together they wandered away from the main part of the house.

Still slightly unnerved, I chose not to say anything to Dov. He stayed on his side of the house, allowing me to finish my work in peace. I tried not to glance up at him, but I couldn't help myself. Most times I found him watching me, his gaze much easier than his family's. A faint smile played at his lips as he watched me work. I could feel myself blushing and tried to let my hair hang in my face to conceal it as I worked.

Unsure of what to do when I finished, I wandered over to the cot and sat down. My eyes were firmly focused on the floor, charting each board and rug in the room.

I stopped breathing as he walked toward me. Counting the steps until he arrived at my side, I waited to see what internal battle I was about to face.

"Thanks for the berries. They were great," he said, sliding down onto the floor by my feet.

"Oh," I replied, not having expected him to bring it up again. "You're welcome."

"They may not have said it—or at least said it well—but Berwyn and Eden were grateful for your contribution as well."

"I'm sure," I muttered.

"Give them time, they'll come around," he encouraged me.

As I sank down to the floor next to him, he pulled a basket out from behind his back. Somehow, I had missed it. Setting it between us, he waited for me to investigate. When I didn't, he reached inside and withdrew its contents, handing me a pile of clothing.

"We're mending," he supplied, retrieving a needle and thread.

I had not been anticipating that turn of events and floundered for a moment. Dov laughed when I hesitated momentarily before thrusting my hand forward to collect the thread. In my overzealous actions, I knocked over a pile of the clothing, nearly toppling the basket.

He took out a second set of tools and began mending with me, another surprise. In the past, I had taken care of Lowell and Shadoe, or if I hadn't been available, one of the women who swarmed after Lowell would see to the work. Dov was remarkably impressive.

"You don't need to do all those chores around here, you know. It's nice that you help, but you shouldn't feel like you need to earn your keep. We don't require you to do anything to find safety here."

I held up the mending work in my hands and raised my eyebrows. Dov laughed, looking down at his own work.

"Truly, Auluria, you don't have to help out here. We're happy to have you...or *I* am. Eden and Berwyn don't really count in this conversation. And as for the mending, that's just something for us to do while we talk."

"But I *want* to help," I insisted.

"I know you do, and I appreciate that," he responded, "but if you're going to do something, don't feel like you have to kill yourself working to stay here."

I couldn't help but smile.

"I know, but Dov, I truly want to help. I'm not doing it out of guilt." Well, maybe a little...or a lot, since I was deceiving his entire family and setting them up for my cousin's plan...but I wanted to help Dov out.

"You're pretty good at this," he commented, motioning to the work in my hands.

"Yes, I suppose I am fine. I am, however, thoroughly impressed with your skills," I said, assessing his work.

"Dad taught me. He thought Berwyn and I should be able to take care of ourselves should we ever need to. I suppose he never realized that would happen so soon." He paused. "Tell me, where did you learn?"

"This? Oh, I don't know. I suppose I grew up knowing. I don't remember ever not being able to do this."

My aunt had taught me at a young age to mend clothing. It was one of the ways she brought in extra money to care for us. As soon as I could, I helped her, anything I could do to support her and take part of the burden.

"I used to help mend clothing when I was younger to bring in extra money for food," I added.

"You're remembering." Dov gave me a small smile.

"Oh. Yes, I guess I am... a little," I covered. We worked in silence for a moment.

"That was kind of you. Selfless, even." Dov nodded.

"It was more about the need to eat to survive. If mending socks for people and guards was the price of living, I could handle that."

"Well, I would have suggested you sew the guards' socks *shut*, but I can't imagine that would have helped your cause," Dov snickered.

"No, I can't imagine it would have. However, sewing them shut with the guards' feet *still in them*...now *that* might have helped my cause."

Dov's head whipped around to face me. He attempted to hold back a laugh but snorted instead before bursting out into that glorious chuckle of his. I laughed along with him as he pretended to sew his own sock onto his leg, his lips quirking up into an amusing grin.

"I was right about you," he announced when he had controlled his laughter.

"How is that?" I asked, returning to my mending work.

"You're trouble." He grinned.

"*Trouble?*" I tried to quip, terrified he knew something.

"If you are willing to put needles through a guard, what else might you do?"

"Well, I *have* been known to beat up men twice my size," I said flirtatiously as if it were a joke. There was nothing humorous about it. Shadoe had trained me well.

"Have you now?"

"I'll have to show you sometime," I replied with a giggle.

"Please, just no broken bones."

No, just a broken heart, if Lowell had it his way.

"Never. I wouldn't dream of it," I said.

"Of course, not," he said, holding my gaze. "But truthfully, maybe we *should* work on your fighting skills, Auluria. It's far too dangerous for you to be out there without having any fighting skills. You need to be able to protect yourself."

If only he knew.

"I can teach you, if you'll let me," he insisted.

"Maybe," I said, trying to stall. There was a very good chance that that was a very bad idea. If I couldn't make it look like I was new to defending myself, or if at any point my reflexes and survival instincts kicked on, I would betray my own secret. He could never know just how well trained I really was.

"Are you nervous about it?" he asked.

"Yes," I answered truthfully, but not for the reasons he thought.

"Just…think about it okay. It would help me be less worried about you," he said awkwardly.

"All right," I agreed.

After a moment, he added, "It would help you to protect the people you care about too."

"Like you?" I asked absentmindedly. I froze when I realized what I had said. I rushed to cover my mistake, attempting to keep my voice calm. "I'll always take care of the people in my life, Dov, you included. I would do anything to protect my friends. Even if that means fighting. Even if it means losing. Whatever the cost is to me, I can take it. I'll take on whatever I have to if it's for the greater good." I took a breath. "You can teach me if you want, but not just yet. I'm not ready for that yet."

"But soon?" he questioned, still watching me.

"Yes, soon. I'll let you know when I'm ready," I agreed.

"You really *would* give up everything for your friends, wouldn't you, Auluria?" he questioned. "You're easy to read. I can see in your eyes and on your face that you meant that. I believe you would sacrifice yourself if it came to that. But Auluria, don't do anything stupid on my account. I can take care of myself. You don't need to worry about me. If for some reason it ever comes to it, just make sure you keep yourself safe."

My *Mission* gave me permission to put myself first. I couldn't believe where this conversation had taken me.

"I'll look out for you, the same way you look out for me, Dov," I replied. "It's nice that you want to protect me, but from where I'm sitting it looks like no one else is looking out for *you*. So, if looking out for you is up to *you and me*, I suppose we had both better do a good job of it."

"You're not going to listen to me on this, are you?"

"Well. there's always the option of sewing your lips closed so I don't have to *not listen*." I raised an eyebrow at him.

"Helping by hurting…so that's how you work then," he mused.

My head went reeling as his words hit true. *I hurt people to help other people. I hurt Dov to help Lowell.* He was absolutely right and didn't have a single clue.

"Yes, well, a lady does what she must." I forced a grin.

"A *lovely* lady at that," he flirted.

My gaze flew to my hands. I could feel myself blush.

He was making it so easy and so difficult all at once.

"Turns out I rescued a pretty special girl," he said, "if she's so willing to give up her freedom to be my friend."

"Not as special as you think, I'm afraid."

"Or perhaps more than she realizes. No one has ever done that for me before, cared enough to focus on me as a person and not me for what I could do for the group. I appreciate it, Auluria. I'm really glad you are here." His words lingered in the air as we both fell back into our work.

We sat in a comfortable silence as we worked.

"Why is your hair so long?" he asked after sitting in quiet for a while.

"What do you mean?" I asked, glancing at him.

"It's longer than most girls," he said thoughtfully. "Eden's hair is only partway down her back, but yours…it's different."

"I suppose," I replied, looking back at my work. "I just like it that way I guess. My mother always had long hair and I always thought it was so beautiful."

He nodded slowly, focusing on the fabric in his hands.

"Are you remembering anything else?"

"Some things," I admitted, trying to guard my words.

"What *do* you remember?" he asked gently.

"Bigger things," I answered. "I remember things about the Society and the government. I remember my family. I remember the way my mother used to sing to me…quietly, as if it were a secret."

I smiled, humming the tune to myself absentmindedly as I worked. Dov's voice joined mine, adding in the words. My breath caught, unbelieving that he knew the very song my mother used to sing to me.

He grinned at me. "Mine too. She used to dance all around the house to it when I was little," he added before continuing the song.

Abruptly, he pulled himself to his feet, extending his hand to me. His voice grew louder as he switched to a livelier song. Without waiting, he pulled me to my feet, causing me to drop my project. It bounced off the floor as he spun me around, respectfully holding both of my hands in his. I was grateful he hadn't tried to hold me as we danced.

I couldn't contain my laughter as he spun us around the room. I tried to shush him, worried his brother and sister-in-law would hear.

"They're out now, Auluria. We're on our own for the time being," he paused to say before singing again.

Circling around the room, we jumped in time with each other, his singing eventually cascading into an uncontainable laughter. When he finally slowed our frivolous display of dancing, my hair crashed into him, wrapping around his back and cradling his shoulder. I pulled away from him and my golden hair dripped down his chest before falling against me.

In between breaths, we laughed again, our chests rising and falling nearly at the same time. He grinned as if he had won something; proving his unspoken point.

Shaking my head, I nearly raced back to my work, throwing myself on the ground. Taking up my task once again, I waited for him to rejoin me. He settled next to me on the floor, still breathing heavily. Brushing back his hair, he picked up the fabric he had been repairing and set back to work.

"Do you dance often?" he finally asked flirtatiously.

Smiling, I gave him a patronizing look. "Oh yes, in all of my spare time, I focus on my studies in the art of dancing for my time in the high society parts of our fine country. Was it not obvious?"

"Not when you stepped on my feet," he grinned, eyes sparkling with a challenge.

"I did no such thing, and even if I had, it would have been your own fault. I had no control of our movements."

"You're saying *I* caused your missteps?" he questioned.

Yes, you are in fact causing my missteps.

"If I had had a different partner, one not tromping us all over the house, I can assure you it would have been more graceful," I said haughtily, tossing him a sly smile.

"Oh, I imagine you are always quite graceful, Auluria," he said, catching my eye. He was going to be a problem.

"Is that so?" I retorted.

"Tell me, where *did* you learn to dance?"

"A very interesting woman taught me not too long ago," I replied, my thoughts drifting back to my training before the mission. Lowell had made sure I was prepared in every way.

"She must have been a good teacher."

"I suppose so." I considered his words for a moment before demanding my thoughts turn back from my time in Lowell's watch.

"The more pressing question, Dov Baer, is where did *you* learn to dance?" I instantly regretted the question as a shadow passed over his face.

"Another story, for another time, my dear Auluria. How is your mending going?" he regained his balance.

"Almost finished. Yours?"

Before he could answer, I sucked in a harsh breath, attempting to cover my gasp.

He was at my side before the blood had time to bubble up out of my skin. I watched as it leaked out of my fringer, red against my pale flesh. Dov gathered my hand in his and pressed it against the fabric in his hand. Holding me until the blood stopped, I sat frozen in place as he watched my hand intently. Neither of us spoke.

Dov removed the cloth, watching for signs of the bleeding to stop. It ended quickly, despite feeling like it was taking an eternity. Releasing my hand, he moved back to his place a few feet away. He never acknowledged our closeness, the way his hand warmed mine as he cared for me.

"Thank you," I whispered quietly.

"Who took care of you, Auluria? Before all this. Who looked after you?" he responded quietly, no longer willing to look me in the eyes.

I looked away, unwilling, perhaps *unable*, to answer. He took my silence as my response and let the moment slip away.

"I'll look out for you, Auluria," he said quietly, making me unable to breathe yet again. "I know I have no right to, but we're friends now, since the day we met in the woods, and I'm going to look out for you."

I started to protest but he continued, cutting me off.

"I know you can care for yourself. That much is obvious, or you wouldn't have made it this far. But you can't go through life alone. It's too hard, trust me. You need people on your side, and I want to be there for you. I don't expect anything from you, but I want you to know you are safe with me. I want to look out for you."

"Dov," I started.

"You don't need to say anything, you don't even have to like it, but I want you to know I am on your side. Whatever you are going through, I am here." He finally looked up at me, convincing me with his eyes. *This man couldn't possibly be real.*

"Just don't go running away on me now, okay?" he joked, but I sensed something more, something stronger behind his words. His easy grin set off butterflies in my stomach, their wings pushing my heart into my throat.

This couldn't possibly get any worse.

This couldn't possibly get any better.

"I won't." I attempted to laugh off his comment, but deep inside I knew, despite Lowell's directives, I didn't want to stray from this man who had become my mission.

"Besides, I'm injured now," I said seriously, holding up my needle-pricked finger. "How far could I really get?"

His somber face held true for only a moment as he nodded before breaking out into a glorious, radiant smile accompanied by that strong, solid laughter I had come to know from him.

"Well, if I knew getting you to stay was that easy, I'd have had you sewing the first day!"

"That worried I'd run off, were you?" I smiled back.

"I admit, I was a little worried at first." He leaned back against the cot. "It is possible that I didn't sleep the first few nights just to make sure you weren't planning on running away in the middle of the night."

Had anyone else said those words, I may have panicked, but I could tell he had been genuinely concerned for my wellbeing.

"I'm not frightening you, am I?" he asked, less enthusiastic. "You know I'm not trying to keep you here against your will. It's just far too dangerous for you—or anyone, really—to be out there on their own."

"Yes, I'm aware," I agreed. "And I'm not worried about your intentions, Dov. Besides, I'm starting to like it here."

"Maybe you still haven't fully recovered from your memory loss… but you *do* remember who the other occupants of this house are, don't you?"

Before I could respond, the door opened on the other side of the house. Dov's eyes darted to the far end of the room and he scooted a bit further away from me as Berwyn walked in.

The older version of Dov glanced at us, eyeing our repair work. I offered him a weak smile that was not returned. He nodded once to his brother before walking off.

"We should probably rest," Dov offered, setting the last of the repair work back in the basket.

I glanced out the window and noticed the stars had come out, peeking through the tree branches as they swayed. It seemed the higher branches always swayed in the place, constantly moving and changing shape.

I set my material down, allowing Dov to help me up. I tried not to smile when his back was turned. Controlling his emotions could have been so easy, but instead, he was controlling mine.

Settling into the cot, my head was whirring with too many thoughts. I fought to control them, willing myself to be still. Sleep, usually one to betray me, welcomed me after a brief time.

Chapter 3

"Come on, we have somewhere to be," Dov's soft voice woke me.

"But it's the middle of the night," I complained, sitting up in bed, keeping the blanket wrapped around my body. I pushed the hair out of my face and struggled to see him in the dark.

"Yeah, I know. But it doesn't change the fact that we have somewhere to be." I swear he was grinning at me, though I still hadn't adjusted enough to see in the dark.

"Fine," I grumbled, rising from the cot. "Where are we going?"

"There's a raid tonight. I have to help, which means you need to come with me."

"Why do *I* have to be involved?"

"Well, first off, I thought you'd like to see what it is we stand for. However, if you're *not* interested, you *could* stay with Berwyn and Eden. They aren't going out until tomorrow."

"What, no second point?"

"What?"

"You said 'first off' but you never had a follow-up."

"I thought that was implied," he said.

"No." I was not amused.

"Not much of a night person, are you?" he teased me.

"Catch me right before sunrise and we'll see who's functioning better, Owl," I scoffed as I found something to change into.

"Uh-huh," he retorted. "Now get a move on."

I changed behind the screen Dov had set up for me. Pulling my hair up into a ponytail, I walked around and grabbed a light overcoat. When I looked up, Dov was watching me.

"Ready?" he asked.

"Lead the way," I motioned and followed him out into the forest cloaked in darkness.

"We're collecting food," Dov explained as we neared the site. "The government has been taking food for years, leaving the people with practically nothing. We," he said, gesturing to the small group we were approaching, "reallocate it."

"Reallocate, huh?"

"Yes, Auluria. We reallocate it. That's what the storehouse is for. We share. Those that are in need can have *what* they need. Not everything there is stolen. We grow our own crops too."

We approached the group and they looked warily at me.

"This is Auluria. She's a friend. She'll be helping us tonight," Dov introduced me, challenging anyone to question him. Berwyn may have been in charge, but Dov was second in command...after Eden, of course.

"We're going in through the south entrance," a boy explained. "There's no one watching that side of the building. If we're quiet, we can sneak in one or two at a time. Everyone will fill their sacks and we'll slip out. Questions?"

He threw a collection of sacks on the ground in front of him.

"I'm on lookout," a petite girl informed us when no one spoke.

Dov nodded, casting a wicked grin at the girl. A rush of jealousy coursed through me. I pushed it aside...I couldn't have feelings like that.

Dov turned back to me and whispered in my ear, "You'll go in with me." Now it was the girl's turn to be jealous.

He stopped and picked up two bags. He handed one to me and I slung it over my shoulder. I started to lead the way toward the entrance, but quickly realized I wasn't supposed to know how to do this, so I slowed and waited for Dov to lead me.

We slipped into the building, old and brown with age. It smelled like mildew and I wanted to cover my nose.

An older girl brushed past me. "Breathe through your mouth. It helps."

Once we were inside, we started collecting items. Some of the stronger boys lifted down heavy crates and broke into them. We took whatever we could fit in the sacks.

I took mostly food, fitting it into my bag as best I could. Then I slipped some small trinkets in around the gaps of food. It was dark inside, but while our eyes were mostly adjusted to the dim lighting from being outside, there was no moonlight inside. I could make out outlines of objects. My fingers told me more about what they were. I felt cold metal pieces a few times. Some items were smooth and others rough and damaging to my fingers.

I worked my hands around the contents of my sack, pushing and reorganizing until I couldn't fit anymore. Dov stayed by my side, brushing against me every so often to be sure we were still together. At one crate, we stood, shoulder to shoulder, foot against foot, and systematically emptied the contents into our sacks.

Just as we were leaving we heard a voice. Everyone froze, inches from the exit. We waited but heard no further noise. A young kid started out the door before we could stop him.

The noise that followed told us he hadn't suffered.

The group panicked, rushing back into the building, searching for another exit. The people outside slammed the entrance closed, blocking us in the room. I scanned the edges of the walls. I wasn't supposed to be able to function in a situation like this one according to the mission plan, but in the moment, I had no choice.

I felt along the wall. With my fingers, I found the weak spot in the wood. The building had been constructed as a temporary house for the goods. The walls had not been reinforced; they were merely pieces of wood nailed together.

I couldn't have been more grateful for the training Lowell and Shadoe had offered me than at that very moment. I may have been young, but Lowell insisted I was ready to take care of myself before I go on any missions. He wanted me working young, so he trained me from the moment he brought me into his fold.

"Here," I shouted, motioning the group over.

I stepped back, moved my skirt to the side and prepared to kick at the rotting wall.

"Wait," Dov said. "Let me."

He kicked to the side, striking the wood where I had pointed. Two other men joined him, taking turns kicking at the decaying material. It shattered. A few more blows and it was wide enough to escape through.

The group poured out into the night, the sounds of our attackers close behind as they realized we had escaped from the other side. I ran as hard as I could, hair whipping behind me as I turned to check on their advances.

I was on my own, running toward the trees. The moon lit my way, casting eerie shadows as we all moved in different directions.

"Get down!" Dov said, pulling me to the forest floor behind some bushes. He had kept his eyes on me as we ran, much to my amazement, and managed to overtake me.

We waited as the guards ran past us, shouting angrily. It wasn't until Dov put his hand on my shoulder that I realized how heavily I was breathing.

"You okay?" he asked.

I nodded. "You?"

"Yeah, I'm fine. You're sure you're okay?" he asked again, brushing a piece of fallen hair behind my ear.

My breath caught. I pulled away before I could think through it.

"Let's go," I said, standing.

He lowered his hand from where it was still resting after moving my hair, words still on his lips. Dov stood without a word and we walked back into the night.

"How could you let that happen?" Berwyn yelled.

He was even more terrifying in the stillness of the night.

"You oversaw the raid. It was your job to know!" He slammed his hand down on the table, causing everyone to jump.

"You got that boy killed tonight, do you realize that? We don't even know if the others made it back yet. How could you be so stupid?" he bellowed.

His next sentence gave me chills.

"Get up," he whispered.

Dov rose from his seat at the table slowly. I wanted to scream, to throw myself in front of him, but Eden stepped in front of me, forcing me to stay in place. They were out the door before I could say anything.

When they had gone, Eden turned to me.

"You might as well get a little rest. They won't be back for a bit." She glanced over her shoulder as she walked away and said coolly, "Just be glad it wasn't you."

It was late morning when Berwyn and Dov finally returned to the house. Berwyn walked in the door, mumbling to himself. He didn't even bother looking at Eden, but she hurried after him anyway.

After a moment, Dov made his way in. His lip was split open. I could see he was nursing several bruises on his stomach and chest as he walked across the room. He winced with every step.

"No," I breathed as my face fell. "Dov, what did he do to you?"

I raced to his side to help him in. I started to reach for him but pulled back, knowing I shouldn't touch him.

"It's fine, Auluria." He tried to push me off.

"It's anything but fine," I insisted, trying to inspect his wounds.

"It's *fine*, Auluria," he shouted. I stepped back as if I'd been the one who had been struck.

"I'm sorry. I didn't mean to yell," he said in a hushed tone.

"Why?" I asked bitterly, looking for an explanation for his injuries.

"Because that boy died last night," he said as if it explained everything.

I must have looked confused because he continued to fill in the gaps for me.

"He died. There had to be some accountability. We went to his father and Berwyn put me in my place."

"He beat you because a raid went sideways?" I couldn't believe anyone could be so cruel.

"It's better than losing a bunch of people when that father went after the people involved," he said. "It's not as bad as it looks."

"Let me at least check it," I begged.

He gave a slight nod and I approached him. I touched his chin, tilting his head up so I could see his split lip. His face was warm in my hand and suddenly I was caught in those blue eyes again as I glanced up at him.

I pulled away and nodded to his shirt. He lifted it and I watched as it revealed his chiseled body. The sight was almost as addictive as his eyes.

"Here, let me help," I said when I saw him wince.

I lifted his shirt the rest of the way, careful not to brush against him, and examined his injuries. I could barely stop myself from touching the wounded skin as I inspected them.

"Turn," I commanded softly.

He obliged and spun for me slowly, allowing me to see his sides and back.

"Well, I don't think anything is broken. You're going to be sore for a while though," I said.

"Really, do you think, Doc?" He smirked and then grimaced.

"Why don't you go rest?" I pointed to the bed. He deserved a good place to sleep now.

He sauntered over to the couch and flopped down gently. He watched me as I watched him for a moment.

I walked over and knelt beside him.

"What do you need?" I asked, concern in my voice. I was going to take care of this man, no matter how hard I tried not to, it seemed.

"Just sit with me for a bit," he said closing his eyes.

"All right," I said, leaning my back against the couch. After a few minutes, I tipped my head back and stared up at the ceiling.

He was brave, I realized. He took a beating he didn't have to take to protect the lives that could potentially be lost later. He was brave and kind and selfless.

I sat with him for two days. We talked when he wasn't sleeping. He told me a bit more about the raids. One night he talked about his family.

"My father started our group," he blurted out. "He wanted to help people. That's why we're doing this—to help."

"What happened to him?" I asked quietly.

"Something went wrong. He tried to take us underground, but they managed to find him anyway. They tried him and hanged him."

I tried not to look horrified.

"What about your mother?" I asked.

He sighed deeply.

"You already know how the Society is fighting that war against our enemy countries. You're aware that they tried to make a deal with them—our food and supplies for our freedom from attack, but those foreign countries took our food and supplies and threaten to attack us anyway. So, the Society takes all our food and supplies to try to appease them, but they still want to get out from under their thumb."

I nodded, knowing all this already.

"Well, they want to raise our population numbers, so we can eventually fight against them. Often, the Society takes young boys—not the ones from rich families, mind you—but they take the boys and send them to training camps. Then they ship them off to the military.

"They take young girls and use them as breeders and then when they're done with them, they, too, end up fighting.

"What you may not know, is not all of the Taken are young. Sometimes, if they find women on their own, they take them too."

I had heard rumors of this but never had any proof.

"They found my mother one day, isolated her, and tried to take her. She fought back and they killed her for it."

"Oh, Dov, I'm so sorry. I shouldn't have asked," I said as a single tear threatened to slip down his cheek. I wanted to reach out and wipe it away, but I forced my hands steady at my sides.

He nodded for a moment, regaining his composure.

"What about your family?

"My parents died in a raid when I was little. I barely remember them. My aunt raised me."

"And is she…?"

"She died, too," I said sadly. "She died so she could take care of me and my older cousin."

"Where's your cousin now?" he asked.

"We were never particularly close." I didn't lie; Lowell and I were never close. I just did what he told me because he was the only family I had left and I was young. I *had* to trust him.

"So. Orphans, then."

"Orphans," I agreed. I almost mentioned that he still had his brother, but then I realized he'd probably be better off without him.

"You're awake," Dov announced a few hours later, the moonlight barely hinting at his face from his place on the couch.

"Yes," I whispered back. "I see you can't sleep either."

"No, I suppose not."

"Why not?" I asked. I knew I had a lot on my mind, but what would be keeping him up?

He shifted uncomfortably, grimacing.

"Oh. You're in pain," I said quietly.

"I'm all right, Auluria," he insisted.

Untangling myself from my blanket I crossed the cool floor and lowered myself by his side. He watched my every move.

"What are you doing?" he asked as I settled myself beside him.

"Making sure you're okay," I answered.

"I'm fine, Auluria. I told you that." He studied me.

"I'm aware of what you said," I replied, staring back at him.

"And yet you're still over here," he observed, leading me to speaking again.

"I know what you said, Dov, but I can also read you. You put on a brave face, but you're hurting. You shouldn't have to hurt alone."

"I can survive on my own." His voice took a harsh turn. I didn't like the hurt in his words.

"I'm sure you can, Dov. But the point is that you don't *have* to." I stopped short of saying more. I wanted to tell him that I would be there for him, that he could depend on me, but the truth was that he *couldn't*. He could never trust me.

He smiled at me as I repeated the sentiments he had not so long ago expressed to me, forcing me to look away. My eyes darted to the floor, the table, the door, the window…anything to avoid connecting with him.

"Tell me, Auluria, where did you come from and how do you know so much?" His words might have scared me if his voice hadn't been so sincere.

"I came from the woods, and I only know enough to survive," I teased. I looked up and saw his eyes drifting to my lips, teasing me in a completely different way.

As I shook my head to look away, a strand of hair fell into my face.

I reached up to move it back, but my hand brushed instead against the warm flesh of Dov's hand. Locking eyes with me, he pushed back the fallen lock, taking his hand away slowly.

"How *have* you survived?" he asked quietly, concern flowing from him.

"I…I don't know," I replied. In truth, I had no idea how I had survived a life without someone like Dov Baer in it.

"Tell me more about your family," he prompted, his hand playing with the blanket that lay over him.

Taking my own piece of the blanket in my hand, mindful to stay as far from his hand as possible, I thought of what possible answer I could give. I refused to outright lie to him; I simply couldn't bring myself to do it. I could have talked my way around the subject—I had been trained to easily do that—but my best option was to avoid it all together.

"Tell me about your mother," I countered.

He looked at me quizzically. His eyebrows quirked up in the moonlight, his face covered in shadows.

"She was kind," he said, keeping his eyes on me. "She was very observant…like you. And she always knew the right thing to say. She was good at keeping Berwyn calm."

"And here I thought no one could keep him in check." I smiled.

"Oh, *she* could. So could my father for that matter. It was only after we'd lost both that…well…you know." He looked away. Staring out the window, he added, "She was quiet, my mother. Always noticing things…noticing people. She knew everything; at least I always thought so.

"She always focused on doing the right thing, even if it was uncomfortable, even if it was hard. She always put us first."

"I don't remember much about my parents," I said, shocked I was allowing myself to speak so freely, "but according to my aunt, they were very much like that too. Selfless."

"What was your aunt like? She mostly raised you, didn't she?" he encouraged me to speak.

Being with Dov was like being given a freedom you didn't know you were missing. He was easy to be near, easy to talk to. His whole presence made me want to trust him. He, simply by existing, made me want to tell him everything, knowing he would care for me once I had finished crying.

I couldn't though. I couldn't tell him the truth. No one could ever forgive me for that. Not even someone as strong as Dov Baer could forgive a betrayal so deep and so calculated.

Still, something inside of me gave me permission to speak. It was as if the window had been thrown open, letting in the warm breeze that forced the words from my mouth.

"But she was strong. She did what she had to do to protect us. She gave up her life to make sure I had enough to survive. She kept me safe from the Society. My aunt always made sure I knew about my parents, though I don't know much and I remember even less. She was a good woman, much like I assume my mother would have been."

"She raised a strong woman…a good person, Auluria. Your parents and your aunt would be proud of you. You have a good heart."

A sharp stabbing pain in my chest nearly forced me to double over at his words. I tightened my grip on the blanket edge. He noticed my change in demeanor and reached for my hand. I dropped it in my lap, tangling it in my hair as it rested against my leg.

"Auluria, do you really not see how special you are?"

"*I'm* special?" I shook my head. "I do believe, Dov, that *you* are the one who voluntarily took a beating to prevent more bloodshed and death. If I'm correct, this isn't the first time either."

I could tell his eyes had grown wide, even with the dark shadows dancing across his face.

"Why, Dov? Why must you always take his wrath?"

"It's not wrath exactly." He chose his words carefully. "Sometimes he is mad, and sometimes he takes it out on me. Other times it's more of a sacrificial thing; a price must be paid and instead of *someone else* paying it, it's better if I do."

"But must it always be *you*?" I asked.

"Better me than them," he replied, tipping his head to the side slightly.

"You're a good man," I replied, but Lowell's words crept into my thoughts, forcing me to wonder just how honest the conversation really was and how one's actions were changed by perception.

"You've done nothing but care for us since you've been here," he redirected the conversation. The moonlight sparkled in his blue eyes. "You've been nothing but selfless."

Selfless? Perhaps selfish, but never selfless.

"Regardless of what it meant for you personally, you've done whatever you could to help the people with you. You've been wonderful."

I supposed, if I stretched the meaning of his words, what I was doing was an act for someone other than myself. Everything I had done and was doing was for Lowell and his cause. And to save Dov.

I was uncomfortable with the attention and praise he was offering me. Lowell would have been furious I had not latched onto it like I had been trained to do.

"*You're* the selfless one, Dov," I murmured.

"Maybe we're more alike than we think," he mused, grimacing. His hand floated to his stomach.

"You should rest," I whispered.

"Goodnight, Auluria." He grinned wickedly, eyes following me as I walked backward away from where he rested.

"Goodnight, Dov."

"You have no idea how…" His whisper drifted off as he chose to keep the rest to himself.

Sleep. Going back to sleep was nothing short of a miraculous occurrence.

"You need to eat," I said the next morning as he stirred on the couch.

I brought a dark bowl over to him. The steam trailed behind me.

"What is it?" he asked.

"It's porridge," I replied. He looked at it skeptically.

"I know, it's not the greatest breakfast. I don't particularly care for it. But it's warm and it will fill you up. You need to get some strength back. Please…just try it."

"It's hot," he protested as I walked away.

"Well, then, let it cool down. Just don't wait too long, or it will get cold."

He looked at me with puppy dog eyes. I sighed and walked back over to the couch, kneeling next to him. I reached out and placed my hand on the rim of the bowl, careful not to touch him. He moved the bowl toward me as I bent down and blew carefully over the steaming food.

I could see him watching me, but I refused to look up. His eyes traced over my hair that fell around my chin, my shoulders, my waist and pooled in my lap in front of me.

"There," I said softly. "Just right."

His eyes flitted back to mine and he gave me a small smile of thanks.

Eden watched me that afternoon as I swept the house. Her eyes followed me every time I hurried to Dov's side when he had trouble breathing or if he asked for something. She allowed me to do the laundry for her.

Berwyn continued to glare at me whenever he walked through the house. I tried to pretend I didn't notice. I needed to be in their favor, whether it was to betray them or to save them.

The next day I heard something fall outside. I looked out the window to see a pile of wood toppled over. When I walked outside to recreate the tower, I found myself being abducted once again.

Shadoe's hand clamped over my mouth and he shushed me as he dragged me away.

"You missed the meeting," he said angrily.

"Something came up."

"You can't just decide to skip a meeting, Lur." He pulled me forward, away from the house. "Lowell wants to see you. *Now.*"

Having no choice, we raced through the woods to where I was summoned. I was grateful Dov was sleeping and hadn't seen me running away. He would have tried to save me and he was still in too much pain for that.

"Auluria," Lowell greeted me, his usual well-mannered demeanor gone.

"Lowell," I greeted him.

Looking at Shadoe, he dismissed him. Shadoe retreated a few steps to the far side of the room we stood in.

"Want to explain to me what's been going on?" he asked.

I raised my eyebrows at him, asking what he meant.

"You've been missing your check-ins. You've barely gathered any intelligence. I know you hit your head, but come on Auluria, give me *something* to work with," he demanded.

"I already told Shadoe about the storehouse," I huffed. "I witnessed a raid the other night, but we were caught. A kid died. I'll have more information after the next one on how they operate though. They trust me." I neglected to tell him it was only Dov who trusted me.

"I need you to do better than that. Usually, you are exceptional at finding information for us. Why can't you now?"

I was silent.

"Oh," he drawled. "Now I see. It's that boy. Dov. You *like* him." He grinned. It made me shiver.

"He's a decent person," I started.

"No, he's not. He's playing you Auluria. I told you he would. *They all do*. You'll see. You know what they did—how they killed all those people years ago. You'll see how they really are." He paced around me in a circle.

"Get your head around him, Auluria, and do your job. We must bring these people down. We are taking down the Society and *those people* are going down with it. Don't get attached. I would hate to lose you at the end of this." He glared at me. "And besides, *Missy*, Shadoe is so devoted to you. Would you really do that to him?"

Shadoe was less devoted to me than to Lowell, but Lowell had paired us together, and Shadoe took that seriously.

"Let me be very clear here, Cousin. I see you need some motivation." He looked me up and down. I didn't like this intimidating side of him. He was never warm toward me, but even in his coolness, he had been respectful.

"Either you pull it together, or Shadoe will become very aware of Dov distracting you. Once Shadoe sets to mind to do something, well, you know how good he is at finishing a mission. I bet that boy won't last the day." His words were jarring.

"And really, while we're pinning this on the Baer family, it doesn't matter *which of them* takes the brunt of it. I was planning on it being Berwyn, but the kid will do just fine."

I could feel myself panicking but I kept my face still and my voice steady.

"That won't be necessary, Lowell, I'll take care of it."

"Good." He nodded in approval. "Now, go make him fall in love with you and then get the information we need. Run along now."

He turned his back on me and left. Shadoe returned to my side and escorted me back through the woods.

My cousin's threatening words followed me all the way back to the house.

I was too aware of Shadoe's presence on the journey back to the Bears' home. When Lowell released me, Shadoe had slipped alongside me, moving in our usual silent way. Since I had first met Shadoe I had felt many different emotions toward him, mostly angry ones, but in all our time together I had come to understand him.

I breathed a sigh of relief when he left me to return to Lowell. He still had other missions to oversee, but Lowell was making sure I was kept in line.

I pulled my dress skirt up to my knees and raced through the forest, having learned the layout of the route on the way to Lowell's meeting place. The small cabin had been abandoned, just the way Lowell liked it to appear. I imagined it had been rarely used, if ever.

I used my time to think of ways to protect Dov from Lowell and Shadoe. I had to make sure Shadoe didn't think Dov was going to be a problem, or he really *would* take care of him. In the time I had spent with Dov, I had learned he was quite capable of taking care of himself, but until I found out the true extent of his training I had no way of knowing if he was a match for my handler and former mentor. Shadoe, on the other hand, I knew to be deadly.

I became hyper aware of everything around me, even more so than I had already been. Every snapping branch seemed louder. Each inhale seemed too vicious and needy. Every exhale promised to give me away.

Certain areas of the woods were light and alive with dancing color as the sun's rays shifted through the branches. Still, other parts bore a darkness that seemed to conceal too many secrets, none of which I could unravel. Though the darkness concealed my movements, the light seemed to force my intentions out into the open. I moved in the illuminated areas, hoping they would force me to realize my own purposes.

I slowed when I neared the Baers' home, stabilizing my breath, ensuring they had no reason to question me. The final minutes of walking toward my temporary housing were almost as painful as if I had ripped each hair from my head in one-by-one strands of gold.

Chapter 4

"Where were you?" Eden asked as I walked in the door.

"Out walking," I said, brushing past her.

I knew she didn't know how long I had been gone and I didn't offer to tell her. She gave me a skeptical look but dropped it. I was grateful she had no idea how long I'd really been gone.

"Hey," Dov mumbled as I lowered myself to the floor by the couch, making sure to stay further back than usual. He opened his eyes, still heavy from sleep.

"Hey," I greeted him back. "How are you feeling?"

"Better. A lot better. In fact, I think it's time for me to get outside and move around. Want to come along?" he asked, sitting up.

"Sure," I said, as monotone as I could.

I wanted to go with him. I also desperately wanted to avoid him. He would get hurt because of me and I wanted to stay as far away as I could. I also didn't know what Lowell and Shadoe had planned for him. I decided the best plan of action was to go with him, to protect him, but stay distant.

"Do I smell or something?" Dov chuckled as we walked.

"What?"

"You're walking all the way over there." He waved his hand at me.

"Oh." I paused. "We're just walking, it's not a big deal."

I hopped over a fallen tree trunk. I could hear the roar of the frogs as we neared a small lake. Cattails sprung up all around the water, concealing it unless you were standing right next to it.

Dov grinned at me mischievously.

"Come on," he said and quickened his stride to the water's edge.

I realized where he was headed.

"Dov! We can't go swimming *now.*" The water looked inviting. But I knew if we went swimming we'd have to leave our clothes on the bank and I couldn't bear to see him shirtless again without staring. Whatever I did, I had to keep him from seeing me stare at him.

Since he had been hurt, once I was sure he was asleep, I'd watch him in the dark. His masculine features rose and fell as he breathed. He slept with his lips open just a touch. They looked so inviting. His dark hair fell in his face, and he would reach up and brush it back as he dreamed; I wanted to reach out and touch his silky locks. Dov's eyelashes were so long and perfect I was jealous. I felt the constant tug of wanting to run my hand along his cheekbones and chin. He could never know I studied his face, his arms, his chest. He could never know how much I wanted to care.

"We're not, only sticking our feet in," he said.

I followed him to a rock near the edge of the water. He rolled up his pant legs and I lifted my blue skirt above my knees. We silently slipped our legs into the cool water.

The ripples flowed out gracefully from where we disturbed the glossy surface. The frogs stopped their calling for a few moments as they watched our approach. When they were certain we weren't a threat, the chorus started again, loudly scolding us for bothering their sanctuary.

"Very few people know about this pond," Dov said. "I've never seen anyone else here. Once I even rigged it by wrapping string around the cattails to see if anyone would disturb it. No one ever did. I like to hide out here sometimes."

"It's a good place to think," I supplied.

I could feel his arm stiffen next to mine. Out of the corner of my eye, I saw his hand deftly move toward mine. The electric buzz pulsed around the back of my hand and wrist. I sucked in a quick breath and froze for only a moment before I leaned forward and dipped my hand into the water.

I saw him pull back, looking hurt, but I pretended not to notice.

"The water feels so refreshing. Do you swim here often?" I asked, still leaning forward, moving my hand in the water.

"Yeah, sometimes," he answered, regaining his composure.

I leaned back and kicked my feet, splashing the water around us. I smiled. It was one of the few things I remember doing with my mother when I was little.

"Well. That was fun," I said after a few minutes. "But we should get going."

I stood, leaving him on the rock. He followed behind me, brushing the water off his legs as he moved. We left our clothing pulled up for a few minutes as we walked so we could air dry.

"We need to stop by the storehouse on the way back. I'm supposed to meet one of the guys there about something," he said, changing direction from the path we were on.

Each step away brought me closer to the path Lowell set me on.

The storehouse was crowded as we entered. A cheer of greeting rose when they saw Dov. Most people ignored me, but some continued to glare at me suspiciously. I was still an outsider.

"Silas," Dov called, waving. He turned to me. "You can look around if you like. See if you want anything."

He walked away from me abruptly, leaving me standing alone in the middle of the walkway.

"Look out, dearie," an older woman croaked as she walked past me.

"Sorry," I mumbled after her.

I watched Dov talk to Silas from a distance. I'd walked down the aisle and pretended to inspect the items, but my mind was about fifty feet away from where I stood, next to a tall, dark-haired man.

"Do you want that?" a voice asked next to me.

I looked down at my hand, realizing I was holding a trinket. I was absentmindedly turning it over, trying to make it look as if I weren't watching Dov and Silas.

"No, you can have it." I handed it over to them, catching a glimpse of their face before they turned and shouted thanks over their shoulder.

A loud sound rocked the floor of the storehouse. Food tumbled from their precarious piles on the tables. Weapons and supplies clattered to the ground. A bright flash blinded us.

I blinked, but couldn't refocus my sight. Stumbling around, I tried to find something familiar. As my vision came back into focus, I saw men rushing into the storehouse.

They yelled and pushed people. The storehouse was being attacked. The old woman from a few minutes ago was pushed to the ground, leaving her in a heap. I rushed to her side and helped her up.

The invaders attacked anyone they could find. They started taking food and supplies. The young men from the storehouse ran at them, trying to defend the building. Dov charged at a man, forgetting his injuries, and knocked him unconscious.

The older people were trying to help the group escape from the invaders. They blocked the exits and only let their own run through, preventing thieves from following.

I ran to help several more people. Pulling them from the floor, I guided them to the door that led to freedom. The attackers ran past me, but never once touched me.

That's when I caught a glimpse of a man charging through the storehouse. I knew who it was immediately, even though his face was covered. Shadoe.

He must have been following me, convinced I couldn't do my job. He had summoned one of his groups and they attacked the storehouse.

"Auluria, get out!" Dov's voice pierced through the noise and reached me.

My head shot up, searching for him. I saw him struggle as a man punched his shoulder near his neck.

My legs moved before I commanded them to. I raced to his side, throwing a punch at the man I didn't recognize. I saw Shadoe's eyes through the opening in his mask when my fist connected. They flashed horror, anger, and finally approval. I was doing as he asked and making the Baers think I was one of them.

The man lost his conviction to ignore me and whipped his hand back, ready to strike. Dov, though injured, lifted his hand, taking the blow for me. I punched the man in the stomach, stomping on his foot, and grabbed the nearest heavy object I could find to send it colliding into his head.

The man fell, unconscious at our feet.

"Come on!" Dov grabbed my arm and wheeled me around toward an exit.

Somewhere, someone had started a fire; they would not let their storehouse be lost to invaders. They would rather burn it to the ground than let them have the upper hand.

The fire crackled, licking up the wooden tables. Smoke filled the room. It became so dense so quickly that we could barely see to escape.

The fresh air felt good on our lungs and we gasped for more of it. The sky was bright blue, not a cloud to be seen. Crickets chirped and birds sang as they flew overhead. Only the sound of the chaos inside ruined the picture.

A voice called loudly from inside the burning storehouse.

"That's not one of ours," Silas said as he came up beside us.

Dov looked at him and then back at me.

"Stay here," he commanded. He was back inside the building before I could process what he said.

"No!" I yelped. Silas held me back.

"He'd want you to wait here. He wants you safe," he said, trying to calm me.

I wouldn't be calmed though. I struggled against him, but he held on tighter. I hadn't been prepared for him to grab me, so he had the upper hand.

"Settle down, miss," he insisted, wrestling me in place.

After what seemed like an eternity, Dov reemerged, a young man walking next to him with his arm slung over his shoulder. Dov practically carried him outside.

I audibly breathed a sigh of relief.

Dov had saved that boy *knowing* he was the opposition. He had run back into a burning underground building to save someone he didn't know. He could have died and all he was worried about was keeping me safe and helping someone in trouble.

Lowell was wrong. Dov didn't deserve what we were doing to him.

Dov coughed as he released the boy. The boy took off, running for his life.

"Let him go," Dov coughed, signaling for his friends to stay put. "He's a kid."

Mercy. In that moment, I realized just how *merciful* the man before me was. He showed kindness and mercy. And *I* was trying to destroy him. No more…I wouldn't.

"We need to separate," Silas announced for Dov who was still having trouble catching his breath. "Go!"

Everyone scattered. I took my place under Dov's arm and helped guide him away from the blazing underground hideaway. His breathing steadied as we moved deeper into the covering of trees.

"What's going to happen now that the storehouse was destroyed?" I asked. I had been hyperaware of watching for anyone following us. Shadoe had been too busy trying to salvage the storehouse to notice my departure.

"There are more storehouses. We only lost that one," he said. "We'll be okay." He gave me a small smile and lifted some of the weight off my shoulders until his arm was simply lying across them.

This would have been nice, walking through the forest with Dov, under ordinary circumstances.

"Dov?" I meant to tell him everything, but when I opened my mouth, I said, "Why did you do that? Run back in?"

"He needed help." He looked confused.

"You didn't know who he was, only that he was trying to hurt us. But you ran in anyway," I said, looking to the ground.

"Auluria, it's about doing what is right. Yes, he was fighting against us, but that doesn't mean he should die."

"It doesn't mean you should die *for* him either," I protested angrily, stopping in my tracks.

I hadn't realized how upset I was that he just risked his life like that.

"*I'm fine*, Auluria," he tried to convince me.

When I didn't speak, he turned to look at me. His face was serious, voice dropping to a tone so low I could barely hear him.

"Auluria…why did you brush me away earlier?"

No answer. I looked at my feet.

"Auluria, why have you been avoiding me?" He stepped closer.

I looked away.

Silence.

Then I felt myself being pushed backward several steps until I landed against a large tree trunk. Dov had my left shoulder in his hand. He stretched his other hand up the trunk above my head and leaned in toward me, his eyes searching mine as he drew close. *Too close.*

He lingered there, inches away from me. The silence made my heartbeats stretch apart.

"Tell me to stop," he breathed and inched his face closer to mine.

I gasped and watched him move. I tore my gaze away.

"Hmm," I whimpered, barely audible. I felt myself breathing heavily. I was desperate for air.

"Tell me to stop," he repeated, his voice low and husky. He moved closer.

"Hmm," I mumbled more forcefully, keeping my sight glued to the fallen leaves on the forest floor. I could feel him grin as I blushed and fought to keep the smile from my lips.

"Look at me," he said softly. A smile played at his lips as he moved closer and repeated in a loud whisper, full of longing, "Tell me to stop."

His words forced me to look at him. His lips hovered above mine. All I had to do was tip my head up and they would connect. I couldn't breathe.

"Tell me to stop," he whispered one last time, his breath moving a few stray hairs across my face, tickling me.

I felt my tongue dancing behind my lips, desperate to say the words that would end this torture and keep me true to my word to protect him, but they stuck behind my teeth. I prayed he would stop, even though I wanted anything *but* for him to stop, for I knew the second he touched me, I would lose indefinitely.

"Don't stop."

He closed the space between us, his lips touching mine. Fire raced through me. He smelled of smoke and his face was smudged with soot, but as he let go of my arm and reached around my waist, clutching my back, all I could think of was how right it felt to be held by him.

His hand ran down the trunk of the tree, scraping against the bark until his hand was tangled in my hair. He cradled the back of my head, pulling me toward him and deepening the kiss.

I slowly raised my limp hands from my side, skimming the sides of his waist before I ran them up his chest and to his collar where I clung desperately to him, holding him against me. I leaned back into the tree and Dov leaned into me. His kisses became more desperate with each passing moment. In that moment, I was desperate too.

He kissed me until we had to pull away for air—though I admit, I thought about letting it end right then and there, allowing us to die happy.

He pulled back just enough that we could catch our breath. I still clung to his collar, clutching it in my nervous hands. He kept his strong arm wrapped around my body, brushing my hair repeatedly with his free hand. He pulled my hair in front of me, wrapping it around his fist. He let it go and untangled it before pushing it back over my shoulder, then pulled it back between us once more.

His eyes danced as he smiled at me, revealing the most gorgeous dimples I had ever seen in my life. His breathing forced my hair back in puffs. I was happy.

He grinned at me and laughed. I laughed too.

"I've been wanting to do that since the day I met you," he said breathlessly.

I laughed again. So, this was what joy was like.

"And tell me, was it worth it?" I asked. Lowell would have been so proud of me for flirting with him, had I not been serious about it.

"Oh, it was worth it." He nodded enthusiastically. He closed his eyes and bent his head, nuzzling my hands still clutching at his collar with his strong chin.

I sighed.

He whipped his head up to look at me when he heard me.

He stared so deeply at me, like he could see everything inside of me. He leaned forward and kissed me three more times. Twice forcefully and passionately, the last time tenderly and slow.

"You're beautiful," he sighed, pulling back slightly.

Suddenly embarrassed, I turned my head and gave a short laugh.

"You are, Auluria. You're beautiful."

"Dov…" I started to protest.

He took my chin in his fingers and forced me to look at him. Biting his lip, he looked harder into my eyes. It made me melt. I knew I was blushing.

He stayed there for a moment, frozen in time, watching me. Finally, he pulled back, releasing me from his manmade prison against the tree. My hands released his collar and momentarily dragged down his strong chest, feeling everything under his shirt. I nearly stumbled when he let go of me.

"Let's go," he said softly and waited for me to take my place under his waiting arm.

I slipped under his shoulder and held myself to his side. I watched him as we walked, letting him guide me as we moved. The smudges on his face even looked handsome.

We stopped by a stream so he could wash off the soot. Dov dipped his hands in and splashed the water on his face. Noticing he had missed some of the dark smudges, I cupped my hands and guided the water to his face, wiping off as much as I could. I tried to be gentle, knowing he was still injured, a thought that didn't occur to me when I was kissing his split lips only minutes before.

Dov reached up and caught my hand as I worked, fastening on to my gaze. I felt myself blush again. This time I didn't look away. I had never felt this way with Shadoe.

He let me finish and took me back under his arm. It was soothing, listening to the birds' chatter as we walked by. All too soon we found our way back to the house.

Chapter 5

"BERWYN?" DOV CALLED AS WE ENTERED THE HOUSE.

"What?" he answered from around back.

"There was a bit of a situation today," Dov called back. "One of the other groups found the storehouse today. We all got out, but we had to torch the place."

"Good," he said coolly. He seemed more relaxed today and less violent. "How much did we lose?"

"I'll check in with Silas tomorrow. We had only just arrived and I didn't get a good look," Dov reported.

Berwyn nodded before turning to me.

"Still want to stay with us, little girl?"

"Well, I don't want to leave," I replied.

"Suit yourself." He shrugged before walking away.

"That was different," I said quietly, looking at Dov out of the corner of my eye as I watched his brother walk away.

"It happens sometimes. He gets angry, but usually he's pretty good at keeping it in check."

"And beating you is 'keeping it in check'?"

"There was a reason behind that, Auluria, you know that."

"And did he have good reasons for the other times too?" I baited him.

I struck a nerve, but he didn't lash out at me. "It's not as bad as you think it was, Auluria. Can we drop it, please?

"Fine," I agreed. "So now what?"

"Now we find out who it was that broke in," he stated.

Another day, another secret to keep from him.

I knew who it was. I wanted desperately to tell him right there on the spot. He trusted me and I wanted to earn that trust. But I also knew that secret was deadly. I needed to wait until I was sure it was safe.

"You know what we need? Something fun," Dov announced, pulling me back to the present.

I gave him a questioning look as he started across the room. He stooped to pick something up, ducking behind the row of cabinets and out of sight.

"Dov?" Berwyn said, entering the room again.

"Yeah?" He popped back up from behind the wall.

"Come on," Berwyn said, motioning as he walked out the door.

Dov started to say something, disappointment spreading throughout his face. He sighed, shoulders sagging.

"I'm sorry," he whispered as he moved past me toward the door. "I promise we'll do it later."

Now *I* was disappointed. I didn't like seeing him go. And I wanted to know what he had planned for us.

I walked around the house for a bit. Finally, I sank onto the couch and curled my feet up under me. I tipped my head to the side and rested my arms on the couch's arm. If I breathed deeply I could smell Dov on his pillow.

I used the solitude to try to make up my mind about what to tell Dov. I needed to figure out how and when to tell him. I prayed he wouldn't be too angry.

Eventually, I fell asleep on the couch, waiting for his return.

Two more days passed before he resurfaced. I was starting to worry, but Eden told me everything was fine. At first, she avoided me, but by the end of the first full day, she came around. By the second day, she tolerated me spending time with her.

"What's your story, Eden? How did you end up here?"

"Same as you, I suppose." She cast me a disparaging glance.

"Meaning?" I pushed, waiting for an answer. She didn't respond.

"Either *you* can tell me, or someone else can," I said casually.

"Fine," she grumbled.

"A few years ago, I was taken from my home. I was there alone and these men broke in and dragged me out. I fought, but I wasn't strong enough. They were going to take me to the camps.

"Some men saw and tried to help me. It gave me enough time to sneak away while they were fighting.

"Unfortunately, not too long after I escaped, the black-market traders found me. Turns out, they were the ones who had freed me. They tracked me down and took me to the underground markets."

I must have looked confused.

"You don't know about the underground markets, then, I see," she continued. "They do all sorts of selling down there, but there's a big market for illegal brides. They find girls and auction them off to be hidden wives. Some of the rich men pay for extra wives because they want more children.

"You know how the higher-ranking officials are deemed more worthy if they have more heirs because it 'leads the way for the people to do that same and rebuild the population,'" she quoted the Society.

"A lot of the time, the rich men don't go themselves, they send discreet workers on their behalf. That, however, makes it easier for unwelcome people to slip in." She grinned.

"One of the men who works with Berwyn got a hold of me and another girl. He told us he was helping us and brought us to a meeting at the storehouse. They questioned us, which was terrifying, but eventually they cleared us.

"Berwyn was one of the men to question us." Now it made sense.

"He took a liking to me after I had been cleared. He tried to help me.

"One of the women took me in, but it only lasted a few months before Berwyn and I were married. He trained me to fight alongside of him. I mirror him in every way, though he's much stronger than me."

"Why do you do this, Eden? You could be happy living your life with Berwyn. Why fight?"

"We're working to help people. And if you hadn't noticed I have a bit of a temper. This is a positive way of letting it out.

"And anyway, there's a lot we can *accomplish,*" she said bitterly.

She might have been right about it being a productive outlet for her anger, but I could see more anger than she was referring to just boiling right under the surface. She was still holding a grudge and with each day it was growing stronger.

"I can see you want to help people, but there's something else," I said. "You want revenge."

"If I can get revenge for what happened to me, then yes, I'll take it. It's not my main goal, but I won't turn it down if the opportunity presents itself either," she confided.

"I don't blame you," I said, finding a new appreciation for Lowell's cause. He had a mission too.

"Honestly, I'd like to burn those camps to the ground, close the illegal trading markets, and hang all of the men who forced people there," she said mostly to herself.

"What about Berwyn? What's his story?" I asked.

"He's recovering from the loss of his father. Griz started the group years ago. He peacefully helped so many people. Then one day an operation went sideways," she started.

"What does that mean?" I asked, brushing back my hair.

The door opened and Berwyn and Dov walked in. Eden stopped talking.

"Hungry, boys?" she asked, back to her cool self.

We made dinner for the group. It was mostly silent as we ate. Dov sat next to me, occasionally, reaching below the table to find my hand. He would brush his hand against mine, tickling my skin, before he pulled away.

It was getting dark when we went our separate ways.

"Dov?" I said when we were alone. "Can I ask you something?"

"Sure," he said, taking a seat near me on the couch.

"Eden and I were talking."

"You what?" he interrupted.

"Eden and I were talking."

"Eden *talked* to you?" he interrupted again, surprise in his voice.

"Yes," I confirmed.

"Well…now you're stuck here forever. You're going to have to *marry* me," he joked, "if *Eden* likes you. I don't think you have any choice," he chuckled.

I smiled, unsure of what to do with myself.

"Go on," he prompted, growing serious again.

"She told me her story," I regained my balance.

"*Ahh*, the kidnapped and out for revenge while simultaneously doing good story. I know it well. She probably left out a few details about her temper and slightly violent tendencies though. You have to watch those."

"Uh-huh. Anyway, she was about to tell me more about Berwyn and what happened to your dad when you walked in."

"I see. Berwyn doesn't like talking about it."

"So, what happened? I know something went wrong, but what was it?" I asked, leaning against his shoulder. I wrapped my fingers around his muscular arm and waited.

He sighed, giving in.

"There was this kid who joined the group. His father died and he wanted to be a part of bringing down the Society. He was good, smart, and he rose in the ranks. My father really liked him and put him in leadership.

"But the kid was bent on a more dramatic type of revenge. He tried to talk Dad into being more violent, causing some 'real' destruction, but Dad wouldn't have any of it. He *thought* the kid was under control.

"Then one day, one of the missions got a little violent. The kid liked it and made the situation worse. Dad reamed him out for it. Secretly, the guy formed a small alliance within the group of people who wanted to perpetuate the problem.

"They sabotaged a mission and people died. Dad tried to take everyone underground, but the guy made sure the Society knew it was Dad's group.

"Eventually they found him, tried him and hanged him, even though it had nothing to do with him.

"He kept the rest of the group safe though," he added.

"And then Berwyn took over."

"Yes, Berwyn took over."

"What happened to the kid?" I asked.

"He disappeared. Formed his own group." He shook his head.

"Do you know where he is?"

"He's around somewhere. We run into his guys from time to time," he offered.

"Dov, I have something to tell you," I started.

"Oh hey! We never had our first date," he suddenly realized, grinning at me mischievously.

"First date?" I asked curiously. "That's what you were doing before you left?"

"We can do it now. I promised you we would."

"It's dark," I protested.

"Then it will be a moonlight picnic," he said, crossing the room and pulling a basket out from a cabinet.

My heart started fluttering. Shadoe had never taken me on a date. Shadoe had never done anything but work with me. Missions hardly counted as dates.

We walked back to the pond, only the crickets serenading us. Dov set out a large blanket near the water. The moon sparkled off the glimmering pond.

Fireflies blinked around us, swirling as we set out our food. A heron swooped down from a tree and glided into the water gracefully.

"What would you like, Auluria?" Dov asked kindly, motioning to the spread before us.

I reached for the strawberries. "Would you like one?" I asked, holding one out for him.

He took it from me, intentionally keeping from touching my skin. He sat back a distance away and leaned back on his hands as he ate. He was tempting me.

I watched his chest rise and fall under his dark blue shirt. Even in the darkness with only the moonlight, his eyes shone a radiant blue color. He offered me bits of other foods and we ate quietly together.

"Why are you so far away?" I finally asked.

"Don't like it?" He raised his eyebrow to me. "Do something about it," he said slyly.

I stared at him for a moment before rising to my knees and

crawling toward him. He waited, unmoving, as I tucked myself against his chest. He shifted his arm just slightly so it was covering my shoulder.

He rested on his free hand and I leaned into him.

"I need to tell you something Dov," I finally forced myself to say. I hated that I was about to ruin this moment.

"Okay," he said. He leaned back, falling to the blanket, dragging me with him so we were lying side by side looking up at the moon and stars.

I had always felt secure under the stars. The way they sparkled and came out of hiding every night, it just comforted me.

I breathed him in. I tried to will myself to speak. He waited for me.

After what seemed like an eternity, I spoke.

"I haven't told you everything," I said so quietly I wasn't sure if he heard me.

After a minute, I felt his hand squeeze my hip. He was waiting.

"I," I started, "I'm really glad you found me that day." I chickened out.

He smiled and it pierced my soul.

"Me too," he whispered, nuzzling my hair.

Chapter 6

WE HAD SLIPPED BACK INTO THE HOUSE UNNOTICED A FEW HOURS AFTER we left. We just stared at the sky until we nearly fell asleep. He roused me and half carried me back to the house.

I barely slept once we got back. I couldn't stop playing that moment over in my head.

I should have told him. It was my chance...my chance to be honest, and I was selfish instead, wanting to keep him all to myself.

I promised myself I would find a way to tell him.

"Auluria!" Berwyn said loudly as he walked into the room.

I nearly dropped the glass I was washing. He had never used my name before.

"Yes?" I asked, trading a look with Dov.

"Come with me," he said and walked toward the door.

I looked to Dov; he stared wide-eyed at me. I saw Eden nod her head to me. Dov turned to look at her and when she nodded to him, he indicated that I should go.

I set the glass down and followed him outside.

We walked in silence for a very long time. I fidgeted with my clothing as we walked.

"You like my brother," he stated, catching me off guard.

"He's a good man," I said, unsure of how to reply.

"You will be the death of him." I reeled back as if he struck me. *How had he found out?*

"He's going to be in a situation where he has to choose between himself and you and he'll choose you. Or even worse, you and the group, and he will, in the end, choose you. You're going to get him, or all of us, killed."

He didn't know.

"That's not my intention, Berwyn," I started, but he cut me off.

"If he wants to be with you, I can't stop him, but I can tell you that I will not let you be the destruction of him. He's the only family I have left, and even though it may not seem like it, I *do* look out for him."

"I know you do." Then I added quietly, "In your own way."

He glared at me but said nothing.

"If you're going to be staying here, you are going to have to learn a few things," he said, quickening his pace.

"You'll have to learn how to protect yourself. It may not seem like it, but even Dov knows how to fight properly.

"You'll also be given a job. You'll have to contribute if you want to stay with us.

"The group must vote you in, so you'll need to start making a good impression now. You'll need to be helpful. Today you'll be meeting our leadership—minus Dov, of course."

So, *that's* where we were going.

"We have a stop to make first," he announced. "Do you know where we're going?"

I thought for a moment before it hit me, remembering Eden's words.

"I have to be interrogated," I said as calmly as I could.

"Smart girl," he answered. "Here."

He handed me a dark sack.

"Put it over your face. You can't see around you, but you'll be able to see directly down so you don't trip," he supplied.

I obliged, lifting the foul-smelling sack over my head. We walked for much longer than I expected. Berwyn guided me around trees, walking directly in front of me. I followed the sounds of his steps. He warned me whenever dangers lay in my path.

Taking my arm, he guided me into what I imagined must be a smaller version of a storehouse. The underground room was cool and damp. The smell of soil was strong and earthy as it assaulted my senses.

The light was dim in the room but my eyes adjusted quickly when he removed the hood. Two men stood before me. Berwyn nodded as he left.

Silas stood against the wall, leaning against his shoulder. He watched me closely, never smiling. The other man was bigger, older. He strode confidently toward me.

"I hear you lost your memory, Auluria. May I ask if you've gained it back?"

"Yes," I said, slightly unsure of myself. Shadoe had practiced interrogations with me. I could confidently answer any question these men asked me, but I knew it was better to come off as being unsure and intimidated by them.

"Good. I'm glad to hear that," he said, a cold edge in his voice.

He placed his hand on the table and leaned on it. After a moment, he pulled out a chair and sat facing me. Watching me, he waited. Silas stayed in his spot against the wall.

"Tell me, Auluria, how did you come to find us?"

"Umm…well, I was out in the woods. I was being chased. Dov found me and he hid me from the men who were following me."

"I see. And who were those men following you, Auluria?"

I didn't like how he kept using my name. Over and over, with every sentence. *Auluria. Auluria.*

"Guards," I answered, casting my eyes downward in shame. I needed him to believe they wanted to take me to one of the camps.

"And what did they want, Auluria?" *My name again.*

"To take me to the camps, I think," I replied, still looking down.

"But you outran them?"

"No, Dov found me. He hid me."

"How did you get so far in the woods before he found you, Auluria?" he questioned, trying to pull apart my story.

"I hid a few times and they ran past me. I went in a different direction, but they managed to catch up to me."

"Where specifically did you come from, Auluria?"

"I lived in town. My parents died when I was young and my aunt took me in. I lived with her until she died."

"Then where did you go?"

"I stayed in her house until it was too dangerous. I did small jobs around the town in exchange for food." It was true enough. I just left out the part about Lowell.

"And then the black-market traders found you?" he tried to trick me.

"No. There were no black-market traders. It was the officials who tried to take me." I frowned.

"Yes, the officials." He nodded.

I saw Silas twitch. The change was about to happen.

The man before me threw his fist against the table, rocking it.

"Who do you work for, Auluria?" he shouted at me, rising out of his chair.

I widened my eyes and sunk backward into my seat.

"Tell me!" he demanded.

I shook my head, choosing not to speak.

I cast my eyes over to Silas as he uneasily stood by the wall. He lifted himself a few inches toward me, but stayed relatively put. As I watched him, I saw the conflicted look in his eyes. Dov was his friend. He wanted to believe in me because he believed in Dov, but he also wanted Dov to be safe and he didn't know if he could trust me.

"Please," I silently mouthed to Silas.

His lips formed a tight line and he almost imperceivably shook his head no.

I looked back to my interrogator.

"Look at me when I talk to you," he yelled. I shook my head up and down.

"You didn't find us by chance, so why are you here?" he asked through clenched teeth.

Somehow, I imagined this would all be more intimidating if it were Berwyn doing the yelling. It might be a challenge for me.

The man stood and walked around the table. He grasped the chair around me and spun me to face him.

"If you ever want to leave this room, start talking," he hissed at me.

"Enough," Silas said, tearing himself away from the wall.

The man set my chair back down and walked to the doorway. I could see his shadow as he waited, just out of sight.

"Auluria," Silas said, cautiously asking me to look at him.

"Silas," I said glumly, not quite making eye contact.

"You remember me then," he stated.

"Yes."

"Then you know I'm friends with Dov. You need to understand I want what is best for him. If that's you, then I'm happy for him. But if you're trying to hurt him, I won't hesitate to take you out of the picture. Do you understand?"

"You're a good friend," I said, finally looking him in the eye. I meant it.

"You need to talk to me."

"I tried to talk to that other man, but he didn't want to listen," I said.

"He wants the truth."

"I gave him the truth. I think you know that."

He smiled, the corners of his mouth just barely tugging up.

"All right, so let's try this again."

He went through all the questions again. Where did I come from? Why was I here? How did I find them? What did I want?

I repeated each of my answers.

Finally, the man walked back in, knife in his hand. Silas glanced at him, eyes large. He shook his head no, but the man jutted his chin out, forcing him back to the sidelines.

I breathed heavily as I watched him. I knew he wouldn't hurt me, but I had to show fear.

He circled the table, walking behind me out of my line of sight. I locked eyes with Silas. The man dragged a finger along my hair, pulling it around to the side. I shivered for real.

The knife felt cold against my neck. The dull edge was pressed against my throat, but to someone who wasn't aware of this tactic, it would have been frightening. He inched it along my skin, making me wince.

Dragging the blade down my shoulder he started speaking.

"If you are lying to me, Auluria, you will feel such pain as you have never known. You see, the Baers are family to me, and if you hurt them, no one will be able to find the pieces of your body." He grinned.

"I'm not trying to hurt them," I said bravely.

"I don't believe you." He knelt in front of me.

He used the tip of the knife to lift my chin to look at him. His icy eyes greeted me. At that point, I had enough of the accusations. Lifting my foot, I kicked his chest hard, knocking him into the table. He cursed and started toward me, fist in the air.

Silas raced forward and caught his hand, forcing him to stop. I scooted the chair back as far as it could go and jumped to my feet.

"Berwyn!" I shouted, hoping he was nearby.

He stomped into the room, looking from me to the men.

"She's cleared, Berwyn. She's cleared," Silas shouted, still holding the man back.

I hurried to Berwyn's side, hoping for protection.

He fixed his gaze on the man, still trembling with anger. After a moment, Berwyn relaxed and nodded to Silas.

I breathed a sigh of relief. I had made it.

"Calm down. She's been cleared," he announced.

Silas watched me as I left. His eyes offered an apology as I walked away.

"That was cruel," I said as I staggered away from the underground interrogation room.

"Everyone has to go through that," he stated simply.

"With a *knife*?" I demanded.

"No, most don't have to be threatened with weapons."

"So, why did *I*?" I asked angrily. I folded my arms over my chest as we walked.

"Because of Dov."

My head snapped up to look at him. My glare demanded more information.

"You're going to get him killed. And if that was your intent, I wasn't going to make it easy for you," was the only explanation he'd offer.

"You will not tell Dov about this," he instructed.

He told me a bit about each of the leaders as we walked to meet them. I tried to remember names when I could—not to help Lowell, though I should have, but to make a good impression when I met them.

I was so lost in my attempts to memorize facts that I didn't see when we were approaching a public area. We had at some point walked out of the woods and into the outskirts of a town.

Many people that worked with the Baers lived in town to keep up appearances. A few of the people that worked for Lowell did as well, though they were mostly spies and contacts.

People bustled about, and suddenly I realized where we were. Many times, I had come to that very spot, often with Shadoe by my side. This was a place for the rebels and the misfits to hide and trade and plan while blending in with the lower classes of Society.

We darted in and out of the walking masses. I followed closely behind Berwyn as he skillfully maneuvered the streets.

"Well, look who we have here," a voice bellowed from behind us.

Berwyn froze and turned slowly on his heels, seething.

"Lowell," he growled.

"And hello to you too, Berwyn," Lowell grinned, stepping toward us.

Berwyn reached in front of me, wrapping his arm around me, and shoved me behind him. I realized he was trying to protect me. I peeked around his strong arms at my cousin facing him down.

"Get out of here Lowell, before I do something I'll regret."

"And scare the little lady? I don't think so, Berwyn." He motioned to me.

"She is none of your concern!" He glowered. "Leave her be."

"Berwyn," I said quietly.

"Stay back," he said in a rough, hushed voice.

"You never did quite manage to figure out how to protect people, did you, Baer?" Lowell laughed maliciously.

I held on to Berwyn's arm, forcing him to stay in place. He tried to shrug me off, but I held tight until Lowell walked away.

"See you 'round, Berwyn." He waved over his shoulder, still laughing.

"Berwyn…" I started.

"You are never to go near that man, Auluria. Do you understand me?"

I looked at him, horrified. "Why?"

"He killed our father."

Chapter 7

THE REALITY OF HIS WORDS SANK INTO ME, SENDING A CHILL DOWN MY spine. The kid that had worked with Griz's team, the one that went violent and turned against him…that was my cousin.

He had lied to me. The Baers didn't cause those deaths, Lowell did.

My head spun as the pieces fell into place. No wonder Lowell wanted the blame on the Baers. He blamed them for kicking him out. It all made sense.

I thought back and remembered bits and pieces from my child-hood when my aunt was still alive. As I thought back, I could finally understand the changes I had seen in my cousin over those years. I watched a man break and then break again.

I saw him come to leadership and form his own group. And then he brought me into his fold. He trained me. He *used me* for this. But he never counted on me questioning him.

I could barely focus as I met the leadership with Berwyn. He kept a close eye out for signs of my cousin, though he was long gone. I knew Lowell had purposely stepped into our path. It was a reminder not only to Berwyn, but to me.

Dov knew something was wrong as soon as he saw us approaching the house. He met me on the path and led me away, leaving his brother to finish his work after he announced I had been cleared.

"What's wrong?" he asked when we were far enough away.

"You didn't tell me about Lowell," I spat out.

"Yes, I did." He looked confused. "Wait, I didn't tell you his name..."

"He was in town today. I thought Berwyn was going to attack him, I had to hold him back."

"Auluria, Lowell is a very bad man. You can't go near him ever again. Do you understand me?" He sounded concerned.

"*You* don't understand *me*," I pleaded with him to listen. "Dov, Lowell is my *cousin*."

The color drained from his face as he processed what I said. He released his grip on my arms and took a step back.

"What?" he asked, shaking his head.

Then he mumbled, "The blond man from your flashback."

"Dov," I said, stepping toward him, "I didn't know."

He pulled away from me.

"How could you not have known?" he gaped.

"He didn't tell me..." I pleaded.

"*Tell* you? *Tell you?*" he shouted, scaring me.

"What *did* he tell you? *Huh?* What did he tell you?" He moved toward me and I stepped back, stumbling.

Tripping over a rock, I fell hard, still looking up at him, never taking my eyes off him.

"Dov, I didn't know. I had no idea, please, believe me," I begged, tears springing to my eyes.

"You are going to tell me everything," he said in a low, quiet voice that sent more fear into me than when he yelled.

I nodded ferociously.

"I tried to tell you. I just…I couldn't bring myself to do it," I whimpered.

I told him everything. How Lowell was the cousin who cared for me when I had no one left. How he took me in and trained me. How I worked for him, knowing no other life. How I thought I was doing the right thing because he was family. How I didn't know anyone had been hurt.

I told him of Lowell's plot to overtake the Society and pin it on his family. That I was supposed to find my way into their lives and get Berwyn to trust me. When we discovered he had been married, I was to target Dov, but I found the good in him and couldn't. I told him how I tried to push him away but he pulled me back in. How I couldn't escape him. I told him of my promise to protect him.

He didn't scoff when I told him how he made me feel, but I saw the brightness in his eyes dim. He didn't believe me. He thought my tears were an act.

"Dov, please," I begged, sobbing. "I never wanted to hurt you. I tried to tell you."

"When, Auluria? When you were kissing me? When you were making me fall for you? *When* were you going to tell me?"

"Last night," I said softly.

"When you said you had something to tell me," he mused softly.

I nodded.

"I just…I didn't want to destroy that. I wanted that moment…for us."

"There is no *us*, Auluria. You lied to me." His words crushed me.

I felt my chest cave in on itself. I couldn't face him. I looked away, tears slipping down my face.

"So now what? You report back to your cousin?" he asked, walking closer.

"No. I have no intention of helping Lowell, especially after finding out what he did to your family already," I said, suddenly feeling stronger.

I stood up and pushed my hair back.

"Then where are you going?" he asked.

He had banished me.

"I'll find somewhere," I said quietly.

"It's dangerous out there," he said quietly, still not able to look me in the eye.

"I'll be okay," I said. "Dov…I'm so sorry."

I stood and turned to go. I wanted to run as far and as fast as I could. I wanted to escape my heart breaking. I tried to leave with the little dignity I had left after throwing myself at his mercy. I walked ten steps before I heard him following me.

"It's dangerous. You shouldn't be out here alone," he said.

He kept ten paces behind me. We didn't speak again.

He despised me and what I'd done to him, but he was a gentleman to the end.

The birds I had loved listening to on our walk only the day before now seemed to be playing a dirge. Their sad and lonely songs filled up the newly opened space in my heart.

I walked without direction, simply moving along until I found somewhere to go.

"You don't have to follow me," I said without looking back—*unable* to look back. "I'll be fine from here."

"Hush," he said quickly.

I turned and started to speak, but the look on his face forced my silence. I listened as he looked around the woods.

A twig snapped and we turned to face it.

The silence was eerie. They rushed forward from all sides, surrounding us. Three men ran at Dov, the remaining two toward me. My hands flew to my face to protect myself as the attack came.

"Run!" Dov shouted, but it was too late.

I heard the sickening thuds, but one of the men had wrenched me around so I couldn't see it. He tried to get my arms pinned behind my back, but I wriggled free. I landed a punch to his face, sending him backward.

The second man kicked my feet out and I toppled to the ground. I kicked back hard, causing the man to curse and backhand me. A scream escaped my lips as he connected.

I heard a loud grunt as Dov lifted a man off his feet and pummeled him to the ground. He hit hard and the air rushed from his lungs. Dov punched one of the men—I recognized him as Jake, from the first day I met Dov.

The man I had hit was back on his feet, coming toward me. Before he could reach me, Dov was by his side. He reached around his neck, cutting off his air supply. The man fell to the ground, unconscious.

Dov wrenched around to face the man holding me. I tried to get away, but he held fast. Dov ran at him, tackling him to the ground. I went down with them, but could roll away as they tumbled over one another. Dov straddled him and slammed his fist into his face, blood splattering with each blow.

"Dov!" I screamed as I watched Marty lower himself and run full force at Dov.

He looked up, but I was already in motion, running as fast as I could toward the man targeting Dov. I crashed into him from the side, sending us both toppling over. He rolled on top of me, pinning me to the ground. He looked at me, wrapping his hand around my throat, and then looked to Dov.

"Don't move," he commanded.

"Marty, let her go," Dov said, hands raised in the air.

"I don't think I will, Dov." He moved his hands around my throat, applying enough pressure to scare me.

"Marty, stop!" Dov begged.

"Get back!" Marty yelped.

Dov retreated, locking his terrified eyes with me.

It was hard to breathe with Marty on my chest.

Marty looked back to me, keeping Dov in his peripheral vision. His eyes traced my hair, my cheek, and settled on my lips. He smirked viciously.

Taking one hand away from my throat, he traced the line his eyes had followed. His hands crept through my hair, over my temple, and along my cheek. He grinned when he reached my mouth, but continued dragging his rough fingers along my chin, across my neck and out onto my shoulder.

A burst of air escaped his nose as he latched onto my collar and ripped it, exposing my shoulder.

"No!" I heard Dov say, but his voice was so far away as panic set in. At some point, my gaze had drifted to the man straddling me and I watched as he looked hungrily at my exposed skin.

"Marty, you leave her alone, or I'll…"

"What?" Marty looked up and shouted. "You'll do what? Because I will kill her before I let you have her back."

Dov stopped, sinking deeply onto his heels. I could see he was fighting everything within him to not run to us. He looked terrified and angry and wild.

"A *golden girl*," he said stroking my hair, "for a *golden boy*."

He looked to Dov to make sure he was watching.

"Get up, darling," he bent low to my ear and whispered.

He started to stand, pulling a knife out from his belt. He held it to my throat as I rose to my feet. I saw Dov suck in a breath of air. I could feel the anger radiating off him even from far away.

"Now don't get any ideas about being a hero, Dov. If I even *think* you're following us, I will kill her." He grinned. "Come along now, darling," he said to me.

We walked backward, away from Dov. I watched him breathing heavily, trying to contain himself. I prayed he would stay put and not come after me, and he did. Marty would surely kill him if he ever saw Dov again.

I stumbled as we walked, the knife at my throat making it hard to move. We trekked through the woods, and Marty whispered cruel things in my ear.

"Looks like it's just us now, darling," he growled quietly. "You and I are going to have a great time together."

He had to be around Dov's age, but he seemed so much older and more menacing to me in those moments.

He breathed heavily into my ear as we walked. "However, do you get your skin so soft, darling?" he cooed.

I cringed with every word. I wished for some rescue. Dov. Shadoe. Even Lowell or Berwyn. But I was alone.

I fought to find a way to get the upper hand without him slicing into my neck. I tried to reposition myself as we walked, hoping to find a more protected angle.

I considered trying to play along but knew that wouldn't end well for me. I let him guide me through the trees and hoped for an opening to escape.

We hadn't been gone more than a few minutes, but there, being subjected to the torture of knowing what was coming, it seemed like a lifetime. I felt myself panicking and tried to calm myself.

I fell fast. Something had crashed into us and sent us careening toward the earth. The knife landed in the soft ground, protruding like it had been jabbed into a heart.

The hand released me, trying to get up and find the weapon, but Dov had him pinned to the ground.

"Go!" he shouted and I ran several paces away.

The two struggled on the ground.

"Don't you *ever* touch her again!" Dov screamed as he hit Marty's face.

He grabbed the man's collar and lifted his head off the ground just enough to slam it back down into it.

"If you ever come anywhere near her *ever* again I will kill you, do you understand me?" He released his anger until the boy stopped struggling.

Marty managed to find the knife with his hand and raised it toward Dov. Dov snatched up a rock and connected with the side of Marty's head. He lay motionless on the ground. Dov felt for a pulse.

"He's alive. For now," he said quietly, taking the knife and turning toward me.

For a moment, he stood there facing me. His shoulders sagged up and down with each labored breath. His mouth hung open, craving oxygen. The knife lay limp in his hand at his side. His feet were spread apart, his stance forcing him to stay upright.

Then he crumpled toward me, caving in on himself and running as fast as he could to me. He crushed me in his arms. He buried himself in my hair and I could feel the tears work their way through my golden strands.

Finally, he pulled back just enough to breathe. "Are you all right?" he asked, his voice thick with emotion.

I held him, trying to be strong.

"I'm safe," I said.

When he didn't let go, I clung to him.

"Are you okay?" he asked in a coarse whisper.

"Dov," I whispered back.

He released his grip on me, pulling his face away. He bent and rested his forehead on mine and breathed me in.

He found his voice again.

"Did he hurt you?" he asked in a strong voice.

"No, you got here in time," I said, realizing he must have run the long way around and looped back on us to have surprised us like that.

"Are *you* hurt?" I asked, suddenly concerned.

"I'm fine. It's you I'm worried about."

"I see that," I stated. "Dov. Why did you protect me? After everything, why did you save me, knowing I could still hurt you?"

"I would never let anyone hurt you," he said, still not looking at me.

"Why did you protect me so fiercely?"

"Because I care about you fiercely." His words filled my soul.

"Why do you care?" I asked softly, needing to know.

"Because you are worth it," he whispered, finally looking at me.

We walked back to the house, standing near each other but not touching. He would need time to heal from my betrayal, but I had the promise that he would soon come to terms with it.

He didn't tell Berwyn about what happened.

Chapter 8

As the days went by, he resigned himself to tolerate my presence. Had he not been forced to confront his feelings for me when he saved me, he may have let me go. He always kept me in his sights but held me at arm's length.

Eventually, he warmed up to me again, though cautiously. I gave him his space. I didn't want to push him away.

"Auluria, we need to talk," he said one day.

"Okay," I replied.

We sat down at the table once he was sure Eden and Berwyn were gone. The space between us felt like a hundred miles. I wanted desperately to reach across and take his hand, but I held back.

"We need to figure out what we're going to do," he said.

"We can be friends for now, if that's what you want," I said quietly, casting my eyes downward.

"I meant about telling Berwyn," he said and I blushed, realizing my mistake.

"You do kind of work for the enemy here, Auluria," he followed up. "But that too, I suppose."

Great, not only had I assumed he would want to talk about our relationship, but I had also neglected the real problem and most likely sabotaged any chance I had of fixing the situation.

"I'll tell him," I offered.

"No, we'll do it together. But we're going to have to come up with a plan to fix it first. If you're not willing to work with us and betray your cousin, we need to get you out of here. Now."

"I have no real connection to Lowell. Apparently, I never did. I don't want to see him hurt, but I'm not going to let him hurt you either," I said, determined to make it true.

"All right then," he said thoughtfully. "We need to find out exactly what he's planning. We could feed him some false information. What were you trying to find out?"

"Locations, meetings, but mostly"—I hesitated—"your weaknesses."

"And did you find those out?" he said coolly.

"No. I don't know them."

"But *I* was supposed to be easy, right? My weakness was supposed to be you." He took my silence as confirmation.

"All right. Then we should make it look like it's working. So, in public, we'll be a couple. We'll make sure they see us together. We'll figure out something for Berwyn."

I hated knowing that'd he'd be touching me, holding my hand, walking with his arm around me, and it would only be for show. That he no longer had feelings for me. But I didn't have a choice.

We discussed the rest of the details and planned our speech for Berwyn.

I was surprised with how well Berwyn took the news. I expected fury and injury. Instead, he had flipped a table and broken some items from around the house.

Eden calmed him down and helped show him the good parts of our plans. Once he settled, he agreed to play along. Discovering he could use me against Lowell made him glow.

Over the next few days, Berwyn sent us out on several missions. These were mostly created so we would be seen together, solidifying our fake relationship.

I made every deadline with Shadoe and gave him the information Berwyn fed to me. Dov had insisted one of them follow me, watching from a safe distance, but I knew better. Shadoe would pick them out instantly, so I was alone when I snuck out to meet my handler.

I made it look like I snuck away from a food gathering trip during one of our meetings. Shadoe held me there an alarmingly long time.

"Have you found anything we can use yet? Something you can take without them noticing?" Shadoe prompted. Lowell had wanted something that belonged to each of the Baers, but in my original search, I hadn't found anything I could easily sneak out. Now that the Baers were aware, they needed me to stall.

"They notice everything, Shadoe, it's not as easy as it sounds."

"You've been able to locate things before. There must be something hidden somewhere." He sounded agitated.

"There's nothing, I searched the house," I confirmed, hoping he believed me. In truth, I never had found anything that would have helped us even before I decided to side with Lowell's enemy.

"We saw you with Dov. You've been swaying his attention?"

"Yes." I nodded.

"Good. Do you have his trust?" he questioned.

"I believe I do."

"He'll follow you then?" His rough voice irritated me. I wished he would release me so I could get back.

"He will," I replied. "He believes I have his best interest at heart. He'd never have any idea I was working with you."

Dov had always thought kindly of me until I told him of my deceptions. He had believed the best in me. Never would he have suspected I had been sent to infiltrate and destroy his group had I not told him of my cause.

"Make sure you keep it that way. We need him to do everything you say without questioning it. He needs to be absolutely devoted to you."

"He is incredibly devoted, Shadoe. Not just to me but to everything he does. Once he commits to something, he devotes himself fully to it and sees nothing other than it. He won't be a problem." I assured him.

"You're not getting too close to him, are you?" he asked, putting his hand on my arm. It was strange to have him touch me so familiarly. Shadoe rarely touched me in our time together, even after Lowell had committed us to each other. In public, he would touch me only to show his claim to me, and in private we were rarely close.

I shrugged him off, letting my anger bubble up slightly. He let his hand fall as I bristled.

"I am very aware of my place with him," I snapped. *There was nothing real between me and Dov, no matter how much I wanted it.*

"Good. You've been trained well. Lowell knows how strong you are. We know we can depend on you to see this through. Your role in your cousin's plan is critical. Without you, this entire operation would fall apart."

I weighed his words. If I simply disappeared, everything would fall apart. I couldn't, of course. I had to help the Baers fight back against Lowell.

"I know my place, Shadoe," I affirmed.

"You and I will help lead together someday, Auluria. This is how we get there."

"We're Lowell's right hands. I know," I sighed.

I refrained from glancing over my shoulder as he continued to speak, far too aware of the passing time. Everything in me screamed to leave and run back to the house tucked far away in the depths of the woods before I was caught. Instead, I stayed planted to the spot, tolerating Shadoe's insistence on running over details of the missions Lowell was running. None of them, however, were helpful to the Baers.

Each minute that passed caused me greater worry. Each minute was one more minute that something could go wrong with my plan. When my mentor finally released me, I ran as quickly as I could, praying I could make up the time.

When I finally made it back, the Baers were just walking back toward their home.

I could feel it the instant we walked in. Something was different. It didn't appear the others noticed, but something made my hair stand on end. I couldn't place what it was. I examined the room carefully, but couldn't see anything out of place. I mentioned it, but they assured me nothing had been displaced.

A smell, maybe?

I wasn't sure what it was.

I kept my eyes open the rest of the day.

"Why did Marty attack us *again*?" I asked Dov, the silence surrounding us in the house so deafening.

"What?"

"He keeps attacking you. Why?"

He shrugged. "They just do that sort of thing."

"That wasn't just for fun, Dov." He still winced every time I spoke his name. "That was personal."

"Fine," he relented. "Do you remember that girl I told you about? The one that betrayed us?"

He spat out the word *betrayed* like it was something bitter in his mouth.

"She was Marty and Jake's friend. They both had feelings for her, but she was sent off to seduce *me*." He looked at me when he said 'seduce', comparing *our* feelings to a directive.

"They hated me for it. But when she was kicked out and sent back, she was interrogated. She stopped giving them information on us, and they weren't happy. She failed, and they weren't happy. Like I said, her body gave out. They blamed us for her death, but Marty and Jake blamed *me*."

"Did you love her, Dov?" I wanted anything but to hear his answer.

"No. I never loved her. She wasn't like…" He stopped and my breath caught.

"Will they ever leave you be?"

"Probably not." He kicked at something invisible on the floor.

"You should be careful, though. Marty was going to hurt you to get to me. He thinks we're together, so he'll be targeting you. He'll do whatever he can to take you away from me."

"Too bad he doesn't know it's all a cover," I said sadly.

"Too bad," he agreed, twisting the knife in my heart.

Dov held my hand as we walked through the crowded streets. I followed along behind him. The town was busy that day. Berwyn and

Eden walked in front of us, stopping to look at different items along the way.

I knew we'd see Lowell that day. That was the entire purpose of the trip. Berwyn wanted Lowell to see me with Dov.

I spotted him out of the corner of my eye as he veered out from an alleyway. He strode purposefully over to us, walking paces behind us until Berwyn finally turned around.

"Get out of here, Lowell," Berwyn growled.

"Hello again, Berwyn. And look, the wife and kids," he grinned.

"Back off, Lowell," Dov snapped as Lowell reached for me. He stepped in front of me and shielded me from my cousin.

"A bit overprotective, aren't we, Dov?" Lowell said. "I just wanted to meet the new girls properly." His gaze lingered on me a moment before turning to Eden. "And what about this pretty lady?"

Eden looked as if she had been slapped. For a moment, something flashed in Lowell's eyes. He smiled again and pulled his hand back.

"Dov, get them out of here," Berwyn commanded.

Dov stood for a moment longer, challenging Lowell. He pushed me back and walked a few steps backward before turning around and walking Eden and I away from the scene.

Dov escorted us back to the tree line. I could see Berwyn and Lowell arguing. Eden stood off to the side, watching her husband and enemy. I had turned to watch the scene but Dov kept moving me backward until I found myself against a tree.

He lifted his hand to my face and buried it in my hair behind my head. He rested his other hand on my far hip as he leaned into me and pressed his lips to mine.

Stiffly he kissed me, and I wished he meant those kisses. They were harsh and foreign and obligated. Just when I thought he would pull back all the way, he lingered. He rocked forward and kissed me again. I'm sure it was to make sure we would be seen, but I could almost swear his kisses changed. They no longer seemed calculated and forceful, but desperate and full of desire and heartbreak.

"I think that's enough," Eden commented, but he didn't stop.

A moment later he leaned away, pulling me from the tree. He wrapped me in a tight embrace, pulling me to his chest tightly. He couldn't even look at me. *This must disgust him,* I thought painfully.

I wanted to run my hands along his chest and up into his hair, forcing him to look at me. I wanted him to talk to me, even if it was to yell at me. I hated the cold silence that often followed us.

Before the conversation came to blows, Lowell walked away from Berwyn. Dov's brother joined us at the tree line.

"Did he see?" I asked.

"He saw," Berwyn confirmed.

At least something was going right.

I silently cried myself to sleep that night. As soon as we were safely in the woods Dov had ripped his arm from around me. He fell back and worked his way to the other side of his family, separating us by what seemed like hundreds of miles as we walked.

He wouldn't take dinner with us. Dov refused to talk to me. He wouldn't look at me. Even Berwyn noticed something was wrong.

The last time I had cried like that was when Lowell told me I would eventually be marrying Shadoe. It wasn't that I didn't like him —he was a nice enough person, very cordial and friendly—but I didn't love him and I never would. We worked well together, but we were better partners than *partners.*

He accepted our fate better than I did. Or if he didn't, he never said anything to me. He had a blind faith in my cousin, though. *That,* I imagine, caused him to not even question the directive.

Dov was different. He cared for me as more than someone to complete a mission. At least, he *had.* Shadoe had kissed me a few times since Lowell had committed us, but they were dry, chaste kisses. There was no passion or feeling like there was with Dov.

Of everyone in the universe, I had to betray Dov. I would never forgive myself for messing that up.

I had nightmares during the little sleep that I did have that night.

Her hair was long, with beautiful curls. She was almost elegant, despite being so young.

I could only see the back of her head as she sat on a bench with my cousin. I watched as they talked, Lowell leading the conversation. She nodded appropriately and waited her turn to speak.

She pulled her hand away as he took it in his, clearly upset at what he had said. He tried to calm her, but she stood, preparing to leave. His next words forced her to stay in place. It took time, but he convinced her to sit again. She crossed her arms and looked away.

"Who is that?" I asked my aunt that cold afternoon.

"That is a friend of Lowell's. Come over here and help me fold these," my aunt chastised.

"Why are they arguing?" I questioned, retreating to her side to assist her.

"People argue sometimes. Lowell fixed it; he's very good at fixing things. Now, don't you be so worried about what your cousin is doing." She waved her hand in my direction, refocusing me to the task at hand.

"Today, I have to go into town. You need to stay here. Don't leave the house," my aunt continued.

"I won't," I replied, setting down the sheet we had folded. I knew better than to leave the house alone. It was far too dangerous outside.

The young girl with Lowell stood, less frustrated, and left. Lowell watched her walk away, clearly no longer as upset as he had been.

He walked away in the opposite direction, not bothering to say goodbye to his mother.

When we had finished, my aunt left to go into town. I knew she was having trouble affording food and we had spent the entire morning looking for items around the house to sell or trade.

The dream jumped ahead several days and I found myself sitting at the table as Lowell burst into the room, yelling something about someone being gone. The blonde girl.

I woke up confused, but with a haunting sense of familiarity. I had forgotten about the blonde girl that day. I knew Lowell had been angry about her, but I never did know why. Something about the girl wouldn't leave my thoughts. I never saw her face, but the dream continued to nag me. She was important to Lowell, I could tell. He never treated any of the girls in his fold like that; had never reacted to them that way. It was such a strange dream. I wondered if it had been only that…a dream I made up and not something I saw once. Perhaps I would never be sure.

I eventually fell back into a restless sleep. When I woke up in the morning, it was with the faint remembering of something long ago.

Everything was fuzzy as if I were still in a dream. I pictured something just out of view, not quite yet in focus. I tried to pull myself together enough to decipher it.

I was still puzzling it out when Berwyn stepped into the room, Eden following on his heels. Dov refused to look at any of us when we sat down to eat, instead keeping his eyes focused on his plate.

As we were cleaning up I gasped.

"That's it!"

Everyone stopped to look at me, even Dov.

"I figured it out. I knew something was wrong the other day. When we walked in and I said something was wrong..." I tried to remind them.

"It was a smell. I knew that smell. It was one of my handlers' trainees. He always had a specific scent to him. I hardly ever saw him, that's why it took me so long to place it." They looked at me.

"He was here," I connected the dots.

"But nothing was missing."

"Something must be, Eden. He was *here*," I insisted.

"Fine, we'll check again." It was the first thing Dov had said since yesterday in town.

A knock pounded on the door.

"Dov!" a voice shouted.

"Silas?" Dov stood and went to the door.

Silas pushed past him. "Berwyn, good. You're both here. Something's happened."

"What is it, Silas? Berwyn asked.

"In the towns," he said. "Something is happening in the towns. We should go."

The men stalked toward the door.

"Wait!" I shouted. "It could be a trap."

"We have to go, Auluria! People might need help," Dov said bitingly.

"Fine, I'm coming too."

"No, stay here," he commanded. I continued walking toward them.

"She's not going to let you stop her, Dov," Berwyn warned. Dov stopped fighting.

We ran through the trees. I could barely keep up with the strong men in front of me. Eden ran with me and we reached the clearing a few moments after the boys did.

What we saw was horrifying.

THERE WAS SMOKE EVERYWHERE AS BUILDINGS BURNED IN THE CENTER of the town. I knew at once it must be the government buildings. This had to be Lowell.

People ran, screaming as they tried to escape. Loud explosions ripped through the air and shook the ground. Although, I barely heard it through my labored breathing and pounding of my heart.

We ran into the center of the chaos, splitting up and looking for ways to help. People ran past us, pushing us out of their way. I stumbled and fell into the side of a building. Berwyn lifted me upright and continued.

The government workers were being attacked from all sides. Their uniforms made them stand out, creating easy targets.

"For Griz!" A cheer went up in the crowd. Fists pumped in the air.

These people weren't working for Griz's group though. They used his name to create violence and chaos and place blame on the family that had taken me in.

I ran to the men I used to work with, begging them to stop. They only laughed at me or called me a traitor. They said Lowell would be furious, but I didn't care.

I ran from group to group looking for someone I could trust, or convince, or get information from. As soon as they discovered I wasn't helping them, they turned on me. No one dare lay a finger on me for fear of retribution from Lowell, but they refused to help me.

I watched as men poured out of a building, fire creeping up its walls. Shadoe ducked around the corner. I followed as quickly as I could.

"What are you doing here?" he hissed when he saw me.

"Shadoe, this is wrong. You have to stop," I insisted.

"Stop? This is just the beginning, Lur, you know that."

"Lur?" a new voice questioned.

"Well, if it isn't the *target*," Shadoe challenged, dropping the act. He pulled me behind him, standing between me and Dov.

"Shadoe, let go." I tried to wrench away, but his grip held firm.

"Let her go," Dov demanded.

"She's not yours, lover boy," he said cruelly.

Realization crept into Dov's devastatingly handsome face as it dawned on him that Shadoe was more than just a handler. He looked betrayed all over again and the conviction nearly caused me to crumble.

"Let her go," he repeated in a steady, strong voice.

"She was never one of you, Dov."

"She was never *yours either*," he spat back at him.

The metallic scent of blood was in the air, mixed with smoke and burning flesh. Everything seemed so still as the two men faced each other down despite the violence going on around us.

I leaned forward and whispered quickly into Shadoe's ear. "Long con."

I kicked the back of his knee, knowing if he thought I was playing Dov, he'd let me leave with him. He hit the ground and stayed there, giving us enough time to escape. He would find out about my betrayal soon enough.

I launched myself at Dov and we careened around the corner of the building. We ran until he stopped me, pulling me tightly against a wall.

"No!" A piercing scream filled the air. Eden.

Dov moved faster than I could and was around the building first. Eden was still screaming as she raced toward a falling building.

"He's in there!" she screeched to Dov.

He overtook her and raced into the flames. She stopped before she reached the door, unable to see inside. I took her arm and moved her several paces back. We searched through the orange-lit smoke, but saw no signs of them.

Eden clung to my arm, tears streaming down her face. I realized I was crying as well. She shouted her husband's name repeatedly.

An eternity passed. People ran around us; we didn't notice any of them. Eden and I looked up just in time to see something fly through a window above us. We pulled away as a chair crashed where we had been standing.

Two figures immediately followed, landing hard on the ground. Eden ran to their sides. I was too shocked to move. I had been trained to escape situations like that, but I'd never thought I'd have to jump from a second story window. I couldn't imagine Dov or Berwyn had been trained to take that kind of fall.

I ran to help Eden as she pulled Berwyn to his feet. I caught Dov's hand just as he lifted himself off the ground. He gave me a grateful look that quickly transformed into something hard and cold when he realized he was holding my hand.

Fire licked up the wall from the window they had just vacated. It crackled and hissed and suddenly the cacophony of the fight erupted around us once again.

Eden and I each supported one side of Berwyn as we fled. Dov hobbled along on his own, leading the way. I looked back just in time to see one of the masked men catch my gaze. If Lowell didn't know already, he would know soon.

"The Society sent in more guards. They killed some of the rebels and took others for interrogation," Silas informed them the next day.

Berwyn and Dov had been committed to the couch since their fall. Eden and I hovered, trying to help.

"They're blaming us," Berwyn said angrily.

"It's not confirmed, but yes, sir, they are."

"This was all a part of his plan. Your cousin…" he growled at me.

"This wasn't *her* fault, Berwyn," Eden snapped at him, cutting off his tirade.

"I'm so sorry," I said, shame filling my voice.

"You didn't do this, Auluria," Dov said without emotion.

My eyes bounced to him. It was the first time I felt like I wasn't being blamed for everything going wrong. Relief washed over me.

"They'll be coming for us," Berwyn said. "We have to move."

Eden sighed and placed a tender hand on Berwyn's shoulder. I'd never seen her so gentle before.

"Where do we go?" Silas asked.

Berwyn shook his head. "This is just like before," he muttered.

"We go underground. For now. We're better prepared this time," he said resolutely.

"We go underground," Lowell had said. I thought back to several months earlier.

"We go under just long enough for them to blame the Baers. Then we come back, stronger than ever, and take out the Society. Or what's left of the Society after the Baers are done fighting back.

"If they think they crushed the people responsible, they won't be looking when we attack and we'll catch them unprepared. We'll have the upper hand and we'll emerge victorious."

"What does it mean, to go underground?" I had asked.

"We have safe houses. We'll stay there. People won't know to look for us there. We just need to have the right evidence to point the Society toward Berwyn and his people. After all they've done, everyone is better off to have them out of the way."

"What did they do, Lowell?" I questioned in my blind ignorance.

"They betrayed us, Auluria. They're the reason so many plans went wrong. They're the reason people died. They've been destroying lives for years. They refuse to listen to people who know what they are talking about, and everything has fallen apart because of them," Lowell seethed.

"Good riddance. They must go. You see that, don't you?" he guided.

Chapter 10

Eden and I packed as quickly as we could. We took only what we thought we'd need the most. Silas put the word out for everyone to gather at the safe houses. Most of the group lived in town and blended in with the rest of society. It would be more dangerous for them to escape. Those whose identities were safe enough to keep were instructed to temporarily cut ties and stay put.

Berwyn leaned on Eden as we walked through the forest to our new hiding place. Eventually Dov dropped back with me, keeping an eye on me.

"You were with him, weren't you?" The agony in his voice nearly froze me in place.

"Not the way you think," I said. "I never chose to be with Shadoe. Lowell said it was to be, so it was. Shadoe trained me, we were partners on missions, but we were barely even friends."

"Did he kiss you?" He sounded afraid to ask.

"Only a few times, but none of them were real. Not like how we kissed."

His jaw clenched and I saw his body freeze up. I wanted to turn to him, but I knew he would only push me away.

"I never wanted him, Dov," I added quietly. "I only ever wanted you."

He slowly inched away from me, not saying anything else. I couldn't blame him.

The safe house was small. Berwyn said there were dozens of them placed among the woods. Most were larger, made to accommodate large groups of people. Since Berwyn was the leader and would be the target of the search efforts, he was isolated, and by extension, so were we.

There was a large mattress and two small mattresses placed on the floor. Dov bent and dragged one to the far wall when we entered the room. I was on the opposite side, a chasm of mistrust placed deep between us.

There was a fully stocked storeroom just off the main room. When we arrived, we found they had stored enough for at least two weeks of coverage.

Even so, Berwyn decided we needed to get as much as possible before the Society decided the attack was the Baers' fault and came looking. We only had a small window of time to move if we needed to.

The four of us crept out of our hidden space. Dov was forced to walk with me as Berwyn and Eden went to a second location. Growing up I had loved silence. I even loved being silent with Dov, knowing we could exist together without needing to talk, but in that moment, I hated it.

The new storehouse wasn't too far off. We silently descended into the earthy room. Silas was waiting for us.

Dov waved me off and turned to talk to his friend. I focused this time on finding supplies. We had brought extra sacks with us to transport our goods in. Once I filled a bag, I slung it over my shoulder. Eventually, there were too many to fit, so I held them on my arm, weighing me down heavily to one side.

As I reached for some dried meats, I felt the weight lifting off my left arm. Silas stood next to me, handing some of the packs to Dov, helping him put them on. He was still recovering from his second story fall.

I felt the corners of my mouth tug up in a half-hearted smile of thanks. Silas had a strange look in his eyes. Disappointment? Kindness? Pride? Realization that I wasn't who he thought I was? Anger?

I didn't know. But I knew Dov had told him of my confession.

"You know," I said.

"I know," he replied.

"I'm sorry I misled you," I offered meekly.

"I trusted you," he said bitterly.

"I know." My voice came out a whisper. Dov still didn't turn to me.

"But you're with us now?" Silas asked.

I looked up at him. "Yes," I said decidedly. "I won't help Lowell knowing what he did."

"Okay."

"Okay?" I said taken aback.

"Okay."

"That's it?" I questioned.

"That's it."

That was it. No questions. No comments. Just acceptance.

Whether it was for my sake or just for Dov's, I didn't care. This man would not hold my transgressions against me.

"Thank you."

The walk back to the safe house took much longer with our heavy packs. Every snapping twig, every rustling leaf seemed louder.

"Auluria…" Dov's unexpected voice startled me. I looked over as we walked.

"Silas told me about the interrogation," he said. "I'm sorry they threatened you like that. They never should have scared you with that knife." The dark-haired boy seemed genuinely concerned over what they had done.

"They didn't scare me, Dov," I said as gently as possible "I knew it was coming."

"Oh," he said, unprepared for my words. Then he realized. "They trained you."

"It might have…scared me…but I knew they wouldn't hurt me, Dov. I knew they wouldn't hurt me because you wouldn't have let them. They were testing me to protect you, but they knew if they hurt me, they'd have to deal with you. You would never let them get away with actually hurting me, so they'd never even try," I said, trying to explain how it was my faith in him that spared me that fear.

"I knew they'd never hurt me, because I knew you'd never *let* them. Because that's the kind of man you are. You're kind and selfless and merciful. You're a good man. You're an incredible man," I concluded.

His eyes softened a bit as I spoke, though he said nothing. But it gave me hope. Hope that maybe someday he'd come back around and give me another chance.

"Dov," I said after a bit, "I know you can't now, but someday, will you…be able to forgive me?"

He stopped walking and looked at me.

"I *do* forgive you. I know why you did what you did, Auluria. You were trying to protect your family. I get that."

"Then why can't you look at me? Why can't you stand to be near me?" I pleaded more than I meant to.

"Because you hurt me. I don't want to go through that again, Auluria. I *can't* go through that again. Not with you." His voice broke on the last word.

"I won't hurt you again," I tried. "I don't ever want to hurt you."

I tried not to cry. I wiped the tears that fell away quickly, hoping he hadn't seen them.

"I know," he whispered.

"You deserve so much better than I gave you. Dov, I'm so sorry." I tried to keep my voice under control, but it was a losing battle. I stopped before I was defeated.

"You deserve better too, Auluria," he said softly after a moment. "Better than I could give you."

Every step, every snap, every rustle was painfully loud.

"I could never find anyone better than you," I finally said.

He closed his eyes but continued walking.

"Just…just tell me that someday we can at least be friends again." I breathed.

"We can be friends again," he answered.

His words made my heart swell and break at the same time.

Chapter 11

WE DROPPED THE SUPPLIES OFF AT THE SAFE HOUSE BEFORE GOING BACK out. Berwyn and Eden were waiting when we arrived. Their location was the closer of the two, giving Berwyn the shorter route to walk. Eden was organizing the room as we left for our second trip out to gather supplies.

Berwyn sent us to collect more water. We had several containers roped over our arms. Despite being light, they stayed quiet when they bumped together.

Dov made an effort to smile at me when he looked to make sure I was okay. True to his word, he was going to try to get to a place where we could be friends again.

We both perked up when we heard a loud noise several yards away. The noises kept coming closer. Before we could move, a young boy stepped out from behind a bank of trees. He saw us before we could move.

"Run!" Dov said, dropping the containers.

He grasped my hand and pulled me away, jumping over tree stumps and roots. The boy turned and yelled behind him.

The chorus of noises rose louder as a group of men joined him. Several of the men rode large horses, their hooves stamping as they stood waiting for instructions.

I heard the dogs barking before I saw them. Their masters followed them, clinging to their leashes. The crowd saw us, focusing on our movements.

Dov's head whipped back and forth as he monitored the men and where we were running. We were far enough away that we wouldn't lead the guards back to the safe house, but in the middle of nowhere, we were trapped.

The dogs came first, howling and barking at us. I knew if they reached us, it would only be moments before they tore into our flesh. I clutched Dov's hand tighter, willing us to disappear into the leaf-covered forest floor.

He lifted my hand and stretched it across his chest until I found it resting in his far hand. As he released me into his distant hand, he wrapped his inside arm around my waist and pulled me along, gripping me tightly. Despite the terror surrounding us, I felt safe in his strong arms.

We ran as quickly as we could, the green leaves blurring around us as we ran. The sunlight filtered through the trees, casting a dappled shadow on every place our feet touched.

Dov lifted me as I slipped on the moss of a rock we were climbing. I shrieked as I felt myself fall. His grip kept me securely at his side though, and he righted me, pulling me forward.

As if we had found our way back to the day we met, Dov and I found ourselves face to face in front of a wide stream. Without hesitation, he ran for it. Our feet left the ground at the same time and we sailed through the air. The wind whipped my hair back, in what I imagine must have been a gloriously golden arc; a banner waving and leading the guards on behind us.

We landed on the other bank, barely making it. Dov and I stumbled and fell, rolling before coming to an abrupt halt. I heard the dogs whining on the opposite shore. They did not follow us.

We stood and began to run. I checked behind us just in time to see the horsemen approaching.

"The horses," I shouted to Dov. He nodded and moved us faster.

Soon the horses had made the leap across the water. Their feet pounded behind us over the uneven terrain. Their beats synced with my heart rate, moving faster with every moment.

The horses approached us from behind. I felt them drawing nearer until they were right behind us. One scooted up alongside of me, the man reaching down and pulling me from Dov's arms. He dragged me across his lap, pinning me in front of him. The man used one arm to restrain me and the other to direct his horse.

I expected him to slow, but instead, he kept charging forward, eventually circling off to the side. I heard Dov yelling in the distance.

The other horses had not been as fast as the beast beneath me. Under normal circumstances, I would have thought him extraordinary, but when he refused to respond to my gestures, I knew how well he really had been trained.

I prayed the other horses were not fast enough to catch Dov as he ducked under branches and wove through the small spaces between the trees.

The man slowed the horse, still using great force to keep me in place.

"Let me go!" I pleaded. "You're hurting me."

"Too bad, princess. We don't take kindly to traitors." His nose tickled my ear uncomfortably.

"Neither do we," I heard Dov's voice say, followed by a loud thud. Once again, I marveled at how Dov had known exactly where to cut us off and catch us.

The man wrenched to the side, his grip slipping on me. Dov's aim was true and the rock hit the man on the side of the head giving me enough time to elbow him. Between the force of the rock and my elbow, he fell, foot tangling in the stirrup.

Dov launched himself in the air, occupying the remaining foothold. He kicked the animal's side and it leapt forward, his master trailing behind him.

We rode for several minutes, the man eventually untangling himself and falling behind. When we reached a large cliff, we dismounted and sent the horse running off into the distance. Dov and I heard the other horses somewhere behind us.

Together we scrambled up the cliff, the rocks biting into us as we moved along. We reached the top only to find a second, taller cliff stretching out before us, hidden by the trees. Dov offered me his hand and boosted me up. He followed along behind me.

I pulled myself over the edge and waited for him to join me. Glancing around, I looked for the best direction to go in. I heard a gasp of air and ran to the edge.

Dov was hanging from one hand, the rocks under his feet giving out. Dangling precariously, he looked up to me and shouted, "Keep going."

He was insane if he thought I'd leave him there. He tried to swing his body up to catch another handhold but his feet slipped as he tried to find a stable place to push himself up.

"Hold on!" I yelled.

The trees that had blocked our view now offered us the protection of concealment. If I could find a way to get Dov over the edge, we might have a chance at escape.

A broken tree branch looked like the best option. I dragged it over to the edge and lowered it down, warning him to be careful.

"It will pull you down. No," he said, refusing to take it.

"No, it won't, now take it."

"I will not have you getting hurt because of me."

"Dov, you've broken my heart, I really don't think there's too much else you can do to me," I said without thinking. I instantly wished I could take it back.

"And anyway, I'm trained, so come on!" I didn't mention my training had never included anything like this.

He swung his arm up and caught the branch. He pulled back and pushed up with his feet. Though he slipped, the branch was enough leverage to start his ascent. He climbed and I pulled. Together, we worked his way up until he sat on the ground beside me.

"Thank you," he said when he caught his breath.

"We need to go," I answered, pulling him to his feet.

We ran as far as we could, knowing they were coming after us. I prayed they wouldn't think we'd be able to climb the dangerous cliffs. When no one approached us, I decided they had gone another way.

"Dov, stop." I stumbled, pitching forward. "I can't breathe."

As I gasped, he slowed us and lowered me onto a large boulder. He sat beside me, arm still wrapped around my waist.

"Are you okay?" he asked.

I nodded, out of breath.

"How are we going to get back?" I asked.

He shook his head.

"Do we even know where we are?"

"No, I don't think so," he responded.

"What do we do?"

"We find shelter. Those men will give up in a few hours and then we can try to find our way back," he suggested.

He rose to his feet. I must have looked terrified because he came back to me.

"I'm just going to look around. I won't leave your line of sight," he said, trying to comfort me.

I nodded, but I didn't want to.

He moved around in a large circle. He studied the ground, the trees, anything he could find.

"I think we should go this way." He pointed.

I stood and followed him, letting him guide us over the decaying surface. We walked for another few minutes before finding a large overgrown mass of a bush. The leaves were dense. The stems and branches formed a barricade around us, opening in the middle, almost like a little nest just for us.

"You did really good out there today," he said as we settled.

"You too."

He sighed and leaned back on his elbows. I did too and we looked up at the bits of light twinkling through the moving leaves.

"We're going to get through this," he said.

I didn't know if he meant being chased or if he meant *us*.

It was nearly dark before we came out of our hiding place. We took turns resting, the other keeping watch. I told him not to, but I know Dov let me sleep longer than he was supposed to.

The trees were so dense we couldn't see the stars. Only a fraction of the moonlight filtered down to us as we walked. Crickets chirped loudly as we moved. A few fireflies danced around us as we snuck through the night.

Dov helped me across a small creek, its glassy moving water shining where the moonlight hit it. He no longer held me now that we weren't running. The sound of his breathing comforted me and I relaxed as we got closer to our hiding place.

Eventually, Dov had figured out where we were and he could guide us back. We signaled before we walked in so we didn't frighten Eden and Berwyn.

"Where were you?" Eden snapped. "We heard the guards."

"They passed right over us, but they didn't find us," Berwyn informed us.

"Thank goodness," I said.

Dov explained how we had been spotted while we were out. We never had accomplished our goal of gathering more supplies. As he lowered himself onto his mattress I could see he was in pain.

I looked at him, hoping he'd let me help, but he shook his head. I stayed on my own side, giving him space.

"Are you okay?" Eden whispered, coming to sit by me. Her skirt rustled against mine.

"Yeah," I sighed, looking away.

"I'm impressed you pulled him up. That was smart to use a branch and not just reach down."

"Thanks," I said, dejection in my voice.

"He's taking longer than you'd like to come back around, huh?"

Eden was observant.

"Yeah."

"Give it time. He'll get over it," she said, touching my knee.

Eden wasn't ordinarily this kind, and never to me. But she had warmed up to me enough to speak civilly to me, and now the almost kindness she was showing restored some faith in her humanity.

"I'm not so sure. He forgave me, but I don't think we'll ever be okay again," I lamented.

"Auluria." She looked at me. "He is head over heels for you. You messed up and you hurt him, you just have to give him a little time."

"I thought I did."

"You crushed him. So what if he needs a bit more time? Don't you owe him that?"

"I owe him everything."

"So then, stop sulking," she chastised me, the switch throwing me off. "Figure out how to deal with it and let him be. When he's ready he'll come back to you. But until then, knock it off."

She stood and walked back to Berwyn who was sleeping in the corner.

I stared at her as she left, shocked.

Eden was a complicated and confusing woman.

Chapter 12

AFTER FOUR DAYS OF BEING LOCKED UP IN THAT TINY SPACE, WE ALL started to go crazy. Berwyn and Eden fought every day. If we had had anything breakable to spare, I'm convinced it would have been shattered.

Dov sat in his corner, scribbling away at something. He rarely looked up, even during the worst part of the fighting. I waited out each verbal storm, braiding and unbraiding sections of my hair.

We hadn't heard the guards again since the first night. Eden and I stayed inside while the men cautiously checked the area. Once they had cleared it, we all stepped outside for fresh air.

It felt good to see the sunlight again. Though it barely peeked through the boughs of the trees, its spotted warmth felt good on my skin. The days were getting cooler as summer ended. I longed to be back at Dov's pond, sitting by the dancing waters with him.

It rained the day before and I could still feel the moisture in the air. It clung to my body and clothes. It invaded my golden locks and refreshed my face. I breathed deeply, letting it reach my very soul.

I wanted to touch everything, to feel the freedom the plants so carefully retained. The bark of a tree felt revitalizing under my hand. Fallen leaves sunk beneath my feet, still wet from the rainfall and the morning dew. I tickled the flowers that grew a few feet from the safe house entrance, running my hands along their undersides causing them to bounce and dance in the glorious morning.

When I turned around, I saw Dov watching me out of the corner of my eye. I couldn't bear to see him turn away, so I was careful not to let him know I saw as I continued my greetings of the environment I found myself in.

The wind picked up and blew my hair in my face, preventing me from being able to see. I struggled to tame it down. The more I tried, the more entangled I became. I was certain I heard Dov smirk. I finally managed to pull my face clear and triumphantly pushed my hair back down. It swung around my waist, hitting my opposite side before resting. I turned into the breeze and it forced my hair back for me.

I picked up my skirt and continued walking on, no longer caring who was watching. I walked as far as I dared, knowing they would call me back and be cross if I strayed too far. I gathered a few blossoms before my return.

Once we stepped out of the wind and into our shelter, I tucked the flowers in my hair. If I was to be condemned to that hole, I at least wanted a little life around me.

Eden raised her eyebrow at me but held her thoughts to herself. I still didn't want to anger her, but I think she was finally starting to get used to me.

On the fifth morning, I woke up and looked around the small room. Eden was sleeping in the corner. Berwyn was in the other room. Dov, however, was nowhere to be found.

"Dov?" I whispered.

I tried again louder, hoping he just hadn't heard me.

"Dov?"

"He's not here," Berwyn said quietly, trying not to wake his wife.

"Where is he?" I couldn't hide the horror in my voice.

"He had something to do. He's fine."

"If he's out there *alone* then he certainly isn't *fine*," I spat back.

"Go back to sleep, Auluria. He'll be back soon."

"Where did he go?" I demanded.

He glared at me, but I wouldn't stop.

"Where is he?"

Eden started to stir and Berwyn came at me fast. I wrenched backward, eyes wide.

"Do not wake her," he commanded, but didn't touch me.

"Where is he?" I whispered.

"Meeting someone."

"Who?" I inquired forcefully.

"It doesn't matter. Leave it be."

"I'm going to find him," I said, standing up and walking toward the exit.

"Oh, no you're not!" He lashed out his arm and caught my hip, dragging me back to the corner. He flung me onto my mattress and pointed his finger in my face.

"If you go out there, you will get yourself killed. You're never going to find him, and in the off chance you happen to catch him coming back while the Society is dragging you away, you know what will happen. So, sit down, shut up, and mind your own business."

I fumed in my corner.

He was right. I had no idea where Dov was. I didn't know when he left. He refused to tell me whom he was meeting, though if I had to guess, I'd bet it was Silas, which offered me a small amount of comfort. I didn't even know how long ago he had left or what direction he was traveling.

Still, waking up to find one of our team members missing was horrifying. I wished Dov had talked to me about it first, just so it wouldn't scare me so. I suppose I forfeited the right to know those things a long time ago, but still, I was there and I should have known.

Waiting has always been a hard thing for me. I'm not good at being patient. After an hour, I was frustrated. Two hours I was furious. Six hours and I was terrified. By nightfall, I was sick with worry. Even Berwyn and Eden were apprehensive.

The knock startled us all. Dov came back in, motioning us to hurry.

"We have to move," he informed us.

"It's bad?" Berwyn asked, pulling sacks from the other room out and handing them to us.

"It's bad," Dov confirmed. "They found a few of us. Lowell's men, the ones that were captured, led them to us, like we knew they would. There have been hangings. The bodies are still swaying from the trees as a warning."

We ran outside into the cool night. Dov and Berwyn led the way.

"It's not just us they are after. They've put a reward out for any rebel. They aren't even asking questions. They interrogate them and then they hang them, guilty or not. Unless they think they're better off sending them to the camps." He glanced back at Eden and me.

He gave Berwyn the names of a few of their group members who had been caught. There was a resolute hardness in his voice, though I know it pained him to talk about it.

After an hour of jogging through the trees, we came to our new resting place. Instead of a small hole in the ground, we found ourselves in one of the other storehouses. Groups of people populated the large space. Families grouped together, huddled in corners.

"We need to be with them to plan," Dov said briefly, the only explanation for the change in venues.

Berwyn and Eden settled in, finding a space on the outer edges for themselves. Dov sat near Silas and a few other young men. I looked around for a place to call my own.

When I found an empty spot near some young girls, I walked over and greeted them.

"Hi," I said tentatively. "I'm Auluria. I need a place to camp out, do you mind if I join you?"

One of the girls looked at me skeptically. The others seemed more friendly.

"Sure," one girl replied to me, moving her blanket to make room for me, "I'm Reyla. This is Katarina, Maylin, and the unwelcoming one is Sharone." She waved her hand at the girl on the end.

"Thanks," I said gratefully.

"So, you're Dov's new girl, huh?" Reyla asked.

"Something like that," I mumbled.

"Well, it's nice to meet you. Have you all been doing okay since this all happened? I know they like to keep Berwyn and Dov separated."

"We've been all right. We all made it here." I tried to be optimistic.

"So how long have you been with Dov? News doesn't always get around as fast as we'd like." The girls giggled.

"Umm...well, we're not really together right now. I've known him for a bit though. He kind of rescued me while I was being chased." I neglected to mention it had been my own people chasing me as part of a plan to force me into the Baers' lives.

"How romantic," Maylin cooed.

"Only if you count being thrown into some bushes, running

around a bunch of trees and then being attacked, yet again, by a couple of thugs, as being *romantic*."

They all laughed.

"I bet he's a good kisser though, right?" Reyla asked glancing over at him.

Before I could come up with a way to avoid answering, she added, "Is there a particular reason he's *way* over there and you're *way* over here?"

"We had a bit of a fight," I answered, hoping to end the conversation.

"And he let you get away?" She clicked her tongue. "Stupid men, they never know what they have until the girl has moved on."

"Well, there's two ways to handle that," Katarina spoke up. "Either make yourself irresistible and he'll come running to beg for forgiveness."

"I don't think that will work."

"Then make him jealous," Katarina said slyly. "Watch this."

She raised herself up and searched the room before calling out a few names. She waved the boys over to us and they obliged, coming quickly to her side.

As they walked across the room I caught a glimpse of the petite girl from the first raid. She was glaring at me across the room. Her head bobbed back and forth between watching me and watching Dov talk to Silas. When she caught my eye, she grinned wickedly at me and intentionally looked to Dov. I didn't like that girl.

"What's up with Gloria?" Maylin asked.

The girls secretly glanced in the direction of the girl who was trying to murder me with her eyes.

"She likes Dov. And she apparently doesn't like me," I supplied.

"Ahh." It made sense.

The boys sat beside us.

"Auluria, this is Ben, Carter, Gregory, and Henry. Boys, this is Auluria. She's new here."

They all greeted me politely, leaning in as they spoke. They kept their eyes fixed on me as they started asking us questions. Gregory told a joke and we all laughed causing the people around us to stare.

When they suggested we play a game, I attempted to just watch, but they would have none of it. I was forced to take part in their fun and soon I forgot where I was or why I was so sad.

"So, tell us, Auluria, how long have you been with our little group?" Gregory asked, moving a card in his hand.

"Not long. Yourself?" I retorted from across the circle.

"Always." He smiled easily and waited for Katarina to put her card down.

"Most of us grew up in the group," she added, glancing at me. "Some of our families joined more recently, like Carter's family, but we all belong here."

"Your hair is incredibly long," Ben pointed out, his eyes sparkling with mischief. "Was that how you found your way in so easily? Because it caught people's attention?"

"Of course not," I snapped before grinning. "I used it as rope to tie the Baers up and force my way in."

Gregory was the first to erupt in laughter after I winked, betraying my joke. The others joined in.

"It looks like gold, could it possibly be that you're wearing a wig made from spun gold?" Gregory asked, placing another card down and disrupting the balance of the game.

"Yes," I said as sincerely as I could. Again, they erupted with laughter.

"We should cut some of it and sell to the Magistrates," Henry added, "Then we could afford an *above ground* hiding place! And maybe some pretty things for the ladies as well."

I watched as he snuck a glance at Katarina, who had purposely looked away. She truly was good at keeping men guessing.

"Oh, don't listen to them," Maylin said. "Men love girls with long hair. I wish mine was half as pretty as your, Auluria."

"Thank you, Maylin, that's so sweet of you to say." I looked down, fighting the urge to brush my hair back out of my face. "Your hair is lovely too."

She tucked her dark brown locks behind her ear and smiled.

"Tell us more about yourself, Auluria," Ben redirected us.

"Well," I said, laying down my card. "I was raised by my aunt. My parents died when I was young."

"Did you have a good childhood?" he asked, setting down his own game piece.

"It was sheltered," I replied. "Tell me more about all of you. Did you enjoy growing up a part of the group?"

"We grew up learning to fight," Gregory said triumphantly as he won the hand we were playing. "That's why I've always been able to beat these guys. I've learned all their secrets."

"Secrets?" I said pleasantly. "Well, now I need to know *everything* you know!"

"*No!*" Henry shouted, glancing up quickly at us. The girls all giggled as he tried to recover.

"Don't forget, Gregory, we have information on you too that you might not want the lady knowing," Carter challenged him.

"Yeah? Like what? Like the time, I fell down the ravine because I was trying to get that flower for Gloria?" He paused, turning toward me. "Yeah, that's how great of a man I am…I risked my life to get her that flower."

My horror for his accidental attempt to take his own life to impress a girl was washed away as he threw me an over exaggerated wink.

"Oh, be serious, Gregory," Reyla interjected, "it was barely a dip in the ground."

"And he *still* managed to nearly break his ankle," Sharone added with a sarcastic laugh. "All for a girl who wasn't even interested in his attempts to get her attention."

She realized she had brought up the fact that Gloria was still eyeing Dov, despite me being there.

"A dip, huh?" I asked, trying to move on from the heaviness that overtook the group.

"It was a chasm," Gregory said, picking up the conversation. "Don't let them fool you. A *chasm*."

"A *chasm* is what's between your ears, buddy," Henry said, forcing even Gregory to double over with laughter.

"When we were children," Henry began, "Griz used to let us go out on missions. Nothing dangerous, mind you, but he'd send us to collect firewood or food from time to time. After the incident happened, all this changed, of course, but back then we were more free."

I tried to keep from cringing when he referred to Dov's father's death. He continued, not noticing.

"We were out working one day when we stumbled across this guy." He pointed to Carter, who nodded his head. "*Gregory* was on another one of his missions to get a girl's attention…who was it that time, Reyla? Katarina?"

"Reyla," Gregory grinned at her before swinging back to look at me as I listened.

"He nearly broke his neck that time too."

"That was my fault," Carter admitted, a toothy grin plastered across his face. "I thought they were a threat so I attacked. I won."

"You did nothing of the sort!" Gregory bellowed good-naturedly.

"Yes, he did," Henry corrected. "You may have started it, but he whooped you good. I had the good sense to stay out of it in case there were more people with him. When there weren't, I propped Gregory up and found out what was really going on. That's how Carter and his family joined us."

"I had the good sense to use my words before threatening a guy over a handful of berries."

"Could I help it if they were her favorite and only grow up on that crest?" he retorted.

"You like giving gifts, huh?" I questioned.

"All women like gifts, Auluria." He wiggled his eyebrows at me.

"Don't mind him." Reyla swatted at him. "The point is that Carter joined us. And a welcome addition, might I add, since before he came along our options were Gregory or running away from home."

I burst out laughing at the thought of these quiet, kind girls running away from the likes of Gregory trying to pursue them.

"How often would you go on these missions?" I asked.

"Every few days they would send us out in groups. Usually, the older boys had to keep an eye on us because even while it wasn't as dangerous as it is now, it was still something the adults worried about," Henry added.

"Once Griz died, everyone became more serious about our training. We were all younger when it happened. Some of us, those higher up like Dov and Silas, were trained from younger ages. The rest of us started seriously training when everything changed," Ben continued.

"Even the girls know how to defend themselves," Sharone said proudly. "We just all have our places when things happen. Mostly the men fight, though there are some women who have stronger training that work with them. We mostly defend the storehouses and safe houses."

"The battles come to us; the men go to the fights," Maylin summarized.

"I see." It was so different than Lowell's flock.

"We've been exceptional at defending ourselves though. We can get quite creative at finding ways to protect our homes and families." Reyla said proudly. I could imagine Reyla being a strong and inventive leader.

"Like the time Reyla and Katarina thought we were breaking in," Gregory started.

"You *were* breaking in," Reyla corrected.

"It was a training exercise," he threw back at her. "They were making sure the girls knew what to do and had us act as if we were attacking them. At first, they thought it was real."

"It was terrifying," Katarina chimed in.

"But then they realized it was us and it was only training."

I saw both girls smile. I really did like those girls.

"It wouldn't have been any fun if we hadn't played along." Katarina said innocently, tossing a look to Henry. He couldn't take his eyes from her.

"We may have been a little *forceful* with our defense." Reyla shrugged and put her card down.

"*May* have?" Carter nearly yelled, voice raising unnaturally high.

"Really, Carter, you shouldn't take it so personally. It's not like you took the brunt of it," Reyla retorted.

"What did you do?" I asked, unable to keep the excitement from my voice. I leaned forward, dying to know.

"It may have involved warm water."

"*Scalding,*" Gregory interjected.

"*Warm,*" Reyla repeated, "We took it off the fire once we knew it was you."

She rolled her eyes and we laughed.

"You threw water at them?" I giggled.

Katarina and Reyla looked at each other conspiratorially.

"What else did you do?" I was already starting to be able to read these girls.

"It is possible that we had a few buckets of pine sap sitting in the house—" Reyla started.

"The weather was turning," Katarina supplied.

"—and Katarina ran out the back for some leaves and pine needles."

"It was incredible," Katarina added.

"You tarred and feathered them?" I asked incredulously.

"It was marvelous," Maylin laughed. "It took them all day to get it off them. I had to help Ben get it out of his hair and I worked on it for over an hour."

"And then they had to cut the sap out," Sharone finished.

"I wish I had seen that!" I chuckled.

"It couldn't have been better if we had known about it in advance. Dov and Silas had the good sense to stay back and just send these fools in after us," Katarina laughed.

"And they truly deserved it. You should have seen what they had planned for us. They were trying to terrify us," Reyla said.

"When was this?" I questioned, picturing a young Dov and Silas standing back and watching the hilarity.

"A few years ago," Reyla said, before adding quietly, "He was just as handsome back then."

She smiled, knowingly.

"Back when it happened, I thought we were going to lose Berwyn and Dov. We all did. Dov really held Berwyn together. Of course, Berwyn used that anger of his to rally everyone and protect them, but Dov was the one that kept him from destroying everyone in his path."

And took most of Berwyn's wrath.

"He was never particularly close with any of us, but we all know he's a good man. I don't know what happened between you, but I can see neither of you are happy about it," she added quietly.

I sighed, my attention jerked back to the group as they roared with laughter over the way the boys had looked after their encounter with the tree sap. Gregory slapped a card down, proclaiming himself the winner yet again.

"You've got to do better than that if you want to beat me," Gregory roared.

I glanced around at the group, the girls not happy over being defeated again by the boys. I grinned and picked up my cards. I hadn't been focused on winning but I decided it was time I put some effort into the game. I won the next two rounds without contest. Gregory, Carter, Ben, and Henry looked shocked. The girls grinned at me triumphantly. Shrugging my shoulders, I gave them the most innocent look I could.

"This is such a fun game, I only wish I knew of it earlier."

Reyla and Katarina tried to suppress their giggles. Maylin was in wonder of me while Sharone smirked. If Henry hadn't been so busy watching Katarina and grinning, he might have looked as shocked as the other boys.

"Beginners luck," Gregory taunted.

"Of course," I drawled, grinning as I picked up a new set of cards.

I made sure Maylin won the next round. She glowed triumphantly when she laid down her final card.

We continued playing, loudly telling outlandish stories to each other that the group members all shot down noisily. I listened and laughed along with my new friends.

I looked up from the cards I was holding in my hands just in time to see Dov duck his head as if he wasn't looking at the group of us along the far wall. Gloria continued to glower at me silently.

The game went on and on. We played so many times we were surprised when we had to stop to eat. The boys kindly told us not to get up. They brought the food right to us, a picnic on the hard floor of a large storehouse.

Katarina shrieked when Henry knocked over his water container. She clutched at her blankets, keeping them dry. Henry and Carter cleaned up the mess, laughing and making fun of her for yelping. Eventually, she laughed with them and settled back on the floor a few inches closer to Henry.

The next time I looked across the storehouse to where Dov was sitting, he was facing me, leaning against a wall. He turned to Silas, but Silas was watching me too. He gave me a look I couldn't quite read. He never looked away from me, but he leaned over and elbowed Dov. I couldn't read his lips that far away, but he pointed at us. Dov shook his head to him, but then looked at me for just a moment before I looked away.

"Don't look now," Reyla leaned over to me and whispered, "but somebody's looking a little jealous."

I refused to look at him. If he wanted to stare, let him. He made the choice not to sit with me, so I would have fun with my new friends and if he wanted to join us, he could.

The card games ran into the night. Once the groups started settling down we had to disband so we didn't keep them up. We decided to play again the next day if circumstances allowed. By the end of the night, even Sharone seemed to accept me.

The next morning, we all lined up for breakfast. We walked the aisles on the near side of the storehouse where everything had been moved and condensed.

I felt someone sidle up next to me, but I didn't look up as I reached for some fruit far across the table. A hand rose in the air next to me, holding an apple to me. As I turned I saw Dov standing beside me, elbow pinned to his side, hand by my shoulder, offering me the fruit he knew I so enjoyed.

He didn't look at me, he didn't even turn, but he held it out to me and I graciously took it from him. I smiled even though I wasn't sure he could see me. He moved on, going his separate way as I went mine.

The boys joined us again on the floor to share breakfast. Ben and Carter regaled us with stories from their heroic past missions. Henry found his way to Katarina's side once again.

"Pst," Reyla whispered and motioned me to lean closer.

I leaned in, tucking myself to her side. She moved my hair off my shoulder and rested her chin on it as she whispered to me.

"Some of the boys want to know what's going on with you and Dov." Her green eyes sparkled as she pulled back to see my reaction.

"You know, I don't know how to answer that," I responded.

"Well, you might want to figure it out soon, because there is some interest." She waited for me to say something. When I didn't, she leaned back in. "Figure it out, or I'll ask Dov *for* you."

She giggled as I swatted at her. I knew she would never actually talk to Dov, but she did so love to tease me about it.

"What about you? Which of these nice boys is going to end up on your arm?" I asked mischievously.

"None of them," she said proudly.

"Oh? And why is that?" I raised my eyebrows to her.

"I already have a man, thank you very much. He's just not here in the storehouse."

"Now I simply *must* know," I giggled, grabbing her arm.

It was nice having female friends. I was orphaned so young and my aunt kept a very protective watch over me. Even though Lowell had women in his group that flitted throughout my life, I mostly spent time with Lowell or Shadoe in training. I talked to some of the girls, but never about anything fun or social. Lowell had his throngs of obsessed girls coming and going, but he never had anyone serious in his life, so I didn't even have those examples to see.

Reyla told me about a boy named Peter that she had known her entire life. He was tall with brown hair and green eyes like hers. He was kind to her and took care of her, but their families were separated when we went into hiding. Everyone was assigned different locations. He sounded wonderful and I was excited to meet him one day.

Some of the younger children wandered over to us when they heard us laughing that morning. Gregory's stories became more amusing each time he told them. The children sat in our laps and played with our hair. They were particularly fascinated with my long locks.

"What's your name?" I asked the little girl raking her fingers through my mane behind me.

"Jaseleen," she said softly, grinning at the ground. "I think you're beautiful."

"Well, thank you, Jaseleen. I think you're beautiful too." I thought for a moment. "Jaseleen, would you like me to do your hair?"

The young girl nodded quickly and came to sit in front of me. I brushed my fingers through her light blonde hair. I forgot how soft children's hair could be. I hummed to her as I worked, letting my fingers take a relaxing pace. I twisted little pieces back and added some small braids, creating an intricate design.

After a while, several other small girls joined us and my new friends took turns dedicating their experience to each girls' hair. The girls squealed with delight as they sat before us. Their mothers offered us silent thanks for the break we were giving them.

Silas nearly scared me when he walked up alongside of me. He placed a large pile of flower blossoms next to me.

"Special delivery," he said quietly.

I looked down to see the flowers on the floor next to me. Catching his eye, I must have looked inquisitive because he offered me a further explanation.

"He thought you might like these for the girls."

I couldn't hide my smile.

Silas grinned back. He stood to leave, but knelt back down.

"You know you're driving him crazy, right?"

"What do you mean?" I asked.

"He's been watching you since you arrived at the storehouse. He can't stop talking about you. I know he's the one keeping you apart, but just go talk to him and tell him to get over it. He wants you back."

Silas stood and threw a wink over his shoulder before he left.

"You're so lucky you get to marry Dov," said a slightly older girl who was sitting in front of Reyla.

My jaw dropped open as I turned to look at her. Before I could stay anything, Reyla jumped in, "Yes, she is."

The two giggled as I shook my head. I finished Jaseleen's hair and tucked several flowers in it. She skipped off to show her mother who waved at me from across the storehouse.

When I turned my attention back to Reyla and her charge, I found them discussing the magnetic draw of Dov's masculine features. Somehow, I had managed to tune them out while I was working and now I was even more embarrassed to reenter the conversation.

I scooped up the flowers next to Reyla and started tucking them in the young girl's hair.

"This one really brings out your eyes," I said placing it behind her ear. "Tell me, do you have a special boy?"

She shook her head and giggled. "I'm too little, silly."

Reyla finished her hair and sent her back to her family.

"It was kind of Dov and Silas to send the flowers over," she mentioned. "What do you think made them think of that?"

"I wore flowers the other day. I suppose Dov noticed."

She lightly bumped into me with her shoulder. I bumped her back, rolling my eyes, and smiled happily.

Chapter 13

BERWYN CALLED A MEETING THAT AFTERNOON. ALL THE MEN JOINED him on one side of the room. The women, even those who fought alongside the men, were left to care for the children and straighten up the storehouse. Once a plan had been decided on, the women would be brought into the conversation.

I walked with the girls around the tables filled with food and supplies. We organized and straightened every pile. Any food that was going bad was discarded.

The men stopped for dinner, putting their conversation on hold. I found Dov off to the side, waiting for his group to get their food first. I took a deep breath and walked up to him.

"Thank you for the flowers this morning. The girls really loved them.

"No problem," he said and offered me a genuine, lazy smile. His eyes told me he was telling the truth.

I wanted to hug him; to thank him for noticing. I almost restrained myself. Almost.

I closed the distance between us and wrapped my arms around his waist, pressing the side of my face against his chest. I only held him for a heartbeat, but it was enough time for him to freeze just slightly before giving in and wrapping his arms around me. I pulled back first, not wanting to press my luck.

I smiled again and turned to leave. I caught Silas's face from the food line. His smile twisted into a smirk, but his eyes cast a questioning look at one of us. He sighed and looked back down at the food table, shrugging heavily.

Silas had a lot to say to one of us.

"Silas wants to know if you did what he asked you to do yet," Maylin ran up to me after dinner.

"Silas needs to take care of *himself*," I replied. She looked as if I had struck her.

"I'm sorry, Maylin. I'm just a little frustrated with Silas right now. He's not exactly being helpful."

She looked unsure.

"He's waiting for you to go back, isn't he?"

She nodded.

"Tell him I did not and that I'm not going to do what he asked of me."

She sighed, shoulders sagging. She clearly didn't want to deliver the bad news. She walked back to him. I turned so I didn't have to watch.

"She likes him," Reyla wandered up beside me.

"Yes, I saw that." I felt myself smile a bit.

With our backs to them, we talked.

"Why doesn't he ask her out?" I asked.

"He's a lot like Dov. They don't just date to date. They flirt with all the girls, but they never commit to any of them. It takes a lot to win those two over. We were all actually pretty surprised when you did it so quickly."

I ignored her.

"How long have they been friends? Dov and Silas?"

"For as long as I can remember," Reyla answered.

"They're good together."

"They are," she agreed.

"Well, come on," I said, turning on my heels. Maylin had stepped away from Silas and I marched us in his direction.

"Where are we going?" she protested.

"To set Silas straight." I grinned.

We marched up to Silas and I halted right in front of him.

"Auluria?" he asked curiously.

"Silas. We need to talk."

"Oh, good. I've been waiting to talk to you." He grabbed my arm and spun me to the side, leading me away.

I motioned Reyla to follow us, Silas looked a bit surprised to see her when he stopped. I cut him off before he could speak.

"You should ask Maylin out," I stated. "She's lovely and she would be very good for you."

"I'm not interested in Maylin," he said. "I am, however, very interested in you and Dov. Or rather, I'm interested in getting you back together so he can focus again."

"Dov's focusing just fine," I retorted. "*You*, however, need to find something to occupy your time. If it's not Maylin, then who is it going to be?"

I started looking around the room trying to find an alternate solution.

"Auluria, we're not talking about me."

"Well, I'm done talking about me. So, choose or I'll do it for you," I said, frustration in my voice.

He shook his head, clearly annoyed with me, and started to walk away. He froze in his tracks when a shout rose near the entrance.

"The southern storehouse has been discovered!" a boy shouted. "They've taken them."

The room was so still for a moment that I could almost hear the breeze moving as the announcer moved further into the room. Someone dropped something that bounced and rolled across the floor. A collective gasp filled the air as everyone remembered to breathe again.

"No one move," Berwyn commanded as he walked quickly to the center of the room. His face was alive with checked fury. As he turned away from me, hiding his face, he looked exactly like an older, slightly taller version his younger brother.

I glanced around looking for Dov. He stood along the sidewall, looking like he was itching to join his brother. He waited to be motioned over. An angry glare from Berwyn told us both he should have followed. Silas quickly joined him at Berwyn's side along with a few of the other men in leadership I had met.

"We're going to rescue them. Most of the men will come with us and some of the women. There will be a small group of men staying here. These men will be responsible for taking care of the storehouse and the people still here. They will also be the second wave if we fail. Most of the women will stay here. All young children will remain in the storehouse. Do not argue with where you are assigned."

"Men, over here," Berwyn motioned them to the far corner. "Women, we will come find you if you have been selected to join us. You can say no if you want, we won't hold it against you."

I watched as Berwyn separated the men. He held a small group out, the group to defend the storehouse. I watched as several of the men walked away from the group going to find the women that would be involved. None of the selected women were small or young. They were clearly well trained and knew what they were doing.

"Dov." I reached out and pulled on his arm as he passed me. "I want to go."

"It's too dangerous," he said, shrugging me off.

"No, it's not. I'm trained for this, remember? Besides, this is Lowell's fault, I have to do something."

"You're right. It's Lowell's fault. But that doesn't make it your responsibility." He shook me off again and walked away.

Silas was only a few steps behind him and had heard the entire conversation.

"I'm going," I told him as he slowed near me. I forced him to stop.

"Find me something else to wear," I said, shaking my dress skirt, "or I will."

He said nothing as he walked away, but I knew he would do that for me. I knew he would do it because he had no choice. I was going whether he or Dov wanted it or not, and if he didn't help me, Dov wouldn't be happy to find I had died because I was tangled in my dress.

Twenty minutes later a pair of trousers and a shirt appeared next to my blankets. Reyla and the girls provided cover for me as I changed.

"I want to come too," Reyla announced, leaning close to my ear.

"No, Reyla, the only reason I'm going is because I'm actually trained. It's dangerous out there and there's a very high likelihood it won't end well."

"Why are you doing this, Auluria? For Dov? He'll be fine, he can take care of himself. You need to stay safe."

"Reyla." I took her elbows in my hand. "I'm not doing this for Dov.

He can take care of himself. I'm doing this because Lowell is my cousin and he got us into this mess. I have to try to fix what he did."

"Lowell is your cousin?" She sounded horrified.

"Yes," I confirmed.

I could see her trying to process the information.

"What Lowell did is awful, but I have to try to stop it, or at least help," I said. "I can't let people get hurt because Lowell framed you all. So, I'm going. And if I died, no one will miss *Lowell's cousin* here," I said, trying to ease her mind.

"I will," she announced. "I will miss you." She threw her arms around me in a tight embrace.

"Thank you, Reyla. I'll miss you too," I said, hugging her back. She was my first real friend.

"Now, you girls have to help me get to the door when it's time," I said a bit louder.

I couldn't allow Dov to see me follow them out. Once I got to the door, I could blend in with the crowd. It was night, so the world would be dark. If I kept away from him, he'd never know. I just had to make it to the door without him knowing. The second he saw me wearing anything but my dress he would know and he'd force me to stay. I knew I'd never catch up if they left before me.

As the departure drew near, the girls quietly slipped toward the doorway. It took half an hour just to cross the room without anyone being suspicious. We stood near the exit, just far enough back to not be noticed.

I felt someone behind me as I waited. He pressed something into my hand before leaving my side. Two cold knives lay in my palm. I slipped one in my belt and the other in my boot.

The men departed. I saw Dov search the crowd for me. I hid myself behind my friends, using their dresses to cover my clothing. They all waved goodbye. When Dov couldn't find me, he stalled, hovering at the doorframe.

"She's there," I heard a sad, defeated voice said. I looked across the people-formed walkway to find Gloria pointing me out to Dov.

He caught my eye and was visibly relieved to see me. He gave me a small smile and a nod before walking away. Before he left, he mouthed the words "I'm sorry" to me.

As the last few men walked out of the room, the girls pulled back and let me escape out with them. No one noticed as I ran alongside the men.

The group moved quickly, led by Berwyn. A scout ran ahead. I could see Silas searching for me but he hadn't found me yet. Dov had no idea I was among the crowd.

My plan had only extended as far as finding a way out of the storehouse, and so far, I had succeeded beautifully. If only Lowell and Shadoe could have seen my plan come together. They surely would have been impressed.

I hated that I still wanted to impress them.

No one seemed to notice as I filtered my way through the crowd, settling somewhere in the middle of the pack. We stopped at a rendezvous point where we were greeted by one of the early scouts Berwyn sent out.

The man shared his information with the group and Berwyn and Dov formed a plan. A few men had joined us from one of the other storehouses, but Berwyn had ordered most of the people to stay in place.

Berwyn walked around, separating us into groups. I prayed he couldn't see faces in the dim moonlight. He lingered in front of me and I knew he noticed. He paused only slightly, deciding what to do, before adding me to a group. I breathed a sigh of relief.

Silas was in my group and I was silently grateful I knew at least one of the people with whom I'd be fighting. Silas'ss group and Berwyn's groups were responsible for breaching the facility where they were holding our people. Dov's group and a few others would then follow behind to free the captives. I was grateful to be among the first wave. It was the deadliest of the jobs, and if someone had to die for Lowell's mistakes, it was better that it would be me.

I stayed hidden behind my groupmates. Whenever Dov came near, I ducked my head, hiding my long hair from him. He wasn't anticipating that I be there, so he wasn't looking for me. If I could blend in, he was unlikely to know.

"Did you tell her?" I overheard Silas ask.

"No," Dov said, sadness in his voice.

"Why didn't you say anything before we left?" he asked, a harshness in his voice. Silas knew I was there—he was doing this on purpose.

"I was leaving her...again. I couldn't do that to her. It will be a miracle if we come back from this, you know that. I couldn't put her through that." I wanted to run to him, but I held my ground.

"You care about her. You didn't even say goodbye."

"She knows I care about her." His voice was ragged.

"What if we don't make it back? What then?"

"She'll be okay. She's strong. She's the strongest person I know," Dov said. Silas waited, making Dov fill the empty space.

"Auluria is amazing, for all her faults, she has handled this entire situation incredibly. She helped us, she warned us, and she's trying to make things right. I haven't made that any easier on her."

"You were hurt," Silas supplied.

"But I shouldn't be ignoring her like I am. She deserves better. I just...I didn't want to go through that again, not with her. I couldn't lose her again. I couldn't survive if I lost her."

"So, what are you going to do about it?" Silas prompted. I didn't like that Dov didn't know I could hear him, but Silas was trying to make a point. I shouldn't do anything stupid.

"I don't know," he paused. "What if I can't get back to her? What if I can't tell her how sorry I am. I never should have let it get this far. What if she never knows?"

"She knows," Silas assured him.

Morning was approaching. The sky turned its tender grey color before the world was alight with color. The early morning birds started their trilling notes, piercing the sky. Soon it would be light and soon I would be discovered.

Dov and Silas walked off a few feet before splitting apart. We continued our journey into the town. The sun was just rising as we crossed over into our enemy's hands.

Chapter 14

D ESPITE MY BEST EFFORTS, I FOUND MYSELF AT THE BACK OF MY GROUP as we started toward the facility. I tried to blend in, but there's only so many ways to hide my long hair.

"No," I heard a loud whisper as we walked away.

Without thinking I looked back. Dov was staring at me, horrified. "No!" he shouted.

He rose from his hiding place to follow, but the man next to him— my former interrogator—slammed him back down, holding him in place.

I nodded to him as he struggled, letting him know it was okay. I had resigned myself to my fate, already having made peace with losing him, and gave him a small placid smile to reassure him it was the right choice.

"It's too late," I heard the man say as I turned to run.

I stopped thinking in that moment and focused only on my movements. Left foot, right foot. Watch that rock. Turn down the street. Head up. Check ahead. No one behind. Move forward. Speed up. Lift feet. Don't stop. Twenty yards. Ten yards. Ten feet. Breech the door. Wait, take out the guard.

A man ran at me, weapon in hand. I reached for my knife resting in my belt. I grabbed for his wrist with my free hand, blocking the knife from coming down on me. Before I could move, a man next to me had pierced the guard. He fell to the ground, blood pouring from his chest wound.

I stepped around him and moved closer to the entrance. A woman sidled up next to me. We stood back to back, protecting each other. "Dov's girl?" she asked. I nodded and she nodded back.

I elbowed a man in the face as he ran at us. He stumbled back as another, taller man approached. He lashed out with his foot, kicking me in the thigh. I crumpled in front of him. The woman was ripped from my side.

Alone, I found myself on the ground, reeling from a second kick to the abdomen. I groaned, trying to roll over. Amazingly I kept the knife firmly pressed into my hand.

I tried to right myself as a third blow was coming, but it never connected. Silas had tackled the man and they rolled on the dirt ground. I moved closer to help, pulling the man away from him. The man turned on me, giving Silas enough time to escape. He took him out with a knife to the back. I watched the life go out of his cold eyes.

I heard the group breaking through the entrance. I saw a guard running to the sound and I took off after him. Silas missed my arm to hold me back. I raced toward him and leapt at him. Landing against his back, I knocked the man to the ground. My fist connected with the side of his face with a sickening thud.

He rolled over on top of me, but I kept the momentum going and straddled him. The large man reached for my throat, but my knife caught his wrists. I held his neck long enough to knock him out.

I watched as the men breeched the door. I hesitated before entering. The early morning sun made everything glow golden as I cast my gaze around the scene outside. I saw the woman who had once stood with me, now dead on the ground, her eyes still open. We had lost a vast part of our small force that morning and we had only just begun.

Inside the facility, we encountered more guards. Our second wave had followed behind us and we spread out. One of the groups waited outside for the guards that would surely be coming to stop the chaos.

Some of the captives were Lowell's men. I recognized them from my training. Others I had never seen before. They all screamed to us, begging for help. Men and women reached through the bars of their cells, praying for rescue.

I searched the body of a guard for keys but came up empty-handed.

"Silas, how do we get them out?" I asked.

He looked frantically around the room.

"Auluria!" a deep, frightened voice shouted.

I turned to see a red-haired boy gesturing to me.

"Pick the lock!" he demanded, pointing to his cell lock.

"What?" I questioned.

"Pick it. Didn't Shadoe ever show you how to pick a lock?" Lowell's soldier asked incredulously.

Shadoe had never taught me, but I had seen him do it before. I looked around for something to use. When I finally found the small pieces of metal I rushed to a cell and tried to open it.

"This isn't working," Silas said after a few minutes, stress filling his usually even voice.

"Almost," I said.

Click.

The door opened.

The people ran out. Silas directed them to the exit where the runner group was waiting to escort them to the woods. I moved on to the next door. Silas was standing at the next cell trying to take the bars off their hinges.

After what seemed to be an eternity, we had set an entire room free. Someone found a key and Silas managed to open several of the other cells. People ran for their lives as we worked to free more people; ours, Lowell's and other unfortunate souls who were trapped there.

The fighting that erupted nearly caused me to jump. I heard the click and stepped back, releasing the prisoners. Silas looked to me and we both knew: they were coming.

The guards rushed into the room, seizing Silas and me. They wrenched our arms behind our back and restrained us. The more we struggled the more painful it became.

We were marched through the building. With every step, my captor held me tighter.

"The camps are lovely this time of year. I have a feeling that you won't find out though. You're going to die pretty, little, lady. But don't worry, we have a special demise for lovely young things like you."

As if to prove his point, I felt a sharp pain in my arm. Blood trickled down my flesh, inching its way toward my wrist. He blew air against the hair on my neck, moving it slowly up and down my skin, making me cringe.

Every muscle in my body tensed. This coming interrogation would be worse than the last one I went through and these people wouldn't hesitate to hurt me.

"Don't you touch her!" Silas struggled, overhearing the conversation.

They hit him between his shoulder and neck, forcing him to stumble.

"No!" I shouted, fighting to get to him.

"Let her go, she's a girl, she has no idea what we forced her to do," he tried again.

"Don't," I said, warning him to stop.

I had chosen to do this. Nothing was going to stop them anyway.

The guards formed a barrier around us. The fighting continued around us, but they wanted at least a few captives alive to be examples. Our people couldn't reach through their barrier of bodies as they made their way through the building.

As we reached the outside, I discovered the sun higher in the sky. The days were cooling down, but it was still warm enough to be nice out. The sun felt good on my skin and I arched up into it, knowing it would probably be for the last time.

I heard footsteps running behind us but I couldn't see what was happening. Silas locked eyes with me, silently telling me how sorry he was that he couldn't protect me. *I* was the one who was sorry I couldn't protect *him*.

A small explosion rocked the ground behind us. Several of the guards with us were injured. Silas moved into action faster than I did. His elbow cut into his captor's face, forcing him back. I stepped as hard as I could on my captor's foot and threw my elbow into his stomach. As I whipped around, I slammed the heel of my palm into his nose. Then I jerked back, punching him one more time. Silas took his man out and latched on to mine, throwing him to the ground.

He reached around my waist, pulling me protectively behind him. I watched for only a moment before I collected myself and turned my back to him.

"They really *did* train you well," he shouted to me above the chaos.

"I told you I could handle it," I replied.

We fought off a few more offenders before running. Several more explosions rocked around us and I couldn't help but think they were meant to aid us.

Silas hid me behind him once again as we were attacked by more guards. With our backs to the woods, if we could just rid ourselves of the men before us, we could easily disappear.

The man closest to us was suddenly flying through the air.

"Go!" Dov shouted as he tackled the man.

I tried to rush forward to help Dov, but Silas shoved me back. I watched as Dov wrestled with the man.

"Dov!" I shrieked when the man pulled the knife. Silas was stronger than I was and he shoved me toward the trees.

"Go!" he demanded, pushing me one last time before running to help his friend.

I ran toward the trees several steps before doubling back. I knew if either of them saw me, they'd try to stop me before helping each other. I kept myself hidden, waiting. Only a moment later, I launched myself toward them, striking at the man closest to me. My spare blade was in my hand, no longer hidden in my boot. He wasn't expecting me and he went down easily.

"You need to go!" Dov struggled to speak. A guard was clutching at his throat.

I picked up a large rock and brought it down to the man's skull. He rolled off Dov and I helped him to his feet.

"I'm not leaving you," I said defiantly.

Dov pulled the man away from Silas. He fell to the ground, unmoving. Silas and Dov fought off the last two men. One ran, unwilling to challenge us.

We turned toward the woods, carnage in our wake.

Chapter 15

"WHAT WERE YOU THINKING?" DOV DEMANDED WHEN WE WERE FAR enough away.

"I needed to help," I replied as coolly as I could. He was looking for a fight.

"You could have died."

"Better *me* than someone Lowell set up," I snapped, suddenly angry.

"He *did* set you up, Auluria, don't you see that?"

"Of course I see that, but it doesn't change the fact that it's my responsibility to fix his mess. I'm sorry it's yours too, but it shouldn't have to be. He did this, not you."

"Not you either," Silas interjected, but at our snapping glares, he retreated a few steps.

"Thank you for protecting her," Dov quieted, turning to his friend.

"She saved me too," he said. "You should have seen her, Dov, she set a lot of those people free. She picked the cell locks. If it weren't for her, half of them would still be in there."

The group had scattered. When the prisoners were set free, they were escorted to the woods where they ran for safety. Those that survived the attempt to rescue our people also scattered. Eventually we were to meet back at the storehouse if we weren't followed. Many of our people died.

Dov dragged his hands across his eyes. He was frustrated, grateful, worried and angry.

"It was the right choice, Dov, and you know that," I said.

He didn't respond.

We moved in silence for a few minutes.

"I heard you," I finally said. "Before the rescue. I heard what you said about me."

The realization that Silas had known washed over him.

"You knew. And you didn't tell me," he said quietly, angrily.

"I had to keep you both safe. She was coming whether we liked it or not. I knew keeping you separated was the only way of keeping you both alive."

"And he also knew making me listen to you would keep me from being reckless," I added. "Don't be mad at him. I forced his hand. He was right, we all would have died if you had tried to stop me and I came anyway."

We had successfully reasoned with him. He didn't fight us on it anymore.

We walked in silence again. After a bit, Dov let out a loud, long, ragged breath before lurching his body around and snatching me into his arms.

He pressed his forehead to mine and closed his eyes tightly.

"I can't lose you, Auluria. I can't."

He held me tightly, frozen in time.

I reached up and stroked his temple. Wrapping my free arm around him, I pulled him close.

"I know," I whispered.

He moved one hand up my back until his was touching my neck and shoulder. He pulled me into the hollow of his neck, leaning down to place his head in mine. He hugged me as a child would hug his mother after being away from her for a long time. Dov clung to me, clutching me closer still. The weight of his entire body was on me, giving all his worry, stress and terror to me. I took it gladly.

I cradled him in my arms, my broken love.

"We need to keep moving." Silas broke us apart.

Dov breathed in, remembering himself, and lifted himself away from me. He kept me tucked between him and Silas as we walked, protecting me from any oncoming dangers.

At some point, he noticed the cut on the fleshy part of my forearm. The long, shallow slice had since stopped bleeding and was now crusted over with deep red. Both Silas and I kept quiet about how it came to exist. I was grateful he spared me that conversation.

Every noise alerted us as we walked back to the storehouse. We didn't know who had survived the rescue attempt. None of us had seen Berwyn after the initial assault.

Dov heard the change in the environment first. He stiffened beside me, listening. Silas and I heard it at the same time and turned to look.

"Run!" a voice called to us. A tall blond man came crashing out of the bushes toward us.

He tackled something in a bush at our sides. A guard fell beneath him, tumbling from his hiding place. We had walked into an ambush. The man wrestled with the guard, a blur of motion I could barely follow.

Silas ran to his aid as Dov scooped me behind him, scanning the entire area, pinning me against his back. A fist collided with a face, but I couldn't tell whose because Dov had turned me around in his effort to secure the perimeter.

When I was finally facing the attacker once again, both he and the man lay lifeless, draped over the tangled roots of a large tree. Silas stood, closing his friend's eyes and joining us again.

"Who was he?"

"His name was Peter," Silas said quietly.

That blond boy, tall and strong and brave, had saved us. He had given his life to protect us, something he didn't have to do.

"Wait," I gasped.

Both boys looked at me. "Was he dating Reyla?"

"Oh, Auluria, I'm sorry. Reyla is your friend," Dov sighed as he realized the connection.

"Oh no," I breathed, stepping backward.

My heart broke for my new friend. The man she loved was dead. She was alone and she didn't even know it yet. She was alone, and it was partly my fault.

All I ever brought was misery.

"This was not your fault," Dov said as if reading my mind.

"I know." I was unconvincing.

"He saved us all. He would have done it for anyone. Peter was a good man."

"Auluria," Silas interjected, "we'll help you tell her. She won't blame you for this."

"I know she won't. That almost makes it worse," I said quietly.

I walked over to Peter's still form. I sank gently to my knees by his side. It was easier to function in the trousers Silas had procured for me than in one of my dresses. I reached gently around his neck and unclasped the medallion that lay crooked on his chest. I placed in it my pocket for Reyla.

"Thank you," I whispered. "She'll know what you did."

An even more oppressive air hung around us as we continued moving toward the storehouse. Peter's death had cast a lingering shadow over our escape. We all knew we had lost people in the rescue attempt, but this was more directly personal to us all.

It was nearly dark when we finally found ourselves nearing the storehouse. I was exhausted from the trek, and so were the boys. My arms hung lifelessly at my sides, weighing me down.

Silas led us in, Dov following after me. The entire storehouse fell silent. A collective sigh rang out, several people rushing toward us. I let someone slip a blanket around my shoulders and lead me down the incline into the main area.

I felt myself being guided to the floor and I didn't resist. My legs gave out below me as I settled onto a blanket. Dov and Silas rested next to me. Several others who had left with us had already returned and were waiting with us. The group surrounded us, asking for answers, wanting information, and offering their assistance.

We all needed time. The three of us sat silently, remembering the details of the day. Many of the rescued were among us, resting quietly on the floor. The little girl, Jaseleen, ran up to me and threw herself in my arms. She let my tears fall in her hair as she clung to my neck. I stroked her locks and rocked her until she was nearly asleep.

Slowly my tears ceased and I found Eden by my side. Jaseleen awoke and ran back to her mother after petting my arm one last time.

"Berwyn's okay," she said quietly. "He's just not here. He had to help another group."

I could see the relief on Dov's handsome face. I was grateful too. He might not treat Dov the way he should, but Dov loved him.

Eden lifted my arm from my lap, inspecting my wound.

"Later," I said quietly, indicating I would explain at some point.

People still straggled in, having escaped the guards and made their way back. Silas and Dov relayed the information we could give the group. They told us what they knew. Once the group had given us some space, I motioned Reyla over.

"Are you okay?" she asked, worry written on her face.

"I have something to tell you," I said, tears threatening to break once again.

She sat in front of me and let me take her hands in mine.

"Reyla, something happened." My voice broke.

She studied my eyes, processing what she saw. Confusion, questioning, understanding, realization.

"Peter," she whispered.

I nodded, tears rolling down my face. Reyla's green eyes filled and poured over. I reached for her and held her as she sobbed. Once we calmed, Silas filled in the missing information. She held me tighter. Dov and Silas watched us, pity in their eyes.

I gave her Peter's necklace and she held it tightly in her hand. We fell asleep next to each other, still crying together over the loss. The last thing I saw was Dov placing a blanket over me.

Chapter 16

EVERYTHING FELT FUZZY WHEN I AWOKE. I FOUND MYSELF CURLED around a tangled blanket. I was facing Reyla, her face still wet with tears, though her breathing was deep.

I moved to untangle myself from my cloth confines only to find my hand pinned behind me. Dov's hand was placed in mine, our fingers woven together. I smiled, pain coursing through my facial muscles.

When I successfully freed myself, I crept away from the people I cared about. Making my way over to where Eden slept, I knelt by her.

She opened her eyes as I gently touched her shoulder.

"Eden?" I whispered. She inhaled deeply and sat up, nodding.

We scooted away from as many people as we could, trying not to disrupt their sleep.

"So, what happened to your arm?" she asked, turning my wrist in her hand.

"A guard got me. Silas and I were caught and they decided they wanted to frighten me. It's nothing."

She gave me a skeptical look but kept quiet.

"Dov saved us."

"You're lucky. If they had succeeded, you would have been in a lot of trouble. Getting caught is always bad, but being a pretty young girl is much worse, especially if they think you're a leader."

"They think I'm a leader?"

"You set all those people free. You were one of the few women there." Eden cocked her head at me. "They think you're a leader. And if they ever find out you're connected to Dov or Berwyn or even me, it's going to be bad for you."

"I suppose you're right," I replied, considering her words.

"I'm impressed you're still wearing *those*," she commented, gesturing to my clothing.

"Oh," I said, glancing down. "I was so tired I didn't even notice."

"Makes it easier to work in, doesn't it?"

"It really does," I replied. "I take it you've tried it?"

"On more than one occasion." She looked around the room at the people starting to wake. "You might want to change before they notice."

I took her advice, preferring my long flowing dress to the trousers anyway. Walking back to my resting place on the floor, I procured a bowl full of food for us to eat. I settled my skirt around me and set the bowl down just as Reyla and the boys were opening their eyes.

"Thanks, Auluria," Silas mumbled, rubbing his eyes.

Dov reached out and took an apple from the bowl.

"Reyla, you have to eat," I said soothingly. "Please?"

I forced her to eat, though she clearly didn't want to. Katarina, Maylin, and Sharone came and brought her back to her place by them. They sat soothing her, rubbing her back and murmuring soft words to their mourning friend.

"You handled that very well last night, Auluria," Silas assured me.

Dov offered me a kind smile and I felt more at ease.

"Do we have a plan yet?" I asked.

They turned to look at me, unsure of what I meant.

"We got our people back." I paused. "Well, some of them, but what are we going to do now? The Society is coming for us and they aren't happy."

Just as I finished speaking, Berwyn walked in, two men flanking him.

"Dov, Silas." He called, motioning them.

I stood with them. Instinctively Dov reached for my hand and pulled me along.

"No," Berwyn said when he saw me.

"Yes," Dov insisted. "She's lived with us, ate our food, slept in our house, she's fought with us, and she's protected us. She is a part of this and she stays."

They stared each other down, Berwyn giving Dov that terrifying look. I was so afraid he might strike him that I nearly started trembling. In the end, Dov won.

"We know what Lowell planted. You were right, Auluria." Berwyn turned to me. "They were in the house that day."

Dov looked to me apologetically.

"They stole some of your father's belongings. The ones you had hidden away in your house," one of the men said to Dov.

"We didn't think to check the hidden compartments," Dov murmured. "Nothing else was out of place or missing."

"Griz's paw," Silas said.

"His what?" I was confused.

"Dad always wore a chain around his neck with a medallion on it. It was a bear paw…because his name was Griz Baer. It was his symbol of sorts," Dov explained.

"They hung it with a confession saying it was retribution for hanging Dad," Berwyn explained. "They started a war using our father's name."

"That explains why they're being so quick to hang us." I hadn't meant to speak out loud. The men looked at me and suddenly I felt like a child who had spoken out of turn.

"So, what are we going to do?" Dov asked, deflecting their looks from me. "If we don't fight, we're siding with the officials. If we *do* fight, we're taking responsibility."

"We have to draw a line somehow. We need to find a way to show it was Lowell, not us, who started this violence. But we also need to protect our people," Silas reasoned.

"Exactly," the taller of the two men said.

"Auluria, you know Lowell best," Berwyn started.

"Are you sure about that?" I muttered. He ignored me.

"What can we do? What is his weakness? Did he ever say *anything* that could help?"

I tried to think back to my time with my cousin. Most of what he said to me was about lessons on my training. He usually didn't discuss his plans with me, just what I needed to know to carry them out.

I must have looked like I was trying too hard to puzzle something out and was failing because Dov interrupted my thoughts.

"I'll work with her. Keep trying to figure out a way to show them it wasn't us."

He pulled me away from the group and took me to the far corner. Everyone moved away and gave us space to work.

"Sit back, Auluria." He motioned me to move back. "Just close your eyes and go through everything. Conversations, training, even things your...*handler* said."

There it was. His jaw clenched and he couldn't look me in the eye. He was still angry about Shadoe.

"Dov," I started to say.

"It's fine, Auluria." But his voice said he was anything *but* fine.

"I never wanted to be with him."

"I know, Lowell paired you. I don't blame you for that."

"But you're angry," I pushed.

His head snapped back up to look at me.

"Of course I'm angry. I hate the idea of him touching you. He has no right to hold you in his arms or kiss your lips." His voice became angrier. "Every time I think of him being near you I want to destroy him. You didn't love him—you didn't even care for him—and for Lowell to throw you together like that..."

His face was hard, so different from Berwyn's anger, but upsetting nonetheless.

"Lowell had no right to treat you like that. He had no right to control your life. What would have happened if you hadn't escaped? Would you be married to a man you didn't love, or even like? What would you have had to do in that life? Right now, at this very moment, if Lowell's plan had succeeded, you could be married to that guy, ruling your cousin's empire, not even realizing all the damage you had caused."

He was right. I was a part of causing the damage.

"Auluria, that life was never meant for you. And if I ever see your handler again, I'll destroy him myself for going along with Lowell's plan."

The look of disgust on his face made my insides turn. Until Dov put it in perspective, I hadn't realized how horrible things had been for me *before*. I never agreed with Lowell's plans for a marriage between Shadoe and me, but it was worse when I thought about the intended outcome. Having it as a far-off possibility was one thing—it was easier to cope with if I pushed it off in my mind—but when confronted with the fact that Shadoe and I were to be close, the way I hoped Dov and I would one day be close, it was too much.

I wanted to reach for Dov's hand, but I held back.

"He didn't touch me, Dov," I said, trying to calm him.

"He kissed you." His eyes bored into me.

I lowered my head and whispered, "Yes."

He didn't respond.

"I didn't know you then, Dov. I would never let him touch me now and I had no choice then."

"It doesn't matter," he said quietly. *But it did.*

Of course, it did.

"We have work to do," he redirected.

I swallowed as I wrapped my hands around my knees against my chest and closed my eyes. I thought back over the last few years of never really knowing Lowell. I pictured his light hair and grey eyes, and the smile that never quite reached them.

When we were younger, he used to watch me with fascination, as if he were studying me and trying to decipher my thoughts. *Why* did I reach for the butterfly? *How many* times would I try before I realized I couldn't do something? *How long* before I gave up. *What* made me stop playing? *Why* was I motivated to win?

I realized Lowell was *always* studying me. He watched me with calculated movements, learning from my every decision.

I remembered how he manipulated situations to see my reaction. He'd give me something and take it away. He'd assign me impossible tasks just to see how far I'd go and how frustrated I'd get. I remembered my mother pulling me away from his games once, scolding him for upsetting me.

He challenged everything I ever did.

My breathing deepened as my thoughts proceeded. I remembered when Lowell first brought me into his fold. I was amazed by the people he had collected.

We never stayed in one spot for very long. We led a nomadic life, constantly moving from one place to the next to avoid detection. He let me travel with him when we moved. We'd often have dinner together. Frequently he was joined by one of the girls that threw themselves at him, and I quietly ate while listening to her talk. None of them stayed for long, so I never worried about learning their names unless I worked with them.

One day, two years earlier, Lowell had brought a chicken and demanded I kill it for dinner. He placed it in my hands and it trembled beneath my grasp. Lowell told me what to do and waited for me to follow his instructions. I couldn't bring myself to do it. The look he gave me frightened me. I had disobeyed him, the first time ever, and he was furious.

He took it from me and snapped its neck. I tried to stay calm until he left, but the moment he was gone I retched. I hid from him that evening, not wanting to see his face. Shadoe gave me a passive look the next time he saw me, having heard that I couldn't do what had been asked of me.

Shadoe tried to teach me to do it several times after that, but each time I refused. I couldn't bring myself to be so callous. I still had nightmares about that moment.

I remembered one day, after a long and exhausting day, Lowell came to sit by me on the porch of the small house we were staying at. I rocked in a chair while the breeze teasingly played with my hair. I had just lifted my face to the sky, letting the wind brush over me and I heard Lowell take the seat next to me. I left my eyes closed as he rocked back and forth.

"Auluria, you know I have great plans for you, don't you?" he asked, almost tenderly.

I nodded, still unwilling to relinquish the small freedom that the breeze and my closed eyes gave me.

"Together, we're going to stop the government. We're going to take back power and they won't be able to hurt us again. You'll marry Shadoe and you will both be my second in command. My little cousin, my right hand," he said almost inspirationally.

"That's nice, Lowell," I murmured, opening my eyes to look at him. I gave him a small smile. I believed he was doing the right thing.

"We're close," he grinned. "We have a plan in motion. You're a part of it, Auluria. You're going to be grand."

I shuddered as I thought of his plans for me. If I had known how sick and twisted he was at the time, I could have ended it right there. There was a knife sitting in my boot. With one flick of my wrist, I could have stopped all the bloodshed.

"He never cared about me," I said. "Just what I could do for him."

"I know. I'm sorry, Auluria," Dov started.

"No. He didn't *care* about me. He only wanted what I could do for him. *This is about power.* He wants the power. So, let's give it to him." I grinned.

I could see him processing my words.

"You want to draw him out and let him think he won." He began to smile. "But how?"

"He needs to think he beat us. So, we let him know where we are

*—which obviously can't be here—*and when he comes to watch us lose, we confront him. Lowell has never been able to resist watching his plans fall into place," I said.

"Now the trick is how to get the right people there to witness it and how we can escape," Dov concluded.

We explained to Berwyn what we had come up with. We agreed it was a good concept, but we had to flesh out the details.

"He will never believe *me* again," I said, "so that won't help."

"How else can we get him to find out?" Silas asked.

The men and Eden tossed around some ideas, none of which would work.

I took a deep breath, knowing my suggestion would not be well received.

"I know how Lowell thinks. But I also know how Shadoe thinks. If we can find the relative area that Lowell's group is in, I know how we can make this work."

"No. If Shadoe is involved, you will not be part of it," Dov protested.

"He's not going to hurt me, Dov. He was supposed to *marry* me."

"And *you betrayed* him…for me."

The corners of Silas's mouth tugged up in a nearly unnoticeable grin. I focused on Dov.

"And that's part of my plan. He hates you too."

"I doubt he hates you," Dov interjected, but I ignored him.

"If we can be where he is, he'll find us. He always does. And he'll follow us back to wherever we set up camp. He'll bring Lowell straight back to us. Lowell has always liked playing with the mice he catches in his traps."

I don't think the group appreciated me comparing them to mice.

"Let's say this works," Eden started. "What then?"

Berwyn explained that we would need witnesses…enough that Lowell couldn't kill them all. One of the men laid out the plan for getting the guards there. We were going to contact them and tell them of our plan. We would ask them to come, knowing that they would plan to betray us. We made an escape plan, a secret get away route that we could use when the chaos ensued, one that we could destroy behind us. Lowell would try to fight his way out, but would only succeed if he didn't try to take on all the men.

Shadoe and his men would likely be with Lowell, eager for revenge, and I only slightly regretted their part in the plan. I had no doubt Lowell would survive, but his men may not share the same fate. Shadoe would fight, but if necessary, he would die for my cousin.

Berwyn, Eden, Dov and I would all be there, waiting for Lowell's game to play out. I wasn't eager to face my cousin or be the cause for his downfall, but I wanted to put this behind us.

We decided the next day we would go to the place Berwyn told us about. It was a small cave that Griz kept for emergencies. He had shown it to his sons a handful of times before his death, in case they ever needed to run.

There was a hidden tunnel in the back. Once we slipped through, we would set off a chain reaction, dropping stones in front of the entrance. When we were far enough down the tunnel we would set off an explosive that would demolish the tunnel, prohibiting anyone from following us. At the far end of the exit, Silas and the men would be waiting, our reinforcements, if necessary.

Once we had escaped, the group would stay underground for as long as we could before resurfacing. The group would then move to other safe houses, making our way to the camps. The ultimate goal would be to set the men and women at the camps free. Our hope was to move on, beyond where the government could reach us.

But it all hinged on exposing Lowell and escaping. The next day came too quickly, and with it, disaster.

Chapter 17

"I don't like that you are doing this," Dov said. "There's no reason for you to be a part of this. It's *us* that he wants. You and Eden should stay."

"You think I could turn on him like that and he'd just let it go? Dov, be serious. At this point, he might want *me* more than he wants *you*. Besides," I continued, "if he really is mad at me, he might use you to get back at me. It's better if I'm right there beside you. You can save me and I don't have to worry about him hurting you worse just to get to me."

He shook his head but held his tongue. I was grateful not to have to argue my point again.

Berwyn and Eden walked ahead of us. Eden look scared to death. Berwyn touched her arm, trying to steady her.

Silas walked alongside of me, keeping me close between him and Dov. A few other men walked near us in a group, ready to take their place at the exit.

"Are you ready for this?" Silas asked.

"Confronting Lowell?" I clarified. "No. I don't ever want to see him again. But I'll be fine."

"I'll be right with you," Dov said, putting his arm around my shoulder. I moved closer to him. It felt good to be talking with him again.

We left Silas and the others half a mile away at the exit to the tunnel. Berwyn and Eden walked through the exit of the tunnel to beat us to the cave, staying hidden. Dov and I took the long way around, moving slightly less carefully than usual.

Our men had discovered word of Shadoe's spies in the area, so we hoped it wouldn't take long to find him. We walked with purpose, though we made several big loops to ensure he saw us.

I caught sight of one of his warning symbols on a tree. When he was young and first training his men, he developed a system with them based on rotating symbols. He hadn't bothered to change it since the abdication of my position with them. I knew he was near.

Dov and I moved toward the cave. If I hadn't known where to look, I may not have noticed Shadoe following us. I could tell Dov noticed too. We led him back to the cave and disappeared.

Eden ran to tell Silas to put the plan into motion. One of the men with him would go through his contact and reach out to the guards. Our people had already connected with them and told them of our plan, so all we had to do was tell them the location. Silas would send one of the men to tell the contact to get the guards. Everyone would arrive soon and it would all be over. One way or another.

I rested my head on Dov's shoulder, his arms wrapped securely around me. He set his chin on my head and we stood, waiting for the inevitable.

"We're sure this is a good idea?" Eden asked.

"No, it's probably a terrible one, but what else are we supposed to do?" Berwyn grumbled.

With each passing minute, I became more and more nervous. I worried about every little possibility. What if Lowell didn't come? What if he showed up with all his people? What if the guards didn't care about Lowell's group and they just came for us? What if one of us got hurt in the fight? What if we had lost before we had even begun? The thoughts were relentless.

The barrage of notions flitted through my mind. I couldn't shut my brain off.

"Hey," Dov whispered. "You okay?"

"Yes," I said, looking up at him. "Just having trouble not over thinking this."

He bent down to me, kissing me softly on the lips. It happened so fast I almost didn't realize until after he pulled away. He gave me a sheepish smile and said, "Does that help?"

I grinned back. It was the first time he had kissed me since he found out that Lowell had sent me. I wished he would do it again.

He waited a few minutes before adding, "Now *I'm* having trouble focusing."

He looked at me expectantly and I obliged, reaching up to grab his collar. I pulled him toward me for a slightly longer kiss. He pulled back and gave me a lazy half smile. He was happy. So was I.

"Well, if it isn't my dear cousin and her *lover*. I'd say that's about enough, *missy*. Get over here *right now*," Lowell commanded, walking into the room.

"Back off, Lowell." Berwyn stepped between us.

"She's *my* responsibility, Berwyn, not yours. And I want her back." The hardness in his voice made my hair stand on end.

"You will not touch her," Dov said, pulling me closer.

"So, young...so naïve. Don't worry baby Baer, you'll learn with time," Lowell smirked. "Isn't that right, Eden?"

I must have looked confused, for he added, "What? They didn't tell you, dear cousin of mine? Eden was supposed to be mine, but I had some trouble holding on to her after she was abducted and turned her back on me."

"That wasn't my choice, Lowell," she spat back at him. "And if I'd known about your little group I never would have married you anyway."

"But you chose to join another group, didn't you?" Lowell said spitefully.

That explained why Eden looked so shocked when he had spoken to her the time we planned to run into Lowell in town.

He looked around the room. "What a nice place you have here."

"Griz built it," Eden defended her father-in-law's hiding place.

"Ahhh, yes. Dear old Griz." He lowered his hands to his sides. "I like what you've done with the place. Do you like what I did with his name?"

Shadoe stood next to him, eyes intently focused on me. I couldn't read his expression. It may have been a mix of anger, determination, resolution, and maybe…jealousy? He couldn't possibly have been jealous of Dov…he never truly cared for me, so it made no sense.

He flinched as I ran my hand up Dov's arm and rested it on his chest. I tucked my elbow against my body. I always found closing in on myself to be comforting.

Berwyn looked like he was ready to hit Lowell. Eden placed a hand on his arm, calming him.

"Why?" he growled, low and fearsome.

"Why?" Lowell repeated in a mocking tone, his voice echoing off the walls. "*Why?* Because your father destroyed me, *that's* why. We could have crippled the Society and taken control of the country, but no! Your father had to have a *conscience*. He didn't like violence…only stealing.

"And when I tried to leave, he made it impossible for me. He destroyed any chance I had at succeeding." His face calmed, almost looking serene with his decision. "So, you see…he had to go."

Berwyn launched himself forward, lashing out at Lowell's face, but Shadoe was too quick. He raked something metal across Berwyn's arm. It came up streaked with blood. I saw the talons protruding from Shadoe's knuckles. It was as if he was wearing bear claws. Five bloody marks ran down Berwyn's arm.

He stumbled backward.

"So why?" Dov spoke up, stepping away from me, keeping himself between me and my former confidants. "Why attack us now?"

"Because, *baby Baer*, I'm about to have what I wanted all those years ago. We're taking the government down and we'll be in charge," he bellowed, confident and strong. "And I *hate* your family. Your father destroyed me, your brother took my place as leader of the group, and you…*you* turned my perfect little agent against me. So, you see Dov, not only will I destroy your family, but I will thoroughly enjoy watching you hang for it."

He looked around Dov to me and added, "Last chance, Auluria. Whatever *I* do to you will be a lot better than what the *Society* will do to you."

"Lur, take it seriously," Shadoe warned. "We'll be more merciful than they will. And we can protect you from the Society better than *they* can." He almost sounded worried, like he was trying to will me back into the safety of being his charge.

"No," I answered. I saw Shadoe visibly deflate at my answer.

"Lur, please, reconsider. I'll keep you safe." He meant from Lowell. He meant Lowell would discipline me, but he wouldn't let him kill me. I didn't care.

"So, what? You launched an attack against the Society, and planted Griz's medallion and then framed my husband?" Eden shrieked, redirecting the conversation where we needed it to be.

"That, *miss*, is precisely what I did," Lowell said stepping toward her menacingly. "And there's nothing you can do about it. They're on their way already."

"Actually," Berwyn said, regaining his footing after reeling from the strike he had taken, "they're already here."

The guards, dressed in their dark uniforms, burst into the room. Lowell turned alongside Shadoe and the two of them lashed out at the men. The people they had with them weren't quite as fast and went down quicker.

Dov, Eden, Berwyn and I ran to the hidden exit, setting off the rockslide and blocking the doorway. Berwyn staggered, his feet slowing.

"Berwyn?" Dov asked.

Berwyn fell to his knees, only steps away from the exit we had just blocked. We only had a moment to reach the point where we could set off the explosive.

Dov ran to his side, dipping under his arm and pulling him forward. I slipped under Berwyn's arm on the opposite side and helped to carry him along. Eden ran ahead to prepare the blast.

The moment we reached Eden she set off the charge, causing a rippling boom to echo off the walls.

"What's wrong with him?" Eden nearly sobbed.

"Looks like there was poison on that thing Shadoe hit him with. We have to get him back…now!" I answered.

We raced through the tunnel, carrying Berwyn as best we could. His feet gave out completely and we dragged him through the dirt walkway.

Eden ran ahead, bringing two of the men back with her. They took Berwyn from us, allowing us to run alone. We raced to the end of the tunnel, breaking free into the refreshing air. With the chaos and danger, a distance away, I finally felt we might have a chance.

The last thing I saw before the explosion was Lowell being

attacked by two guards. I no longer felt I owed him my allegiance. I had absolutely no doubt that it wouldn't be the last time I saw him.

Chapter 18

WE RAN TOWARD THE CLOSEST OF THE SAFE HOUSES, THE MEN dragging Berwyn along. I clamped my hand around Eden's arm and forced her to stay upright as we struggled along the path.

When the path split, so did we. The men took Berwyn to a safe house for medical attention while the rest of us kept running. Dov and Silas repositioned themselves so that Dov was guiding me and Silas looked after Eden. She sobbed as we left Berwyn fighting for his life.

It was eerily silent in the woods. No birds, no crickets, no frogs. Something felt wrong. I tried to keep a careful watch, letting Dov pull me along, but I couldn't seem to focus on what was bothering me.

Dov and Silas kept turning to look behind us, watching for signs of the oncoming guards. I imagine Lowell and Shadoe kept them busy for a few minutes, long enough to give us a brief head start, extended even longer by using the tunnel.

The moment I opened my mouth I knew it was too late. I screamed my warning anyway, but the last words were ripped out of my mouth as we were catapulted into the air by a net strung from the trees. The air rushed from my lungs as we bounced wildly up and down.

Eden had just missed being swept up in the net. Silas's arm was ripped from Eden's hand as he was caught up in the ropes. The guards were on top of Eden so quickly we hadn't even had time to see her reaction. They forced her to her knees and bound her hands behind her back. Fear radiated from her eyes.

"No!" I screamed as they kicked her back, sending her tumbling to the ground.

"And who do we have here?" a strong, tall man called out.

"Let me go!" Eden yelled viciously, struggling against the man pulling her upright again.

"Don't touch her!" I chorused, causing the men to turn their attention to me.

"You must be the one." He pointed at me. "We've been looking for you, *missy.*"

At the sound of that name, I realized Lowell had told them about me. He specifically sent them after me. Whether they captured him or not, he wanted me to know he had won.

The men cut us down, surrounding us to prevent escape. There were too many of them to fight. Surrender was our only option. Once we had fallen and struggled to our feet, Dov gently placed his hand on my shoulder and pushed me to my knees. He didn't want me to fight. I looked at him, begging for some sign of rebellion, but his eyes had lost their light.

"No," I whispered, pleading for him to not ask me to do this.

"Please," he whispered back.

I sank to my knees and the men roughly tied my hands behind me.

"I was told to be gentle with you," my guard said once the boys had been secured.

I saw Dov and Silas tense, straightening their spine and lifting themselves as high as they could, knees planted firmly on the ground. Neither spoke.

Their guards pulled them to their feet, not caring to be gentle with them. They marched us forward, back the way we had come.

"Where are you taking us?" I asked in a monotone voice.

"To interrogation," one of them answered me. I hadn't expected an answer.

"And then to die," another added, laughing gleefully.

The others joined him in the celebration. They knew who we were. They knew what our capture meant.

My guard jabbed me in the back, nearly causing me to fall forward. Dov clenched his jaw, but he continued to stay quiet. When I righted myself, I intentionally changed my gait, giving me just enough time to "accidentally" step on my guard's foot, hard. He let out a yelp and grabbed my arm. Spinning me around, he slapped me across my face.

I tried not to shriek, but I couldn't hold it back. I whimpered as he pulled me close. "Don't you ever do that again, *Missy!*"

He pushed my shoulder, turning me away from him and propelled me forward. I could feel the side of my face swelling. I refused to cry.

Eden threw her head back, crashing into her guard. He saw her moving and caught her around her waist before she had fully moved and he clung on even after the blow. She lifted both feet and sent them crashing into his knees. They buckled beneath him and he pulled her to the ground with him. Two guards rushed to his aid, plucking Eden from the moss-covered ground. She struggled against them, but they held her in place.

Before Dov and Silas could do anything, I saw the blade. "Stop! No!" I shouted. "They'll stop, don't hurt them!"

A young boy put his hand on the older man's forearm and brought the knife down. In that moment, he stopped our massacre. He glared at us, hatred in his eyes, but I silently thanked him anyway.

I confirmed our compliance for the rest of the journey, assuring them we wouldn't try anything else. Dov, Silas, and Eden agreed reluctantly.

We walked with our heads down, bent low as our captors had demanded. When we reached the tree line, we were told not to make eye contact with anyone in the town. The guards formed a barricade around us and marched us through the city.

Finally, we arrived at a stately building. We were escorted inside where we found ourselves standing in the middle of a large indoor courtyard.

"The Baers," an amused voice boomed, deep and solid. "I see you've decided to join us."

We all looked up at the same time. The man sitting before us was probably older than Griz would have been if he were still alive. His graying hair was parted in the middle, combed to each side. His short beard framed his face, the whiskers sticking out at all angles. He wore a robe of vibrant reds.

"I am Magistrate Canton and *we* have been looking for you for a great many years, *Mr. Baer.* Since the day your father killed all those people."

"That wasn't my father who did that," Dov protested.

"I told you he would lie," a voice from the shadows called.

I turned to find Lowell, hidden in the dark confines of the over-hang. He was bound and being watched by several guards.

"He would say anything to save his neck," Lowell continued.

"Lowell killed them, Sir," Dov said, jerking his head toward my cousin.

"It doesn't matter to me who did what. You're all going to die for it. The Society wants you gone and since it was my men who captured you, I'm the one who will get the credit for ridding the world of the likes of all of you." He rose from his chair and walked toward us.

He walked to Eden and lifted her chin. She restrained herself from biting him, but just barely.

"Tomorrow you'll all be interrogated. The people want answers. This will go on for several days. In a week's time, there will be a lavish ceremony held in your honor. Well, in honor of your deaths. Public execution will be a fitting end to you all."

He walked past the boys to me. He cupped my chin in his hands and bent down in front of me. The man tilted my chin up and inspected me before speaking.

"I've been told you are quite the nasty one, girl. Betraying your lover, betraying your family, betraying your country." He clucked his tongue at me. "We really can't trust you, now can we? What shall we do about that?"

He paused to think.

"I know. We have a special plan for you." He stood and backed away from me, smiling.

"Now, off to your cells. The interrogators will be here in a few hours and you wouldn't want to be too tired for your questioning, now, would you?"

His laugh echoed off the courtyard walls and followed us down the hall. I was sure I heard it follow us down into the cold stone chambers we were hidden in.

Water dripped down the sides of our cells. Eden and I sat in one small cell together while Silas and Dov were held in the cell next to ours. We were isolated from the rest of the prisoners.

The bars were strong enough that we couldn't bend them, no

matter how many times we kicked them. They were close enough together that not even Eden could slip out.

I sat near the bars, my back against the wall. On the opposite side of the wall, Dov sat, mirroring me. We stretched our hands as far as we could through the bars and around the walls, holding onto each other.

Eden took up the opposite corner wanting her space. Her tears had long since dried and now the anger had taken a hold of her. If any of us had been able to break through the metal bars, it would have been Eden with her rage spurring her on.

"I'm so sorry you got caught up in this," Dov said softly to me. There was no privacy but there were things to be said.

"It isn't your fault," I said. "In fact, it's more my fault than your fault."

"Let's not do this," he begged. "Please, let's not talk about that."

"What else are we going to talk about, Dov? We're going to die within a week. Tomorrow they're going to separate us and interrogate us. What are the chances we'll ever see each other again?"

"We'll see each other again."

"How can you be so sure?" I questioned.

"Auluria," he said slowly, in a measured voice, "they want us to suffer. They want *me* to suffer. There's no better way to do that than to make me watch you being hurt and killed."

That horrible realization sunk in as he spoke the words. They would torture us just to make the other suffer.

"This is going to be bad, isn't it?" I breathed.

"I'm so sorry," he whispered, his voice catching.

"No." I squeezed his hand. "I don't want you to worry about me. Don't think about it. When it happens, promise me you won't watch. Promise me, no matter what, you'll look away."

"I won't do that, Auluria. I won't leave you to suffer alone."

"Dov, promise me."

"Auluria, you know he won't do that. He'll do whatever he has to do to make your suffering stop," Silas said from somewhere in the cell next to me.

"This is a nightmare," I said, letting my head fall to my raised knees.

"I'll protect you," Dov said softly.

"You can't, Dov," I replied, giving up. "And I don't want you to. I want you to take care of yourself. Don't worry about me."

"I can't do that, Auluria. You know that."

I sighed. I knew.

"We'll do whatever we can to protect you, girls," Silas confirmed.

"Silas, don't. Eden and I will be fine. You need to focus on protecting yourselves. Don't worry about us." I knew I would be fine. I wasn't so sure about Eden, but I knew if the boys could find a way to escape, they'd come back for the others or at least they would be able to warn the people that weren't with us. I wanted them to focus enough to escape.

"Auluria..." Dov started, clearly wanting to say something.

"I know," I breathed. "I know."

He tightened his grip on my hand. We both knew.

"Eden?" he asked. "Are you doing okay?"

"I'm fine, considering." Her voice was angry. Softening it, she added, "Are you okay?"

"Yeah."

"Dov," Eden started again. "I'm sorry."

She never said for what.

"Thanks," he replied.

"Silas..." I started, aware that we were beginning our goodbyes. "Thank you. For everything. For looking out for us and helping us and standing by us."

"Anytime, Auluria." He let out a short, hard chuckle. "I knew you two belonged together."

"Oh, is that right?" I questioned with a laugh. "It seems to me someone who looked a lot like you doubted that awhile back."

"I didn't doubt it," he retorted. "Just making sure you understood what it meant."

I laughed.

"You should have heard the way he pushed for us back in that storehouse, Auluria." I could hear the smile in Dov's voice.

"Yeah, I bet he was...really annoying." I smiled.

"Yes," Dov agreed.

"Knock it off." He joked, "I'm the one who got you two back together, and don't you forget it."

"Okay, buddy, okay," Dov replied.

"Are you ever going to tell me who that girl is, Silas?" I asked.

"Nope," he said.

"Dov?"

"Sorry, babe. I can't."

I squeezed his hand, but he still wouldn't relent.

Just then we heard the footsteps approaching.

Chapter 19

I WAS THE FIRST ONE TAKEN. TWO MEN PULLED ME KICKING AND screaming from my cell. I saw them lead Eden away. She didn't fight. In my thrashing, I saw Dov and Silas at the cell bars, reaching for us, but I couldn't hear them over my struggling.

We hadn't expected them to come for us so soon.

I was thrown into a chair, my wrists tied to the armrests, my feet fastened to the legs. I pulled against my restraints to no avail.

"Before we begin, there's someone who would like a word with you," the guard said.

The lighting was dim in the room, there were no windows, so it was flooded only by candlelight, most of which had burnt out. It was cold. If I was there for long, I knew I would begin to shiver.

"I told you not to betray me. I told you to focus. But you just couldn't listen, could you?" the sharp voice said.

His blond hair was matted with blood. The grey of his eyes was accentuated by the dark print from a fist surrounding it. His lip was split open, blood crusting over where it dribbled down his chin.

He was restrained, though not to the chair. He guided himself into the room, sitting across from me.

"What you did was wrong, Lowell," I said.

"We would have been just fine, cousin, had you not changed the plan. And not only did you disobey me, but you also sold me out. You blamed me for all this,"

"It was *your* fault," I interrupted.

If he hadn't been tied, he would have struck me.

"Well, now I suppose we'll die together. Mom would have been so proud we saw each other through until the end." His sarcasm set a fire in my soul. I strained against my bindings, hoping to lash out at him.

"But don't worry, I'm always true to my word. I'll see to it that your precious little Dov is to blame for all of this. I'll see to it he suffers. But you are still my cousin, so I'll give you a choice, Auluria." He looked up at the guard to make sure he still had time.

"There are two ways to hurt you both: either you get hurt and he has to watch, or he gets hurt and you watch. Choose."

It was an impossible choice. I couldn't bear the thought of him being hurt; his handsome body being torn to pieces. But I knew how painful it would be for him to watch me. In the end, I couldn't take the thought of him in physical pain more than forcing him to watch my own pain.

"Hurt me," I said, looking down at the ground.

"What?" he demanded.

"Hurt me," I said louder, looking up at him. "Hurt me."

"All right then." He grinned that twisted grin I'd come to see often since being sent on my last mission. He glanced to the guard who nodded once. How Lowell had a guard on his payroll, I might never know.

"And not a word to Lover Boy"—he paused only slightly—"or any of them for that matter, or you'll only make it worse on all of them."

"Lowell," I yelped, trying to make a deal. "Make it quick for them. Draw mine out if you want, but don't make them suffer."

Lowell stood and walked to the door. "Goodbye, *missy*."

I sat in silence after he left. My mouth felt dry and my throat was scratchy. This was the end of us.

No one else came for me. A guard took me back to the cell. Eden was already there. I caught a glimpse of Dov and Silas as I walked back into my cell. Both had taken a few punches while I was gone.

"Are you okay?" Dov raced to the front of the cell as soon as the men were gone.

"Yes." I quickly changed the subject. "Eden, are you all right?"

"Fine," she answered.

"They just asked her questions. What about you?" Dov supplied.

"Uh-huh," I mumbled, unwilling to answer.

"They're coming back in a bit for us," Dov said.

That worried me. I knew they would come back more broken than before.

Before anything else could be said, the guards were back for them. I watched as they dragged them away. Dov locked eyes with me and refused to look away, even as they strangled him back.

Eden came crawling over to me and leaned against the wall. We sat quietly until we were sure we were alone. She raised her head up to my ear.

"They didn't question you. What happened?" She used our hair to block our conversation.

"It doesn't matter Eden," I whispered back. She was an intuitive woman to have figured that out so quickly.

"Yes, it does. What happened?"

"*Lowell* happened. He has one of the guards in his pocket and he wanted to talk to me."

"I sat in a cell by myself. A man came in and asked two questions and then they dragged me back here and told me not to talk," she said. "What did Lowell want?"

"We made a deal. I think. I suffer…you all don't. Simple as that."

"Dov suffers. If he must watch you suffer, he suffers. It's revenge on you both."

"I know. But the more physical pain I take, the less he has to endure."

"That's brave of you."

"I couldn't let them hurt all of you. We're not normal, by any means, but I care about you all. I can't let you get hurt."

"I have news for you, Auluria. We're all about to experience the worst pain of our lives. When they're done with us, we'll be begging to die. That's how it works, and you, Dov, and I…we're the *special cases*. And Silas by proxy. It's going to be so much worse."

"They aren't going to be able to rescue us, are they?"

She shook her head.

I felt her shudder against me. It was a hard fate to accept.

The next time we were removed from our cells was to be brought before the Magistrate. He wore his shaded robe. It flowed out behind him as he walked. Dov and Silas were in chains in the center of the room as Eden and I were escorted in.

At the far end of the room, several moveable walls had been set up and a man stood by each. I fell hard as my knees were kicked out from behind me. I couldn't take my eyes from the partitions as I fell.

"And so, it begins. Welcome to your trial," Magistrate Canton formally announced.

High-ranking officials stood on either side of us. They were here to witness our pain. The magistrate smiled, looking down on us.

"Now...who's first?"

The guards lifted each of us to our feet and forced us toward the freestanding walls. The backside did not have a wall, leaving it an open entrance. In each makeshift room, there was a chair, a long table, and a small table with something under a piece of fabric.

Eden was pushed into the first room, terror on her face. Dov was given the next room. I was led into the third and Silas was taken to the last room.

We could hear each other, but we had no way of seeing each other. I promised myself whatever happened, I would try to stay quiet for Dov's sake. I didn't want him hearing my screams.

I was led to the table. A man, my interrogator, walked in behind me. He forcefully pushed me against the table. As my back bent over, he scooped up my legs and deposited me on the metallic surface. With one swift movement, he strapped down my wrists and ankles. My skirt fell at an uncomfortable angle off the table, exposing my lower legs below my knees.

It was cold and I was terrified. I heard Dov struggling against something in the room next to mine. The voices of the interrogators started, but they barely waited for a response before they inflicted the pain.

Eden cried out first, her piercing shriek startling us.

"Eden!" Dov yelled out. I could hear him fighting the restraints.

I tried to hold still. I tried to block out the noise. Her shattering screams rocked me to my very core.

She quieted as they started to question her. She answered what she could, but she refused to give up the group. The pain they were inflicting was less, after the initial shock of trauma meant to scare her…and us.

Silas and Dov cried out as their interrogators turned on them. The Magistrate walked into my room, watching my reaction.

"Don't worry," he said, petting my hair. "Your time is coming. We just need him to be focused."

I watched as the man took out sharp utensils from under the fabric. He held them up, inspecting each one before setting them down. The light glinted off them.

I forced my tears back as I listened to my friends scream.

The sudden noise of the wall being moved frightened me. They only removed the wall that separated Dov from me. As the men unveiled him, I saw his perfect, beautiful face had been destroyed. His arms were covered in blood.

He looked to me, slightly dazed. His eyes registered me and it brought him back to an alert state.

"Don't hurt her, please," he begged.

"We're not," the Magistrate answered. "Not yet."

They forced me to watch as they mutilated Dov's body. Shallow knife marks ran over his chest and spilled around to his back. They took a long, sharp object and forced it under his skin, lifting it and piercing out in a second location. They twisted it and lifted it in the air, dragging the body part along with it. I would have retched if I had had any food in my stomach.

He had begged me to turn away, pleaded with me not to look, but I wouldn't look away. He focused his eyes on me, as if trying to remain calm for me. He tried to tell me he was fine in our silent way, but I knew he wasn't. I could see the damage they were causing.

Finally, they turned to me. I had never been so grateful.

"No!" he said, alert again. He struggled against the restraints, his wounded skin hanging off his arm in places.

"It's okay," I said. Over and over I repeated it as the man walked toward me.

Suddenly I was aware that I could no longer hear Silas and Eden. I prayed they had stopped to make them hear this.

The man held up the long tool Dov's interrogator had used to pierce his flesh. He dragged it up and down my arms. Back and forth from the tips of my fingers to my shoulder, across my chest, and back down the opposite arm.

When it punctured my upper arm, I thought I might pass out. I held back my scream, but I saw Dov's eyes widen in horror. With every entry into my body, I fought against unconsciousness. Lowell wanted me hurt, and if it wasn't good enough, they'd move back to Dov.

"Is this not painful enough?" the Magistrate asked, stroking his beard. "She's barely making a sound. See what else you can do."

"No!" Dov said, straining toward them. "Auluria, you have to scream. Stop holding back."

I couldn't. I couldn't do that to him. I had to take this punishment.

"Auluria, please!" he gasped as the interrogator began to saw off a piece of flesh from my upper arm. *"Please!"*

I felt the knife, dull and sharp at the same time. Blood rushed from my incision. I faltered.

With Dov's last scream for mercy, I released my pain. A blood-curdling scream that made even the Magistrate duck his head filled the room.

I couldn't bring myself to look at Dov. I knew the pain I'd see there. My interrogator smiled, enjoying the moment. He moved down my body, letting the chunk of flesh hang off my arm, not bothering to finish cutting it off.

He clasped my foot and ran his hand up my leg. Moving my skirt aside, he pushed his hand up along my thigh. I struggled to kick at him as Dov threatened him from his table. I could hear Silas and Eden yelling over the walls, begging for compassion.

He dragged the knife along my inner leg, careful to avoid the artery that would end my life too quickly. I screamed again, giving into their demands.

He picked up a small object, replacing the knife in his hand. When he placed it against my leg I didn't feel it at first. My flesh became warm and then instantly burned, the object searing into my skin. The smell of burning flesh filled the room as the object sizzled.

Again, and again, he placed the object against me. Tears were streaming down Dov's face. In between my screams, I shouted how sorry I was to Dov. He leaned to me, fighting to protect me.

Dov begged them to stop, to take my punishment himself. No one listened. Even Silas volunteered his flesh for my pain. I remember slipping into blackness.

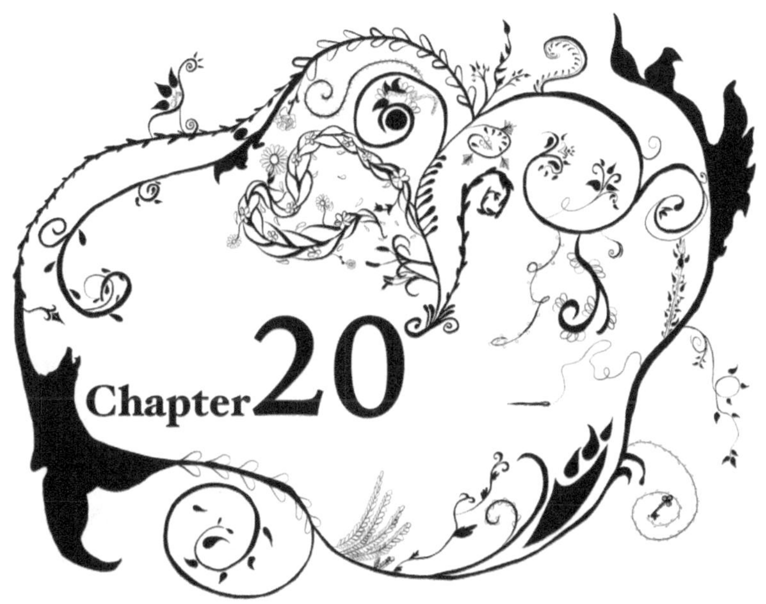

Chapter 20

DAYS PASSED. THE MAGISTRATE DECIDED TO WAIT AN EXTRA FEW DAYS before the execution to give us time to heal. My interrogator had done such a harsh job on me, I couldn't even stay conscious, though some of that was my own pretending.

Eden tried to care for me, but in our cell, there wasn't much she could do but sit with me. Even that was a comfort.

After a week, my scars were starting to heal. Dov and Silas said they were healing as well. Eden, thankfully, had taken the least abuse.

The dark burn marks would have been a constant, lifelong reminder of that day, had we not been scheduled for execution. It still hurt to touch them. Most of them ran along my legs, but he had managed to burn through my dress on my hip once, and he branded my left wrist; a twisted mark of darkly burned flesh as a constant reminder of our pending death.

They allowed us some bandages to wrap our bodies in. I gave most of mine to Dov to help rebind his skin to his arms and chest. My wounds, while painful, had not been as dramatic as his.

I listened to the sound of my friends breathing as they slept. It was the only time they were at ease. I prayed for it to be easy for them when the time came.

One night the guard informed us that the following day, the leaders of the Society would arrive. They would speak to us briefly before sentencing us and carrying out the hanging.

Five men gathered outside of our cells, watching us.

"So, this is the son of the Great Griz Baer," they sneered. "Not what we were expecting."

Dov didn't say anything.

"Where is your brother?" they asked.

"I don't know. Let me out and I'll go find him," Dov said, his voice dripping with sarcasm.

"And this is the wife?" they said, pointing at Eden.

She rose to her feet and walked calmly over to the bars. She placed one hand on the bars, leaning toward the men. Her free hand snaked out, catching one by the collar. She forcefully pulled him toward her, slamming his skull into the metal. His friends pulled him away and stabilized him.

I laughed. I couldn't help myself. In a place where everything was going so wrong, I found her small act of hatred to be hilarious.

I couldn't stop laughing. Everyone froze in horror as I continued to laugh. Eden stared at me, shocked at my response. After a moment Dov joined me. Then Silas picked up the chuckling chant. Even Eden turned back to face the men she had fought against and laughed. We couldn't stop.

Eden came and joined me on the floor and we laughed together, knowing our end was near. She took my hand and laid her head on my shoulder and we laughed until there were tears. The officials were so frustrated they finally left, causing us to laugh even harder.

Eventually, we quieted, and then the silent void crept in.

It was nearly dark the next day when they came for us. We had resigned ourselves to our deaths and walked into it with our heads held high. We did not give them the dignity of acknowledging them.

We shrugged their hands off and walked ourselves to where the guards directed us.

Four ropes hung on four corners of a platform. Each had a trap door, but they also had the option to raise the ropes by hand, extending the death sentence.

I locked eyes with Dov, trying to communicate all the things left unsaid. I wanted him to know how much I cared for him. I needed him to know how much he changed my life. And I needed him to know I would die for him...though I didn't want him to know *that* was exactly what I was trying to do at that very moment.

A second, smaller platform stood to the right of the one we stood on. A single post rose from the center. Underneath it stood Lowell, awaiting his sentence. He glowered at me.

Looking at him, awaiting his death, hating me every moment for ruining his precious plan, I realized what he was. Lowell was a wolf, a vicious, menacing wolf. He played his part and wore many masks. And when he was ready, he attacked, maimed and destroyed. I regretted how long it took me to see him for who he really was.

We were escorted to our posts, each step more horrifying than the next. The rope grated against the soft skin of my neck as they positioned me to die. Our charges were read as the procession began, the tall man with a deep voice finalizing our lives. It seemed like an eternity went by as the officials read our crimes and told the people of our impending fate. The crowd consisted mostly of officials and guards, though there were townspeople in the back, forced to watch to remove any foolish ideas from them. Future uprisings would not be tolerated.

Dov's eyes nearly broke my heart. Those deep blue eyes that awakened me that first day in his house and caused my heart to melt every day since, watched me from our separate posts. He held such remorse in those eyes. Together we played out what our lives could have been, mourning the moments we would never have.

He swallowed hard, his throat bobbing with the effort. I held my tears at bay. I didn't want to lose this man I had come to care for so intensely. I didn't want to lose his smile or his laugh, his kindness and compassion, his integrity and character. The world would be such a wasted place without Dov in it to make it better.

The officials finally stopped and turned back to us. They took their places on seats near the platform. Ropes tightened around our necks, causing us to stand taller to alleviate the pressure. The guards pulled the ropes as tightly as they could before it was our turn. None of us could move. We stood, suspended in place, knowing it was coming.

The Baer family was supposed to suffer for their crimes. Eden was a woman so they would end it quickly for her. Dov would be made to suffer through my execution.

The others watched as my rope was pulled again. I was forced onto the tips of my toes. The restraints on my wrist were cut, giving me the freedom to clutch at the ropes around my neck as they lifted me higher.

I couldn't breathe. I felt the world swirling around me, as I was lifted bit by bit from the ground. I struggled to keep a foot on the wooden paneling to hold myself up.

Dov fought to get to me, but they held him in place. The others were still restrained and caught in their ropes, but they all tried to get to me to save their friend. Everyone but Lowell.

I felt my life slipping away. All the sounds were blocked out, everything slowed down. I felt the rope being pulled and I was off the ground. I tried to pull myself up, but I couldn't. I fought and I lost.

When I opened my eyes again I saw a white grey brightness floating above me. I moved my eyes downward, tipping my head back to its normal position to find I was in a pile on the ground. I gasped for air. The trees and grass came into focus even in the darkening hour.

I looked up and saw Dov's panicked eyes as he jerked his head for me to get up. He wanted me to run.

Chaos surrounded us. Guards were running at some oncoming foe. The officials were scrambling to find safety. I tried standing only to fall back down. On my second try, I managed to get to my feet and I staggered over to Dov as he violently shook his head.

I threw my arms around his waist, trying to lift him out of his rope necklace. Between his struggling and my near ability to lift him, he freed himself. Somehow, he managed to land on his feet. I raced to Eden, still stumbling from oxygen deprivation, and freed her. Dov had knelt in front of Silas, hands still bound and Silas stepped on his back to lift and free himself.

I tackled a guard who was running by the platform. Surprising him, I grabbed his knife with one hand while simultaneously, grabbing a rock with my other hand and pummeling it into his head, leaving him where he lay. I cut the chords around my companions' wrists.

"What is going on?" Eden gasped as we tried to run.

"Lowell," Silas said. "His people were here to save him."

"How ironic," I laughed bitterly. "Lowell sent us to die and yet he's the one who saved us."

We raced away from the guards and into the town. They'd find us instantly in the woods, knowing we'd run there.

"Be careful. If they were here to free Lowell, that means Shadoe's here somewhere." I trusted him even less than I trusted Lowell at that point.

We ducked around homes and buildings. People jumped out of the way as we crashed by them. Dov and Silas grabbed anything we could use as a weapon as we ran by it. Metal poles, bottles, anything we could use to defend ourselves, were collected during our run.

We were all still recovering from our wounds, so we moved slower than we would have liked, but we refused to let that stop us. Even Eden pushed forward, knowing our lives were on the line.

Everything blurred by me as we ran, but my training kicked in, forcing me to identify buildings and streets. Remembering my way back was something Lowell and Shadoe would expect of me, and while I didn't want to be what they taught me to be, I knew it was sound training. Should we need to escape or evade soldiers, it would be important to know where we had been. I took careful note as we ran, storing every dark building, every dilapidated side street, and every foreboding structure in my mind. Shadoe taught me well and I would use this experience to survive and help protect my friends.

Eden stayed by my side as we moved, racing past people. We held up our skirts to avoid tripping, though I'm not sure how much good it did. Silas followed behind us as Dov led our race, pushing us to our limits and further.

We were out of breath when we finally reached the end of the town. Dov slipped into an alleyway between two dark buildings and we stopped to catch our breath. I felt like I could collapse.

"Are you okay?" he demanded as soon as he could speak.

He raced the few feet to my side and pulled me to his warm body. I leaned into him, my tears refusing to come.

"I thought I had lost you," he whispered into my ear. He kissed my head, working his way from the top to my ear. He kissed my jaw line through my golden locks. Pushing his forehead to mine, our noses touched as we breathed each other in. He was about to kiss me when we were startled by a noise.

Dov pulled away, grasping my hand and dragging me behind him. Silas and Eden ran with us as we escaped the alleyway, running from the sound. Together we scaled a large hill, the barrier between the towns. We crept down the opposite side and slunk into the unfamiliar area.

The four of us hid between buildings as people walked by, residing in the shadows. The sun had gone down and the moon was the only light to see by.

Our injuries forced us to slow our pace. Dov kept a firm grip on my waist, still worried about my earlier suffocation. I had a hard time remembering what had happened before we ran.

"Dov, how did I get down?" I suddenly asked.

"What?" he asked, distracted.

"How did I get down from the rope? I was in the air. How did I end up on the platform?"

"Someone cut you down."

"Someone just randomly cut me down?" I repeated.

"I don't know who, Auluria. It was an arrow, shot from somewhere near the woods. It released you and then they attacked."

It made no sense to me but I didn't care. It happened and we got away.

"Here," Silas whispered, motioning us toward him.

We followed him into an empty building. It was small and dark. The place looked like one of the old shacks the government used to store the food they collected from the people. It was standing unused, only a few crates littering the floor.

"Look," Silas said as he broke into one. "Food."

He passed out the dried meat and we hungrily ate. Our captors had only given us enough rations to keep us alive in our cells. It was almost humorous that they wanted us to live long enough to be executed.

Food had never tasted so good...except for the picnic Dov once made for us. We ate quickly, trying to regain our strength. Our flight was far from over.

"Where are we going?" Eden finally said.

Silas and Dov looked to each other. At some point, they had formed a plan without telling us.

"The wall," Dov said.

"The wall?" Eden asked in disbelief.

"You want us to leave?" I asked wondering if the boys had also suffered through the ropes cutting off their ability to breathe earlier that day that would cause them to decide on such a dangerous idea.

"Yes," he stated.

"But we don't know what's out there, Dov. Those people on the other side of the wall are the ones that started this mess in the first place. They tried to attack us, and now *because* of *them*, the Society is going after its own people. We have no idea what we're walking into on the other side of that wall." Eden protested. "Besides, what about Berwyn."

"Berwyn will find us," Dov said.

"You don't…"

"I *do* know, Eden," he interjected. "It was his plan all along. If we ever escape and can't go back, we go over."

"We don't even know if he's still alive," Eden choked.

"Berwyn is strong, Eden. He'll make it," Silas reassured her.

"How far away is the wall?" I asked.

"We still have a few towns to get through," Dov answered. "It will take a few days."

"What is our plan then?" I feared the wall, but I feared staying more.

"We need to sleep for a few hours. We should be safe here," Silas said. "We'll sleep in shifts. We need to leave while it's still dark though."

"I'll take first watch," I announced, knowing that if anything happened, the boys needed the rest more than I did. It would be easier for them to help me along than for Eden and me to drag the boys along.

After some protesting, they let me take the first watch. I spent the entire night replaying the day, knowing if the arrow had missed by even the slightest bit, I wouldn't have been awake to think about it.

Chapter 21

MY FEET DRAGGED ALONG AS WE LEFT OUR HIDING PLACE SEVERAL hours later. The sleep had helped a little, but I was still exhausted. My companions showed the wear of the past several days as well.

The early morning was quiet. It was cool against my skin and I wished I had a wrap with me. I shivered as we walked along the streets.

The sun had risen as we crossed over into the next town. This one, thankfully, was more spread out than the last. The distance between buildings was further which meant less cover, but it also meant less people.

We picked our way through the fields, now starting to wilt and decay. We stopped by a small stream to drink water, a blessing during our journey. Dov helped me over the stream when we finished.

We found an area of tall grass late in the afternoon and chose to rest in its covering. We took turns sleeping again, always leaving someone to keep watch. The wind gently blew the grass towering over us, a wild mass of weeds growing in the bountiful land.

I rearranged my skirt around my feet and looked at the clouds that peaked between the stalks of swaying grass. The clouds moved quickly in the sky as I rubbed my hand over my knees.

"How bad is it?" a soft voice asked.

I turned to find Dov staring at me. He propped himself up on one elbow next to me on the ground and watched me.

"How bad is what?" I asked, unsure of his question.

His eyes fell to my legs. Last night he held my hand in his, his finger resting gently over the scar on my wrist, circling around it in a soothing motion.

"It's fine," I said.

"Auluria, you can tell me," he tried again, even softer.

I moved the bottom of my skirt so he could see my lower leg.

"See? It's fine."

"What you went through wasn't *fine*, Auluria," he said, moving to capture my wrist. He brought my burn to his lips and kissed it. "I'm so sorry you had to go through that."

"How are your arms?" I asked, motioning to his wounds.

"They're healing," he said. "The skin reattached and I didn't lose anything, so I'd count it as a victory." He tried to smile at me.

Reaching forward, I stroked his dark hair. I pushed back a piece that fell in his eyes.

"At least we match," I offered.

He smiled, more genuine and relaxed this time. I guided his head to my lap, stroking his hair as he drifted back to sleep.

It was evening when we weaved our way out of the grassy maze. We walked the entire night, not encountering anyone. We made it through the town and the town next to that, just entering a third as the sun rose.

"Hey!" a voice called harshly, trying to keep quiet.

We froze.

"Don't move," the voice commanded. "I'm a friend."

A man circled around us. His light brown hair was going grey and his clothes were old and worn from work. He held a knife to us, still wary of the four strangers who were trespassing near his home.

"You're Griz's kid, aren't you?" he asked.

Dread washed over me. We had been recognized.

"You look just like him," he pointed at Dov. I took a step closer to Dov, wrapping my hand around his arm gently to avoid hurting him.

"Your dad helped me out once. You were just a boy. Let's see… Bernie or something, right?"

"Dov, actually. I'm the younger one," Dov surprised me by answering.

"And his name is Berwyn," Eden said spitefully.

"I heard they were looking for you," he said, still pointing his knife. "The way I see it, your father helped a lot of good people out of tough places in his day. Now it's time to return the favor. From what I hear, they aren't headed this way yet. Come on, you can stay with me for a bit."

He turned and walked away. Unsure of what to do, we looked to each other. Finally, Dov made the decision for us, and we followed him as he walked after the man.

His house was small, but it was nice to be in a real home again.

"My name is Barone," he said. "Are you hungry?"

We nodded and he started looking for something to feed us. He told us about how Griz had stolen food for his family and found supplies for Barone's sick daughter. She had eventually died, but Griz had helped to prolong the life she had.

"So, you're the oldest son's wife," he said, pointing at Eden.

"Yes," she replied.

"And you're how old?"

"Twenty-three."

"And he is…?"

She sighed in frustration. "Twenty-four."

"And *you're* with *him*." He pointed from me to Dov. "But not married."

"No, we've only known each other for a little while," Dov confirmed.

"So, who are you?" He looked to Silas.

"I'm the friend, co-worker," he started before Dov cut him off.

"Co-*leader*," Dov corrected.

"…match maker, and all around good person to have on your team," Silas finished, grinning

"Interesting," Barone murmured.

He stood and walked toward the door. "I'm going to see what I can find out about the guards. Stay here until I get back."

"We can trust him, right?" Eden asked.

"I think so," Dov said.

"I think so too," Silas agreed.

"Okay, then we stay. But, only until he comes back with news," I said.

Everyone nodded. We took the time to change our bandages and inspect our injuries. Despite the deplorable conditions in our cells, we seemed to be healing better than we expected.

A few hours later Barone came back while Silas was on watch. He woke us as he heard the man approaching. I was just sitting up when he closed the door behind him.

"I have news," he stated.

We looked at him expectantly.

"They know you ran into the towns and not the woods. They're working their way through the towns looking for you. There is a reward being offered for your capture.

"I heard there are also men looking for you who aren't the guards."

"Our people?" Silas mused.

"Or not," Dov said, his voice concerned.

"I wouldn't wait around to find out. I heard the non-government men had a head start. They could catch up to you at any time. The Society folks aren't too far behind either.

"We should go," Eden said.

"Thank you for your kindness, Barone," I said, remembering my manners.

"Here." He stopped us. "Take this."

He scooped up a sack and filled it with the remaining food. I was certain it was all he had left in the entire house. "I owe Griz," he insisted, forcing us to take it. Something told me he would have helped us even if Griz hadn't helped that little girl all those years before.

Silas carried the pack on his back. His torture had not been as extreme as Dov's had been. I offered to help, as did Eden, but he refused. We moved as quickly as we could, standing out in the broad daylight. The afternoon sun cast harsh shadows against everything it touched.

A stray cat jumped in front of us, scaring us as we moved. Silas beat Dov to me and swooped me behind his back. Eden was several steps away, making me the closest one to protect. I was grateful that they were looking after me, but I was more than a little tired of being pushed to safety.

The cat wandered away, flicking its tail as it walked. It reminded me of a grey cat that used to visit me at one of our campsites a few years earlier. Every night, he'd come looking for my dinner and often I obliged, grateful for the company. He'd arch his back into my hand as I pet his sleek back. Once he was finished eating he'd run off into the night. I was never fond of cats, but I liked that one.

At the edge of the town, we found ourselves on a weed-infested road. We followed the pebbled path until the buildings came into view. Many of them were made from stone in this area.

The sun was setting once again and we decided to keep walking with the setting light. We wove our way around carts that had been left outside, blocking the walkways. Eden nearly tripped over a wooden bucket left in the road as she tried to skirt one of the carts.

We found ourselves along the edge of the town. The trees weren't more than thirty feet away. The group decided to take shelter in the woods we had come to trust. Just inside the tree line, where we couldn't be seen, we settled for a few hours of rest.

Leaning against Dov, I rested my head on his shoulder. Softly I placed my hand gently on his chest, hoping it didn't hurt him. He took the first watch as I fell asleep in his arms. The rise and fall of his frame was comforting as it lulled me into a deep sleep. He stroked my hair and murmured soft things in my ear. I dreamed of my childhood with Lowell, everything taking a strange new turn toward the reality I had only recently discovered.

Two hours later I was awake again, still leaning against Dov as he slept. Eden would be next on the watch rotation, but for now, she slept peacefully. My mind wandered as I listened for any unwanted guests.

I thought back to the first day I had met Dov. He was so full of life, despite everything he had gone through. He took beatings to protect people. He saved those he could. He cared for me. How I had even possibly stumbled into his life was beyond me. He would never know how truly changed I was because of him.

I thought of Berwyn and Eden and how much they too had

changed since I had come to know them only a few short months before. I admired them in some ways. I pitied them in others.

The moving grass caught my attention before I heard it. I reached out and shook Dov and Silas awake. They snapped to attention just as the men came into the small clearing.

"Well, if it isn't the *golden girl* and her *golden boy,*" Marty sneered.

Chapter 22

I was genuinely surprised to see Marty alive. I had been certain he wouldn't survive our last encounter. He had recovered better than I expected him to, though Jake seemed like the one who was ready for a fight. Another boy their age stood behind them.

"Looks like you really *are* a Golden Girl, *Sweetie*," Marty said as he eyed my arms wrapped around Dov. "You're going to make us very rich men."

"There's a reward for you, you know," Jake supplied. "We figure you owe us. Now get up."

Jake started toward me and I kicked him hard in the shin before I had time to think it through. Dov was on his feet the moment after I struck Jake. He kneed him in the abdomen, forcing him to double over. Silas threw his weight against Marty.

Eden was furious over yet another intrusion and she took out her frustration on the third boy. Her fist made a sickening thud as it collided with the boy's nose. Blood poured down his lip as his hand flew to his face. Eden didn't stop though, she chased him several feet back, hitting and kicking with each step. Marty whirled around, grabbing Eden's arm before she could throw another punch and tossed her to the ground. Dov, defending his sister-in-law, kicked Marty in the back, sending him to the dirt as well.

I took the opportunity to pick up the sack the third boy had dropped on the ground. I searched through it finding several knives, rope, and some rations.

Leaping on to Marty's back, I wrenched his hands around, fastening them with the rope. Dov looked impressed as I twisted the rope and secured it. I did the same with Jake and the other boy. We tied them to a tree, preventing them from leaving.

The four of us took off with their knives and rations in tow, leaving our rivals behind.

"How did they find us?" Eden asked.

"They were very motivated," Dov said. "I bet they tracked us this whole time. They probably found a way to watch the execution too."

"I'm sure they did," Silas said. "You okay, Eden?"

"Yeah," she panted, "just getting…. a little…tired."

I was tired too and I had more training than Eden ever did. Shadoe had demanded that I be ready to hold my own if a mission went sideways. He ran drills with me until I wanted to complain to Lowell. I never did.

"We probably should have knocked them out before we left," Silas said.

"We gagged them," I offered.

"It's nice that they planned on gagging us when they caught us," Eden commented making me smile.

"We need a plan for when we get over the wall," Silas changed the subject.

"We don't even know what is out there, how could we possibly make a plan?" I questioned.

"That's true, but we need some kind of idea about what we're doing. What happens if we get over and find ourselves in danger over there too? What are we going to do?" he replied.

"What happens if everything the Society told us is a lie? What if there is nothing? *Or* what if it's somewhere *safe*?" Dov countered.

I interrupted, listing off steps in a clipped voice.

"We need to stay together, assess the situation as we go, try to agree on a plan, and once a plan is made, we stick to it," I said too hastily. *"There. Plan made."*

"Sounds like Lowell did a number on you," Silas said, glancing at me from the corner of his eye.

"Shadoe, actually. Lowell didn't handle my training," I replied.

"I *really despise* that guy," Dov muttered.

"I know," I sighed.

"We *all* know," Silas and Eden said at the same time, prompting Dov and me to turn to them.

"How much farther is the wall, anyway?" Eden asked again.

"We should reach it by tomorrow afternoon," Dov said.

Eden sighed as she panted. We were all tired of running.

We sat behind a stone wall on the outskirts of the town. Everyone was breathing heavily as we sank back against the stone. Eden had stepped in a hole, twisting her ankle. The boys had to help move her over to the stonewall, preparing to carry her over. Silas bent, lifting her into his arms as he handed her to Dov on the other side. Dov set her down and we joined them.

"It will be fine in a few minutes," she assured us as she tested the injury. When she was done, we took a seat on the ground, using the stonewall as a covering to protect us from sight.

I had no doubt that even if she *wasn't*, she would push through it. She took Dov's hand in hers as we sat.

Silence stretched between us, not for lack of things to say, but because we were still so close to the town. The wall was only a short distance away, a half hour's walk from our resting place.

I was itching to start again, but I knew it was important to give Eden a break. She rubbed at her ankle. I could already tell it was going to swell.

"Can I wrap it for you?" I asked quietly. She nodded. Dov handed me one of the wraps he had taken off a few hours earlier from his arms. I bandaged the wound for Berwyn's young bride.

"We're close," she said, her voice lifting.

"We're close." I smiled back.

Within a few minutes, Eden decided she wanted to try walking again. Silas checked the area to make sure it was clear. Dov helped Eden to her feet. Sitting on the edge of the stonewall, she swung her legs over and righted herself on opposite side, back on the path we had started on, no longer needing the veil of the stone barrier.

I followed her over and waited on the other side for Dov. We could hear the noises from the town not too far away, but we stayed as far from them as we could, even if it added a few minutes to our journey.

Eden limped, gradually working out the pain in her leg. Eventually, she could walk closer to her normal walking speed. She stayed tucked between Silas and Dov in case she needed to lean on them for support. I walked behind her, keeping the group in my sights, watching behind us for any signs of followers.

With each step, I grew more optimistic. Each foot further was one step closer to the wall and the freedom it promised. Whatever freedom we found on the other side, I was willing to accept it. Whether we were to find ourselves truly free or on the run yet again, I was prepared to take that step.

Even the sky seemed more blue as the clouds floated silently by. Hope was a funny thing, the way it changed your outlook down to the very colors you saw. It pierced and stabbed at my heart, echoing "you're free, you're free." It quickened every heartbeat. It made each step lighter. Hope was a funny thing.

"There," Dov said, pointing ahead.

I stretched up to look around Eden. There, in the distance, so far I could barely distinguish what it was, stood a small black line stretching across the horizon. The wall.

Chapter 23

I SMILED.

It was real. I could see it. If I could have run at that moment I would have. I would have run and thrown myself at the wall and leapt over it and run. I would have run as far as I could and never looked back.

Instead, we inched toward the wall. Each step was more torturous than the last, for we could finally see the finish line of our journey but couldn't reach it yet.

"Look," Dov said, pointing away from the wall.

Tall walls rose into the air. Guards were everywhere, forming a human wall around the fortress we could only distinguish because of their uniforms.

"The camps," I said. "Which one?"

"That's a boys' camp. They train them there to fight," Silas explained as if it was all new to me.

"How many boys must they keep there?" I asked astonished at its size.

"More than we'll ever know, I imagine," Dov said sadly. "Between the boys they *take* and the boys they get from the breeding program, there's no telling how many are in there. We don't even know what age groups that one houses."

As we walked, we saw a line of tiny dots being marched from one building to the next. The compound was comprised of several large buildings surrounded by a fence. The bottom part was a wall, holding them in and preventing their escape. Metal rose high, like an iron gate, on top of the stone.

The dots were taken into another building just as a second string of dots exited a different structure. They were stopped off to the side, we assumed for training. I counted at least thirty boys in each row.

We followed the line of the hill and descended too low to see the camp. I felt like I was abandoning them. They had no idea we had witnessed them that day, but I wish they could have known someone knew them and would remember them.

"We'll come back for them one day," Dov said quietly. "We won't just leave them there."

Dov; a heart of gold.

I wrapped my arm around him, hoping he knew I admired that golden heart that always put others first.

He wrapped his hand around my hair, pulling it down slightly. I tipped my head to accommodate his grip, but I didn't mind the adjustment.

We were so close to our escape. I could almost see some of the larger detailing in the wall. I felt the mood shift in the group as we drew close.

Something heavy clinked off Dov's back as we walked. He lurched forward as it clattered to the ground. The knife's metallic rattling drew our attention. Someone had thrown a knife at Dov and by some miracle, the wrong end slammed against him.

He dropped down and claimed the knife. We turned, trying to identify our attackers. Dov's grip tightened around the knife as I reached for the one in his belt we had acquired earlier.

They appeared so quickly, as if they came out of the wind itself. They were less in numbers than we expected would follow us, but still a surprising number. They stalked toward us, ready to fight.

"Silas!" Dov shouted, as if initiating some silently made protocol.

Silas moved into action, taking Eden and moving her away from us. Dov ushered me in the opposite direction. We were splitting up. I lost sight of Silas and Eden as we ran. Dov kept himself between me and the guards as we ran at an angle from them.

I prayed the distant trees would give Silas and Eden some covering. We were familiar with the woods, more familiar than the guards were. Perhaps if they had a head start, they could bury themselves within the confines of the greenery.

Dov and I ran toward the camp. It was still far off in the distance and I couldn't imagine we'd find refuge there. The camp guards would join in the pursuit and we'd be dead within minutes. The area was expansive and open.

My tall companion pulled me back toward the town, championing our race. His hair was disheveled as he turned to look over his shoulder. He was frustratingly handsome, even then, as fear gripped us both.

The Society's man had thrown his knife too early, alerting us to their presence and giving us the advantage. It might have been our only hope for survival. He gave us the gift of distance.

Time stretched out as we ran back toward the town. The group had split, sending a smaller number after us. Even so, if they caught up to us, there was little chance we would win.

We pulled carts into their path, throwing the small objects we could find at them. They pressed onward, only allowing our distractions to slow them a little.

Crashing through the town, we changed course often, hoping to misdirect them.

"Stay here," Dov whispered harshly as he pushed me to the ground.

"No." I pulled myself back up. "Together. Captured or not."

I wrapped my arms around his neck, fastening myself to him. He embraced me and begged me to listen to him.

"No," I insisted.

I watched as he deflated in my arms. He would not win this battle. I would not leave his side.

He leaned to me and kissed me, the kiss I had waited so long to have once again. Dov placed his hands on my hips and pulled me close. His kiss was rough and harsh and passionate. Heat radiated across my body as his breath feathered over my cheek and neck. My vision clouded for a moment, swirling around us in this stolen moment.

"Auluria."

"Dov." We breathed in the same moment.

Dov pulled back first, pulling my wrist with him. The guards had run past our hiding place and this was our only chance. Freedom was just beyond the town buildings, through the fields and past the wall. Liberty was heartbeats away.

With my hand in his, I felt like we could make it. I put all thoughts of everyone else out of my mind and focused only on the steps ahead of us. Dov pulled me along, his stride lengthening my own.

We made it down the hill before we were spotted. I heard them approaching. Dov heard them too, his grip tightening on me.

"When we get there, I'm going to put my hands out for you. Step in them and I'll boost you over. I'll follow right behind," he added before I could protest.

"Okay," I gasped, short of breath.

"It's the only way we'll make it. Once we get over, we must run. As soon as your feet touch the ground, go. I can catch up to you."

I knew it made sense; he was faster than me and could easily overtake me, even if I had the lead. This time I would do as he asked, without question and without the hesitation that might get us killed.

I registered the set of footsteps that approached faster than the others, even over our own noise. It came so near I knew they were on top of us.

"Get a move on, Lur," he shouted as he ran up behind me.

He maneuvered himself to my free side, running his hand along my back. I felt his grip tighten around me and propel me forward. I nearly lost my footing.

Between Dov and Shadoe's strong guidance, I was running faster than ever as they nearly carried me to the wall.

"Shadoe," Dov growled, his eyes turning fierce.

We were only feet from the wall now, and I felt Dov slow as he prepared to lift me over. The wall wasn't what it appeared from a distance. Up close it was more of a large metallic fence. Rocks lined the bottom on both sides, keeping it in place. There were holes, allowing air to pass through from one side to the next. Its frame was large. The top was flat, strong enough to hold a person on top. I decided it must be in case the government ever needed to use it to defend the land; it was a perch for soldiers.

"I was the one who cut you down, Lur. It was my arrow," Shadoe said, loud enough for Dov to hear. He was trying to gain our trust.

While Dov slowed, Shadoe removed his hand from me and launched himself forward. He threw himself at the wall, clinging to its high grips. He scrambled to the perch just as the guards caught up to us.

We were trapped between the metal wall and the human wall. The guards sneered at us, weapons ready. We must have been wanted alive or they would have killed us already.

Dov pinned me against the wall behind him, protecting me.

"You can't save her, Dov," Shadoe shouted. *"She's not yours."*

"Yes, *she is*. She'll *always* be mine," Dov shouted back. My heart swelled.

I was his.

In my peripheral vision, I saw something fly through the sky, coming from behind me. Shadoe had thrown an explosive device behind the guards, not close enough to *us* to hurt me, but enough to disorient the guards.

In that moment Dov turned. He bent before me, cupping his hands. I grabbed his shoulders and set my foot in his waiting fingers. He lifted me and I watched the top of his dark hair leave me. I reached up as Shadoe grasped my arm, pulling me to the perch alongside of him.

"Go!" Dov shouted as the guards ran toward him.

I struggled to get back down to help him. Shadoe threw me to the ground on the opposite side of the high wall. I landed hard, knocking the wind from my lungs.

Dov turned around one last time as I regained my footing. Through the openings in the metal wall, he shouted to me.

"I *will* find you!" He turned to Shadoe. "Get her out of here!"

He no more trusted Shadoe than he trusted the guards attacking us, but he knew it was the safest option for me in that moment. Dov knew that I knew his reservations about Shadoe helping me and that I wouldn't let my guard down. My best chance for survival was with only one opponent on the far side of the wall. Dov faced our attackers alone. One raised his baton, about to bring it down over Dov's head. I screamed as Shadoe pulled me away, refusing to let me turn back as Dov fought to keep the guards from me.

I was on my own with a man I had never loved and no longer trusted. Dov was alone, at the Society's mercy. Eden and Silas were out of my sights. No one knew what had become of Berwyn or the groups in the safe houses. I didn't know of Lowell's fate.

In those short few months, I had learned to love the Baer family. I had lived with them, shared their food and their home. I had talked with them and grown to know them. And yes, ultimately, Dov chased me away, forcing me to leave to *save me*, just like they say I was chased away from the people I had come to know.

I was the girl who couldn't be saved. He was the man who couldn't help but save me.

The wall, with all its promises of protection and freedom, stood uncaring as we were all dragged away to our own separate, desolate isolations.

But I was Dov's and he was mine. And somehow, I'd find a way back to him. No matter the cost.

Shadoe violently dragged me along.

No matter the cost.

ACKNOWLEDGMENTS

My beautiful readers, thank you so much for going on this journey with me. I hope you don't hate me too much. I know my beta readers spent quite some time live-texting comments to me…mainly yelling, some tears, and some happiness…so I can only imagine what you are thinking right now.

Before you go getting too upset with me, don't worry—I know there are unanswered questions. I promise you, you will find out how Goldilocks got her name early on in the second book, but that's all I'm telling you. There's so much more to her story, and we'll be exploring that in books two and three, as well as the prequel. I can't wait to share the rest of this journey with you!

Special thanks to my amazing beta readers! You were so incredibly helpful and I absolutely loved the live text reactions to what you were reading. I will always cherish the screen snaps of those conversations!

To my mom and dad, I know it was a bit surprising when I

dropped *"Hey, I wrote some books and one of them looks like it is going to be published!"* so thanks for rolling with that and being supportive!

To my little sister, Susie, thank you for giving me permission to not be nervous during the early stages of all this and for listening to me while I was talking myself through it. You've definitely improved on your secret-keeping skills since we were kids!

To Alexis Johnson, I have no words to express how much our friendship means to me. You've done so much for me and for Reading Transforms and I cannot thank you enough. This book would not be what it is without you and your stunning interior artwork. I am in awe of all you do.

To Jenny Pang, the first person to call Dov bae. I'm so grateful for your live messages as you read Golden, it was so affirming and an amazing experience. I'm sorry I *"broke your heart in pieces"* and made you yell *"why"* a lot. Actually…I'm really not sorry at all, Cupcake. *To Option A, my friend, to Option A!*

To Charlotte Selby, thank you for your friendship, Peaches! You've been so wonderful and so supportive. One day we will cause complete chaos when we meet half way. I'll bring the floaties, you bring the math.

A big thank you to Awnna Marie Evans, my lovely friend and the first person who tried to find Auluria and Dov a home, thank you from the bottom of my heart for believing in Golden. Your jokes always make me laugh. I'm so thrilled to have been able to work with you and I'm so grateful we met! I truly appreciate your confidence in me!

I'm so grateful to have found a caring and supportive home with Snowy Wings Publishing.

To the amazing street teams with Snowy Wings Publishing, The Snow Angels, and to my own street team, The Robins, thank you for all of your hard work and effort. I truly appreciate everything you have done to help me get the word out about *Golden*!

To my fabulous readers, thank you for going on this journey with me. I cannot wait to tell you more about Auluria and Dov in the rest of the series.

Thank you, thank you, thank you.

LOCKED

BOOK TWO OF THE GOLDEN TRILOGY

To those who fight for what is right, even when it costs them. It's not easy to put yourself last in order to take care of others. Well done. I'm proud of you. Keep going!

Goldilocks, having been separated from her love, the young Baer, is forced to work with her enemy to fight her way back to her people and country. She must decide who to trust and just how far she is willing to go to get back to where she belongs. Goldilocks was supposed to have a simple story, but that couldn't be further from the truth.

The stories never mention the war we had to fight, both in our country and on the other side of the wall. People neglect to talk about how enemies had to choose to unite or work to tear each other apart and destroy any hope of survival. They always ignore the part where I found myself trapped on the far side of the wall and what it took for me to return. They never talk about how many lives would be lost along the way.

My name is Auluria, and I won't stop until I've found out whether or not the Baers are still alive and I've brought the Society to its knees.

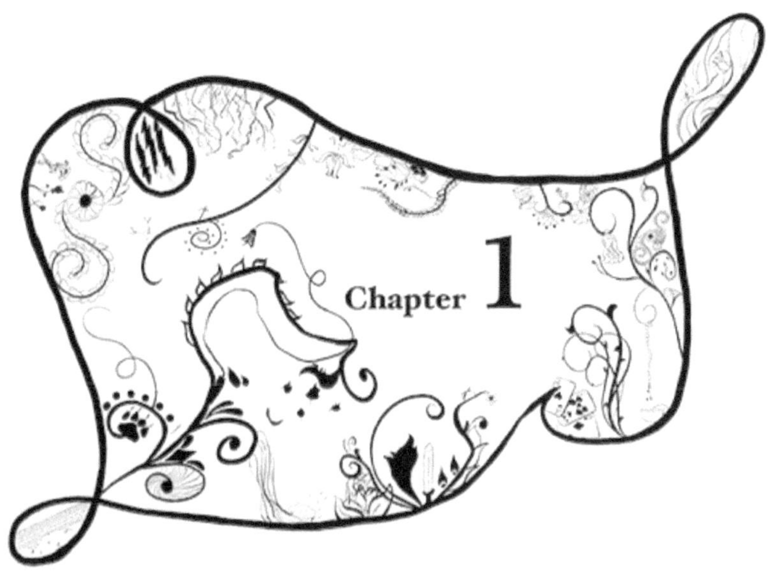

Chapter 1

THE MOMENTS BETWEEN *KNOWING* THE PAIN IS COMING AND ACTUALLY *feeling* it are the most agonizing. As soon as I heard it—the low, vicious growl—I stopped moving. I held in my gasp, as I had been trained to do.

Before I could turn to confront my attacker, I heard the collision as body met body. The wolf that had been crouching behind me flailed in the grass. It hissed and snarled as it tried to attack Shadoe.

He held the beast back, trying to strangle it. Without thinking, I picked up a large branch and brought it down on the gray wolf's head, silencing it. Shadoe made sure the job was done.

It had been a week since Shadoe and I escaped over the wall. Dov, the man I cared for, was still trapped somewhere in the Society. He gave himself up to save me, as he had been doing since the day I met him all those months ago.

Shadoe, my former handler, and I had been traveling together since that day. I didn't trust him, but we still work as well together as the day we started training. I relaxed enough to work with him without fearing for my life.

The day we escaped, I learned a great deal of information from Shadoe as he attempted to convince me not to run. Every day since, he tried to show me he was not a threat. We both worked for my older cousin Lowell, following his every command. His mission was to take down the Society by framing Dov Baer, his older brother Berwyn, and Berwyn's wife, Eden, along with their entire group. Knowing I could never be a part of that once I met Dov, I betrayed Lowell.

Shadoe remained loyal to Lowell, despite the fact that he was gone. Just before our escape, the government was going to hang us. In an effort to save Lowell, his men unintentionally gave us the opportunity to escape. When the soldiers finally caught up with us, we split up. Silas and Eden ran toward the woods. Dov and I ran toward the town. Shadoe found us at the wall and helped Dov to save me. The last thing I saw was the soldiers capturing the man who stayed behind to protect me.

Shadoe and I had rabbit meat, having saved our meal from the wolf. A meal of anything more than tiny birds was more than I could ask for. My former handler and I set up camp in the wastelands that lie between our nation and the foreign nations that attacked our people. With our camp being only a few miles outside of the closest foreign town, we had the perfect opportunity to spy on them while staying far enough away to keep from being discovered.

Each day, we crept toward the city. Each day, we got a little closer, pushing our luck and challenging them to notice our approach. The next day we planned to go into the city. I prayed it wouldn't be our last.

"Are you ready Lur?" Shadoe asked me.

I tucked the last bit of my long, golden hair under my wrap and nodded to him.

Shadoe and I carried sacks of food we had gathered to trade. We decided the best thing we could do was disguise ourselves as traders to get around the city without much notice. Some of the rabbit meat was tucked away in our bags, ready to be bartered for supplies. I was grateful we could hunt in the wastelands.

"What do you have, dearie?" A woman clutched my arm and held up several strings of beads.

The glittering crystals caught my eye as they shimmered. For a moment I was lost in their beauty.

"They're beautiful, but not today, thank you." I shook her off.

"We need more weapons." Shadoe muttered.

Shadoe had always been practical. For as long as I'd known him, he always made the dependable choice. Shadoe had been assigned to me since the day my cousin brought me into his fold. He had been my trainer, my partner, and even the man I was supposed to marry. Together, we were to lead as Lowell's next in command.

I glanced around, looking at the goods for sale. This town was much freer than where Shadoe and I came from. People came and went as they pleased. There was still an oppressive feeling over the town, but the fear was not as great. I concluded it must be because they were so far away from the people controlling them.

"Shadoe… " I nodded to a nearby man.

He eyed the short man before stepping over to speak with him. I stood near, my back to his. I pretended to scan the area for trades, but really, I was watching for oncoming attacks.

I imagined they must have been hunting us by now. The Society was furious with me. They may not know Shadoe, but *I* had escaped. They would be coming for me. Over the years I worked with Shadoe, he had trained me well; our reactions to each other came instinctively.

We walked away with several knives, having traded for the rabbit meat and several small birds. I put a knife in each crumbling boot, grateful to have it securely against my skin. My hand brushed over the knife in my belt.

I watched as children ran through the streets. They reminded me of the little ones from the storehouse. I hoped they were all safe under Berwyn's watch.

I still didn't know of Berwyn's fate. He had been poisoned during our plan to show the government it was Lowell who had attacked them, rather than the Baers. I still hadn't worked up the courage to ask Shadoe what he dosed Berwyn with. My sight bounced to Shadoe's hip where the dangerous metal claw hung, just out of sight under his shirt.

Shadoe nudged me and I looked away from the children's game. Just inside a small doorway sat a row of boots, ready for sale. We cautiously approached the illuminated doorway, warm with candle-light, even in the day.

"Welcome. Welcome." An older man eyed us. "Freshly made boots, perfect for long journeys and hard labor."

His eyes swept from my wrapped hair all the way down to my

boots. He grimaced at the sight of them. They were the same boots I had had when I started Lowell's mission all those months ago. Somehow they survived every attack and murder attempt. They served me well, but I was in desperate need of a new pair.

"What do you have?" he asked, and Shadoe showed him the remainder of our trade items. "Not enough, but for the pretty lady, I'll take it."

I shook my head at Shadoe. It was way too much and we hadn't finished gathering our supplies yet. I started to walk away when I heard the man speak again.

"Which pair would you like?"

I turned to see Shadoe handing everything we had left to the man.

"No." I shook my head again.

"Be practical, Lur. You need this. We can come back another day."

I tipped my head at him, trying to read him. On one hand, I couldn't imagine Shadoe ever paying such a steep price for something as simple as everyday boots. On the other hand, I really needed them. I hadn't complained, but I knew he could tell that it was getting too bad for me to continue in them.

Sighing, I reached down to inspect them. I tried several on before selecting a pair. I used my skirt to block my knives as I tested them. The man never knew I had them safely hidden around my ankles.

"Thank you," I said as we left.

"You needed them," was all he said.

Shadoe had always been a man of few words…at least to me.

We hunted again that afternoon. I never had the stomach for killing, so I helped Shadoe track, but allowed him to take them down. It made me sick each time, but I knew it was the only reason we were able to survive.

The sky was dark that night. The clouds blocked the moon, allowing us slivers of passing light as we lay on the ground next to the fire. On our journey we had seen several nomadic groups roaming about, so we felt safe enough to have the flames at night.

The days were growing short and the air was getting cooler as summer slipped into fall. The leaves dropped off of the trees and swirled around our feet.

"Tomorrow we'll go back again. We need to be seen. The more familiar they become with us, the more they will let their guard down." Shadoe said absent-mindedly.

"Shadoe?" I asked. "What's the plan?"

He looked at me as if I was crazy. "The plan is to get information, Lur, you know that."

"I mean the long-term plan. We escaped, but all those people are still back there. What are we going to do?"

"Auluria." He demanded my full attention. "We're not going to *do* anything. You're safe. Now we just have to survive."

Now it was my turn to look shocked.

"Shadoe, I'm not just leaving them there. I'm going back for them, whether you help me or not. It's just a matter of when and how."

I couldn't read his expression as he gave me a strange look.

"The guards took him, Lur. If they didn't kill him on the spot, they have surely hung him by this point."

I felt like I had been punched in the gut. Not even the pain of the torture I had received only weeks earlier compared to the notion of Dov being dead.

"He's not dead. He can't be." I said quietly.

Shadoe sighed at me and rolled over, ending the discussion.

But I didn't care. I would find a way back. I'd save Dov and Eden, Silas and Berwyn. I'd save all of the Baers' group. I wouldn't give up on them.

I brushed my hair back with my cold hand and forced the tears back into their deep wells.

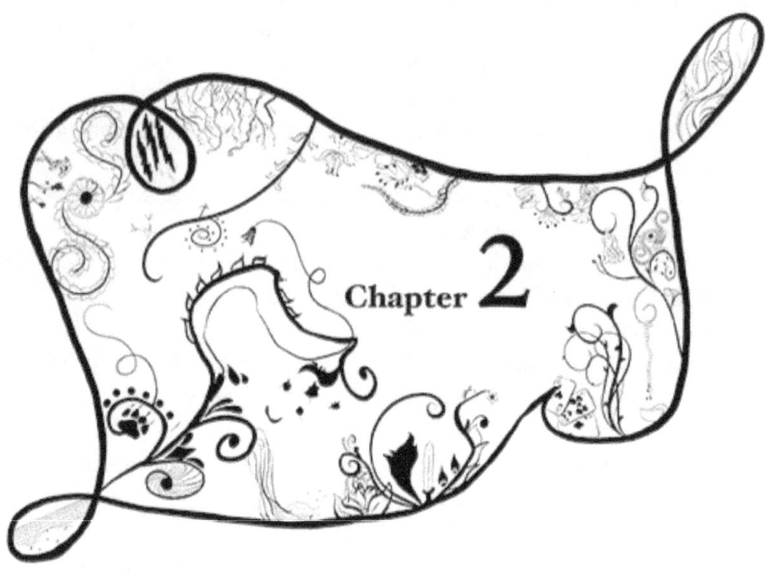

Chapter 2

By morning I had a plan. I'd learn my way around the city. I would find alliances if I could. I'd find a way to provide for myself, and then, if need be, I'd slip away from Shadoe and run. I knew it was very likely that he'd find me and drag me back away from the wall, but I had to try.

The town was full of people again. They bumped and jostled into each other as they walked. I watched carefully for every move they made.

"Hello again, dearie," an old lady said—the woman with the beads.

This time she carried a small cart behind her. "Help an old woman, dearie, and I'll let you have one of these." She held up a sparkling necklace.

"What do you need?" I asked kindly.

"I need to be across town." She looked down to her cart, heavy with bottles, jars and crates.

I nodded to Shadoe, indicating he should let me be. He branched off and went to trade. I picked up the handles and followed behind the woman.

"What's your name, dearie?" she questioned me.

"Au… " I caught myself. "Lur. My name is Lur."

"That's an unusual name, dearie. *Lur.*" She grinned as she tried out my name. "I'm Necesta. As you can see, I'm a bit of a medicine woman. Nothing other-worldly, mind you, but herbs and natural remedies. And the beads, of course." She chuckled to herself.

"You seem to be quite experienced." I remarked, trying to keep the conversation going.

"Oh yes, dearie. I've been doing this since before your parents were even born."

"Where are you taking all this?" I asked.

"Across town where I set up shop once a month. If people need me, they find me, but I try to make myself available in different locations when I can," she croaked, still chuckling.

I could tell as she walked that she was stronger than she appeared to be. I had no doubt she had been about to haul the load by herself. It made me wary.

Once we arrived, she asked me to help set up. It was almost like a small shack, similar the ones the Baers had in back of their house—only this was missing a side. The front had been removed, leaving it open to the world. There were several chairs and a table waiting.

She set out a few things but left most of her work in her cart.

"Sit, dearie, you could learn a thing or two." She winked at me.

I obliged out of curiosity, but my hand sat on the knife in my belt as I leaned away from her.

Almost immediately people started making their way toward the shack. Necesta called out ingredients for me to fetch for her. I examined each one before handing it to her. Watching, I waited as she set a young boy's broken arm. I helped her as she wrapped the hand of a man who had lost a finger, barely stomaching the blood.

Within a few hours, I felt strangely at peace around the woman.

"Necesta, thank you for letting me help you today. I've truly enjoyed it." I said. "Let me help you take your cart back."

I stood and picked up the handles. She nodded and we walked together back to her side of the city. Most of the cart's contents were gone, making the trip lighter.

"Where's that friend of yours, dearie?" she asked as we drew close to the street we met on. "Is he your lover?"

Her question nearly pulled me to a halt, but I caught myself and continued with only a slight hesitation in my step.

"No, he's not. He's a friend."

"I thought so. You didn't seem too worried when he left your side. *Him*, on the other hand, *he likes you*."

I gathered that Necesta was a woman of many talents. She was very perceptive, even if she was a little off.

"You'll both come to dinner, and then I'll pay you for your help."

"Oh no, Necesta, you don't have to pay me, I enjoyed it. And we don't want to impose… "

"Oh, nonsense, dearie. Go find your companion and let's get on with it," she demanded, scuttling into a small house.

Shadoe appeared, as if on cue.

"You were watching," I said without turning to him.

"Of course," he grumbled.

"Did you get anything accomplished today?" I asked.

"Yes." He seemed cross. "I stayed close in case you needed me, but I didn't watch you all day. You're trained well enough to take care of yourself. I just wanted to be sure you were all right; this *is* a new place, after all."

"Necesta wants us to stay."

He raised his eyebrows at me.

"She's feeding us. Just don't be rude." I said stomping off toward Necesta's door.

Shadoe followed me. The house was small, but the warmth of the fire was like heaven. She pointed to the table where she had already started setting out food.

"So, young man," Necesta started. "I have already met *Goldilocks* here, but I haven't had the pleasure of meeting her *young male* companion yet."

"I'm Shadoe, ma'am." He introduced himself as she bustled about the room.

"Ma'am," she mocked. "*Ma'am*. I may be an old grandma, young man, but you will call me Necesta, understood?"

"Yes," Shadoe confirmed rigidly.

"Yes?" she prompted, hands on hips.

"Yes, Necesta."

"That's better." She proclaimed, "Now, tell me. Where are you two from? It's not around here, that's for sure. And it's not from *our* country… Now don't worry," she said glancing at us, "no one else knows that. I'm just a perceptive old lady who's been around long enough to know who's from here and who ain't."

Shadoe and I were both horrified but managed to keep straight faces. I felt him stiffen, preparing to run if needed.

"Relax, young man, I'm not telling anyone. I'm only saying if you and your pretty lady friend were to have come from over that wall"—

She pointed in the direction of the wall—"then I'd just be obliged to tell you that there are those of us who wouldn't mind it. That's all. *Apple?*"

I sat stunned for a moment before reaching for the red apple in her hand. *How had she known? Did she know who I really was?*

"You aren't the first to run, dearie," she said, eyeing me.

"*You... ?*" I couldn't stop myself in time.

"Yes, dearie. I was once just like you. I jumped the wall and escaped. I found refuge here, though hardly anyone knows it. Don't worry; I'm on your side. Tell me, how has it been?"

"How did you survive?" Shadoe interrupted, unwilling to give her any information.

"Same as you will. I made friends. I learned to blend in. I made myself important." She nodded as she started to eat. "You'll find this place, while still controlled by violence and fear, to be a much easier place to live. Only, though, because we're so far removed from the capitol. Once they want something from us, which is still often, it can be very deadly. On days like today, when there is no oversight, we're free." She smiled thoughtfully.

I was beginning to like this woman. She was a no-nonsense, down-to-business, incredibly perceptive person. I had no doubt she was a good person to know in this town.

We finished our meal without upsetting Shadoe any further. We thanked Necesta and walked back to our campsite. Shadoe checked behind us every few steps the entire way back.

"I like her," I announced. "I think she's going to be helpful to us."

I touched the necklace around my throat. I insisted Necesta keep it, but she forced me to try it on and then pushed me out the door. I took it off and put it in my pocket.

"Keep it on, dearie," she had said, "so they know you're one of my friends. It will keep you safe here."

The next day when we went back to the town, I would wear it for her to see. Its jewels sparkled in the firelight before I dropped them into my pocket.

"We'll be careful," I said, "but I think we can trust her."

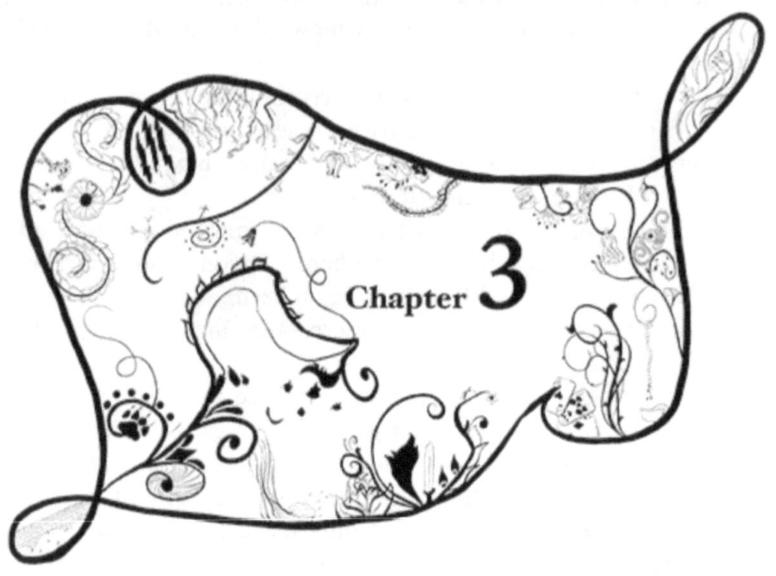

Chapter 3

SLEEP NEVER CAME EASY. FACES FLITTED THROUGH MY DREAMS, vanishing and reappearing. I watched as Dov was murdered a hundred different ways. I woke up screaming, Shadoe at my side. He said nothing, but watched over me as I tried to shed the tension in my body.

I stared at Eden's hollow eyes as the Society dragged her away time after time. I saw Berwyn crumpling under the force of the poison. I watched Silas being carved apart. I even saw myself being forced to watch their torture.

At times, I pictured Reyla and the girls I met in the storehouse. Reyla's face fell in my dreams as it did the day I told her that her beloved Peter was dead. Other times, I saw little Jaseleen and the other children, terrified, as we all went off to war.

Gone were the times I dreamed of happy memories from the past few months. Only the unanswered questions haunted me. Had any of us survived?

I dreamed of Dov that night. My precious Dov, who sacrificed his life for me, who saved me and protected me. My Dov, who took a beating to protect the lives of his people and his enemies. My darling Dov, who right now was with the people who hated us most… if he was alive at all. I would have given anything to just know what became of him after he chased me to safety that day.

I dreamed he was sitting in his cell—the same awful cell we had been forced into weeks earlier after our capture. In my twisted nightmare, the skin hung off his arm, even worse than the very real torture he had endured in my presence. I saw him covered with knife wounds and blood was everywhere. He blinked but he couldn't see me.

In my dream, I stood, just out of reach, screaming to him, but he never heard me. Suddenly Berwyn, Eden, Silas, Reyla, Gloria, and the others were standing there. They blamed me. They screamed and accused and mocked me.

Lowell stepped out from the crowd, grinning at me. "At least I paid you back, *Missy.*"

Shadoe stepped from behind him in my dream. "He was never yours anyway."

Marty, my vicious attacker, moved forward. "Not a golden boy anymore, is he? Nice work, golden girl." He laughed.

I tried to push past them, attempting to get to Dov. I screamed his name. When he finally turned to me, it wasn't his deep blue eyes I loved, but murky, dead eyes. His head lolled to the side as I slipped in his blood and fell at his feet.

The crowd behind me whispered, "You."

Somehow, even though I knew it couldn't happen, I found his dead hand grasping mine.

As I had each night before, I woke up screaming. Shadoe shushed me. He kept watch as I cried. Under normal circumstances, Shadoe would have never tolerated me showing this kind of emotion. I suppose I didn't give him much of a choice.

"Dearie, dearie!" I heard the old woman cry as Shadoe and I walked down the streets the next morning. He stiffened next to me but didn't hold me back as I walked toward Necesta.

She embraced me tightly, an action I wasn't expecting. I saw Shadoe reach for his weapon, but he held steady as the old woman pulled away. She grabbed my arm and pulled me toward her house. I glanced back to Shadoe, and he followed us through the streets.

She swung the door open and I saw several people sitting around the table we had occupied the night before.

"*There*, dearie, are your friends," she explained. "They escaped, too."

They all nodded and said hello. I could tell Shadoe wasn't happy.

"Come, sit. Sit." She demanded kindly.

"What is all this Necesta?" I asked.

"This, dearie, is what you've been looking for." She grinned at me.

"And what have I been looking for?" I played along. Maybe she was a bit more unstable than I thought.

"Oh, dearie, you've been looking for a way out. And we're it." She spread her arms wide, motioning at the people in the room.

I must have looked confused because one of the men jumped in to explain.

"I'm Raselin," a stocky, brown-haired man said. He had to have been at least twenty years older than I was. "What Necesta is trying to say is that we all know what it's like over the wall. We came looking for freedom too. While we found oppression, it's slightly better here. But not one of us *wouldn't* choose to go back if we thought we could fix the Society.

"There are groups over there, working to fix things—we know this as fact. We also know that the majority of this town would jump the fence to be rid of this place if there was some promise of life over there.

"Necesta says you want to go back. So do we." He motioned around the room. "And we think, if we can band the town together, we can help overthrow the Society and start again."

"We'll need training, of course." A woman who looked to be a bit younger than Raselin said.

"And that's where you come in, dearies." Necesta concluded. "And don't even try to tell me you haven't been trained. I may be old, but I'm not blind," she said. Dropping her voice she added, "And even if I was, I could fix that."

She had tenacity.

"And what do you want from us?" Shadoe said gruffly.

"Train us. Turn us into an army," the woman said. "We'll fight."

"We are strong in numbers," Raselin added. "We, ourselves, can overtake the Society. If we can get the resistance groups to join us, there's no way the Society will survive."

"I need a word." I stood to my feet so quickly I actually may have scared Shadoe.

I pulled him into another room before turning on him.

"Shadoe, this could be our chance."

"Lur, this could be a trap. We don't know these people," he argued.

"They want to go back. They want to fight," I insisted.

"They want to use us. And who knows, they may actually know about us and want to collect the reward. Lur, this is insane."

"Maybe it *is* insane." I would not stop. "But who cares? This is our chance to set things right. This is our chance to fix what Lowell did."

He paled and his face became taut.

"We can undo this mess. We can help save both of our groups and save the innocent people who got caught up in all this." I formulated a plan with every syllable I spoke.

I would lead these people. I would train them if Shadoe didn't. I knew enough. We'd cross the wall and take out the guards. We'd head straight for the center city and take out the leadership. Once we took over, I'd personally see to the agonizing pain of Magistrate Canton for what he did to us. We'd set the camps free. The people would be able to take care of themselves again.

There would be bloodshed, but there would also be freedom.

"We're doing this," I announced.

Without waiting for him to answer, I slipped under his arm and ran back to the group waiting for me. Shadoe clutched at my arm but I shook him off.

"I'll do it." I clamored. "I'll train you and we'll fight the Society together."

Their faces radiated with elation. I knew I had made the right choice.

"Now, how can we tell who is on our side?" I asked.

"Give us a few days, Goldilocks." Necesta said smiling, "We'll get them ready for you."

I was ready.

"Move over, Raselin, give Goldilocks some room. She has a lot to plan and her boyfriend is none too happy about it." She pointed a finger at Shadoe.

"*Clearly* not her boyfriend," Shadoe said under his breath. I almost didn't hear him.

I kept my eyes on Necesta, refusing to look at Shadoe. I didn't care what he was thinking or feeling. He could sit there and sulk for all I cared.

A chorus of screams rose up from the streets. Raselin was the first to the door, Necesta at his heels. I heard a loud crash as I ran to the window to see. I pulled the curtains away just in time to see several men who looked to be in uniform pushing several carts on their sides and rolling them over.

"Stay back, dearie." Necesta hissed at me when she caught sight of me at the window.

I ducked low, but held the curtain back just enough that I could still see out. Shadoe was crouched by my side, his hand near my foot. He sighed, shifting the curtains slightly.

"This can't be good." He huffed in a whisper.

The men in uniform jumped up on the overturned carts and started addressing the crowd. We had to strain to hear the men at the end of the street.

"...time... you all will... no one... by order of... " I made out a few words from the speech.

I watched as Necesta closed her eyes, clearly worried. She brushed back her graying hair, her other hand grasping the doorframe.

"Heavens." She breathed.

We waited for the men to leave, the minutes stretching on until my legs started to cramp. Necesta swayed back, rocking onto her heels when they finally moved on.

Her slight nod prompted us to stand, knowing it was clear of the uniformed men.

"Well, this changes things," Raselin said as soon as he shut the door.

"What happened? I rushed toward him, eager to find out what I had missed.

"The government is changing how they do things." Raselin explained. "They are now demanding even more of our people to go fight for them. We have one month before they are coming back for the selected. They're posting names in the city center now."

"Guess it's not too much different than home, now is it?" Shadoe remarked.

"At least they have the decency to warn their people first," I muttered.

"I imagine that will add a few people to our list," Necesta quipped, almost looking happy.

I gave her a look and she just winked back at me. I knew in that instant that I would never truly figure out Necesta.

"Well, off with you all now." Necesta waved us off. "You clearly have a lot to do."

She escorted us all out of the house and shut the door behind her.

"Come back tomorrow," Raselin whispered to me before branching off in a different direction. "We'll be ready for you."

"Shadoe, this is a good thing," I tried convincing him.

He walked several paces ahead of me, not even stopping to trade. As soon as we left Necesta's house he stormed off toward our campsite.

"Can we just talk about this?" I asked.

"Talk about what?" He fumed. "Auluria, I did not pull you over that wall and get you this far just to go back."

"I thought you would want to go back." I shot back at him, "The rest of Lowell's team is still there, and who knows what has happened to them?"

"They'll be fine on their own," he said spitefully. "They're trained to survive."

"Well maybe you don't have people you care about, but I do!" I said forcefully. I felt the anger in me rising. "How could you not care about them?"

He cut me off. "I *do* care, *Lur*. You think I don't care? If I didn't care, I never would have saved you. I would have saved Lowell, or if I couldn't, I'd have stayed behind and run the group. Instead, I came after *you*. You're my… partner." He faltered, then added slowly, "I had to make sure you were all right."

So, Shadoe, who never seemed to actually care about me a day in his life, had formed an attachment to me.

"If you care about me, then help me. We're partners. I'd like to be in this together." I said softly.

"It's not a good idea." He tried to persuade me. When I wouldn't relent, he gave in. "Fine."

I felt a smile tugging at the corner of my lips. I nodded my head instead.

"Thank you."

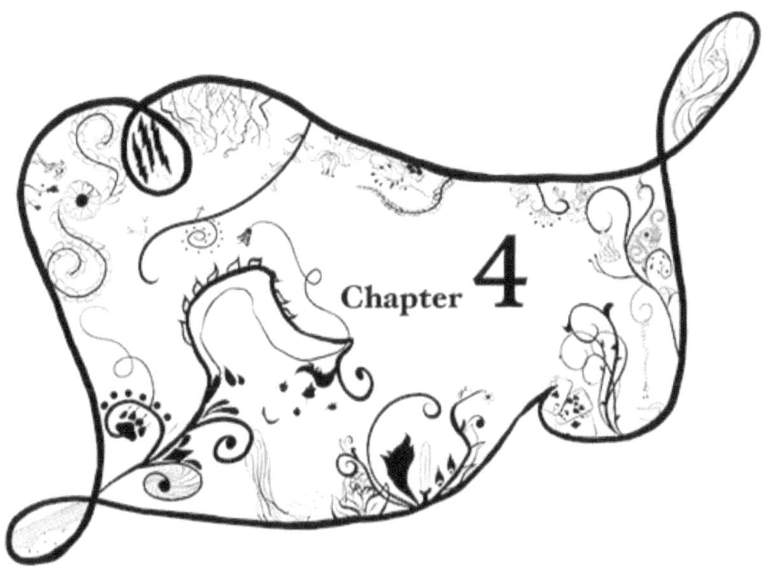

Chapter 4

Necesta and Raselin greeted us alone in her house the next day.

"Where is everyone?" I asked.

Raselin motioned us forward. Without saying a word we followed our two new friends down the streets, winding around people and buildings. The wind blew my hair out of my face as we walked and I arched up into the breeze. I allowed my eyes to slip closed for just a moment and Dov's face flashed through my mind. An aching stab clenched my chest, but I refused to let it hold me back.

When we reached our destination, we found ourselves in the woods. I felt Shadoe come alive as we entered the bark-covered fortress, both our bodies humming in anticipation. The woods gave us safety.

We wandered a bit into the depths of the trees. I watched as Shadoe's eyes swept across the terrain. He pointed just before Raselin held back a tangled clump of vines.

Of course he noticed.

Shadoe and I slipped in after Raselin and Necesta. The opening to the hidden place was small, good for deterring unwanted guests. Once we got passed the tight opening, we found ourselves in a spacious cave. I decided we must be mostly underground, not having seen much space on the surface.

A large crowd greeted us, turning in unison as we approached. Many of them nodded to us.

"This is Lur and Shadoe," Raselin announced. "They're here to help train us. Do everything they say."

Everyone nodded, eager to begin.

"We'll split into groups. You'll all work with one of us and we'll rotate often. Be ready, this will not be easy. Once we finish our training, we not only have to breech the wall, but we also have to defeat the Society from our neighboring country. Some of us come from there and are familiar with the cities and towns. For those of you that aren't, we'll do our best to prepare you." The crowd watched intently as Raselin addressed them.

"Anything is better than staying here!" a voice shouted.

"It's going to be dangerous there." Raselin said. "But if we succeed, and help take control of the Society there, we have a chance at a better life."

They cheered.

"We will work hard and learn to fight. We'll succeed in our mission and give good lives to our children. Now, break up into your groups."

They started splitting up as Raselin turned back to us. "Lur, you'll go over there, and Shadoe, you'll… "

Shadoe stopped him. "No, we're staying together."

"We need smaller groups and more leaders. You can be near each other, but you each need to train people."

"That's fine," I said before Shadoe could object.

"For the first few days we'll work on fighting. After that, we can make a plan to rotate and teach them the other skills they will need," he said. "As you can see, we already have some trained fighters, just not quite as finessed as you both."

"We can work on that." I assured him.

Stepping to my left, I found a small group of older men and women. I waved my hand toward another group—made of mostly young people—that Shadoe should focus on.

He positioned himself so he could see my every move and began. His sharp tone did nothing to encourage the youths, but my glare softened his words.

We spent the next few hours training our different groups.

Raselin rotated them out, allowing each group time to practice while we worked with a new group.

I walked around the men and women, watching for the correct positioning. Repositioning elbows, I gave strength. Moving feet into the proper stance, I gave power.

Shadoe watched as I demonstrated proper techniques to the group, working hard not to overwhelm them on their first day. Some were better than I anticipated, others stronger than they looked.

I ignored Shadoe as I worked, talking to the group I was overseeing. Soon, I blocked him out entirely and focused on the sound of elbows striking flesh as the fighters practiced.

By the end of the day I felt certain that with the proper training and planning, we could accomplish our goal. Raselin motioned for us to join him when he dismissed the people for the day, and I quickly joined him standing by Necesta.

"You didn't train with me today," I said to the older women, sad she hadn't worked with me.

"No dearie, that's coming." She nodded to me, eyes searching the length of Shadoe as he approached slowly.

"What did you think?" Raselin asked us.

"I think they have potential," I started to say.

"I think this is a suicide mission," Shadoe muttered under his breath, just loud enough for me to hear him.

Raselin shot him a look, but obviously missed what Shadoe had said.

"Lur, you seem to be the sensible one, how do you want to proceed with this?"

"I think you're right. Spend a few days exclusively on fighting and then we can start adding in the other elements. We have to move quickly, but we still need to assess where they stand."

"Good, I'm glad you feel that way." He nodded to me.

"Lur and I will work on a plan and we'll have it ready for you tomorrow," Shadoe said.

"Excellent," Raselin said.

"So you can go now." Shadoe dismissed him.

I gaped at him, but Raselin only held a hand up, telling me not to start a fight.

Raselin and Necesta turned and left.

"Shadoe!" I scolded. "They're trying to help us get our home back, you have no right to speak to them—"

"*Save it*, Lur. We have too much to do to argue over manners."

Before I realized what he was doing, his hand slammed into my arm, and I stumbled back. Readying myself, I attacked in retaliation and we locked in a battle of wills.

"I'll take charge of the physical training," Shadoe said as he attempted to kick my knee out from under me. "You oversee the spy training and manipulation lessons."

"Of course," I said sarcastically as I slammed my fist into the side of his head.

We spent several minutes arguing over what to teach them and when to teach it, but by the end of our sparring match we had a plan, and we were both exhausted. Collapsing on the ground, we tried to catch our breath. I may not have liked Shadoe, but he certainly was a good trainer.

"Lur?" he said quietly. "You know this is going to get us both killed, don't you?"

"Yeah." I sighed. "I'm pretty sure it will."

The bells jingled as the young girl reached into the test pocket.

"Like this." I showed her again how to use two fingers to slide into the pocket I was pretending to pick. She gave an exasperated sigh when I pulled my fingers back in silence.

"Like this, dear." Necesta brushed passt her and reached for the pocket. She deftly reached inside and pulled out the coin.

I smiled at the older woman. Her eyes glittered mischievously.

"Don't look at me like that, Goldilocks. I know my way around the spy world." She chuckled.

"I see that. Why don't you take over here and I'll move on to my other group?"

She nodded and I walked quickly to my team a few feet away. I watched as they practice the flirtation techniques I described to them. Brittella had trained me well when Lowell had put me in her charge so very long ago. It was strange to think of her now after all this time has passed since my training with her.

I had no doubt she had survived whatever the Society had thrown at her since I had last seen her.

"Very good. Now, let's try something else," I said, entering the circle.

I described ways of being seen without really being noticed and sent them off to practice observing quietly around the room, an art only the best could master. Shadoe continued to push the trainees to their limits, giving them the same coldness he had once offered to me. His face softened when he saw me watching him, but only enough that someone who knew him very well could tell.

Shadoe started walking toward me and I met him halfway.

"It's been three weeks, Lur. How much more time can we spare?" he asked, glancing around the room.

"Not long, but we can't risk sending them in too early. We just have to see this through," I said.

He nodded gruffly.

"Go spar with him. I need to see what he's doing wrong."

I looked as a man about our age stood in the center of Shadoe's training space. He was much larger than me as I stepped up to him.

"Lur's going to help us for a moment; I need to see how you do against someone of her level."

I waited for the boy to make the first strike. When he didn't, I moved first, kicking his leg out from under him. Before he could stand up, a voice sounded from behind us.

"You're not pitting them against Lur, are you?" Raselin asked. "Shouldn't you partner her with someone more matched to her skills?"

"Like you?" Shadoe said skeptically. He waves his hand dismissively, gesturing toward me. "If you want to fight her… go ahead."

Raselin eyed me, asking for permission. At my nod, he stepped forward as the boy on the floor scrambled out of the way. I noticed the other groups eyeing us as we size each other up. They moved so slowly, but it seemed they were at our side so quickly. Everyone gathered around to watch.

He circled around me and I matched his steps, keeping on the opposite side of our invisible circle. Shadoe's eyes lingered on me as I moved deftly around the ring created by the people we were training. We both seemed to be waiting for the other to begin the sparring match.

When he finally ran at me, I flipped him over my back. Raselin slammed into the ground, air rushing from his lungs. I quickly met him on the floor as he kicked me so hard in retaliation, I was convinced something had broken. Raselin rolled on top of me, attempting to pin me down, but I managed to slip my leg under him, pushing to throw him off balance.

We were on our feet at the same time, fists swinging in calculated motions. I held back my yelp as he connected with the side of my face. Shouts went up all around us and I blocked out the noise, focusing only on my opponent. Soon, I no longer even saw Shadoe in the crowd.

Dov's face filled my thoughts, distracting me momentarily. *Where was he? Was he alive?*

The searing pain stretching from my jaw to my ear brought me back to life. With a few quick swings, I connected and sent Raselin to the floor, ending the match. He reached out his hand and I helped him up.

"That, ladies and gentlemen, is how we will win this." He grinned at me.

Shaking my hand, he turned to challenge someone else. For a moment I'm worried he had slipped into thinking it was something fun, but I realized he was only keeping morale up. Turning it into something less terrifying than it really was made it easier for everyone to cope.

"That was amusing," Shadoe grumbled as he slipped to my side.

"You've been wanting to hit him for days… Here I thought you'd be happy," I mumbled back as I watched Raselin begin his next match.

"I *am* happy you hit him. Wish it could have been me. But this spectacle… this is ridiculous." His eyes glanced around the room, unappreciative of the hard work we had been putting in the last few weeks.

"It's better than what you did to me, Shadoe," I snipped before I realized what I was saying.

Instead of lecturing me, he stalked back to his group. I went to check on the group I had been training.

Two hours later I noticed someone run into the training room. The young man whispered something to Raselin who immediately looked concerned. When he glanced up at me, I knew whatever it was couldn't be good. He had the same look on his face that Berwyn had in the storehouse when he found out about our people being captured. *Our people.* I wasn't sure when I had considered the Baers as mine, but I knew how right that thought was.

Raselin swung around to face me.

"Okay, everyone, that's enough for today. Go home. Eat something and rest. Meet back here tomorrow." He announced, holding my gaze.

When the room cleared, Raselin walked over to a table set up on the side of the room. Only the leadership remained after training. Pulling out the table, we sat, waiting for an update.

Necesta set out the food for us. I knew I needed to eat after everything that day, but I couldn't think of anything but the information our spy had brought back to us.

I waited for him to speak but he took his time, thanking Necesta for all her hard work with the food.

"Our spy has just returned from the other side of the wall." Raselin started. "He arrived with much news. It seems the government has been spending their time and resources tracking several large resistance groups throughout the country."

I looked to Shadoe. We both knew who they were. The Baers... Lowell's men... Marty and Jake's group. *We* were the people they were tracking.

"You know something," Raselin started to say, eyeing us.

"We have an idea of who they are," Shadoe replied. "Keep going."

"They're focused on finding these groups and exterminating them. I'd almost guess that they're willing to remove the older men and women and send the younger ones to the camps. Trouble within their borders makes it harder to fight the monsters outside."

"Are we the monsters outside?" Necesta laughed darkly.

"For now." Raselin glanced at her. "But not for long. We'll be over the wall soon, and then we'll be the monsters inside... One more group for them to fight against. Hopefully with being pulled in so many directions, they won't notice us until it's too late."

"What else did Devin say, Raselin?" I asked, redirecting the conversation. "Do we know what groups they are going after or why?"

"I'm afraid I don't have much news on that front. Devin went into the heart of the Society, so he only learned what the townspeople could tell him, and even then, they didn't have much information."

"We learned never to talk," Shadoe muttered.

"Which is why we only have a vague idea of what was happening with these groups. As far as we can tell, they all want to destroy the Society. Can you confirm this?"

"Yes, basically," I answer before Shadoe can.

"So we can get them on our side."

"Of course we can. Goldilocks can be very convincing when she wants to be, can't you, dearie?" Necesta turned to me and cupped my chin in her hand.

She watched me for a moment, as if trying to tell me something. Backing away, she let her hand fall as she turned back to Raselin.

"What else? Give us all the details." Her voice settled into a hum as she sat beside me.

"The man in charge, at least in charge of that area, is Magistrate Canton."

"We know him," I interrupted, shuddering.

The group's eyes swung toward me, waiting for an explanation.

"He captured Lur for a time," Shadoe supplied, unwilling to give details to the group.

He held Raselin's gaze, challenging him to push for answers. I slowly lowered my eyelids in a signal that was blocked from Shadoe's sight by my hair flowing in front of me. I would give details later, without the entire leadership group watching.

"From what Devin gathered," Raselin continued, "Canton is working on something big."

Just then Devin stepped back into the room, as if on cue, his arm in a sling that hadn't been there earlier.

"Devin, come tell the team what you learned."

Devin settled on the bench across the table, his injured arm resting on the table as Necesta pushed her plate toward him.

"I was in the town, talking to people, trying to find answers. I met a few men who weren't bright enough to know not to talk to me, fortunately.

"Magistrate Canton, the man in charge, is searching for survivors from rebel groups he is trying to dismantle. I hear that not too long ago, he took out key leaders of two of these groups, but I also hear there was an escape attempt and not everyone was killed. From what I could tell, it seems like the Society hasn't been able to locate some of these leaders and it's believed that they are creating an even stronger resistance group.

"I also heard that Canton has some kind of a plan. He managed to get a few hostages and is holding them to try to manipulate the leaders of the groups he is searching for."

Shadoe elbowed me and my gasp turned into a grimace.

"I've been told that one of the people Canton is holding is a woman. No further details," he said, slipping into a militaristic recount of what he had learned. "A man is being held. He's older and they aren't sure how he is connected, but he's being held on suspicion. Based on the conversations I overheard, 'being held on suspicion' is code for being submitted to torture.

"I know there is someone else they are holding, too. A younger man; a leader. They confirmed his identity as one of the men who runs one of the main groups they are fighting with.

"While I was there, they paraded him out in front of the crowds of people forced to watched. His clothes were torn and he looked like he had been dragged off of the front lines of the war.

"The soldiers shouted about his crimes and warned the people that their fate would be the same if they tried to rebel against the Society. They beat him in front of everyone and told the people to spread the word that if his family surrendered, they'd let him live," Devin said, his hand moving toward the sling his damaged arm rested in on the table, suddenly uncomfortable as he picked at the fabric.

"Devin, you saw this man?" I asked.

"Yes." His eyes swept up from their mark on the table in front of his arm. "From a distance."

"What did he look like?" I held my breath.

Shadoe straightened his back, waiting for the answer.

"He was tall, but it was hard to see his features after the beating he had obviously taken before they brought him out in public. They shoved him into the middle of a stage, surrounded by what looked to be places where they could set up gallows."

"But what did he *look* like, Devin?" I erupted in a rush of words, causing the entire table to look to me.

"Oh, my dear." Necesta said in a low, breathy voice. "It's him, isn't it? The one you left."

How Necesta could have guessed that there was a man in my life besides Shadoe was beyond me, but she had figured it out.

"Devin," she said quietly when she noticed the tears forming in my eyes, "Go on."

"He was tall…" he said quietly, unsure of himself. Tears always made men unsure of themselves—Brittella had taught me that— though this was by no means an attempt to elicit information by crying. I fought to stop.

"He was tall," he said again. "He had dark hair and the soldiers were calling him an animal. I think it must be his group's symbol or something."

"What was it?" Shadoe asked, his voice filled with loathing, already knowing the answer.

"He said to tell the bears they had their cub."

I closed my eyes so hard it hurt. Dov was alive, or had been when Devin was there.

I knew the Society had him—there had been no way for him to escape them once he sent me over the wall—but the confirmation of his capture made it real. Until that point, I could have at least hoped that Dov hadn't been hurt, but Devin's account confirmed otherwise.

"Your young man?" Necesta asked.

"You have a… Never mind." Raselin caught his curiosity.

"Not bear the animal," I choked, "Baer the last name. And his first name is Dov, and yes, he is mine. He sent me over the wall to protect me and they captured him."

"He's still alive," Devin said quickly, trying to silence the tears I was keeping at bay.

"Canton is trying to call the Baers out." Shadoe mused.

"But why is he targeting them?" I turned to Shadoe and dropped my voice. The group casually looked away to give us a moment, as if they couldn't hear everything we were saying.

"Is it just because they have Dov and they don't have any of Lowell's men, or is there a reason?"

"I don't know," he answered, tipping his head toward me, adding to the illusion of privacy.

"We need to get him out of there."

"We need to find out why they're keeping him and not executing him," Shadoe countered, confronting me with the deadly reality of the situation.

If Canton and his men had Dov and hadn't killed him yet, there was a reason.

Whatever the reason was, he was using Dov to get to someone —*me? Eden?* Had Eden survived? Did he have her too? Could she be the woman Devin was talking about?

"Who is he targeting?" I wondered out loud.

"We'll find out, I suppose," Shadoe said reluctantly.

"We need to find out why Canton has Dov." I turned back to the group, their attention immediately on me. I saw Necesta's eyes light up at the mention of Dov's name. I would likely regret giving her that information.

"He tried to kill us once. If he's holding Dov, there is a reason."

"Canton has a plan. He always has a plan. But we're smarter than him. We'll figure it out and beat him at his own game," Shadoe announced.

"It's time," Raselin said, ignoring the conversation. "We need to start running missions over the wall. We need to test what we're up against. Small groups at first; a few men at a time. We need to know how quickly they will discover us."

"I'll go," I volunteered.

"No," Shadoe said next to me, leaning toward Raselin and nodding once. He was trying to intimidate the man.

Raselin raised an eyebrow at my former handler, deciding whether to challenge him or not. Shadoe and I had the upper hand, our training far outweighing his experience, but which of us would he side with?

"I'm going; they need people who know the land," I repeated.

"You will get too distracted. You'll try to run in and save your precious boyfriend and we can't afford that. You're not going."

"*You* trained me. Are you saying my training isn't good enough to stay focused?" I challenged him.

His face grew red, and I could see him fighting between the two options, wrestling with them privately before he answered. Pride won out.

"You will stay with me the entire time. You will not run off to help him. We stick to the plan."

"Is the team ready?" Devin asked, interrupting the impending battle.

"No," Shadoe and I answered together.

"But not everyone is going on the test missions," I added. "We'll only take those who are ready. The rest will continue to train here with Raselin."

"Oh, no." He raised a hand, stopping me. "I'm coming along too. There's no way I'm letting you out there with this one alone—he might not let you come back."

Shadoe scowled as the man nodded toward him. Pulling me out of the mission was a distinct possibility, especially if we managed to sneak back into the Society's side of the wall and could get back to Lowell's group. I was suddenly very grateful for Raselin's involvement in this mission.

"Fine." I practically jumped out of my seat to ensure Shadoe wouldn't resist. "When do we leave?"

"We spend tomorrow preparing," Shadoe said, taking the lead on the mission. "We'll leave the next day. We'll be back within two weeks."

He stood up and swung his leg over the bench we sat on at the table. I took a deep breath, knowing this wouldn't be pleasant.

"Should we discuss who you're taking with you?" Necesta asked politely, waiting for Shadoe to sit down.

Had anyone but the older woman asked, Shadoe would have walked away. By some miracle, he sat down next to me, locking eyes with me. He waited for me to give him a name.

"Well, Devin is injured," I said, glancing at the man. "It's probably wise that he stays here and heals. Besides, the town just saw him. It might not help our cause if they see him with us lurking around."

Necesta reached over the table and fussed with the sling. Standing, she walked away from the group as Devin watched curiously.

"What about Fitch?" Raselin suggested. "He seems to be doing very well during training. And I trust him with my life."

"Fitch would be a good asset to have. His strength might be helpful," I said, thinking of the way he nearly put Devin's brother, Justin, through a wall two days ago during a sparring match.

"Send Justin," Devin interjected, obviously reading my mind.

"Justin is acceptable." Shadoe nodded. "Reed, too."

"Here, try this," Necesta interrupted, bringing a cup to Devin's place at the table. "This will reduce the swelling."

Devin glanced at the cup, taking a quick breath, and lifted it to his lips.

"Thank you, ma'am," he said after swallowing. Another drink and the cup was empty.

She pressed something into his injured hand.

"For later." She winked at him and returned to her seat. "You're taking Nian, right?"

"I think that's a good choice." Raselin waited for more suggestions.

Several minutes later we had completed our team. Devin was sent to gather the men while we discussed what we would need to do to prepare and who would be in charge while we were gone.

"Lydia can help Necesta while we're gone. Fitch has been training her to fight since before we started her training and she's got a good handle on things," I suggest.

"Lydia is a good girl. She'll be missing her husband while he's with you on the mission, so this will give her something to do." Necesta smiled conspiratorially at me.

"You summoned?" Nian asked as he walked back into the training room. Reed followed behind him, joining him where Devin sat earlier.

"We're going on a mission," Raselin informed them. He looked to the door, indicating that we were waiting for more members before we gave out details.

Fitch sauntered in a moment later, with Devin and Justin in his wake. It always struck me how similar Justin and Devin looked, despite their age difference. It reminded me of how similar Dov and Berwyn were.

The men stood behind the benches and waited for directions. Raselin stood at the head of the table to address them.

"Men, we're going on a mission. We need to test our limits over the wall. Devin just arrived back with valuable information for us and it's time that we start to make our move. The team as a whole isn't ready yet, which is why we're taking a select group of you over the wall with us to run a few test missions.

"We need to know the Society's response time. Our job will be to map the area, figure out how they respond to things, and determine what their goals are." He turned to face our side of the table. "Lur...?"

I stared blankly at him, unsure of how to respond.

"Would you like to tell them what you know?"

I continued to stare.

"About your friend?" he waited for me to catch on.

"Oh." I caught on. "The man in charge, Magistrate Canton, has our friend. He captured him when he helped us to escape. He gave himself up to save us."

I motioned to Shadoe as he glared at me. In his opinion, Dov had never saved him. I knew the truth, but Shadoe would never accept that Dov sacrificed for him too.

"The point, gentlemen, is that Canton would never let this man live if there wasn't a reason," Raselin added, making me realize I had trailed off while trying to decipher Shadoe's resistance to the fact that Dov had saved us.

"He had sentenced us all to hang. Actually, that's how we escaped." I glanced around the group, noting their reactions. "It's a long story. But Dov wouldn't be alive if Canton didn't have some purpose. Devin said he was using him as bait. We just have to figure out who he's using him against and what his plan is once he gets what he wants from them."

"This is a rescue mission?" Reed asked.

"No; this is a scouting mission. If we find an opportunity to help people along the way, we will. It would be in our best interest to recover this boy. If Canton wants him, he's valuable to have with us."

"I also imagine it will motivate Goldilocks a bit more, too,"

Necesta prattled and rocked forward to look at me. She played the frail, meddling, old woman well, but I knew she was very direct in her methods.

"I don't mind saving the kid," Fitch said, shrugging a shoulder.

"I heard he wasn't someone you wanted to mess with while I was over there," Devin added, grinning at me. "Tough guy."

Why Devin decided to show me this small mercy, I didn't know, but I'd happily accept any hope he could give me of Dov's resilience.

"We'll see if we get that close," Raselin said, glancing at Shadoe. "Now, let's talk about tomorrow and what we need to do."

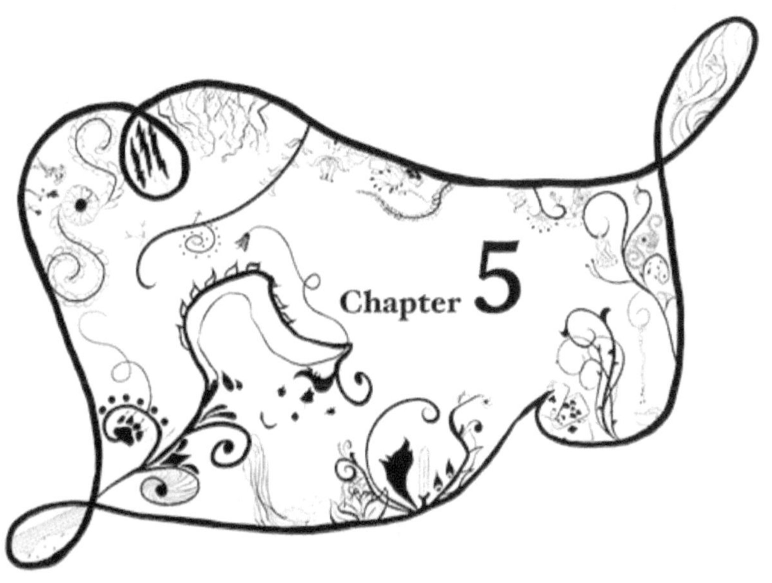

Chapter **5**

"Lur?" Shadoe called into the room.

"Back here," I replied, lifting the basket to my hip.

He eyed the woven container balanced between my body and hand. Walking forward, he glanced at the contents.

"Beads?" he asked.

"I'm moving them for Necesta. She's got something back there she said could help."

"What's that?"

"I don't know yet. Help me move the boards."

He lowered himself to the ground and reached forward to move the boards. For a moment, I braced myself for him to turn and attack like he did during my time training with him… I was never to let my guard down. The strike never came.

We were no longer in training.

I stepped backwards, setting the beads down carefully to avoid spilling them. When I turned around, the first board popped free of the wall.

"Careful, dearie," Necesta said, walking in the room. "That's fragile."

Shadoe cautiously reached inside the wall. When he drew back, he held two small vials. The clinking indicated there were more hidden in the recess.

Necesta brushed past me, her clothing catching against mine, creating friction against my arm. She took the glass from him and turned her back to Shadoe to face me.

"Take these with you." She handed me the vials, but pulled back suddenly. "No, not that one."

Bending down, she leaned into the hole in the wall and moved things softly. Her back bent low, unnaturally hunched over to reach what she was looking for. When she returned to her normal posture, she held a few small containers.

"Goldilocks," she said softly, waving her hand to indicate that I should join her on the floor.

Gathering my skirt in my hands, I settled myself on the ground next to her. Her glance at Shadoe was meant to dismiss him, but he waited, arms crossed across his chest, raising his shirt just enough for me to see the metallic claw that hung there.

Berwyn.

His face flashed in front of me again. I should ask Shadoe. I should know what became of my friend.

Friend. When Berwyn had become a friend, I didn't know, but there it was. I was worried about him for more than Dov's sake.

"Take these with you, Goldilocks. You might need them." The old woman handed me several vials. "Put them in that pouch of yours."

"What are these for, Necesta?"

Holding them up to inspect them, the first sparkled in the light as it passed through the clear liquid.

"That's for injury. But only use it if it's bad. You can't afford to waste that."

I nodded, setting it in my skirt to rest. The second vial was dark, filled with murky liquid that reminded me of the mud out in the woods I was trained in.

"That one is for poison." She touched my knee with the tips of her fingers, as if impressing great wisdom upon me. "It counteracts the effects of most poisons, dearie. Use it wisely."

She waited for me to make eye contact and nodded slightly.

Dov. This was for Dov.

Did she know something? Had Devin told her something he didn't tell the rest of us?

One side of her face hitched up into a half grin, her eyelids lowering just slightly in sympathy. She was guessing what might have been happening to Dov; she would tell me if she knew.

She placed a few other vials in my hands, explaining how to use each one before pointing a long finger at the pouch attached to my hip. I placed each container in, committing their uses to memory.

"Don't mix them up."

Her warning prompted Shadoe into action.

"She won't." He grabbed my elbow and lifted me up. "We need to go."

"You're coming back with us, right, Necesta?" I asked as I scrambled to pull my feet under me to alleviate the pressure on my arm.

"Yes, dearie. We just needed to collect the things from the house."

She waited on the floor for me to reach down and help her up. The woman was surprisingly solid for how tiny she looked—another of her quiet deceptions.

Shadoe reached out to steady her as she stood, offering his arm to the woman. Necesta looped her arm around his elbow once she was on her feet, refusing to relinquish it. Shadoe grumbled, but stopped trying to pull away once he realized she wouldn't let go. She let him lead her the entire way back to the training facility, leaning heavily on him for support that she didn't actually need.

I followed along side of them and she prattled on as she had the day I helped her with her cart: an act for the town. Once we reached the hidden door, Shadoe allowed her to go first, casting me a look when she stepped ahead of him. I rolled my eyes, which annoyed him even more.

Underground was cooler than outside, the shade from the sun making it easier to work in. I hadn't realized it when I was in the storehouse with the Baers, but thinking back, that had been cooler too, despite the large number of people staying there during our time in hiding from Lowell's men.

Glancing around the room, I notice Lydia helping Fitch packing a bag. Talley, the woman I had met in Necesta's house the day I met Raselin, stood nearby, talking to Justin and Devin.

They glanced up as I approached.

"Hello, Lur." Justin nodded to me. "You ready to go?"

I took a deep breath.

"Yes, I think so."

Rather than follow me, Shadoe walked over to Raselin.

"What's his deal?" Lydia asked, nodding to my former fiancé.

"Is he always like that?" Devin asked.

"From what I've seen." Talley's voice was low as she answered.

"It makes him a good soldier." Fitch responded, his deep voice hushed so that it didn't project around the room. "We don't need *feelings* on this mission; we need level headed people who can be practical in bad situations. Emotions have no place here."

He glanced at me.

"Did he cut you down when you escaped, Lur?" Talley said. "Sounds a little emotional to me."

"Being a decent human being, doesn't mean he's emotional, Talley." Necesta joined us. "He's fond of Goldilocks. That's not a bad thing. It means he will protect her… We need her more than we need the rest."

"How so?" Devin asked, a touch of resentment in his voice.

"She's connected to the one Canton has. Somewhere in all of this mess, that's going to be leverage." She stepped closer. "So you see, we need her. And if he's the one to protect her until that comes into play, then let him have his little attachment, and you lot stay out of it."

"You're important too, big brother." Justin reached over and patted Devin's uninjured shoulder.

"Shove off," Devin replied, grinning as he pushed his sibling's hand back.

"Don't make me separate you two," Talley added, joining in with them. They both rolled their eyes at her and grumbled to each other about how she always tried to mother them.

"Don't let the power go to your head while I'm gone, sis." Justin joked. He turned to instruct Devin. "If she gets a big ego while I'm gone, do something about it."

"And how is he supposed to do that with a bum arm?" She challenged her younger brothers.

"All right," Lydia interjected, "Enough. Devin, we're running the show, so no arguments, and Justin… Just don't die out there, okay?"

"Wow, such confidence." Fitch laughed.

"Now, Fitch, you know I didn't mean you. It's not *you* I'm worried about."

Justin's eyes grew wide until he caught her smile and realized she was teasing.

"Oh, don't worry, Lydia, I'll protect your man while we're gone." He glanced at the man twice his size. "I've got your back, buddy."

"I feel so safe." Fitch replied in a monotone voice, making everyone laugh.

Maybe this mission wouldn't be as serious as I thought. The

banter made me miss Reyla and her group of friends. I wondered what they were doing to try to save Dov. I knew they'd never leave him in the hands of Magistrate Canton.

"All set?" Nian joined the group, dropping a bag of supplies at his feet.

"Almost," Necesta replied. "Goldilocks, join me for a moment."

We walked along the edge of the room, eyes roaming over the men and women continuing to train without us.

"They're doing well," she commented.

"They are," I agreed, wondering what she was up to.

"By the time you return, they might be ready."

"You'll have to work hard with them."

"Lydia and Talley will work hard with them." She slowed her steps. "Now, Goldilocks, there's something you must do for me."

I nod.

"Take this." She handed me a brass necklace, tarnished from years of ware.

"Necesta, I don't think it's wise to wear—"

"You must." She stopped me, closing my hands around the beads. "Just like you have your secrets locked inside that pretty golden head of yours, these beads hold secrets too. Look."

She guided me to turn to fully face her, using my long hair to block the beads from the sight of the room. She nodded and motioned for me to get on with it when I shot her a questioning look.

Bringing the necklace closer, I saw that each bead had the ability to open.

"Not yet, dearie." She placed her hand over mine. "Look here. You'll notice the tarnishing on each is a bit different. That's how you tell them apart. These three here are poison. Those four are antidote. These two heal."

She turned the necklace, explaining each of the beads' particular mixture of life, death, and power. I counted each with her, from left to right, start to finish.

"They match the ones I gave you earlier. The bottles, the colors, the liquids... They all match. Remember one, remember them both." She concludes. "Now, dearie, don't use these unless you don't have a choice. I've had these for a long time and have never had to resort to exposing the necklace. It's old and decaying, at least it looks that way, so no one should question you about it. Keep it under your clothing, though. Don't give them any reason to be suspicious."

"I will," I said, slipping it around my neck. I tucked it under my dress.

"Are you wearing that out?" She appraised my outfit.

"I fit into a crowd better in the dresses. I'll save the pants for when we're running." I smiled, knowing she already knew that.

"We best be getting you back to your young friend." She nodded toward Shadoe and Raselin as they start to walk toward the others.

Necesta and I walked over to join the group as they reached down to pick up their packs that had been resting on the floor. Shadoe handed one to me, barely waiting for me to take hold before he released it.

"Necesta, you are in charge of overseeing everything that happens here while we're gone. Lydia and Talley answer to you." Raselin turned to the younger women. "You ladies are in charge. Make sure they are prepared by the time we return. Do not come looking for us if something goes wrong. Keep the people protected, no matter what that means."

They nodded, Lydia slipping her arm through her husband's in their final moments together before we left for our trial mission. Talley glanced at her brothers, standing on either side of her. Devin would be safe, still in her care, but Justin would be with us. She glanced at Devin's sling before looking to her youngest brother.

"Am I clear, Devin?" Raselin asked. "You are not to come after us."

He opened his mouth to speak, but quickly closed it.

"Devin," Raselin warned, "You are not to come after us. Talley will need you here to help protect the people. Your obligation is to them, do you understand?"

"Yes, sir," he finally responded, refusing to make eye contact as a touch of red crept into his cheeks at being called out.

Raselin gave specific instructions on how things were to be run while we were gone, Shadoe adding a few harsh directions on training. When they were finished, we said our goodbyes.

Justin hugged his siblings, promising to return safely and reminding his brother to keep Talley level headed. Lydia and Fitch stepped away for a private moment, while Nian and Reed said goodbye to their people as well.

"Take care of each other, dearies," Necesta said, turning to where I stood beside Shadoe. She winked at me, whispering, "Bring that young man of yours home."

Shadoe turned and walked away. I watched as he made his way to the door.

"He'll be fine," Necesta sang as she walked away from me, tossing her words over her shoulder. "So will you, Goldilocks. Take care."

Alone, I decided to follow Shadoe. Once through the tunnel, I stepped out into the fall air. The smell of slowly dying leaves permeated the breeze and floated around us in gentle waves.

"You know we likely won't make it out this time, don't you?" Shadoe said without turning to me, kicking a leaf out of his way. It was just beginning to turn yellow.

"I know."

"We probably won't even make it through this trial mission. You know Canton is looking for us. *Specifically* for us."

"You mean *for me.*" I corrected.

"Yes, for you. You're the one that escaped. He doesn't actually know about me. He never saw me, and the only ones that could have were too preoccupied with your boyfriend at the wall."

"And yet, we'll both probably die."

"Yes."

"What are you going to do when we get over the wall, Shadoe?" I asked, knowing he must have a plan.

"I don't know yet, truthfully." He looked up from the leaf he was moving with his boot and surveyed the land in front of us. "I'll have to see what we encounter when we get over there. From what Devin said, things have changed, Lur."

"You're going to help me save them, aren't you?" I asked tentatively.

Before he could answer, the rest of the team joined us, the sound of their boots announcing their arrival. Raselin stepped to my side and nodded to me and then to Shadoe.

Shadoe led the team without a word. We followed quietly behind until we reached the edge of the town.

One at a time, we slipped onto the crowded streets of merchants selling their wares, trying to survive on what little money they could make. Raselin went first, judging the atmosphere of the town he had known for years. The men followed behind, several minutes between each, until only Shadoe and I were left standing in the tall grass.

"Go," he said.

I thought about using the opportunity to talk to him, but when he pushed me out into the street, I had no choice but to move. Wandering through the area, I looked at packages of food and bolts of material.

A shout rose up a few yards away, claiming my attention.

Someone had called Justin into the commotion, putting him on display.

"I really need to go," he said, attempting to step back.

"Justin!" a woman screeched, reaching for him over the table she stood behind.

The look on his face might have been hilarious, had we not been trying to keep a low profile as we made our way through the town. The woman was angry, obviously wanting Justin to return to her table. He glanced around, looking for escape when he caught sight of me. He leaned forward just enough for me to get the picture.

Walking toward them, I added a bounce to my step, acting oblivious to the chaos around us.

"There you are," I said as I approached. Looping my arm through his, I weaved our fingers together, making his breath catch. "I got separated from you. I'm sorry, darling. Did you find anything for my parents? We really need to find the perfect gift for them…"

I trailed off, pretending to wait for an answer. I locked eyes with him, willing him to not look away. I had stunned the woman into silence, but if he engaged with her again, I didn't know how I could slip away with him.

"Oh, you did!" I gushed before he could speak. "Show me!"

I pushed him back, turning Justin away from the rogue woman who was beginning to collect herself. As I moved him farther away, I uncoiled myself from his arm and moved closely against his hip, wrapping myself around his back to hold his hip, claiming him.

Her gasp told me I had succeeded, but I pressed on, forcing us forward. Three steps and I sped up. Another three steps and I quickened our pace again as he leaned in and whispered in my ear.

"You decided making her jealous was a good thing?" he teased.

"Was that a bad call?" I asked.

"No." He shrugged as he wound his arm around me possessively. "It gets her off *my* case. She used to have a thing for Devin, but when he ignored her, she moved on to me. Aren't I so lucky?"

"Clearly," I said, shrugging him off once we made it around a corner. "We need to move."

"Before she sends the soldiers after you?"

I stopped in my tracks, hair whipping me in the face as I turned to look at him.

"Relax, Lur. The soldiers won't be around for at least a few more days. By then, we'll be long gone." He laughed.

I blinked a few times, trying to decide if he was joking about her sending the soldiers or if she was the type that really would do that to someone she was mad at.

"Hurry, before Shadoe finds us." His words spurred me into motion. "Besides, there were lots of witnesses. If anything happened to you, they could come forward and tell them it was her and not you."

"You really think they'd stand for me if it came down to it?" I questioned as we walked faster.

"You probably didn't notice this because you were so busy focusing on me," he grinned, "but all those men back there had their eyes glued to you. They'd step up to help the pretty girl."

"Would they now?"

He nodded.

"You'd have to marry one of them, but they'd certainly speak on your behalf." He grinned; reminding me of Gregory that night I played cards with the boys and Reyla's friends at the storehouse. If we made it over the wall and survived, my goal would be to find the Baers' group and see what had become of the others.

"Hurry." Justin's voice changed, his arm tugging at me, as the noise rose behind us.

We scurried down the alley, exiting behind the buildings onto another street. I held my hand up, motioning my companion to wait while I cleared the area. Tentatively I stepped out and swept my eyes around, looking for people in our way. When I found no one, I nodded to him.

A few minutes later, we arrived at the meeting point; the field on the opposite side of town that would lead us to the hill Shadoe and I camped on when we first approached the community. Shadoe arrived a moment later, making me wonder how much of our display he had seen.

"Lur," Shadoe said, taking his place next to me. He waited for me to respond to the wordless command he had given.

"Fine." I didn't bother to hide the exasperation in my voice. I didn't like him telling me what to do, even though I knew it was the smart move.

"Where are you going?" Raselin asked as I started to walk away.

"She shouldn't be traveling in a dress." Shadoe answered for me.

I slipped behind a tree even though I had my pants on under my skirt, prepared to make an easy switch. Dropping the skirt, I adjusted the waistband of the trousers and scooped up the fabric I had left on the ground. I rolled up the skirt and tucked it in my bag as I rejoined the group.

"That was fast." Nian looked shocked.

"I was prepared." I smiled demurely. I was going to enjoy surprising these men.

"Prepared to waste time?" Shadoe grumbled so only I could hear him, knowing I didn't actually need to step away to change.

We walked up the hill, away from the town. Each step carried me closer to the wall where I had last seen Dov. I had to force myself to keep pace with the men and not run ahead. I would have run all the way to Canton's prisons if I could have.

I was exhausted by the time we stopped. We would arrive at the wall the next day if we kept pace, a point Reed brought up as we sat around the fire.

"We'll arrive by nightfall. Should we wait until morning to cross over into the Society?" Nian asked, brushing his hair out of his eyes.

My entire body screamed at the thought of waiting longer.

"No. Nightfall," Shadoe calmly answered instead. "The dark will be our cover."

"I agree. Our best shot at not being noticed is after dark. Do we know where to go once we breach the barrier?" Raselin looked to me.

"Toward the woods." Shadoe replied, dashing my hopes of attempting an immediate rescue. My judgment was being clouded; Lowell would have destroyed me for it.

I straightened at the thought and Shadoe stiffened beside me, wary of whatever had caused my change in posture. When he decided that I hadn't been alerted to a potential threat, he relaxed, letting his shoulders lean toward the fire. I nodded once to affirm nothing was wrong, and he continued to eat the bread we had brought with us.

"I asked if you were familiar with the woods." Fitch's voice grounded me.

"Yes, I know the woods," Shadoe said as if he hadn't ignored the man a moment earlier. "Lur will easily be able to navigate it as well. She's never had a problem finding her way around."

"And just what do we hope to get out of traipsing around in the woods?" Reed reached for his mug. "Shouldn't we go to the city?"

"We will have the upper hand in the woods," Shadoe said by way of explanation.

"We need to stay hidden. We can watch from the woods," I added, "set up our home base there. Then we can go into the towns and cities as needed. It's the best choice."

Raselin nodded, as did Fitch.

"Okay. Tomorrow we go to the wall and come evening, we make our way to the woods." Justin announced, looking around the circle. "I'll take first watch."

I prayed the woods would bring answers.

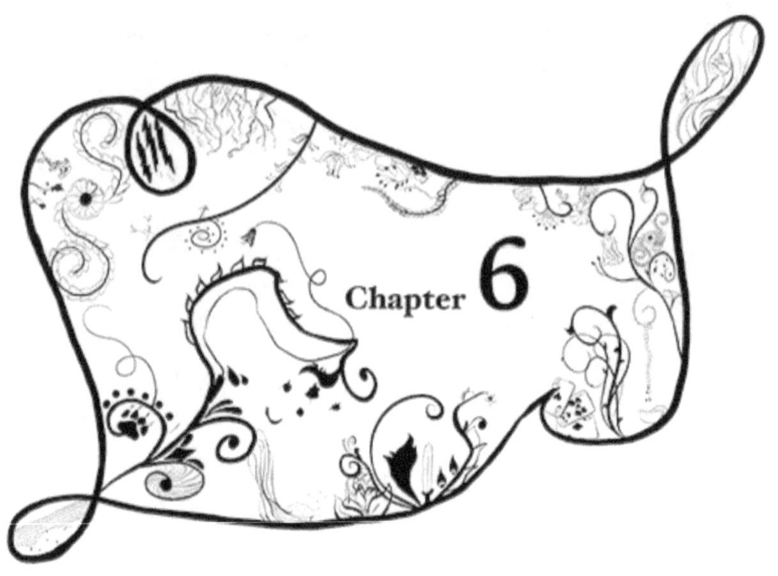

Chapter 6

In the distance, I could see the wall, as dark and small as the first time I had laid eyes on it. The closer we walked, the further away it seemed. Eventually, it loomed above us, not nearly as tall as I remembered it.

Fitch was the first to climb it, just before we lost our light. He peered over, checking for signs of Society soldiers. Dropping down on the other side, he walked in both directions, checking for an ambush. Three taps gave us permission to join him.

Shadoe walked to the wall and readied himself for my approach. Once he was in position, I crouched and ran at him, letting him lift me off the ground, high into the air. My fingers grasped the edge and I realized how much work Shadoe had actually done to pull me up as Dov worked to ensure my safety.

I struggled to swing my leg up over the wall, my boot slipping against the divider. Using my arms, I pulled myself further over the barrier and tried to move my leg again, this time managing to perch on the top of the wall.

I dropped down into the dying grass on the Society side of the wall. *Home.*

Nian dropped to my left, stumbling a bit as he hit the ground. He caught himself, brushing his hair back, and straightened. Shadoe deftly landed to my right, immediately steering me toward the woods as if he were afraid I might run. I slapped his hand away and guided myself to the tree line.

"It's like we never even left," Raselin said, making me wonder if he meant here or there.

"Come on." Shadoe stepped in front of everyone. "Let's get an hour or two in and make camp."

The remaining bits of daylight in the far distance faded away under the covering of branches and leaves, leaving bits of moon to filter down to us. I caught sight of the stars when we came to a small clearing in the forest, the small dots sparkling and disappearing in the night sky.

My eyes grew heavy, having taken the last watch shift before we moved that morning. Each step left me more tired than the last and more committed to taking the next step, because each foot forward brought me closer to answers.

I inched closer to Raselin, knowing he'd be better support than Shadoe would as I felt my body slow. He noticed my forced movements and matched his to mine, slowing our rate.

"I give it another twenty minutes and we rest for the night." He looked at the group for approval. Shadoe nodded along with the others. Even someone with his strength needed to rest.

We made it another mile before we stopped to set up camp. Shadoe took his place near me as we slept, telling me he would wake me for my watch in a few hours. We had to be up with the sun, so we wouldn't get much rest.

I slept without dreaming, so deeply that Shadoe had to shake me awake.

"I'm not covering your shift, Lur," he said gruffly as I grasped consciousness.

Sitting up, I surveyed the area, familiarizing myself with the landscape. Once I was confident in its memorization in limited lighting, I looked up. The stars once again greeted me, darting in and out of the clouds.

Nian snored quietly across from the fire, his hair falling in his eyes again. I would have to encourage him to cut it back if it would interfere with our missions. The last thing we needed was for someone to die because their hair blocked their sight.

Shadoe fell asleep quickly. I watched his shoulders rise up and lower as he breathed evenly, as I had often watched Dov sleep from across the room. These men were nothing alike.

A noise caught my attention, a far off animal replying. Their game continued, moving further away as they spoke to one another.

I twisted my hair in my hands as they sat in my lap. Whenever I needed to move and couldn't, I twirled my hair through my fingers. The movement was so slight most people rarely noticed, as it calmed and focused me. I pulled my locks through my fingers over and over again, weaving it around my hand.

The crickets slowly stopped chirping, their chorus dying away so slowly I didn't notice until it was profoundly silent. My fingers found their way to the necklace tucked below my shirt. For as tarnished as they looked, they certainly didn't feel that way.

My eyes traced over the outline of the trees, searching for signs of Silas and Eden. I knew I wouldn't find evidence here, even if they had been through this area. The last time I saw them, they had been running toward the woods. I only hoped that Dov had drawn the soldiers away from his sister-in-law and best friend as much as he had drawn them away from me. Dov would want his capture to matter.

I hated his selfless streak as much as I adored it.

"Lur? You ready to switch?" Justin's voice made me jump.

"Is it time already?" I asked, trying to distinguish how long I had been lost in thought.

"I'm guessing so," he replied, dragging himself into an upright position. "You should rest."

"What is it like to have siblings?"

"What?" He adjusted his shirt and ran a hand through his hair.

I shrugged, unsure why I had asked.

Justin raised an eyebrow at me, weighing my words.

"It's not the worst thing in the world." He offered me a half smile. "But also not the best. Don't get me wrong, I love them, but that's part of the problem. It's hard to leave them like this, or worse, to have *them* leave. Devin came back injured, but it could have been worse. I worry.

"It's great because you always have people to rely on, but it gets a bit overwhelming at times, trying to protect them. I imagine it's worse for them, since they're older. I know they've spent a lot of time protecting me.

"Do you have siblings, Lur?"

"Auluria."

"What?" His eyes pinched together at the change in the direction of the conversation.

"My name. It's Auluria. And no, no siblings."

"But…"

"We didn't know you. It was safer. Only Shadoe calls me Lur, and I hate it."

"Auluria." He said my name gently, nodding.

"Good night, Justin." I turned to lie down, closing my eyes.

"Auluria is prettier anyway. It suits you," he murmured as I drifted back to sleep

"There's a stream over here, Auluria." Justin waved me over in the morning.

Raselin turned to face us, but said nothing. I walked toward Justin, looking forward to cleaning up. Down a small embankment ran a creek flowing to the brim with water.

Dropping to my knees, I dipped a hand into the cool water. I held in a gasp as my fingers penetrated the surface, a chill running through my body. I brushed the dirt off my hands, pulling the water up my arms until it met my sleeves.

It tasted amazing as I raised my hands to my lips. Justin dipped his container into the water alongside of me.

"Auluria, fill your canteen," Raselin reminded me, having caught on to the switch of names.

I reached behind me, waiting for him to hand his to me as well. When I felt it touch my dripping hands, I pulled back, dipping it in the water for him.

A gasp made me turn. Fitch pulled his face back from his hands where the cold water had hit his skin.

"A warning would have been nice," he commented, throwing us a look.

"It's fall, Fitch, what did you expect?" Raselin chastised him playfully.

We finished rinsing our visible skin off, the cold water terrorizing our systems. I raked my wet hands through my hair, pushing it back. It was as good as it was going to get.

Walking up the embankment, we found Shadoe dropping out of a tree. He joined us, telling us where we had ended up during the night.

"There's a town two miles from here. We can reach it within the hour and make a supply run," he announced, lifting his chin as if he'd won some kind of competition.

Nian's hair dripped in his eyes as he walked up beside me and cocked his head.

"So what's the plan?" he asked.

"We need to see what the town is like first, but two of us should probably go in and gather some more food and scout the area." Shadoe looked at me as I started to speak. "Not you."

The syllable I squeaked out before he narrowed his eyes to threaten me meant nothing. I considered kicking his leg out from under him, but I knew that would only result in an unnecessary beating for both of us as we battled wills.

"Auluria will stay behind for now." Fitch's deep voice ended the discussion. "Shadoe, are you going or staying?"

He was silent for a moment, weighing his options. "I'll go. Reed, you can come with me. You'll be the least likely to be remembered."

Reed's lips pursed at the veiled insult, but he didn't say anything. I considered stomping on Shadoe's foot.

We started walking in the direction of the town, Shadoe took the lead, Reed trailing behind him, unwilling to show his pride was wounded. Justin sidled up next to me, nodding toward Shadoe.

"Has a way with words, doesn't he?"

I sighed, knowing if I said anything at all, I'd tell him everything. He shrugs.

"When you get tired of him, just let me know and Dev and I will take him out for you," he volunteered, pulling away from me and continuing the journey a few feet from me.

A bird trilled in the distance when we reached a place where we could see the town on the horizon. Shadoe and Reed left their packs with us, taking just a few things to trade in the town. Before they left, Shadoe checked to make sure Reed had his knives properly hidden in his boots, aggravating the man yet again.

I watched as they jogged toward the road. Once they reached the end of the trees, they slowed, ducking out into the quiet road. I turned my back once they were in public.

"Now what?" Justin asked.

"Now we work," Raselin said, grabbing his pack. "Nian, stay here. We'll be back before they are, but cover for us in case."

My grin was unintentional. I hadn't pegged Raselin for this much of a rule breaker, but I could work with it. Grabbing my pack, I jumped to my feet from where I was sitting on a giant tree root.

"Lead on."

The other men followed suit, tucking their packs behind them and turning from the town.

"Now we're talking," Fitch said. "Where are we going, boss?"

"We need to know what's here. Auluria?" His hand gestured for me to take the lead.

"Me?"

"No one knows these woods like you do, even Shadoe said so. Lead the way."

I took a tentative step forward. Somewhere along the way I had forgotten the girl Shadoe had trained me to be while I was busy following his lead. I wasn't the girl Lowell had taken in after her aunt died. I wasn't Lur, the girl Shadoe had trained to destroy. I was Auluria, the woman who fought for the family she chose, who decided to love instead of go after revenge, who was going to save the man she cared for and her people. I wasn't just *a* leader; I was *their* leader.

After a few dozen yards, I announced over my shoulder that we would be splitting up to cover more ground.

"Raselin, you and Fitch go to the right. Justin and I will go to the left. Meet back in one hour. Check in with Nian if anything comes up."

Once we were far enough away, I turned to Justin.

"You ready to do some running?" I challenged.

"Oh, so *that's* why you brought me along instead of Raselin." He grinned, shrugging one shoulder. "I could run."

"Good." I took off.

"Are we looking for anything in particular?" he asked after a moment.

"Signs of life? I mean, my people are exceptional at covering their tracks. Well, both of my groups, actually. But some of the others aren't.

"Look for good places to shelter. Look for food. Just *look*."

"Should we split up?" Justin suggested.

"Not a bad idea, just stay within shouting distance. We can cover more ground this way." I split off from him and ran toward an embankment, dipping down below tree branches as I descended. Justin ran out of view, covering the higher ground.

I leapt over a small stream, barely worth the effort to jump. A branch hit me in the head as I attempted to duck mid-leap, the soft pine needles brushing against my cheek. I landed harder than I anticipated, but kept running, knowing I needed to keep up with Justin.

The sun filtering through the trees was blinding. A golden color settled around me, illuminating the area with a metallic tone. It glistened off of the bark and flashed off the water as I propelled my feet forward.

Sprinting around a large rock, I corrected my course. My eyes darted back and forth as I moved, looking for things I should take account of.

A branch behind me cracked, bringing me to a halt. Whipping around, I looked for Justin. He wasn't there.

I took a few steps backward, watching for movement in the bushes. I saw nothing, but I could sense it. Someone was there.

Turning, I ran, not worrying about kicking up the dirt and brush behind me. They knew I was there, they didn't need to track me, they would just follow me.

My arms pumped at my sides and fear coursed through my body. I pushed myself faster, harder. I would escape. I needed to warn Justin. I attempted to control my breathing, trying to reserve enough air to yell out.

Crashing through the underbrush, I forced myself forward as a bird shrieked above us. No one followed me, but that gave me no security.

Ahead, I saw a bush. Going around it would take far too much time. Through was my only option. I lowered my stance, hoping to gain more power in my steps.

I didn't know what was on the other side of the bush, but it didn't matter; it was my escape. My hope waved its branches in front of me, beckoning me to enter its realm of protection. I accepted its offer and crashed into its greenery.

Far too late, I realized that it was a drop off. I plummeted downward, crashing into the short ledge the size of a tall man during my descent. Rocks embedded themselves into my arms. The exposed roots of plants tangled in my hair, ripping pieces out as I slid down in the dirt.

I righted myself once I hit the ground. Without checking for injuries, I pushed myself to my feet and took off. The trees reached out for me as I fled, demanding I stop and confront my unexpected company. I had to get to Justin, though, and I refused to stop.

"Justin!" I screamed his name, praying he could hear me, wherever he was.

I crashed past another set of trees and slammed into a tall bush made mostly of tangled vine-like branches. My foot caught, forcing me to leap over the edge of the brush.

I saw the second stream before I landed, my foot getting caught on a rock as I tried to avoid tumbling into the water. Overshooting the water, I slammed into something else.

Arms wrapped around me, body heat enveloping me as we swung around together. I knocked the breath out of my captor and he grunted as our collision slowed. Throwing myself back, I tried to escape his grasp.

"Auluria?" a voice barked.

A flash of blue, then black jumped into my line of sight as I made eye contact with the man holding me. *Dov.*

No...Berwyn.

"You're alive?" I gasped, throwing myself at him, knocking him off balance once again. I couldn't stop my tears.

He roughly pushed me back.

"What are you doing here?" he asked, anger in his voice.

"You survived." My words frustrated him even more.

"Auluria! What are you doing here?" he shouted.

My eyes dragged the length of him, focusing on his arm that Shadoe cut with his claw-like blade.

"The poison didn't kill you," I concluded.

"No it didn't, now why are you here?" He shook me, trying to get me to focus.

"Where is Dov?" I demanded.

"Canton has him. He's using him as bait to try to get the rest of us," Berwyn confirmed. "Where is Eden?"

"You don't know?" I asked in horror.

"I haven't seen her since we split up. I had heard some of you made it over the wall. I was hoping she was with you."

I shook my head.

"Dov gave himself up so we could get away. Eden and Silas ran toward the woods."

"Why are you here if you made it over the wall?" he asked, looking for information.

"It's just as bad over there, Berwyn. We've come back to help bring down the Society once and for all."

"We?" He looked at me skeptically.

"I have a team, Berwyn. There are men and women. They are trained and ready to fight. Some of them are from here and escaped to look for a better life. Some just want freedom, but they're here Berwyn, and they're ready."

"And just where are they?" He nearly sounded like Lowell, casual, but searching for answers he didn't believe were there.

"Most of them are on the other side of the wall," I admit. "I came with a small team as a trial run. We've had spies here the last few weeks. We know Canton has Dov, or at least he did the last time our spy saw him."

"And just how many people do you have on this team?"

"There are seven of us." I said. "Berwyn, there's something you should know."

He waits for me to continue.

"Shadoe is with me." I cringe as I say it.

Berwyn flinches and my eyes dart to his arm, the wound still visible; a dark red color.

"He helped me escape." I tried to assuage his anger before it built up.

"Did he help *Dov* escape?" *Too late.*

"He did what Dov instructed him to do. He's stayed with me this entire time; he even trained the people from the other side of the wall."

"And you think he won't return to his group now that he's here?" Berwyn challenged.

"I don't know. He's loyal to Lowell; he always has been. If Lowell wants him back, he'll probably go."

"Lowell is dead, Auluria," he said bluntly. "He was the only one that didn't escape, I'm told."

"Shadoe thought that might have happened," I said, trying to digest the information. Lowell was really gone. I should have known if *Shadoe*, his most loyal follower, thought Lowell was dead, than he had to be gone.

"Shadoe was the one who cut me down." I glanced at him, hoping that would win him some points with Berwyn.

He raised his eyebrows again, as if asking if that was supposed to be a good thing.

"If he hadn't cut me down, there wouldn't have been chaos, and Dov, Eden and Silas would have died too."

"You don't know that they haven't," Berwyn challenged. "*You* don't have Eden and Silas, *I* don't have Eden and Silas... And Dov is only partially alive, from what I hear."

"Have you seen him?" I asked, his words slapping me as I stepped closer.

"No. I haven't. I'm on my way to the city now. We're going to rescue him, but we need some information first."

We.

It was Berwyn's people that I had been running from.

"You brought a team."

I nodded.

Berwyn shook his head once, realizing his people were waiting.

"It's fine," he announced, with a flick of his wrist.

Several people stepped out. One man in particular caught my attention—the man who had interrogated me when I first joined Berwyn's group. He was the last man I wanted to see—other than Lowell, who would no longer be a problem.

"And *you* made me stop." The tall man turned to Berwyn when he realized I was there.

"It's not her fault, Arin." Berwyn silenced him. "She didn't do this to us, and even though she escaped, she came back to help us."

I fought to keep my face from twitching. *This was not the Berwyn Baer I knew.*

He turned back to me and glared.

Or maybe he was.

"Sir!" A voice interrupted, followed by the heavy footsteps of the man it belonged to.

The man joined us, his eyes widening and his brow dropping at the sight of me.

"You're back," he said to me. "You're not with them."

"With who?" Berwyn asked skeptically.

"Your wife, sir." The man turned to face Berwyn.

"You found her?" he asks, astonished, dropping the glare from his face as a hunger for information takes over.

"Yes, sir. She's alive, as is Silas." The man confirms quickly. "Wallace has her."

"Berwyn…" I turned back to him.

"What do you know?" He commanded me to speak, his voice a deep growl.

"Marty and Jake ambushed us while we were escaping. They wanted to capture us for the reward. We tied them up but…"

"But they must have found a way to untie themselves and captured Eden and Silas after you split up." He finished for me.

I nodded miserably.

A metallic thud sounded behind Berwyn. We both turned to find a knife bouncing in the dirt, settling a few feet behind him. I turned to see who had thrown it.

"Auluria, run!" Justin shouted.

"No, wait!" I moved toward the voice, trying to prevent him from actually hitting someone with the next knife. "It's safe! Stand down. It's safe."

I repeated my words until Justin stood, popping up slowly out of the bushes. He looked skeptically at me until I waved him forward.

Berwyn stood, weapon in hand, ready to assault the man approaching us. Arin and the others were poised for action.

"Everyone stand down. He's with us."

I knew Berwyn's men would never unnecessarily hurt someone—that wasn't who they were—but I rushed to Justin's side anyway, bringing him safely into the group.

"This is Justin. He's part of the team I brought here to run our trial mission. Justin, these are my people." I motioned around at the group.

He hesitated a moment before smiling.

"Nice to meet you all. I take it we'll be working together?"

Berwyn flinched.

"Maybe," he replied.

"Sir," the scout interrupted quietly. "We need more men, if you want to rescue Eden *and* Dov."

"He's right, Berwyn. The Society doesn't know about my team, but they're actively looking for your group. It gives us the ability to surprise them," I tried to encourage him.

"What else do we know about Eden?" Berwyn turned back to the scout.

"Nothing. I can only confirm that Wallace has them."

"Why hasn't he made this known yet?" Berwyn mumbled to himself.

"Maybe he doesn't want to tip his hand yet... Maybe he has a plan." I suggested.

"What is happening?" Justin finally asked in a clipped voice, prompting me to quickly explain what we had just learned.

"We need to get our people here." Justin said, confident that we could assist Berwyn. "We can help you, but you have to help us first. We need to get our people over the wall and we need to do it quickly."

"What are you proposing?" Berwyn crossed his arms, leveling a glare at Justin.

"If you want to save your wife and your brother, you need more backup that the Society doesn't know about. It seems like you've kept most of your group hidden from what I can tell, but the more people you have, the more likely you will be able to overtake the Society.

"If we can free your people, we can combine our forces and take out the Society once and for all. We can all live here, free of the threats we live under. If we can take out your government, then we can rally the entire country and take out the government on *our* side of the wall. Our countries can live in peace. We could even knock down the wall entirely and form a bigger, stronger nation to keep the others from coming after us."

Berwyn tipped his head, thinking through the implications of teaming up.

"Who exactly is in charge of your little band of men?" Berwyn asked.

"Auluria." Justin crossed his arms and tipped his chin up, mimicking Berwyn. "Auluria is in charge, along with Raselin, Necesta, and Shadoe."

"Shadoe?" Berwyn gapped before turning on me. "You let *Shadoe* have any say in—"

"Yes. Shadoe has a say." I cut him off. "He has just as much right as any of us, and he's the best trainer we have. He trained *me*—"

"Because that means so much," he snapped.

"When have I ever failed, Berwyn? I'm still alive, aren't I? I did every job you asked me to do, didn't I?"

"He tried to *kill* me, Auluria," he shouted, holding his scarred arm out to me. "He nearly did!"

Arin jumped into the conversation, yelling his distaste for me and for Shadoe. The scout tried to calm everyone, but no one listened.

"Are you sure this is a good idea?" Justin hissed in my ear, leaning close so I could hear him over the argument. "Maybe we should do this on our own."

"We are not doing this on our own!" I yell, swinging to face him as I disrupted the fight. "We are going to save Eden and Silas, then we are going to save Dov, and then we're going to bring the Society down once and for all, and the Baers are our best chance of making that happen and surviving it all."

I refused to back down.

"Berwyn, enough," I lectured. "This is happening. You are working with these men and women. You need help. We need help too. Canton won't kill Dov yet because he's too useful, so that means our first job is to get our people over the wall and go after Eden and Silas. We'll probably need them anyway. Then we go straight for Dov. Once we have him, we bring Canton down and use him to dismantle the Society. Now move!"

I turned on my heels and marched away, Justin following immediately behind me. I could sense Berwyn hesitate, but only because he wasn't in the lead. He knew my plan was the smart move.

He stomped behind me until he caught up with me. I kept a brisk pace, forcing everyone back toward our rendezvous point where I would introduce him to Raselin.

Eventually I broke the silence.

"What happened to you after we left?" I asked quietly, hoping the others wouldn't notice.

"I barely survived. The men got me back to the storehouse and by some miracle, they extracted some of the poison. They had almost given up on me when I started to pull out of it. Whatever they gave me counteracted the drugs.

"He meant to kill me, Auluria. How can you work with him?"

"He's been protecting me. He's done what I asked. He saved me from dying with a noose around my neck," I replied. "I don't trust him, not like I trust you, but I will work with him, because I'd rather have him on our team where I can watch him, than possibly working against us somewhere else.

"He could change, Berwyn. It's possible, especially now that Lowell is gone."

"You think he won't go back to them and take Lowell's place?" Berwyn scoffed. "I think that's exactly what he plans to do, and he'll probably try to drag you with him."

"I would never leave Dov," I said, trying once again to prove my loyalties.

"We'll see."

"We should go ahead and warn Nian and Raselin," Justin interrupted.

"Go ahead. I'll stay with the men to guide them." I nodded at him as he held my gaze. "Go."

Justin took off, running ahead to prepare our team.

"What's that all about?" Berwyn asked, nodding toward Justin's disappearing figure.

"He's a good guy, Berwyn. His family is a lot like yours. I think you'll like them."

He grumbled as we continued to walk.

"We just need to get them back." Berwyn finally said.

"We will," I insisted. "We'll save them. We'll get Eden and Silas, and then we'll go get Dov."

My voice cracked. I missed him.

Berwyn looked at me out of the corner of his eye but didn't comment.

"What do we have here?" Raselin greeted us, clearly having walked out to meet us away from the meeting point.

"Berwyn, this is Raselin. He's one of the leaders from the other side of the wall."

Raselin reached out to shake his hand. After a moment, Berwyn accepted it.

"I'm Berwyn Baer. I hear you want to take down the Society as badly as we do." He removed his hand and placed it on the knife on his belt, tightening his fingers around it.

"We do," Raselin confirmed. "And if Auluria trusts you, so do we. I hope you feel as though her confidence in us will allow you to trust us as well."

Berwyn appraised the man who was just a bit younger than his father, Griz, would have been, had he lived.

"Auluria says she trained you." He avoided the question.

"She did. She and Shadoe are strong leaders."

Berwyn tensed at Shadoe's name. I could tell he would blame Shadoe for what was happening to Eden. He needed a target, and for once, it couldn't be me. He needed me too much, and for Dov's sake, he had to accept me.

"We have a strong group of men and women who are ready to fight. We've spent many years on the outskirts of our government's reach because we were so close to the wall. We've lived more privileged lives than many of our countrymen, but it's getting worse.

"It's only a matter of time before they force us to work for them. In fact, it's already starting, though not nearly as bad as it is here. We want to preemptively strike back and end this before it gets out of hand."

"And you're willing to take down *our* government to do that?"

"Some of us started out here, Berwyn, but even those that didn't know how effective it will be to take down your government first. Ours is much stronger and we need your people to overtake our oppressors. If we help free you of your reign of tyranny, you can help us. We can have a country united, working for peace.

"Justin told me about your wife, and Auluria informed us about your brother. We were already planning on making him one of our priorities, hoping that he would bring his people to join us.

"Now that we have you on our team, our priority is to restore him to leadership in your group. The faster we have our people in place, the easier it will be to take them by surprise when we strike."

"*Baer?*" A dark, piercing voice filled the air, shattering the quiet I hadn't noticed until that point.

Berwyn looked beyond Raselin at Shadoe's approaching form.

"You should be dead," Shadoe threatened.

"Yet here I am." Berwyn scowled at him, the muscles in his arms tightening.

"Not as easy to kill as your father, I see." Shadoe sneered, looking eerily like Lowell.

Berwyn ran at him, stopping only because Raselin injected himself into his path, blocking him from murdering Shadoe.

I lurched forward, grabbing Berwyn's arm to pull him back. He turned on me, hand ready to strike as he had once struck Dov. Catching himself, he bit down, grinding his teeth in an effort to control his rage.

Rocking back, I saw him deflate slightly, and I released his elbow where my nails dug into his skin.

Turning, I marched over to Shadoe, his eyes tracking me as I moved. Every moment of anger I had felt toward Shadoe in the time since we scaled the wall built up in my steps. My hand flew from my side, wrapping in front of me. I brought my elbow back to his face with as much force as I could, intentionally aiming for his cheek and not his nose.

The sharp crack made the spectators gasp. Shadoe stumbled back, not having expected my attack, his hand on his face. His eyes flashed, rage turning them dark.

Berwyn marched up behind me, getting dangerously close. He stopped just behind my shoulder blade, leaning around my body.

"She was *never* yours." He hissed, echoing the words Dov had once said to Shadoe when my handler claimed me.

He must have told his brother about the encounter. What else had he told Berwyn?

He pulled away from me, the sudden force causing my hair to move in the breeze he created with his movements. Satisfied that he had won the conversation, he stalked back to his team, arms crossed, and waited.

Shadoe stared, wide-eyed at the scene. He glanced to me, but I had no intention of lending him my support. He deserved all that and more.

"Wallace has Eden and Silas. We're going to get them back," I announced, breaking the tense silence.

Raselin and Fitch stood back, watching, waiting for the moment they would have to intercede and quell whatever fight might break out. Reed looked worried one might, slowly reaching for his knife. Nian brushed his hair back, his amused smirk matching Justin's. Arin looked ready to kill on Berwyn's behalf.

"Wallace?" Shadoe grunted. "You had to go and involve him, didn't you, Baer?"

"If anyone is at fault here, it's you, leech."

"Leech?" Shadoe demanded.

"What else would you call someone who hung onto that wolf like you did?"

"Enough!" I shouted, stepping between them.

Shadoe lowered his hand and a nasty welt surrounded the bloody cut I had created. I turned to him.

"Berwyn will help us get our people across the wall and into the Society. We will help extract Eden and Silas before Wallace can hurt them and then we'll go after the Society."

"You think we can get them out of Wallace's hands before anything happens to them? He's probably already torturing them. You thought those boys who attacked you were bad, Lur? You have no idea what Wallace will do to them."

Arin's quick movement reminded Berwyn to restrain himself as he angled his shoulder in front of his leader.

"Then we'll have to move quickly, won't we?" I replied.

"Excuse me," Raselin interrupted, "but for those of us who don't know, what *exactly* is this Wallace capable of?"

Berwyn's scout gave him a brief outline of what he knew of Wallace's group, avoiding any discussion on what he might be doing to them. For all of Lowell's faults, he was far less reckless than Wallace. My cousin didn't destroy just for the fun of it.

"Bit of a wildcard, isn't he?" Raselin ventured.

"Which is why we need to move quickly." Berwyn confirmed. "Wallace knows how we operate. He will be watching for us."

"We need our people," Raselin said, motioning for us to start walking. "They'll have to be ready."

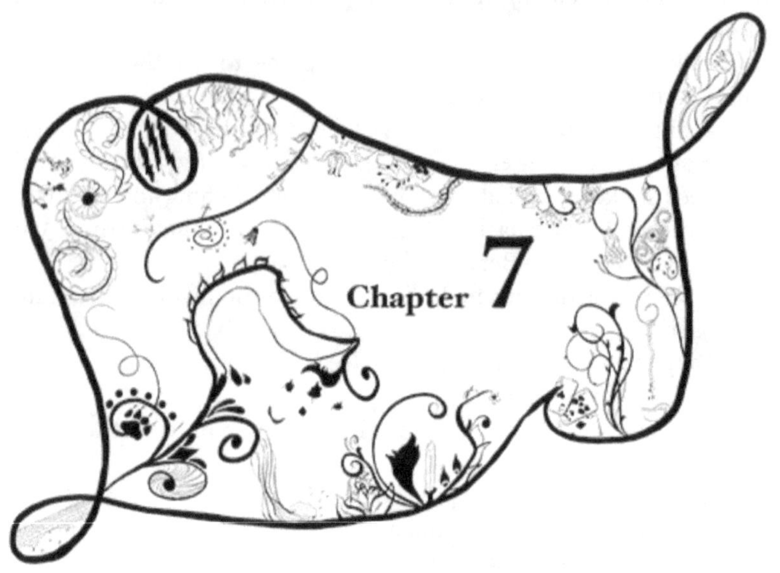

Chapter 7

"YOU'VE CHECKED ALL OF THESE PEOPLE OUT?" BERWYN ASKED, slipping away from the group when we stopped at the stream.

"Yes, Berwyn. I trust them."

"You trusted Lowell once, too."

"So did you," I countered, reminding him that Lowell had once belonged to the Baers' group, working alongside Griz.

"And you trust the man we sent ahead? Fitch?" Berwyn ignored my comment.

"Yes, his wife is there. He wants to protect her." I tried giving him a reason to feel more secure. "He won't betray us."

"How do you propose we get them over the wall?" He asked, filling his canteen with water.

"I was hoping *you'd* have an idea." I squirmed under his watchful eyes. "It's not going to be easy getting that many people over the wall without being noticed."

"Well." He considered our options. "We could create a distraction. Send some of the boys to the town and draw the soldiers away. That should give us more time."

"Can we risk that?"

"I don't think we have much of a choice." We discussed our options.

Berwyn walked over to his men and instructed them where to go.

"We have a plan?" Raselin asked, walking up behind me.

"We do. Berwyn is going to send some of our men into the town to distract the soldiers. They will be tasked with leading the men away from the wall for a day or two. That should give our people enough time to get to the wall and climb over it."

"Why not just lead them away when it's time? Why have them go early?"

"The soldiers will be suspicious. They'll investigate when our men start causing problems. If they start early, the men will look into it and find nothing, so by the time we're actually doing something, they won't be watching as closely because they'll think the threat has passed."

"Interesting."

We watched as Berwyn's men branched off, taking a more direct route toward the town. One of his men walked back the way we came.

"He's going to the storehouse," Berwyn said as he approached. "Did you fill him in?"

"She did." Raselin answered. "Interesting plan. Now the question is how we're going to get everyone over."

"Most of them can climb the wall. A few people, like Necesta, will need help."

"Fitch will help with that," Justin said, joining the group. "I've seen him carry full grown men around when they're injured. Last fall he carried Reed's cousin clear across town when the soldier's ran him over as they marched through."

"I'm sure he's already thought about that." Raselin nodded. "He's had the entire journey back without anyone to talk to. I'm sure he's come up with at least a few solutions.

"Let's get moving, boys." Arin stomped into the circle, glancing at me. "We have a lot of ground to cover."

The stars were out when we finally arrived.

I woke up a few feet from Reed. Nian slept on my other side, hair once again in his eyes. During the night, I moved to the far side of the fire, instructing Raselin to stay between Berwyn and Shadoe as they fought over who should be watching out for me.

"Did you sleep well?" Reed whispered.

"Not at all." I raked my hands through my hair, pulling it out of my face. "You?"

"Kind of," he said, sitting up. "What's the plan for today?"

"Not much we *can* do. We can't move anyone until nightfall."

"So we're just going to wait around all day?"

"Are you volunteering to go back over the wall and wait for them to arrive?"

"Is that an option?" he asked casually.

"It is if you want it to be."

We let the others sleep, knowing it would be a long day and they'd need all the rest they could get. The sun cast shadows through the trees when they started to stir.

Reed slipped over the wall late that afternoon, after the entire team stared at the open space between the town and the wall for over an hour, watching for movement.

Once he disappeared beyond the barrier, we did our best to keep ourselves occupied. It was immediately clear that staying together was a bad choice given the impending fight between Shadoe and Berwyn.

Spacing out, we each moved off on our own. Shadoe sharpened his knives, gaze moving between where I paced and Berwyn's location a dozen yards away as he talked with Arin.

The minutes were agonizing. I stretched my arms above my head, bringing them down to my neck as I tried to work out a knot, succeeding only in tangling them in my hair. Flipping my head over, I let my hair fall in front of me. It fell to the ground, brushing over the grass as I massaged my neck.

"Wow, girl. That is some hair." Justin smirked, coming to sit on a log near me.

"It's taken you this long to notice?" I straightened and moved to take a seat by him.

"It's on the ground, Auluria. It didn't look that long when you were beating us in the training."

"Auluria, a word." Berwyn approached, waiting for Justin to leave. Mysteriously, Shadoe appeared behind him, glaring at Justin.

Justin glanced at me, assuming if both men were there to see me, it couldn't be good. I smiled tightly, telling him to go. The man stood and walked away, giving us space.

"Leave, Shadoe." Berwyn instructed.

"*You* leave, Baer."

"I'll leave," I volunteer, standing to make a quick exit.

"No," they respond in unison.

The men faced off once again, squaring their shoulders until Raselin called for Shadoe. I was grateful for his choice.

"What are you doing?" Berwyn whispered harshly once we were alone.

"What do you mean?"

"That boy."

"That *boy* is *your age*, Berwyn," I pointed out.

"Dov is being held captive and you're—"

"Whoa!" I cut him off, fist clenched, daring him to say another word.

We wait to see who will break first. He wins.

"I've known Justin for a few weeks. We didn't even talk much until this mission. He's a nice guy. He reminds me of Silas, actually, but that's all. So stop seeing things where nothing is there."

"That better be all it is." He cautioned me.

"Is that why Shadoe came over here too? Because of Justin?"

"I assume so." He glanced over his shoulder at his enemy. "He nearly beat me over here. Just one more time I bested him."

He grinned to himself.

"Shadoe isn't as clever as he thinks, and you'd do well to remember that, Auluria."

"I've known him a lot longer than you have, Berwyn."

Berwyn spent the next hour detailing the plan to break into Wallace's camp, partially to pass the time, but mainly to keep Shadoe away. If Dov couldn't be there to protect me, Berwyn was going to make it his mission to get between us.

I waited in the trees as the next group of people ran as quietly as they could through the tall grass.

"Keep going. One hundred yards and you'll find Nian. He's

waiting with everyone else." I pointed in the direction they should run as people filed past me.

Finally, Shadoe, Berwyn, and Raselin reached my checkpoint.

"That's everyone," Raselin said, Necesta on his arm.

"Hello there, Goldilocks," She crooned, eyeing me.

Berwyn frowned, but I ignored him.

Lydia hung on Fitch's arm, Talley trailing behind her, head darting back and forth as she looked for Devin.

"He's already with Nian," I said as she neared.

Justin stayed close by to appease his sister's nervousness. He nodded as he walked by, but didn't try to speak to me after what had happened earlier.

Once we reached the group, Berwyn addressed them, informing them that we'd be going as far as we could during the night. We needed to move them away from the wall. We'd head straight for the storehouse. I was anxious to arrive.

We planned to regroup at Berwyn's hiding place, something he had been reluctant to give up in Shadoe's presence. The children and young people would be staying at the storehouse, along with the adults who weren't trained enough yet. Berwyn would select the best of the teenage boys to continue their training while we worked to free Eden and Silas.

The night dragged on well into the early morning hours before we broke for camp. I made sure to stay close to Berwyn from the time the new members joined us to show my trust for Berwyn and the Baers. If the people had to choose between Shadoe and Berwyn, I wanted the choice to be clear.

He chose when to stop. He chose when to go. I always yielded to Berwyn. By the time we rested, the group surrounding us was looking to him. Raselin's approval solidified their acceptance of this new leader.

"Auluria, are you ready for this?" Berwyn asked as we sat.

"I need you to promise me something, Berwyn." I tucked my hair behind my ear and focused on the fire's flames.

"What?"

"No matter what, you get Dov out," I requested, knowing my chances of survival going up against Marty and Jake one more time. I had pushed grace too far with those two; this time I very well might not survive it.

He raised an eyebrow at me.

"We'll get Dov," he said, "but you don't get to die for my wife, Auluria. Not now."

I attempted to grin.

"Maybe I'll die for Silas."

"You keep trying that, from what you told me. It hasn't worked so far."

"Suddenly you care, Berwyn? I didn't know you had it in you," I teased, desperately wanting something more than the dread that was washing over me.

"I sent people to look for you too, Auluria," he said quietly.

"You did that for Dov."

"I did for *you*. I might not like you, but I still respect you. I don't want to see you hurt." He took a deep breath. "Besides, Dov would kill me if I didn't."

I tried to hide my smile. Dov would definitely kill him if he didn't step up while Dov couldn't.

"Seriously, Berwyn, promise me you'll get him out of there."

"I'm not going to abandon my brother, Auluria," he said tersely.

"I know, I just…"

"You'll be fine. *He'll* be fine. We'll make it through this. We survived Lowell. We can survive Canton too. And now we have back up. So stop sulking and get your head in the right space," Berwyn snapped, reminding me of my little talks with his wife. Those two were definitely suited for each other.

He turned away and ended the conversation.

Definitely like Eden.

I just hoped Eden was still like Eden when we found her.

Shadoe claimed me as we walked the next morning, refusing to leave my side. I waved Berwyn away, knowing I needed to make sure I didn't isolate Shadoe. As long as he stayed on our side, we might actually survive this rescue attempt, but if he went out on his own, there was no telling what type of damage he would create.

His hatred of Berwyn was evident. I decided to play on his remaining loyalty to Lowell, working the Society's potential destruction into the conversation as much as I could while we walked. Convincing him that Berwyn could be useful in its downfall wasn't an easy task.

Shadoe remained quiet most of the walk, only speaking when he noticed people watching, an attempt to keep them from approaching us. My former fiancé had never been a man of many words. I knew the conversation must have been killing him by the way he ground his teeth each time I started a new branch of the conversation. Something about that knowledge delighted me.

"Enough, Lur." He finally tried silencing me. "I've heard you. Enough."

"So you'll put this nonsense behind you and work with the Baers?"

"I will do what we need to do to finish Lowell's mission. The Society will fall. Whatever it takes to accomplish that, I'll deal with."

"Good." I replied, only slightly satisfied that he had relented.

"There." Shadoe pointed ahead.

Once again he had selected the entrance to the hidden underground storehouse. The man had a knack for knowing these things. I was surprised he hadn't stumbled on any of the Baers' storehouses before.

The tunnel was cool, the temperature dropping as the earthy smell enveloped us in its embrace. I trailed my hands along the tunnel walls, momentarily forgetting they were made of dirt. I brushed my palms along my pants, knocking off the loose dirt.

The room brightened as we stepped out of the entrance and into the main room. It was filled with life. People moved around the room, changing locations to create space for the newcomers.

"Auluria?" Katarina's surprised voice floated above the crowd.

"Auluria?" A second voice sounded from the other side of the room. "*Auluria!*"

Reyla slammed into me, knocking me into Shadoe as she wrapped her arms around me, tears in her eyes. Maylin followed closely behind her, throwing her arms around me as well.

Katarina quickly walked over to join us, swaying her hips as she moved. She commanded to be observed. Henry stepped up next to her, keeping pace, forcing several men to look away.

Sharone made her way through the crowd, finishing the group of girls surrounding me.

"You're alive," Reyla squealed. "We were so worried."

"We heard they hung you." Maylin informed me. "They thought you got away, but we weren't sure…"

"We escaped." I nodded, still holding on to them.

"They have Dov." Katarina said gently, as if she were unsure if I knew.

"I know. One of the men I met on the other side of the wall saw him. He was alive last we knew."

"We'll save him." Reyla said quietly.

"Well, look who is back!" Gregory bellowed, joining the group.

"The team is back together at last." Carter grinned.

"I don't see how any of you can celebrate." Gloria cast us a disparaging look. "Dov *and* Silas are still gone."

She curled her fingernails into her palms as she walked past us, looking Shadoe up and down. She blamed me for Dov's imprisonment, and she didn't trust Shadoe.

Just then, the group noticed my former mentor standing behind me, scowling. They turned in unison from him to me.

"This is Shadoe." I saw Reyla mouth his name as I spoke, making the connection before I told her. Her face paled.

"He is the man who trained me before I joined you all. He managed to cut me down when Canton took us to the gallows and has been helping me train the people from the other side of the wall." I tried to calm their tension.

Reyla dug her nails into my arm, questioning why I would let him anywhere near me. I appreciated her worry over my safety, but she had also never seen me on a mission. I had confided in her about my training, but she would be shocked to see just how capable I really was.

I pried her hand off of my arm.

"He's working with us to bring down the Society. Shadoe, these are—"

"It doesn't matter," Shadoe announced, walking away.

Everyone turned to look at me, eyes wide.

"He takes some getting used to?" I phrase it as a question.

"Are you '*used to*' him yet?" Gregory challenged with a smirk.

"More than I'm used to you, Gregory," I teased.

"Oh, please, you adore me." He acted offended, placing his hand over his heart. He winked at me, a low growl escaping as he jutted his chin at me.

"Go find some other girl to harass, Gregory." Reyla pushed him.

"Really, Gregory. Are you that desperate?" Katarina asked, winking at Henry.

"I wouldn't do that if I were you." Justin leaned into the conversation. "Shadoe will probably murder you in your sleep."

"Hilarious," Gregory said sarcastically. His face dropped when I didn't laugh along. "Seriously?"

"Probably." I thought about softening it with a smile or laugh, but when it came to Shadoe, they really needed to know the risks.

The boys tentatively took a step back.

"Okay."

"Got it."

"Distance is our friend." They chorused.

I sent them off to find me something to eat before we started on our new mission, leaving the girls by my side.

Reyla looped her arm through mine and leaned close as she stared at Shadoe across the room.

"You were really engaged to him?" she asked, her nose turned up a touch.

"You what?" Katarina asked, demanding a further explanation.

"Not by choice," I assured her. "My cousin came up with the idea."

"Did you… Kiss him?" She looked horrified, her face matching Sharone's.

"But what about Dov?" Maylin asked.

"I wasn't with Shadoe by choice. We were never a real couple. I'm with Dov. End of discussion," I replied.

"No wonder you came running to us," Reyla said, still watching Shadoe.

"I don't know. He's kind of cute, in that standoffish way," Sharone said.

"I guess I can see it," Katarina mused, "but I'm still Team Dov."

"Aren't we all?" I accidentally said out loud. The girls looked at me before breaking into laughter.

Together, we wandered over to where the boys had procured food and found a seat on the ground. In the few minutes we had to talk, I told them what I had been through since I left them, and they regaled me with tales of their heroics while I was gone. The girls attempted to keep Gregory's wild stories in check.

"Auluria, we need to talk," Berwyn interrupted.

I cast the group a look. This was goodbye again. Their faces fell as fast as mine had.

"Berwyn, I'm coming too." Reyla stood with me.

"No, you're not, Reyla." Berwyn turned to walk away.

"I am. Peter gave his life up to protect your brother, so the way I see it, you owe me. This is what I want," she said defiantly.

Berwyn continued to walk away. Reyla grabbed my arm and

followed behind him. When we reached his inner circle, he didn't stop her.

Being in the inner circle without Dov and Silas felt wrong. I hesitated as I approached, but this was my place now. I was a leader. Raselin stepped up beside me. I felt Shadoe's presence behind me, but even *he* didn't have the gall to separate me from Reyla.

"We have a plan." Berwyn announced, turning to me. "You will be bait."

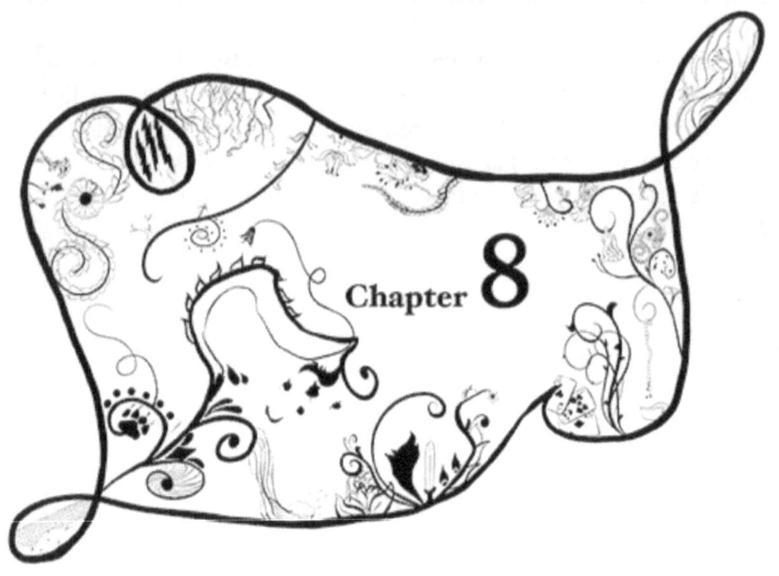

Chapter **8**

MY EYES GREW WIDE. ONCE AGAIN BERWYN PLANNED TO DANGLE ME IN front of someone to get what he wanted.

Reyla swallowed hard. "And me. Where she goes, I go."

"Fine," Shadoe said, not giving Berwyn a chance to object. "Wallace will be thrilled to get his hands on them and I imagine Marty and Jake won't be too upset about it either."

I didn't like the idea of Reyla being anywhere near Marty or Jake after all of my accidental run-ins with them. I knew I couldn't convince her to stay any more than she had been able to convince me not to clean up Lowell's mess. Protecting her would be a distraction. Shadoe had to know that.

"We'll get as close as we can to Wallace's territory without being suspicious," Berwyn said. "He will likely take the girls to where Eden and Silas are being held. We'll track them there and finalize the plan from there based on the conditions we find them in.

"If we all strike at once, we should be able to overwhelm Wallace's people, especially if they don't see us coming." He ignored the part where things likely wouldn't go as planned.

Shadoe and I took turns adding to the plan, tweaking the Baers' mission until we were all satisfied it was the best of the choices we had. Reyla quietly stood next to me, taking it all in.

"This is going to be bad, isn't it?" she asked once the group broke apart, tucking her hair behind her nervously.

"You don't have to do this Reyla."

"The last time you went off on your own, you didn't come back, Auluria. That's not happening again."

"You're not trained, Reyla," I said. "Not well enough for this."

"I'll be fine. Peter used to teach me things. I know more than I let on." She tried putting on a brave face. "Silas is our friend, and Eden is our leader. We need them back, and like Shadoe said, two of us are better than one. Besides, would they really believe they captured *you*? You've escaped Marty how many times now?"

I tipped my head, wishing she would listen to me.

"If they catch us both, they'll actually believe it. They'll also assume they can use me as leverage. You'll have to listen to them to protect me."

"I want you to be safe," I protested.

"I know. But I'll be fine. Right now the priority is rescuing our people, so stop arguing and let's go. The faster we get moving, the better."

"Fine. Here," I said, bending down to show her how to hide a knife in her boot. "They're going to take this from you when they search us, but it will be more believable that way.

"You ladies ready?" Raselin asked, eyeing me as I stood up.

"Almost." I glanced down at my clothing. "This isn't going to do me any favors."

"I remember not too long ago we had to work to get you out of here in those," Reyla nodded to the trousers I was wearing. "Now look at you, trying to get out in a dress."

I couldn't stop a giggle from escaping my lips. We'd come full circle, and this time, Reyla was jumping in with me.

"There." I stiffened. "Get ready."

I continued to adjust the snare I was setting. Reyla calmly reached out for the one she was working on.

"Is this right?" she asked casually enough that even *I* was impressed.

I lifted my head, leaning over to see what she was doing. It was perfect, but I stood up as if I were going to help her adjust it. Before I made it to her, a fallen branch snapped loudly.

"Well, well. What do we have here?"

We both turned to face the man watching us.

"Are we in your way?" I asked tersely. There was no need to play coy. They would know who I was soon enough, and being polite would be out of character once Marty saw me after our capture.

"You are." He stepped closer.

"We can leave," Reyla said quickly, grabbing my arm as if to tug me away.

"No, I don't think you can, young lady. You see, this is our land." He gestured around him. "And when you enter our land, you answer to us."

"We don't answer to you." I glanced around, looking for a branch to use as a weapon. I spotted one a few feet away.

"No, you answer to my boss." He sneered. "Boys..."

Five men advanced from the bushes and trees, surrounding us. I dove for the branch, whipping it above my shoulder, ready to swing. As the first man came at me, I swung, connecting with his shoulder. I intentionally avoided his face. I had to make the fight look good, but not good enough that we could have escaped.

The man fell backward as Reyla screamed. One of the men plucked her off the ground, arms around her waist as she kicked. A sickening thud echoed off the trees as her heel connected with his knee, forcing him to drop her. She kicked at his other leg, knocking him to the ground and she scrambled to get up.

Hitting another man with my branch, I cracked it in half. I dropped it, knowing I would have to fight with my fists.

The man caught Reyla by the arm, whipping her around to face him. He backhanded her, sending her reeling to the ground once more, red cascading over her face.

Anger boiled inside me as I ran to her side. I lifted my leg up, drawing all my strength, and slammed into the man's knee from the side. He shrieked as badly as my friends and I had when Canton tortured us. I knew it would be the only injury I would be able to get away with during the attack, but I wasn't sad about wasting it on him after he hit Reyla like that.

The men converged on us, blocking us in a tight circle as the injured man pulled himself far enough back from the group that he wouldn't accidentally be stepped on as they captured us. Hands grasped my arms, wrenching them behind my back.

My skirt tangled around my ankles as they turned me to tie my hands, and I pitched forward. The men holding me kept me upright, the force straining my bones from their sockets. Before it could cause more than pain, they righted me and I stood on my own.

The ropes bit into my wrists as we walked, but none of the men recognized me. Reyla walked quietly beside me, the only tear stains on her cheeks from her eyes watering after being hit. She was brave, holding herself together after the attack, but the worst was yet to come.

When we arrived, we were pushed into the center of their camp. I watched for signs of our friends but found nothing. Noise fluttered all around us, the waves crashing and subsiding as we moved along.

"Where do you want them?" one of the men shouted, his unexpectedly loud voice making me jump.

"Take them to Wallace," someone shouted in the distance.

"Are we taking them to Wallace?" the man holding Reyla's bound wrists asked quietly.

"Might as well. He has to see them at some point anyway. We'll just have to drag them back out again if he doesn't see them now." The man behind me answered.

When we arrived, Wallace was sitting inside a large area with many tables that appeared to be a dining area. Groups of people milled about, finishing their food and conversations.

"What is this?" He had the same presence Lowell had, but there was something far more reckless about him. His hair, while combed, was wild. His movements had an edge to them like a cornered animal.

He stood, walking over to appraise us.

"Who are you?" he asked us.

Reyla looked tentatively at me. I made eye contact before turning back to stare at Wallace. Aggravating him would be easy, though it would have been easier to play nice. That version of Auluria wouldn't be the one Marty and Jake had built up though. I had to stay true to the girl they believed I was and had likely told their people to explain why I had escaped so many times.

"Who are you?" Wallace demanded again.

The men behind us kicked the back of our legs down, bringing us to our knees. Reyla crouched low, ready to submit to their questioning, just as I had told her to do. The man behind me gripped my hair, pulling back, forcing me to look up.

"Who are you?" He bellowed one more time.

"It can't be!" a voice in the crowd said.

Jake.

He pushed his way through.

"Wallace, that's her. That's the one that was helping the Baers." He pointed an accusatory finger at me.

Wallace whipped his head back to look at me.

"Well, seems we caught another Baer." He walked forward until he was standing an arm's length in front of us. "You too?"

Reyla nodded slightly, looking miserable. She was better than I expected.

Wallace grinned gleefully.

"We have your friends. Would you like to see them?"

The men lifted us up, pulling once again on our shoulders painfully.

"I think it's about time we reached out to Berwyn Baer, don't you?" He bellowed for the crowd, as if it were a joke. They all laughed.

"We have his wife. Now we have the little one's woman. What more could we ask for?" He flicked his wrist, dismissing us. He lowered his voice so only the group surrounding him could hear. "I'll be by to talk to you soon. Eden and I need to have a little conversation anyway."

A body nearly slammed into me as we walked. He careened out of an alleyway into our path.

"So it's true," Marty said, astonished. He quickly collected himself. "The golden girl is back again."

He leaned as close as he dared, but with my hands tied behind my back, it was far too close. I felt his breath crawl over me as he tipped his head, watching me.

"Too bad your golden boy isn't here to save you." He baited me.

From my peripheral vision, Reyla looked ready to take him out. She would have shattered him in two if she could have, but she held back as Eden screamed my name.

Glancing beyond Marty, I saw Eden's hands wrapped around the bars of a holding cell. She was deep in the heart of a building, only visible because the main door was opened for us to enter. It glowed a yellow color as the sky itself dimmed for the show.

Eden looked horrified as she pulled on the bars, trying to escape. Silas was quickly by her side, slamming his open palm into the bars, yelling my name once along with her.

"Marty, don't you touch her!" He threatened from his cage.

He grinned at me.

"Reyla?" Silas noticed my companion.

"Oh no." Eden breathed out, suddenly aware that it wasn't just me she needed to worry about. *"Marty!"*

She screamed as she slammed her hands against the bars.

"Move." My captor commanded. "We don't have time for this."

"We're not done yet," Marty said roughly, sliding to the side so we could pass.

He argued that I couldn't be in the same cell as Silas and Eden, but the men didn't listen. One of the men stepped around us to unlock the door and I tried to signal Silas not to do anything stupid. I could see him preparing to run at the men as soon as the door was open. Reyla's gasp was the only thing that stopped him as the door swung open.

At her throat sat a knife: the controlling factor in our obedience. I was pushed into the cell, tripping into Eden.

"Slowly." The man cautioned as he eased Reyla forward. "That's it, slow."

Once they reached the door, he pulled back the knife before throwing Reyla inside and slamming the bars shut. They left as quickly as they could, forcing Marty away as well.

Eden turned to me, throwing herself around my shoulders. I could feel the bones through her skin. Hollow eyes looked back at me. Tears pricked at my eyes.

"Oh, Silas," Reyla said, looking over the damage.

He was in rough shape too, bruised from an obvious beating.

"Silas," I said, reaching for him.

"I'm fine." He brushed me off. "Why are you here?"

I grinned.

"A rescue, of course. We only have a few minutes." I turned to Eden. "Berwyn is fine. He's alive."

Her face crumbled as the news overwhelmed her.

"You've seen him?" she asked.

"I just left him."

"Dov?" Silas interrupted.

"Canton has him. He's using Dov against us, but once we get out of here, that's our next mission."

Crashing outside told me it was time to move.

"Listen carefully," I said as I darted to the door to try to open it. "I went over the wall. I brought back a team I trained. There will be people you don't know helping us."

Eden rushed to my side to try to help. We both knew it was useless. Silas would have found a way out a long time ago if there had been one.

"Shadoe is helping me," I confessed. Silas and Eden froze.

"What?" Confusion won out in Silas' voice.

"Excuse me?" Eden demanded.

"It's a long story, just don't kill him." Reyla snapped. "Now let's get moving and we can handle the rest later."

Chaos erupted outside. I was a bit surprised that Berwyn hadn't held back until it was later in the evening, but I'm sure he wanted to get Eden back to safety as quickly as possible.

The main door flew open, revealing a figure illuminated only by the lights outside the entrance. We waited for our savior to unlock the door and free us.

We all backed up to allow the door to swing open. The man's hand shot out, grabbing onto me as he pulled me out. The force moved me so quickly I stumbled out into his waiting arms. He pulled the door behind me shut, blocking the others.

Looking up, I saw not one of our men, but Marty.

"I told you we weren't done."

My friends yelled behind me, fighting against the door once more. Throwing myself toward Marty, I struggled to get the keys he held. We grappled, each trying to get the upper hand. I was thrown against the wall, slamming my head into the rock. I slid down, preparing myself for the next attack.

He yelped when I kicked him. The keys fell to the floor. Dirt crammed under my nails as I clawed at the keys, trying to beat him to them. Marty pulled me back, digging his fingers into my leg where I had been burned. If I didn't have scars before, he certainly would have created some.

Lifting my elbow back, I slammed into his face, making him reel back. I caught the keys as he tangled his fist in my hair, dragging me to my feet. I dangled in the air for a moment before he kicked my knees out, sending me back to the dirt, shrieking.

I made eye contact with Silas just long enough to know my scream took him back to Canton's torture. He slammed into the door again, trying to free them.

Whipping my head back, I connected with Marty's chin, giving me just long enough to throw the keys. My opponent reached around my stomach, clutching me under his arm. I was off the ground and unable to get the leverage I needed to escape. Twirling, he threw me into the wall, making me dizzy enough to be unable to regain my balance.

He dragged me outside as the others fought to get the correct angle to get the key into the door. Marty forced me past people fighting; Berwyn's men taking on the people holding their leaders captive.

I raked my fingers down his arm, leaving bloody gashes that barely deterred him.

"I owe your golden boy for a few things," he hissed in my ear, throwing me face first into a tree as we neared a line of denser forest. "This time, he doesn't get to win."

"Canton has him, I hardly call that winning," I shouted back, throwing a fist at him.

The second he released me into the tree, I knew it was my only chance to fight. I swung, readying my elbow for his recourse. He came at me, but I ducked to the side, allowing him to overstep and hit the tree smeared with my blood.

He struck, landing a tight fist to my chin, snapping my head back. I moved my arm as if to jab him, but instead pulled back, and attacked with my foot. I slammed into his boot, wishing Wallace's men hadn't taken my knife when they tied us up.

In response, Marty brandished a knife from his belt, slashing it through the air at me. I attempted to take the cut on my arm rather than my face. I moved just enough that he missed, barely slicing my skin. When he swung again, I stepped just out of range. He crashed into another tree, arm high above his head as he collided into the bark.

Red rained from the sky as a scream so fierce I thought the world was ending rang out. Marty's knife toppled to the ground, still wrapped in his hand.

My scream nearly shattered the world.

Shadoe pulled Marty's trembling body away from the tree, turning him to look into his eyes. Shadoe used the entire force of his body to slam Marty into the tree.

"You will never touch her again, or next time, I won't let you live." Shadoe took his knife and slowly buried it into Marty's shoulder, slicing flat down his back, so that it missed the bones but separated the skin in an agonizing way. One more reminder of who held the power.

"Shadoe!" I screamed, hoping to deter him.

My eyes fixated on Marty's hand lying on the ground. Shadoe stooped to pick up the knife. He stood, wiping the blood from his blade on Marty's shirt as he shivered in shock against the pine.

Shadoe turned back as he started to leave. He picked up Marty's hand, avoiding the bloody stump. Opening the man's hand, he placed the missing one in it.

"Dov and I wish you a nice day." Shadoe leaned forward, growling. "*She is not yours.*"

With that final reminder, Shadoe turned back to me. I stood frozen, watching the scene before me. He gently turned my body away, making me walk back toward the cell.

"Do you want to save your friends or not?" he hissed, handing me Marty's knife as he shrieked in the background, writhing on the ground where he had slipped down when Shadoe walked away.

Another scream filled the air, this time far more fragile and feminine. *Reyla.*

Her cry sprang me into action, Shadoe following along side me. Having regained my equilibrium, I sprang over small objects in my way, not bothering to go around them. Shadoe followed suit when he needed to.

We arrived just in time to see Berwyn push a man off his knife, Eden behind him. The man crumpled to the ground, his shoulder gushing blood. I had never seen Berwyn look so tall or bulky in my life. He looked like his namesake as he towered above the man and I expected to hear him growl a warning to the others to stay away from his wife.

"Berwyn!" I shouted, announcing our approach to ensure he didn't mistake us for the enemy in his rage.

Eden wheeled around to face one of Wallace's men, rage burning in her eyes. Her hair flew behind her as she lashed out, kicking the man. She quietly reeled back in pain. Berwyn turned, landing a hard punch to her attacker, knocking him out.

I smiled at the scene, happy Berwyn and Eden were together again, but the moment only lasted until I heard another shout.

"Where is Reyla?" I shrieked, racing toward Dov's family.

Eden's eyes darted around wildly, searching for the girl.

"Where is she?" she echoed as Berwyn joined the search.

"There." He pointed.

In the darkness, Silas struggled forward, painfully taking each step. A body sagged in his arms.

Berwyn rushed forward. I followed quickly behind. The leader of the Baers took Reyla's broken body from Silas' careful grip and he nearly stumbled forward as the weight was transferred from his arms. I caught him, slipping under his arm to keep him steady.

Blood covered him, but I couldn't tell where it was from as it dripped off of him. Silas attempted to rush after Berwyn. Eden caught his other arm, ducking under it to stabilize him. He kept his weight on me, ensuring he didn't hurt Eden further. Shadoe waited where we had left him, not bothering to help.

"We need to go," Berwyn said, carefully positioning Reyla in his arms. He shouted to the team that it was time to leave. "Fall back!"

Eden and I hurried Silas after Berwyn, Shadoe taking a position behind us to watch for Wallace's people behind us. Raselin appeared, moving alongside Berwyn in case he needed assistance.

Wallace's men backed up, unwilling to face us in light of Marty's accusatory screams as he charged his companions to take Shadoe out in revenge. Berwyn's men had already taken out the high ranking men watching the cells, leaving only the underlings to fight us off. They didn't risk it.

Berwyn led the way away from Wallace's camp. Fitch took Reyla from his arms when he joined us in the dense trees as we retreated, relieving Berwyn. I could tell he was still struggling to bounce back from the effects of the claw Shadoe had used to shred his arm in the cave before we were split up.

"You're hurt." Silas said quietly, eyeing me as he stumbled forward.

"Look who's talking…"

"Nah, this is all surface-level." He tried to grin, wincing. "What happened?"

"Made it to the wall before they cornered us. Shadoe showed up and Dov pushed me up to him. He gave himself up to make sure we made it over."

"Sounds like Dov." He shook his head. "And Canton has him?"

I nodded, reliving Devin's report once again.

"Reyla?" he asked, nodding ahead of us.

"I don't know."

"Silas, what happened?" Eden asked, joining the conversation.

"They attacked us. It all happened so fast." He struggled to catch his breath at the pace we were forcing him to move at. "She fought hard. She looked like you, Auluria. If her hair were more like yours, I might have thought it *was* you for a second. You would have been proud."

I *was* proud—of both of them.

"And you thought carrying her while you were this beat up was wise?" Eden chastised.

"We had to move, Eden." He said, not joking back. Whatever had happened, the gravity of the situation weighed on Silas. I had never seen him unable to find levity in a situation afterward.

Eden cast me a worried look as she moved a bit closer to Silas' side.

"I'm fine, Eden." He insisted as he attempted to walk more on his own. He failed.

Ahead, Reyla started to move in Fitch's arms.

"Reyla." I said when I noticed, lurching forward before I remembered I was holding up Silas.

"Go," he said, obviously worried about her.

Reyla's head lolled back as she fell unconscious again.

"She's out, don't bother," Fitch called over his shoulder.

"I didn't realize we were so loud," I mumbled, looking at the distance between us.

"I have good ears." Fitch replied, hearing even my quiet muttering. Eden's face fell.

"Who is that?" She resorted to whispering.

"Fitch. He's one of my guys from over the wall." I replied. "He's been a real asset to us. You'll like his wife, Lydia, too."

"Less talking," Shadoe demanded, reminding me he was behind us.

We continued our harsh pace, trying to put as much distance between us and Wallace as possible.

The quiet should have been my first indication that something was wrong. It was hard to hear it over the soft crunching of leaves and branches under our feet, but it was there, screaming at us to take notice.

I failed to listen.

The attack was brutal as the Society soldiers divided us. We were far enough ahead that we weren't touched. The back of our team, however didn't fare as well.

We moved our injured men as far away as we could, sheltering them from the soldiers as we heard the fighting in the distance. Our secondary team heard the commotion from where they waited for us a mile away.

They ran to aid us. Berwyn sent them back to help as we pressed forward toward the storehouse. We had to hide our men before we were caught.

When our men made it back, they brought a story of horror with them. The soldiers had cut them off from the group. The secondary team was able to fight them back, causing a retreat.

"They have them, Berwyn," Henry said. "We couldn't get to them. We only managed to get a few of the men on your team back."

"The soldiers captured at least a dozen of our men," Gregory confirmed, glancing at Silas where he leaned against me in the circle.

Silas insisted on being there, even though he needed medical attention. He swayed against me.

"Okay, that's enough. You're getting looked at now," I insisted. Glancing at Shadoe, I decided to ask for help. "Justin, help me."

Justin moved to Silas's side and together we forced him to a small room in the storehouse where Eden was recovering. Reyla had been given a separate, tiny room because her injuries were far more severe.

"Do not let him move," I directed the woman watching over them. I turned to place him under a stricter charge. "Eden."

Pointing my finger at her was probably a bad idea, but she didn't snap at me. Instead, she watched Silas closely as the women helped lower him to a cot.

"What happened?" Eden asked softly.

"They captured our men. We're planning a rescue," I answered.

Justin hovered outside the room.

"Auluria, we should get back."

"How many?" Eden asked.

"A dozen." Silas winced, and he moved back on the cot. "We'll get them. They got us out, this won't be too much harder."

"I'm going to go back and help with the plan." I cut Eden off when she opened her mouth to speak. "I'll come back with details. I'll probably even beat Berwyn."

It was surprising that Berwyn wasn't sitting next to Eden to conduct the meeting from the tiny room. He always put his loyalty to the group first and this was no exception it seemed.

"Hang on," I said to Justin once we left the room.

I detoured to the next room where Reyla was lying on a mattress.

Her body was hidden under a blanket, but I saw her chest rising and falling in a steady pattern.

"Reyla," I whispered into the quiet room.

Her eyes fluttered open, and she inhaled deeply.

"Can I get you anything?" I asked, kneeling by her cot.

I brushed her hair back and waited for her to think about the question. Her lip was broken open under a swollen cheek. A small cut by the side of her eye was already starting to scab over.

"Are you okay?" she asked. "Did he hurt you?"

"I'm fine. Marty didn't get very far."

"Don't worry, Shadoe lent him a hand." Justin said dryly.

"What happened?" Reyla's eyes grew as round as mine.

"Marty pulled a knife on me." I paused. "Shadoe didn't take that well."

"What did he do?" the brunette prompted when I didn't continue.

"He might have, um, cut off his hand." I looked down, guilt flooding me, tightening in my chest.

Reyla looked horrified.

"He…?"

"He cut off his hand," I confirmed.

"The poor thing." Her hand flinched under the sheet.

"The important thing is that Auluria is safe." Justin chimed in, refocusing us.

"Did everyone get out?" She clenched the sheet in her hand nervously.

"We got Silas and Eden out," I replied. "But the Society found us. I'm assuming Wallace had something to do with that. I wouldn't be surprised if he had a few men in his pocket like Lowell did. They got a dozen of our men. We're staging a rescue now. We want to strike before they're ready for us."

"You should go," Reyla insisted. "I'll be fine."

It only took a minute of arguing before she kicked us out.

"Hey, Rey?" I paused at the door. "You did really good. Silas even said you looked like me while you were off fighting the bad guys."

I grinned from the door. She smiled, her tiny attempt at a giggle radiating pain that made her body seize up.

"Yes, I made the bad guys run for their lives." She gave me a sad look. "Go get our men back. I expect flowers when you return, Auluria."

She managed to yell the last part loud enough for me to hear it as I walked away. Necesta nodded to me as she slipped into Reyla's room, a satchel in her hands. I knew my friend was in good hands.

"A girl with priorities," Justin mused.

"She certainly has those." I smirked. "Are you going on the mission?"

"Have I missed one yet?"

"No, you haven't. Is Devin coming?"

"Probably. They let him help with the backup group today, and I imagine Berwyn and Raselin are going to want as many hands as possible."

Berwyn nodded to us as we approached, finishing what he was saying to the group.

"Auluria, you and Shadoe are in charge of a team. Arin and Raselin will be leading a team. Fitch and I will be leading the first team," he said, mixing up the team to ensure he had one of his trusted people with each group.

"Are you sure it's such a good idea you lead the initial strike, Berwyn? You're still recovering," I say softly, hoping only Berwyn could hear.

He turned sharply to glare at me.

"I'm just saying, maybe Shadoe and I should go in first. You can follow with the second wave." I held my hands up as if I was trying to calm an angry animal. "*One* of us needs to make it back, Berwyn."

"We'll go," Arin said, stepping into the conversation. "She's right… All of you have been through a lot recently, but my team hasn't sustained as much damage. Let us go in first, and you act as our back up."

He rolled his eyes when we agreed that I had a point. It was amazing how the man still didn't trust me. He leered at Shadoe for a moment. Maybe I wasn't the only one he didn't trust.

All eyes were on Berwyn when he reluctantly agreed to Arin's plan. But even with a solid plan, I knew nothing ever worked the way the Baers planned it to, and I wondered how many more we would lose in an attempt to save lives.

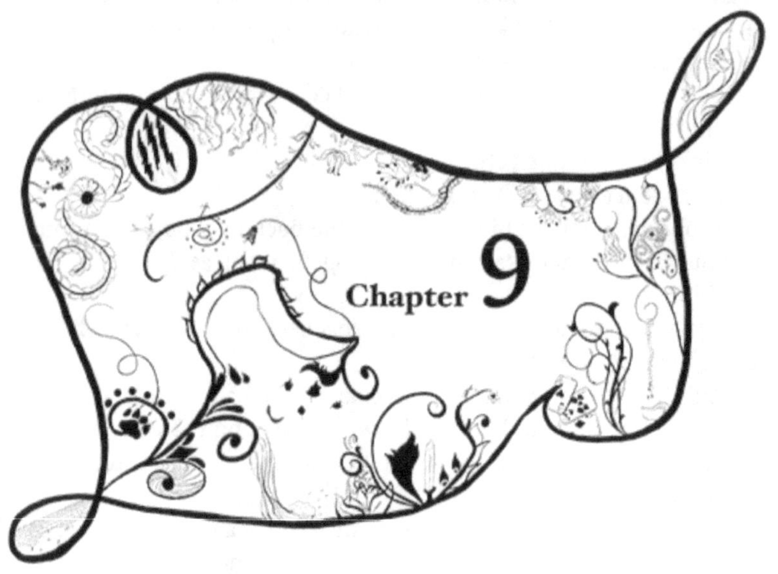

Chapter 9

THE SOLDIERS WERE WAITING FOR US WHEN WE ARRIVED. WE NEVER made it into the town. They lined the streets facing the woods. It didn't matter where they were—they knew we would find them.

Our captured men were lined up, each the length of two men apart, spreading the group out over a great distance. The soldiers had them on their knees, resting in the dirt uncomfortably. Rocks dug into one man's knees as I watched from a distance.

When our lookout delivered the news of the stand off, the team leaders raced ahead to assess the situation. Their men were watching for us, alerting the soldier in charge when they saw us at the tree line.

"This is what happens when you work against the Society. Magistrate Canton has found these men are guilty of treason." The soldier quickly listed the charges against our people. "The sentence is death."

Before any of us could move, the soldiers pulled knives from their belts and ran them across the throats of twelve of our men. They fell at their feet, blood pooling around their bodies. Shadoe clamped his hand around my mouth to keep me from screaming, his strong arms holding me back as I tried to push forward to help the lost cause.

Berwyn's eyes were glassy as his fists tightened so hard I thought they might break. Raselin wore a shocked expression, realizing, perhaps, that taking down the Society would not be as easy as he thought, despite our numbers.

"Tell your leaders," the soldier shouted, "that if they give this battle up and work under Magistrate Canton's command, they can prevent this from happening again."

He waved his hand at the bodies as he stepped forward to kick the corpse of a man around Justin and Devin's age. The body moved slightly with the impact, jostling his hair out of place, making me nauseous.

"Run along, little spies. Or you'll join them."

They thought we were spies. They didn't realize we had come with a team. Surprisingly, they had missed our actual spy. We would have to remember to let him take the lead on spy missions from then on.

"Go." Berwyn whispered harshly.

We retreated quickly, running back to the waiting teams. Before we reached them, we gave them the signal to retreat. After a few miles, we stopped to tell them what had happened. Everyone was devastated.

"They expect us to retreat," Berwyn said. "They want us to disappear. The Society wants us to submit to their will and fight their wars. But today we will do what they do not expect. Today we will bring the war to them."

His voice rose in power as he spoke until he was shouting. He grew taller, rising up on his feet, taking up as much space as he could. Berwyn leading not by emotion, but by some master plan he had conjured up in the few miles we had traveled.

"We're going back," he said, a wild smile slipping onto his face. "They took our people, now we will take theirs."

"Berwyn!" I was horrified.

He looked to me, but never faltered.

"We're going into the Society to find their men. We will take their leaders and question them. We can't get Canton, but we can get the men who work for him. They'll never suspect we're coming for them. We've never dared to abduct their men before."

I was catching on to his plan.

"We will take Canton's men and find out what his plans are. Once we have information, we'll release them and Canton will never know."

"You want to release them?" Justin said incredulously. "They'll run straight to Canton."

"No they won't," Arin said, a darkness encapsulating his voice.

No one questioned him further.

Berwyn divided the team, sending many of them back to the storehouse. I didn't question him when he directed me to return.

Shadoe watched long enough to concern me before he turned and left with Arin. I started to shake once they were out of sight.

"I know you're upset," Berwyn said, slipping his injured arm under mine, "but you have to keep it together."

I tried to nod, but my body rebelled.

"I know Lowell and Shadoe trained you to withstand interrogation, but did they ever teach you how to extract information from a person?"

"In a way." My voice quivered.

"In the time I've known you, I've watched you coerce your way into our group, manipulate your cousin, withstand Canton's torture, and rally an entire division of men and women to follow you over the wall.

"I think you've seen enough in your lifetime to handle getting information from one of the Society's men, don't you?"

I glanced up at him as we walked back to the storehouse.

"You have the motive, Auluria. You're using the men we capture now to find Dov."

The spark caught. My head whipped up to look at the tall man who was guiding my steps, fire racing through me.

This was how I would get Dov back.

"And that's all you needed to know." He smiled at me as I stopped shaking, dropping his arm from mine. He wandered away, leaving me to consider my moves the rest of the way back.

I didn't speak to anyone when I returned, brushing off Sharone when she raced up to me.

"Later," I promised, not knowing if I could keep my word.

I paced in one of the rooms that was hidden off of the main area; formerly a storage area, transformed into a multipurpose room that was used for medical needs, private meetings, or as a place to hide from the crowd.

I debated going to Silas. I even considered teaming up with

Shadoe, but I knew his tactics would not sit well with me. No, this was something I had to do on my own.

I played with my thoughts, running through every possible tactic I could think of, but nothing felt right. Lowell had trained me to be smart. Shadoe had trained me to be fierce. But in the end, Brittella's manipulation training won out. I knew what I had to do. I would need to be patient.

Eventually the men returned, four of Magistrate Canton's underlings in their possession. I watched quietly as they brought the men, bound and blindfolded, into the storehouse through the main entrance.

Everyone was silent as we guided the men down a separate set of tunnels, keeping them far away from the main storehouse. We gave no indication of how many of us were walking alongside them.

Each man was given a room far enough away that they couldn't communicate with each other, but close enough should we need them to overhear the screams of their friends.

Shadoe, Arin, Berwyn, and another of Berwyn's men followed into the rooms. Berwyn had agreed to work with my plan, substituting his extra man in for the fourth captive. I waited, listening to the grumblings that came from behind the closed doors as the men interrogated Canton's people.

Knowing I didn't want to oversee Shadoe's work, I asked Raselin to monitor him. Fitch stood between Berwyn and the fourth man's cells, while I wandered over to Arin's, looking in the window.

He stalked around the man much as he had done the day he questioned me. His knife glinted in his hand as Arin walked quietly around the terrified man. He looked like he never spent a day outside of his fancy home in his entire life.

When the interrogator walked back into his line of sight, he leapt forward, throwing his hand against the table, creating a noise that must have made the man in Shadoe's room jump as well. Arin yelled at him, demanding information. The tiny man shook, tears forming in the corners of his eyes. Arin had a system for his interrogations and he did not deviate.

"Are you okay?" Raselin asked from a few feet away. He leaned back against the wall, arms folded across his chest.

"I've been on the receiving end of one of Arin's interrogations. Shadoe trained me well enough to play along, but Arin certainly has this guy worked up."

Berwyn stepped out of his room, motioning us to follow. We left our posts and walked out into the hallway. A moment later, Arin and the other man joined us.

"We managed to get some low level intelligence out of them, but we're not done yet." Berwyn said after each man had told the group what they had learned.

They debated whether it would be wise to continue to work with the same captive or to switch out the interrogators, eventually deciding to attempt to work with different Society men. Berwyn went to inform Shadoe.

"Auluria," Berwyn called to me before opening the door. There was an edge to his voice that I couldn't convince myself wasn't there.

I reached the window just as Shadoe stepped out.

"What did you do?" I said, horrified.

Berwyn held me back, blocking my path with his arm. He grunted as my stomach collided with his mostly healed cuts.

"Not yet," he cautioned. "You have a good plan, you just have to get the timing right."

Shadoe eyed me, knowing what I planned to do.

"He will be ready for you," he said, wiping his blade.

He must have removed the gag the man was wearing while he used the knife on him. We wouldn't have missed what must have been pained screams otherwise. I cringed thinking of the pain my former handler had inflicted, my thoughts floating back to Canton's presence.

"It's nothing he wouldn't have done to you," Shadoe said. Dropping his voice, he added, "And far less than Canton *did* to you."

Was this retribution?

"Give it a few minutes and then go in," Berwyn instructed.

I took the time to gather a few rags and bandages. My hand floated to the necklace Necesta had demanded I hide below my clothing. This man would not be receiving that kind of help today.

Stepping inside, I adopted a demure demeanor, walking over to the man gently. Bending down, I dropped to my knees and dipped a rag in a small bin of water I brought with me. He hissed when it touched his open wound.

I continued to say nothing as I worked, waiting for him to speak first. As I started bandaging his arm, he broke his silence.

"Who are you?" he demanded as I continued to work, wrapping gauze around his forearm. "Where are we?"

His body grew tenser the longer I went without speaking.

"Look at me, girl," he demanded, flexing his fingers in an attempt to grab me. His attempts were in vain as his wrists were tied to the arms of the chair.

Berwyn burst into the room, stomping over to where I knelt on the floor.

"You're not done yet?" he bellowed, grabbing my hair and throwing me to the floor. "We don't have time for you to waste."

He stormed out of the room, leaving me to pick myself up.

"Are you being held here against your will?" the man hissed, hoping to convince me to help him.

"I can't help you," I said quietly.

"We can help each other," he said, gaining strength, as he leaned forward to formulate a plan.

I finished wrapping his cuts as he spit out idea after idea.

"Even if I could get you out, where would we go?" I finally hissed at him.

He smiled.

By the time I reached the fourth cell, playing the game with each one, I had answers. I wiped the blood off my finger where I pinched down on Shadoe's victim's injuries. I let it sit through all of my interrogations as a terror tactic, and it sickened me.

Each man wanted the same thing: escape. Each captive reacted differently as I played the part of a helpless woman they thought they could manipulate. It was too late by the time their other interrogator walked in: I had enough information to use against them.

When I switched from innocent, naïve girl, to strategic interrogator in front of their eyes, they were terrified, desperately trying to convince me they had lied. They had no grace as they flailed about, trying not to pay for their ignorance. By the time I left their cells, they were more afraid of me than they were of the men in the room.

They gave up everything they could about the Society's plans. We knew more about where they were keeping Dov than we had been able to find out since they took him. The men gave up information about the war over the wall, the camps, and the soldiers than we had ever had access to in the years we had been working against them.

Berwyn was elated. Shadoe looked proud of me for the first time ever as he took up his place at my side.

"Looks like Lowell was right about you. You are a leader. I think we owe Brittella a debut of gratitude too. This was her doing, wasn't it?"

"I thought you hated Brittella." I walked along side him back to the main storehouse.

"I hate what she teaches, though I see its importance. Just don't ever use that stuff on me."

I refused to test what I had learned from the woman out on Shadoe when she had first educated me, and I refused to do it now.

"We have a problem, though," Berwyn said loudly once we rounded the corner. "We can't send them back. Not after the damage Shadoe did to Justice Kenton."

"There will be retribution," Fitch said. "Are we ready for that?"

"We'll have to be." Berwyn glowered at Shadoe.

Shadoe glared back, refusing to justify his actions to anyone. I wanted to slap him again. It was a stupid move; one that would likely cost us. We had lost too many lives already.

"Can we use them to negotiate Dov's release?" Fitch asked.

"I don't know," Berwyn replied, "Right now the Society doesn't know what their men have told us. We have the upper hand. But if we trade, they'll interrogate their men too, probably kill them afterward, and they'll know exactly what we know and can change their plan."

"They didn't have enough information for us to bring down the Society, Berwyn, just to mess up Canton's plans," I commented, unsure of how I felt about releasing the men as a trade.

"We're not done talking to them yet." Raselin turned to us as we walked. "Let's give it a few days to see how desperate the Society is to get their men back."

Unfortunately, giving the Society time was a mistake.

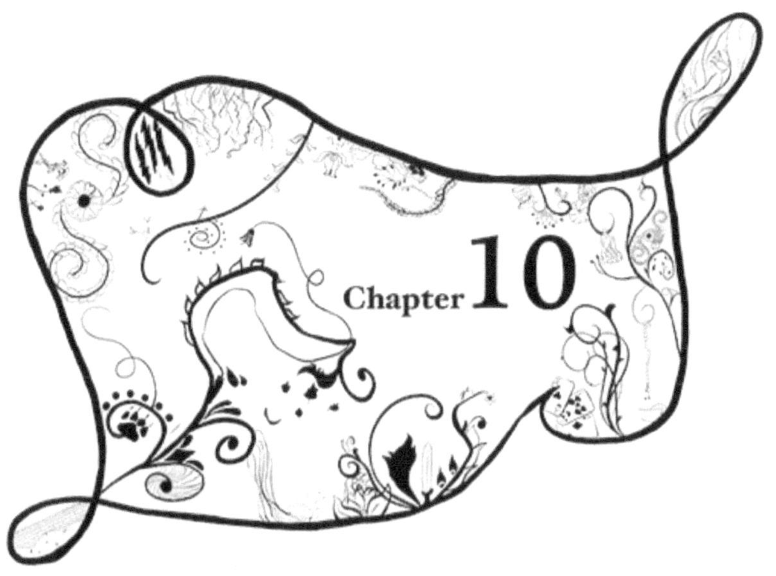

Chapter 10

T̲HE CROWD WAS CHARGED WITH TENSION AS WE SNUCK INTO THE masses, weaving our way through hordes of people. The air seemed to crackle with each step I took. I moved my hand to brush my hair back, but I had tied it down earlier in an effort to keep it hidden. I was too well known in the city after my escape.

Four days after capturing Canton's men, he had retaliated. Our men found word of a public spectacle, but we knew he wouldn't kill Dov. He wanted a trade. We also knew he would never trade Dov, but rather use it as a ploy to get us to come out of hiding and release his men. We quietly snuck into the city, waiting for what would happen next.

I crept forward, making my way to the same stage I had once stood on, noose around my neck. The noise of voices hummed around me as spectators guessed the extent the Society would go to this time.

My breath caught as they dragged him out. He stumbled up the steps, tripping as he walked out onto the stage between two guards. His hair was matted with dried blood, the color drained from his face. Bruises covered his body as they threw him to his knees.

A fixture had been placed toward the front of the stage. They pulled Dov's hands from behind him and fastened them to the device he knelt in front of. He leaned forward, placing his weight on his arms.

Magistrate Canton walked on stage, his robe flowing behind him as he walked. Taking his place slightly in front of Dov, he stared at the audience.

"Where are they?" Canton asked.

"I don't know," Dov croaked, sounding as though he hadn't had water all day.

"Where is your brother?" he inquired.

Dov grunted in response, trying to adjust his hands into a more comfortable position.

"One more time. Where are your people?" Canton queried.

"I don't know," Dov said, looking up at him.

The lash came down on his back, making a horrific sound. The entire gallery gasped.

"Dov Baer, you have been charged with crimes against the Society, as have your brother, sister-in-law, and entire group. Tell us where to find them and we won't kill any more than we have to. We'll give them the chance to confess and surrender."

"I do not know where they are." Dov glared at him.

The soldier with the lash reached out and kicked Dov in the stomach. He wasn't prepared to be hit from that angle, assuming he would be lashed again, and he crumpled in on himself. His shirt dangled in front of him, a hole torn by the man's boot exposing his flesh.

"Where is your brother?" Canton turned to look at him.

"You won't win, Canton." Dov said as fiercely as he could in his state.

The guard kicked his hip, tossing Dov to the ground. I could almost feel his shoulders pop as his body moved away from where his hands were tied. He struggled to right himself quickly to avoid another blow that might actually dislocate his shoulder.

Once he had positioned himself on his knees, he stared out into the crowd.

"Where is the girl?"

"What girl?" Dov challenged, his eyes taking a sad turn.

"The one that works for Lowell. Where is she?"

"She's gone. You'll never get your hands on her." Dov smiled just enough to infuriate Canton.

"We'll find her, Baer," Canton tormented him. "When we do, we'll do a lot worse than the last time we had her."

"Good luck with that," Dov offered. "You'll never hurt her again."

Canton fumed. He rushed around behind Dov, to the man with the whip. Ripping it from his hand, he towered over Dov.

Dov's entire body stilled as he found me in the crowd. My hair was back, I had covered as much of myself as possible, but he held my gaze, questioning me. I nodded just enough that he could confirm it was me, and his entire body went tense.

"Where is she?" Canton demanded, hand raised in the air.

Dov watched me. He never moved from where he held my gaze. The lash came down again, ripping into him. The second hit forced him to fight against squeezing his eyes shut so he wouldn't lose sight of me.

I stood, frozen, knowing I couldn't move or I would give him away. My jaw clenched with every strike, but I didn't look away.

Canton kicked him, knocking Dov off balance. He fell to the ground again, angling his head to see me.

We're coming, I mouthed, hoping he had seen.

"Where are they?" Canton yelled as he stepped back for the soldier to take over.

Dov remained on the ground. When the guard neared him, he kicked, pushing the man over. The crowd hummed.

Canton nodded to another soldier. He and his partner stepped forward quickly. The second man reached out, untying Dov from the fixture he was bound to. The first man pulled Dov up by his chin, wrapping a hand in front of him to force him up, while his dominant hand held a knife to Dov's throat.

I was about to rush forward when Canton roared.

"This is the last chance you will have. You have one week to give yourselves over, or I will kill him."

The soldiers dragged Dov away. His face was tipped up so high he couldn't have seen me if he tried. The man holding him practically carried him off the stage.

Canton turned back to the crowd.

"Anyone found helping the Baers from this point on will be executed on the spot. If you have contact with them, get word to them today that this is their last chance. They know what we want in addition to their surrender.

"The Society has always worked to protect its people, both from forces outside the wall and threats in our own country like the Baers. We will not stand for any more loss of life because of these people!" Canton roared to the masses.

"If they come after any more of our people, I will see to it that their leaders are sentenced to death for this. There will be no mercy for them. If their people give themselves up now, we will rehabilitate them and welcome them back into our community."

He gave his speech pledging benevolence we knew would never come. If he got his hands on our people, they would be sent to the camps, if they weren't exterminated.

"If anyone attempts to harm my men again, I will send Dov Baer back in pieces!" he threatened, anger radiating off of him matching his red flowing robes.

"Now go!" the magistrate demanded, charging the crowd to find and turn over the Baers.

"We have to go." Devin tugged on my arm.

When I didn't move, he tried again.

"Auluria, please. We have to go." He pulled harder. "*Lur!*"

I snapped out of it and allowed him to drape an arm over me as if I belonged to him—sister, lover, wife—I didn't know. He guided me away from the crowd.

"He's worried for his own safety. He doesn't care about his men. He thinks we're going to come for him," Berwyn said when we reached him where he waited out of sight at Raselin's suggestion.

"If we're going to survive this, we need more people," Raselin insisted as we evaluated our options. "We have your group and ours, but Canton has an army bigger than I thought. We don't have any other choice."

The two men looked at each other, silently communicating. Their eyes argued, back and forth, over a conversation the rest of us were not privy to.

"We have to, Berwyn."

Our leader looked reluctantly at Raselin. He turned to face us.

"We need your men," he said to Shadoe. "Go get Lowell's men and bring them here."

My heart dropped.

"We will send a few men with you," Raselin said, reminding us that Shadoe would be watched. "You were second in command to Lowell, which means these are your people now."

"No one has heard much from them since Lowell died. They have no leadership that we can tell." Berwyn added painfully, "You are their leader now, Shadoe."

I knew once Shadoe returned to his men, he would not be helping the Baers. He was only there for me.

"We need to take the Society out, once and for all. This is the only way we will ever be free of them." Raselin played into Shadoe's vanity. "After we bring them down, you will be responsible for your people and their wellbeing. But until then, we need to work together to stop Canton and bring down the entire government structure."

Shadoe stood in silence for a moment. He looked to me, considering my role in this.

"She comes with me," he announced boldly.

I was about to refuse, demanding to stay with the Baers, when they stopped me.

"You will go with him, Auluria," Raselin informed me. "Lowell wanted you both in charge, and now you are. Go do your duty and bring your men here."

I started to argue until Berwyn pulled me aside.

"Listen," he demanded. "We have to get Dov out now. Canton isn't going to draw this out much more. We need Lowell's men, and right now that means we need Shadoe to lead them. If we give him free reign, he'll probably resort back to Lowell's tactics, but *you* can control him.

"Pull yourself together and go get them."

"They won't accept me, Berwyn, I betrayed them." I insisted.

"They will do anything Shadoe says. They know Lowell trained him to take over. If he brings you back to them, they will have to accept you.

"The faster you find them, the faster we can save Dov and take down the Society. I don't care what you have to do, just do it, and get those people back here and ready to fight. I don't care if they kill every Society man along the way if they have to at this point. We are saving Dov and getting control of Canton."

"Auluria," he softened. "I know this won't be easy for you. I understand that we're asking you to walk into a bad situation, but you won't be alone."

"Auluria." Silas puts his hand on my shoulder as he approaches from behind me. "I'm not going to leave you alone with them. You'll be safe."

He looked to be almost back to his normal self. Necesta's brightly colored little jars had worked miracles. He stood at my shoulder, waiting for an answer.

"No one will force you to do this, Auluria," he said softly, "but from where I stand, this is the only way I can see for all of us to survive this. I promise, I won't leave you. We'll save Dov together, and if that means we use Lowell's people to do it, so be it."

"What good can come from following Lowell's plan?" I asked.

"But we're *not*. You'll be in leadership, just like he wanted, but that's all. You'll never run his group the way he wanted you to.

"Besides," he added, "that's not the wedding we're planning here."

Berwyn's jaw dropped as far as mine did. I turned so quickly I nearly collided with Silas.

"We were all thinking it." He shrugged, grinning.

Berwyn sputtered.

"Time to go." Silas wheeled me around. "We'll be back with reinforcements, Berwyn."

"No," Shadoe said when we arrived at the tree he had retreated to to wait by.

"She's not going alone," Silas insisted.

"You're not coming," Shadoe forbade him.

"You don't get a choice," I interjected. "Silas is coming with us. It's one of my conditions."

"You don't get to *have* conditions," Shadoe challenged me.

"Oh, yes I do, Shadoe. Lowell put us *both* in charge. You and me; together. If you showed up by yourself, maybe they'd follow you. But what happens when I show up too?

"Let's just say for a moment that I walk into the camp with an elaborate story about how Lowell instructed me to continue on with the ruse even to the point of us hanging. I mean, how else would anyone be able to explain the fact that you cut me down or that you climbed the wall with me?

"I'll tell them all about what Lowell had planned and how you didn't follow his strategy."

"I have followed—"

"Followed *what*, Shadoe? Are you and I married? Are you and I together? Here's a hint: *we're not!*"

I dropped my voice the way Brittella had taught me to do, sounding sad and meek.

"I couldn't help it that you didn't want to follow through with Lowell's plan." I pouted, "But it turns out *Silas* could be bought."

For a moment, Silas looked like I had slapped him. He grinned, leaning an elbow on my shoulder and pretended to examine his hands.

"Yeah. You heard the lady… Money talks." Silas looked up to catch Shadoe's eye before pointing at me. "And I'd bet money that this little lady can spin a better tale than you can, Shadoe. So I suggest you be practical if you want to keep control of your group."

"Not sure what's happening here," Talley said as she joined us, "but I'll side with Auluria. Seems she has a way of beating the odds around here."

"Not you, too," Shadoe complained.

"Yes, *me.* Devin, Fitch and Lydia, and Nian, too," she responded. "And before you go protesting, we're here in case you have trouble taking back command from whoever is overseeing your people at the moment."

I turned back to Shadoe and nodded. Surrounding myself with friends was a wise choice, especially if I was about to step into unfriendly territory.

"Fine," Shadoe grunted. "Let's move."

A day and a half later, we walked into the temporary camp Lowell's men were using. Their transient lifestyle made them hard to find, but Shadoe and I watched for the markers they left that only people from Lowell's fold would be able to decipher.

The men overseeing the group quickly turned over power to Shadoe… after he broke a few bones in the scuffle. Their new leader explained that we had been following Lowell's plan, escaping over the wall and rallying more fighters. Shadoe told the plan of working with the Baers to bring down the Society as if it had been his own idea. He didn't mention the part about saving Dov.

My former colleagues had torn down the camp and were ready to move within hours. They begrudgingly accepted me back into the fold, having no choice but to listen to Shadoe as he forced them into submission.

Several of the men I had known from my time training with Shadoe watched curiously as I stayed between Silas and their new leader. Shadoe did nothing to claim me and Silas refused to leave my side, leaving the group unsure of my standing.

The group followed behind Shadoe toward the place we would meet the Baers. It took several hours before we reached the location. We moved the group into the burned out storehouse the Baers used before Shadoe had torched the place to prove a point. Dov's pond was within walking distance, but I couldn't risk the excursion.

Berwyn and Eden were waiting when we arrived, surrounded by

their best fighters. They walked out to meet us, allowing Shadoe's people to file into the storehouse while the leaders talked outside.

"We're leaving tonight." Berwyn said, Raselin and Eden taking equal positions on either side of him, their arms crossed. "We're almost out of time."

"We're not ready to take on the Society yet," Shadoe countered.

"We need to get Dov out."

"If you want to go after your kid brother, fine, but my men are not getting involved.," Shadoe pressed.

I knew he would pull something like that.

"Our job is to bring down Canton and destroy the Society. Not to rescue your family."

"He saved you, Shadoe," I protested.

"No, he saved *you*." Shadoe turned on me. "I was already on the wall. He stayed behind for *you. I* owe him nothing."

"He saved your *fianceé*." I reminded him.

"*Are* you?" he leered at me. "Are you my fianceé, Lur? Because I'm pretty sure fiancés aren't allowed to kiss other men."

His lecture might have hurt if I had cared.

"*They* don't know that," I said, pointing to the storehouse entrance. "So in their eyes, you *do* owe him. Don't forget, I still hold some power here. You *will* help us rescue him."

"I insist," Berwyn said. "Or else I can easily block your men in the storehouse right now and turn them over to Canton as a peace offering. Don't you think he'd be willing to trade my brother for *all* of those people in there? And then where would you be? You can't take down the government without an army."

"He's right, Shadoe," Raselin said. "We're all in this, and we will win or lose by what we choose now."

I wrenched myself closer to him and whispered in his ear, "You help us now, and we'll help you later. You're going to need something later on, and this will be your bargaining chip."

He pushed me away. I stumbled back into Silas, catching myself on his arm.

"Fine. But we do this my way." Shadoe took authority over the situation. "My men will be the distraction. They will not be taking the risks for one of you."

"Fine," Berwyn said.

"We'll rescue him while you draw the soldiers away," I confirmed.

"No." He stopped me. "*They'll* rescue him while *we* draw the guards away."

I furrowed my brows, ready to correct him.

"I'm helping save Dov." I tried to keep my voice even.

"Yes, by being a distraction with your team," he corrected me. "That was part of this deal. I'd go back to lead Lowell's men and you would be alongside me, and together, you and I would lend our people to *him* to defeat the Society."

He jutted his chin out at Berwyn.

"Baer wanted our group back together so we could help him. You are the price he paid for that. You're back with your people. If you want to help your precious Dov, you do it with *us*. Otherwise, we conveniently slip away during this little distraction mission and the soldiers return right in the middle of your jailbreak and ruin any chance you have of getting him out."

Eden looked like she was ready to pummel Shadoe. I wished she would have. I wish *I* could have.

Silas stepped up behind me, taking my wrist gently between his fingers. His arm brushed against me, every muscle in his body pulled tightly in anger, but his fingers held loosely onto me without hurting me.

"I'm staying with your team, in that case," he said, voice low and dangerous.

"You can't," I whispered. "They need you. Dov needs you."

"You are not going to do this alone," he insisted quietly. "Dov wouldn't let you and neither will I."

"Dov is not going to pay the price for this," I hissed back, instantly regretting my tone. "Dov gave himself up to save me; now it's my turn. I'll be fine. When this is all over, we'll handle it. But right now, Berwyn and Eden need your help. Between the three of you, you'll get him back."

"Auluria," Silas insisted.

"Silas. This is how it's going to be." I stepped away from him.

Shadoe practically beamed, grinning over his victory at Berwyn as I approached him and turned to face the Baers. He cast Silas a withering look that would make a lesser man back down.

Three leaders watched one another. Three groups faced off in a circle of wills. Shadoe's team would be a distraction, entering the city first and drawing the guards away. Berwyn's men would breach the city and retrieve Dov. Raselin's team would assist, acting as the hidden second wave that would stop any soldiers that chased Berwyn's men.

The three men watched each other, Eden and Silas with Berwyn,

Fitch with Raselin, and myself standing by Shadoe. The leaders of three very distinct groups, with very clear lines drawn, stood on opposite sides of the circle, all willing to work toward one goal, despite the conditions and the mistrust. The very thing Lowell had lost everything over was happening: the Society was going to burn at the hands of enemies.

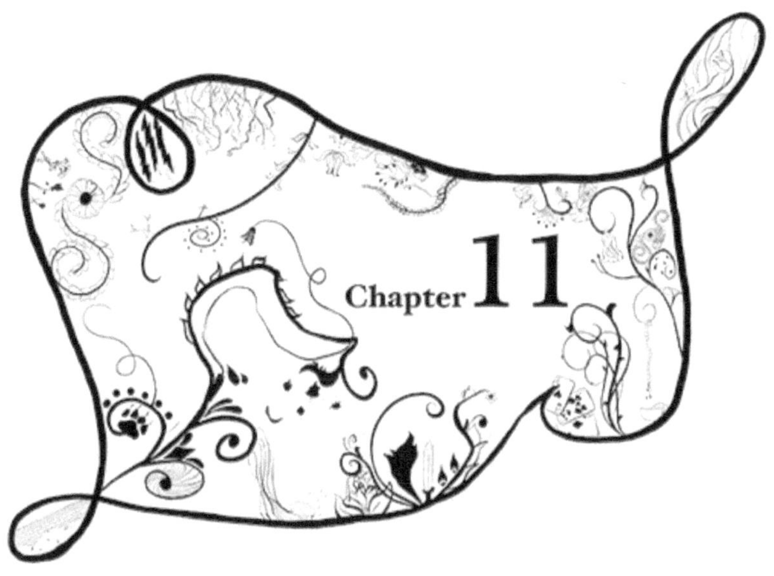

Chapter 11

"Now," I whispered to myself, begging Shadoe to be thinking the same thing.

My hand gripped the wooden crate, a sliver of metal icily touching the tip of my little finger. I tensed my muscles, waiting to push. Rocking on my toes, I tried to see around the box, hoping Shadoe was ready.

This has to be now.

Movement caught my eye as Shadoe stepped back just enough that I could see his hand fall.

Now.

Without bothering to inhale, I pushed, toppling the crate. The metal latch broke open, toppling the contents out. Food spilled out, bouncing across the floor. I kicked a piece out of the way as I started to run.

I threw myself at the entrance, grabbing the door frame to swing myself out into the fresh air. It was a relief to be out of the stale stench of the makeshift building that housed the boxes we were destroying.

Shadoe had several of his men carrying boxes with unknown content. One didn't need to know what was inside when one was planning to drop it along the way.

Locust, a boy I met while training with Shadoe, held a crate with another man. It bounced between them, slamming into their legs as they ran out of sync.

"Pick up the pace, boys," one of the women shouted as she raced by.

"You try running with a crate and an idiot," Locust snapped.

"Move!" I shouted, not waiting to see if they would find their footing.

"Stop!" the soldiers shouted as they rounded the corner, hearing the commotion. Shadoe had timed it perfectly so that they could hear our escape, but were not close enough to do any real damage.

A moment later, I heard a crash as the crate Locust and the man were carrying fell to the ground. It splintered, wood cracking as it slammed at their feet. The boys kept running.

The group shouted to each other, making it seem as if we had been accidentally discovered and the dropped crates were actual losses. The Society men kept running.

We wove through the city, spreading out through alleys, hiding in houses. Shadoe's men forced their way into hiding, quietly holding families hostage for minutes at a time until it was safe to run again. Shadoe ran ahead as I darted into a quiet alley, hiding in the shadows.

I breathed heavily as the soldiers ran past the entrance, casting long, dark shadows down the walkway, cutting off the glimpses of gold the setting sun threw into my walkway. Pressing against the wall, I waited. I glanced down, noticing my hair had fallen from where I had tied it back.

A loud thud at the mouth of the alley screamed for my attention. A soldier slammed a boy into the wall. The guard was surprised when I appeared at his side, kicking him into the road. He sprawled in the dirt while I leapt over him, the boy's hand in mine as I dragged him away.

I threw him ahead of me, turning to face the soldier. I found him still in the dirt.

"Go!" I commanded, letting Shadoe's man run ahead.

When I felt it was secure, I ran, focusing on the path ahead of me in a desperate attempt not to worry about Dov. Each pounding step urged me to focus more. The woods loomed ahead of me, our meeting point once we had lost the guards. I sprinted for the trees, prepared to dive into the tall grass that separated the tree line from the roads of the city. I skirted around the city onto the gravel road that outlined the space.

Before I could reach where Shadoe stood just behind a tree, watching, I was forced to a stop. My team struggled against an unexpected attack by the Society. A small group of men appeared from the neighboring town line, striking our men.

They struggled, drawing blood as knives were brandished. I raced forward to help, knowing if we could use our numbers, we could survive. A hand clamped around my arm stopped me, swinging me back into the arms of a young man with red hair.

"You have to go," he hissed, checking to see where our team was. "He's not watching, you need to go."

"What are you talking about?" I struggled to pull away.

"Shadoe is fighting. Go save your boyfriend," the man hissed.

The minute his eyes connected with mine, I remembered a scared, redheaded boy held in the cells of the Society as I broke out members of the Baers' team before Silas and I were temporarily captured.

"Just go!" he hissed, repaying the debt he never owed me in the first place.

Without thinking through the implications of betraying Shadoe, I ran. My breaths felt heavy as I forced my way through the streets, back the way I had come. I raced to the center of the city, hiding from the soldiers I nearly met along the way.

"Please let me make it in time," I whispered. "Please let us get him out."

The sun glinted fiercely off of roads and buildings alike. I could barely see as I charged into a haze of yellow, arms pumping furiously by my body.

"What are you doing here?" Arin yelled, seeing me approach.

"Where are they?" I shouted back.

"I don't know. Eden was separated from us. Berwyn is looking for her. That way." He pointed to where I was running as he took the opposite direction, rushing after soldiers we could hear around the corner.

I wanted to burn the buildings to the ground to create a path for myself. Instead, I leapt over carts and darted around buildings as I sped forward. At the break in the buildings, I paused, determining which way to go out in the open space.

Chaos was everywhere and Berwyn's men fought to keep control as their leaders fought their way into the prison where they held Dov.

"Eden?" Berwyn shouted in the distance, not close enough to where Dov was being held.

I saw the stage I had once graced and turned, angling for the entrance. I saw something out of the corner of my eye as I ran. My feet were pulled out from under me, nearly flipping me over the arms of a soldier who grabbed me. Smoke burned my eyes as he tried to subdue me.

"Eden!" Berwyn shouted again, closer to where I was being held captive.

"Berwyn!" I tried to scream. The man muffled my cry.

I bit down, forcing *him* to scream instead.

A second man pushed in between us, revealing the first. I struggled against him in vain as another man joined him to restrain me.

All I could hear was yelling. Soldiers, rescuers, and people inside the prison all shouted out in an orchestrated attempt to survive and win. The men behind me stilled.

Looking away from where they held onto me I saw what had stopped them. I watched in horror.

A single figure ran out of the prison, taking on three men. The soldiers were cut down, one at a time. They flew into the air or dropped dead to the ground. Eden systematically took them out, beating them with her fists and cutting them with her weapon. She lifted one and threw him farther than I imagined even Berwyn was capable of throwing a man.

Turning, the blond woman, having cleared a path, ran back into the prison, returning instantly with a battered and limping Dov Baer.

Fighting, I slammed my head into the men behind me, trying to knock them off balance. The man I bit was running toward where Eden was, far across the yard. She turned and threw her knife, sinking it in the man's chest.

Dragging Dov with her, she retrieved it and hurriedly guided him away. Eden blocked a soldier who ran at them, slamming her knife at him. He backed up, barely avoiding her strike. He readied himself to strike, but Eden moved quicker, breaking something in his hand loud enough for me to hear it all the way across the yard.

She scooped Dov up off the ground, slinging his arm around her shoulder. They moved further away, my heart cheering them to run, while, at the same time, breaking as Dov was moving further away from me.

A sharp hand on my shoulder reminded me I was being held. The men came to their senses, realizing they had me in their possession, and forced me toward the cells. Digging my feet into the ground, I tried to counteract their movements. The two men worked together to push me ahead of them, digging up the ground in the process.

I heard a grunt before I was propelled into the ground. My arms, now free, jerked in front of me to protect my face. I hit the ground, hair flying out in front of me in a massive wave of gold, covering my arms and tangling in my outstretched fingers.

"Move!" Berwyn shouted, pulling hard on my arm under my shoulder.

"Berwyn?" I gasped as his fingers dug into the soft flesh under my arm. I tried to point. "Eden…"

"I saw." He looked shocked that his wife had just defeated multiple Society soldiers and managed to carry his brother away from the prison. "We have to go."

He shook his head to refocus himself. Dropping his shoulders, he ran toward his wife. I limped after him, having twisted my ankle when I fell. Halfway across the yard, I figured out how to move without causing too much pain and picked up my pace.

"Berwyn!" I screamed, seeing the oncoming soldiers that ran into the yard after he had passed.

He turned, looking at the men. Berwyn reached them before I did, engaging in battle. A fist struck him, causing him to rear back. He lashed out, looking like Shadoe the day he had cut Berwyn with his clawed contraption. His eyes were deadly, holding no remorse.

Ignoring my ankle, I attacked. The man turned to me, weapon in hand. Reaching down, I grabbed my extra knife from my boot. I cut deep into his arm as he attempted to drag his knife through me. He was tall, tall enough that my knife easily found its way into the flesh on his chest.

Blood trickled out of his wound as his hand clutched it. A moment later he toppled to his left, a hand appearing where he once stood.

"I heard things went sideways." Justin appeared next to me. "A couple of us left the backup group to come help.

"Time to move, *Goldilocks*," he said, pushing me until I was running with him.

"Spending time with Necesta again?" I asked.

"Simple rule, Auluria: never turn down time with Necesta. You'd be amazed what you will learn."

"The fact that she was taking care of a couple of pretty ladies the last few days didn't hurt either, I'm guessing."

"What can I say? I'm a sucker for unavailable women."

At least I wouldn't have to remind him that Eden was married and Reyla was in mourning. I added Justin to the list of men I had to find girlfriends for, right after Silas.

"I have some good news though," he said, ducking as we ran under a tree branch as we reached the tree line. "Eden brought Dov out. At least, I'm assuming it was him. We were running pretty fast and she was having a hard time keeping him upright, so I basically just saw a guy having trouble running."

"We saw." Berwyn said as he caught up to us. "We need to get to them."

His voice caught, making him cut off his words. We raced around trees, deeper into the woods. Raselin's men were waiting as the soldiers followed us. Berwyn and I didn't stop as Justin turned back to help his team.

"You saw him, right?" Berwyn asked when we were alone.

"He looked terrible, Berwyn." I cringed. "Do you think he will be okay?"

"I don't know." The seriousness in his voice made my blood run cold. I sprinted faster.

"At least Eden got him out," I responded. "How did she even do that?"

"Serious motivation?" Berwyn suggested. His voice turned dark again. "She's wanted to get back at the Society for a long time, Auluria. I think that, mixed with her fear over losing Dov, resulted in what we saw. I don't think she could have physically done that otherwise."

"Berwyn, I don't think *you* could have done what your wife did today."

He smiled softly for a moment before it iced over.

"He didn't look right, did he? Something was really wrong…"

"Something was wrong," I whispered, tearing up.

"I can't lose him too." Berwyn mumbled as we ran.

"We won't." I said my wish as a promise, hoping it would be true.

"Sit down." Eden pushed me back, forcing me against the wall. "You will wait your turn."

For suffering at the hands of Wallace's men not too long ago, Eden had gained incredible strength, much of which I assumed must be credited to Necesta.

"You *will* sit down or so help me—"

"How will you stop me?" I threatened, trying to stand up as she pinned me against the wall, forcing me to bend my knees in an effort not to fall to the ground.

Indignation rolled across her face, darker than any storm cloud I had ever seen. She looked ready to slap me. We were in public so I knew she wouldn't, but I wanted to dare her too, just to have reason to escape.

Instead, she held me there, with the same strength she used to rescue Dov hours earlier.

"You will allow his brother to do whatever he needs to do. He will not leave his side until he is ready and you will *not* interfere." She struggled against me as people watched our argument.

Justin looked sympathetically at me, Devin hovering close by. I was one of them; Eden was not, but even though they wanted to help me, they knew whose house we were in. What the Baers said was law.

Silas stood by the door of the room Berwyn had entered, guarding his friend as Necesta scurried in and out. Maylin quietly fetched items for her. They were a good fit.

I wouldn't see anything through the door when it briefly opened for an entrance or exit. No bed, not glimpses of even his feet or a hand hanging out of the cot. I couldn't even tell where Berwyn was situated in the room.

"*You* got to see him," I protested, near tears.

Silas looked pained as he watched me grapple against Eden's wishes. I cast him a pleading look, begging him to speak to Eden. He would be the only one other than Berwyn she would listen to.

He shook his head slightly, telling me there was nothing he could do. I turned back to Eden, not above begging.

"I got to see him because I dragged him back. You'll see him when Berwyn is done talking to him."

"At least tell me *something*, Eden, please," I implored. "*Please.*"

"I don't know anything, Auluria, or I'd tell you just to get you to shut up. Sit down!" She shoved me hard on the ground. "He was messed up, that's all I know. That woman kicked me out as soon as we arrived. No one has been in there since, except for Berwyn."

I pushed against her.

"I *will* hit you to get you to calm down." She leaned in to hiss at me. "Now settle down. You're causing undue stress out *here,* which certainly isn't helping in *there.*"

I calmed, knowing I had used up the last of her grace. I had taken too many hits recently; I knew I couldn't survive whatever blow the back of Eden's hand would deliver should I speak again.

Sharone and the girls inched closer to me, trying to make eye contact in an attempt to support me. I continually looked away, knowing it would be my undoing.

Shadoe's gaze made me wither. He judged me as he had judged the weak, young girl he had met the day Lowell brought me into his fold. Vulnerability was a blemish on one's record, a stain on life meant to be rubbed out and replaced with strength and cold valor. Trembling on the ground, I was everything Shadoe despised. His perfect creation, the girl built to destroy, sat wrecked on the ground, leaving his reputation as a trainer in her wake.

He couldn't stand to look at me, pulling his eyes from me whenever I looked at him. I didn't blame him. Lowell would have been ashamed.

Each time the door opened, I flinched so hard Eden looked like she was prepared to pummel me to the ground just to keep me from moving. I didn't try to stand, but every fiber of my being was being drawn to that room.

When Berwyn finally stepped out, Eden held me in place until he approached.

"What did she say?" Eden asked through her teeth and she tightened her grip on me.

"He's been drugged. That's why he couldn't walk or stay upright. Necesta is working to remove the toxins now. She's bandaging his wounds."

"Berwyn, can I see him?" I pleaded, interrupting the account of what had happened.

"He's not really with us right now. I'm not sure…"

"Berwyn, *please!*" My tears burst from my eyes like an angry waterfall, misting as they hit my legs and chest as I hunched over myself. I rocked forward, hands gripping my calves so tightly I thought I'd do more damage than the Society people had. I choked. *"Please!"*

He looked away. "Go."

I scrambled to my feet, falling along the way. My hand touched the floor halfway to Silas, who was no longer at his post. I pushed myself upright, refusing to fall all the way.

Silas heard me coming, crashing as I raced to Dov's door. He stepped outside just as I entered. I heard him pull the door closed as I fell on the floor inside the threshold.

He was sitting up in the bed, propped against the wall, his breathing labored. I crawled over to him, quickly and slowly all at once. I didn't want to spook him; I knew I had to be careful. He watched my every move, tracking me with his eyes as I approached him.

He looked so tired, dark circles forming deeply beneath his eyes. His hair was wild, like the day he ran out of the storehouse fire...the day he first kissed me. His eyes held a certain weariness in them and I could see the pain written across his face from the torture he had endured.

Moving closer to him, my only intent was to make sure he was all right, but I longed to touch him. My fingers itched to reach out and trace his face, his lips. I couldn't help myself; I moved closer.

My hand found its way to his shoulder, resting gently near the side of his handsome face. His gaze held mine, finding recognition, then traveling to my lips for only a moment. I could see the hesitation in his eyes as I inched closer and closer still.

So much time has passed. I didn't know this new Dov; the broken man before me. He didn't know me, this leader who was willing to compromise everything and work with the enemy to get him back. We were strangers; so familiar with each other's touch and yet, so fragile that the slightest rebuff might break us.

I knew he needed time. I knew *I* needed time. But time was something I wanted to bind up and cast aside, banishing it for the remainder of our lives, so that this moment would only be me and the man I cared for and once knew so well.

I leaned in as he stared, motionless. He felt so warm beneath my touch. Everything in me sparked to life under his gaze. He called to me without a word.

"Tell me to stop," I whisper, closing the space between us until I rested over him, lips just out of reach, waiting for him to lean into me.

His throat made dry clicking sounds as he breathed out in response, eyes still fixed on me.

"Dov, tell me to stop," I whispered. His eyes dilated as he registered how much I desperately needed him in that moment, to know that he was still in there behind the drugs that made him hazy.

I waited as he swallowed hard, the moment causing his eyelids to close slightly in pain. We breathed together, heavy and deep, waiting. His hand found its way to my hip, his touch so weak, but his grip firm.

"Tell me to stop," I whispered so quietly I doubted he could hear me.

Dov pulled me to his chest, leaning against the wall for support. I supported myself, propping my knees along side of his hip, leaning against him only enough to let him feel my presence against him. My movements were careful and protective.

His touch was so weak, yet full of more power than I'd ever seen from him. Such strength existed in his broken and damaged hands.

Everything I loved about Dov that I thought must have been stripped away during his beatings still existed, just beneath the surface, hovering under his bruised skin. His scars reminded me that every one of them had been for me.

I kissed him, driving our lips together again and again. He let me explore him as he rested against the wall, my mouth tracing his jaw, his neck, his shoulders. His hands traced up my back sending a shudder racing through me.

"Auluria," Dov whispered as my mouth found its way to his jaw again.

I couldn't think.

"Come here." He groaned, pulling me against him so that I was no longer supporting myself, my dress tangling around me.

The effort it took for him to reach up and tangle his hands in my hair nearly broke me. I hated seeing Dov in pain. I willed my kisses to heal his defeated body, removing all of the scars I had left there in my wake.

Instead, his lips cleansed me, purifying my transgressions against him. Forgiveness so sweet I could cry coursed through his lips, pressing into my very soul.

I loved this man.

I loved him, I loved him, I loved him.

Reaching my hands up to his hair, I wrapped my fingers around him, cradling his head between the wall and me. He fought to keep me close, forcing me to abandon any ideas of pulling back to keep him from hurting. His hands tugged at my hips and my back, bringing me as near as possible.

"Auluria," he breathed again, forcing me to lean back just enough that he could see me. I lingered with my eyes closed, not wanting to be present for fear the communion might end.

"I thought… " he started, his words lost. "I thought… how… how do I have you here, with me, now? How is this possible?"

His anxious eyes betrayed him, screaming to me how Dov had thought he had lost me for good.

"I will never leave you, Dov, never," I replied softly… forcefully, as I clutched at his face with my hands. I stroked the sides of his face, brushing his hair down, as he stared at my lips.

"I never want you to," he sighed, and everything in me broke. I wasn't sure he'd want me back, not after everything, but he had admitted it… *committed* to it. I was his and always would be. Nothing could break us.

"Shadoe!" Silas called from outside a moment before the door swung open.

"Let's go." Shadoe grumbled, crossing the small room as he reached for my arm.

His nostrils flared as he saw me perched on the cot by Dov's side. Dov started as Shadoe burst into the room, lurching forward in surprise. My hands, resting on his shoulders, gently pushed him back against the wall as Shadoe latched on to me.

"Out!" Silas commanded, following Shadoe into the room.

"We are leaving. We have a mission," Shadoe growled.

Silas clamped onto Shadoe's shirt, dragging him to the door. Turning, he pushed hard, sending him into the doorframe. I knew Silas would pay for that later.

Dov was wild-eyed when I turned back to him, hands still resting on his arms.

"Why was he here? We have to get you away." He tried to get up.

"Dov." My voice silenced him. "He's working with us now. Shadoe and Berwyn made a deal. We needed Lowell's men to help rescue you, and we're planning to take down the Society."

"We can't trust him," Dov insisted.

"We're not," I promised him. "But, Dov, we have an agreement with him."

I cringed.

"I'm so sorry, Dov. I have to go with him right now."

"No." Worry filled his blue eyes.

"Dov, listen." My hand found its way to his cheek. I stroked it gently, trying to sooth him. "Shadoe wouldn't reclaim Lowell's group unless I was there too. And, honestly, I had to go to make sure he actually did what he promised. Lowell's men listen to me…kind of."

"Auluria, no." Dov shook his head sadly.

"It's okay." I sounded like I was talking to tiny Jasleen. "We just have to defeat the Society. Once we do, I can come back. I don't have to help Shadoe anymore."

"I saw his body." Dov said.

"What?"

"Lowell." He looked away. "They brought his body by my cell to show me what would happen to you if they caught you without me turning you over. They threatened Berwyn and Eden, too."

"But you didn't, Dov. You stayed strong." I moved closer to him.

"Every day they told me they had found you. Every night they questioned me about where you were." His voice was heartbreakingly sad.

A bang on the door told me I had to move quickly.

I leaned in, kissing Dov again.

"I have to go," I whispered. "I'll be back as soon as I can. I'll be okay. Shadoe will keep me safe. He's trying to prove a point.

"As soon as we can bring down Canton, we can be together again."

He nodded, understanding.

"Don't go," Dov whispered.

"I have to." I smiled at him softly, hoping he would let me go.

Instead, he pulled me in, kissing me. He nodded when I pulled back, saying goodbye.

The door flew open just as I reached for it.

"Let's go." I pushed past Shadoe.

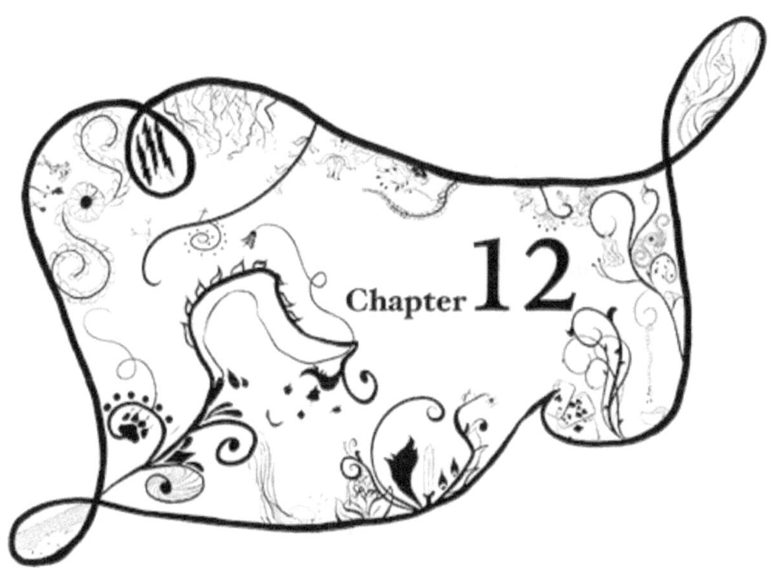

Chapter 12

THE DENSE AIR SEEMED TO WEIGH ME DOWN AS I WALKED THROUGH THE light fog bank. Moisture rolled over the ground, pale and thin at my feet. The area was illuminated with it in the early morning hours as light in the atmosphere reflected off the bank of clouds. It grew thicker the further I looked out, blocking things from sight.

The fallen leaves on the ground were a dull color, muted by the opaque fog. They crunched quietly with each step as we crept forward.

Shadoe had sent most of his men back to the burned out storehouse Berwyn had provided as shelter. His elite team and backup group stayed by his side, moving strategically toward the city. Shadoe's mission was to gain intelligence on Magistrate Canton in the hours after the escape when the Society soldiers would assume everyone had fled.

"Martin," Shadoe whispered, flicking a wrist to the left, instructing the man to go around the outskirts of the city to enter. Hopefully he would hold his temper if he ran into any of the Society men.

Locust crept to the right, careful to avoid me. He clicked his tongue to get Shadoe's attention as he nodded to the right. Our leader dipped his chin down once, giving the man permission to split off.

I followed along beside him, fighting to keep focused on the task at hand and not the tiny room on the right side of the storehouse that held my heart. I dug my nails into the side of my legs every time I found my thoughts straying, using the temporary pain to bring me back.

Slowly the group disbanded, taking different routes into the city. Shadoe stayed by my side as we walked.

"Ready to put your training to good use?" he asked unexpectedly.

"Sure," I said lifelessly.

"You're going to have to do better than that," he chastised me, scowling.

I turned to him sharply, working a smile onto my face.

"There. Happy." I said, sarcastically playing the happy girl who was out walking with her fiancé.

I threw my shoulders down, elongating my neck, and leaned over to him, wrapping my arm through his. Shadoe had never been one for physical contact with a person unless it was in combat, so I didn't mind making him uncomfortable as we moved through the city.

It took a while to see the dark smoke rising up in the air after we heard the deafening collision of rock meeting rock as a building was being ripped apart several streets over. An explosion rocked the ground, making it tremble beneath my feet. Shadoe's arm unexpectedly steadied me.

He looked to me and for the first time I saw fear. It reminded me of the day I made him believe he had drowned me during my training, though this time, I was the only one he knew *was* safe.

We ran, darting to the scene of the explosion. My ankle caught again, pain jabbing into me where I had twisted it not a day before. Limping was not an option, so I kept up with Shadoe, despite the pull I felt.

Smoke poured from the rubble, casting a black trail into the sky, outlined by the white fog in a slow motion version of life. It drifted in front of us, commanding our movements.

"No," Shadoe whispered harshly under his breath. "He didn't."

"Who?" I looked at him, furious that he knew what was going on.

"Martin," he said. "He's been talking about this for ages. Lowell always said no."

"He wanted to blow something up?" I asked.

"He wanted revenge for his sister. They took her when he was too young to stop them." He looked at me. "You're aware that he has anger issues."

Eden had anger issues. *Berwyn* had anger issues. *Martin* beat people for the fun of it.

My fingers glided to my stomach, remembering my encounter with him during one of my tests in training.

"So he did *this*?"

"And destroyed any hope we had of capturing Canton."

"Wait," I paused. "We were *capturing* Canton?"

"Not *technically*." He rolled his eyes, pulling me away. "But had the opportunity presented itself…"

The opportunity would have presented itself. Shadoe would have seen to that.

A second explosion cut through the air, another building in Martin's wake. Pieces of wood and debris flew all around us as we retreated. The heat was overwhelming as I fell to the ground.

Lifting myself up, shards of wood tumbled out of my hair. Miraculously it remained tied back. It was just like my hair to stay in place the *one time* I would have granted it an excuse to fall out of place.

Shadoe was on his feet, engaged in battle with two soldiers. His silver claw lashed out at the men, striping their arms with bloody streaks. I wondered if he had had time to dose his prize before the attack. As the men began to react as Berwyn had when he had been struck, I knew he must have laced the metal contraption.

My lungs burned as smoke filled the air. A sharp pain shot through my right shoulder that, I assume, had taken the brunt of the fall. I rolled to the left, hoping to prop myself up with my good arm. My eyes rolled back in my head with the pain of the effort.

"Stay down," Shadoe yelled, trying to keep me from being noticed by the soldiers that were running to join the onslaught against him.

I waited for the men to pass me before I stood up. Finding a wood board ripped loose in the blast, I staggered to my feet. My balance was off.

Taking aim, I slammed the board into one of the soldier's heads. He fell unconscious at my feet. His partner turned to me, seeing his friend fall, and attacked. I swung hard, striking his arm with a loud crack. His knife toppled to the ground.

He looked at me, daring me to go for the weapon. I lurched

forward as if I were going to stoop to retrieve it. When he bent to catch it, I slammed the board into the back of his skull. Taking his knife was easy while he lay sprawled out on the ground.

Standing back up was not so easy.

Nausea crashed over me. My head felt like it was floating.

"Come on," Locust said, appearing out of nowhere.

He grabbed my arm and guided me to Shadoe. Together, they killed the soldiers that had been fighting our leader, returning to me. They braced me between them, running from the city.

"Did you see anything?" Shadoe yelled as we ran.

"No, the explosion hit before we could get close enough." He yelled over the roar of noise. "What happened?"

"Martin happened," Shadoe said, righting me as I stumbled.

Despite my efforts to watch the ground as it raced by under my feet, I could see the boys share a look over my head. Either Locust had risen in the ranks since I had left, or Martin had become a big enough problem that most of Lowell's men had heard about while I was gone.

"We don't have a choice, Shadoe," Locust said, pulling me faster. "We have to call it off... for now."

I knew Shadoe well enough to know he wanted to argue, but he knew I was in no position to fight.

"I know." He admitted coarsely. "We have to get out of here."

The soldiers burst out of a walkway in front of us, forcing us to stop in our tracks. My feet kept moving, nearly flipping me forward as my chaperones slammed to a halt.

"Back," Shadoe commanded as he stepped in reverse, quickly wheeling us around to run in the opposite direction, just as I had started to regain my balance.

They ran with me, half carrying me as we moved, taking a street that brought us to a new part of the city.

"Go," Shadoe instructed, shoving me toward Locust.

He caught me as I pitched forward, increasing our speed as I gained my strength back. Shadoe turned, knives in hand, and took out our attackers. I heard at least one of his men join him, executing the other soldiers that followed us.

Locust slowed us, hearing it as well. He leaned me against a wall, holding my shoulder to brace me, as if I would fall, as he leaned out to check the status of his friends. He looked back at me, nodding twice as he sighed in relief. For all of Locust's faults, he wasn't *entirely* bad.

Then he grinned at me and I lost my faith in him yet again.

"Let's move," Shadoe commanded, Sherman and Ella trailing behind him.

I pushed Locust off, considering stealing one of his knives in the process. I knew I would feel miserable if he ended up needing it and I had stolen it, so I left it in place. I considered running alongside Ella, one of the women just a few years older than me, but she was still angry with me over my work with Lowell, so instead, I lagged behind Shadoe, watching everything that surrounded me in the city.

Sherman, one of Shadoe's elites, broke off from us a mile later, taking care of a Society man. The sound was sickening as he beat the man's head into a wall. Shadoe grumbled under his breath, distracting me momentarily.

Eventually we made it to the meeting point in the woods. Most of Shadoe's team was there, waiting for our arrival.

"Was anyone followed?" Shadoe looked at the group.

"None that made it this far." One of the men answered, a hint of achievement in his voice. Lowell's careless appreciation of life had infiltrated the majority of his flock.

Once he was sure we weren't being followed, Shadoe led us back toward the storehouse. We climbed the side of the hill, ducking under low tree branches and crawling over enormous roots that grew into tangled nests above the ground. The wind felt good on my face, bringing me back to life after what had happened in the heart of the city.

Shadoe glowered the entire trip, fuming at losing his shot at capturing Canton from the Society. I assumed his plan was to use the man against the government; something Lowell's training would have encouraged *me* to do also had I been calling the shots. I wondered if Shadoe had discussed this with Berwyn.

The group quieted as we reached the top of the mound, cresting at the line of trees that formed a sad attempt at a wall. Shadoe glanced to the edge as the rest of the group followed behind us, using the exposed roots as ropes to scale the steep incline.

We walked, high above the world, for a mile. Forming several lines, we walked behind each other in groups of no more than three. Shadoe let several of the others take the lead, falling further back with me where I had planted myself toward the far end of the middle of the team, decidedly far from Locust and Ella.

The birds sang overhead, reminding me that soon I would be back with Dov. I would survive until then. The scream made me rethink that.

Shadoe launched himself out of the line, toward the precipice, carrying Martin with him. The boy struggled, Shadoe's hand around his throat as he propelled him backward.

"Shadoe!" I screamed, pushing a woman out of my way.

He pushed Martin further toward the drop off and I prayed he was only trying to scare him.

"Lowell never would have tolerated this," Shadoe bellowed loud enough for the entire group to fear him. "You will never disrespect me or my decisions again."

He pushed the boy again and he stumbled on the edge, teetering several inches out before flinging his body back at Shadoe. I had hoped Shadoe had been talking to Martin; he had been speaking to the group, warning them that their actions had consequences. He glanced back at them to make sure they were listening as I pushed past another team member, knocking them to the ground.

"Shadoe, don't!"

He focused his speech on Martin again.

"You jeopardized our plan. You risked our lives. *For what? Revenge?*" Shadoe taunted him, tightening his grip on his throat. "Never again."

Shadoe pushed him just as I reached them. Grabbing onto Martin however I could, I fought to pull him back. His hands flailed, digging into my flesh like a cat might, clawing to get to safety.

I threw myself back, hoping to counteract the fall. His foot slipped, jerking him backward as I pulled to save him. Martin's foot caught, finding a steady step. He pulled himself up on my arm quickly, finding his footing so fast that it threw me off balance. He stepped forward, throwing me past Shadoe, over the edge.

I saw panic on Shadoe's face as I pitched over the edge and plummeted. I wasn't sure if I screamed, but my hands flew out, desperate to grab anything that could sustain me. I registered the pain of sliding down the face of the cliff, but didn't have time to think. I saw brown, likely dirt, as I slid.

Shadoe had attempted to catch me, scratching at me in the air. His hand hit mine at some point, pulling me back enough that I skidded down the face of the cliff instead of free falling several feet away.

Suddenly, I jerked to a stop, crashing into something. I paused for a moment, before feeling the wind rush around me again. Another hesitation in my fall, an interruption in my descent, and I found myself cascading again, clawing at the earth and air.

A final body-shaking stop ended it.

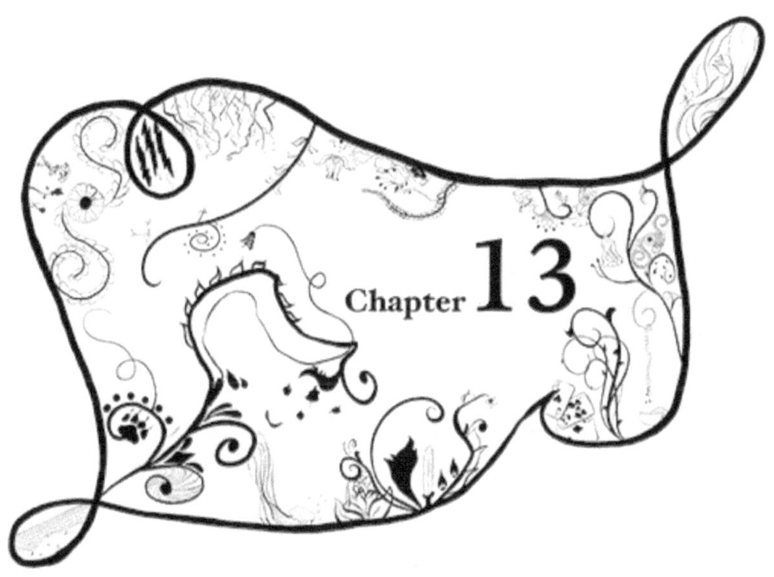

"THERE NOW," A SOFT VOICE SAID, "GOOD GIRL. TAKE IT EASY."

A hand, much less soft than the voice, touched my face. I held still, not opening my eyes until I figured out what was happening.

"Now, now, dearie. Don't be like that. I know you're there."

I inhaled the much needed air, letting my lungs expand. My eyes shot open when I realized if I was with Necesta, I must also be with Dov.

"Where is he?" I demanded, pain shooting through my body.

"Sit back." Necesta growled at me, the first time I had ever seen her annoyed with me. "If you're talking about your young man, he's fine. If you're talking about the young man you saved, he's fine too. If you're talking about Silas, he's outside."

"Where is Dov?" My voice sounded gravelly and harsh.

"He's at the storehouse," she responded, picking up a bottle of something.

My eyes clicked from her, to my lap, to the wall, to the door. She handed me something, but I didn't move to take it.

"Where are *we*, then?"

She studied me for a moment, then paused to force-feed me the liquid in the bottle she held.

"You thought we were in the storehouse?" she asked. "Well, we are.

Just not *your* storehouse. They brought you back after your fall. The Baers were so intent on figuring out what to do next and taking care of your young man, that they didn't hear about the incident right away. When they did, they sent Silas and a few men to check on you all.

"Shadoe's physicians looked at you, but they're nothing compared to this old girl. Silas was smart enough to come get me and bring me here.

"You took a nasty fall. You've been in and out for days. You've spoken to me a few times. Do you remember that?"

I shook my head.

"I didn't think so." She smiled at me. "You'll be fine, though. You're body just had a great deal of trauma. Sleep helps the body heal, Goldilocks. You'll be fine soon. You just need to rest."

"Is she awake?" Silas asked, sticking his head in the door. He grinned when he saw me, relief washing over his face.

"Nice to see you, Sleeping Beauty."

"Wow, you *have* been hanging around Eden too much." I tried to laugh and ended up coughing.

"Easy," he said, slipping quietly into the room.

Necesta nodded to him and walked toward the door. Silas took a seat in the chair near the bed.

"So you thought going back and forth to the storehouses was a good idea, but you didn't think to just take *me* to *them*...?" I goaded him.

"Dov may be in the business of carrying women around after injuries, but I, madam, am not."

"Reyla might think differently." I raised an eyebrow to him, challenging him to disagree.

He smirked.

"You were in no condition to be traveling." Necesta added.

"Oh, *Auluria*..." He sighed. "You just had to go and be noble, didn't you? What were you thinking? You nearly died."

I stared at him.

"Oh, don't give me that look. You know he'd say the same thing."

"How is he?"

"You threw yourself off a cliff, Auluria, how do you think he is?"

I could feel the color draining from my face.

"*He knows*? Why would you tell him that?"

"Because you almost died, Auluria." He dragged his hand down the side of his face. "But to be honest, we didn't at first. We knew he would try to get to you and he was still in no condition to be traveling so far.

"I brought Necesta here first, and once she determined that she could help, we told him what had happened. You have no idea how hard it was to convince him to stay." He paused. "Necesta might have had to knock him out."

My face fell.

"Just until I could get out of there." He held up his hands against whatever verbal attack I might launch at him. "No one bothered to tell him where you were. If he couldn't track us, he couldn't find you."

It was sound logic.

"Go tell him I'm okay," I said, attempting to lean up.

"No." He laughed at me.

"Excuse me?"

I attempted a second time to sit.

"I'm up. Go tell him I'm fine."

"You are not fine, Auluria, you can't even sit up." He reached out a hand for me to pull myself up on, his other slipping behind my shoulder to assist me. "I'm not leaving you alone with him."

"Necesta's here," I insisted, my hair catching as Silas lifted me up.

He gave me a doubtful look.

"Yes, and how will she protect you?" He questioned. "By throwing bottles of medicine at him?"

"She knocked Dov out," I pointed out.

"Dov was only partially conscious to begin with." He patronized me. "Shadoe is *fully* awake and very much aware that the Baers are furious with him. I doubt he's slept at all for fear of retribution for throwing you off a cliff."

"He didn't throw me off a cliff... He tried to throw *Martin* off a cliff." I made a vague attempt at rolling my eyes. "And Shadoe isn't scared of anyone."

"You're defending him?" He looked shocked. "In all this time, haven't you figured this out yet, Auluria? Shadoe is not the good guy here."

"I'm aware of that. You don't think I know that?" I was annoyed. "But he didn't intentionally try to hurt me. In fact, he tried to catch me. He almost did and, frankly, he's the only reason I survived. He pulled me into the cliff enough that I was able to partially break my fall."

"I'm still not leaving you alone with him." Silas said stubbornly.

"And how did you manage that with all the running back and forth between the storehouses, Silas?"

The storm in his eyes cleared, flashing a brilliant green, as his smile returned.

"Please," he said smugly. "You don't think I'm here alone, do you?"

I gave him a quizzical look.

"Talley is here. And Devin and Justin. They haven't left your door this entire time. Shadoe may still be in charge around here, but they haven't let him anywhere near you without one of them outside the door and the door left open."

I sat still for a moment, deciding whether to be annoyed that I had babysitters or grateful that they cared enough to watch over me.

"You can go," I said. He looked at me until I continued. "If they are here, that means you can go to Dov."

An inner war played out across his face as he debated whether or not to listen to me. I waited, as I had been taught, until he had had enough time for my words to sink in.

"It's me or him, Silas. You know I'm going to be okay. But he doesn't know that, and you're the only one that can tell him. Don't you think he will focus more on getting better if he's not stressed out over me?" I said calmly, focusing him on my goal.

"I won't talk to Shadoe, if that makes you feel better." I grinned, knowing I was winning him over.

"Don't look at me like that." He grinned back. I knew I had him.

"Seriously, I'll be fine. Go take care of Dov. It can be a race to see which of us heals first." I hesitated. "Silas, how is he?"

"Worried about you." His smile didn't slip. "He's getting better. I don't know what Necesta learned on her side of the wall, but she's better than anyone I've seen over here."

"When I first met her, I watched her work. She was magnificent," I agreed.

"You're going to have to fill me in on your time over the wall sometime."

"I'll fill you *both* in. But, Silas, you've got to get one of us to the other."

"I'm working on it, Goldilocks." He laughed. "I'm working on it."

I tipped my head, unimpressed that he picked up Necesta's nickname for me.

"Don't."

"Don't?" he smirked. "Don't get you and Dov back together? Doesn't it seem like that's all I ever do these days?"

He squinted his eyes at me, daring me to play along.

"Don't call me that." I didn't rise to the bait. "That's Necesta's name."

"I'm going to tell Dov. We'll see how you like it after that." He winked, making me giggle.

"Time to let me work, young man." Necesta entered, carrying a bowl.

"I'll come back soon," Silas promised. He stood to go.

"No you won't," Necesta said, setting the bowl down on the small table beside the bed. "You have work to do over there."

She turned to me and dipped her head as if she was about to say something important and needed me to listen.

"You and I need to have a little talk, Goldilocks. He's not going to be back for awhile, so say your goodbyes." She leaned back and waited patiently in her chair.

Silas shrugged.

"Don't sass me, young man," Necesta said without looking back. Silas' eyes grew wide.

"I..."

"Yes, you did." She grinned conspiratorially at me. "Now go. Berwyn and Raselin need your help. Take the bag I left outside the door for Dov. That should help. Twice a day, Silas. Don't forget."

"Yes, ma'am." Silas said, stepping toward the door. "Auluria, if you need *anything*, send one of guys to come get me. Berwyn will send an army if you need us."

"I know." And I *did* know.

"He's a fine young man," Necesta said. "All of the Baers' group is, so it seems."

"How is Reyla?" I asked.

"She's fine, dearie. She was nearly back to normal when I came to you. Silas, as you saw, has recovered nicely."

"And quickly," I pointed out.

"She followed my instructions well—like you did." She grinned. "But we'll get back to that. Reyla is a strong girl. She'll be fine.

"Poor thing... She told me about that young man of hers. How terrible. You're a good friend to her.

"Your friends are quite lovely, really," she crooned, rocking forward in her chair. "I especially like that young man of yours.

"I think you'll be impressed to know that his family took very good care of him. He and I had a little chat after you left and before I came here. He had some old scars that were of particular interest to me."

She reached forward to the table, something scraping along the wood. She handed the beads to me, waiting for me to take them.

"Before I forget," she commented, "just like I said. You're a good listener."

I gave her a questioning look, but she waved me off.

"His family, like I said, took very good care of him. Eden and Berwyn stayed by his side the entire time. They were about as adamant as your other friends were about staying by Reyla's side. Maylin, Katarina, Gregory… Silas refused to leave her side unless he was allowed to go in to see Dov for a few minutes. Prying those Baers away from him was harder than climbing that wall. They all took wonderful care of both Reyla and Dov. You'd be very proud of how they handled themselves."

"So it would seem." I didn't need Necesta to tell me how helpful they had been, but I was glad she had.

"Now, we need to talk, dearie." She grew more serious. "There are two things we need to discuss. The first is what happened out there. What do you remember?"

"Martin caused an explosion," I started, leaning my head back against the wall. "He destroyed Shadoe's plan and nearly got us killed. I got hurt in the second blast."

"How so?"

"I was very dizzy. Shadoe and Locust had to help me back. I'm sure I had a concussion…it certainly wasn't my first.

"When we finally escaped the city, we went to the rendezvous point. We had to walk for a while. When we reached the cliff, Shadoe decided to make a point.

"Martin nearly got us all killed *and* he possibly cost us an opportunity to defeat the Society."

I paused, shocked I hadn't realized it yet.

"Necesta," I said urgently, "Where is Martin?"

"He's fine, Goldilocks. He's locked up with the Baers. Berwyn didn't trust Shadoe enough to leave him in his care. Shadoe couldn't argue at that point because they could have accused him of throwing you off that cliff. He didn't, did he?"

"No." I attempted to shake my head only to be met with searing pain.

"Don't do that, Goldilocks," she chastised as I flinched.

"It's probably wise that Berwyn is in control of the situation. Arin is probably busy terrifying him as we speak."

"Something like that," she murmured. "Goldilocks, do you know what happened after you fell?"

I tried to think back, but only my hands grasping at dirt came to mind. I blinked at her blankly, refusing to shake my head again.

She eyed the necklace around my neck. I absentmindedly reached up to brush it with my fingers.

"Somewhere along the line, you told Shadoe how to use it. It probably saved you," she said, admiring her handiwork. "They brought you back here and eventually Silas and a convoy came to see what had happened. When he saw you, he left all of his men to guard you and came immediately for me."

She explained what she knew, most of which I had already learned from Silas. I waited patiently, not telling her Silas had already explained it to me, but she kept it brief.

"Now, Goldilocks, we need to talk about something else," she said gently. I waited for her to continue. "Your scars, dearie."

Suddenly self-conscious, my fingers inched their way to the burn marks on my thighs, remembering the marks Canton's interrogator had inflicted on me in front of Dov. The twisted feeling in my stomach returned, sharp and metallic, reminding me of every painful thing I had ever endured.

"Canton's men did that. They wanted information, but really, they just wanted to torture us. They made us listen to each other being hurt; Eden, Silas, Dov, and me.

"Lowell got involved, and the Society realized Dov and I were more than just members of the same group. They made us watch each other being tortured."

"Ahh, so that's where some of those came from. He didn't give much detail," Necesta said knowingly, tapping her arm where the men had sliced Dov. "Unfortunately, there's not much I can do for scars. We can help them to fade a bit, if that's any consolation."

"Get back!" Justin's voice rang out on the other side of the door.

"I imagine that would be your intended," Necesta frowned.

I groaned. I didn't want to see Shadoe after he had nearly murdered Martin to make a point. Necesta stood, walking to the door.

I could hear Talley arguing as Necesta reached for the door.

"Now or later, dearie? You'll have to get it over with at some point."

I sighed, knowing she was right.

"Now."

She opened the door, stepping outside to talk to my keepers. I could feel the tense pause where they all considered Necesta's request to let Shadoe inside.

"It's fine," I attempted to call out.

After a moment Shadoe stepped in. He attempted to close the door, but forceful hands held it open, reminding Shadoe once again that in the struggle for power, he did not have the upper hand.

He stood by the cot, until I motioned for him to sit. He refused until I flicked my eyes at the chair again, daring him to provoke me as I lay wounded in a bed due to his choices. He sat.

"Are you okay?" he asked, the moment eerily similar to the time he had checked on me after I was beaten at the hands of his men as part of Lowell's initiation.

"Do I look okay?" I challenged, refusing to break eye contact.

"Necesta says you're healing."

"I am." Hostility took over, tensing every muscle in my body. "What do you want?"

"To check on you. They haven't let me near you."

"You think that's a bad thing? You think it's unwarranted?"

"Lur." His voice grew icy.

"No, Shadoe," I interrupted. "You tried to kill Martin. What were you thinking?"

"He nearly got us killed," Shadoe protested. "He's never going to listen. He will always try to do things his own way, and it would always cost us."

"Shadoe, do you even hear yourself? How can you be so judgmental when that is *exactly* what Lowell did to the Baers?" I asked. "Or didn't you know that? When Lowell wanted to do things his own way, what happened? He split off from Griz, got people killed, and started his own group. All of this was because of that, and you sold your life to it.

"You've done the same things Martin has done. Even when we went on your mission to find Canton... Was that something Berwyn was okay with, or did you do that on your own?" I demanded. "Considering I knew nothing about that part of the mission, I'm willing to bet the Baers knew nothing about it."

I waited for him to deny it.

"We have an obligation to Lowell's—"

"No," I interrupted him forcefully. "We don't."

He glared at me, returning my own furious gaze.

"We owe Lowell *nothing*. Lowell didn't care about any of us. Even when I was locked up in that prison with him, his own flesh and blood, he had his inside men work to punish me. He didn't attempt to help me. He didn't attempt to save the little cousin he helped to raise. He didn't do one thing to honor his mother's last wishes about protecting me.

"Shadoe, he never cared. Not about me, not about you, not about anything other than his revenge mission!

"He was sick and twisted, and he is dead, Shadoe. He's gone. We don't have to listen to him anymore. You're in charge now. Be a man and make decisions for yourself.

"You *have to* know that this isn't right. The *only thing* Lowell ever got right was that we needed to bring the Society down. Lowell wanted to do it so he could be in charge, but you... You know we need to bring them down to save this country. You know these people need help. *Our* people need help Shadoe. The only way we can do that is if we stop thinking about ourselves and actually work together to stop the Society. Canton is only the start, but if we can use him to destroy the government, we have to be smart about it."

Shadoe fumed, the muscles in his face clenching so tightly, I thought his lower jaw might burst through the top of his head, sending teeth shattering everywhere. He leaned forward viciously.

"You of all people should remain loyal to Lowell. He kept you alive. I know those Baers have you sucked into their world, and I don't know how Dov managed to seduce you into his illogical little plan, but you're smarter than this. You know being nice isn't going to win this war.

"Martin is a threat to our standing in this war. Any smart leader would have cut it off at the head. Don't you blame me for putting our entire group of men and women ahead of one misguided life, Auluria."

"Lowell thought I was a misguided life," I provoked, letting a small laugh escape my lips. "And you went against him and saved me. He died while you saved *me*, remember? You chose *my life* over *his* and his mission."

"Maybe I shouldn't have," he said quietly, ensuring no one but me heard. "Maybe I would do it differently now."

"But you didn't. You're turning into Lowell. His ideals cost him his life. Is that a price you're willing to pay?"

"I've always been willing to pay that." He sat back in the chair, deflating, looking at his folded hands.

"You are not Lowell," I said quietly. "You can still be redeemed."

His head shot up to look at me, anger rippling through him.

"You have no idea what you're talking about, Auluria. You are a confused and foolish girl. We never should have let you go to the Baers. We should have trusted Anetta to go. She, at least, was loyal.

"You have been nothing but a disappointment."

He stood to leave, but I wasn't finished.

"I'm not the one who let Lowell die."

"You're the entire reason he is dead," Shadoe whipped back to me, roaring loudly enough to propel Justin, Devin, and Talley into the room, hands on their knives. "We will work with the Baers, because you're right, we need to take the Society down, but mark my words, Lur, you will *never* be going back to them. This is the price you will all pay for this."

Shadoe stalked out of the room. I knew he was right. We had all agreed this was the price, and Shadoe would never let me leave. He had too much of a point to prove now. He was a man who was true to his word: he would work with the Baers and I would never again leave the fold.

Devin, Talley, and Justin stared blankly.

"That is incredible." Justin laughed, dropping a card on the pile at the edge of my cot. "I can't believe they actually pulled that off."

"What did you expect?" I laughed, tossing my own card on top.

"I really need to spend more time with those two when we get back." Justin wiped at a tear in his eye as Talley placed a card on the pile.

"They seem nice." Talley smiled, brushing back her blonde hair. "You really found yourself a good crowd of people to run with, Auluria."

"I don't know how, but I really did."

Dov had sent the cards over a few days ago when he sent Silas to check on me, flowers carefully tucked away in the small package. They sat on the table next to my cot. Justin had pushed away the chair, giving himself and his sister room to sit on the floor for our game.

"It's really not fair that I don't get to play." Devin leaned over from where he was sitting on the floor outside the room, hovering over the threshold.

"No one said you couldn't come in, Devin." I motioned for him to enter.

"I'm on duty," he complained, grinning.

"This is silly," I said, loud enough for him to hear me. "No one is going to try to come in with the three of you here. Just come inside."

"Nope," Devin said, turning back around to face outside.

"You might trust them, Auluria, but we don't," Talley said, putting another card down when it was her turn.

"What do you think they're going to do, lock us in here?"

"Yes," the siblings said at the same time.

"And just what will that achieve?" I asked.

"World domination?" Justin asked.

"Hostages," Talley murmured.

"Test subjects for whatever mind control project your cousin passed on to him," Devin leaned in and shouted into the room, careful to make sure Shadoe's men weren't listening.

We had been very careful to keep a buffer around the room. Shadoe's men kept their distance. He hadn't returned after I had yelled at him. No one bothered us. I guessed it had something to do with Shadoe keeping them away from me—I still had cards to play that wouldn't be found in his favor.

I laughed at Devin's suggestion.

"Manipulation and persuasive power of speech do not equate to mind control." I rolled my eyes. "Lowell just found the right people at the right time and knew how to talk to them. Once he had a handful of people, it was easy to convince other people he was right."

Getting people to believe in something was always easier when there were people to back it up. An idea on it's own was simply that: an idea. But an idea with force to stabilize it and give it roots was practically unstoppable.

Lowell showed the world people believed in his way of doing things. One follower lead to another follower, and eventually he amassed a following so large it rivaled the one he had left.

When people feel they have permission to think and act in a certain way because it is perceived as accepted by others, there is no stopping the wildfire that started from one tiny spark.

It is how evil and goodness continue to exist in our world. One man or woman convinces a second and third person that what they are doing is right, and the entire world is transformed because of it.

Lowell did it when he convinced his people to go after the Baers. Raselin and Necesta did it when they persuaded their people to band together to fight back against their government and ours. I did it when I convinced Dov to trust me. Dov did it when he showed the world his goodness and they too gave selflessly like he did for them.

Even Shadoe was doing it now, as he made his choices for his new command. Every action, every step, every choice gave the people he interacted with permission to do things, one way or the other.

"Auluria?" Justin sang, breaking my thoughts. "You with us, Goldilocks?"

"Seriously, you have *got* to stop calling me that," I said, shaking my head, for the first time without much pain. "What did I miss?"

"Where were you?" Talley prompted softly, moving her legs so one was in the air under her elbow and the other was wrapped around it, reaching her opposite hip.

"I was thinking about Lowell."

"Your cousin?" Talley asked, settling in for a conversation.

"He manipulated people. He manipulated me," I confessed what they already knew. "But I did that too. Lowell trained me to manipulate. Shadoe trained me to manipulate. They even sent me off to a woman specifically for manipulation training. She did a bang up job too." I glanced down, thinking of all the people I had exploited in the last few months.

"You weren't trying to hurt people, Auluria."

"Wasn't I? I mean, I didn't *want* to hurt people, but I wanted to help my cousin. I did what he told me to do and that involved hurting Dov and Berwyn. I willfully did that."

"That doesn't make you the same," Justin said earnestly, sitting forward. "You were protecting your family. Any of us would do the same thing."

"Doesn't that make us all just as bad?" I could see him questioning himself.

"None of us are guiltless in this, Auluria." Talley leaned her chin on her hands as they rested on her knee in front of her. "You and I, we both have flaws. We've both made bad choices. But we've also both made choices to protect our families.

"What Lowell did was wrong, and he paid for that. Somewhere along the line, doing what he thought was right crossed the line to hurting people. I'm sure that wasn't his intention starting out, though, do you think? Just like it was never your intention to hurt people when you started out. The difference is that you realized it and did something about it."

"We all mess up, Auluria." Justin said. "You're thinking about Shadoe right now, I can tell. He's at that place where he has some very big choices to make. We can't make them for him. It's up to him to decide what side of this he will fall on."

"But you *can* influence him." Talley picked up. "He's watching you. He's *been* watching you, and I'll wager he's been watching you since the day you met him. He's seen your choices during all this.

"You've saved the Baers. You were willing to give your life for them. You fought when you didn't have to. You honored your word to Shadoe and Lowell about caring for this group." She motioned to the door. "You came back to help, even when you were safe over the wall. And here you are, sitting in a bed, recovering from falling off a cliff, because you would rather die than let someone who nearly got you killed die. I promise you, Shadoe sees all of that."

"Just keep making the right choices," Justin chimed in, "or fixing them when you make the wrong ones. Your actions affect everyone else... you can either influence them for the better or for the worse."

"That was deep," I joked, making him crack up.

"He gets that way when delivering the truth. Even as a kid, he'd have these deep conversations with the others and send them crying to their mothers." Talley laughed.

"And then Talley would have to console him because all his friends ran away." Devin leaned back into the room, laughing.

"I had more friends than you did," Justin retorted.

"Necesta doesn't count." Devin tried to keep a straight face.

"You're just jealous because she thought I was more adorable than you." Justin smirked at his older brother, turning back to wink at me.

"Because you were a child." He emphasized the last word.

"Necesta was good to us all," Talley interrupted, quelling the fake fight. She turned back to me. "She watched out for us when we lost our mother right after we climbed over the wall. It wasn't easy being so young and in charge of these two monsters."

Justin acted offended, clutching his hand to his heart.

"That is harsh, sister."

"That is *Hersh*, brother." Talley played off of their last name. "And *you* try raising two little hooligans *and* make enough money to survive. Thank goodness Necesta let you two hang around while I was working at the market."

She turned back to me to finish her story.

"Necesta would set up next to me and the boys would run between us. When I had to go to the far side of the city, she would watch them closer to home for me, especially when I had to go to the rougher areas."

"Hey! *I* was helpful." Devin glanced back to the main room before spinning to partially face us. He leaned forward on his crossed legs, looking like he was Jasleen's age.

"If you say so, baby brother."

"Ten years is not that much younger," he quipped.

"I can't really talk here; she's fifteen years older than me." Justin shrugged.

"Necesta was very kind to us." Talley tucked a strand of hair behind her ear.

"When will she be back?" I asked.

"A few days, assuming everything is fine at the other storehouse," Devin said from the doorway.

I had sent one of the flowers Dov had sent me back with Necesta that morning as she traveled back to the Baers' storehouse. It had started to die, withering away, when Necesta helped me to dry it. She carried it back with a message of well wishes from me as she checked on his progress.

"Okay, enough of this." Devin stood up, hand on the back of his neck. "My neck is killing me. Justin, out. It's your turn to keep watch."

Justin reluctantly stood up, winking at me. "We've got your back."

His hand shook the cot as he used it to balance himself. Devin took his seat as Justin settled on the ground outside, back against the doorframe.

"Just don't leave me out this time," he called in to us as we giggled over lowering our voices the day before so even when he strained he couldn't be a part of the conversation.

"Okay," I called, before dropping my voice to a whisper. "Let the games begin."

Shadoe sulked in the main area, skulking past my line of sight every so often. He scowled whenever he saw me talking to one of the Hersh siblings.

The days dragged on, each one bringing more strength back to my body. Necesta's bottles worked wonders, though I might have felt better than I actually was.

"I just want to talk to her," a voice outside said.

Talley glanced inside, waiting for approval. I nodded and she stepped back to let Anetta inside. She walked in, tall and graceful, standing several feet from the cot. I swung my feet over the edge, keeping the blanket draped over me.

"Hello," I said cautiously.

"Hello, Auluria," she said tentatively.

I watched as she hovered, rocking onto her heels.

"What is it, Anetta?" I encouraged her to speak.

Her eyes dragged the length of me, reminding me of how Lowell used to examine me before a test. Perhaps she had learned this technique from him during her time with him.

"Was any of it true?" she finally questioned. "Did you ever care?"

"What do you mean?" I was confused.

"Did you ever actually try to help Lowell?" she said, accusation in her voice.

"Of course I did. I did everything he asked, Anetta."

"Then why is he dead?" she whined.

"Lowell made some bad choices, Anetta. His goal of taking down the Society was admirable, but he let his revenge get in the way of actually helping people. How many people did we lose during his campaign of retribution against Griz Baer? You lost friends, I remember it happening."

"But Lowell didn't have to die," she persisted.

"No, but Lowell made his choice. His revenge was worth more to him than surviving."

"You could have helped him." She sounded like she was pleading.

"How?" I waited for her to answer. Tears started to drip down her face.

"Why did this happen?" she asked as she sunk to the floor, a puddle of tears forming in her lap.

I remembered once thinking it would be nice if any of Lowell's friends had taken an interest in me. Now one finally had and it was *still* all about my cousin.

"Your aunt would be so ashamed," Anetta sobbed. I wondered if she had ever met my aunt. I didn't think Lowell had ever introduced any of the girls to my aunt.

"Yes, she would, but not of me," I addressed her. "She never would have been okay with what Lowell was doing had she known."

"She was okay with the food and money Lowell brought you." She looked up at me defiantly. She wiped her eyes. "She never questioned that."

"She couldn't question that. Lowell was her son. She had to trust him or she had nothing. I heard her questioning it to herself once. She knew something was strange, but he was her son and he was taking care of her. She didn't want to push him away; he needed her. And she needed to take care of me."

"She would be horrified that you turned your back on your family."

"I didn't turn my back on Lowell; I tried to get him to stop the disaster he was creating. Lowell turned his back on me though. Do you have any idea what happened once we were caught, Anetta?"

She stared at me, daring me to go on.

"When Magistrate Canton had us in our cells, we were taken out for interrogation. Lowell had at least one of the soldiers in his pocket. Instead of bribing them to get him out, he traded for an empty room alone with me.

"He used his time to threaten me. He made me choose who would be hurt worse—Dov Baer or me. Anetta, he had so much power that Magistrate Canton actually listened to him when it came to our torture. You think a man like that couldn't have found a way out of all of this?

"He used his opportunity on revenge. That was his choice."

She looked furious, realizing that Lowell had done this to himself without a thought for his people...or her.

"His mother would have been heartbroken to see what he had become. He was always cold, but he changed once he left the Baers. My aunt never would have been okay with what he did to me or how he betrayed me. When I didn't do what he wanted, he threw me away.

"Lowell didn't care about anyone other than himself. I'm not even sure he truly cared about my aunt. Everything he did for her was a show of power."

"He loved her," she said. "He talked about her all the time. That's why he took you in. He had promised her he would look after you."

So Lowell wasn't completely heartless.

"Did he *ever* care about me, Anetta?" I asked quietly. "I mean, more than for what I could do for his mission?"

"I don't know." She breathed deeply, another tear falling off her cheek into the ocean that sat in her lap. She dragged a hand through her blonde hair. "I honestly don't think I know anything anymore."

"Did you love him?" I asked.

"Yes," she replied. "But, then, we all did. He didn't love me; I know that. But I think he was fond of me."

"I think he was too." I smiled. "I think I saw more of you than any of the other girls."

"Except Marjorie." She smiled ruefully.

"You two always did spend a lot of time with him."

"He was obsessed with you while you were gone, if that's any help," she suggested, hoping that would mean something to me. It didn't.

"Thank you, Anetta."

"He talked about your aunt all the time. He really felt that she would be proud of him."

"She would have been, even though she wouldn't have agreed with him. She loved him, even if they didn't see eye to eye. She would have loved him unconditionally, even in the face of all this."

"She must have been very special."

"She was." I paused. "I still love Lowell, Anetta. He was my cousin, and even though I didn't agree with him, I still love him because he is my family."

She glanced up quickly at me.

"I couldn't support the choices he made, but that didn't make him less of a person to me, or less of a relative. We get to make our own choices, Anetta, but we can still love and respect people as humans even though we don't see things the same way."

After a moment, she nodded. Anetta crawled over to the cot, putting her head on the mattress by my knee. I stroked her hair as she cried.

"I'm sorry he left you, Anetta. But you're strong." I smiled at her as she looked up at me. "I've seen you fight. You'll be okay."

"Maybe," she mumbled.

"You will," I insisted.

"I'm sorry you lost your cousin," she whispered.

Tears sprung to my eyes.

I had lost a cousin. I had lost my only remaining family.

We cried together as I forgave him.

Chapter 14

"NECESTA IS HERE." TALLEY GRINNED AS SHE REACHED AROUND THE doorframe.

I pushed myself up, arranging my skirt in front of me as I stood to show Necesta my progress in the week and a half that she had been gone. The dark fabric fell in front of me, cascading around my feet. She took an exceptionally long time reaching the door and I assumed she had stopped to talk to someone.

Talley walked away from the door in my line of sight, Devin and Justin going with her. My protection detail left me. Fear washed over me. They hadn't left my side since they arrived. Something was wrong.

Coldness crept over me and I looked for something to defend myself with. Footsteps approached the door. Twenty feet away, a figure stepped into my line of sight. The man approached quickly, coming straight for the door.

I nearly fell when I recognized the face. I shouldn't have been seeing him, but he was there.

My breath caught as he reached the door. It was real. *He* was real.

Blue eyes, so deep and true, moved slowly toward me. His smile hitched up on one side, showing his dimples as his hands tangled in my hair.

Dov's lips touched mine, as soft as I remembered them. He panted slightly in pain as I reached up his back and embraced him, accidentally touching his injuries. I pulled back, breathing in as I released him. Dov held me in place.

"It's okay," he whispered, finding my lips again.

His hands found my hips as he smiled against my mouth.

"Auluria," he sighed.

I reached a hand to his face, cradling it as he kissed me.

"Are you okay?" he asked between kisses.

"Mmm," I murmured against his lips.

I ran my hand up his arm, making him shiver. I jumped when he touched my shoulder and neck with his mouth. His warm breath rippled through my body as I quivered.

I stepped toward him, forcing him back. He moved with me, letting me guide his steps.

The door had closed at some point, giving us a modicum of privacy. He found the wall beside the door, leaning against it. I rested my hands on his shoulders, wanting to work out the knots, but terrified I would hurt him. He pulled at my back, moving me closer.

I pulled back, unable to breath, and watched him through half closed eyes. It was like a dream. He smiled at me, one hand in my hair, the other possessively on my hip.

"Took long enough," he finally said, making both of us burst into laughter.

"Sorry, the other side of the wall was a bit of an obstacle course." I giggled.

"From what I hear, it was *this* side that tripped you up." He smirked.

"Less tripping, more tangling," I corrected appreciatively, brushing his cheek with my fingertips.

"I think we need to work out a better plan next time—one that avoids cliffs. We seem to be making that a trend here." His moved his face to hover over mine again.

"And prisons. Let's avoid those too," I added.

"And that awful stage in the center of the city. That's the worst of it all."

"Agreed." I nodded, nearly bumping his nose. I thought twice and nudged his nose with mine.

He pulled me toward him, kissing me.

"How are you here? Shouldn't you be resting?" I asked when he pulled away.

"I have my ways." He shot me a flirtatious look. "But I've been holding out on them, so we can't wait too long to go back."

"What do you mean?" I pulled back and guided him to the chair.

He pulled it close to the cot as he sat, our knees touching.

"We have to come up with a plan. They aren't doing anything until you and I are back on our feet, but I intentionally stayed pretty quiet about what happened while I was gone, otherwise Berwyn never would have let me come." His smile faded into one a little sadder. "Silas knows, just in case we needed the information."

"Silas always plays a hand in everything, doesn't he?"

"I can't even imagine a life without Silas knowing everything before we do." Dov laughed.

A fist pounded against the door as we chuckled.

"Okay you two, that's about enough, we're coming in."

The door swung open to reveal Silas and Reyla. I jumped up so fast, Dov nearly toppled backward off the chair. He grinned as I raced past him into Reyla's arms.

"How are you here?" Tears pricked my eyes, more from the surprise of seeing her than the pain that pierced through my back.

"I was better off than Dov was, and he's here." She frowned. "They couldn't have kept me away if they tried. I tried to come the last time Silas was here too, but he wouldn't let me."

"You weren't ready yet. You needed to heal," he told her quietly. "But she's here now."

"I'm doing much better, and apparently, you are too." Reyla nodded to the cot before guiding us there.

I moved the pillow against the wall to give us more room. Reyla sat at the foot of the bed, leaving me to sit near Dov's chair at the head of the cot. Silas sat on the floor near Dov. As we sat there, I realized just how much each of us had endured.

Talley and her brothers resumed their posts outside of the door as we settled in to catch up. She closed the door over again, giving us space to openly talk.

"Auluria, what happened?" Reyla said urgently as soon as the door was closed.

I glanced to Silas to see what he had told them. He raised his hands in the air.

"I told them everything you said," he offered.

"I know what Silas said, but what *really* happened with Shadoe?" she persisted.

"Nothing. He was trying to teach someone a lesson and I interfered. He had nothing to do with it ending badly. Martin pulled himself up and landed poorly enough that it swung me out over the cliff. Shadoe tried to reach me." I noticed Dov grimace as I spoke. "But at least he pulled me closer to the face of the cliff so I could slow my fall. I just couldn't catch myself."

Reyla looked horrified.

"I don't like him," she pushed.

"I know," I said at the same time the boys said they didn't either.

"He hasn't come near me since I woke up, if that helps."

"Because you told him off," Silas added, his smug look suggesting I should consider him helpful.

Dov pursed his lips, a grin tugging the corners up. I wanted to kiss it off. I got lost staring at him, making him grin for real.

"Should we leave you two alone?" Silas smirked.

"Yes," we both said, refusing to break eye contact. Silas gaped at us until we laughed.

"So what is our plan here?" I finally asked when we calmed down.

"For what?" Silas asked, indicating there was a lot we should probably be discussing.

"For handling Canton. For reigning in Shadoe. For all if it."

"Well... I'm pretty sure *you're* the only one who can handle Shadoe at this point," Silas pointed out as Dov scowled.

"I don't like this," Dov said.

"Well, of course not," Reyla jumped in. "That's a terrible idea. She shouldn't be anywhere near Shadoe without some of us there."

"I agree. I don't want you alone with him," Dov said, reaching for my hand.

"I've been alone with him this whole time. I'll be fine," I said softly, trying not to upset him. I knew Shadoe was a sore spot for Dov. I brushed my thumb over the top of his hand.

"But he's angry now."

"Isn't he always angry?" Reyla asked.

"I think that's called 'personality.'" Silas answered.

"What about Canton?" I redirected, glaring at Silas's joke.

"Well, we've been talking about that," Dov said, glancing at Silas. "We think Shadoe is right. We need Canton. If we can get our hands on him, we can use him against the Society to bring them down."

"Dov knows his way around inside Canton's mansion," Silas supplied, looking between Reyla and me. "He can create maps for us."

"They dragged me around enough while I was there," he said sheepishly, not wanting to discuss what had happened to him in

Canton's possession. I'd have to ask him about it later. "There are ways we can get our people in."

"The trick is getting close enough to get in," Silas said.

"So what do we need to do?" Reyla asked, hand running through her hair. She leaned over and started brushing her fingers through mine, beginning to work it into an intricate design, needing something to occupy her.

"We're not sure yet. We really need to discuss most of this with Berwyn and Raselin." Dov hedged.

"But you have *something*?" I prompted.

"We have our people already planted in the city," he started. "And we're pretty sure Lowell has people planted as well…"

"He does, but not as many as you. At least, not that I know of. More like people he paid off and worked with. Shadoe probably knows more about that though."

"We're thinking maybe we could slip in. We could hide with our people and slowly start to, umm, replace the soldiers." He coughed, glancing down.

"Define 'replace,'" Reyla said.

"We would isolate a soldier or two and have our people inside the city hold them. We'd take their uniforms and pose as them for awhile," Silas informed us, looking as unsure as Dov.

"And then what?" I nudged Dov's foot with mine.

"Once we're all in place, we make our way to the mansion. We slip inside, try to avoid anyone who might figure out that we aren't really soldiers, and take over the soldier's duties inside the mansion," Dov finished.

"How do we get *inside* if we're the *outside* soldiers?" I asked.

"Turns out they rotate them every two weeks. If we're involved with the soldiers outside, we'll get rotated into the mansion. Once we're inside, we can get a hold of Canton and use him to control the soldiers.

"Once we rotate again, we can imprison the soldiers that we switched with. They won't think anything of being sent to the cells on their way back in. We'll lock them up and then pose as them again, with the end goal of using Canton in his position of power to bring down the Society." Dov grinned.

"And because no one will even realize the soldiers have been replaced by *our* people, no one will be the wiser." Silas looked between us, waiting for approval.

"So we quietly invade his precious mansion as his own men, and then coerce Canton into doing whatever we say, because no one will be there to stop us. Guys, this is brilliant."

"Can it really work?" Reyla hesitated.

"I think so," Dov replied. "I saw a lot while I was there. Canton dragged me all over that place. I might have acted a little more out of it than I really was."

Dov locked eyes with me.

"You were spying the entire time." I laughed. "I knew there was a reason I liked you."

"You like me for my charming personality." He smirked.

"And maybe a few other things too," I hinted.

"Reyla?" Silas interrupted.

"They already had their time together." Reyla shook her head jokingly. "Besides, I'm not done with her hair yet."

I hadn't even realized she was still braiding little pieces of my hair back, I was so absorbed in Dov's plan.

"We need to learn the layout of the mansion. Once our men are inside, we have to make it look like they know what they are doing. How much of it do you know, Dov?"

"Not everything, but enough to make it look good. Canton had me locked in different rooms. He was pretty paranoid that you all were coming for me."

"We were," Silas and Reyla said together. They glanced at me.

"I was dealing with a wall," I said in mock exasperation. "I got there eventually."

"Speaking of which, that *was* you that day, wasn't it? In the courtyard by the stage? I wasn't making that up, right?"

"No, that was me."

"I was pretty proud of you not running up to take another beating."

I always noticed how long Dov's lashes were when he was having meaningful discussions with me. They made me jealous. Everything about his eyes made me jealous.

"Yeah, well, they wouldn't let me. I tried," I teased back. "Devin had a pretty good grip on me at that point. I would have ended Canton had I made my way up there."

"Well, then I like this Devin guy."

"Have you met them yet?" I asked, glancing back at the door. "Devin and Justin and their sister, Talley?"

"Not really."

"I like them!" Silas says. "You'll like them too. I trust them."

"Oh I trust them. You left them to watch Auluria. I won't ever question them if you trusted them that much."

"I really did." Silas nodded. "But a lot of that came from Auluria's trust of them. She had a lot of faith in Raselin and his men."

"They've worked as hard as any of the teams I've worked with. Shadoe trusts them too, or at least as much as Shadoe trusts anyone," I added.

"How are we going to get Shadoe to go along with this?" Reyla picked up on his name.

"He wants to take down the Society. This is a good way to do it. He just has to understand that he can't try to go solo again. We all have to work together." Dov reached up to brush his hair out of his face, wincing when he reached high enough to tug on one of his injuries.

I started to lean forward to reach out to him, but that wasn't the place. He looked disappointed when I pulled back. I lowered my eyelids slowly, opening them back up to lock on him as I flirted from a distance. Brittella had taught me how to use my eyes to communicate when I was still in Lowell's care. Her lessons were paying off. His breath caught quietly as Silas smirked at his best friend.

"When are we going to tell *him* that?" Reyla brought up another good point.

"Soon," Dov said. "He's going to have to come back with us."

"We're going back?" I asked excitedly. I didn't know when I'd get to see any of my friends again with Shadoe's new rule. "When?"

"When Necesta says you can," Reyla cautioned. "And not before."

"Where is she?" I suddenly realized I hadn't seen her. "Talley said she was here and then you all showed up."

"Relax there, babe. She's outside with the others," Dov said soothingly. He tried to keep from smiling, but his lips quirked up, making me fight my own smile.

"She said she would give us a few minutes once Devin told us you were doing better," Silas added. "We should probably let her in though."

Silas stood, offering his hand to Reyla to help her up. I reached out and took Dov's hand. He stayed in the chair.

"Fine." Silas laughed. "We'll get Necesta."

They walked to the door, opening it enough to slip out. Necesta walked in, beaming.

"I've been waiting awhile for this scene," she said, motioning me to lie down. "Now, dearie, what do we have here?"

"I'm feeling a lot better." I tried to look confident enough for her to release me from the room.

"I'm sure." She hushed me. "But that doesn't mean anything. Your man is back… You're on top of the moon right now."

She glanced at Dov. He smiled back. He would have no problem convincing her that he was fine. Probably.

"Have you been taking this?" She motioned to the bottle sitting on the table next to me.

"Yes, ma'am." My hair bunched next to my face as I tried to nod against the pillow.

"And you're standing and walking now?"

"I am," I confirmed.

"You two are a matching set," she said, looking from Dov's arms to my legs, both hiding the scars with clothing. "Now get out, I have to check over Goldilocks here."

Dov smirked, standing. I wanted to say he could stay and just turn around while she checked over my injuries, but I knew I shouldn't. He leaned down, carefully hiding his pain as he bent over, and kissed my hand that he was still holding.

"Soon," he whispered, meaning so many different things.

As soon as the door was closed, Necesta nodded for me to move the fabric of my skirt. She examined me, running her fingers over my damaged skin. I wound myself up so tightly to avoid reacting to her touch that she lectured me.

She made me stand and walk around the room. I did better than I thought I would. By the end of her overview, she gave me permission to walk around the storehouse. If I could handle functioning normally over the next few days, we could go back to the main storehouse and put our plan into action.

Dov's laughter was deep and careless as he leaned into me. I doubled over, folding into his shoulder as tears filled my eyes. The last time he had been this care free, we were dancing in his house, long before he ever found out Lowell had sent me to him.

Justin righted himself, wiping a tear. Devin slapped him on the shoulder, nearly choking as he laughed.

"You can't blame me for that, Necesta," Justin claimed. "I was seven, how was I supposed to know?"

"Oh, dearie, I can," the older woman said knowingly.

"Can we please talk about Devin?" Justin grumbled, feigning embarrassment.

"I'm not as amusing as you, baby brother," Devin rumbled, smirking.

Justin shot him a look, winking at him, hidden meaning in his actions. Devin looked affronted.

"I'm going to let that go because we are in the presence of ladies." Devin gestured to where Reyla and I sat. "Anyway, here comes Talley."

Talley sat down next to us, asking what we had been laughing about. Necesta briefly filled her in on the stories she had been telling us from their childhood.

"It's time," she said when we settled down. "We need to get back. This needs to happen."

We collectively sighed. Shadoe had avoided us the last two days as we created our own camp around the room that used to be my cage. Dov, Reyla, and Silas didn't leave my side as we worked on the maps of the mansion and strategized how to get in.

I glanced at Dov, trying to decide how he would take my next statement.

"I'll go talk to him."

Dov's hand on my wrist stopped me from standing up.

"*We* will talk to him." He said.

"You know he won't respond well to you. He's been waiting for you to confront him since you got here."

"Auluria, the only way I'll be talking to him is if you are present. Otherwise, I'll kill him." He said. He meant it.

"Auluria, he's going to have to deal with us one way or the other, and if it's not with the rest of you around, Dov and I can't promise he will come back in one piece." Silas shifted, as if getting ready to jump up and catch me if I tried to make an escape.

"He needs to see that we're a united front, Auluria." Dov added. "He's going to have to work with all of us to get through this, and when he does, it's you and me, together."

"But it's not, Dov. It's you and your family, and me and him. That was the deal. Like it or not, he and I have to work together on this. For now at least, these people are my people." I swung my arms around, motioning to the group. "I'm responsible for them. Shadoe and I are leading them together."

"Shadoe doesn't need you. We do." Dov nodded as if it would help me understand.

"No, Dov. You don't. Your people have you. They have your brother and Eden. They have Silas. They have so many good people watching out for them and leading them. You keep them safe.

"But these people… They don't have anyone. Shadoe is as blind as Lowell was in his ambition. He only sees the mission; he doesn't see the people.

"He's still thinking like Lowell. He stepped off Lowell's path to help me, but now that we're back on this side of the wall, he's right back on it–minus the revenge part, of course. He's going after the Society to bring them to their knees and he's willing to play whatever part he needs to in order to accomplish that.

"Be honest. Do you really think Shadoe is going to make the best choices here?"

Everyone shook their head. I prepared myself.

"I have to stay with him," I said. Dov looked like I had slapped him. "I have to help him lead until we bring down the Society. He won't listen to anyone else while he's still listening to Lowell. My cousin put him in charge *with* me, so I'm the only one who can keep him in check."

Dov stood, taking my hand. He pulled me into the tiny room where I had been recuperating and closed the door.

"Auluria, please," he begged. "We cannot trust him and we certainly can't leave you with him."

"We don't have a choice," I argued.

"There is always a choice," he disagreed. "We can keep him in check while you're with us. Berwyn and Raselin will help. It's two major factions against one. He has to work with us or the entire operation will fail. You don't *have to* be with him."

"Dov, you don't understand."

"What don't I understand?" he challenged, eyes flashing.

I stared at him, unsure of what to say.

"Has something changed, Auluria?" He finally broke the silence. "Is something different? Because you've been spending a lot of time with him since we were separated."

"That wasn't by choice," I lectured. "You're the one that sent me over the wall with him, Dov. I didn't want to go."

"I wasn't about to leave you to be captured." He argued, raking a hand through his hair.

"You should have let me stay with you," I said quietly. "We could have fought."

"We did fight. You rallied more troops and I spied on Canton."

"And nearly died because of it."

"Better me than you." He tipped his chin at me as if proving a point.

"Haven't we been here before?" I asked, exasperated.

"Like we never left." He was short with me.

It was apparently the only thing that hadn't changed in our time apart. He looked the same, as did I, but scars covered everything we once knew.

"What are we supposed to do from here?" he asked quietly.

"I don't know."

"I trust you, you know that, right?" he asked, stepping forward. He took my hands in his. "This isn't about you, Auluria. I trust you. But I can't trust him; not after everything.

"I didn't want to leave you with him, but you know I knew you could protect yourself against him and you'd never be able to fight off all those Society men. I didn't want to leave you, but I couldn't see another way."

"I know." I couldn't tell if his hands felt familiar or foreign in mine as I answered.

"Please don't do this," he begged softly.

"I can't see any other way," I whispered, looking at the ground.

"Auluria."

His voice tore at my heart as I was breaking his.

I stepped closer to him, reaching up to kiss him. We stood, holding hands, my lips on his, trying to convince him to let me go, at least for now. I released my right hand and it climbed up his chest to his neck, pulling him harder against my face.

It hurt so much knowing that I had to walk away.

His free arm reached up, cradling my head. He was nervous, I could feel it in the hand he kept in mine. I was nervous too.

Pushing him back, we stepped deeper into the room. Slowly he moved, bringing me with him. I didn't want to stop kissing him as he worked to convince me to stay.

His shoulder rose in surprise as he inhaled once I had stepped away. I moved quickly, leaving him frozen in place.

"I'm sorry. I'll come back to you," I promised, slamming the door. I turned to Silas who was as shocked as Dov had been. "Do not let him out of here, it's for his own good."

Dov was at the door, attempting to open it. Justin leapt to his feet, locking it.

"Do what she says," he commanded Silas.

"You know I have to do this," I pleaded with him.

"Silas," Reyla said quietly, urging him to help me.

He nodded once and I ran.

"Dov, she has to do this," I heard him trying to explain as Dov shouted through the door. I hoped he wouldn't hurt himself trying to get out.

I heard him begging Silas to go with me as I rounded the corner created by the long supply table. I hurried faster.

"Where is he?" I asked Marjorie.

"Who?" she snapped at me.

"Shadoe, where is he?" I asked, not slowing.

"I don't know."

"He's outside, Auluria," Anetta intervened from far enough away that I hadn't seen her.

Marjorie glared as I nodded to thank her. I turned, making my way outside. Speeding through the tunnel, I nearly crashed into Shadoe as I exited into the light.

"Go," I commanded the people surrounding him, finding my voice as their leader.

They shifted uncomfortably, looking to Shadoe.

"Now." I left the dangerous tone in my voice. I was Lowell's blood and I would not let them forget it.

They retreated without another question, wandering back inside the storehouse.

"We need to talk."

Shadoe crossed his arms, narrowing his eyes at me.

"You wanted me to lead, well, now I'm leading." I crossed my arms. "We have a plan, Shadoe, and you *will* listen to me.

"We're breaking into the Society and taking control of Canton."

"I'm listening," he finally agreed.

"Sit down," I said, nodding to a fallen tree.

"Lowell had contacts inside the city, right?" I waited for him to nod. "Do you know them? We need to use them."

"Yes, I know who they are."

"You need to contact them. We're going to reach out to the people the Baers have planted in the city too."

"Why?"

"We're sneaking into the city. We're going in a few at a time and hiding with our people. The goal is to quietly switch places with the soldiers and make our way to the mansion.

"Dov knows the layout of the building. He knows how to get us in. Once we're inside, we can get control of Canton and use him to play the Society. Shadoe, this is going to work."

"How do you propose we do this?" He questioned, looking skeptical.

"We've been working on the plan, but you and I have to go back and talk to Berwyn and Raselin about it."

He looked impressed that I had aligned myself with him.

"But we have to go soon—today or tomorrow if we can. We have to time it right so that we can sneak into the mansion."

"And where do our people fall into all this?" he asked.

"We're all going in. We'll send a large initial group to pose as soldiers. Once we're inside and we handle the other soldiers, we can bring everyone else in. The Society won't have any idea that we replaced their men."

"Where do you and I fit into this?" He pushed, face stone cold.

"I'm honoring my word, Shadoe. I'm here to help you and our people."

The smug look on his face only lasted a moment as Dov burst into the forest, Silas and Reyla following behind him. Justin and Devin joined them as Dov stalked over to us.

Shadoe slammed into the ground, the cracking sound from where Dov's fist collided with his jaw reaching me just as my own jaw fell.

"Dov!" I shouted, turning to see where Shadoe had landed.

"You will not touch her," Dov threatened quietly, as terrifying as his brother.

He leaned over the fallen tree to where Shadoe was lying. Shadoe lunged, kicking out at the tree, shaking it so hard that I was propelled off of it. It slammed into Dov's legs, moving him backward. I caught his arm and steadied us both.

Shadoe jumped to his feet, ready for a fight. I didn't know if Dov could withstand Shadoe in this condition. He still hadn't fully healed.

I eyed the claw that sat on Shadoe's hip, an ever-present reminder that he was willing to do whatever it took to succeed. It swung, catching the light as he stood.

I attempted to stand between them, but Dov reached around me and moved me off to the side. I pulled at him, hoping he would let me go.

"You will not touch her. You will not upset her. You will never be alone with her." Dov grew louder, listing his demands. "One of us will be with her at all times."

"You still don't get it, Baer," Shadoe sneered. "She is still not someone you can control."

"I'm not controlling her, I'm keeping *you* from hurting her or *any* of my people."

"This is why Lowell always had the upper hand on your kind." Shadoe stepped closer.

"Dov," I hissed, hoping it would cause him to back down.

"You live by the rules, Baer, but out here, there are no rules. The Society doesn't play by rules. Rules will get you killed."

"Rules will get *you* killed if you don't play by them, Shadoe. Auluria almost died because of your recklessness. I will not allow that to happen again."

"How will you stop me?" Shadoe taunted smugly.

Dov stepped forward, prompting Shadoe to look to me. He waited.

I had to choose.

I wasn't about to let Shadoe win, but I knew I had to side with him. I stepped in front of Dov so quickly he didn't realize I was moving. I kissed him longer than I should have, making it uncomfortable for anyone watching, before I stepped back to align myself with Shadoe.

His hands trailed after me, latching on as they moved from my back, to my hips, down my elbows and arms, to my hands. We held each other, separated by a chasm, clinging to each other with Shadoe by my side.

"We're going to see Berwyn and Raselin." I turned my face toward Shadoe without breaking eye contact with Dov. "Get the group ready."

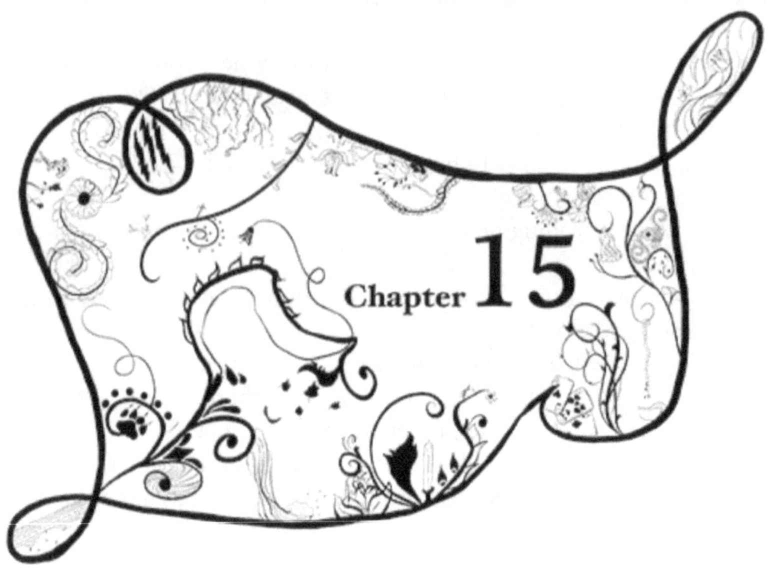

IT WAS STRANGE TO SEE DOV STALKING THROUGH THE FOREST, STILL livid as we neared the storehouse that housed his people. He glared at Shadoe every few feet, making sure he kept his distance.

Reyla stayed next to me, frequently wrapping her arm around mine to keep step with me. She and Silas kept Shadoe from me, forcing him to the far end of the chain. The Hersh siblings and Necesta walked behind us, mixed with Shadoe's men. The rest of his team would be joining us a day later after they had packed.

Shadoe refused to let Necesta look him over after Dov attacked him. I think his pride was hurt more than anything. His chin was swollen where he had taken the punch.

"Auluria," a friendly voice greeted me. I looked up to find Henry walking out from behind a tree where he was keeping his sparkling green eyes on things. "Nice to see you back. The girls will be thrilled."

His eye flitted between Dov and Shadoe and his face grew reserved. Shifting, he turned his shoulders, aligning himself with Dov. He nodded to Shadoe briefly, letting everyone know where his alliance rested.

"Anything you need?" he asked Dov, giving him a forced smile.

"No, Henry, thank you. Please let the others know the rest of Shadoe's men will be on their way shortly."

Henry nodded. I had a feeling Gregory, Ben, and Carter would be joining us shortly. He glanced at Silas before we walked past him.

Dov and Silas walked slightly heavier as we moved toward the storehouse entrance. It took me a moment to realize they were trying to cover the sound of Henry moving quickly away to enter the storehouse before we arrived through a secret entrance. He was going to warn Berwyn. I walked harder.

Once inside, Berwyn was waiting for us, arms crossed.

"You're back."

Eden walked up behind him, eyes moving from Shadoe, to Dov, to Silas before coming to rest on me. Apparently I was the one she wanted to telepathically communicate with. I moved my eyes to the side, letting her know something was going on with Shadoe.

"We have a plan, Berwyn," Dov said, pulling the maps out of the supply bag he was carrying them in. "We need to talk. Now."

Berwyn nodded, eager to hear what his kid brother had worked out. We all started to follow when he stopped us.

"Just him. Then you."

Dov hesitated, hovering in place for only a moment before following his brother, leaving Silas, Justin, and Devin a warning glance.

We walked through the tunnel to the main area, Eden leading the way. Reyla stayed close by my side, ensuring Dov's wishes were followed.

"What is this idea?" Eden said once we reached the main area.

Shadoe's men broke off, eager to find food. Talley went to find Lydia while Necesta made her way to Raselin to fill him in on the situation. Devin and Justin took positions very close to Shadoe, allowing Reyla to be my bodyguard as Silas oversaw the production.

"You're back!" A tiny voice shouted as it collided with my legs. "Mommy said she didn't know if you were coming back, but I knew you were."

"Well, hello, Jasleen." I bent down to see her, scooping her up in my arms. "Your hair is so pretty today. Did Katarina help you with that?"

She giggled, running her hand through my hair. The boys watched me curiously as I bounced the little girl around and talked to her.

"Where is Dov?" she asked sheepishly.

"He's in a meeting with Berwyn."

"Why aren't you there?"

"I wanted to come see you, of course."

She caught sight of Silas and ducked her head into my shoulder, suddenly shy.

"Do you want to say hi?"

She shook her head against me, tossing her hair in my face. Silas laughed.

"Hi, Jasleen," he called softly.

She swooned against me as I tried to suppress a laugh. Reyla leaned over, grinning viciously.

"But we know who you like better," she teased just loud enough for the three of us to hear. "*Dov.*"

Reyla stretched out his name, sending Jasleen into a fit of giggles as her tiny fists balled in my hair. She shook her head violently, begging Reyla to stop, grinning against my shoulder.

"Oh, I see. Somebody thought she could steal my man while I was gone, did she?" I asked quietly.

Even Shadoe looked amused as I looked up to catch the others smirking at what we had done to the little girl. She giggled as I set her down, letting her run off to her mother.

"What did you say to her?" Silas asked once she was gone.

"Nothing," Reyla and I replied in unison, as innocently as we could.

"Oh, please," Eden scoffed. "She's been pining over Dov since he got back."

They all looked at her in surprise.

"Since he *got back?*" Reyla yelped, making us turn back to her. "She's been obsessed with him since the day she decided she wanted to be Auluria when she grew up.

"No offense, Silas." She winked at him, taking away the sting of falling in second place. She looked to the other men standing with us. "Don't worry boys, I'm sure she'll find a place in her heart for you all too. Or maybe some of her friends will adopt you as their crushes. It's amazing how crushes race through the little ones."

Reyla and I giggled as male eyes grew wide. Eden laughed only long enough to change the subject.

"Speaking of which, I think it's time Auluria and I had a little talk."

She guided me away from the group, Reyla keeping a watchful eye on Shadoe as she moved out to find our friends. Justin and Devin stayed by his side, leaving Silas to be a little less obvious about his surveillance.

"Speak," Eden instructed once we were alone.

"Hello to you too, Eden. Nice to see you again."

The look she gave me so deeply resembled her husband's that I knew she had been spending far too much time with him. Her hands found her hips as she jutted one out to emphasize her point of who was in charge.

I quickly recounted everything that had happened from the time I left her until we walked in the door, giving her as many details about Dov's place as I had. She listened intently, making comments as I talked, her blonde hair bobbing as she nodded.

"Once we have Canton, then what? What is our plan?" she asked. "Even with all three of our groups working together, are we really going to be able to control the entire Society?"

"If we do it strategically, I think we can, yes," I said carefully.

"But what if we can't?"

"Do we have a choice?" I shrugged. "This is the best we've got, Eden."

"So, we capture Canton, use him against the Society, somehow manage to control the soldiers in the entire country, and then live happily ever after?" Eden mocked.

"Those of us who make it, I suppose. I can't imagine we'll all live through this." My realistic side, well groomed by Shadoe, made an appearance.

"And those of us that *do* survive… What do they do?" she inquired.

"They run the government, I guess. No more dictatorships. They handle our enemies on the other side of the walls. We already know we have to free Raselin's people, so that will be the first thing.

"They'll need to train our people," I continued. "And free the camps. We'll have to have something in place to help the people trapped in the camps."

Eden's face grew dark, brows furrowing as one of her curls fell in her face. She blinked several times, processing something.

"What if we didn't free the camps after?" she asked, to my horror.

"What?"

Her head snapped up to me.

"What if we didn't free the camps after we defeat the Society?" She grinned wickedly. "What if we got them out before?"

I inhaled sharply. *What if we did?*

"Think about it…the boys are sent to camps to learn to fight and then sent off to war. They would be incredible assets to us. The girls could learn to fight or do things around the country to be assets to us. Auluria, this could be huge! You know how many camps there are."

Her eyes were animated as her hands flew through the air while she was speaking. Excitement overtook us as both a brilliant idea and one of her revenge plans fell into place. She had wanted to destroy the camps for a long time.

"We can't force them to fight for us." I shook my head. "We have to give them the option of how they help us. These kids and people they send to the camps haven't asked for any of this. We free them, but they have the option of helping us bring down the Society that did this to them or not. We have to let them choose or we're no different than Canton and the Society."

She dimmed a little, but understood my words.

"We're not them," she agreed. "But they'll want to help. If we can take down the Society, then we can take down our enemies, and then we'll all truly be free."

"We need to talk to the boys." I gave us direction.

"Right." She grabbed my hand and pulled me back toward where Berwyn was meeting with Dov.

Arin let us pass without question as we approached. Berwyn and Dov were deep in conversation, looking over the maps Dov had created of Magistrate Canton's mansion. Dov sat in a chair as Berwyn towered over the table where the maps sat.

"We need to free the camps," Eden said, not taking the time to announce our entrance. She walked up to the table and slammed a pointed finger on one of the maps.

"We will, Eden," Berwyn assured her.

"No, we need to do it now."

"We'll free them as soon as we have the Society under control. We can't give away our plan this early. The Society can't know we're working together or how strong our numbers are."

"Do you really think we have enough men to control this entire country, even if we follow this plan, Berwyn? It's a good plan, but we have to have every advantage."

"If we free the camps," I added quietly, "don't you think most of those men and women will want to join us?"

"Eden, Auluria, the Society will know if we free the camps. There is no coming back from that. Right now we will be able to slip in and not draw too much suspicion. We have to do this now," Berwyn said gently, trying to convince his wife it was better to wait.

"What if," Dov said, drawing out his words, "we get into the mansion and gain control of Canton, get all of our people on the inside, and then handle the camps before we take on the rest of the Society?"

Everyone paused to think through the implications. In theory, it was a solid plan.

"That way we don't lose our ability to rule through Canton, but we still have the numbers to back us up when it's time for the real battle." I concluded.

"That could work..." Berwyn turned back to the maps, moving them to uncover the Society maps below. He charted the locations as Dov stood to join us, hovering over the pages.

We spent an hour working out patterns, deciding what the most strategic order to free the camps would be before we sent for Raselin and Shadoe. They, and a select group of their top people, joined us in the small room.

Shadoe forced his way in after Raselin, making his way to my side. Eden and Dov stood across the table watching as I was pinned between Shadoe and Berwyn. Silas slipped in, taking his post by Dov and Eden.

Raselin, the Hersh siblings, Reed, Fitch and Lydia, and Nian rounded out the far end of the table as everyone leaned in to see. Berwyn pointed out locations and Dov took charge, explaining the plan to everyone. Shadoe and Raselin each took turns challenging pieces until they were satisfied, tweaks being made to what we had worked on without them.

Eventually, we all stepped away to consult with our teams in private. Raselin led his men out before Shadoe and I followed, his men behind us. We convened down the hall, dark shadows falling across our faces from the lights on the walls.

Shadoe made comments. I responded. Everyone else complied. After a few moments, we decided to agree with the Baers' plan, as if it hadn't been a given.

"We have to get into the city unnoticed. Our men will hide with the people Lowell planted in the city. We can bribe the rest of his contacts, although they may be willing to join us to avoid having to work under the Society for much longer." Shadoe nodded to each of us. "We need to move immediately. It will take a week to sneak us all in."

"We should get started," Nikko said. Shadoe glanced at him.

"Should we establish the order we send our men in before we go back to the leadership?" Sherman asked.

"Yes," Shadoe acknowledged them. "We need everything in order before we go back."

I had a feeling I wasn't going to like where that ended.

The first wave of people had already left. The second wave would be following. A third group remained in the storehouse, prepared to join us inside the city once we had taken over Canton's stronghold. I dropped the curtain, moving away from the window before I was lectured. Dov would arrive soon enough.

Shadoe had insisted we go with the first group of rebels, finding shelter in the house of a man Lowell once traded with. He left the residences of our trusted contacts for our lesser-skilled fighters. Should any of the contacts we bribed turn on us, Shadoe would deal with them swiftly.

Ella turned to me, ready for an argument.

"I know." I cut her off.

"Leave her be, Ella." Anetta snapped, walking in the door. "I brought us food."

She shed the gray jacket the Society soldiers wear, dropping it on the back of a chair. Shadoe followed behind her. He placed a Society weapon on the table accompanied by a knife with barbed edges, like the back of a fish with a prickly spine. Definitely not Society issued.

I joined them at the table, happy to see food. I picked up the bread, ripping a piece off. Anetta glanced at me before looking down. She seemed to be warming up to me after all this time. Marjorie still glowered from a corner.

"Tomorrow we're moving to the mansion. We have to make sure everything is ready," Shadoe explained, joining in eating. "Is everything in order here?"

"Yes," Ella responded, not giving details.

"Ella and I will go on patrol when we're done here," I said, taking another bite of the bread.

"I will not. I've already been on patrol today. We're not supposed to go back out until tomorrow," she protested, looking to Shadoe for support.

"I'll go back out," Anetta volunteered. "It's better than sitting around here all night. I don't like being cooped up like this."

She waved her hand around the house. Lowell had trained his fold to be mobile, constantly moving from location to location. It's what made it so hard for the Society to catch us. Staying inside houses for prolonged periods of time was suffocating to some of these people.

"Anetta and I will go," I said before Shadoe could protest.

He grumbled but knew he couldn't argue with me in front of everyone. When we were finished with our food, we slipped back into the Society uniforms we had stolen and stepped outside.

I tugged the cold weather hood up over my hair, concealing my long mane. Anetta did the same, tucking her short hair back so it wouldn't be noticed.

"Which way do you want to go?" I asked, walking out onto a main street.

"Whichever way we need to go to meet him," she said casually.

"What?" I questioned, turning to her. "Meet who?"

"You don't think I know you're out here looking for your boyfriend?" She warned me not to question her. "I saw you watching out the window as we walked up. "It's been two days and you're pining."

I stared at her and she started to walk.

"Which way?" Anetta demanded.

I guided us left, hoping I was correct. I didn't know where Dov was, or even if I'd see him, but if he was coming through, it would be in this direction. She kept step with me.

"Does he care about you?" she finally asked.

"Yes."

"It's more than Lowell ever did for me, so I say don't let it go." Her voice was quiet, as if reluctant to admit it.

"I don't intend on letting him go." I smiled, making her smile back.

"I'm sorry I ignored you back then," she admitted. "I shouldn't have done that. I was wrapped up in your cousin and you were just another thing to take his attention away from me."

"I never understood why you competed for his attention," I divulged. "He really wasn't worth it."

"No, he wasn't. But what girl doesn't want to be seen that way by the most important man she knows?" She made her point. "Speaking of..."

She pulled me off to the side of the street, a precaution in case it wasn't our people joining us. Only a few Society men roamed the streets, the last of the second wave of our men would replace them soon. We walked together with intentionality, hoping we wouldn't be questioned.

A small group approached us, not wearing uniforms. They drew closer, detail starting to take form. It would have been easy for Shadoe to have stopped the oncoming group and question them, adding credibility to our deception. As women, we had to remain quiet to avoid suspicion.

The group kept their heads down, huddling on the far side of the road. One chanced a look, eyes raking across us for information so quickly I wasn't sure I had seen it.

"Justin," I said when my brain had processed what I had seen.

He stopped, recognizing my voice. The group halted, waiting for us to cross the street and join them. Reed grinned as we stepped in front of them.

"Do you know where you're going?" I asked quickly, knowing we couldn't stay long.

"Yes, we're near you… one street over. Berwyn has a family there that will take us in. Why are you out here?" Justin questioned.

"We're patrolling," I explained.

"He's not here," Justin said quietly when he noticed Anetta looking around. I wanted to smack her.

"Where is he?" she asked, not bothering to hide what she was doing.

"Dov is in the next group," Nian said, moving his hair. I should have insisted he fix that before we started the mission.

A branch cracked. We turned, realizing someone was approaching. Justin's team darted into the trees. I grabbed Anetta's arm and propelled her forward. We walked down the road, faces tipped down. The team would be fine in the trees until the people had passed by. I was tempted to look back once the man walked by us, but resisted.

The road was quiet for the next ten minutes, each moment slowly dragging by. I counted leaves as they fell, turning the deep colors of the forest in fall. Each noise frightened us as we reigned ourselves in to keep from being noticed.

Two figures approached us, casually walking the road. Leave it to Dov and Silas to remain nonchalant in a time of crisis. They both nodded as they passed by, stopping only after they had walked by us, realizing it was me.

"You're safe," Dov said, breaking from his act.

"So far," I replied with a smile.

"Is everything going according to plan?" Dov asked, staying business-oriented even as his hand slipped around my wrist.

"Yes. We're just waiting for the last of you tonight, and in the morning, we'll breech the mansion. Shadoe acquired some extra weapons for us. He's been getting them to the men that are already here. He will give the rest out tomorrow."

"Nasty looking things," Anetta commented.

"But effective, I'm sure." Silas knew how Shadoe operated.

"Do you know where you're going?" I asked Dov.

"Yes, we've got another mile to go, but we'll catch up with you tomorrow at the mansion. You and Shadoe are going to meet us in the study once we get there, right?"

"We'll be there," I confirmed.

Dov looked over my shoulder. I stiffened before slowly turning. Society men were about to discover us. With no time to hide the boys, I pushed Dov around, facing away from the men. With his hand behind his back, I nudged the back of his knee, indicating he should fall.

Anetta saw what I was doing and reached for Silas. Slightly confused, she had to kick his knee out for him to understand.

"Be our voices." I hissed at them, knowing Society soldiers could not sound like women.

Dov and Silas slipped into commanding roles, shouting for themselves to get on the ground as if our roles were reversed. They were about to get their Society uniforms much quicker than expected.

"Get on the ground!" Dov yelled as he pretended to struggle against me.

"I said cooperate…and maybe we won't try you for treason!" Silas echoed back, effortlessly straining against Anetta.

Dov threw his elbow back, nearly catching me by surprise. I ducked just in time, missing the painful blow, but Dov made a gasping sound as if I had been hit. Silas wrenched around, making it look like an escape attempt.

We heard the men running over the noise of the fake brawl, attempting to assist us. I tossed a look over my shoulder in the dwindling light for good measure.

"You there, help us," Dov lured the Society men to our aid.

The men shouted, raising their weapons.

"Put those away and help us," Silas shouted.

As they approached, Anetta and I realeased our grip on the men and turned on the soldiers. I threw my elbow into one's face, crunching something. Kicking out, I connected with his stomach, doubling him over. From above, I brought my hand down on the back of his shoulder, making him fall to the ground.

Quickly, I dropped to my knees, touching the sensitive part of his neck that rendered him unconscious. When I turned, Dov stood, his face a mixture of shock and pride. I stepped over and helped Anetta knock the second soldier out.

"Well, gentlemen, I think we found your uniforms for this little event." I grinned.

"I think we have." Dov smiled back.

We helped lift the unconscious bodies to the side of the road, stepping back into view of anyone who was watching to block the scene as Dov and Silas swapped outfits with the men. Once the change was complete, we helped tie the men up to be taken to the house where Dov and Silas would be staying. If anyone saw, four Society soldiers were taking prisoners for questioning. We gagged the men to prevent them from talking.

I walked alongside Dov as he led one of the disguised soldiers down the street. Anetta walked beside Silas. If we were approached, we would let them speak.

We stayed silent as we moved, avoiding conversation to prevent the Society men from learning anything from us. When we arrived, they stopped on the street, allowing me to approach the house so we didn't scare the owner. Dov and Silas weren't meant to be dressed in Society uniforms yet, nor should they have prisoners.

I knocked on the door, waiting for the owner to greet me. I gave the signal, indicating we were on the same team, and waited for him to step back.

"Well, it's about time," Fitch said from the back of the house.

"Fitch," I said, smiling. "Is Lydia here too?"

"Back here." A hand waved from behind a counter as she climbed out of the cabinet she was hiding in.

I turned, waving the rest of my group in. They hurried up the path and into the house, making sure no one was watching us. We explained what had happened.

"Well, at least you won't have to go back out tonight to find uniforms." Fitch smirked as his eyes made their way over to the soldiers tied up on the middle of the floor where Silas and Dov had dropped them. "I guess we should put these two away."

He stood, grabbing each man by an arm, and lifted them into the air. Lydia's eyes grew wide in appreciation of her husband. She winked at me, making me giggle.

Fitch locked the men in a cellar below the house, concealed in the floorboards so no one could easily find it. The family that Berwyn had planted here would watch them while we ran our mission to the mansion the next day.

"You were great today," Dov said when we found a moment alone in the corner. "You knew just what to do."

"Well, I tried." I giggled.

"You saved us…again, Auluria." He inched closer. "You never cease to amaze me."

"We need to find time to talk, Dov." I grew serious. "We can't keep going like this."

"I know," he whispered back. "Soon. Once we get into the mansion, we'll find time to talk and get all of this figured out."

He reached up and brushed a strand of my hair back.

"Besides, Goldilocks, we have a few other things to discuss too."

I batted his hand away at that name.

"Why haven't you forgotten about that yet?"

"Everyone has told me about that, Auluria. Did you really think it's not burned into my brain?" he teased as I rolled my eyes. "Besides, it suits you. *Goldilocks.*"

I gave up trying to suppress my smirk and stepped closer to touch his hair. He froze, waiting for me to move.

"Speaking of the whole 'golden girl' and 'golden boy' thing… Did you hear about Marty?"

"About Shadoe taking his hand off for touching you?" Ice crept into his words. "It's about the only thing I can think of to redeem him."

His hand wrapped around my wrist as I played with his hair.

"Are you okay after all that?" His eyes pierced into me, searching every inch of my soul for an answer.

"I'm okay. We need to talk about it though." I moved my finger around a wave of his hair, making his eyes flutter. "But for now I'm fine. I'm not hurt, so it can wait until after."

"Okay," he agreed, nodding his head. "I know this is going to be a battle, but I promise, we will find time to reconnect. I know we need to go through everything we've been through."

"I don't want any of this to come between us."

"We have enough working against us as it is, but we won't let all of this be one of those things. We'll get through this. Besides, if Silas and Reyla have it their way, we won't be apart for very long."

"Of course not. We really need to find Silas something else to do with his free time." I laughed.

Dov chuckled, his face lighting up.

"Reyla too."

"Reyla is still in mourning, we can forgive her on this one." I paused. *"For a bit."*

Dov laughed, as loud and free as we had in his house before he found out I was working with Lowell and Shadoe. I stepped into his arms, holding him. He felt good; he felt safe.

I inhaled, every feeling I had while we were apart came flooding back. He wrapped himself around me, protecting me. When he pulled back, he rested his forehead on mine.

"I'm not giving up on us," he promised. "Not after all this."

"Good," I murmured.

"And you're both making me sick." Anetta stomped across the room. "Time to go, Auluria."

She flipped her hood over her head and put her hand on the doorknob. I turned back to Dov.

"See you tomorrow?" I asked, running a finger down his jaw to his chin.

"See you tomorrow," he confirmed. "Will you be okay out there?"

He knew better than to ask to walk me. We couldn't afford to have him out there any more than necessary tonight. He also knew Anetta and I could take care of ourselves if need be.

Instead, he walked me to the door. I waved goodbye to everyone and stepped into the darkness.

Chapter 16

WE WAITED IN THE COURTYARD AS SOLDIERS PASSED US. EACH ONE OF their steps felt like a nail being pounded into a board next to us, inching closer. My soul wanted to jump with each slam of their feet, but I willed myself still. Even Shadoe's training had not prepared me for this anxiety.

The men emptied out of the mansion, walking past us to the streets to their patrols. Our lines slowly started filing into the gates, branching out in different directions. Our men made their way to their posts, attempting to make it look as though they were doing their jobs for Magistrate Canton. I was near the front, only a few dozen men in front of me.

Stepping inside was like being captured again. Every feeling I had had when I was brought before Canton the first time washed over me. Shadoe had no idea the terror that grasped me inside these walls. He made his way quietly over to me from his position a few lines away.

"This way," he mumbled softly.

We branched off, following the hallways Dov had marked for us on a map. Up a flight of stairs, we took a right, entering into one of the Great Rooms in the mansion. Red, like the robes he wore during our sentencing, filled the space. I almost wanted to stop and admire the tapestries and banners hanging from ceiling to floor, but I remembered why we were there.

The only men we saw along the way were our own as they hurried to find their stations. Dov had carefully chosen a route for us that would avoid the main areas that Canton might be occupying upon our arrival. Neither of us trusted Shadoe not to change the plan.

Footsteps echoed along the hallway as we drew closer to the study where we were meeting the other leaders. Raselin nodded to us as he slipped in the door down the hall. Shadoe and I approached cautiously, making sure no one was around to see us follow him inside.

Raselin stood in the room alone, weapon in hand. Shadoe and I swept the room, ensuring no one was there to hinder our success. Fitch tentatively stepped inside, only relaxing once Raselin nodded to him that everything was fine.

Eden's blonde curls gave her away as she entered. She took a position by me as we waited in silence. She tucked her hair back under her hood.

Silas and Berwyn arrived a few minutes later, having been toward the back of our lineup of men and women. They nodded to Raselin and Shadoe before coming to stand by Eden.

"Anything?" Berwyn asked quietly.

Most of us had been sent in different directions, an attempt at ascertaining where Canton was at that given moment. We all shook our heads.

"Hopefully Dov found something."

As if on cue, Dov bounded in the door, closing it behind him. He put a finger to his lips, warning us. He tipped his ear back toward the door, pressing it against the frame to listen. I watched his shoulders move as he breathed, waiting for him to tell us it was safe.

Berwyn started to lean forward, ready to move to the door for answers if Dov didn't release us soon. Raselin and Fitch traded nervous glances while Shadoe's fingers inched toward his knife. Realizing the Baers didn't have Shadoe's new toys yet, I held my hand out, collecting them from him while we waited.

Finally, Dov released us. Every shoulder in the room lowered an inch in relief. Walking to Dov and Berwyn, I held out the new knives.

"Shadoe found them. Just go with it," I instructed, handing them the weapons.

"He's in the weapons room," Dov reported.

"Of course he is," Berwyn groaned.

"As if the day weren't hard enough," Raselin echoed his sentiments.

"He has a few men with him. We're going to have to neutralize them," Dov added.

"We'll hit hard and fast," Shadoe said, pushing his way into the conversation. "They won't see us coming. We'll need to get Canton isolated and then we can interrogate him."

"We can't hurt him, Shadoe," Berwyn instructed. "The people will have to see him. He can't be injured or they will know something is wrong."

"I'm aware, Baer," Shadoe sneered. "That doesn't change the fact that we need information."

"We'll get it." Raselin tried to calm everyone. "Let's just focus on getting him under our control. We can focus on getting information later."

"We need to focus on it now," Shadoe protested. "If we can't hurt him, we have to make him fear us. This is a man who is willing to sell out his own people to protect himself. If he thinks he can find help when we let him address people, or address the Society, than he will take whatever chance he gets."

"He's right." I take a deep breath. "We can never control Canton unless there is a reason for him to do what we say. If he thinks he can win, he will try anything. He has to know the only way he survives this is if he plays along."

"Auluria and I will take care of that," Shadoe announced.

I look to him, unsure what he meant. He refused to look at me.

"Leave it to us. Now," he continued before anyone could stop him, "we need to go. We know where he is. This is the time to strike."

Standing outside the weapons room door was like waiting for my aunt to die—painful and unending. She fought with every breath to stay alive and it seemed as though the door before us was prepared to fight to stand its ground too.

Silent breaths filled the air as we waited, listening for the proper moment to break in. From what we could tell, six men were with Canton. We assumed they were high-level soldiers.

We all came to life when Dov turned back to us, ready to signal our entrance. Fear prickled through me, rushing through my veins. Eden brushed against me as she leaned forward on her toes.

Dov motioned for us to prepare ourselves. Counting down, Fitch burst through the door, surprising everyone inside. Canton wheeled around, his red robe dusting the floor. Shock flashed over his face until he recognized Dov.

"Kill them," he instructed his men. "But not the girl."

His men looked to me, recognizing me as we attacked. Dov and Berwyn worked as a team, taking on the brunt of the attack. I heard an arm break, the soldier's scream filling the room, as I engaged with a man at Shadoe's side.

"Silas," Eden warned her partner over the noise of the fight.

I blocked the soldier who swung a knife at me, striking so fast he didn't have time to protect himself. He doubled over as Shadoe kicked him hard enough to knock him out.

We moved to help Fitch and Raselin as they battled two strong soldiers. The first was no match for Fitch as he slammed him into a wall, knocking the ax he had pulled from the wall display out of his hand. The second man reached for something along the weapons room displays, throwing it toward Raselin. A knife buried itself into his upper arm, causing him to cry out in pain.

"Look out!" Dov shouted, warning one of us. A spear flew past me, landing in a display of what I could only assume was something that was meant to restrain people during torture. It clattered into it, knocking the display down.

Metal crashed to the floor, bouncing in all directions as Fitch pushed the soldier back into the displays against the wall. I wheeled around to see who needed help as Shadoe helped Raselin.

"Don't move," Eden said, her words precise and calculated. She held her knife out at Canton, circling slowly like a wolf looking at its enemy.

He laughed nervously.

"Now, now, Mrs. Baer. Do you really think you hold any power here?" He held up his hands as if trying to appease an upset child.

"I do," she answered. Berwyn shifted to glance at her.

"There's..." He scanned the room quickly. "Oh, Mrs. Baer, there's only eight of you here. I don't know how you got in, but you certainly have no chance of making it out of here alive. Even if you do hold me hostage, my men far outnumber you."

"That's where you're wrong, Canton." Dov called from across the room. "You're men aren't here."

Another snap followed by a loud cry and a painful whimper signified the last of his soldiers losing control to us. Canton looked around nervously.

"You've won for the moment, but moments only last so long, young Baer."

Fitch moved to pick up the shackles that had been thrown to the floor during the struggle. We had brought rope to tie them with, but it seemed less effective now. We began binding the soldiers, chaining them to the heavy pieces of equipment in the corners. Raselin, Fitch and Shadoe moved everything around them, isolating each man in a separate place.

"Here." Canton held out his hands. "I surrender."

His self-preservation skills were on par with the skills of his torturer: unquestionable.

Eden, Silas, Dov, Berwyn, and I surrounded him, forming a half circle in front of him. He eyed us, waiting for us to strike. His face changed when he noticed Berwyn.

"The great Berwyn Baer. We meet at last." He chuckled, tormenting Berwyn. "As you know, I've met your *beautiful* wife and kid brother…"

Berwyn stepped forward, ready to hit him.

"No, Baer." Shadoe's voice cut through the room as viciously as his barbed knife had through one of the soldier's arms. "It's my turn."

Shadoe stepped toward us, daring Berwyn to fight him.

"Out. Auluria and I have work to do." He challenged Berwyn and Dov to argue. "Stand guard."

Raselin nodded, walking over to put a hand on Berwyn's arm.

"Let him," he whispered. "Let him do what we cannot."

Berwyn hated backing down, his temper radiating across his movements in stiff, angry motions. Silas turned Eden, convincing her to go. Berwyn followed her out.

"Don't hurt him," Dov warned Shadoe before leaving. He held my gaze, asking me to walk out with him.

When the room was empty of anything but Canton's men chained to walls, Shadoe stepped forward. Canton sat in the center of the room, fiddling with the shackles Fitch had placed on his wrists before he left. His legs tangled in his robe, making him sit awkwardly while he watched us.

I waited for Shadoe to give me an indication of what we would be doing since he couldn't torture Canton. After a long time—an intimidation tactic he used to throw Canton off—he nodded to one of the soldiers. He was the least injured of all the men, sitting directly to Shadoe's right.

My heart raced as Shadoe took careful steps toward the man, maintaining eye contact with the magistrate.

"Up." He instructed the man.

He scrambled to his feet, stooping because the chain holding him in place wasn't long enough to stand upright.

"Not a sound." Shadoe whispered in the man's ear, but I knew his words were for me as he held my gaze.

The man whimpered as Shadoe brought his knife up the side of his arm, quietly brushing the metal against his skin to terrify him. I waited for Shadoe to draw blood, slicing off a layer of his arm. I knew Canton had to be as mortified as I was, but the thin layer of skin never fell to the floor, because, instead, Shadoe suddenly raised the knife to the man's throat and slowly dragged it across.

Blood pooled out in a dripping line. Canton gasped but I couldn't look away. It felt like a year before Shadoe dropped the man to the ground, sliced so deeply that I couldn't save him.

I gaped, shoulders shaking in horror.

"Not a word," Shadoe instructed before striding over to Canton.

My eye stayed on the dead soldier until I realized how dangerously close Shadoe had moved next to Canton.

"Shadoe!" I prayed my voice would halt him. Instead, it spurred him on.

He walked within feet of the man. Canton cowered to the ground, holding a shaking hand out to protect himself as the other soldiers gasped in fear for their leader. Shadoe watched him closely. He stopped quickly, convincing both of us that Canton was about to suffer.

Whipping a hand out, he threw his knife at the man across the room. Canton paled even more as he realized the knife had been thrown over his shoulder at one of his men. He blanched as the guard toppled over, the others crying out, begging for leniency.

Before I could reach him, Shadoe lashed out again, knives flying so quickly I didn't have time to look back from the target before the next had struck. All six men bled from chests, abdomens or faces.

Canton nearly passed out, the only thing reviving him was Shadoe's hand as he struck him.

"Oh no, you don't get to leave yet," Shadoe said. He knelt down to whisper instructions in his ear.

A man stirred; a survivor.

I rushed to him. Knowing not to pull out the blade, I tore off my uniform jacket and wrapped it around, attempting to slow the bleeding. I grappled for the beads around my neck, praying it would save him, or at least give him the ability to last until Necesta could help.

I heard Shadoe in the background as I spoke to the man, telling him what I was doing. Canton whimpered, squirming at Shadoe's proximity as he told him what happened to Justice Kenton and his other men in our custody.

"Yes, yes, I understand!" he yelped, surprising me. I jumped, knocking into the man.

It was as if I was breathing again, oxygen filling my lungs as I realized the carnage I sat in. A man was dying in my hands. Five others lay as sacrifices to our mission in the mere minutes the rest of the team had been outside.

"Berwyn!" I screamed, still holding onto the bloody mess of a man at my feet.

The door slammed opened, Dov racing inside. The others entered behind him, pausing to see the horror that had befallen the room. Six sets of eyes blinked, processing the scene.

"How?" Berwyn asked slowly, not sure if he could trust his eyes.

"I need help." I pocketed the necklace until I could put it back on, Silas rushing to my side as Dov and Berwyn approached Shadoe with Raselin and Fitch backing them up.

"Eden," I begged, nodding for her to check the other men. She scrambled forward, nearly tripping over herself to rush to them.

"Help me," I said quietly to Silas as the men argued in the center of the room. "We have to stop the bleeding."

Silas pushed down as the man groaned.

"Where is Necesta?" I asked, hoping she was nearby.

The man started to gurgle, and Silas shook his head.

"Go," he whispered, not wanting me to see the end.

I refused, staying where I was. Eden checked the man behind Silas, obviously not finding anyone alive.

"Eden." Silas's voice carried just enough to get her attention.

When she arrived, he nodded to me. Eden glanced at the dying man, realizing what our friend wanted. She dragged me away with the same force she used rescuing Dov. I couldn't escape as she forced me to the back of the room.

I watched Canton's back as he trembled in front of the men. Dov eyed me but held his ground in front of Canton and Shadoe. A battle of wills played out, but in the end, we could not change the fates of the dead men in the room.

Silas joined us and overwhelming sadness hit me so hard I couldn't catch my breath. Silas and Eden took my hands in theirs, comforting me.

Berwyn nodded to Fitch, who stepped forward and lifted Canton to his feet, a sobbing mess. He nodded at every instruction, doing exactly what he was told to do. He flinched when Shadoe looked at him.

I didn't realize I had tears streaming down my face until they were gone, Berwyn, Raselin, and Shadoe following behind Fitch. Dov rushed over to us, dropping to his knees in front of me.

"Auluria." He wrapped me in his arms, pulling me to his chest as I cried.

I sensed Eden squirming, uncomfortable with emotions. Dov let me cry and I soon found myself mourning more than just the loss of the man who I couldn't save.

When I looked up, tears were in Dov's eyes too. I reached out to hold him again, wrapping my arms tightly around his neck. He murmured soft things in my ear as I looked between Eden and Silas, realizing it was the first time we had been together like this since the last time we were in Canton's dwelling.

I rose, Dov standing with me. Reaching out, I pulled Silas to my side. Eden wrinkled her nose, questioning my change in demeanor.

"We beat him," I said softly, eyes drifting from Silas, to Eden, to Dov.

When it clicked, Eden joined us, her body language changing completely. She put a hand on Dov's shoulder before both of the boys pulled her in.

"We did." Dov grinned. We had beaten Canton. We had all survived.

"But now the real work begins," Silas reminded us. "We survived him once, but now we have to survive the Society."

"And whatever torture we endured here before will be nothing compared to what we're about to go through," Eden added harshly.

"Are we ready for this?" I asked, refusing to relinquish my hold on Dov and Silas.

"We have to be," Eden said.

"We have Canton now," Dov reminded us. "Whatever Shadoe did, he is now in control. I'd say we have a pretty good chance of getting through at least the next part of this."

"We should go make sure they gave our men the signal to sweep the grounds," I commented, realizing we had left Berwyn, Raselin, Fitch, and Shadoe to handle everything.

"She makes a point." Silas nodded to Dov, smirking.

"Indeed, she does." He smiled at his friend before ducking his head back to me.

"Oh get over yourselves." Eden pushed Dov, releasing herself from the circle. He crashed into me, sending us stumbling back.

Silas was concerned for a second until we got our footing before he laughed at us.

"*She's* got a point *too.*"

"You're just giving me more incentive to find you a girlfriend, Silas," I teased. "If you've been reduced to agreeing with Eden, then it's definitely time to find you new people to hang out with.

"Shut up." Eden shook her head at me and tried to glare, not quite convincingly enough. Eden was starting to lose her ability to stay icy toward me.

Dov wrapped his arm around my waist and we walked toward the door.

Canton slouched in the corner, wrapping his arms around his legs pressed tightly against his chest. Like a cornered rabbit, his eyes darted from one person to the next, assessing their threat level.

We ignored him as Talley reported back to us. Our people had made it inside, neutralizing the few soldiers that remained on the grounds. They patrolled the area, ensuring Canton had no friends to save him. We took turns peering over to make sure he wasn't trying anything, though the chains on his wrists and feet gave us a certain assurance.

"We'll keep him quiet for a few days. No one will think anything of it if they don't see him for three days," Berwyn said, formulating a plan.

"And after that?" Raselin asked, wondering what we would use the man for to convince people he was acting of his own free will.

"After that, he will have his own personal guard helping him." Berwyn nodded to Shadoe. "You can never be too careful these days, especially with all the rebels breaking out of prison."

"Berwyn?" I realized something. "Do you think they'll question that? I mean, Canton has lost *all* of us...more than once. The only one he actually managed to stop was Lowell. He lost Dov *twice*. Don't you think the Society is going to have something to say about that?"

"Probably. We'll handle that when it gets here. For now, it just lends credibility to the fact that he wants a personal guard to follow him around." He turned, raising his voice to the man in the corner. "Doesn't it?"

Canton looked up and nodded. At least he was cooperating.

"I think it's time we find out a little more about what he knows." Raselin said. "Like if the Society has been questioning his abilities."

Arin stepped forward, walking menacingly toward Magistrate Canton.

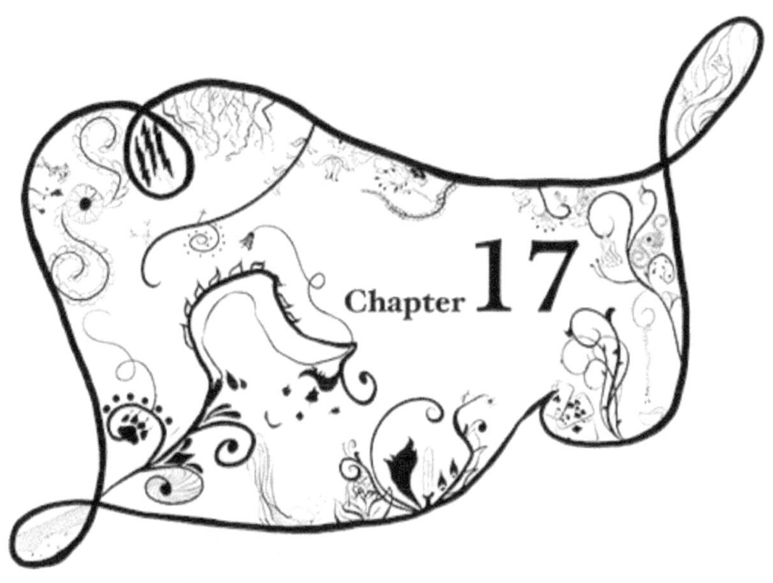

Chapter 17

"Sir, there's something wrong outside." Reed ran into the room an hour later.

"What do you mean?" Dov asked, rising from the chair in the study where he was pouring over Canton's record books.

"I don't know. Something is happening in the courtyard. There are no soldiers."

"What?"

"There are no Society men outside. Everything is empty. It's never empty out there. Everything is closed up tight, and since it's Canton's men outside, we thought we should get you first." Reed tried to catch his breath.

"Have you found Berwyn yet?"

"No, you're the first one I found."

Dov nodded, motioning me to follow.

"Go find Berwyn, Raselin, and Shadoe and have them meet us by the entrance to the south courtyard."

Reed raced out the door ahead of us.

"Silas," Dov called once we were in the hallway.

"In here." A voice came from a few doors down.

Dov paused at the door where our friend was searching the room and explained what was happening. Silas set down the papers he was riffling through and followed.

"Dov, over here." Gregory waved us over to a window once we exited the stairs.

He stepped back, giving us space to see.

"Do you see anything?" I asked, squinting to make sure I didn't miss any sign of movement or life.

It was quiet. Far *too* quiet for the Society. Had they found out?

"Missing something?" a jovial voice asked. It was exactly how Lowell would have spoken had he been there.

"Wallace?" Dov asked as we turned.

He was surrounded by a group of his men. Jake found me in the crowd and grinned. Marty, likely still learning to cope after his loss, was nowhere to be found.

"Little Baer," he greeted Dov. "You really didn't think I wouldn't find out about this, did you?"

"Why are you here, Wallace?" Dov growled as he stepped forward.

Henry, Ben, and Carter filed behind Dov and Silas, ready to assist. I was getting a little tired of Marty and Jake's crew.

"Where are the soldiers?" Dov demanded, holding his ground even in the face of Wallace's intimidating weapons.

"Dead." Wallace shrugged. "They were in the way. You left all of your men inside, so it was easy to pick off the few that maintained the grounds. You didn't do your math right, tiny Baer."

He must have hidden the bodies out of view from the mansion windows. I wondered where that meant he had concealed them.

"Wallace." Berwyn rushed down the stairs, ready to face his enemy. "Why are you here?"

"Berwyn," he leered. "So nice of you to join us. I imagine by now you have Canton under your control. I want you to give him to me."

"No." Berwyn looked amused. Crossing his arms, he added, "Why on earth would I do that?"

Wallace beamed as two of his men stepped out from the back of the crowd. They held Anetta and Marjorie, arms behind their backs. The women struggled to free themselves as the men clamped dirt-covered hands over their mouths to keep them from talking.

Anetta struggled wildly, catching my gaze. Her eyes kept darting to Marjorie and then back to me, trying hopelessly to communicate. Knives were held to their throats by the men assisting their captors, making it impossible to struggle too much. Marjorie flinched as the man stepped closer, her red hair falling in her face like it used to when Shadoe had to save me from countless dinners with Lowell and his friends.

Shadoe burst into the room, assessing the scene. Anger washed over his face when he saw Wallace occupying the room, darkness trembling through his every step. When he noticed Wallace was holding our people captive, a flicker of fear crossed over his face, melting into deeper hatred for the man. He stopped where he stood, waiting.

"That's what I thought," Wallace proclaimed victoriously. "Now, I see that you're trying to take control of the Society, and I admit, none of us alone have the numbers for that. So, I understand your little plan here, but I don't like being left out."

His voice changed from jovial to cold and dangerous.

"Now, you're going to go get Canton and bring him here. You will work *with* me and support *my* plan for this, or we'll kill your people. Not just these two, but all of them. My men are hiding all over this mansion. They'll never see us coming."

"How did you get your men in here without anyone seeing?" Shadoe challenged.

"Wouldn't you like to know?" Wallace sneered. "Now where is he?"

"Not one of our people would ever let you near Canton," Berwyn refused.

"No? Then how did I get in, Berwyn?" Wallace waved his arms around. "If your security is so good that you believed the Society couldn't get in, how did I do it?"

We all realized at the same moment that we had a spy in our midst. *But who?*

Just then Anetta stomped on the foot of her captor, causing him to pitch forward with her. The man with the knife leapt back as they lurched forward, barely nicking Anetta's neck and shoulder, just enough to see little bubbles of blood prick through her skin. She threw her blond head backwards, a flash of white, as she slammed into her captor's face.

"Marjorie!" she yelped to her friend.

I started to rush forward to help them as Anetta toppled onto the ground. She kicked out at the man, trying to knock him over.

"No, Auluria!" she screamed at me, panic in her voice.

Before I could reach her, Marjorie was free. She rushed to her friend, bending low. She held a knife in her hand.

Anetta's eyes were wild as the redhead held the blade to her already bloody neck. I froze.

"What is this?" Locust asked from his place behind Shadoe as he surveyed the scene.

"Marjorie is a spy," I responded quietly, wondering how I had never seen it. I found my voice, demanding information. "When?"

"Always," she sneered, no longer the flirtatious ladder-climber I had always known her to be. "You don't honestly think I would have hung around Lowell all that time without a purpose, do you?"

"Flirting your way to power seemed like a pretty good goal."

"It *did* seem that way, didn't it?" She laughed like it was all a joke. "Wallace is pretty good about picking his spies."

"Lowell took care of you. So has Shadoe. And the Baers have never hurt you. Why turn on us?" I asked, hoping to find a way to break her and free Anetta.

"Oh, little girl. You're wrong there. Speaking of which, let's make a little trade." She pulled Anetta to her feet.

Anetta's face was pulled tight as she raged inside against the woman she once trusted. I willed her to stay calm.

"Dov Baer," she turned to address the youngest Baer leader. "Your life for hers."

"No," I yelped unintentionally.

"Fine," Dov said, stepping forward. It was remarkable how good he looked in the Society's uniform. It seemed perfectly streamlined for his body. "Let her go."

Anetta tried to get his attention with a small shake of her head but he ignored her. He stepped forward slowly, trying not to spook Wallace's men.

"Let her go."

"Why him?" I snapped. "Take me instead. You've never liked me. If you want to make a point, make it with me."

"I don't want you, Auluria, but make no mistake, I'll come for you later. Funny, I have a feeling that Lowell wouldn't mind one bit." She laughed, enjoying herself. "But right now, I want *him* to die."

Jake stepped forward ready to assist. Moving to Marjorie's side, he took control of Anetta, in a move I hoped would give her a better chance of escape.

"Thank you, lamb," she said to Jake, almost adoringly, before turning to Dov. "Do you know who I am?"

"No," Dov said, not pretending.

"Look closer," she instructed.

Wallace looked amused as he watched the scene.

"No, no, big brother," he sang when he saw Berwyn start to inch forward, forcing him to hold his ground.

Dov studied the girl, trying to puzzle out who she was. When it clicked, his face fell.

"Oh, and he figured it out!" Wallace shouted, as if it were a game. "Your turn, Berwyn. Have a go!"

"No," Eden said in disbelief, understanding before her husband.

"That's bad," Silas whispered.

I shot him a questioning look, pleading for an answer.

"Wallace sent *her* to *us* and sent *you* to Lowell. He was playing us both."

I felt like I had been kicked as I realized Dov was talking about the girl that had been sent to win him over before I came along. It was the same girl who was discovered and sent back to Wallace's men, where she died from her interrogation. She was the entire reason Marty and Jake came after us so mercilessly.

"And here we thought we were special," Berwyn growled.

"When your sister left us," Dov addressed her, hands up to prove he wasn't being aggressive, "she was fine. She was very much alive. Wallace is the one that hurt her."

"Oh, I know," Marjorie said. Taking a step back, she moved her hand sharply behind her, digging her knife into Wallace's stomach.

His eye grew wide as he realized what was happening. Falling to his knees, his men all rushed forward to help. Marjorie stepped forward, nodding to Jake who was willing to turn his back on his leader to get revenge for the girl he had cared about.

"But he's not the only one who will pay." She lunged forward at Dov, attempting to cut him.

Dov moved quickly, grasping her wrist before she could bring her knife down. She fought, pulling his hair to whip his head around. Using her head, she crashed into Dov's face, making him gasp. She clawed at the hand holding her wrist.

Berwyn reached them first, assisting his brother. Everyone else rushed forward, engaging with Wallace's men. Anetta grappled with Jake until I arrived. Having had enough with the man, I didn't hold back. He lay unconscious on the floor, badly injured by the time Berwyn and Dov had Marjorie under control.

"Are you okay?" Anetta asked, kicking Jake once for good measure.

"I'm fine. Are you—" My words faded as she ran at Marjorie who was kneeling on the ground in front of the Baers.

"How could you?" Anetta screamed, accosting her former friend. She ranted about how Lowell protected them, how they were friends, and how she had trusted her.

Everyone gave her a moment to handle her feelings. She got in a few good punches before Dov dragged her back.

"Enough," he said quietly, allowing the older girl to collapse against him as Marjorie screamed about her sister.

He made Eden take a sobbing Anetta from him, making her uneasiness show as she patted the girl's back. Her eyes caught mine, begging for help. I continued to guard Jake, leaving her responsible for the crying woman.

Dov knelt down in front of Marjorie.

"I'm sorry," he apologized. "I know you don't believe this, but I was heartbroken when I found out what they had done to her.

"I tried to protect her and I couldn't. If I could have changed what happened, I would have. If I could have taken the punishment for her, I would have, but there was nothing I could have done."

Shadoe joined him, kneeling beside them. Fear raced through me, knowing what he was capable of.

"You betrayed Lowell," he started.

It was the worst sin she could commit.

"Shadoe…" Dov cautioned.

He stared at her as I counted his breaths. One, two, ten, fifteen. He waited long enough to scare her. She was no fool.

"Lock her up," Shadoe finally said, standing. "Take the others."

Devin had arrived, helping to stop any uprising Wallace's men had considered pushing after the death of their leader. Silas confirmed he was no longer a problem before instructing his friends to take the new prisoners to the cells. With all the extra bodies, we'd be out of space before long.

Anetta stumbled back to me as Carter and Ben picked Jake up off the floor. They carried him out of the room with the others.

"I should have known."

"You couldn't have. Even Lowell didn't know. You honestly think any of us could have guessed it if Lowell hadn't?"

"I've lost Lowell. I've lost my closest friend," she lamented.

"You still have all of us, Anetta. We'll be your friends. And we still have a mission to carry out, so don't give up yet," I reminded her.

"We have a problem," Eden's voice rang out, forcing all of us to look toward the door.

"Hoods!" Dov hissed as he saw what was approaching.

I peered out from behind the mantle, the fabric once again hiding my hair. I walked quickly to fall into line; the perfect soldier doing their daily tasks around the mansion.

"Where is Magistrate Canton?" a frantic soldier asked.

The foyer was filled with panicked men. They searched for someone to address.

"In his study." Raselin responded. "He is not to be disturbed. What is it?"

"Bodies." The scared soldier answered. "They're all dead."

"Who?" Berwyn inquired.

"The men outside. They're all dead. The courtyard is empty. We found the bodies while on patrol and brought the men back. Is everything okay inside?"

Wallace's disruption had cost us our plan. The soldiers were about to discover what we had done.

"Everything is fine." Raselin guided the conversation. "Nothing is out of place."

The door slammed open, revealing an army of Society men. They jostled in the door.

"Everything is fine." Raselin raised his hands. "We've already patrolled the mansion, there is nothing out of place."

Canton appeared at the top of the stairs, hiding behind the banister. He stood taller than I had seen him since we arrived. The man looked calm as he placed his hands on the railing.

"Everything is fine. Stand your ground outside. Look for the rebels who did this on the grounds," Canton ordered.

He shifted, revealing Justin standing behind him. I assumed he had him at knifepoint.

They waited until most of the soldiers had returned outside. I saw Justin whispering to him, giving him direction. He had risked bringing Canton in front of his men, but it had paid off.

The soldier who addressed us began to argue, unwilling to let it go so easily. He grabbed a hold of Raselin, trying to force him to listen. Raselin tossed him off, sending him into the group of men that stayed with him. They pushed him back, angry at being overlooked in the situation.

The man swung at Raselin, one of his coworkers swinging toward

Berwyn. The soldiers started to yell as Canton was backed off of the landing, presumably to go back to where we had him locked up.

A soldier stumbled forward, crashing into Anetta. She knocked into me, swiping my hood off. I rushed to cover myself, but it was too late.

"It's her," one of them gasped, as visions of our plan to release the camps, take on the Society, and free our enemy countries on the other side of the wall flashed through my mind as quickly as memories of Dov had when I was waiting to hang. Everything slipped away.

We had been discovered, and no matter what we did now, the Society had the upper hand.

They attacked.

ACKNOWLEDGMENTS

Two down, one to go. Sorry I hit you with a cliffhanger again, but did you really expect anything less from me at this point? You know I'm kind of mean to characters and readers!

In all honesty, there were some things I didn't see coming in this one, and I'm happily surprised by the appearance of a few new characters. *Oh, do I have plans* for them! I hope you enjoyed meeting them as much as I did.

The thing I love most about this book is that we really see Auluria grow into her new role. In Golden, Dov was this strong, selfless character that did whatever he had to do to save the people he cared about, and Auluria had a bit of trouble making some of her decisions in the first book. Dov's selflessness clearly brushed off on Auluria in Locked as she fights to save not only Dov, but an entire country from the Society. I love seeing Auluria really step into her own in this story.

Don't worry, we still have one more piece of this story to go and I have some major things planned for this ending. Get ready, this is going to be the wildest ride of them all. Here's to the finale!

Thank you to Alexis, my amazing interior artist. You never cease to amaze me with your talent, hard work, and creativity. I appreciate you more than words can say. Thanks, yet again, for being the first to read my new babies. I love when you gush over my characters and help make sure everything is just right!

Special thanks to Awnna Marie Evans, my stunning editor. Words cannot express how grateful I am to have you in my life, both as a friend and as a colleague. I appreciate you helping me to *level up*!

Thank you to Lyssa Chiavari for your friendship, guidance, and all your hard work on the beautiful formatting for the printed book. I truly appreciate you.

Thank you to Sissy and Jess for all of your help! This story wouldn't be what it is without you!

Major shout out to my beautiful Elite Street Team—you all make life so much better! I'm so grateful for your friendship and all your hard work! Danna, Yentl, Jess, Sissy, Alexis, you ladies are the best!

Thank you to my awesome Street Team—your help, encouragement, and involvement are so appreciated! You rock!

Of course, special thanks to you, dear reader, for sticking with me on this journey. Auluria and Dov's story has always been so important to me and I couldn't be more grateful that you're experiencing it with me. I can't wait to wrap this up with you in the third book. Edge is going to be interesting to say the least. Let's do this!

EDGE

BOOK THREE OF THE GOLDEN TRILOGY

One spark can light your entire universe on fire. One choice, one action, one word can give permission to change the way a life is lived.
To those of you who are unintentional world changers-spark the world for good.

My story ends like this:

Having been discovered, Goldilocks is forced to fight for her life, clawing her way away from the enemy. With her new family by her side, she runs into the war to free her people, but not everyone will survive. As she discovers that every choice she makes, she will be held accountable for, she must do everything in her power to survive the consequences of her actions.

But the stories of Goldilocks and the Three Baers never mentioned just how deadly my story really was. No one ever said I would lose people on both sides of the war. They always forget to mention that I would have to do horrifying things just to survive and protect the people that I love.

My name is Auluria, but the world knows me as Goldilocks, and I won't stop until the entire Society has heard my name and taken a stand…one way or another. The Society will fall.

<h1>Chapter 1</h1>

MY FINGERS FAILED ME, TANGLING IN MY HAIR. EVERYTHING WAS muffled as I struggled to hide myself. Voices echoed inside my head, but I couldn't make out what they were saying.

Suddenly, I was snapped forward, jolted back to reality. Fixing my hood no longer mattered. Anetta tried to support me as I crashed into her. I came alive, realizing that we were under attack.

The Society men lunged toward us in the foyer of the mansion. I was suddenly grateful Canton had been led away before the soldiers realized who I was. Justin had good timing.

The noise of the fight dulled over the loud tearing of fabric. A red tapestry boasted a long tear, threatening to topple from its place on the wall. The ripping cloth drew my attention when it shouldn't have, making me involuntarily turn. A rough hand on my shoulder forced me to reach for the knife resting on my hip, its jagged edges begging to be used.

I sliced the man's arm, silently hoping that it was the worst damage I would have to do. Blood bubbled up on his skin as his eyes grew narrow and fiery. The man's nails dug into me in what I assumed would end in yet another scar on my body which was already marred by so many tales.

Gregory took the man down just as I drew back to attack once more. He nodded at me solemnly; the first time I'd ever seen him anything less than flirtatious.

"Behind you," he nodded.

I spun on my heels to confront whatever waited for me, my hair splaying out with my movements. Instead of being confronted with an attack, I found Shadoe grappling with a soldier.

"Here," I announced just loudly enough for my former handler to hear me.

I stepped beside him, taking a defensive position. Before I could help, Shadoe leaped forward and snapped the man's neck. Shock waved over me in the two seconds between the dead man hitting the floor and another soldier rolling over my shoulder as I ducked, tossing him effortlessly as he attacked.

Shadoe looked impressed as I stood back up, having felt the man's approach and flipped him over. I turned away from Shadoe to see where else I could help and was immediately confronted with Dov's eyes, ten feet away. They were wide and surprised, but that same brilliant shade of deep blue.

I smiled to let him know I wasn't hurt, but it immediately faded as a soldier approached him. I jerked my head to the side to give him warning before I raised my hands, using my left arm to steady myself, and released my knife at the soldier. It embedded itself in the man just before Dov attacked.

"Auluria!" Silas shouted a warning, looking beyond me. "*Anetta.*"

I followed his gaze to where Anetta was fighting off two soldiers and failing. One grabbed her around the waist, attempting to lift her off the ground. Eden launched herself at the second man, kicking him so hard in the hip that I thought I heard it crunch. He toppled into a man beside him, taking them both to the ground. Shadoe and Locust appeared out of nowhere, slicing the soldiers' throats.

I ran to Anetta as she kicked in the air. She bit down on the man's hand, making him shriek and swear. I pulled an extra knife from my boot, plunging it into her captor's arm. The blond fell to the floor, bouncing up as soon as she hit the stone. Pulling her own knife, she drove it into the soldier's leg. His boot helped to protect him from her attack. He grabbed Anetta's hair, ripping it out from under the hood that only partially covered her head.

Locust—having finished off the men Eden had kicked down—stood up and took three wide steps forward. His hand dug into the soldier's wrist as he held him in place. His grip forced the man to release Anetta. He pulled back, preparing to hit the man as I turned.

"Fancy seeing you here." The low voice sent tingles up my spine.

The knife glistened in his hand as it moved toward me. The blood had been wiped off, though only so much could be removed from the strange, jagged blade without a proper cleaning. My sight traveled up the length of his arm to his face.

"Your knife, my lady." Dov smiled before growing serious. "Are you okay, Auluria?"

I took the blade from him, heat exploding through my hand when our skin touched. Tucking my backup weapon away in my boot, I opted to keep the knife Shadoe had provided for us.

"So far," I replied. "You?"

"Yeah," he mumbled before another soldier moved toward us.

I moved behind him, taking a position to cover his back. Hearing Dov fighting without being able to see him made me slow as I focused on what *he* was doing. I forced myself to block him out of my thoughts in order to protect him.

I kicked a soldier causing a sharp pain to crawl up my ankle where I had injured it before the attack on the mansion. I sucked in a deep breath, trying to control the burn creeping through my leg.

The soldier came at me again, yelling something I blocked out. I lowered my stance just enough to get a secure footing, putting as much weight as I could on my uninjured leg without throwing myself off balance. When he moved, I elbowed him in the nose. Blood gushed down his face.

He stepped forward again, undeterred by my hit. I prepared to strike, but suddenly, he fell at my feet. Silas lowered his weapon, having used it to hit the man in the head, knocking him out.

"Miss me?" he asked as he turned our two-person team into a trio.

"Nice to see you haven't died," I could hear the grin in Dov's voice as he called over his shoulder.

"Reinforcements are here," Silas informed us.

I glanced around, noticing that most of our team was in the foyer. Berwyn had made his way to Eden and Anetta, who appeared to have formed a partnership during the fight. Ben and Carter must have finished securing Wallace's men if they were available to join the combat, leaving us one less thing to worry about during the battle.

"You all okay?" Raselin yelled from a few feet away as he fought with a soldier.

I stepped ahead, darting my good leg out to sweep the Society man's feet out from under him. He crashed forward, nearly taking Raselin down with him. A tooth bounced across the ground, looking like a horrifying white bug skittering across the forest floor. I heard every ding and scrape it made as it moved.

Raselin nodded and shrugged when the man didn't get up.

"Works for me," he added.

"Shadoe!" Dov warned loudly.

"Shadoe, no!" I echoed when I saw that my former fiancé was doing as much damage as he had when he threatened Canton in the weapons room. Bodies littered the floor. "We need them."

Nikko took out another Society soldier before looking to Shadoe for direction. I searched for Ella but didn't see her in the room. I tried not to think about what mission Shadoe had sent her on that would have prevented her from joining the fight.

Shadoe nodded, knowing he had to play by the rules in a room filled with people who would not tolerate his deadly behavior. Berwyn's people and Raselin's group would work together to outnumber Shadoe's team if anything were to happen.

"Give up now and you won't get hurt." Berwyn's voice filled the room, giving the remaining Society men an option.

Most of the soldiers relented and stopped fighting, knowing they were outnumbered. One man rushed forward, refusing to back down. He launched himself at Devin. I leaped forward, despite knowing I would not be able to reach him in enough time to help. Devin tossed the man over his shoulder, protecting his newly-healed arm. He kicked the man's arm, making him cringe into himself. Carter stooped down to bind the man's wrists behind him.

I found Silas and Dov giving me questioning looks when I turned back to them, having only made it a few feet forward to help Devin.

"You didn't actually think you were going to help that situation, did you?" Eden scoffed from behind me.

"I was going to try," I growled back at her, knowing she wasn't being malicious, but also not caring of her intentions.

"Get these men taken care of," Berwyn announced. "Quickly. We still have to handle the men outside."

"This isn't over yet," Raselin added.

We quickly scrambled to determine who was awake, unconscious, or dead. The men who gave themselves up were bound and taken to the cells. I walked a man down the dark corridors with Eden and her charge as Dov and Silas carried an unconscious man behind us.

The cells were as bad as I remembered. The chill seeped into my bones as the hollow silence filled every space in my body. The last time I was there, I was meant to die, and my cousin, Lowell, had been the one to sentence me. The walls held the memory of my last conversation with my cousin.

Eden tensed next to me, her gait becoming stiff. She pushed the soldier forward with sharp fingers to his back between his shoulder blades. I forbade my muscles from tightening around my captive's hands; he didn't need to know my terror.

Dov and Silas looked less concerned about being in the space. I assumed they had been down here since our arrival. Dov had spent so much time in the mansion during his captivity that it was practically his second home. It didn't seem to affect them to be back in the cells... or they hid it well.

"Right," Dov instructed as we neared the end of the hall.

We turned, finding another series of hallways.

"Take the first one," Silas said, his voice strained under the weight of the unconscious man he was helping to carry.

We steered our charges down the walkway and found ourselves in an entirely new wing of cells.

"I didn't realize this was down here," Eden mumbled.

The man in front of me started to say something. My nails dug into his wrists silencing him before he could start.

We locked the men up, keeping them bound to prevent them from helping each other inside the cells. Dov and Silas checked all the locks on the prison doors before we left.

"We didn't either until we explored once we got in," Silas explained, "once we were away from the Society men."

"*I* didn't even see all of this," Dov commented as I slipped an arm around his waist, tucking myself under his arm as we walked through the muted gray lights of the cell passageways.

Shadoe and Raselin walked toward us, carrying another unconscious man. I expected Shadoe to try to talk to me, but instead, he locked eyes with Dov. They held each other's gaze until we passed, continuing to the foyer to see if we needed to move more Society bodies.

Several of our people filed past us, moving the Society prisoners to their new living quarters deep below the magistrate's mansion. I watched for my friends as we moved.

"You okay?" Dov whispered quietly in my ear, his lips tangling in my hair.

I nodded, not trusting myself to answer out loud. His hand tightened against my hip, pulling me closer. I leaned toward him, resting my head on his shoulder for a moment before stepping into the foyer.

Berwyn noticed us as we stepped into the light, motioning us to join him. Eden hurried to take her spot by her husband. His fingers slipped around her hand quietly at their sides so that only our tight circle could see.

"We have control of the mansion again, but we're going to need to handle the soldiers outside," Berwyn guided the conversation, his angry tone ever-present. "We're going to have to use Canton to deal with the courtyard."

"Can we trust him?" Eden asked before I could open my mouth to speak.

"Where is he?" I followed up.

"Justin is still guarding him. Apparently, he got Canton to a cell and kept him ready in case we needed to use him to end the fight down here." Berwyn grimaced at the thought of coming so far only to play our hand before we were ready. "He's still with him…I'm assuming because he's thinking what we're all thinking—Shadoe will do something reckless."

"No surprise there." Silas and Dov murmured at the same time.

"What's the plan?" I asked, knowing I probably wouldn't like it. I wasn't fond of not knowing the next step. It reminded me too much of my time with Lowell.

"We're going to have to take Canton out and have him calm the courtyard." Dov took my hand, mirroring Berwyn and Eden. "And, once we've done that, we have to get a stronghold in the towns."

Dov glanced at Berwyn.

"One of us is going to have to go out and tell the people what is going on. They'll side with us, but right now, they have no idea what's going on here. Once we do that, then we can start to use Canton against the Society."

"And who is going to go out into the towns to do that?" I asked.

Dov's eyes shifted to me.

"No," I forbade it. "You are not going out there. Someone else can go."

"It has to be one of us," Dov tried to persuade me. "Berwyn can't go. He needs to stay here and lead everyone. If it can't be him, it has to be me."

"What if *I* go?" I insist, trying to find another way.

"No offense, Auluria," Silas interjected. "But even though people have heard about you, you still worked for Lowell, and Lowell is dead. They might not know which side you are on."

"Despite the fact that you did all this, babe, the famous Goldilocks is still not as well-known as the sons of Griz Baer." Dov grinned, teasing me.

"That's not fair."

"We can't all be famous, Auluria." Dov's eyes sparkled as much as they did the time we sat on the floor of his house, mending socks and fantasizing about taking on the Society soldiers.

"*Auluria* might not be famous, but Necesta has been awfully quick to start spreading tales of *Goldilocks*," Raselin said, sidling up to the group, running his fingers through his dark brown hair. "Don't underestimate her…she knows what she's doing."

"Which one?" Silas smirked.

"Both." Raselin leveled a glare at him, removing Silas's joking grin.

"The point is," Berwyn growled, "That we need to handle making Canton cooperate first."

"Are we considering letting Shadoe handle this?" Raselin asked with concern. "He seems to be the one the Magistrate fears, but do we really want to let him oversee Canton?"

"Do we have a choice?" I asked. I trusted him more than the others did, but I still didn't like what Shadoe was turning into.

"Can Justin handle it? He did well before the fight." Silas suggested.

"He can handle it," Dov, Raselin, and I all said in unison.

"The better question is whether we can afford to have Justin be Canton's handler and lose him for everything else."

"Would it be better to let Shadoe oversee Canton and let Justin help with the missions we're running?" Eden added, tucking a lock of hair back over her shoulder. It caught on the hood of her uniform as it lay on her back, leaving the strand of hair at a strange angle.

The group took a collective breath, puzzling out the best choice for the good of the team. It was quickly interrupted as Talley walked up.

"Whatever we're planning on doing, we need to do it now. The Society men outside are not going to wait any longer," she announced. "What's the strategy?"

The tall woman glanced at me, then to Raselin, looking for an answer. When we didn't speak, she turned to Berwyn.

"Well?" she prompted.

"Do we have a plan yet?" Devin bounded up next to his sister, looking out of breath.

"Are you okay?" I asked as he leaned forward to calm his rapid breathing.

"Yeah, I just ran from Justin to find out what's going on."

"Is he okay up there with Canton?" Talley asked, concern filling her voice.

"He's fine. Canton is behaving. But Shadoe is up there, so we'd better get moving if you weren't the ones to send him."

Everyone turned, sprinting toward the flight of stairs. Deep red carpet covered the stair, so soft it felt like layers of moss piled on top of each other.

"Time to vote," Berwyn said. "Who do we leave in charge of Canton?"

"Justin." Eden cast her vote first.

"Justin," Talley added, assuming her vote counted as part of the leadership vote.

"Justin," Devin echoed a vote for his brother.

"Shadoe." I shocked the Hersh siblings into looking at me. "We need Justin elsewhere and this will give Shadoe something less destructive to do. Plus, Canton is already under his thumb. He's terrified of him."

"She makes a good point," Raselin nodded. "Shadoe."

"Shadoe." Silas grimaced.

Dov only sighed and nodded once.

"Shadoe," Berwyn finished the count.

"You're not moving him." Justin's voice rang out as we approached the room Canton was being held in.

"Get out of the way, Hersh. We don't have time for this." Shadoe threatened.

"You're not taking him until I have confirmation that he is really supposed to be moved," Justin argued.

"Are you really going to take me on?" Shadoe's strong voice filled the hallway.

"Enough," I shouted, still far enough away that I wouldn't be able to step between the men, even if I wanted to.

I rounded the corner to find Shadoe and Justin facing off, chest puffed out and standing at full height. Canton leaned against the corner as I peeked over Berwyn's tall shoulder. The magistrate looked defeated as he slumped against the wall, eyes bouncing back and forth between his captors. He perked up when he saw the top of my head peering at him from behind Berwyn.

"Stand down," Raselin said from alongside Berwyn. "Shadoe, we need you to handle the magistrate's announcement. Justin, you're working with these three."

He nodded to me, indicating Justin should follow us. My friend's eyes bounced from Raselin, to me, to his siblings, and back to me. I nodded, hoping he would cooperate.

Reluctantly, he stepped aside, moving toward the door. Shadoe turned toward Canton.

"Up," Shadoe commanded.

Canton scrambled to his feet, locking eyes with Shadoe, ready to obey.

"Excuse me," Justin said quietly, slipping through the door once Berwyn and Raselin had stepped inside to give Canton directions.

Devin and Justin traded a look. Talley looked unimpressed with her brother's decision to take on Shadoe.

"What's the plan?" Justin asked.

"You and Dov are leaving. Now," Eden said before anyone else could speak. "They're handling Canton and quelling the soldiers outside. You two are sneaking out while the men are distracted by the announcement and you're going to rally the townspeople. We need them on our side."

Justin nodded.

"And the rest of you?"

"We have things to do here. There really isn't time to explain. You need to go." Eden reached out and put a hand on his arm, pulling him into motion. Dov followed quickly behind.

It took everything inside of me to force myself not to argue. Dov needed to do this—it was the only rational way. I had to stay and keep Shadoe in check. I was the only one that could.

"We'll be back in a few hours," Dov whispered quietly. "I'm not that easy to get rid of."

He grinned before surprising me with a quick kiss.

"Don't let this get out of hand." He took my hand and placed it on his chest when we reached the door.

"I'll watch him," I assured him.

"Don't get caught," Talley said a few feet away. She patted her brother on the shoulder.

"Come on," Justin said, nodding to Dov. "Let's get moving before the announcement starts."

The two men slipped out the door into the bright light of day. The white light bounced off the mansion floor. The light colors reflected the white light harshly, temporarily adding a green haze to my vision as I watched the people I cared about disappear into the world.

"They'll be fine," Talley acted as the voice of reason. "They're both very good at this."

"Justin will watch out for Dov." I murmured, knowing that he would.

"He knows to watch for Dov's injuries. He's not quite back to himself yet. Besides, unlike the rest of you, Justin isn't well-known. He can blend in and watch, where Dov will likely be recognized. They'll make a good team."

"Auluria," Eden's voice echoed from the stairway. "Get up here!"

Chapter 2

"HAPPY?" SHADOE ASKED SARCASTICALLY.

"Yes," I responded as he came to a stop in front of me. He squared his feet with his shoulders and glared at me from behind crossed arms.

He watched me as if hoping I could guess what he wanted me to say. I didn't care enough to try.

Shadoe had forced Canton onto a balcony overlooking his soldiers. He quietly stood just behind the magistrate's shoulder, off to the side, acting as his personal guard. Every word was precisely spoken to planned perfection as the man convinced his minions to do his bidding. In the aftermath of his announcement, he cowered in the next room over under Devin's watch.

"What?" I shouted, demanding my handler say something as I looked up from the map I was studying.

He continued to stare for a moment before storming off. I considered going after him, but after everything that had happened that day, I needed a few minutes to myself.

The paper crinkled under my fingers as I gazed at it. My eyes traced the town lines. I followed the length of the Wall surrounding the Society, marking each place I thought we should begin the teardown process once we had defeated the Society. Liberating Raselin's country to the northeast would be the next thing we needed to do.

"Learning anything important?" Silas's voice frightened me.

Two deep breaths and I banished my shock, returning my shoulders to their normal position after gasping. Anetta smirked as she took a seat across from me at the table.

"We need to free the camps." I redirected.

"I know," Silas agreed.

Anetta shifted her focus to the window on the side of the room. Her eyes bounced slightly as she focused on something. I turned to glance outside. In the dark, small green lights flickered on and off.

"Didn't you see enough of those with Lowell?" I teased.

"I like fireflies." She shrugged.

Silas moved his chair closer to mine, leaning into my space to look at the map.

"Here," he pointed. "This is the route Dov would have taken. He's starting here, then here, and here."

His fingers traced along the towns, showing me where my boyfriend would be completing his mission. My gaze moved outward to the other towns. We needed a plan to reach them.

"The first step," Silas said as if reading my mind, "is to get control of the justices in these towns. If we can gain control there, we've got a shot."

"Once we handle that, we should be able to get at least two of the other magistrates," I added.

"And if we can get them, we've got them all. We know, we know." Anetta rolled her eyes, turning back from the scene outside the window. "But how do we get them?"

"Once we have the towns and the camps with us, it shouldn't be hard to do exactly what we did here." Silas looked up from the map briefly to address her.

"This one," I said, pointing at the piece of paper, making it crinkle again. "We need this one."

Silas inspected it.

"You're right," he said, making me grateful for Shadoe's training. "We need that one first. We have the best chance of getting in there unnoticed."

"But we also need the rest of them."

"Or at least most of them." Silas nodded. "We'll have to send out multiple teams."

"What are we going to do about Marjorie?" Anetta interrupted, demanding answers.

We both looked up, slightly surprised at her outburst.

"She'll stay locked up in the cells," I answered, "For now, anyway."

"But she *will* answer for this?" she pressed.

"She will. Just not today." I felt Silas's leg tense next to mine as he spoke. I bumped his foot with mine, assuring him he didn't need to prepare to stop Anetta from running down to the cells and taking her revenge on her former best friend.

"Just how do you plan on breaking into the camps?" She changed the topic.

"We have a few ideas," Silas said, glancing at me, telling me he and Dov already had a plan. "You probably won't like them."

It was light when I woke up, still early, but not early enough to be up before visibility entered the room. I moved the covers off my body, remaining warm for only a moment before the rush of air beat against my skin.

I looked back, the pillow re-inflated, erasing the dip where my head had been resting. I brought the covers back up over the top of the bed, something I hadn't had to do since fleeing the Baer's cabin. I paused, wondering what had become of their family home.

I moved to the curtains, drawing them back just enough to see outside. It was quiet out. A few Society soldiers stood at their posts, but nothing concerning. I half expected a war to be raging three floors below me as I looked past the curtains.

Turning back, the bed caught my attention. As a child, I had slept in a small bed at my aunt's house, though nothing like ones in the Magistrate's mansion. My aunt's house had been small and safe. The mansion was bigger than anything I had ever seen. All of the comforts of this life invaded the space, cloaked in deep reds. I wondered if red was the color of all of the magistrates or if Canton just had a thing for that hue.

I crept to the door, still cautious to stay quiet. I paused, listening at the door. After a moment, I turned the handle, peering into the hallway.

"Morning, Goldilocks," Nian said as he stepped into the hallway from the landing.

I raised an eyebrow.

"You should go downstairs," he waved his hand toward the door.

In his signature move, he reached up and brushed back his bangs. "There's food down there, and we've got a long day."

"Thanks," I answered, walking past him to the stairs.

The marble was cool against my hand as it glided over the banister. I pulled my hand away and raked it through my hair, trying to untangle it before I reached the bottom of the stairs.

I heard Dov and Silas talking before I walked into the dining room. They were seated at one end of the table, plates of food in front of them. Maps sat beyond the plates, toward the center of the far end of the table. Dov had a knife in his hand, slicing the apple that rested in his other palm.

They both looked up when I entered, Dov jumping to his feet. He grinned.

"Told you I'd be back."

"Yeah, yeah." I brushed him off with the wave of a hand, taking a seat next to him.

"I brought you a present." He handed a slice of apple to me.

"Just what I always wanted," I grinned as I bit into the slice.

"The present brought *herself*, thank you," a voice said behind me.

"Reyla!" I unintentionally yelped when I realized to whom the voice belonged.

"Sit," she commanded before I could rush to her. She slipped into the seat next to me. "The girls are with me. Dov figured we'd need some reinforcements for storming the camps."

I glanced at Dov, giving him a pleased look.

"It's less about needing our help getting in, of course," she teased, "and more about having other females to comfort those poor girls in the camps once we break them out."

"Good point," I said, accepting another apple slice from Dov. He leaned closer.

"The boys pretty much have everything covered," she added.

"Did you expect anything less from these two?" Katarina swayed into the room, making her way to the opposite side of the table. She took a seat by Silas as I beamed. The whole team was coming back together.

"Well, good morning, Sleeping Beauty," Justin walked in and caught sight of me. His head swung around taking in the sight of the newcomers. "Well, well. If it isn't the prettiest ladies from the Baer clan."

Grabbing an apple off the table, he rubbed it against his shirt as if to clean it. Katarina noticed appreciatively while Reyla bit back her smirk. Silas gave him a strange look as he sat next to Katarina. Justin eyed the maps. He turned to Dov, waiting for an explanation.

"Camps," Dov said by way of an explanation.

"I get to go too, right?" Justin prompted.

"Yes," Dov nodded. "And your brother and Talley, too, if they want. Fitch is coming as well."

"Shadoe?" I asked, risking a look up at Dov.

"That's up to him, I suppose." Dov shrugged. "He's going to have to decide what is more important."

"Does he know about this yet?"

"Yes, he found us on the way in."

Reyla leaned toward me, adding quietly, "You might want to go help him with that little decision."

Her eyes told me more than her words. I needed to go see Shadoe. I ducked my head, mumbling confirmation that I would help him work out what he needed to do behind the veil of my hair, blocking my face from the others.

Berwyn ambled into the room, eyeing the food we were all picking at.

"Nice that Canton had so much ready for us."

"He had a lot of people to feed," Silas replied.

"Don't forget, now *we* have to take care of all those people," Eden said, following Berwyn into the room. "Speaking of…has anyone checked on our visitors in the cells today?"

"Raselin is down there now. He took Arin and Fitch with him, so I'm assuming they're looking for information," Justin answered, leaning back in his chair. "I think Talley was on her way to check on them when I passed her in the hall."

"We need to leave quickly," Dov reminded us. "Not all of the teams can leave at once. The ones going to the camps on the edge of the Society need to leave immediately so we can strike at the same time."

"Berwyn and I worked out a list of the teams last night," Silas offered.

I glanced at him. It must have been after I had fallen asleep.

"Once Arin and Raslin are done with the interrogations downstairs, hopefully, we'll have a little more information about how to get into the camps. The only thing left is to talk to Canton." Berwyn's response sounded more like he was grumbling.

Dov subtly shifted closer to me. I liked having him back.

"We're going to the Wall," he whispered.

I nodded quietly, trying not to draw too much attention from the other people seated around the table. I picked up a piece of food and popped it into my mouth, not taking the time to taste it. I was pleased that I had confirmation that I wouldn't be held back to watch over Shadoe, should he end up remaining in the mansion to keep Canton under control.

We finished eating as Berwyn, Dov, and Silas ran over details of the mission. They'd have to do it again for the larger groups, but they used this time to work out the details with the inner circle. I found my hand in Dov's by the end of the meeting, resting against his knee under the table. I had to force myself to not lean my head against his shoulder.

Raselin, Talley, and Arin joined us, revealing what they had learned about the camps. The Society soldiers had proved helpful enough, giving us locations and details we needed to make decisions.

"Hello, Goldilocks," a voice crooned in my ear, making me jump. "Your friend needs to see you."

Necesta pulled back, taking a few strands of my hair along with her. They didn't detach from her sweater until I turned to face her, pulling them away.

"You too, Charming," she nodded that Dov should follow.

We stood, excusing ourselves from the meeting and followed Necesta out into the hallway. I noticed how strong she looked now that she wasn't trying to deceive her own community into thinking she was frail and helpless. She still walked with the weight of her maturity, but she acted at least ten years younger than the appearance she had projected when I had first met her. Even her posture was straighter than I had ever seen her stand on her side of the Wall.

"Your young friend has a choice to make, and I don't think he's making it well," Necesta explained. "You need to go talk some sense into him."

She glanced at Dov, looking him up and down.

"And she shouldn't be doing the convincing alone."

"Do you have a preference on whether he stays or goes?" I tried to withhold my smirk at Necesta's oversight on the matter.

"Whichever is best, dearie," she shrugged. "You know more about this situation than I do. I just don't want him to meltdown before a decision is even made. He looks like he's about to burn so hot that he will melt right into a puddle on the floor."

"Well, that can't be good," I mumbled, picking up the pace.

Ella glared at me as we approached. She was leaning against the doorframe, arms crossed harshly over her chest. Her hair sliced into the line of her arm, falling halfway between her shoulder and elbow in a vicious straight line. I had no doubt if she whipped her hair toward an oncoming enemy, it would decapitate them where they stood.

"Where is Shadoe?" I tried to keep the edge from my voice.

"With Nikko and Sherman," she huffed.

Refusing to let her try to intimidate me, I raised my eyebrow at her, mirroring her glare. She relented after a moment, nodding across and down the hall. Necesta paused to engage the girl in conversation while Dov followed me to the door.

The handle felt cold in my hand, threatening to send a tingling chill through my spine. I forced it down and swung the door open. All three men looked up, scowling at the sight of me, then looking downright murderous when Dov followed me into the room.

"Have you made a decision?" I asked.

"I get a choice?" Shadoe's voice teetered between anger and shock.

"Of course," Dov said. "You're a leader here too, Shadoe. We're all working together on this."

"You're just going to support me, whichever way I choose?" Shadoe challenged.

"On this, we are," Dov put his hand on the small of my back, creating a united front. I hoped it didn't set Shadoe off. "There are benefits and downfalls to both staying and going. You need to be the one to make this choice. Do you think you will help the group better if you stay and control Canton or if you come with us to help free the camps? It's up to you."

Shadoe stayed quiet for a moment, collecting his thoughts.

"I'm not sure yet."

Sherman looked like he wanted to say something, but out of loyalty to Shadoe, he remained quiet. I took that as my cue.

"Yes, you are," I softly prompted. "You know what you need to do...you just don't like it."

Shadoe flushed a shade of red.

"Shadoe, where do you need to be?" I took a step forward, hoping to show him that I was on his team with this. "What is the best strategy here?"

"I need to stay," he said reluctantly. "I need to stay here and control Canton because if anything goes wrong at the camps, the other justices and magistrates are going to need answers, and Canton needs to be the one to give them to them. I have to be here to oversee him."

"Okay," I confirmed his plan.

"Our men need to go," Shadoe insisted hurriedly. "They need to go and bring down the camps. Even if I have to stay, our people need to go."

"Okay," I agreed to his terms.

"I want a say on who goes," he pushed.

"Okay," Dov nodded.

"I want to help plan the attacks."

"Okay." I was starting to get annoyed. "Shadoe, we're not cutting you out of this. You can be involved in everything. Berwyn and Silas were working on a strategy last night, and Raselin and Arin interrogated the soldiers in the cells this morning. You can go to them right now and help plan."

"Well, there is one thing we need you to do first," Dov halted the conversation.

"Canton," Shadoe snarled.

"Ready?" Fitch asked, ambling up beside me, his wife trailing behind him.

"We have to be."

I glanced up at the top of the staircase to where my former handler stood. The moonlight filtered in from the high circular window, cascading just to the left of where Shadoe stood. Dust floated in the air, spinning at odd angles in the light.

Shadoe glared at my boots, asking without words if I had extra weapons with me. I tapped the toe of my boot once, letting him know I was annoyed he was asking such an amateur question.

He shifted his gaze, locking onto Nikko as he stood a few feet to my left. Shadoe didn't look at me again. He had left oversight of Lowell's team in my hands…assuming Nikko was unavailable.

Reyla used her hip to bump into me, reminding me not to roll my eyes. The last thing we needed was to upset Shadoe before we left him behind.

A cool breeze filled the room as the door opened. The changing weather took away any hope of warmth in the evenings, sending even the crickets into hiding. I stepped into the pale night.

Through Canton, Shadoe had commanded the rest of the Society men into cells, adding another full wing of men to the confined rooms below the mansion. Our own people patrolled the courtyard, nodding as we made our escape into the night.

Fifty men and women from three different groups converged together to form one rescue party as we set out for the camps near the Wall where Dov and I had once said goodbye. We had control of the area, but were still cautious, wearing Society uniforms and breaking into small groups to travel, with intervals in between our departures. We set up several checkpoints along the way, but we each had to find our own path to the same destination.

"I still don't understand how you tolerate these things," Katarina grumbled before branching off with Henry and Carter's group. She glared at the trousers she was wearing.

"She'll never get used to them," Reyla smirked under her breath. "They aren't *terrible*, but they wouldn't be my first choice."

"I know," I cast her a sympathetic look.

"This is where we split up," Fitch announced, looking around at the group. "See you all tomorrow at the checkpoint."

He nodded to the group surrounding him and they took off, jogging out of sight. Twenty minutes later, it was our turn to follow. Reyla stayed by my side as we moved out, Dov keeping a watchful eye on us.

The stars sparkled in the sky, darting in and out of the wispy gray clouds trailing our steps. Like shadows in the sky, they moved along with us. The warmth of Dov's hand in mine kept me focused on the journey and not the heavens above.

"It's nicer when we aren't running, isn't it?" Dov leaned toward me an hour into our journey.

"Can you tell in the dark?" I questioned, giggling. "Oh, that's right. I forgot…owls can function in the dark."

"Still not an owl," I smirked, running his free hand the length of my arm.

"Lovebirds," Silas coughed harshly, sending Reyla into a fit of giggles. She looped her arm through his.

"We should probably start taking bets on this," she motioned to us.

"On what?" I asked.

"We should," Silas ducked his head toward her conspiratorially. Together, they examined us.

"Looking for a show?" Dov stopped walking. He pulled me close, wrapping his arm around my waist.

"Oh, gross," Silas teased as Dov kissed me.

Reyla laughed, her voice only catching on the last note of her melodic giggle. She was probably thinking about Peter, the love she lost in a Society attack. I pulled back, wanting to spare her feelings. I swirled my thumb over Dov's hip twice to let him know I wasn't pulling back because of him. He flawlessly bounced back into step, hand falling to intertwine with mine.

"Jealous." I saw Dov mouth the word to Silas, mercifully keeping quiet in front of Reyla. He must have noticed too.

Silas glared at him before rolling his eyes and shaking his head. I would find out what girl he liked if it was the death of me.

"So, you all ran all this way?" Reyla started up a conversation. "That must have been awful."

"Well, it wasn't fun," I remarked.

"It certainly wasn't," Dov agreed. "Speaking of which, we should check in on Barone if we can. I'd like to make sure he's okay. I heard rumors about a man being hurt for helping us, but I never knew if it was true or if it was some device Canton was using to try to break me."

"Let's hope it was a ruse." I realized I hadn't even had time to think about the man who had helped us escape since I returned from the other side of the Wall. "Hopefully, he'll be safe in his home and we can rest there for an hour and tell him what's going on."

"I'm excited to meet him. He sounds lovely," Reyla chirped cheerfully, echoing the first bird of morning in the distance.

"We should probably pick up the pace if we're going to make it to the checkpoint before it gets too bright out," Silas reminded us. We broke into a jog down the main street of a sleeping town.

Twenty minutes later, we slowed, pausing our steps by the side of the road. The trees hung out over the street. Silas and Dov jumped, trying to reach the apples on the lower branches. My eyes darted to Reyla before sprinting to the tree trunk. Taking a running start, I threw myself at the bark, praying my foot would give me enough resistance against it to propel myself to a branch. I clawed in the air, miraculously grasping onto the rough bough. Scrambling up, I moved onto the branch.

I inched my way out on the thick arm of the tree as the boys managed to rip off an apple.

"Heads up," I said before releasing two apples above them.

Dov and Silas caught them, tossing them quickly to Reyla.

"Get enough to take for the others," Dov quietly shouted up to me.

I heard Reyla shuffling things around in the bag she had brought, transferring the contents to Silas' bag. Each apple I dropped smacked into waiting hands, only to be transferred with a thud into the sack.

"That's all we can fit, babe," Dov stopped me. I pulled four more apples and dropped them below for us to eat on the way. "Do you need a hand?"

"No, just step back," I cautioned, preparing to drop down out of the tree.

I positioned myself to sit on the branch, suddenly grateful I wasn't in a skirt that could get tangled in my descent. Inhaling, I kicked my feet out, pushing myself off the branch, only catching my body with a hand wrapped around my former seat. My body jarred to a stop as my grip prevented me from falling. My feet swung with the momentum of the sudden movements, and I paused long enough to glance down to make sure I wouldn't hit anyone when I let go.

I landed on the ground, surprisingly avoiding hurting my ankle. Suddenly I thought of Eden and was exceptionally thankful I wouldn't be hobbling to the Wall like she had the last time we went there. Everyone looked impressed that I had remained upright. I had been prepared to fall and roll and felt like a part of myself was missing when I didn't complete that part of my self-assigned mission.

I held my hand out for my apple, realizing they had cleared out Dov's bag as well to make room for more food. The more we gathered like this, the less we had to acquire from the towns and cities we passed through.

My teeth broke into the skin of the apple. A sharp, sweetness raced over my tongue and lanced into my ears, painful for just the first second as the taste exploded against my lips. My tongue recoiled against my back teeth, attempting to quell the unexpected feeling. The second bite was gentler.

"These are really good," Silas commented.

"The checkpoint should be just a few streets that way." Dov pointed to the left, apple still in his hand.

When we rounded the corner, my hair bristled. One street to go and something was wrong.

"Stop!" the voice behind us commanded.

Chapter 3

I CLENCHED THE APPLE CORE IN MY HAND, WISHING I HADN'T EATEN IT so quickly. Even with my non-dominate hand, I was certain my aim would be true if I needed to throw it at the soldier's face.

We turned to find a group of men standing behind us. Their clothes were worn, covered in dirt. One man had a tear in his shirt. They held brooms and shovels that I had no doubt were meant to give a plausible reason for having a weapon at the ready.

"Who are you?" the same voice asked.

"Who are *you*?" Dov said authoritatively.

We hadn't expected townspeople to stop us.

"Wait," the man studied us. "I know you."

His eyes flitted from Dov to me, locking onto my hair.

"You're Barone's friends," he loosened his grip on his shovel.

"You know Barone?" Silas asked cautiously, aware that Barone was still a town over.

"You're Griz's kid," the man continued.

The entire group of men relaxed. Ordinarily, I would assume it was a trap—a clever way of getting us to let our guard down—but the feeling that normally resided in my chest when bad things were about to happen refused to make an appearance.

"Who are you?" I asked.

"Name's Chester. We're on your side. Word has been going around that you're rallying troops," he paused when my eyes grew wide.

400

"Worry not, miss; it's all being kept very quiet. We all want this to end as badly as you do. We're ready to help."

He motioned to the group as they all nodded.

"Barone and I are cousins. You can trust me," he placed a hand over his heart. Leaning forward, he added, "He told me you stayed with him once."

He looked us over before nodding to each of us.

"You, and you, and you." He identified us as the people Barone had described to him before assessing Reyla. "You look a bit young to be—"

"She's not," Dov, Silas, and I answered, confirming that she wasn't Eden.

"Ah," he recovered. "Well, he told me most of you stayed with him. Your father was kind to him back in the day."

Dov nodded, relaxing beside me. *Another ally.*

"Where do you need to go?" Chester asked.

"We're meeting our team," Dov explained.

"And you're going to the camps?" Chester questioned. "We'll go with you. You're going to need all the help you can get. How many people do you have with you?"

"Fifty," Silas confirmed. "We'll never turn down help, though."

"Good, I'd hate to have to argue with you. Come on," he said, pushing by us. His men followed.

At the end of the street, they let us take the lead, not wanting to frighten our team.

"Everyone safe?" Fitch asked, greeting us.

"We're all here," Dov confirmed. "Did the other groups make it?"

"Almost, just waiting on Nian's group to show."

Dov explained about the recruits we had picked up along the way. Several of the new men raced home to tell their families what they were doing. They would catch up along the way.

Reyla and I passed out the apples we had collected to the team.

"Well, isn't this sweet?" Justin grinned.

"The apple or Auluria?" Reyla questioned as she transferred the contents of her bag back into her sack.

"The apple, but Goldilocks too, I guess," he teased.

"Is there a particular reason you're here, sunshine?" I asked, throwing out the first nickname I could think of.

"Food," he replied, crunching into the apple.

"Where are your siblings?" I pretended to snap with a grin.

"Devin is over there," he nodded. "Talley is…somewhere. I don't know. She's fine."

"Talley is probably the most capable of you Hersh kids anyway," I commented, watching his eyes spark, ready to challenge me.

"Just be glad you aren't one of us…you'd never hack it," he smiled triumphantly.

"I'm pretty sure she could give you a beat down, baby brother," Talley joined us, slinging her arm around Justin's shoulders.

"Which is why I like *her* best of all," I taunted.

"I'm wounded," Justin flailed around like I had stabbed him in the heart.

"What, did she tell you that you're not pretty enough, baby bro?" Devin grabbed his brother's chin and shook it playfully while dropping his insult in a baby voice.

"Oh no," Talley said in a deadpan voice. "Don't tell him he's not pretty."

She glanced sideways at her youngest brother. Justin gaped at her, shocked that she had gone there.

"Why do I talk to you all?" he yelped playfully.

"Well, I think you talk to Auluria because she's pretty." Reyla sounded like Katarina. "I have no idea why you talk to your siblings."

She shrugged, slinging the pack over her shoulder.

"Awww, it's okay, big guy," I chattered. "You're still prettier than me." I patted his shoulder, attempting to stifle a giggle.

"Do I need to be worried?" Dov asked, joining the group.

"Oh, be careful, Auluria," Reyla leaned in and whispered loud enough for just the small group to hear. "Gloria is over there. You don't want her swooping in on your man."

Dov looked more affronted than I did, making Justin and Devin burst into laughter.

"Relax, I think she's finally given up," Reyla said apologetically.

"Don't you give me that look, Dov Baer. I distinctly remember you flirting with her the night you took me on that raid," I chastised.

"*Reallocation project,*" Dov corrected with a smirk. "Besides, she couldn't win me over even if she tried."

He stepped forward and drew me into his arms as the rest of the group hassled us. His arms felt extra warm around my waist as I pulled him closer.

"It's a good thing you came first, Baer, or we'd have to beat you up for doing that," Justin added.

"Really," Devin said as if we made him gag.

"I think they're cute," Talley interjected, bumping Reyla with her shoulder as if they were on the same team.

"I guess I can see it," Devin relented.

"Fine, whatever," Justin sighed, rolling his eyes. "But seriously, enough with the kissy face."

"Oh, leave them alone, Justin," Katarina waltzed over. She moved quickly to Justin's side and looped her arm through his to lead him away as Henry paled. "If they want to kiss, I say we let them. None of us get much of a chance to do that these days."

"Shame," Justin said grinning wickedly at her.

Suddenly, as if propelled by some unseen force, Henry darted forward and latched on to Katarina's arm. He whipped her back so quickly that she collided with him, nearly sending them both crashing to the ground.

Everyone froze, watching the scene unfold.

He stared at her in his arms as she blinked quickly at him. Her face melted out of her shock and into a radiant smile.

"About time, Henry," she said in a low, quiet voice.

He kissed her and Reyla and I accidentally cheered out loud. It didn't deter them one bit. Devin and Justin joined in, clapping enthusiastically.

"You kids can thank me later," Justin joked.

"Who knew you were the key to solving everyone's relationship problems, Justin?" Devin clapped his brother on the back. "You hang out with Katarina, and she gets together with Henry. You hang out with Auluria, and she gets back together with Dov—"

"Hey, now! To be clear, she was getting back together with Dov long before I came along."

"And for the record, he never tried to steal her," Talley quickly interjected, wanting to make sure her brothers didn't inadvertently get themselves in trouble with their leader.

"Never thought he did," Dov said confidentially. "But even if she had, my girl never would have fallen for it."

He winked at me.

"They're here…" Silas trailed off as he jogged over to the group. "What did I miss?"

We all nodded toward the newly official couple. Katarina snuggled into Henry's chest as he held her protectively. Silas beamed.

"About time, buddy. Well done," he turned back to Dov. "They're here. Time to move out. I think Fitch is done grilling Chester, by the way."

"I assume he cleared?" Dov said, turning to follow Silas as he nodded.

"There's something you need to know, Baer," Chester said, meeting him halfway.

Dov waited quietly for Chester to proceed.

"We're going to Barone's next, right?" he asked cautiously. "You should know that he isn't quite the same as when you left him."

"What do you mean?" I asked, stepping alongside of Dov.

"Once you left, you see," he said as he wrung his hands nervously, "Magistrate Canton wanted information. He sent soldiers looking for anyone who might have seen you. Someone must have figured it out because they came for him."

"Oh no." My face fell.

"He withstood the beating, but…"

"But what?" Dov asked somberly.

"He's missing a few pieces, that's all," Chester replied, looking down at his hands again.

"What do you mean?" Silas stared.

"He means that there are always consequences, Silas," Fitch interceded. "We've all learned that the hard way over the years."

"No one gets out unscathed," I murmured, catching Dov's attention. It was something my aunt used to say, more as a warning than anything else.

"You lot will come with me to see him," Chester informed us. He nodded toward Raselin. "He thought it would be best if we didn't overwhelm Barone."

"The rest of us will go on as planned and you'll meet us at the next location," Fitch concluded. "Raselin will be joining you."

Lowell's voice in my head argued that we didn't have time for a side trip, that we were wasting valuable time. Basic humanity quickly won out, elbowing my cousin out of my head. He was dead, and his vicious agenda should be too.

I was grateful Raselin would be joining us. He would keep us on track—it would be far too easy for us to get distracted. Reyla might not have met Barone, but she would react the same way we would, wanting to stay and fix the problem we had created. Raselin would have to act as our clear head.

Dov nodded as Fitch glanced over my shoulder.

"Time to head out," he murmured.

"We should go, too," Chester echoed quietly. He turned on his heels and started out.

"Time to go," I muttered to Reyla as we fell into step.

"I'm going." Barone raised his voice.

"I don't think that's a good idea, cousin," Chester pleaded with him.

"We finally have a chance to do something about those camps, and you expect me to sit here and do nothing?" the older man argued.

"Barone," Chester's voice retreated to a whimper.

"I'm going," he said, placing his stump of a hand on the table. He lifted himself off the bench with great effort. It scraped across the floor, echoing loudly in the silent room.

I saw Dov take a deep breath, preparing to engage in the battle to convince Barone to stay. Barone's foot hung limply as he held his weight on his good leg, bracing himself with his arms against the table. He was in no shape to travel.

"Barone," Raselin interjected, directing the man's attention away from his fight. "Chester said you had information for us…"

"Yes," he said, shifting more weight onto his hands. He looked to Dov before continuing. "I know the guard schedule."

"What?" Silas tipped his head.

"At the camps, boy," Barone leaned forward, shifting his weight again. He needed to sit down. "I know when the guards come and go."

Realization crept over Dov, Silas, and Raselin's faces. Barone wanted to come along, and he might withhold information to do so. I stepped forward, taking a seat on the bench across the table from him as he eyed me. Placing a hand on the table, I tried to draw his attention in enough to quietly convince him to sit.

"Barone, how did you find this information out?" I asked quietly.

From the corner of my eye, I could see Dov and Silas visibly relax as I took control of the situation. Lowell would have been thrilled that I was putting my training to good use.

"How did you find out?" I repeated as the older man watched me with hesitation. I patted the table, inviting him to take a seat and join me in conversation.

Slowly, he lowered himself to sit, leaving his remaining hand on the table. Three fingers stared back at me. Searing pain crept into my own fingers just looking at the mutilation the Society had caused. When we returned, I would be having a conversation with Magistrate Canton on behalf of Barone's missing pieces.

"I watched them," he started, leaning forward sadly. "After I lost my family, I started watching the soldiers. I watched the camps, looking for an opportunity, but I never had the manpower to do anything.

"That day you stumbled into my house… I had just returned from another mission to scout the soldiers who were on their way to the camps. I haven't been able to go, but a few of my people have been watching it. It hasn't changed in all these years.

"The Society is arrogant. They think no one can overtake them—and so far, they've been right. None of us have been able to get the upper hand. But now…. Now we stand a chance. Now that we're all working together, now that we have more people," he paused to nod to Raselin, "Now we can fight and win.

"But they don't know that. The Society has no clue that we can stand against them. Their imperiousness has left them with a false sense of security, and they've become apathetic. Their systems haven't changed in years. We know their game, and now we can win it."

"It hasn't changed at all in years?" I asked. "Not even after we escaped Canton?"

"Not even then." Barone forced a smile that looked more like a grimace. He swallowed hard.

"Your people have confirmed this?" I confirmed.

"They have," he nodded, finding a less painful smile. "We can get you in."

"Barone," I said as I placed a hand on his. He flinched in surprise, his remaining fingers flexing instinctually under mine. "I know you want to help, but do you think you can really make it all the way to the camps? I see the way you're shifting your weight when you stand. Your leg is injured."

"I'll be fine," he grumbled but didn't shift away from me.

"May I look at it?" I asked. "There was a woman I met, a friend of ours, who helped to take care of me when I was hurt. She taught me a few things."

Barone suddenly looked concerned when he heard I had been injured, a fatherly look slipping over his face.

"What happened?" he demanded.

"May I look at your leg?" I asked again, hoping to keep him on track.

"What happened?" he repeated, looking to Dov.

Dov nodded to his leg, indicating that we would fill him in as I examined him. He acquiesced and pushed the bench back. A pebble dug into my knee when I knelt on the floor to the side of the table. I brushed it away, adjusting my position in an attempt not to wince. I worried about adding validity to Dov's account of my injuries as he filled the man in on what had happened.

Necesta's training offered me little help. I could tell something was clearly wrong, but I didn't have the skills to properly assess the damage. I glanced at Reyla. She was watching me examine the leg, well aware that I was clueless. The best I could do was to offer some peace from the pain.

"Here," I said taking a small vial from my pouch. "I don't know enough to really help—I'm sorry—but this should make it a little less uncomfortable."

"What is it?"

"It's for pain," I responded, unsure of how to answer. "We've all used it, and it's been a great help."

Dov, Silas, and Reyla nodded in response.

Barone nodded sharply and opened the vial, quickly swallowing its contents without argument. He set the container on the table.

"You're not going to let me go, are you?"

"No," I said quietly, looking down.

He sighed.

"It's time we had a talk."

Dov tucked the maps inside his uniform, shielding them from unwanted eyes. Each paper contained small marks, a code that they had developed in case the papers fell into the wrong hands. The marks spelled out everything we needed to remember to find the right locations to break in once we arrived.

Walking away from Barone was nearly as difficult as walking away from my aunt's home with Lowell when he took me in after her death. He leaned against the door, watching us go, knowing there was nothing he could do to help us. The Society had taken everything from him, including the ability to fight back. I had no doubt that wouldn't stop him from hindering the Society's efforts on a more local level though.

"We have to get the timing right," Silas said, talking to Dov about how to split up our forces. "If we hit all at once, they won't be able to get their feet under them in time to stop us."

"I want to verify this first," Dov replied, hand slipping to his chest where the papers were hidden inside his pocket. "We need to watch them just to confirm."

"Agreed," Silas nodded.

"I think we need to split up," Dov directed the conversation.

"I think we need to split up *intentionally*," Silas glanced meaningfully at him, indicating that Dov and I shouldn't be in a position to be a distraction to each other.

"I'd say there is some merit in that for *everyone*," Raselin mused. I wondered if he knew something I didn't. The secrets were starting to frustrate me.

"Look," I glared at them, "I know you two have issues being separated, but I think you can manage one mission apart. I promise I'll take good care of Dov."

"And I'll take care of Silas," Reyla grinned, reaching up to grab his chin like she was talking to a child. "We won't let either of you do anything foolish that will get you killed and ruin your friendship."

"That's not—" Silas tried to interject, making a face.

"Oh, but it is," Reyla stopped him. "That's exactly what you meant because we know you *of all people* weren't trying to say Dov and Auluria are too emotionally invested to work together."

Raselin opened his mouth to say something, but Dov and Silas cut him off, making him suppress a grin. The brunette shook his head, refusing to give anything away, when I squinted at him, silently begging for more information.

"We'll be fine," Dov said definitively.

"I don't think it's a good idea," Silas countered. "Auluria and I work well together; I think we should partner up."

Reyla looked down at the ground, deciding to stay out of it as we walked

"We could each lead our own team if that's what it's going to come to..." I supplied.

"Do you honestly think we need so many teams?" Dov asked, raising an eyebrow at me.

"Four isn't bad," I insisted. "Reyla and I can lead a team. We'll be fine."

"I believe in true love," Reyla jumped back into the conversation, "but I'm also totally fine with working with Auluria."

"Aww, did we just turn into these two?" I asked, pointing at our leader and his right hand.

"I think we did," Reyla nodded seriously.

"Well, you can't break up the team, now can you, boys?" I asked, challenging them.

"I don't think it's a bad idea," Raselin said as we slipped off the road, entering the forest. He ducked under a branch that nearly snapped back and hit Silas in the face.

He caught it, holding it up for Reyla to duck under while I walked around it.

"I still don't think we need an extra division," Silas added.

"I agree. I'd rather have Auluria and Reyla supporting us."

"Fine, but I'm working with Dov," I respond. "I'm tired of being separated."

"Me too," Dov said softly.

"Silas and I have always worked well together, so I guess that's settled." Reyla finalized our plans.

We stayed near the edge of the woods, watching the town, as the wind tugged at our uniforms. I reached back to adjust my hood, attempting to make it lay more comfortably. Hoods and long hair did not mix when the goal was to hide the hair. A gust of wind knocked into the side of my head making the fabric grate harshly against my ear.

"Well, maybe the noise from the wind will cover up our approach," Silas smirked.

"Can anything keep you from being noticed, Silas?" Reyla teased.

Before I could jump in, Raselin's step faltered.

"There they are."

On the horizon, sitting on a fallen tree, were Justin and Talley. They perked up when they saw us, Talley raising her hand in greeting as Justin jumped to his feet.

"I see you made it," Talley welcomed us. "They're all waiting over there."

She pointed deeper into the woods where everyone was setting up camp for the night, far out of sight. Justin stared directly at me until I gave him a small smile, letting him know I had survived seeing Barone in such a shattered state.

We changed course, walking further into the cover we had become so familiar with over the years. Leaves rattled on the trees as the wind slammed into them, growing softer as we continued forward, only to spring back up as we let our guard down against it.

"You good?" Justin sidled up next to me, bumping his arm against mine.

"Yeah, I'm good. Where's Devin?"

"He's at the camp."

"Didn't want to spend too much time with you, huh?" I grinned.

"Nope." Talley came up behind us, pushing her brother's head forward good-naturedly. "So I got stuck with him."

"Barone had some interesting information for us," I added once I finished rolling my eyes at their antics. "He knew the guard schedule at the camps. We know when and where to hit to get in."

"That's great," Talley said somberly.

"We're dividing into three main groups, and we'll take on the camp from there," Dov instructed. "One from the front, one from the back, and the last group will follow once we're in to help with any resistance we encounter."

"Sounds like a smart plan," Justin nodded.

"Have you figured out the teams yet?" Talley asked, reaching up to push back her hair.

"Yes, on our way here," Dov nodded. "You're all together with Auluria and me."

"I can work with that," Talley agreed. "Justin?"

"Works for me," he concurred. "What about you, Rey?"

"I'm with Silas' team on this one," Reyla smiled. "We're taking the opposite side of the camp from you."

"My team will be the follow-up," Raselin added. "We'll be taking point on the girls' camp, though."

Ahead, I could begin to see signs of our team. The quiet murmur of voices was momentarily carried to us on the breeze, mixed with the scent of smoke. A colorful leaf chased after it, landing at my feet. I stepped around it, not wanting to crush the pretty thing.

"You're back. Everything okay?" Carter called down from a tree, making Reyla startle.

"We're good," Dov tipped his head up to see his friend through the leaves. "Everything look okay up there?"

"Yes, sir. We're good," Carter nodded, shifting on the branch where he was perched, legs stretched out and crossed at the ankle. He leaned casually against the trunk of the tree, hands folded on his lap, but he was clearly alert and watching for signs of intruders.

We continued walking toward the campsite, eerily feeling like I was stepping back into my transient life with my cousin before he had sent me to the Baers. We paused to nod as we walked by more of our scouts, hidden quietly in the trees.

"Hey, *Goldilocks*," Gregory said slyly as we passed.

"Probably a good thing you're up in that tree, Gregory," Dov taunted, nodding toward me. "I don't think you'd fair well if you were within arm-range."

He chuckled, grinning at me.

"I'm sure you're right, Dov. That's why I'm doing it from up here!" Gregory laughed hard enough to nearly knock himself off balance. He quickly reached down, grabbing onto the branch to steady himself.

"You know, I don't actually feel bad about that," Dov laughed, raising his hand to wave as we continued.

"Would have served him right," Reyla giggled.

"Oh please, you would have been the first one by his side had he fallen," Silas teased.

"Are you really insinuating that I'm faster than Auluria is?" her eyes sparkled.

"That...is a good point," Silas bowed his head in defeat. "I don't think anyone could outdo the legend of Goldilocks at this point."

"Really? It's come to this?" I mocked, rolling my eyes.

"I think you're just going to have to accept this, Auluria," Dov wrapped his arm around me, pulling me close.

"Necesta has done me no favors with this," I muttered.

"She kept you safe and built you a name," Dov replied quietly. "And even if you don't think it's helped you, it's helped us. People have heard about Goldilocks. They've heard about the Baers. We have a reputation, and that's definitely helping this situation."

"What if it gets us killed?" I posed the darker side.

"Auluria, we were going to die anyway," Dov grinned. "Need I remind you of our little tangle with the noose not too terribly long ago? The Society knew who we were long before your name was ever known, and they've known about the three of us Baers for longer than that. But now the *people* know too. It doesn't change our fate either way, so why not live the glory?"

"I guess that's a decent point," I relented "Speaking of points and legacies, you and I still need to find time to talk."

"We will, I promise," Dov assured me, running his fingers down my arm as we walked. I fought against the shiver that movement made course through my body.

"Welcome back," Fitch greeted us as we walked into the space littered with campfires and supplies. The people resting looked up to see us, some raising a hand in greeting. "What did you find?"

"Answers," Raselin slapped his friend on the back. "We found answers."

"Come with us," a sharp whisper hissed in my ear as a hand latched onto my arm.

Ella tugged me away, nearly causing me to trip. I waved Reyla off as she started to follow me, wide-eyed. The girl dragged me away from the crowd, beyond the fires, to a quieter location, Locust in tow.

"What do you want, Ella?" I demanded, yanking my arm from her piercing grip. When I looked down, I saw the nail marks on my forearm.

Ella stepped back, glaring at me as Locust took the lead.

"We're going to have a little conversation, *Goldilocks*." He grinned lecherously at me now that we were away from the others.

Ella rolled her eyes. Crossing her arms, she kicked her hip out to the side, placing all her weight on her left leg, locking her knees to hold her pose. Her eyes traveled the length of my body, judging me. Dissatisfied with what she saw, she sneered at me, wrinkling her nose.

"You need to see Brittella," he informed me.

"What?" I asked in surprise.

"Brittella," Locust snapped. "You remember her, don't you? She trained you back in the day."

"Of course, I remember Brittella," I snapped accidentally.

"Shadoe said she's here, in the town. You need to go find her and bring her into this," he insisted. "She's stayed neutral all these years, but we don't have time for that anymore. You know her better than the rest of us, and we need her on our team. So, go get her."

"And do what?" I barked. "Just what is she supposed to do to help us?"

"You know exactly what Brittella is capable of," Ella reentered the conversation, growling. "And she has contacts that we need. Go get her and get her to work with us."

"We don't have time to waste," Locust grabbed my arm, turning me back to face him. "Get her here before we move out. She won't stay long. She hasn't stayed in one place for longer than a few days in a long time."

"She's not staying at her house?" I asked, trying to piece together a new picture of the woman I once knew.

I tried shaking him off, creating enough of a disturbance that people noticed. In the distance, I saw Reyla stretch up to see what was happening before turning away to point us out to Dov and Silas. They cautiously started to approach, giving me space to handle the situation before rushing to my aid.

"No, even Brittella knows when to get out. She may own half the people she comes in contact with, but she's smart enough to know when things are no longer safe." Ella answered.

"So then, how do we know she's here?" I challenged. "If she's on the move, why would she be here?"

"Shadoe has informants everywhere," Locust replied, "maybe he knows one of her people. Who knows? It doesn't really matter. Shadoe said you're going to do this, so you're going to do this."

Ella looked at me skeptically, waiting for me to step out of line so she could put me in my place. I owed Shadoe, and although I didn't understand his reasoning or know where his information came from, I knew I needed to play along. Having Brittella wouldn't hurt anything, and she *was* a master at manipulation and getting her way. I was willing to give this one to Shadoe and avoid a fight with his people—*our* people.

"Do you know where she is located?" I asked, backing them down as my friends drew closer, watching the scene.

"Locust," Ella warned when she noticed the approach.

He glanced sideways, noting my boyfriend. I could see his eyes twitch as he decided his next move. For a moment, I thought he would try to swear me to secrecy, but I judged wrong.

"Besides," he said, stepping back from me in a grand sweeping motion. "Your boyfriend needs to thank her. After all, it's the entire reason you're together."

He grinned at me, swaggering away. Ella pushed away from her post, still angrily crossing her arms over her chest. She turned when she reached his side, eyeing me once again.

"You really owe Brittella for everything she taught you," Locust continued. "You'd probably be dead by now if you weren't able to seduce all those people like that to get out of all of those situations… or into them."

"Better hurry, Lur. We have a lot to accomplish," Ella grinned smugly before turning her sights on Dov.

The two walked away, leaving me to deal with the fallout.

"You'll know where to find her," Locust shouted over his shoulder as he slinked away.

"That was…interesting," Dov turned to me, waiting for an answer.

"They want me to find Brittella. She was one of the people who trained me before I was sent to you," I responded, annoyed.

"Trained you to do what?" Silas asked in horror, having heard their comments.

"Umm, to read people and respond to them in a way that would get them to do what I needed to do," I said carefully.

"She trained you to seduce Dov?" Reyla leaned in, whispering quickly in my ear so the boys couldn't hear.

"No," I yelped sharply. "Kind of…maybe. I guess. But not just that."

Dov patiently waited for me to finish panicking.

"She taught me persuasion tactics," I tried again.

"When was this?" Dov asked.

"Before you," I answered, hoping he wouldn't press for more. I clamped my teeth together, hoping to control the red flush tingling in my cheeks.

"And how did you meet this woman?"

"Lowell sent me to work with her." My entire body flushed with embarrassment.

"She worked with Lowell?" he asked skeptically.

"No," I quickly looked up. "She didn't work with him. He knew her, but she didn't work with him."

"Then what was it?"

I paused, unsure of how to answer.

"She was a woman he knew who had many talents and would occasionally train people. I'm not sure how many people Lowell sent to her, but I think the two of them were more like informants for each other. My cousin had information she wanted, and she had information he wanted."

"Interesting," Dov mused. "Just how often do you find yourself using what she taught you?"

"I…" I faltered. "She taught me how to get information out of people, so, I guess I use it enough."

"And who have you used this on?"

I searched his eyes, trying to figure out what he was asking.

"Just when I need information. She taught me to identify what a person wants or needs and use that to my advantage."

"As a female who could bat her eyelashes and get what she wants?" Silas offered, making me turn red again.

"Sometimes, yes."

"She was pretty good in practice," Locust yelled, making me whip around to look. I hadn't realized he stayed close by.

"I *never* did any of that *anywhere near* you!" I shouted angrily, making him smirk.

"But you did practice, didn't you?" Dov said a little sadly.

"No. Only with Brittella listening but not directly with anyone, and never that." I quickly said.

"No? So how did you get so good when it came to me?" Dov stepped closer, flirtatiously putting his hand on my hip. I hoped Locust saw and felt like it was a punch to the gut.

"I wasn't very good," I commented.

"Well, if *that's* what *'not very good'* is like, Auluria, I *can't wait* to see how you handle yourself with a bit more practice." He ducked his forehead to mine, lips a mere inch away. "You can practice on *me* any*time."

Silas snorted, trying to keep in his laughter while Reyla swooned.

"Stop it, Silas," she hissed, "That was the most gorgeous thing I've ever heard a man say and if you ruin this moment for them, I'll…do something horrible to make you regret it."

He laughed as her threat petered out. Silas let Reyla slip her hand through his arm as she guided him away. She peeked back over her shoulder, winking at me.

"You're willing to be my test subject?" I asked, locking eyes with him.

"If you really need one, I think I can help out," he grinned.

He tipped his head just slightly before pulling back.

"You didn't kiss him, did you?" He nodded toward the onlookers just enough so that I could see it, but not enough that they could.

"*Him?*" I gasped, horrified. "No. Never."

"Shadoe?" he asked sadly.

"No, never him either," I assured him. I unintentionally gripped his arms tighter.

"But you…"

"I kissed him, but never for that." I couldn't help the disgusted face I was making. "Even Brittella knew that."

"So, we have to go…what, rescue her?" He redirected.

"No, she's fine. She will *always* be fine," I answered. "She's Brittella. She's the only one of us who can pick either side and actually end up as the right-hand to the person in power without ever changing her allegiances. I don't know what it is about her, but she has the power."

"Then we are…?"

"We are asking her to join us. Apparently, she's in town."

"To what end?" Dov questioned. I reached up and tucked back a piece of his dark hair.

"She'll be an asset to us. She understands people more than any of us do." I let my fingers fall to his collarbone, grasping the edge of his uniform fabric. "I don't know why Shadoe wants her, but if nothing else, she'll be able to help us convince the people from the camps to join us. She's really good at convincing people to do things, but never takes away their free choice. She's kind of magical to watch."

I gave him a small smile. I respected the woman, though I didn't always like her tactics. I *certainly* didn't like her hold over my cousin...or maybe I did. It was nice to see him so out of sorts with her.

"Well, I guess we have to go see a woman about a membership to the club." He grinned. "But first..."

He leaned forward, closing the space between us.

Reaching up my back, he pulled me closer, tangling his hands in my hair. My tresses shifted, tickling the back of my neck, adding to the sensation of his hand searing into the skin between my shoulders and my head.

I pulled on his collar the way I had the day he kissed me after the fire. For an instant, I could smell the smoke from that day, but quickly realized it was a more present scent, directed to us by the wind as it carried the campfire smoke to us. It was mixed with the smell of cooking food, and Dov's lips crashed into mine faster, as if he were starving.

I waited, letting him dictate our moves, before making my own. Knowing we were very much in the open, I allowed myself one small moment to use some of the tricks my mentor had taught me on the man kissing me. He responded by grinning and playing into my every move.

"Well, that's more like it, Goldilocks." His eyes lingered on my lips as he slowly pulled away. "Any chance we can try more of that?"

"Are you going to keep calling me Goldilocks?" I taunted him.

He grunted with a nod before leaning back in to kiss me.

When we finally looked up, Silas was elbowing Reyla from where they had chased away Locust and Ella. They grinned at us, happy to see Dov and me back to a bit of normalcy.

"We should go," Dov said, brushing his nose against my hair.

"We should," I agree, standing there.

He smiled and sighed, pulling me into motion.

"Always making me do the hard work, huh?" he teased.

"Hey now," I challenged. "I recall a certain one of us pulling the other up a cliff once."

"And *throwing herself off a cliff once…*" he continued to tease.

I slapped his arm good-naturedly, using the other to pull him closer.

"Glad to see you two back to normal," Silas grinned.

"Should I even ask if you set that up, Silas?"

"No, Auluria, you should not," he started to walk away. "But for the record, I did no such thing. And quite honestly, I don't think it should be *me* that you're asking."

He glanced at Reyla, making her sputter.

"I would never!" she exclaimed.

"Would never meddle?" Silas threw a look at her. "No, of course not."

"Says the one overseeing everything!" Reyla spit back.

"Wait, what is this?" I asked, realizing there was more than met the eye.

"Nothing," Silas insisted.

"Nothing but a plan to get you two to a *happily ever after* like you were headed to before," Reyla informed us. "Don't you think for a second he hasn't been working behind the scenes on this."

"We, my dear, have been working on this," he said, "Credit where credit is due."

"Fine, thank you both," I said, shocking them.

"You're not going to fight us on this?" Silas asked.

"No," I leaned over and kissed Dov's shoulder as we walked.

"That was unexpected," Silas breathed. With a shrug, he added, "I'll take it."

"You two want to come with us to go find this Brittella?" Dov asked, glancing over at his friends.

"Actually, I think Reyla and I should go alone," I interrupted.

"Why?" Dov looked at me, concerned.

"Just trust me on this one."

"I'm in," Reyla smirked. "I like a good girls' mission."

"We'll be fine, you just wait for us by the edge of town," I said, grabbing Reyla's arm, darting away from Dov and Silas.

"By the edge of the town!" Dov shouted after us, mandating that we be there. I could feel him restraining himself from running after us.

"Edge of the town!" I confirmed, not looking back.

Chapter 4

BRITTELLA WAS PERCHED AGAINST A BOOTH, HER HIP LEANING AGAINST the edge of the counter. She leaned forward, speaking quietly to the man on the opposite side. The woman reached out and stroked the man's arm as she talked. He nearly swooned under her gaze.

"Really?" Reyla murmured as she noticed the woman commanding attention from every man within a twenty-foot radius.

She looked closer, watching Brittella maneuver the conversation.

"How does she do that?" Reyla turned to look at me. "Wait, can *you* do that?"

"I have no idea, I've never tried," I admitted.

"But she taught you how to do that?" Reyla pushed.

"She did."

"I'm not sure if I should be impressed or concerned," Reyla added.

"I'm not either," I sighed. "We should go get her."

"How do you propose we do that?"

"Wait here; she'll come to me when she sees me."

Reyla nodded, allowing me to go without protest.

I slipped around a few stands, ignoring the meager goods for sale and trade. Something spicy hit my nose, and for a moment, I thought about looking for food. My hand trailed along the booth as I left the thought behind.

Angling myself, I wandered into Brittella's line of sight. I turned, enough so she could see me, but not far enough to make it obvious. I would make her come to me.

She took a slightly longer breath when she noticed me, just enough to be noticed by someone watching for a shift in demeanor, but not enough to concern her entourage. Brittella swayed back, still engaged in conversation. I could hear the final strains of her laughter as it filtered over the crowd. She swayed again, and the crowd of men moved with her, mirroring her every move. Pulling back into herself, she ducked her chin to her shoulder, petting her dark mane as it fell across her chest.

She detached herself from the group skillfully, leaving them wanting more of her attention. They finally wandered off when she waved them away. The woman made her way through the tables, finding her way slowly to a place where she had easier access to me.

"Auluria," she purred, looking down at a table. Her fingers traced over a string of decorative beads, similar to the ones she was wearing. "Where *have* you been all this time, my dear?"

"Shadoe sent me." I ignored her question.

"Ah," she moved closer. "Your young man has stepped up since Lowell's passing."

"You know?" I confirmed with her.

"I know everything, Auluria." She smiled softly, a wistful look on her face. "The benefit of being me. Now, I asked you a question."

"I've been on Lowell's little mission," I tried not to sneer.

"Still?"

"New mission," I answered.

"With the Baers?" She picked up the beads, leaving a coin on the table. The owner kept his distance, allowing us to talk.

"And others, yes," I said cautiously.

"Why are you here?" She purred again.

"Shadoe sent me to find you."

"But why?" She finally turned, making eye contact with me.

"He would like you to work with us. Here is not the place to talk." I waited for her to respond.

"So, you and your friend have come to take me where?" She glanced at Reyla who was still waiting where I left her. "She's very pretty by the way. Have you trained her?"

"No," I frowned, wishing she would cooperate.

"Well, I've always loved a good conversation. Let's get on with it." She motioned that we should walk.

We walked together past the tables. She nodded to a few people as we moved through the area to the main road where Reyla joined us after I signaled her. Brittella had clearly been there long enough for them to become familiar with her, though I guessed not long enough to truly know anything about her. She was good at making friends and better at making contacts.

"Reyla, this is Brittella," I started.

"Reyla…" Brittella interrupted me, looking my friend up and down. "Beautiful name. I'm pleased to meet you."

She turned to me, an aware smile crossing her lips.

"This one has seen love," she nodded to her other side where Reyla walked. "I see you have too. Quite the change."

Reyla's eyes widened, but she said nothing.

"Who is he?" my former mentor asked. "Not that boy you were sent after?"

"His name is Dov."

"So, the rumors are true," she said lightly. "You're working with the Baers. You're the famous Goldilocks. How quaint. Lowell would have some thoughts on this."

"Lowell is dead," I reminded her.

"Yes," she paused. "Shame."

She ran her hand through her hair, letting it fall in front of her.

"Do we like this new man?"

"We do."

"We *really* do," Reyla added with a smile. Brittella glanced at her.

"I suppose I'll get to meet this man?" she asked.

"Sooner than you think," Reyla muttered, stepping around a stone in the road.

"Ah, we're going to meet him," Brittella reflected. "How delightful. I look forward to meeting the young man who persuaded you away from your loyalties. I admire that, mind you. You took care of yourself. That's what I taught you to do."

"You did," I agreed. "And now I'm Goldilocks."

"The most well-known woman in the Society, I'd wager." She surprised me when she put her hand on my back. "At least that's the way I've heard it in my travels."

"Why did you leave, Brittella?" I had planned to wait to ask, but I took the opportunity. "What made you walk away?"

"Safety, Auluria. Alliances are shifting, as you well know. Lowell's men and the Baers working together? A warrior girl rising up in gold? All signs that it was time to manage my situation. I can tell when it's time to change allegiances, my dear. I've lived on my own, taken care of myself for so long, but I got comfortable, and comfort leads to carelessness. I couldn't have that.

"I knew I'd need new resources, new people to count on in times of war. War is coming, Auluria, but you know that. Safety is in the unexpected. Moving, changing, presenting myself to new people and disappearing…it's all unexpected. I'll survive this and so will the two of you. I'll help you."

"You'll help the two of us, or you'll help all of us?" I suddenly noticed every stone, every pebble, every piece of dirt in the street as I waited.

"I will help you," she said cautiously. "You're working against the Society, and right now, they are my only enemy—or at least my most important enemy. I'll help however you need me to. What is your plan?"

We quieted, moving as quickly as we could without raising suspicion. It felt strange to be in a dress again after so many days of wearing the Society uniform. The hem of my dark skirt brushed against my ankles softly. We would need to change back into our uniforms soon, but for the moment I relished it.

The two women and I neared the edge of the town, making our way to a silent street away from the crowds. Once we were far enough away, I told Brittella about our plan to overtake the camps.

"I see," she followed my reasoning, responding quietly. "And I'm going to help convince them to join you, I take it?"

"I had hoped so, yes."

"You think you can't do that on your own?"

"Oh, I know she can," Reyla interjected, "but it never hurts to have more help. Auluria can't be everywhere at once. She also can't stay."

"You expect me to stay?" Brittella asked, surprised.

"No, just perhaps a little longer than we'll be staying," I replied.

"You're bringing me there and then leaving?" the tall woman remarked. "What could Shadoe possibly want me for then?

"We'll see when you return. I wasn't notified of this plan until a few hours ago."

"He's running his own strategy, then?" she bowed her head in thought. "That doesn't seem very productive, nor does it seem particularly helpful to your mission.

"Auluria, I've studied you for a long time. Even when you were younger, Lowell would tell me about you. I've also studied your friend. If I was a betting woman—and I have been, just not with the stakes most men lean on—my beautiful jewels wouldn't be placed on his plan.

"He's calculating, that's a given, but his strategy is single-minded. He has an objective, and he takes the straightest, most true path. It's quicker, perhaps, but messier and more treacherous.

"His plan isn't your plan, nor is it the Baer's plan. I can tell."

"I don't know his plan," I admitted.

"I can tell that too. But he's still allowing you to be a part of it, whatever it is. There are pieces I'm missing though. I can't form a clear picture.

"Is he here?" she inquired about Shadoe's whereabouts.

"No, he's not." Reyla supplied.

"We have control of Magistrate Canton. He's watching over him."

"He's controlling him, you mean," Brittella corrected. "A man like Canton requires fear. Fear must be brought in a way Canton doesn't think he can escape and only Lowell's man can provide that level of insurance."

She grinned at the slight shock that crept into my face.

"You forget that I knew your cousin well, Auluria. Who do you think helped him with his little schemes? I may not have been one of his fold, but I certainly understood his game, and I knew how his people operated. You were the wildcard, my dear. You were the only unknown in his little enterprise. The rest of them all fit into a neat little box.

"Auluria, is that your man?" Brittella abruptly changed the topic, surprising me.

I looked up to find Dov and Silas standing above the tall grass at the side of the road. It waved around their waists like a river of light brown fuzz as the wind kicked up.

"Yes, that's Dov and our friend, Silas."

"Charming." Her purr was back.

She pulled her shoulders down and forward, making her collarbone pop out sharply as she held her upper arms taut against her body. Dipping her chin, she prepared to meet the boys—something she did every time she wanted to appear demure and fragile.

As we approached, I saw their eyes grow wide. My stomach dropped, worried it would be Lowell all over again. I couldn't bear the thought of my men following Brittella around like lost puppies.

"Hello," Brittella dropped her voice. As she neared, she held out her hand, waiting for them to take it.

Dov and Silas remembered themselves, adjusting their faces into a smile.

"You must be Brittella," Dov said, reaching politely for her hand.

"You must be the one she practiced on," Brittella said flirtatiously. Dov faltered, sneaking a glance at me. "It's easy enough to see, young one; she didn't have to tell me. It's nice to meet you, Mr. Baer."

"And this is Silas," I supplied, relieving Dov of responsibility of talking.

"Ma'am," Silas extended his hand for hers as well.

"Hmmm," she raised her eyebrows, staring at him intentionally until he squirmed. Only then did she release him from her hold. "Interesting. We should be on our way, gentlemen."

Her abrupt change in tone threw the boys, but they recovered quickly and led us deeper into the woods. They explained the plan as we returned to the camp, giving her only as many main details as were essential.

Once again, we were greeted by the scent of smoke on the wind long before reaching the site. A few crickets gathered, the last that remained so late in the year.

Locust was waiting by the edge of the camp. He disappeared into the darkness once he confirmed Brittella was with us, pausing for only a moment to leer at Reyla and I standing in our dresses. I made a note to change into our uniforms immediately.

The camp was bathed in an orange glow, and twisted gray smoke climbed into the sky. A fire sparked, dropping orange flecks to the ground as we made our way to where Raselin and Fitch were waiting. Lydia sat by her husband, clinging on to his arm that was nearly as wide as she was. She smiled when she saw us approach.

Raselin turned when Fitch nodded toward us, glancing over his shoulder. When he saw us, he leaped to his feet.

"Brittella?" His jaw fell.

"Raselin," the woman faltered. I had never seen Brittella so out of sorts.

"They told me they were picking up a contact..." Raselin trailed off.

"It's been far too long," Brittella recovered gracefully, rearranging her face into a gracious smile. "I see you made it back."

"I did." Raselin returned her grin as Fitch's eyebrows shot up behind him in the background.

"I always wondered what had happened to you," Brittella murmured. "Shall we sit?"

Raselin suddenly backed up, making room for her to sit next to him on the log near the fire. He gestured for her to join him as Britella gracefully swooped in to take a seat. She reached out her hand, allowing him to steady her descent.

"We'll let you talk," Reed said, standing. He nodded to Nian who joined him.

"After you," Dov murmured, guiding me to a seat near Brittella. Reyla and Silas settled opposite us as I gazed across the flames.

Heat enveloped me, and I realized how cold I had been.

"How have you been, Raselin, darling?" Brittella took his hands in hers, patting the top of them.

"We've come to free us from the Society," he told her as if she didn't already know.

"So I see," she smiled pleasantly at him. "And you brought reinforcements, how lovely."

"I take it that you'll be helping us?" Raselin asked. "Is that the plan?"

He leaned forward, looking around Brittella to me.

"It is."

"Tomorrow we'll be entering the boys' camp," he settled back, speaking to Brittella again. "We have a plan for getting inside."

"So I've heard," she purred. I didn't realize humans could sound so much like cats.

She removed her top hand, bringing it back to her shoulder where she stroked her hair, dipping her body backward with a swaying motion for a moment. She was good.

My eyes grew wide as Fitch and Lydia caught on to Brittella's flirtation. Horror raced through my body, knowing they'd figure out I had been trained to do that as well. I relaxed when Lydia stifled a giggle.

"How have you been, Brittella?" Raselin lowered his voice.

I clamped down on my back teeth, willing my face to remain calm. I tried as hard as Lydia did not to laugh at the scene. Maybe bringing Brittella with us was a good thing after all, and, *perhaps* Raselin had the ability to control her a bit. Lowell certainly hadn't.

The two fell into discussion, catching each other up on the missing years. Reyla and Silas talked quietly, giving them space. I attempted to listen in, letting Dov murmur quietly to me, knowing I was spying. Brittella was too smart for that and kept her voice low.

When we finally separated for the night, arranging our bags on the ground to sleep, she slipped off with Reyla and me to change into a Society uniform.

"I like him," she whispered into my ear loud enough for Reyla to also hear.

"Raselin?" I questioned.

"Dov." She drew out his name slowly. "I like him."

She slipped her dress over her head and dropped it next to her, picking up the uniform we had provided her. Brittella made a face mixed with judgment and disgust.

"Unlike Shadoe," she continued, "he's better for you."

"We know," Reyla said, winking at me.

"And then there's *you*," Brittella turned her attention to Reyla as she shrugged on the uniform, pulling her hair out from between her shoulder and the sleeves.

Reyla shifted to a nervous posture. I knew she wouldn't want to talk about losing Peter, so I commandeered the conversation.

"How long have you known Raselin?" I asked.

"Since long before he went over the Wall."

"You were friends?" I hinted, hoping she'd give us more information.

"We were," she smiled, settling her hair back in place, cascading down the front of her chest. "I suppose I won't be able to keep this down."

I shook my head.

"Ah, well," she sighed, tucking her mane behind her. She popped the hood over her head to try it, grimacing. Brittella glanced at us, likely wondering how we could be so comfortable in pants.

"You'll get used to it," I assured her.

"Lowell did a number on *you*, Auluria," she shook her head. "I should have taken you away while I had the chance."

"Well, I for one, am glad you didn't," Reyla jumped in. "I like having her around, and if Lowell hadn't messed her up, we wouldn't have her. And Dov would be very lonely."

"What do you really anticipate me doing tomorrow, ladies?" She asked, tucking a piece of hair back inside her hood. "I don't fight. I can't imagine I'll need to do much sweet-talking. After all, the soldiers will be under your control by the time I'm brought in and the boys will likely side with you.

"Besides," she continued, "they're much more likely to follow along after a rousing speech from you and Dov, don't you think? You're closer to their age, my dear, and you're the ones leading them to victory and freedom."

"What are you proposing?"

"I think I should work with the women, my dear. They're going to need me more than you will. I can train them when the time comes."

Reyla glanced over at me to see what I thought. I nodded softly, considering her words. It made sense, though I wondered how helpful she might be with Magistrate Canton and his friends.

"Don't give me that look, young lady. I want nothing to do with that man," she chided.

"Who?" Reyla asked.

"Canton." I assumed Brittella knew everything I was thinking all of the time.

Brittella looked Reyla over yet again. "I could teach you a thing or two, you know. Come see me after tomorrow and we'll talk."

She grinned wickedly, tipping her head to the side.

"Oh, I don't know—"

"I'm really not sure—"

"Auluria, please. If you haven't figured it out by now—" Brittella snapped at me before being cut off.

"Everything okay?" Lydia asked, walking around the group of trees we were using as cover. "The boys were wondering where you ladies ran off to. It seems you were taking long enough that they thought you might have become lost."

"Not quite, Lydia," I smiled.

She quirked her lips up, smiling back at me before extending her hands to Brittella.

"We haven't had a chance to talk yet. May I walk back with you?" She slipped her arm through Brittella's and they walked together, chatting like old friends.

"Will that be us someday?" Reyla giggled, looping her arm through mine.

"You really think we'll both live through this?" I asked with a teasing grin. "One of us, maybe, but do you honestly think I'm going to make it?"

Reyla slapped my arm.

"Yes! I'm expecting little Dov and Auluria nieces and nephews, my friend. Don't you deny me becoming an aunt!" Reyla pointed an accusatory finger at me, feigning shock.

"Reyla!" I yelped loud enough to cause Lydia and Brittella to turn around to look at us.

She cast me a look, daring me to protest again. With a deep breath, I relented and turned to step forward.

"I mean it, Auluria. Babies. When this is all over, I want a big, lavish wedding, followed by nieces and nephews, preferably living next door."

"Wouldn't you get bored living next to me?"

"Have you seen the way you live, Auluria? I doubt any of us will *ever* be bored," she smirked. "I'm just hoping you calm Dov down and he calms you down. All this nonsense involving you running into burning buildings and escaping the hangman's noose is getting old.

"I want you settled and happy," she finished.

"Fine, but only if you're happy too," I said, making it a condition in the agreement.

"Having nieces and nephews will make me very happy," she informed me. "Maybe we can get Katarina and Henry on that too once this is all over and done with. You'll obviously be getting married first, but your kids can play together."

"That's assuming they get to that point," I reminded her.

"Trust me, I've known them a lot longer than you have," she replied, "They will."

I reached over and took her hand. I knew she wouldn't be ready to move on from Peter for a long time, but I desperately wanted her to find someone to be happy with. One day, when she was ready, I would make her my new mission.

She smiled and patted my hand, knowing.

"It will be fine," she reminded me. "Speaking of gorgeous men…"

She nodded toward the fire where everyone was preparing to rest.

"Let's just hope we all make it out tomorrow," I sighed, taking in the image of the people I cared about resting around the golden flames before finding a place to rest.

"Ready?" Dov asked, taking a deep breath.

"Ready," I confirmed, turning to signal our people.

Justin and Devin winked at me at the same time, their hands mirroring each other as they pushed off their knees to stand. I slowly rose in front of them.

The youngest Baer brother led the way as I quickly rallied behind him. A moment later, Justin and Devin followed behind us. Quietly, we moved forward, allowing the rest of our team to slip in behind us. We kept a safe distance between us, giving us space should anything happen.

We waited for the guard to round the corner, then slipped along the cold edges of the building. It was cold in the shadows, but I was grateful it masked our movements. The sun might have kept us from shivering, but it also exposed us in its deep orange glow.

I paused behind Dov, waiting for his signal to move forward. I kept my sight trained over his shoulder, looking where he wasn't. I tapped his shoulder, indicating that it was clear.

He risked a glance back at me before turning around, his back to the wall, weapon ready. I mimicked him, ready to protect Justin as he stepped between us, preparing to break into the entrance to the camp. Devin carried a second tool to help break in. Together, they quietly tried to break in, a harsh, metallic sound filling the air. I held my breath.

Talley sidled up next to me, a third layer of protection for her brothers. Her jaw was set in a harsh line, her eyes furrowed. She forced a breath out of her nose, the rush of air making a small snorting noise as a form of communication with me. I did it back, confirming it was all clear.

A loud bang sounded. My eyes darted around, checking for signs of guards.

"We're in," Devin whispered. He moved next to Talley, taking my place as Dov and I stepped backward, ready to lead the raid into the compound.

Justin took a place to my right as we stepped inside. It felt bitterly cold inside the building; worse than the wind outside. We hurried down the hall, finding places to wait. Any empty pocket, recess, or room was occupied by as many of our people as could fit.

Dov and I took the last place, tucking ourselves away in a dark corner hidden around a closed off room. His fingers found their way to mine as we waited. We stood, chest to chest, waiting in the silence.

For a long time, he watched me, staring into my eyes. Finally, the smallest of smiles crept onto his lips. His deep blue eyes wrinkled just enough to notice that he was restraining his grin.

I rolled my eyes, making him smirk.

My breath caught as someone entered the hallway.

A second set of footsteps joined the first, padding down the hall-way. They talked quietly, mumbling as they went. My eyes bore into the ground to my left, watching for them to pass. Society uniforms flashed by, safely passing us. I waited for them to reach the end of the hall, praying they didn't notice any of our people lurking just an arm's length away.

The door to the outside world shut with a soft click halfway down the hall. They hadn't gone far enough to notice our entry point.

Impulsively, Dov leaned forward and brushed a kiss against my lips. I looked away, grinning, trying to remain focused. When I looked back, he was stifling his own smile.

He was going to get us all killed.

I shook my head, looking at him. Darting forward, I surprised him, brushing my lips against his. When I pulled back, he stared so intently at me, I knew he was forgetting where we were. The voices dragged us back to reality.

Multiple footsteps sounded, filling the hall with a soft padding noise. A row of men shuffled past us in drab grey clothing. The boys.

We waited for them to pass, attempting to count how many filed through. Once it was quiet again, we held our positions long enough to feel like it was safe.

Dov was the first to venture out, stepping cautiously into the walkway. He held my hand, letting his linger behind the wall. When it was clear, he tugged me forward. Crossing my path, he guided me toward the door, while he moved deeper into the building, pulling our people out of hiding. If we were caught, it was all over.

Once everyone was in the hall, we moved en mass toward the door. Silas and his team would be on the other side of the building, waiting to exit as well.

Talley placed her hand on the door, waiting for Dov's signal. Outside, the boys were training, as they did every day. We nodded to Talley to open the door just enough to see outside. Waiting, we watched as she peeked out, counting the guards and waiting for the patrolling Society man to pass by.

She held up her fingers, counting down. On cue, she threw her arm back, yanking the door open as she crushed herself against the wall to get out of our way.

Without wasting time, Dov walked through the door, into the sunlight which was now much higher in the sky. We calmly walked into the yard, the boys barely taking notice. Unlike the captives, the guards took note of the intrusion.

"Surrender now, and we won't hurt you," Dov announced.

Our people spread out, surrounding the front building. Confusion broke out among the Society men, trying to decipher who we were and why we were there. One man finally activated the rest, spurring them into action.

They shouted to their captives as they ran drills, forcing them to turn their weapons on us. The boys carefully stepped toward us, reluctant to go into battle as their trainers launched an attack, leaving the boys with their training weapons as their only defense.

"My name is Dov Baer, I am the son of Griz Baer. My father died fighting to free this country. Join us and help us overthrow the Society," Dov addressed them, standing tall.

"Dov?" a voice in the crowd carried to us.

Dov searched the crowd, looking for the source.

"We can trust him," the voice cried.

"He's Society!" screamed another. "Look at him. It's a training tactic."

The voice muscled his way forward.

"He's with us."

"We're here to free you. Our people are at all the camps as we speak, starting the first wave of assaults," he said, neglecting to tell them that we also had the upper hand with Canton and the magistrates.

"Lur?" another voice pierced the noise of the training yard.

I knocked my hood off, exposing my hair. Dov had given himself up, so why not me? It fell around my waist in a wave of gold.

"I know her," he said. He was young. Lowell didn't usually let such young people join; perhaps it had something to do with Shadoe.

"You know us. If not personally, you know our people...our families. We're just like you; the Society is willing to throw us all away to get what they want," I said. "But we have a plan to free the camps and rise up against the magistrates and take back our country!"

A guard ran at us, coming from my side. I stepped toward him, blocking him from Dov, allowing him to continue to talk. The blade Shadoe had given me tore into the man's forearm, forcing him to drop the knife he attempted to plunge into my chest. Blood quietly dripped to the ground, like the beginning of a rainstorm, one small, intentional drop at a time.

"We promise to tell you everything once we, together, have taken control of the camp away from the Society," Dov yelled over the screaming guards, "and we promise you a free choice in whether or not you join us, but for now, we ask you to help us in this fight—right here—and bring this camp to its knees."

Four boys stepped forward, running at their captors. Another half a dozen followed behind, engaging in battle against the men who whipped them when they stepped out of line. The rest of the young men being trained against their will stepped forward, encouraged by our bravado.

Glancing around, I took stock of the scene.

I registered Dov shouting to tie the men up as I watched two men brawl. One was young; still a teenager. His opponent was tall with dark hair covering his face.

I ran at them, determined to take the knife from the man. My foot lashed out, striking him in the hip, turning him over as he toppled from where he straddled the boy.

"Nope," I muttered under my breath as I reached for his hand. He grappled with me, trying to get the knife back.

The man cursed at me, attempting to claw at my face. I kicked at his arm, trying to block him. His bone shattered. The man wrenched over in pain, shrieking in agony. My eyes grew wide. I didn't realize I had put that much force into my kick.

"Auluria?" Dov called.

"Not me," I answered back. The knife sat in my hand as I darted away. I was surprised I had scooped it up from the ground without realizing it. Shadoe would be proud.

The young boys worked together, taking on their trainers. More men joined from inside the building, but the boys outnumbered the men who were overseeing them. Without time to plan, their efforts were disjointed.

A metallic scent filled the air as blood pooled on the ground. I hated the carnage. The boys held at the camp had been taught to succeed in battle. Their skills were focused on causing destruction. Their aim was to defend their battleground and take down as many opponents as possible. The Society had planned to quell any uprising from inside the camp long before it started, and end any intruders before they entered. They hadn't planned for rebels to get inside and start a coup.

"Lur!" a voice shouted, causing me to duck.

A large man tripped over me. I lifted my shoulders as he collided against my side, dropping him on the ground beyond. The boy was by my side—knife in hand—ready to slit the man's throat.

"No!" I yelped, blocking his arm. It crashed into mine as I gritted my teeth against the immediate pain. "I know Lowell's mission was less careful about life, but he doesn't need to die."

The man groaned on the dirt, shifting. I reached down, clamping my fingers around his thick wrist. I started to instruct the boy to tie him up when he looked at me, annoyance written across his face. He grunted but turned the knife in his hand so that the blade faced away. With a quick movement, he brought the hilt down on the man's temple, knocking him out.

"I can live with that," I nodded. "But tie him up."

The boy nodded back.

"What happened to you?" he asked, working quickly as chaos continued to erupt around us.

"When did they catch you, before or after Lowell?"

"Lowell is dead?" his eyes widened.

"Yes, Shadoe and I are in charge now." I made sure he knew whom to respect. "We combined our forces with two other groups: the Baers and a faction from beyond the Wall.

"Can you get the other boys to work with us?" I asked, hoping he had some influence.

He took a deep breath, studying me.

"What exactly is the plan?" he asked over the shouting. For a moment, the world quieted and it was just the two of us.

"We're bringing down the camps…all of them. We're shutting them down simultaneously and making it look like they're still functioning. We're going to move as many people inside the Society as possible." I decided to trust him, even though I shouldn't. "We have control of Canton. They won't even know what hit them."

The boy's eyes grew wide at Canton's name. He tipped his head, considering my words as someone grunted beside us.

"You okay there, Goldilocks?" Justin grinned as he grappled with a trainer. He pushed the man backward, but the Society guard got his feet under him and pushed back, moving Justin a few feet.

"Goldilocks?" the boy asked incredulously.

"It's a…thing." I shook my head, dismissing it. I turned to Justin. "Do you need help?"

Justin pushed forward again, this time shoving the man hard enough for him to lose his balance. Talley stepped up behind him, catching the pressure point on the man's neck between her fingers. He dropped to the ground.

"Nope," Justin shrugged. His grin fell as he eyed us. "What's this?"

"I'm one of her men," the boy straightened, addressing Justin like the loyal soldier Lowell or Shadoe had trained him to be before he was taken. He spun on his heels to face me. "I'll help you."

"Good, start getting these men organized." I glanced around, noting that we clearly had the upper hand. "I'm going around to the other side to check on Silas' group."

"I'll come with you," Justin announced, nodding to his sister to stay. She turned to see where she could help. "Come on."

The scream in the distance prompted us to run faster.

Chapter 5

"Go," I instructed, "Help her."

Justin split off from me, racing toward where Reyla held her ground. She was cornered, but not giving up.

I ran toward Henry and Katarina, throwing myself into the man rushing at them. He was more solid than I had anticipated, sending me rocking backward. A jolt of pain coursed through my body as I stumbled, catching myself after a few staggering paces.

I lashed out at him, using the knife Shadoe had procured for me. It sliced across his arm, only serving to anger him more. He stepped toward me menacingly. Perhaps I couldn't stop him.

I braced myself, waiting for him to lower his stance and barrel at me. I gripped my knives tightly in my hands, hoping to be faster than he was.

"I always knew I'd be the one to save you," Gregory said, stepping up to my side. "Prince Charming, at your service."

The man's eyes widened as he continued to move toward us. His steps slowed for a moment before he toppled toward us. Henry stood with a bloody knife as Katarina lowered her foot. They had turned around to discover I had joined them and used the opportunity to take down the threat while we distracted the man.

Katarina grinned smugly, crossing her arms over her chest.

"I believe that's prince and *princess* to *you*." She pointed between herself and her boyfriend. She batted her eyelashes at Gregory to tease him.

Henry's face dropped suddenly.

"Look out!" he warned.

I whipped around, elbow ready to crash into any face I may find behind me. Gregory acted quickly, taking on the assault himself. When I was sure he had it under control, I maneuvered around to see where I could help.

The light shifted, moving from day to evening despite the early hour. The world seemed to mute as light and sound went dull. I had seen the switch before. I knew what it meant.

A moment later, without any time to react, the sky opened up, dousing us in rain. It fell hard and fast, angled so strangely I almost thought it had to be a part of the Society's plan. The one thing they *couldn't* control was the weather…aside from us, anyway.

As if taking a collective breath, the entire training yard paused to glance up. A few men grimaced as raindrops hit their unprotected eyes. Just as quickly as everyone had stopped, they started again, growling and slashing at each other.

Nikko ran by me, happily taking on anyone who got in his way. Not far behind, Ella took her time picking off Society trainers until we had the upper hand.

"Auluria," Reyla said, announcing herself before she could frighten me as she approached from behind.

"Is everything okay out front?" Silas asked, following behind her.

"Yeah, I came around to check on your team," I replied, glad that the fight was dying down. "Have you secured the boys over here?"

"I think so," Silas said. "Reyla did a great job."

I grinned, nodding to my best friend.

The rain fell harder, soaking through my hair. Reyla wrinkled her nose as she tucked a stray piece of hair back into her hood. My fingers fumbled as I attempted to pull my own hood back up. Reyla reached over to help me as I fought to push all of my hair inside.

"Graceful," Silas commented, smirking before he took off to help Justin.

"He's just mad that he couldn't help you like Dov would have," Reyla teased.

"Oh?" I rolled my eyes. "And just how would that have been?"

"Very, very slowly, I imagine." She brushed her fingers down my arm and laughed. Reyla delighted in teasing me.

"We should move everyone inside," I commented, watching puddles grow on the ground.

"At least the rain will help hide all the blood," Reyla grew serious.

"Go get Justin and tell Silas we're going to clear the building," I instructed her.

I made my way to Henry and Katarina to explain the plan.

"Find Dov and tell him I'm taking a small team in to clear the building. If you can, send a few of his people in to help us," I pointed around the side of the building. "As soon as things are under control, get everyone to the same side of the building and move them inside."

"On it," Henry said. He pulled at Katarina's hand and guided her quickly along the building.

Reyla made her way over with Justin in tow. Silas waved from where he stood, directing his team to let me know he approved of the plan.

Locust appeared alongside Anetta, Reed, Gregory, and a few others. I quickly explained that we needed to clear the building and split the group up into pairs.

Justin and I took the lead, entering through the back entrance. We swept the bottom floor, quickly moving on to the second floor, as Gregory and Reyla did a more thorough search. Locust and Anetta branched off, looking for Society men to the left.

"Clear," Justin whispered, backing out of the room as I waited in the hallway.

"*Clear*," Locust said harshly from down the hall. His voice echoed, making me cringe. I could almost feel Anetta's glare against my back.

I took the next room. Swinging the door open, I prepared for confrontation. The room was empty, a small set of shelves against the walls. Books sat at odd angles. A few maps were tucked away between books, an occasional page spilling out of a pile, cascading down over the shelf below it.

Once satisfied, I stepped back.

"Clear," I whispered.

Justin moved down to the next door, preparing to check it as I took my place behind him. I tapped his shoulder to let him know I was on my mark. The door opened, revealing a similar room to the one I had just swept.

Justin tensed. A man stood by the window inside. The sky outside had brightened a little since we made our way inside the building. It illuminated him, wrapping light around his figure just enough to see his features. The backlight was harsh against the dark shadows that played across his face.

"I've been waiting for you," he said, sadly.

Justin rocked forward, waiting to make his move.

"I take it this means we lost," the man said. He placed a hand on the windowsill behind him. "You know the magistrates won't take kindly to that."

"I do believe that's the point," Justin replied dryly.

The man sighed.

"You realize I'm supposed to put up a fight..." His lips turned down as he spoke.

"Oh? Why is that?" Justin asked.

"Part of the job description," he tipped his head sideways, studying Justin. "I have a family and I'm sure the magistrates would take it out on them."

"What if we could help them?" I asked, stretching up to be seen over Justin's shoulder.

"You can't." He looked defeated.

"What if—" Justin tried to push.

"No, this is how it has to be."

The man lunged toward Justin, nearly tripping over himself as he crossed the room. Justin reacted, moving far enough back to move us both out of the way. He caught the man as he propelled forward. The man didn't stop.

Throwing his elbow back, he collided with Justin's shoulder, making my friend yell in pain. Locust and Anetta shuffled in the hall, coming to investigate. I latched onto the man's wrist, forcing his knife away from Justin.

The man was strong. As I clung to him, I had to use my full body weight to drag him down, and even then, it was a fight. Justin wrenched one hand behind the man's back. His kick to the man's leg was his undoing, sending him crashing to the ground. I was tugged along in his fall, forcing me to the ground. My knee slammed against the floor making me cry out.

Anetta burst through the door, eyes frantically searching the scene. She found us in a messy heap on the floor as Justin wrestled the man into submission. I clawed back his hand that I had managed to keep a hold on.

"Want me to kick him?" Anetta asked. She took a terrifying step toward us, preparing to slam her boot into the Society man's face.

"No!" I yelped, hoping she would drop back.

"Let her, Lur," Locust said over his shoulder as he watched the hallway. "We need to keep going and don't have time to deal with him conscious."

"No," I held a hand up to stop her.

She studied me, deciding between listening to Locust and her intuition, or me. She backed down, moving back toward the door.

"You better handle this," she said, giving me the space to deal with the situation.

Justin accepted responsibility, reaching forward to knock the man out. The man's head smacked against the floor. We held him for a moment longer to make sure he was really out.

"You okay?" Justin asked quietly, glancing at Anetta and Locust in the doorway.

"I'm fine," I answered. "Are you okay?"

"I'm good." He put his hands on the ground to push himself up. Once standing he added, "What are we going to do with him?"

He used the tip of his boot to push the man's leg, rolling it slightly. I shrugged, wondering if there was a safe place to tie him up.

"What if we put him in the room down the hall? We could block him in the closet." Justin suggested. "Put a chair in front of it and he won't be able to get it open even if he *does* wake up before we get back to him."

"Locust," I called. "I need you to help Justin move him to the room down the hall."

I traded places with him, temporarily partnering with Anetta. Justin and Locust lifted the man, dragging him out the door as we covered them in case anyone should unexpectedly appear in our path.

Inside the room, we maneuvered the Society trainer into the closet. Justin tried to position the man so that it wouldn't be too painful when he woke up, but there was only so much he could do. They tied the man's wrists under his knees where they bent to fit inside the small closet.

Closing the door, Justin waited for me to bring him the chair. He wedged it under the door handle, tipping the chair on its back legs.

"Good luck getting out of there, buddy."

"They're here," Anetta said from the doorway, relaxing her stance. She nodded inside the room.

A moment later, Dov stepped around her.

"Should I ask?"

"Creative jail?" Justin shrugged from the corner of the room, nodding to the barrier outside the door.

"I'm not going to ask," Dov looked amused. "Everyone okay?"

"We're good. Are they sweeping the rest of the building?" Justin joined our small circle.

"They are," Dov confirmed, wrapping his arms around my waist. "The good news is that the rooms where they keep the boys all lock from the outside, so we can lock the trainers in there. We've got the boys partnered with our people and they're overseeing the Society trainers.

"The bad news is that we definitely have a few bodies."

"Any of ours?" I asked.

"No," Raselin rounded the corner, expanding our group. "A few injuries, but no deaths, thankfully."

"Most of the bodies are from when the boys initially turned on the trainers before we talked them down," Dov said. "We need to talk to them."

"There's a dining room downstairs," I added. "We could hold a meeting there."

"That's a good idea," Dov agreed, flipping a piece of hair out of his eyes. "Let's get all of the boys down there. Fitch can oversee watching the prisoners."

"Good idea. We don't need everyone in the meeting," Raselin put his hand on Dov's shoulder. "Go get your people, Dov. We'll meet in fifteen minutes."

"We should work with them," the blond boy shouted from where he stood by his chair. "We've been trained to fight, and they need fighters. They're working against the Society, which is something we *all* want to do.

"Just look what the Society has done to us!" he bellowed, holding out his arms to expose the scars. "This is our chance to get them back for destroying our lives!"

"And our family's lives!" Another added, standing to his feet.

"But we could be free," a third boy argued.

I resisted the urge to find a wall to lean against as they talked within their group. The blond boy looked at me, begging for me to be as vicious as Lowell had me trained to be. Fire was one thing; destruction was another.

One hundred boys sat around the tables, hovering between revenge and freedom. They looked like scared mice ready to bolt at any moment. The blond kid looked to me again, trying to motivate me into action. Dov's hand on my back was the only thing that prompted me to speak.

"Our goal is for all of us to be free." I forced my hands to remain at my sides instead of crossing them over my chest. "But not just *you*. We want the entire country to be free of the Society.

"In theory, we now have control of all of the boys' camps. The next step is to free the girls. Right now, as we speak, our leaders have control of certain factions of the Society. We want to make it look like everything is business as usual around here, and then sneak most of you in with us."

Dov stepped up next to me. I hadn't realized I had moved forward while speaking to the boys.

"By the time the Society realizes we hold all the power, it will be too late. They won't be able to recover," Dov smiled convincingly. "We're going to arrest the people who are working against us."

He held up a hand before the boys protested and chuckled.

"I know that seems counterproductive. We need these men alive though. We need to question them. These men have been running the Society since long before any of us were born. They know everything about it, and more importantly, about what's going on outside of the Wall.

"You see, once we've freed ourselves from the magistrates' control, we still have to protect ourselves from the outside. This all started specifically because the outsiders came for us. Our leaders bent to their will in an effort to save us originally, but continued to bow to them in order to protect themselves."

The slight pressure on my hip indicated that it was my turn to jump in.

"That threat doesn't go away just because we take down the Society," I said, shifting my foot to touch Dov's. "Our immediate goal is to close down the camps and take power from the magistrates. We have leaders set in place to facilitate this—"

"I thought *you* were our leader," someone interrupted.

"We are part of the leadership, yes," I agreed. "We have leadership from the Baers, from my cousin, Lowell's, group, and from a faction from over the Wall."

I nodded to Dov, Raselin, and myself.

"We aren't the only ones. There are many of us. And before you ask, we are not keeping the power when this is all done. We're only overseeing things until we bring the Society down. We'll stay on after to bring down the Wall and end the threat from other countries if that helps, but after that, it will be up to the country to decide."

"No one is that *good*," someone said, "Certainly not *Lowell's* people. He wanted power."

Dov's hand tightened around me, ready to back the boy down for me.

"Yes, he did," I said before Dov could speak. "My cousin only wanted power, and he didn't care what he had to do to get it. But where is Lowell now?"

I shrugged, waiting for them to speak. When they didn't, I continued.

"Lowell is dead. His greed and deceit lead to his downfall. My cousin was willing to do anything to get power. He used me and threw me away when I was no longer useful. I watched him do it for years. He wouldn't hesitate to use each and every one of you right now and let you die to get him the power he wanted.

"We don't want to use you. We want you to stand with us, but even if you don't, we'll still fight for you." A few of the boys perked up, resonating with my words.

"You don't have to help us," Dov added. "You will get your freedom either way if we win."

He paused, tipping his head. "It would be a lot easier to win if you'd help."

The boy who remembered me from my time with Lowell looked affronted. He must not have known me well even back then if he thought I would sweep into the compound and order a massacre of my enemies.

"We are not the Society. We don't need to be like them," I looked directly at the boy, hoping my words would mean something. "We want to be free of them, not bring in a new generation of them."

The group nodded all at once, surprising me.

"Okay," one boy murmured. The others followed, creating a soft echo.

"If you don't want to help, that's fine," Dov said, pulling his hand off my hip to emphasize his words. "We'll show you where to go to be safe until this is all over.

"If you *are* joining us, we're going to need a few of you to stay here to run the compound. You'll need to make it look like the camp is still operational and keep an eye on the trainers we have locked up. The rest of you will be coming with us."

Dov took a breath, preparing to direct people.

"If you don't want to stay, stand up now and move to the door. Silas is going to help you prepare to leave. He'll show you where to go and will give you some supplies to get you started."

He paused, allowing three boys to stand and make their way over to Silas. The rest remained seated. I grinned.

"I'm glad to see some of you want to stay and help." Dov shifted forward. "I know most of you probably want to take the fight to the Society, so I'm going to ask for volunteers to stay here and protect our cover."

"If you stay," I added, "you'll be responsible for handling your former trainers. You are not allowed to hurt them. Remember, we're going to need them once we have control of the magistrates. They'll all be held accountable for their crimes. If you stay here, we have to be able to trust you."

"Some of our men will be staying to help you. There's a plan in place for handling these trainers. They're also prepared to handle anyone who may show up unexpectedly." Dov nodded to one of the men who stood against the outside wall. "Who can we trust to stay and handle things here?"

Dov surveyed the room, waiting for volunteers. When no one stood, my heart stopped. I pressed my tongue against the back of my teeth to keep my worry in check. I didn't need my face betraying my confidence in the mission.

"I'll stay," the blond boy said, standing to his feet. He looked right at me. "If this is our mission, I'll stay."

He was a soldier through and through. Lowell would have been proud.

A dozen others stood, joining him. Progress.

"Good men," Dov praised them. "Come with me and I'll introduce you to your new leader."

Dov led the boys across the room, quietly explaining their new mission. They listened intently as he shifted their attention over to one of Berwyn's men that would be overseeing the camp.

I turned my attention back to the main group.

"Tomorrow we're going to the girls' camp. We need to break them out. The ones that can, will be joining us. Many of them will not be able to."

"Why?" one of the youngest boys asked. He couldn't have been more than twelve.

"Many of the girls will be carrying babies. They train you to fight and they took the girls so they could create new fighters. Did any of you come directly from a camp?" I asked, knowing I'd hate the answer.

Many of them nodded. They had been taken from their mothers; created and raised specifically to be added to the training camps. They had never known any other life.

"We're going to make sure they're all safe. We'll need some of you to stay there to help protect them if the Society figures out what we're doing. We'll need volunteers for that too."

Several of the boys jumped up, looking furious.

"I'll protect them," one of the boys who had just admitted to being raised in a camp said.

"My sister was taken to a camp," another proclaimed. "I'll stay with the girls."

"Good, we'll need everyone we can get," I smiled. "We'll set out for the camp tomorrow. Tonight, we need to get you all fed and ready to move out.

"I need you all to help us gather supplies."

The boys listened as I rattled off a list of things we'd need them to bring. I kept them seated as Dov returned.

"Meet back here in one hour. At that point, we'll share a meal together and go over the plan," Dov instructed.

They all filed out, ready to collect supplies. Dov and I watched them go, waiting until the room cleared.

"Time to talk," Dov said.

Chapter 6

DOV TUGGED AT MY HAND, GUIDING ME INTO THE ROOM. IT WAS QUIET despite the shuffling out in the hall. Brilliant orange lit the space, bits of gold adding pops of glitter as it glared through the window. The rain had ended.

"Took long enough," Silas smirked from the chair.

"Did you find anything?" Dov asked, taking the seat opposite his friend.

"The building plans for the girls' camp." Silas pushed a piece of paper across the study table.

"This seems too easy," Dov joked, shaking his head.

"Everything else has been incredibly hard, Dov," I reminded him as I perched on the arm of his plush chair. "Accept a moment of ease."

"Good point." He took my hand in his, bringing it to his lips.

The sunset glinted off their hair as I looked over from where I sat, highlighting them both beautifully. We'd been through so much together in the months we had known each other. I could barely remember my life before Dov and Silas. My world would be so empty without them...even without Berwyn and Eden.

I couldn't help myself when I reached out to touch Dov's hair when they finished discussing the papers in front of them. He ducked, not expecting my touch. Even Silas' eyes were wide when I giggled.

"I honestly don't know where I'd be without you two."

"Dead," Silas smirked.

"Still with your cousin," Dov suggested.

"Probably a killer," Silas offered with a shrug. "What, you know he would have pushed for that."

"Not my girl," Dov said, reaching up to tuck my hair back. It caught the orange glow, lighting it up like fire.

"You two really did save me," I commented, my voice laced with contentment.

"And you saved us," Silas said, making Dov grin. "Well, *him* at least…and the others. I totally had this, though."

"Give her a little credit, Silas." Dov's eyes sparkled mischievously. "She's not done yet. You know she's going to make it happen."

"Make what happen?" I sat up straighter.

"I know no such thing," Silas disagreed playfully.

"Make *what* happen?" I persisted.

Dov locked eyes with Silas, challenging him.

"*Don't,*" Silas cautioned.

"I'm going to have to tell her sometime," Dov shrugged, leaning back in the chair. "Wouldn't hurt to be today."

"It would be a distraction," Silas corrected him with a glare. "We need everyone on top of their game."

Dov sighed dramatically, nearly knocking me off the chair arm. I scooted closer, wrapping my arms around the back of the chair.

"Fine," he teased. "But you really should stop putting it off."

"Oh, Silas," I shook my head. "You know I already know."

He studied me, trying to decide if I was bluffing. I raised an eyebrow at him, daring him to call me out.

"I really have no idea if you do or don't right now," Silas admitted, struggling to read me.

"Brittella trained you well," Dov turned to me, pride radiating across his face. "Speaking of…"

"Well if *that's* where this is headed, I'm out." Silas laughed, standing up. The dwindling orange light raced across his face, darting in and out of the shadows as he moved. "I'll check in with Raselin and Fitch."

He walked toward the door, turning back to add, "Don't be long, we have things to do."

"*Yes, Dad,*" Dov teased as Silas closed the door behind him.

When the door clicked, Dov turned to me. His face was covered in dark shadows, making his skin almost blue. A bit of light bounced off my own skin, illuminating his eyes as he pursed his lips.

"I've been promising you a conversation," he spoke softly.

"You have," I agreed.

I reached out, tangling my fingers in his hair. He responded by reaching around my hips and roughly pulling me onto his lap. I managed to work my knees around his during the short fall so that I didn't get caught. My left hand left its spot on my thigh and wrapped around Dov's neck.

He leaned forward quickly, holding me to avoid throwing us off balance. He breathed in as he approached me. The sunset danced behind my eyelids as Dov kissed me.

His lips were warm against my skin as he trailed down my neck. I leaned into him, burying my face in his hair. A laugh bubbled up to his lips as I tickled his ear with my nose. Dov dragged me closer.

"Playing dirty, are we?" he growled as he pressed his fingers against my back.

"I was never trained to play fair." I dropped my voice as I ran my hand over a lock of hair that had fallen between us. "Take it or leave it."

"Oh, I'll take it." His voice rumbled deep in his chest.

I beat him this time, closing the distance between us. His fingers found their way to my chin, caressing my skin with each kiss. He tilted my face, anticipating each move so that we would fit perfectly together each time we touched. I tugged on his hair, encouraging him.

"Auluria," Dov breathed against my neck, his voice hitching.

I pulled my knees up, moving my feet from the floor as I let them fall on the chair next to Dov's hip, curling into myself. His arm wrapped around my legs, pulling me close. I leaned in, desperately wanting to be closer.

When I finally pulled back, the sun was perfectly aligned with the horizon outside, glaring in through the study window. It bathed Dov in a radiant golden light.

My eyes, tired from lack of oxygen, rested half-closed as I watched him. He stared at me like I was brand new to him.

"I love you, Auluria." He smiled, drawing small circles on my back.

I watched him for another moment before leaning in to brush our lips together.

"I loved you from the moment I first saw you, Dov Baer."

He tried to keep from smirking as he gave me a look, challenging my statement.

"Fine, maybe not the first moment," I said, thinking back to the time I crashed into him in the woods, "But definitely when you sat me down at your kitchen table."

"That's more believable," he grinned, "The *first* time you saw me, you threw things at me and hurt my feelings."

"Oh," I pretended to be sorry. "I should make up for that."

"You should," he nodded.

"But first," I added, shattering his plans, "that talk."

"Yeah," he sighed, "that."

"That." I traced his jaw with my finger, making him tip his lips to kiss it.

He watched me, trying to decide what to say.

"Dov, when you—"

The knock at the door scared me so much that I jumped, making Dov jump as well. He closed his eyes, sucking in a deep breath to steady himself. I threw myself to my feet as the doorknob twisted.

Brittella entered, giving me a knowing look as she locked eyes with me. She stepped aside, making way for the blond boy from earlier.

"Sorry to interrupt your meeting, my dears, but Eli wanted to say something," Brittella said, holding no remorse in her voice. She looked like she was enjoying the moment.

Eli's face was hard as he stepped forward. Dov stood from the chair, joining me near the table.

"I know who you are now," Eli started. He held Dov's gaze. "You saved my brother."

Dov squinted at him.

"What do you mean?"

"You pulled him out of a fire, and then you let him escape. Anyone else would have tortured him for information." His words implied that he meant Lowell would have tortured him. "Had it been Wallace, he might have killed him just for the fun of it. But you let him go.

"It took me awhile to make the connection, but they were talking about you downstairs. That was you, wasn't it?"

"The storehouse," I whispered, realizing it was the boy Dov had pulled from Shadoe's failed mission to attack the Baers' storehouse not long after I joined the Baers. It was right before Dov kissed me for the first time.

"I remember him," Dov confirmed. "Was he…okay?"

"Yes, he made it back," he looked down, kicking at an imaginary rock. "It wasn't long after he returned that I was captured and sent here."

Dov nodded, allowing him to continue.

"I owe you," the boy finally said.

"You don't owe me, Eli," Dov said gently. "I was happy to help your brother."

"He wouldn't have helped you," Eli finally looked up. "I wouldn't have either."

"You have a chance to change that now," Dov said, trying to encourage him. "You volunteered to help the girls, didn't you?"

"I did that because of Lur. She needed volunteers, and she's my leader now that Lowell is gone."

"So you're a good soldier," Dov said cautiously, "but you also have the opportunity to be a good person.

"Many of the girls we will free tomorrow won't be able to take care of themselves. Many of them will be with child or will have young children. Your job is to protect them if the Society comes for them, and to help them if they need anything while you're there."

"It may be your job, Eli, but it's also your choice," I added.

"I helped your brother when no one else could," Dov continued. "Now you can help people that no one else can. I have faith in you."

"I do too," I told him.

Eli's gaze shifted away as if lost in thought. Suddenly he turned back, straightening. He threw his shoulder back as if he were preparing to speak to Lowell or Shadoe.

"Thank you for helping my brother." He spun on his heels and exited the room.

Brittella took that as her cue. She sauntered across the room, batting her eyelashes.

"And what have we here?"

"Did you need something, Brittella?" I asked, trying to keep from sounding terse.

"A word," she purred before smiling at Dov. "Run along, Mr. Baer. I believe your friends are looking for you."

Dov eyed me but sidestepped around Brittella to make his way to the door. He closed the door over behind him.

"Have a seat, Auluria." She motioned with her hand as she took the chair Dov and I had just occupied. "I have one more thing to teach you."

With the recruits organized, supplies in order, and the camp trainers under heavy guard, it should have been easy to sleep. Reyla and I spent the entire night fighting to turn our minds off and rest.

"This isn't going well," Reyla whispered quietly after hearing me sigh in defeat.

"Nope," I whispered back. I propped myself up on an elbow before pushing myself to my feet. "Come on."

She quietly followed me out of the room, making our way to the hall. Sounds of snoring and soft breathing hit my ears as we passed by each open door. I shivered in the cold.

"Couldn't sleep?" Lydia asked as we walked into the study.

"You couldn't either?" I asked, lowering myself to the floor to the right of the window. I pulled my knees to my chest, securing them in place with my arms.

"I don't like being away from Fitch," she admitted, leaning back into the chair. "I've also never felt anything so luxurious in my life, so spending the night in this chair isn't the worst thing ever."

I smiled, giggling as she scrunched herself up in the chair.

"These are pretty wonderful," Reyla sighed. "What shall we talk about, ladies?"

"How do you think Canton is behaving? Do you think Shadoe is keeping him under control?" Lydia asked.

"If Shadoe can't, no one can," I replied. "I'm worried about what Canton might do when he gets around the other magistrates though."

"Have we found out how Raselin and Brittella know each other yet?" Reyla interrupted. We turned to her a little shocked. "Well, do we?"

Her persistence made us giggle.

"They grew up together from what I can tell," Lydia informed us with a knowing look. "No connections other than that as far as I can tell."

"Back to your matchmaking ways, Rey?" I smirked.

"I handled you and Dov, didn't I? I need a new project."

"I volunteer Jasleen," I offered.

"Auluria, she's five." Reyla rolled her eyes.

"Precisely, that should keep you away from everyone else's love lives for a while." I paused. "Actually, new assignment: Silas and Justin need girlfriends. They're your new projects."

"Hmm," she tapped her chin. "I can work with that."

"Talking about my brother?" Talley said sleepily, ducking into the room. Her hair stuck out on one side She noticed us looking and reached up to straighten it. "I saw you two slip out and got bored, so I decided to follow you."

"Join the party," Reyla said, stretching out her hand to wave her in.

Talley slid down the wall next to me, dropping her head on my shoulder. She mimicked my pose, wrapping her arms around her knees.

"I really don't have a preference on which girl you get to marry Justin, as long as you get him out of my hair," she teased. "While you're at it, Devin, too, please."

"Talley, I'm going to need your help tomorrow," I lowered my voice as Lydia and Reyla discussed possible girlfriends for Silas, Justin, and Devin. "We need to make sure the girls can handle themselves before we go bringing them into battle. Many of them will have been at the camps for a long time, and while I'm sure some of them can fight, we have to make sure their skills are still sharp enough that they won't get hurt when we take on the Society."

"I can help with that." Talley nodded, sending her hair tumbling over her ear where she tucked it and into her face. She let out a short, sharp breath and blew the strands back. "What do you want to do?"

"We need to see them work. If they feel like they can join us, we need to see them in action. I'm sure they'll feel better if they're fighting us than any of the guys. I'm also a little worried they might take their frustration out on the guys and we don't need any of them getting hurt before we take on the Society men."

"Assuming everything is going well at Canton's mansion, we should be able to get in without too many problems."

"Hopefully," I commented. "We'll have Dov, Silas, Reyla, and Fitch help us decide about the girls tomorrow. I have a feeling Lowell's former girls will opt to come with us because Lowell has always trained them to handle the mission first. We may actually have a fight on our hands with some of them if they can't come for some reason."

"You'll reason with them," Talley assured me.

"Auluria doesn't do reason," Reyla joined the conversation. "Auluria does impulsive."

"*Hey!*" I shouted.

"She has a point," Talley teased.

"Really, you're all turning against me?" I questioned, looking each of them in the eyes.

"Yes," they all chorused.

"Careful," I warned them, "I might just be inspired to leave you all to guard the girls' camp tomorrow."

They rolled their eyes, chuckling.

"Auluria," a small voice at the door made us all look up. Maylin and Katarina stepped in. "I want to stay tomorrow."

"You want to stay?" I questioned.

"Necesta has been teaching me," Maylin looked down as if she were embarrassed. "I don't know much, but I think I can help."

She glanced up, waiting for my permission. I studied her in the doorway. She was soft and sweet. Fighting was no place for a girl like Maylin, but Necesta knew that long before we left.

"I think you would be a great asset, Maylin. I imagine Necesta sent a few things with you?"

"She did." Maylin pulled her pack off her shoulders and gently set it at her feet. "I think she planned this."

"I have a feeling she did," Katarina agreed as she patted Maylin's shoulder.

"You have to agree to come back to us once this is all over though, Maylin," I instruct the girl. "We can give you up for a little while, but we can't have you leave us forever."

Maylin smiled. "Okay," she promised. "When it's all over and the girls are safe, and their babies are all okay, I'll come back."

"I'm just pointing out," Katarina swayed over to Reyla and sat on her armrest. "*I* wasn't the one who had to make that mandate."

She winked at Maylin.

"We'll all happily benefit from it though," Reyla added.

"Since you know what you're doing, Maylin, maybe now is a good time to teach us what we should be looking for tomorrow," I suggested.

Maylin glanced at the way Katarina was perched on the chair before confidently walking over to the edge of the table closest to the window. She sat on the edge, testing it cautiously as she put her hand back to guide herself. She walked us through what Necesta had shared with her before we all fell asleep for a few hours before we left for the camp.

"Can I get you anything?" I asked the girl. She rested in a bed, looking like she could give birth at any moment.

Raselin's team had breached the camp without needing any backup from the other groups. We quickly flooded the halls, letting the girls know what was happening.

"I'm fine, thank you," she smiled sweetly at me. "Could you send Katarina over when she has a moment?"

"Do you know her?" I asked, glancing across the room to where Katarina attended to another young girl.

"I did." Her nod was stiff against her pillow. It moved her hair behind her, causing it to stick up at a strange angle. "She hasn't seen me yet though…or maybe she doesn't recognize me."

She reached up, attempting to fix her hair. Once it was successfully tucked back under her head, she added, "I hope she remembers me."

I quietly slipped away and crossed the room. I tapped Katarina on the shoulder.

"You're needed over there," I tried to suppress my mischievous grin.

She gave me a curious look before walking away. Katarina glanced over her shoulder, waiting for me to indicate that she was going in the right direction.

"Hannah!" she shrieked when she saw the girl.

Katarina raced the rest of the way, throwing herself onto the edge of the small bed. She burst into tears and the two talked incoherently.

"What's that about?" Reyla asked as she joined me, squinting to try to make out the scene.

"That would be a girl named Hannah," I replied, still watching the old friends reunite.

"Hannah?" Reyla gasped, nearly dropping the glass of water she was holding. She managed to shove it in my hands and mumble to get Silas and Dov before racing across the room.

It took a moment for me to return to my senses. I found the girl the water was meant for, and set out in search for Dov and Silas. They stood in the hallway, lecturing Ella for being too harsh with one of the girls.

"Gentlemen," I interrupted, "I was sent to find you."

Dov sent Ella off. I could feel her roll her eyes as soon as her back was turned.

"Ella," I lectured sharply. The girl froze for a moment. She plastered a smile on and turned over her shoulder enough for me to see. "Please tell Anetta I need to speak with her. It's no rush."

Ella bounced off as I dismissed her, brown hair swaying behind her.

"Any chance we can leave her here?" Silas complained.

"Haven't these poor girls suffered enough?" I joked, putting my hand on his elbow in mock sincerity.

"What did you need us for, Auluria?" Dov called us back to the mission.

"Oh," I shook my head to refocus. "Reyla told me to come get you. We found a girl I'm assuming used to be one of yours. Katarina and Reyla were both in tears, so I'm guessing that's a good thing. Her name is Hannah."

Neither Dov nor Silas looked like they were breathing. The moment stretched on so long that I began to worry.

"Hannah's alive?" Dov breathed before his slack face came back to life.

"She's alive?" Silas repeated, still in shock.

"Guys, who is Hannah?" I asked, feeling very left out.

"Sharone's sister. She went missing…years ago. We thought she had died." Dov informed me, still not moving.

"There was so much blood," Silas remembered.

"She's in there," I pointed down the hall. "She's very pregnant, but she seems to be in good spirits. Do you want to see her?"

They nodded but didn't move. I tugged on their wrists, guiding them toward the door. After a few steps, they moved quicker. I left them to check in on Sharone's sister while I looked in on the other girls.

"Auluria," Anetta stepped up behind me after a few minutes. "You wanted to see me?"

"I wanted to see how you were doing," I started, "I was wondering if you wanted to stay here or come with us tomorrow.

"I'm not done with the Society yet," she said, sounding slightly offended that I had asked. "I found some of Lowell's girls though. They'll probably want to see you. Ella's with them now."

"Of course she is," I muttered.

"Ella will get over herself soon enough," Anetta assured me. "Shadoe's not the only one in charge around here. She'll just have to deal with that."

"Have you found anyone who can fight with us yet?" I asked as she led me down the grey halls.

"I found the *children.*" She wrinkled her nose as she spoke.

"Where are they?" I stopped walking.

"Downstairs. I'll show you in a minute. We're going to go annoy Ella first." I continued to follow her down the hall. "I don't think many of them will be going with us. They're all either pregnant or have small children."

"I had a feeling…"

Ella looked up as we entered. She nodded tersely at me.

"You all remember, Lowell's cousin, Lur," Anetta announced loudly. "She's in charge now."

A few of the young girls looked pained at Lowell's name. Anetta must have told them he died before she came to see me. Some of the girls looked angry, others seemed devastated by the news, while still others didn't care. They must not have been from Lowell's fold.

"Are you all okay?" I asked. "Can I do anything for you?"

"Let us fight," one girl sat up in her bed.

"You're not fighting," I cut off the discussion as I surveyed her bulging stomach. "Nice try."

"She's in charge and you will listen," Anetta declared.

It took me a moment to work out that she had just placed herself as my right hand. She was a much-less-deadly Shadoe to my Lowell. I realized I was always going to need back up with Lowell's people and having one of his favorite women by my side was a wise choice. They all knew Anetta was close with Lowell. They would respect her.

"Your jobs are to protect your children," I remind them. I couldn't help but feel like Reyla was having an easier time convincing the girls in her room to stay put.

"We'll only be taking those of you with us who are able to fight," I explained our plan to the girl, telling them how we would be taking on the Society from within.

"Lur, what about when it's all over? What will happen to us?" a girl I vaguely recognized asked.

"We'll come back for you all. We'll move you into the towns and out of this camp.

"Once we bring down Canton and his men, we'll still have to take care of the people outside of the Wall. You'll all have your chance to participate then if that's what you want."

After answering a few questions, Anetta inserted herself back into the conversation, announcing that I had to go check on the children but would return later. I whispered a word of thanks under my breath as we slipped back into the hallway.

"You do better with the Baers' people," she said as she bumped into me with her hip.

"Did you *just* figure that out?"

"Figure what out?" Dov asked, nearly colliding with us.

"We're going to see the children," Anetta commandeered the conversation, "Want to come?"

She led the way down the stairs to where the children were housed. The noise grew with each step we took.

"Sorry, they're not usually this loud," an older woman greeted us at the bottom of the stairs. "They're usually required to be quiet, but their mothers wanted them to play, now that you have control of the camp."

"That's okay. They should be able to play." Dov returned her smile. A few steps away, he pointed to a small girl, "That one looks like Jasleen."

"She does." I laughed. I missed that little girl.

Small children toddled around the room. A few grasped the hands of their mothers or nurses as they attempted to walk. I looked down when Dov suddenly tipped his face toward the ground. He smiled brilliantly as he scooped up the little boy clinging to his leg.

"Hello," he said softly. "Who might you be?"

The toddler reached out, lightly taping Dov's face. His fingers bounced over Dov's lips as he fearlessly explored his new friend. Dov shifted the child to sit on his hip as we walked around the room.

"Do you need anything? How can we help?" He took the time to speak to each woman in the room, making sure they were taken care of before continuing.

I finally sat down with a group of children to give the mothers a break. A few wandered off to walk around, but the majority of them stayed in the room, allowing me to watch their babies for them for a few moments.

I quietly sang a song my aunt had taught me long ago, hoping no one else could hear me. A few of the children stopped to listen, but most kept playing.

The noise ebbed and flowed as the toddlers and young children moved around the room. Occasionally one would burst into tears. The nurses ran over quicker than I could ever reach the child, after all their years of being forced to keep the facility a quiet place for the doctors and overseers of the camp.

Dov took a seat next to me after making the rounds.

"You're good with them." His voice made me quiver.

"So are you, I see."

He waved to the little girl who sat in my lap, pulling on my hair that surrounded her.

"Hi there, little girl," he cooed. Picking up a strand of my hair, he dangled it in front of her as she tried to catch it. The tiny girl giggled each time she missed it.

"Is this our future, Auluria?" he asked, dropping my hair in front of her again.

"What?" I asked, afraid to move.

"You and me and a little one. Is this our future?" Blue eyes glanced up at me. He smiled and winked before flicking his fingers to send my hair into my face.

His laugh was so deep and genuine when I closed my eyes to try to avoid being hit with my own mane, that everything inside of me jumped. Dov tipped my chin toward him.

"If this is what our life will be like then I will be a completely happy man." He paused. "I know we've needed to talk, Auluria, but this is what I want to talk about the most. What do you want for us?"

The small child squirmed in my arms, upset that Dov had stopped playing.

"Hey, little girl," he turned back to her for a moment, dangling my hair once more. I had a moment to process. "I didn't forget about you."

I waited for him to pacify the little girl, giving her enough attention to satisfy her. My hand darted out, mimicking Dov's motions when he pulled my face to look at him, pulling his face back to me.

"Yes," I nodded, an inch from his lips. "This. I want this. I want *you*."

I was overwhelmed by the scent of him as he kissed me. No one else could ever wear that sweet, spicy scent as well as Dov could. The moment was quick, but it said more than any other kiss we had ever had.

He pulled back, holding my lower lip between his. My heart went into overdrive. When I opened my eyes, he was watching me, grinning around biting his lip.

"I was hoping you'd say that."

"How will your brother feel about this?" Nervousness took root in my stomach, shooting through my legs. The little girl looked at me, feeling the switch in my posture.

"He's coming around, Auluria, you know that."

The little girl's nurse came over, lifting her from my lap. She quickly thanked us and walked away. Dov stood, holding his hand out to pull me to my feet.

"What does this mean for us?" I asked as he escorted me to a room with the older children to check on them.

"It means we get through this, take down the Society, and then… we make sure we don't get separated again." He lifted my hand to his lips. "I promise."

"Dov Baer?" a voice interrupted.

He lowered my hand, reluctantly looking away.

"You're the one everyone is talking about?" The boy looked about ten. I couldn't tell if he was impressed or skeptical.

"I suppose I am." Dov leaned down to be more on his eye level.

"What are those?" The boy nodded to Dov's arms. We both glanced down.

"Oh," Dov realized, pushing his sleeve up further. "Those are scars."

"Why?" he asked, crossing his arms.

"Why…do I have them?" Dov tried to figure out his question.

"Gregory, don't ask things like that," a woman scolded.

Dov and I looked at each other, trying not to laugh.

"I have a friend who has the same name as you," Dov was on the verge of breaking down. "He would ask a question like that too.

"I got these because some bad people didn't want me to help some good people."

"He got those saving us, Gregory. You should thank him. He took that pain so that we didn't have to," his mother said. She leaned over to me and added, "From what I hear, you did, too. Thank you."

"How did you get them?" the boy pushed.

"Trust me, you don't want to know. It was pretty painful," I tried to sway him away from that line of questioning.

"Gregory, go get your brother." His mother shooed him with a wave of her hand. She waited for him to walk away. "Some of the girls who were recently brought in arrived with stories of Goldilocks and the three Baers. I assume that's you?"

She picked up some of her son's skepticism. The woman waited for us to explain our glorious past.

"A recent nickname," I shrugged.

"No tales of unrealistic heroics?" She placed a hand on her hip.

"Afraid not," Dov chuckled.

"No shiny promises of riches for all?" She wasn't going to let us off easy.

"None whatsoever," Dov replied. "All we want is to get out from under the rule of the Society and then help our allies over the Wall get their freedom as well. We're willing to fight for that."

"The scars are proof of that," I added.

"So the stories aren't true?" She asked, almost looking disappointed.

"We haven't heard any of the stories, so we don't know," I confided in her. "What I *do* know is that we're going to take down the Society and end these camps."

"What's your plan for us when this is all over?"

"You can go wherever you like. Home…or you can make a new home."

"Well, with a future like that looming ahead, I guess you'd better win. I think they're looking for you." She nodded behind us before walking off to catch up to her son.

"You'd better come upstairs," Reyla announced, latching onto my arm. She dragged me across the room.

"What's going on?"

"Anetta and Ella are going at it," Reyla's voice was high-pitched as she moved us faster than a normal walking pace.

"The*y're fighting*? Why?" Dov asked, wrapping his hand in mine temporarily.

"I have an idea…" I quickly explained what had happened earlier when Anetta had sided with me over Ella.

"Great, are we going to face this when we get back too?" Dov shook his head.

"Haven't we been?" I gave him a frustrated look.

"You're in charge; Ella is not. Time to handle this," Reyla didn't bother to hide the exasperation in her voice.

Something slammed ahead. We ran faster.

Chapter 7

"This doesn't concern you, Baer." Nikko's voice was dangerously low and rough.

"You can't kick us out," I challenged him.

"No one said *you* had to go, *your majesty*," Locust scoffed. "But this has nothing to do with *them*."

He jutted his chin out at Dov and Reyla.

"We're not just going to leave, Locust," Reyla snipped, her fierce side coming out. "You don't get a say in this any more then you had a say in what happened before we all decided to work together."

"You, *little girl*, have *no idea* what I did or did not do when Lowell was still alive." He took a menacing step toward Reyla as Ella took another swing at Anetta. "But you're right. I had no say in joining forces with *you*."

"That's because *she's* in charge." Reyla pointed to me. "And Shadoe. Not you."

"We did what *Shadoe* said," Ella glared at Anetta.

"Auluria is just as much responsible for Lowell's people as Shadoe is," Anetta challenged her. "You answer to her too."

"Do you honestly think once this is all over that we'll answer to anyone but Shadoe?" Ella circled the blonde.

"Back off, Locust," Dov said sharply as Locust stepped dangerously close to Reyla. She stood her ground, but I could see the panic in her eyes.

459

I connected with Dov long enough to indicate that I'd handle the girls and he could deal with Locust. Dov turned to take on Locust at Reyla's side. Nikko followed me.

"Leave it alone, Lur. You know this is how Lowell handled things." Nikko warned me, to prove myself worthy of taking my cousin's place.

"You so quickly turned your back on Lowell?" Ella shouted hysterically. "You know he despised her."

"He only turned on her when she decided not to obey his every command." Anetta threw back at her, blocking a punch. She missed the kick and cried out in pain as Ella connected.

"You followed his every command, but so suddenly you're willing to walk away?" Ella pushed harder, lashing out again with her foot. Had she been coming after me, I would have used that move against her the way Shadoe had trained me to...but she also wouldn't have been able to walk back to the mansion.

The room filled with noise as Ella and Anetta shouted at each other. Nikko chimed in, cheering Ella on. Reyla's voice mixed into the sound in the room, but even through the chaos, I heard Dov's voice above them all. I shut it out, forcing myself to listen to the girls in front of me. When they didn't relent, I attempted to control the situation.

"Stop," I said, mustering as much of my cousin as I could, keeping my voice low and even. When they didn't break apart, I tried again. "Enough."

Anetta ducked a punch, her movements far more agile than I remembered her to be. Furious, Ella attempted another attack, this time landing a kick to Anetta's hip. She crumpled on the floor before kicking back, sending Ella staggering several feet.

"Let them be," Nikko said, reminding me of Shadoe.

"Enough!" I shouted louder.

Anetta was on her feet again. She held her hands up to yield to my angry intrusion. Ella didn't stop.

"Fine, we'll do this the hard way."

I stepped forward, ready for a fight. Gripping her elbow, I spun her to face me.

"I said enough," I gave her one more warning. Ella didn't take the hint.

She threw a punch at my face, anger sizzling off her. I was prepared for her outburst and ducked, taking her foot out in the process. She hit the ground and rolled, bouncing back up.

Ella moved to try to hit me again, but I moved faster. It was easy to block her move. She wasn't expecting the elbow to the face and she went down.

"Really?" Nikko criticized. He reached down to help Ella up, but pulled away at the last second, attempting to backhand me.

I reared back, kicking him as hard as I could, anger overtaking me.

"What is going on here?" Justin shrieked as he ran to my side. I nearly turned to him to defend myself, but I realized who he was in time.

Nikko stumbled over Ella, crashing into the floor. She stood up, ready to take me on again. Furious, I circled her.

"You want a hand, Goldilocks?" Justin asked, laughter in his voice.

Dov's shouting distracted me, allowing Ella to strike. My lip broke open as she connected.

Anetta glowered, moving in to help me. Nikko recovered, ready to side with Ella. I wanted desperately to turn around so I could see what Dov's scuffle was about.

"He's fine," Justin murmured, knowing where my head was at. "Can I help now?"

"Stay out of this," Anetta and I both responded as if it had been planned.

"You did *what?*" Dov's voice broke my concentration again. A loud thud sounded, but Shadoe's training snapped me back to the fight where I was already engaged. Dov could hold his own, and with competition like Locust, I doubted the fight would last long.

I maneuvered my body to flip Nikko when he launched himself at me, using the proximity to my advantage. Anetta took on Ella again, slamming the bottom of her boot into Ella's shin. Justin snorted in amusement.

"Enough, Ella," Nikko finally said. "Shadoe's not going to like this."

"I'm still in charge here, Nikko. If you had done this to Lowell, he would have destroyed you." My shoulders moved rapidly as I tried to control my breathing.

"You're not Lowell," he sneered. He used his wrist to wipe the blood trickling down his forehead.

Justin deftly stepped forward. He grabbed Nikko's shoulders and spun him around, slamming him into a wall face first as he threw me a playful wink. He mouthed, "I got you."

Nikko bounced off the wall, new blood trickling down his face. He sputtered at Justin as Justin arranged a scowl on his face.

"*She's* Lowell," he bellowed, pointing to me. "*I'm* Shadoe. *You* are *nothing* but an underling.

"*You come at her, and you come at me. For as easily as she could take you down, I can do a lot more damage, a lot faster than she can. Don't try me and don't test her.*" Justin growled, making Nikko blanch.

"Don't forget, Nikko, not only did I train directly under Lowell and Shadoe, but I also trained under the Baers *and* Brittella. In case you've forgotten, I started a war and escaped death more times than you've ever even seen it." I matched Justin's ferocity. "When this is all over, I have the power to decide if you go or stay. More importantly, I have the power to decide your position within this leadership structure. I suggest you choose wisely."

I played into Justin's attempts to position me in authority over them.

"*Dov!*" Reyla screamed, making us all turn.

Locust brandished a knife, playing by Lowell's handbook. Reyla looked terrified as Dov prepared himself to disarm the man, tugging up his sleeve so it wouldn't get in the way.

The last thing we needed was for Dov to be hurt before we returned to Canton's mansion. Tension rolled off of them. Justin flinched just enough to let me know he was going to involve himself in the confrontation, risking another of our top men. I inserted myself into the situation before he could.

"Locust." I dropped my voice seductively as I called his name. It set him off balance. I stepped toward him to further distract him.

Dov rushed forward, wrenching the knife from his hand. Locust looked around, shocked.

"If you *ever*," I continued speaking the way Brittella had taught me, taking slow, deliberate steps forward to upset him, "try to hurt my boyfriend again, I will make you suffer a worse fate than *anything* my cousin could have dreamed up for you.

"If you are incredibly fortunate enough *to earn your way back* into my good graces before we get back to the mansion, I *might* consider not telling Shadoe. But you *will* suffer whatever consequences *I* deem appropriate for an offense like this.

"Dov is your leader. *I* am your leader. To try to hurt either of us is treason, and you know what happens to traitors in the Society.

"You have no Shadoe to cut you down at the last second, Locust. You only have me. I am your judge, jury, and executioner, and you have made me *very* angry."

The closer I got, the wider his eyes became.

"You will pay for trying to hurt your leader, Locust, mark my words. Before the end of the day, you will pay for your actions. Nikko can't save you. Ella can't save you. No one but I can save you."

Locust looked cornered as I moved closer. Everyone but Dov had already started inching away from me as I revealed a side they didn't know I had. Locust took it as his cue to move away too, stepping back each time I took a step until he reached the wall. His throat bobbed when he realized he couldn't move away any farther.

"I suggest you come up with a very compelling apology and a plan for making this up to us before I give you my verdict, Locust. I suggest you think very, very hard."

My tone took an icy edge by the end of my speech; another tactic Brittella had taught me during my time with her. I hadn't realized it until that moment, but she had trained me to be Lowell's successor. She knew I would never be like him, but she gave me the ability to *sound* like him when I needed to protect myself with his people. I could practically feel Lowell's words breathing down my neck.

"Get out of sight and be back here in one hour for your sentencing, Locust," I commanded him. "If you try to run, I'll have Nikko hunt you down, and I promise you, he won't be kind. We tolerate deserters almost as well as we do traitors."

Locust scampered out of the room as quickly as possible. I turned, drawing on everything Brittella had taught me to do. I summoned a knowing smile as I found Nikko in the crowd.

"If he runs, you will hunt him down and bring him back to me. He will stand trial, and I don't care if we're in the middle of a war with the Society, he will live by Lowell's law. Do you understand?"

"Maybe you *do* have a little of Lowell in you after all," he commented. Blood still dripped down his forehead.

"Watch him." I jerked my head toward the door. "Help him make the right decision."

I waited for Nikko to nod. He and Ella followed Locust through the door.

"You want to explain that?" Dov looked as if he had never seen me before.

I dropped the look, relaxing my body.

"Brittella," I shook my head. "She knew one day I'd need to sound like Lowell to be effective with his people, so she taught me. I didn't realize it until just now, but she was smart enough to have the foresight to protect me, even back then. She might have recently reminded me."

"So that was all just an act?" Justin asked, looking slightly concerned.

"I'm not really going to have them hurt him," I rolled my eyes. "But now Locust fears me and Nikko respects me. I don't think Ella will ever care about me, but Nikko will keep her in check."

I paused, looking at each of them. Anetta shook her head slightly when I glanced at her, arranging a softer look over her features. She had known Lowell better than Dov had. For a second, she looked as if she had seen his ghost. Maybe I took it too far.

"At least they'll listen to me until we get back to the mansion now," I smiled, looking away from her.

"I'm going to have to talk to Brittella," Anetta teased, adding a grin as she re-joined the land of the living.

"I've seen you in action, *honey.*" Brittella posed in the doorway, having slipped in unnoticed. "I have nothing to teach you. I *do*, however, have some things to teach the young ladies here."

"Brittella," I tried not to gasp. "How long have you been here?"

She smiled coyly, ignoring my question.

"I believe you wanted a report, Auluria." She nodded for Anetta and me to follow. "You too."

"I did. Just a moment." I turned to Dov, needing answers before I left. "What was that all about?"

"He found out that lecherous Lowell-devotee tried to get too touchy with you before your mission," Brittella answered for him. "*Don't give me that look*, Auluria. Of *course*, I heard everything. How else do you think I got so good at my job?"

Brittella traded in secrets. I had always assumed she acquired them by way of her influence over people, but a smart woman also knows how to find answers without the help of man or minion.

I turned back to Dov, sliding my hand from his elbow, to his wrist, down to his hand where I entwined our fingers. I wanted a moment with him, but, surrounded by people, that was the best I could get.

"Thank you for defending me," I said, appreciating his effort to protect me. "Locust never touched me."

"Shadoe wouldn't let him," Dov mumbled.

"No. Well, yes. Neither would Lowell. Actually, Lowell saw pretty quickly to that when he pronounced my engagement. But even so, do you honestly think I couldn't hold my own against *that*?"

"I only faced off against him for a few minutes," Dov chuckled, "Just imagine what *you* would have done to him."

"Oh, I think you did a pretty good number on him from the looks of things. Did you hit him with a bag of rocks?"

Locust looked like he had gone a few rounds against Arin in the interrogation room.

"Too much?" He winced.

"We probably could have done without the facial injuries. Might be a little hard to sneak him back into the mansion." I laughed.

"I can fix that," Brittella said with a wave of her hand. She stepped closer as if she was about to approach Dov. "As for *you*, kiss your girlfriend goodbye and go check on your little friend down the hall; she's been moping around about not being able to go help her sister... Foolish girl."

She turned on her heels to face Justin, shocking him. Her hand darted up to his chest as she eyed the length of him. Her lips quirked up into a gentle smile meant only for him as she dropped her hand. Finishing her examination, she let out a small *hmm* before walking away. She paused at the door.

"Ladies," Brittella grimaced when I approached, noting my split lip. "You should clean that up."

Reyla attached herself to my side, even though she hadn't been invited. She giggled at the look of terror that seemed permanently etched across Justin's face. I had a feeling that's the look all of Brittella's contacts had when she started grooming them to work for her. I turned back and shrugged, offering him a playful wink that made Dov snort as he tried to hold in his laughter. I'm sure he was grateful that it wasn't him.

I had to force myself to keep walking. Reyla looped her arm through mine, knowing I wanted to turn back and take my place at Dov's side. It was beginning to seem like every time something big happened, Dov and I were ripped apart.

"I've managed to find a few girls that I believe will work well on your team," Brittella noted as we walked. "They're the more recent girls who have no responsibilities around here yet, nor do they appear to be carrying a child.

"Here we are," she said, turning left into a small room. Seven girls stood as we walked in.

"Of course, you'll have to see for yourselves, but I'd certainly take them on for training were we not fighting a war." Her eyes sparkled as she spoke. "They have many of your talents, my dear, but they still need work. Perhaps you could train them."

"Perhaps we need to reevaluate where we place Brittella," I whispered to Reyla. "I think she might need to come with us and teach our spies."

"Do you think she'd do more good here or there?" Anetta whispered.

"I really have no taste for war, ladies," Brittella interjected. "I see I was misguided in thinking I had nothing to teach you, Anetta. Clearly, the art of a gentle whisper is not among your talents. You should pay more attention to Auluria; her training is flawless. At least, my part of it, anyway."

The girls looked wary of the conversation, fidgeting across the room. I could already tell which one of them was Brittella's favorite. She stood straight, balancing her weight on one foot, the other stretched lightly across her knee, giving her a graceful curve. Her face was soft as she gave the appearance of having a light touch. She would be a perfect student for Brittella.

"Have any of you been trained to fight?" I waited as all seven nodded. "Good, time to see what you can do."

I had never seen Brittella look out of sorts before, but standing near the wall in the nearly empty room we occupied, she looked more uncomfortable than Justin had half an hour earlier. She swallowed hard, attempting to stifle a gasp.

I refocused my attention, watching the young girl face off against Anetta. The blonde easily stalked around the young girl while she held her ground.

"Not bad," I mumbled.

"I think it's time you and I had a little talk, Reyla. Come along." Brittella tugged at Reyla's sleeve.

"Umm, okay…" Reyla tripped after her, caught in Brittella's death grip.

"Have fun," I said, unsure of what Brittella had in store for my friend.

Knowing it was time to change the game, I silently slipped up behind the girl we were testing as the other girls watched. Anetta saw my approach and held a swing, giving me an opportunity to surprise the girl.

She whipped around, sensing my presence and tried to take me on. Dov, Silas, and Devin stood near the door, watching quietly as we tested the girls to make sure they would survive when we attacked the Society.

The girl was vicious; Wallace's men had trained her well. She growled as she threw her full weight at me, taking her aggression out. The girl claimed she had no allegiance to Wallace's men because they hadn't rescued her. Based on her reaction when we told her about Wallace's death, I believed her.

My name was muttered a few times by the men near the door, but the pounding of blood in my ears prevented me from hearing more. I angled myself to see them over the girl's shoulder and found them all grinning at me.

Justin timidly stepped inside. He relaxed when he realized Brittella was no longer in the room. He nodded for us to join them.

"He's back," he informed us quietly.

Anetta and I had a silent conversation with our eyes before we both nodded in agreement. I turned to the girls, wishing Talley had been there to help test them.

"Congratulations, we're confident that you all will be great assets to us. We'll give you instructions in the morning. Be prepared to leave early with us." I dismissed them. The girls filed out of the room, pleased with themselves.

"Have you decided what to do yet?" Dov asked.

"Yes." I took a breath to steady myself.

Locust stood in the middle of the room when we arrived looking like a man about to be hung. Under Lowell's reign, he might have been. Nikko, having weighed his options, stood with his arms crossed as he faced me. He nodded to show he would cooperate. Ella was nowhere to be seen.

Dov, Silas, Anetta, Reyla, Raselin, Fitch, Devin, Justin, Talley, and a few others filed in and stood next to me, creating a line of judges for Locust to face.

"Do you have anything to say, young man?" Raselin asked.

Locust looked like he was about to be sick.

"I'm sorry for my actions," Locust mumbled. "I felt threatened and my reaction was to defend myself and I should have made a different choice because I know you weren't going to escalate the fight like that."

His eyes were focused on the floor in front of our feet, hands behind his back. He shifted as if he were twisting his fingers.

"How do we know we can trust you not to pull a knife on one of us again?" Talley asked, staring him down. Locust looked up, surprised to hear her voice.

"I won't," he stated.

"You shouldn't have the first time," Talley countered.

Raselin nodded to me, giving me the floor. I took a few paces forward, putting myself between Locust and the group.

"I am not my cousin, Locust, but I can be if I need to. I don't like being like Lowell, so the fact that you've made me step into his shoes isn't helping your case.

"That said, I've come up with something that I can live with."

I stepped back toward the group as Locust watched me, trying to figure out my angle. My eyes never left him.

"Locust, because of your actions, you will never be allowed to rise in the ranks. You will never achieve a position higher than the one you have now. Once we return, after we're done handling the Society, Shadoe will be responsible for deciding if you can stay or if you will be dismissed from our command."

"You're telling Shadoe?" Concern made his voice lift higher than usual.

"He needs to know. We have to be able to trust you and I can't be impartial on that. Shadoe will be the one who decides if you stay or leave, but I won't tell him until after we bring down the Society. That way you'll have a fair chance to prove yourself valuable to him."

"I suggest you thank her for her benevolence, young man," Raselin added quickly, crossing his arms defensively. "That could have been much worse."

He remained silent, looking down. No one spoke, waiting for him to summon the ability to speak again.

"Thank you for giving me another chance, Lur. I'm sorry." He looked at me on the last sentence.

"Nikko will be responsible for overseeing you until we get back. Don't do anything to make me regret this second chance."

Everyone turned to watch him as he walked out of the room, Nikko in his wake. The group turned to me as if it were my job to tell them what to do next.

"You should go say goodbye to Hannah," I waved to Reyla, Dov, and Silas. "You probably won't see her in the morning before we leave."

"Do you want to come?" Dov asked, holding his hand out to me.

"No, you go ahead. I'm sure I'll get to know her later on, but this should be for her friends." He gave me an understanding smile before following his best friend and Reyla.

Raselin led the others out to get them set up for the night, but the Hershs lingered.

"You okay, Goldilocks?" Justin asked, sidling up next to me.

"Yeah, I'm okay."

"What are you thinking about?" Devin asked. He blinked as he looked at me.

"I'm not sure," I answered, suddenly feeling exhausted.

"Want to sit with us for a few minutes?" Talley suggested, motioning to the floor. When I nodded, she slipped down to the floor across from me.

"Sharone's going to be so excited to hear her sister is okay..." Devin started.

"I'm sure she will," Talley's head bobbed as she spoke. "It would be like getting one of you back...although I doubt Hannah is a monster like you two."

"Hey!" the boys protested together.

"Hannah is older than Sharone, so really, it would be like *us* getting *you* back." Justin corrected her.

"Well, in that case, Hannah might want to rethink going back," Talley teased.

"You couldn't leave us if you tried, sis." Devin wrinkled his nose at her.

I watched their playful banter, fiercely jealous of them. Justin noticed and stopped laughing.

"What?"

"Nothing, I was just thinking about how nice it must be to have siblings."

"Aww, Auluria," Justin gave me a sad smile. "Haven't you figured it out by now?"

"Figured what out?" I frowned, waiting for him to turn it into a joke.

"You're one of us now, Auluria," Devin grinned as Justin leaned over and slung his arm over my shoulders.

"Auluria, please. We adopted you almost from the moment we met you," Talley said from across the circle. "Why do you think we keep hanging around with you?"

My heart swelled.

"You don't think we stayed in that storehouse with you all that time because it was our *job*, did you?" Devin asked. "You realize there were much more productive uses for our talents at that point in time, don't you?"

"We had to talk them into letting us watch over you. They wanted us out scouting and surveying the towns." Talley informed me, reaching out to rest her hand on my knee.

"Like it or not, you're stuck with us, Goldilocks." Justin pulled me in for a side hug. "And don't you forget that when it comes to who gets to walk you down the aisle in this upcoming wedding of yours."

"Yeah, me," Devin announced.

"Wedding?" I felt the color drain from my face.

"Oh, don't try to deny it, Auluria," Talley laughed. "We *all* know it's coming."

"I feel like I'm always the last to know these things," I said, letting out a nervous laugh.

"Don't be so naïve, Goldilocks," Justin winked at me, scooting closer. "And the answer is me. I'm the one walking you down the aisle."

"No," Devin protested, prompting a full argument over what their roles would be.

"Don't worry about trying to explain this to Dov," Talley leaned in and quietly said over her brothers' fight. "We've already had this conversation with him."

Justin and Devin bolted to their feet, upsetting the conversation. The two moved behind me, arguing loudly, arms in the air. Justin lunged at Devin, locking him in a chokehold. The two wrestled until they were in a heap on the ground.

"This is your one and only chance to get out, Auluria," Talley whispered. "Take it or leave it."

"I'm good," I replied.

Our attention was pulled in the direction of the two men yelping on the floor, alternating between threats and laughter.

"And tomorrow, we go back to the mansion."

"Here's hoping it's how we left it," Talley added.

Chapter 8

THE HOODED MAN TURNED, REVEALING HIS FACE, AS OUR SMALL GROUP approached the mansion. Arin shook his head, warning us off. We changed directions, moving to the right as we entered the building, not acknowledging him. A few minutes later, he joined us in a small room we had quietly snuck into.

"We have to be careful getting everyone in," he said gruffly. "The other magistrates are here and will know if something is off."

"Why are they here?" Silas asked, brow furrowed.

"They must have figured out something was up. They've been asking a lot of questions." Arin replied, looking over his shoulder at the door.

"Has Shadoe been able to keep Canton in check?" I asked, praying he had.

"Canton's been behaving himself, but we're also keeping him away from the other magistrates. I'm sure they find it suspicious."

"Where's Berwyn?" Dov asked.

"I can go find him." Arin started to back away. "You should warn the others."

"I'll go," Ben volunteered, looking to Dov for approval.

"Thanks, Ben. Have Fitch help you sneak them in a few at a time and make sure Raselin knows to come right away. Tell him we'll meet in the study."

"On it," Ben said, slipping out behind Arin.

"Now we have to get to the study," Silas murmured. "I have a feeling that won't be as easy as it sounds."

"Doubtful," Dov said heavily. "This intrusion could really change the course of our plans. I hadn't anticipated the magistrates coming here. I thought we would take the fight to them."

"We'll adapt," Silas offered. "We always do."

"Gloria, can you—" Dov was cut off.

"Yes." She dashed off.

"Where did she go?" I asked, wondering how she knew what he wanted. Then I remembered my first mission with Dov. He and Gloria used to work well together before I appeared in his life.

"She's doing a little reconnaissance. She'll be back." Silas brushed his hair back. "You ready?"

"Let's go."

We followed behind Silas and Reed, walking two at a time in line. Silas nodded when we passed a group of our people moving in the opposite direction. I searched for Sharone in the crowd but didn't see her.

We took a back staircase, hoping to avoid the magistrates and their people. Distinguishing their people from our own team would be difficult while wearing the Society uniforms to blend in.

Berwyn was waiting in the study when we arrived, Eden, Shadoe, and Necesta by his side. He looked annoyed as we entered.

"Well?" he asked once the door was closed.

"The camps are ours," Dov reported. "Have any of the others returned?"

"Two of the teams are already back," Berwyn said, explaining what had happened. We had lost a number of men on one team but had been successful at capturing all of the camps. "The last teams should return any time now."

"What are we doing about the magistrates?" I asked out of turn.

Berwyn's icy gaze turned to me. I resisted the urge to shrink back.

"We need to take them out," Shadoe grumbled. He clenched his teeth when he looked at me.

"We can't; they brought soldiers with them," Berwyn protested.

"And now our men are back," Shadoe argued.

"You think at least of a few of them won't escape and warn the others?" Berwyn raised his voice for a moment, forgetting to be quiet. He immediately dropped it to a harsh whisper. "We're so close. We can't ruin this now. We will *not* risk this."

"You think they aren't going to figure this out while we're

standing around, waiting, Baer?" Shadoe sneered. "You're a bigger fool than I thought."

"We need to strike *now* before they see it coming."

"Glad to see things haven't changed much," I muttered to Silas, who, for once, didn't laugh at my joke.

"Our priority right now needs to be to get our people back inside the mansion," Dov mediated. "How many soldiers did the magistrates bring?"

"Five hundred men and they're all asking questions."

"How many of the magistrates are here?" Silas asked, attempting to get a better view of the situation.

Dust floated in the air, sparkling in the late afternoon sunlight pouring in through the window, catching my eye. It changed direction in swirling clouds of sparkling matter each time someone spoke with their hands.

"Twelve magistrates and fourteen justices," Shadoe informed us, looking as if it were taking all of his mental restraint to keep from snapping at us.

Necesta reached out and put her hand through Shadoe's elbow. He looked as if he wanted to turn and yell at her, but he held steady.

"We will work a plan out now that our people are back home, but they're right. Our first priority, dearie, needs to be to get them back inside the mansion. Goldilocks, where is Raselin?"

"He should be here soon, Necesta. He was in the second group." A thought occurred to me as I spoke, quickly adding, "How have none of the magistrates' soldiers found the soldiers in the cells yet?"

"We haven't let them downstairs. We've kept them very busy up here," Eden answered, finally speaking. "We've even sent some of them on missions just to get them away from the mansion."

"Any chance we can just swap some of the magistrates' men out for our people?" I ventured a guess at a plan.

"They're too familiar with the people in their own groups. They'll notice if someone goes missing and is replaced." Berwyn voiced my worry.

"Where are the new recruits?"

"Raselin," Necesta crooned, looking at the door. She released Shadoe and joined her friend. "You made it back in one piece."

"Most of us did," he replied sadly. "We met one of the other teams on the way in. There were losses."

He quickly explained what he had learned. Berwyn added in that he had made arrangements for the people who had joined our forces from the camps to be hidden in the town since the magistrates were already in place once they arrived.

"We'll send for them when we're ready," Eden added, giving a pointed look at Shadoe. She scowled at him, looking as if she were prepared to shred him on the spot, cutting bit by bit away until he was nothing.

A loud knock sounded at the door. The sharp sound made us all flinch.

"Sir, Magistrate Canton is asking for you." I recognized Sherman's voice on the other side of the door.

I grabbed hold of his arm as he brushed by me, apparently still behaving like my cousin. "Later," I mouthed to him. His face twitched with surprise as he wrenched himself away from me.

When I turned back, Eden was staring at me. I couldn't read her expression before she tore her gaze away, her curls bouncing with the motion.

"We need a plan," Raselin whispered, unsure if any soldiers lingered outside the door.

"Come with me," Berwyn waved his hand as he backed up.

He led us to the wall. Lifting a table, he set it a few feet to the left. Berwyn turned back to the right, stepping over to a bookcase. He gently pulled on a board, moving it out just an inch. His other hand slipped behind it as a click sounded. The wall opened.

"Canton had a few security measures put in place. After a few days, he told Shadoe everything." He pushed the board back in place, grabbing the door so it wouldn't close. "Hurry."

Dov tugged at my hand as I stood motionless, worrying about what Shadoe had done to acquire that information. We all slipped into the crowded hallway behind the room, barely big enough for one person to fit through.

"Keep going," Berwyn whispered loudly as we followed Eden.

She stopped at another door and placed her face against the wall, where I assumed there was a hole to check the room before entering. Her fingers climbed the side of the wall as she observed the room until she found what she was looking for. The door opened to reveal a dimly lit room.

Eden opened the curtains, letting in the muted reflection of light that came from the other side of the building. Books sat out on the tables. Maps littered the room. Knives and weapons were scattered about on the furniture and floor.

"As far as we can tell, this room isn't accessible any way but the hallway," Eden said softly.

I glanced around and realized there was no door.

"Is it wise to be in here if *that's* the only way out?" I asked. *Shadoe couldn't have approved this meeting place.*

"Probably not, but it's the only place we're sure the magistrates' men can't hear us." Berwyn shook his head.

The other team leaders who had returned joined us and we recounted the takeover of the camps, going over our losses and gains. The boys from the camps waited in the towns, hidden with the people who had sided with us thanks to Dov's efforts before Canton's men caught us.

We talked until evening, coming up with a plan to get the magistrates to leave. We would send our teams ahead, to each of their districts to wait for their arrival. The idea was to strike as they arrived, not giving them time to prepare.

The wind howled against the outside wall, but without windows, we couldn't see if it was storming or if it was just blustery. The walls creaked each time the noise crept up, crackling through the ceiling.

"Auluria, walk with me," Necesta said, pulling me from the table. "You too, Dov."

Berwyn waved us off, wrapping up the meeting. We followed Necesta to the wall, stepping into the narrow hallway where she released my elbow. She clutched my hand, guiding me.

"You need to have a conversation with your friend," she said flatly.

"Which friend?" I asked.

"Shadoe, of course." She glanced back at me over her shoulder. "You left him here for all this time without anyone to keep him in check. He barely managed."

"What do you mean?" Dov asked skeptically.

"I mean, he's managed to restrain himself, but it's only because he knew you were coming back. That, and your brother can be rather frightening when he wants to be," Necesta squeezed my hand as she glanced at Dov. "But, dearie, I can see the strands starting to snap, one by one. He's untethered. You are the one holding him in place. You're the one keeping him from ending up like your cousin. You need to talk to him."

"Did he do something while we were gone, Necesta?" My body tensed up as I asked the question, dreading the answer.

"Not that I know of, but it's only a matter of time." She stopped abruptly. Dov collided with me as I avoided crashing into the older woman in front of me.

She rapped on the wall once before opening the door. We stepped into Canton's chambers. A fire crackled in the fireplace along the far wall. Canton sat in a chair, slinking back into the cushions. Shadoe stood in front of him menacingly. He flashed the smallest smile at the man before turning to face us. Canton's skin blanched.

Necesta patted my back before exiting. Shadoe waited for me to address him. I eyed the magistrate as he carefully watched me.

"Go," Shadoe said, prompting Canton to stand and scurry into a large closet. He closed the door behind him. "He's fine."

"Why did you get called out of the meeting?" I asked.

"One of the magistrates wanted to speak to Canton. We'd been putting the conversation off since yesterday."

"What did they want?" I inquired.

"A plan," he straightened his shoulders. "They wanted to know how Canton was planning on finding you two and your brother. We gave them one."

That should have horrified me, but I knew it was meant to put the magistrates where we wanted them for battle.

"I take it they'll be helping Canton destroy us?" I offered, walking to sit on the settee at the end of Canton's grand bed. Shadoe took Canton's chair as Dov gently sat next to me.

"Are you going to tell me what happened out there?" Shadoe redirected.

"What do you mean?" I asked, trying not to sound confrontational as Dov put a hand on the small of my back, sending a shiver up my spine.

He raised an eyebrow at me, challenging me. I jutted my chin out, silently communicating with him.

"So you haven't completely changed, Lur." He smiled sarcastically at us. "I knew it would come back to you sooner or later.

"We need to talk about this stupid plan of your brother's. Striking now is the best option. We need to take them out while they're still here—"

"Enough, Shadoe," Dov intervened. "We've all agreed that we need to get control of them in their own districts. There's too much that could go wrong taking control of them here and having to transport them back."

"You aren't listening, Baer—" Shadoe protested.

"You've discussed this with Berwyn and the others?" Dov held up a hand to silence him.

"They don't understand," Shadoe insisted.

"Do you want to talk to Berwyn and Raselin one more time?" Dov shook his head but reluctantly offered Shadoe one last opportunity to make his case.

"Well you two certainly aren't going to listen to me, so why would they?"

"Present your case, Shadoe. It can't hurt." I shrugged. "You and Dov can go now. I'll watch Canton."

"Are you sure you shouldn't come with us?" Dov hedges.

"Go, I'll be fine."

"I'll send Sherman," Shadoe announced as he stood. "Keep him in the closet."

Shadoe stalked over to the door, preparing to throw it open.

"Shadoe," he paused at my words. "I brought Brittella back."

"Good for you," he muttered over his shoulder.

"Why did you send me for her?"

"We needed her. I assume she got the job done?" Without waiting for me to confirm that she had helped us, he added, "Then it was a successful mission."

He continued stalking toward the closet where Canton had taken refuge, refusing to say anything else on the topic. When he opened the door, we saw he had shackled himself in place. Shadoe had trained him well.

Canton was perched on a settee similar to the one I had just occupied. He gritted his teeth as Shadoe checked the chains on his wrists.

"Cooperate," he instructed the magistrate. Shadoe turned back to Dov. "Let's go."

Dov gave me one more look before following Shadoe through the hidden doorway. I sat back down, propping my elbow on my knee. My mind drifted to where I could feel my knife hidden in my boot, checking to make sure it was still there just in case I needed it.

"Hello again, Auluria," Canton said once he was sure the others were gone.

"I'm not talking to you." I glared at him, leaning forward, putting more of my weight on my knee.

"But you should," he crooned, shifting the way he held himself. The scared man faded away as the magistrate came forward. "You see, I know things you don't want me to know."

I refused to respond to him.

"Oh, Auluria, you don't think I didn't learn about you before hanging you, do you?" He smiled at me. "Don't be absurd. Your cousin told me all sorts of stories. But more than that, I know *you*, Auluria. I saw what you did."

That got my attention.

"What did I do?" I asked, hoping to sound uninterested.

"I saw you try to save my guard. You're not like the rest of them," he insisted, trying to use my actions against me. "You won't let them do this to me."

"Of course, I will." I blinked a few times, wondering why he thought he could leverage those particular actions.

"They're going to murder me, Auluria. You know you're going to help me, so why not use it to your advantage? We could help each other."

"Magistrate Canton, the last man who tried to use that line on me didn't like the end results of his efforts. I'd refer you to the bloody mess that was—*is*—Justice Kenton, but I don't think you really want to see that right now." I smirked at my intentional slip of words.

"You didn't." His face slipped.

"No," I quickly agree. "*I* didn't—of course not—I would never. Shadoe did. Just like Shadoe killed all of your men...but he already told you that."

"You won't just hand me over to him," Canton tried to remind me. "You don't have it in you."

"I already did," I snapped. "Who do you think left you under his charge?"

"The Baers," he snarled at me, beginning to lose hope that he could coerce me.

"Where do you think they got that idea from? Remember, Canton; I'm part of two groups. They all listen to *me*. I'm the one who left you with Shadoe, and I'll leave you there again if you don't prove useful."

He started to stand up, his red robes fluttering as he moved, only to be stopped by his chains. He growled in frustration.

"You're not like Lowell or Shadoe. You can't just do this."

"Magistrate, you tried to have me hanged. You tortured my boyfriend and friends. You're lucky you're alive at all." I answered him. "Isn't this all getting a little old? You've tried this before."

The secret door opened as Sherman stepped into the room. He stalked to the closet, raising his weapon. The hilt of his knife slammed into Canton's arm, making him crumple in pain.

"No talking," Sherman demanded. He turned and glared at me.

I sat in silence as Canton sniffled from the closet. Sherman glowered outside the closet door as he waited for Shadoe's return. I held still, watching as Sherman glowered.

Eventually, Shadoe stormed in alone, rage vibrating off his arms.

"I knew that was pointless," he said quietly.

I stood, walking to the hallway.

"I'm sorry. I think they're right though, Shadoe. I think it's the best course of action." I walked backward, letting him guide me.

"You're wrong this time, Lur, but that's never stopped you before."

"Can we talk about this?" I requested.

"Go to bed, Lur." He collided with me as he tried to brush past me.

"Shadoe," I tried calming him.

He slammed me against the wall and slipped past me.

"Not tonight, Lur."

Shadoe stormed off, leaving me to find my own way out of the hallway.

Chapter 9

"GET UP," HIS FRIGHTENED VOICE STARTLED ME AWAKE. I JOLTED upright, nearly colliding with him.

"We have a problem, Lur." Red flooded my vision as the boy came into focus in the soft light filtering in through the window.

"What is going on?" I breathed deeply, trying to get enough oxygen to fully wake up and process his words as he continued to shake my shoulders.

"It's Shadoe," he said, rendering me fully awake.

"What happened?" I pushed him away and jumped to my feet, looking for Dov. He sat up next to where I had been sleeping, looking tired.

"During the night," the red-haired boy panted, "he left. He took a group of people and went to get the new recruits."

"He *what?*" Dov bellowed, fully conscious. He slammed his hand into Silas' sleeping form, startling him awake.

"Shadoe took us into the town," the boy clarified. "He found the boys from the camp and brought them here."

Berwyn sat up, wide-eyed.

"*What did he do?*" Berwyn growled. Eden placed a hand on his arm.

"Wait, I know you," I tried to process what was happening.

"Yes, I'm Louis. We've met before." He sounded annoyed as he tried to rush me.

Images of the boy Silas and I freed from the Society cells, then again when he helped me to free Dov from Canton's captivity flashed through my mind. He worked for Lowell, and now, for Shadoe.

"They're downstairs," Louis said. "You'd better come."

"Berwyn!" Nian shouted as he raced into the room. His moves were frantic. "Berwyn, Shadoe brought the recruits. It's a bloodbath, Berwyn."

We raced to the door, tripping over each other to get there.

"Wait, weapons," Dov reminded us, skidding to a stop.

"You won't need them," Nian turned back to us. "It's all over now."

The main floor was littered with bodies. Society guards lay in their own blood, mixed with a few boys from the camps. Carnage was everywhere.

"No," I breathed, ready to cry. Dov gripped my fingers tightly.

Raselin gasped behind us as he joined our group on the landing.

"How did this happen?" he asked.

"It doesn't matter," Berwyn cut him off. "We have to make sure we have everyone before they manage to escape."

"If anyone is still alive, take them prisoner," Dov instructed.

Eden leaned over to me, whispering, "They look just like their father when they stand together like that. Griz would be so proud of those two."

I wondered what Griz was like. I had heard stories from the brothers and Eden about him—even Reyla and the others had told me stories—but I wished I had been able to meet the leader of the Baers' group. It was just one more thing Canton had taken from us.

The sounds of a fight outside filtered into the room.

"We need to get help outside," Berwyn turned to direct people.

"I'll go," Raselin pointed for Berwyn to go down the hall. "You handle inside the mansion; I'll take reinforcements outside."

Berwyn nodded as Raselin bolted down the stairs, calling to our people to follow him as they spilled into the foyer. The oldest Baer turned back to us.

"Split up. Find all of the magistrates and justices," Berwyn shouted as he moved down the hall. "Be careful."

"Come on," Eden hissed at me, declaring me her partner. She brushed a piece of her hair back into her hood, tucking it behind her ear. Our opposition may be dead, but it was best to use our cover until we had the magistrates and justices in our custody.

The small group crept down the hall to the guest wing, lingering behind Berwyn, Silas, Dov, and the others. We each took a door, bursting into the rooms simultaneously. In the distance, I heard our people running outside, engaging with the enemy as they fought in the courtyard.

A fire quietly crackled, warming the drafty room. The embers glowed as the breeze from the door made the flames sway. Red curtains hung heavily over the window, blocking the muted early morning light from entering.

My eyes swept from the curtains, across the floor, following drops of blood. A hand sat motionless on the floor, palm up. The rest of the corpse was hidden by the bed. My body was drenched in a cold spark of nerves, but my eyes kept traveling up, over the comforter to where feet sat quietly below the blanket. It appeared undisturbed until it reached the man's waist. The comforter began to twist, as if in the middle of being ripped away and thrown to the side.

Blood soaked through the red color, staining it even darker. Hollow eyes stared up at the ceiling, grasping onto the man's last view. The magistrate was dead.

Eden stiffened next to me, lost somewhere between horror and happiness. She despised the Society for what they did to her and her people, but the tragedy of death wasn't lessened by her hatred of the men that hurt our people.

I forced myself around the bed, finding two other soldiers also dead on the ground. Shadoe's men had been thorough.

Taking in the scene, I realized how much trouble Shadoe would be in for going behind our backs. It was an errant tactical move on his part—one that Lowell would have made—and perhaps it *could have* worked. But going behind our backs and specifically working against the team's orders...I didn't know how Berwyn and Raselin would respond to that.

I also knew that we couldn't afford to lose someone as skilled as Shadoe. For as highly trained as the Baers were, Shadoe was better. His training had been harsher. His work was more punishing than theirs. No one could get the results Shadoe could get.

I needed to find him.

"Auluria," Eden's voice pulled me back into the moment. She waved me out of the room.

In the hallway, Berwyn asked for a report.

"Dead," I responded. "The magistrate and three of his men."

Berwyn shook his head as everyone reported at least one death in the room they had checked. Several reported deaths from our own ranks as well.

Shadoe must have snuck the boys in and blitz attacked the sleeping Magistrates.

"We need reinforcements down here," Henry called from the foyer downstairs. We all rushed to the stairs.

I clung to the banister as I flew down the steps, moving far faster than I should have been going with a weapon in my hand. With each step, the noise grew louder.

The Magistrate's men raged against us, but unsure of who belonged to the resistance and who belonged to a different magistrate, they occasionally turned on themselves.

It was hard to see in the early morning hours, but the blood on the ground was distinctly darker than the stone beneath it. I tried to avoid stepping in it. A Society man ran at me, not noticing the liquid on the ground, and made my job easier as he fell before reaching me.

A second man charged at me. I lowered myself, flipping him over my back. Ben took him out for me.

"You okay?" He asked quickly. When I nodded, he turned his attention back to the fight.

"Auluria," Dov called, warning me. I turned in time to plunge my knife into the stomach of a Society soldier. He crumpled, eyes wide, as I pulled my blade back. I kicked his weapon away, close enough that Dov could pick it up, before retreating.

I gritted my teeth, trying not to think about the way he fell after I struck him. My head felt light, but I didn't have time to waste thinking about it.

"Hey," I said lightly as I moved along side Dov.

"Hey," he said, offering an apologetic smile.

"Dov?" Berwyn yelled, his back to us as he and Eden fought side-by-side.

"We're fine," Dov shouted back.

"No, please!" a frightened voice was cut off behind us in the crowd. When I turned, I saw Shadoe.

I was accustomed to Shadoe looking smug when one of his missions succeeded, but his gaze infuriated me more than usual, the carnage he created in my peripheral vision. His arm lashed out, taking down another Society man, but he kept his eyes latched onto mine. He would see his mission through, even though it cost our men their lives.

Dov breathed deeply beside me. "Go help him," he said reluctantly.

"Are you sure?" I questioned.

"Yes."

I tentatively took a step. Shadoe *did* need me; Dov was right.

"I'm here," I announced, taking my place by his side.

"How bad?" he asked as he took on another soldier. Berwyn and Raselin were furious at him, but Shadoe was willing to take their anger for this victory.

"Pretty bad," I slashed at an approaching Society man.

A light mist danced into the courtyard, slowly filling the space as we fought. The light bounced off of it, making it brighter than it usually was that time of day. The toxic scent of spilled blood permeated the air, sharply piercing our senses.

At last, the fighting dwindled, leaving a handful of Society man alive and captured, and far too many of our own dead. I surveyed the area. Lowell would have been pleased.

"Shadoe, what did you do?" I asked, turning to him.

"I made sure of our place here, Lur. I handed us the victory. When this is all done, they can't cut us out."

"They wouldn't have done that, Shadoe." I couldn't believe his reasoning.

"Report," Shadoe yelled, making me jump out of my skin. His leaders ran toward us.

I tolerated them as they gave individualized reports to Shadoe as Berwyn and Dov looked on. Raselin had ended up inside after the battle ended and watched from a window, Justin and Talley at his side.

I stood, arms behind my back, feet apart, waiting for it to end. The death count was higher than I had anticipated.

"The magistrates and justices?" Shadoe pompously inquired to the group.

"We checked their rooms before we came down to the courtyard," I jumped in, finally speaking. "It was a massacre."

Shadoe forced a smile down, silently congratulating himself on winning over Berwyn and Raselin. I stood miserably, watching him gloat.

"Two magistrates escaped with a handful of their guards," Nikko supplied, attempting to prove he was loyal to me. It was smart thinking, considering how bad this was about to get for Shadoe.

My jaw fell.

Shadoe's smug look faltered as he realized his mistake and what it would likely cost him.

From the corner of my eye, I saw Berwyn, Dov, Eden, and Silas collectively straighten taller, leaning in at my expression. They knew something was wrong even from that distance. Raselin, still standing in the window, leaned forward, putting his palm on the glass. Talley stretched up, placing her hand on Justin's shoulder to try to see over her tall brother. Justin's jaw dropped, matching mine.

"What?" I breathed.

"We couldn't stop them," Nikko added, willing us to believe they had tried.

"Where did they go?" I growled. My hands flew to my sides as I dropped the soldier-like pose I had been maintaining.

I looked up, sharply jerking my head to indicate that the others should join Shadoe's celebratory party.

"Dismissed," I hissed at our people, sending them scattering away. Nikko stayed behind.

"What?" Berwyn's voice was dangerously deep.

Raselin raced through the foyer and out into the courtyard, skidding to a stop as he caught himself on Dov's shoulder, Justin right behind him.

"They escaped," I screeched, accidentally sounding more frantic than I meant to.

"Who?" Concern flooded Dov's voice.

"Three of the magistrates."

Everyone looked as if they might be sick. Raselin stumbled backward. Justin offered a hand to steady him.

Shadoe swallowed hard before locking his jaw. His eyes narrowed as he processed the news and tried to work out an escape plan.

"How could this happen?" Eden wailed, hands in her hair as she curled in on herself.

"They'll be coming for us now," Berwyn's voice wavered.

"It will take them time," Dov said, steadying himself as much as steadying us. "It will take them time to return to their towns and then more time to return here. We have time."

"How could you do this, Shadoe?" Arin asked, having followed Berwyn over. He looked ready to kill Shadoe on the spot.

Shadoe remained quiet. I'd never seen him like that before; not even when Lowell lectured him. Not even when he nearly killed me on that cliff.

Necesta ambled into the courtyard, quickly making her way over to the group. She heard Arin's tirade and hurried to Shadoe's side.

"Now, you owe him," she urgently reminded us, wrapping a protective hand around Shadoe's arm. He was still in shock. "You owe him for helping to save Dov's life. Now is the time to repay him."

She glared defiantly at anyone who looked like they were going to question her.

"He is one of our leaders. He made a judgment call, albeit a poor one. He initiated a tactical strike and it failed. It was a mistake," she insisted. "You owe him."

"We owe him," I repeated, seeing my chance to keep him from suffering whatever retribution Arin would likely come up with *and* take away anything else we might owe Shadoe.

Color started returning to Shadoe's face.

"Berwyn," I said cautiously. "Berwyn, please."

The oldest Baer stared at Shadoe and I worried that he was seeing Lowell—the man who had killed his father—instead.

"He will be okay, Auluria," Dov promised. "But we need to get this handled."

He turned and motioned everyone over. They crowded around, stepping over bodies.

"How *could* you?" Eden suddenly screamed. She ran at Shadoe, slamming into him with her open hands as she pushed him.

Shadoe stumbled backward but didn't retaliate. Eden kicked him just below his knee. He grunted loudly, anger flashing across his face.

"How could you put us all at risk like that?" Eden screeched. Everyone was too stunned to stop her.

She swung her arm, attempting to slap him. Shadoe reached up, grabbing her wrist roughly. Eden used her other hand to connect with his face, the blow sounding so loudly that it echoed off of the mansion walls as the sun started to peek up over the landscape.

Eden's hair flew wildly as she continued her brutal attack. Shadoe blocked most of her efforts but allowed her to get a few good punches in.

"You nearly killed Berwyn," she dissolved into tears as she continued to fight against him. "You're going to get us all killed! You're as bad as Lowell!"

"Eden," Berwyn finally called his wife. She didn't react, continuing her outburst. He tried again. "Eden."

She summoned all of her strength, suddenly looking like the woman that had dragged Dov across the mansion courtyard the day we rescued him from Canton. It terrified me.

Letting out a war cry, she scratched at his face. Her foot slammed into his as she landed a punch to the gut. Shadoe was enraged but managed to control himself as he grabbed onto her shoulders and swung her around. He didn't say a word, but his eyes were murderous.

"Shadoe, let her go," I warned.

Eden spat every vicious accusation she could think of at him, calling him out on every infraction. Berwyn wrestled her away and she lit into Shadoe about nearly killing me on the cliff.

"Eden," her husband said softly, burying his face in her hair near her ear. It broke her. She settled back against his chest.

"How could you?" she whispered.

Dov squeezed my hand. I hadn't noticed he had picked it up. Looking down, I realized Silas held my elbow. The two of them had restrained me from interfering in Eden's moment. I was grateful they kept me from involving myself. I honestly wasn't sure which one I was hoping to protect—Shadoe or Eden.

Berwyn turned his wife to face him, running his hand over her back to soothe her.

"I'm okay," he murmured to her, reminding her that he had survived the poisoning. She calmed. She sniffled into his arms as he held her.

After a moment, she realized what she was doing and straightened her shoulders. Turning back, she glared at Shadoe. I couldn't remember if his lip was split open before Eden had gone after him or not.

He clenched his fist, glaring back. I knew Shadoe well enough to know in that moment he was reevaluating every decision he had made since Lowell died. His jaw ticked.

Necesta took her place at Shadoe's side again, lending him her allegiance. She wouldn't let anyone's feelings cloud the group's judgment on what should happen to Shadoe for picking the wrong battle.

"Have you had your say, dearie?" she asked Eden.

Eden tried to hide her shudder. She let out a forceful breath but didn't speak.

"Good," Necesta proclaimed, "Time to move on."

"We can't let this distract us from handling this situation," Raselin added.

Dov moved into action.

"Reed, Nian, Anetta, collect all of the weapons and take them inside. Henry, Ben, Carter, Gregory, Devin, Justin, Fitch, Sherman, handle the bodies if you can." He turned to see who else was nearby. "Nikko, we need information about the magistrates that escaped. Go see what you can find."

Everyone rushed to start their assignments, working as quickly as they could.

"Reyla, get the girls and start preparing supplies. We don't know what we'll need yet, but collect everything you can." He paused as Reyla rushed off. He pointed at Louis before adding, "Help her."

"Canton," I murmured, reminding him.

"Sherman, get Brittella and take her to oversee Canton until we get this all worked out. Don't tell him what happened yet."

Sherman nodded and strode toward the entrance to the mansion to find Brittella. Next to Shadoe, she was likely our best chance at controlling the magistrate. She wasn't going to like it.

"Talley, go check on the prisoners downstairs—"

"Don't bother," Shadoe interjected, coming back to life.

"Why not?" Dov's voice trailed off as he realized Shadoe had slaughtered those men as well. He swallowed hard, trying to stay calm.

"Berwyn, Raselin, take Necesta and Talley and have a conversation with Shadoe. I have an idea. I'm going to take Auluria and Silas and try to work it out. Come meet us when you're through. Eden, you stay with us."

I trusted Necesta to keep the peace in Shadoe's hearing and Talley to follow through.

"Just go," I murmured to Shadoe. He moved forward rigidly, ready to accept his punishment like the good soldier Lowell had trained him to be.

Berwyn looked torn, divide between needing to come up with a solution to our new problem and wanting to destroy Shadoe.

"Berwyn, go. Let me handle this," Dov pushed gently. His brother finally nodded gruffly before kissing Eden's hand and spinning to walk into the mansion.

Eden shuffled over to us, looking drained. We paused long enough to let the others get inside before Dov turned to us.

"What's the plan?" Silas asked before Dov could speak.

"They know we're here," Dov started, thinking it through before he spoke. "If we stay here, they have the advantage, and they'll have us cornered."

"You want to take the fight to them…" Silas mused, processing his words.

"If we clear out now, we can hide in the towns. We can surprise them as they try to get through. It will be smaller groups for us to handle and they won't be expecting us."

"The towns are already with us," Silas added. "You saw to that before."

"We could set up strategic places within the towns and create choke points," I continued, pushing the plan forward. "They'll never see it coming, especially if we do it immediately and meet them closer to their territory. If we move soon, we'd only be a few hours behind them."

"By the time they get there, rally their troops, and try to return, we'll already be waiting for them." Dov's eyes lit up as he spoke.

"We'll hit before they get organized," Silas concluded.

"You're sure we can do this?" I asked.

"I think it's our only chance, Auluria." Dov wrapped an arm around me, pulling me close.

"Are you okay?" I asked Eden. She nodded.

"I shouldn't have done that," she muttered under her breath.

"It was bound to happen," Silas gave her a half smile. "I'm surprised you held it in so long."

"I really don't like that guy." She glared at the mansion doors as if he were still standing there. "I don't know how you put up with him for so long."

"Just think," Dov snorted. "She was supposed to *marry* him. She would have had to endure him for her entire life."

Eden mimicked Dov's snort. "And instead, you get *this one*."

She dropped a hand on his head, messing up his hair like Talley occasionally did to Devin and Justin. He looked as shocked as I felt.

"Did you just give your approval, Eden?" Silas drawled.

Realizing what she had just said, Eden looked at me, wide-eyed.

"*Maybe*," she snapped. "Don't we need to look at some maps or something?"

"No," Dov chuckled as he shook his head.

"Don't think so," Silas shrugged, grinning so widely I thought his face might break.

"*I* don't need to," I shook my head, smiling at her.

She huffed, rolling her eyes.

"We need to leave the bodies," Eden said abruptly.

"What?" Silas questioned.

"If we're abandoning the mansion, we need to leave a message for anyone who approaches it. We don't want the Society taking it back and using it as a stronghold against us.

"If we leave the bodies out, it's a warning. At the very least, it creates too much of a problem for them to be able to easily use the mansion. We can handle it when we get back...assuming we make it back."

"Let's talk to Fitch," Dov agreed. "I don't like it, but it's a good plan."

"We need to get moving if we're going to abandon this place by this afternoon," Silas commented, motioning us back to the mansion. "This won't be easy."

Chapter 10

My skirt brushed against my legs as I walked hand-in-hand with Dov. He casually strode next to me, acting as if he were examining the wares on a table in the market on the outskirts of town.

I relished being in a dress again. It had been far too long.

Eden, along with Berwyn, mingled with the crowd. Her voice floated over the hum of people talking as she bartered for a loaf of bread. Reyla slipped her arm through Justin's as they walked down the street.

Dov did most of the talking, drawing people's attention and quietly telling them about the plan, while I looked for anyone I could identify. He chuckled merrily with a man selling gloves in preparation for the impending winter.

"And is this your lovely bride?" The man's voice we deep and warm.

"Not just yet, but we're getting there," Dov flashed him a mischievous smile as I looked back to the conversation. The man grinned at me, laughing heartily.

"We're working on that one," Silas strolled by, Gloria at his side. She made a face and pulled him along.

"You can't be serious?" Devin raised his voice, arguing over the price of boots at a table on the other side of the street. Talley glanced around, acting embarrassed by her brother.

Our contact had told us the entire town was willing to support us in our mission to rid the Society of the magistrates and their soldiers. All we had to do was quickly inform them of our plans.

We had been welcomed into many homes over the past two days, staying only long enough to rest and move on. There was one town between us and our final destination.

A woman gasped loudly behind us. I turned to find her several tables down, standing across a makeshift table from Berwyn. Her husband was engaged in conversation with the Baers, looking like they were talking to long-lost friends.

Her gaze traveled beyond Berwyn and Eden, falling first on Dov, then on me. He waved just as the woman's face fell. Tears welled up in her eyes as she grabbed her skirt and maneuvered herself around the table. It wasn't until she was halfway to us that I recognized her.

"Oh no," I breathed.

"Auluria?" Dov asked.

Silas skidded out of the way to avoid being run over by the woman. Gloria looked horrified as he crashed into her.

"It's you," she said, coming up to me. "It's you, isn't it?"

Everything spun, like my world unraveling before me. Dov steadied me.

"Auluria? You know her?" Dov whispered.

My eyes felt wild. I tried desperately to tame them, but I knew I failed. My hands groped for something to ground me, finding Dov's forearm. He knew something was wrong.

He turned to me, placing his hands on my elbows.

"What's going on?" he demanded.

"I…" I stumbled.

I couldn't tell them. I *had* to tell them.

"Hello," I said to the woman, my voice shaking. "Yes, it's me."

"Whatever is wrong?" The woman looked nervous.

Her husband trailed behind her, Berwyn and Eden looking over his shoulder.

"Is this…?" He gaped at me. "It is, isn't? You're that girl."

"What girl?" Berwyn growled.

"We took her in for a night once," the wife explained. "She hurt herself outside our home and she spent the night with us."

"She tried to run away a few times, but we finally convinced her to stay," the husband added.

Berwyn and Eden slowly turned to me with exaggerated looks of accusation. Dov's gaze was one of shock and curiosity.

"You should know that I've been working with the Baers all this time," I tried to preface what I was about to admit, hoping it would soften their reaction. "I'm so sorry."

They watched me, eagerly awaiting an explanation.

"My cousin sent me to you," I looked down at the ground, wishing I could melt into it. "You were so kind to me and I'm so sorry."

Berwyn cleared his throat as I babbled.

"My cousin knew you worked with…I'm assuming the Baers," I glanced at Berwyn for confirmation. "I didn't know that then, nor did I know what my cousin had planned."

"She's Lowell's cousin," Berwyn supplied, evoking shock and outrage from the couple. They didn't say anything though.

"I'm so sorry; I didn't know," I begged them to forgive me. "Lowell sent me to you—"

"Why?" the husband asked.

"Papers." I looked down again.

"You weren't hurt?" the wife sounded wounded. "You stole from us?"

"I'm so sorry." I tried reaching out to her, but she pulled back.

"What were the papers?" Dov asked gently, trying to help.

"I don't know," I admitted.

"They were your location," the husband said. "It was the only thing we had that she could have found."

"So," Dov's face morphed into a grin. "You brought Auluria to us… to *me*." He took my hand, placing it over his heart. "I owe you a great debt of gratitude, in that case."

The couple looked shocked for a moment.

"We can't thank you enough for the kindness you showed Auluria that day," Dov praised them. "Without you, she never would have come to us, and without her, we'd still be under the control of the Society."

"We still *are* under the control of the Society," Berwyn reminded him.

"Not for much longer," Dov beamed. "We're almost free."

"I know what I did was wrong, and I'm so sorry for betraying you," I tried one more time. "But I hope you can forgive me."

They hesitated for a moment.

"It all worked out in the end," the wife said. "And if it got you away from that vicious Lowell, then it was worth it."

The husband looked at his wife, willing to agree with anything she said. He nodded to me, accepting my apology.

"Thank you," I sighed.

"When this is all over," the husband said, turning to his wife, "We need to figure out how we were compromised."

"Lowell had many resources," I recalled, "but we're all on the same side now."

"So we see," the wife smiled politely.

Dov's fingers flinched over mine where it still rested on his chest. He smiled at me when our eyes connected.

"The good news is that we have one more bit of information for you," the husband smiled.

I huddled against Dov, wishing the cold away. The wind swept a piece of my hair up, tossing it into Reyla's face as she curled against my shoulder.

"Do you mind?" she teased playfully.

Dov reached up for me, pulling the stray piece back down. He tucked it between us as he kissed the tip of my nose.

"I know we wanted you two back together, but do you think you could cut back on the lack of public awareness?" Silas groaned.

"Be quiet, Silas," Reyla shook her head at him, "They are adorable. Don't be jealous."

"He's very jealous," Dov grinned at his friend.

Shadoe grumbled from his place alongside Raselin at the next fire over.

"Remind me why we didn't stay in the town?" I mumbled, shivering as the wind picked up again.

I heard the log behind us creak. Using my hair to block my face from onlookers, I mouthed his brother's name to Dov. He nodded slightly and I made a face, pretending I hadn't spoken. The log creaked again, letting me know Berwyn had turned back around as he monitored Shadoe. Canton sat on the ground far enough away to not be able to hear us, under constant supervision. The trainer from the camp sat far enough away that they couldn't communicate, also under guard.

"We're only staying for a little while," Dov whispered.

"And it's safer to move through the woods than the town at this time of night," I whispered in a nagging voice. "I know, I know."

"Are you okay, Rey?" Silas squinted to see her across the flames. "You look like you might shiver right off that log."

"I'm freezing, Silas," she admitted.

He pouted at her, making me laugh.

"So helpful, aren't you, Silas?"

"Usually," he grinned. "Want an extra shoulder, Rey?"

She nodded and he stood up, walking around the flames to join her. We all moved down, barely fitting on the overturned tree trunk. He wrapped an arm around her shoulders, bumping into me with his hand.

"How come *I* wasn't invited to the party?" Justin pouted as he walked over with a piece of bread in his hand.

Reyla batted her eyelashes. "*I couldn't say,*" she taunted.

"Don't look at me," I added. I tried to hold a hand up in innocence, but it was tangled in Dov's, and I inadvertently raised our hands together.

"Thanks a lot, *Auluria*. See if I invite *you* to the next family outing." Justin teased, taking Silas' seat.

"You have to—it's mandatory now," I reminded him.

"Have the scouts come back yet?" Justin asked, changing the direction of the conversation. I wanted to see if the information the couple had given us had helped.

"No, not that I know of," Dov replied. He tucked my hand between his to warm it for me.

"I hate having to wait around for Devin," Justin mumbled, biting into the bread. "Oh, this is amazing."

"I just have this feeling that tomorrow is going to be the day," I said, my thumb tracing circles on Dov's skin with the hand he wasn't holding. I wasn't sure if I was prepared for what we would find.

"I have that same feeling," Raselin said from behind where he sat by Shadoe. "Shadoe?"

"It's likely," Shadoe replied. "By now, I'm sure they've made it back and have rallied their troops. If it were me, I'd already have my men on the move."

"Should we leave earlier than we had planned?" Eden asked begrudgingly. She was still angry that Shadoe had been allowed to not only stay, but also participate.

"That might be wise," Berwyn nodded.

"That *would* be wise," Devin announced, joining the group. "It sounds like tomorrow is the day."

He dropped down next to Justin, stealing the last of his bread.

"Hey," Justin protested, looking shocked.

"*Hey nothing.*" Devin popped a piece of bread in his mouth. "I've been out all night while you sat around here. Go get me more food, little brother."

The two argued until I stood up. "I'll go," I said, walking away.

With the warmth of Dov's body gone, my body went into an extra cold state as I wove my way through the different fires. Necesta fell into step beside me.

"Now you listen here, Goldilocks," she started, matching my movements. "You need to be careful when we take on the Society. Do you still have your necklace?"

I pulled it out from under my collar to show her.

"Good, good," she crooned. "Get Devin some food—the poor boy —and then you're coming with me. We have to refill that before the fight."

"You can refill it?" I questioned, fingering the necklace.

"Well, part of it, anyway. I found a few ingredients along the way, but I need your help."

She steered me toward where the food was being cooked and warmed. I collected a few things for Devin and the others. Necesta walked me back to the group.

"Where are you going?" Dov asked, sounding a little desperate. I touched his cheek, cupping his jaw in my palm.

"I'll be back soon. Necesta just needs me for something."

He turned his face into my hand, kissing me. "Hurry back."

I followed Necesta to the edge of the fires, our shadows casting long, dark figures ahead of us. She sat down, patting the rock next to her.

"Can you see all right?" she asked gently.

"Yes." I watched her pull a small bowl from her satchel. "What are we doing?"

"Grind this." She forced the bowl into my hands.

She retrieved a second bowl, adding in more ingredients. We worked in silence as the wind tugged at our hoods and whipped our skirts around our ankles.

"Oh, Goldilocks," she sighed. "You've come so far."

"Have I?" The corners of my mouth tugged up.

"I imagine even more than I know," she grinned at me. "I've only been with you on part of this journey. Are you the same little girl your cousin took in all those years ago?"

"No," I laughed, shaking my head. "I most certainly am not."

"Are you the same girl engaged to your handler?"

"Definitely not," I shook my head rapidly.

"I should hope not." She winked.

"You're not the same girl sent to seduce a Baer, nor are you the girl who had to choose between your family and your people. Goldilocks," she stopped her work to turn to me. "You have changed the face of your reality, but not only that—you've also changed each and every person here.

"Without you, dearie, none of this would be happening. The Baers would still be living their quiet existence in the woods, simply trying to survive. Your cousin would have done something stupid and you would likely be dead. Shadoe wouldn't have the slightest conscience —though I'm not sure how much of one he has now—and we most certainly wouldn't have come over the Wall to find our freedom. You're the key here, Auluria."

She set her bowl down, motioning for me to do the same, and took my hands in hers. She smiled a toothy grin.

"I knew the girl I met that day in the market was special," she praised me. "I knew you would do great things. I want to thank you, Auluria, for bringing this old woman *home*."

"Don't sound so grim, Necesta," Brittella's voice floated over to us. She flounced over, taking a seat behind me. "You sound like you're dying and trying to say goodbye."

"Who knows what tomorrow will bring, Brittella," Necesta chastised good-naturedly.

Brittella chuckled, picking up my bowl.

"What are we making, my darlings?"

"Oh, just a few things for tomorrow," Necesta quickly explained each one. "Now, Goldilocks. Should you need any of this, I've been teaching Maylin. You can ask her if you ever need something done quickly and I'm not around to do it for you."

"I'll keep that in mind."

"Dearie," Necesta continued, "I've given the girl all of my notes. I knew she would stay at the camps to help and I wanted her to be prepared. She's been a good student. Sharone too, though I'm sure she'll be preoccupied now that she knows her sister is alive and she's about to become an aunt."

She glanced at Brittella, adding, "Like this, dearie."

We worked in silence for a few moments, letting the wind whisper secrets to us. The two women watched each other, one magnificently dressed, the other looking like a quiet grandmother, and polar opposites. Brittella finally paused.

"I think we're going to be good friends, Necesta."

"Perhaps we shall," Necesta answered with a grin.

"By the way," Brittella murmured as she looked back down to her work. "I saw what you did back there."

"What was that, dearie?" she asked innocently.

Brittella's eyes sparkled as she looked back up, giving her the same knowing smile she frequently gave me. Necesta chuckled as she looked back down. They were both women of many secrets.

When we finished and Necesta had replenished my store of antidotes and medicines, she sent me back to the group so the two of them could talk alone—likely about me.

"Come on." His eyes were still fiercely blue, deep and intense, even in the shadows from the fire. I blinked, bringing him into focus.

"What's happening?" I murmured as he smiled.

"I'll explain, just come along," he whispered back.

"Are we leaving?" I stumbled along behind him. He practically sprinted around the fires and sleeping people.

"Not yet." He turned, glancing over his shoulder with a wicked smile.

His dark hair moved in the breeze as he tugged me forward. I fixated on it as we moved, reminding me of the day I woke up in his house, unsure of who he was. It fell over his eyes each time he looked back at me.

"Dov, what are we doing?" I had accepted his spontaneity, giggling by the time he slowed.

"We've only had a few dates, Auluria, and I will not go marching off to start a war tomorrow without at least one more."

"Oh," I blushed, giggling like little Jasleen when she got around a handsome man.

"Sit with me." Dov leaned against a tree, holding out his hand.

He wrapped his legs around me as I leaned against him, my back against his chest. Heat radiated off of him, warming me as I curled into his embrace. Together, we stared up through the trees in silence, watching the stars. Each time a wicked wind rose up, he pulled me tighter to his chest, protecting me from it.

"Have you ever doubted me, Auluria?" Dov murmured in my ear.

"What do you mean?"

"I don't want you to ever doubt my feelings for you," Dov said softly. "I know it's been hard for us. It started out as a deception, and then I kept us apart because I didn't trust you. When we finally found our way back together, Canton ripped us apart, and I sent you off with Shadoe—and then he nearly killed you—"

"And *you* nearly died," I reminded him.

"That too," he nodded into my hair. "I just want to make sure you feel like you can trust me and that you know I'll always be here for you."

"What, no more cold shoulder?" I teased. "I was kind of getting used to the silence…and Silas' interference."

"You hated Silas' interference," he reminded me. Dov paused before adding, "Do you honestly not know who he likes?"

"Everyone in this world knows who he likes except for me," I grumbled.

Dov leaned forward, whispering a name in my ear.

"No," I whispered in disbelief.

"Yep," Dov leaned back against the tree, dragging me back with him.

"I can work with that," I finally said, trying to keep from glowing at how simple my job would be.

"It won't be that easy," he smirked, knowing what I was thinking.

"Of course it will be," I grinned back at him as the leaves jumped to life overhead. A shower of dying leaves cascaded around us, swarming our vision as if they had been fireflies in the summer. The pieces swirled around us, more beautiful than I had ever seen fallen leaves before.

"I love you, Auluria," Dov whispered, reaching an arm around in front of me to tangle in my hair, reaching across my chest. I turned to him, catching his lips with the side of mine.

Kissing backward was no easy task. I turned to the side, trying to make it easier on us. Finally, he scooped up my legs, lifting them over his knee so that they sat between his raised leg and hip. Dov cradled me in his embrace, pulling my hair as he tangled his fingers in my mane.

"I promise I won't lock you out again," he murmured between kisses.

"I promise I won't deceive you," I responded, my hand running up and down his chest, making his breath catch.

"I promise to always listen and believe you," he continued, using his feet to pull my body closer.

"I'll never try to manipulate you again," I committed as he kissed me again.

"Oh, you can manipulate me into doing your bidding anytime you want," he panted as the kissing grew more intense. His left hand wrapped around my waist, pulling at my hip.

I freed my arm from where it was pinned between our bodies and caressed his chin, guiding him back to me each time our lips broke apart.

"I will spend the rest of my life making sure you are safe and taken care of," he opened his eyes, watching me as I leaned in to kiss him. He moaned softly as I touched his lips, begging me not to pull away.

I leaned back, trying to get a different angle as I wrapped my arms around his neck. Every muscle in his shoulders was pulled taut. His arms went under mine, lifting me into a more comfortable position as I settled onto his abdomen and upper leg, forming a wedge for me to sit on.

"I'll always be there to take care of you too," I promised my allegiance to him.

He brushed my hair with his hand, pulling it back and forth over my shoulder as we stared at each other's lips, trying to catch our breath.

I relaxed my body, realizing how rigid I had gone while kissing him. Sliding down, I curled up against him, nestling into his neck. I didn't mind when my breath moved his hair, tickling him. My heart jumped as his eyes fluttered shut, trying to keep them from rolling back at the sensation.

"This is an interesting date," I commented, barely able to move my cheek to smile from resting it so hard against Dov's shoulder.

"I didn't even get to the best part yet," Dov murmured.

"*That* wasn't the best part?" I looked up, shocked.

"Oh, my dear Auluria," he grinned at me, "No, no it wasn't."

He reached into his pocket, nearly tipping me over. He withdrew his hand, carefully hiding something.

"I have something for you," he smiled at me.

"I can see that," I crooned, waiting.

The wind shook the trees above us again, showering us once more in leaves. They danced in brilliant oranges and reds in the muted firelight from the camp just close enough to still give us light.

"I know this hasn't always been easy for either of us, and I didn't want to do this until after, just in case, but I can't wait any longer." His eyes glittered even more than the stars in the sky above us. "Auluria, I fell hard for you the moment I met you. I got so caught up in you that I couldn't see anything else but you, but you wouldn't let me get away with that.

"You made sure that I not only saw you, but I saw myself and everyone else around me. You made me into such a better man than I ever thought I could be—"

"You were perfect," I interjected, jumping forward to kiss his nose. "You took care of everyone Dov. I, in no way, could have *ever* made you a better man than the one I met, who ran into fires and took beatings for people. You've always been the best man, my love."

"I'm not finished, ma'am." His eyes were soft as he gazed at me. "I love you with the very depths of my being and I'd be lost without you.

"You've taught me something very important, Auluria."

"Hmm?" I watched him carefully.

"One spark can light the entire universe on fire. One choice, one action, one word can give permission to change the way a life is lived. You've irrevocably changed me, Auluria. You set my world on fire—literally, once or twice—" he smirked, eyes sparkling, "and you've completely changed the way I'm living my life. I'll always be grateful for that.

"Berwyn gave our mother's ring to Eden when they were married, so I want to give you this." He unfolded his hand, revealing a silver medallion on a black cord.

"I thought the Society had this," I gasped, fingering the paw that rested in his hands.

"They turned it over to Canton," he smiled slyly. "We may have found it and reallocated it."

"Well, you *do* like reallocating things," I smirked.

"I want you to have this, Auluria," he whispered earnestly. For a moment, I thought to insist he keep his father's medallion, but I knew what this meant to him. "Marry me."

He said it like a statement, for there was never any question.

I touched it one more time before looking at him. Tipping my head sideways, feeling like I was in a dream, I pursed my lips.

"Yes." I teared up.

Dov reached through my hair, securing the medallion around my neck, before crashing against my lips once more. My fingers wove their way through his hair, as my lips became more swollen from kissing him.

Our movements were happy and frenzied, colliding with each other again and again. When they finally slowed, I found myself standing, pinned against a tree. I had no memory of moving, but I didn't need one. All I needed was Dov's arms wrapped around me. I whimpered when he pulled away to gaze at me.

My hair caught in the bark as I leaned forward, pieces dragging behind me. Dov brushed them down, leaning around me to rest his arm on the trunk of the tree as he had done before.

"Auluria," he breathed gently, making me shudder.

I sighed, enjoying the moment.

"Dov!" a piercing voice shouted, echoing in the forest, jolting us both into action.

Chapter 11

"Dov!" Berwyn yelled again as we crashed toward the campsite.

"What happened?" Dov asked as we skidded to a stop in front of Berwyn and Eden.

"We have to move," Berwyn looked frantic. "Now. They're coming."

"They're moving already?" Dov looked shocked as he brushed his hair back, reminding me for a moment of Nian.

"They must not have wanted to wait until morning." Berwyn turned, guiding us through the camp. "Whatever they have planned, they must think it's important to enact it sooner rather than later."

Eden eyed the necklace around my neck.

"Better put that away for now," she mumbled. I tucked the medallion inside my dress alongside Necesta's.

Everyone was quickly packing their bags. Justin tossed me my pack as he pulled on an extra layer of clothing. Silas doused the fire, making sure the embers no longer glowed as Reyla quickly tamed her hair back into a braid that she could quickly release if she needed to, should the enemy try to use it against her.

Berwyn paced, checking to see if anyone needed help. It reminded me of those first few days in the Baers' cabin as he stalked about. Eden kept a watchful eye on him as she gathered supplies and hid extra weapons in her boots.

"Reyla," I whispered as I sidled up next to her, adding weapons to my own boots."

"Hmm?" She looked down to where I was bent over.

"I have something to tell you."

"Already?" Silas yelped a few feet away. Reyla and I both looked over to find him grinning wildly at Dov. Dov nodded enthusiastically before they both looked at me.

I shot straight up, knowing I needed to tell Reyla before they gave it away. My hands flew to my neckline, fishing out the medallion. I held it between my fingers to show her.

It took her a moment to realize what it was, then to register that I was wearing it, and finally, her jaw dropped as she realized *why* I was wearing it. Reyla slammed her jaw closed, swallowed her words—hard—and tried to suppress a squeal.

My best friend bit back a grin, nodding sharply once, before turning away.

"Good," she said in a clipped voice, trying to contain her joy. "But we're celebrating this later."

"Celebrating what?" Justin asked.

I quickly tucked the medallion away. "Nothing."

Justin looked back and forth between Reyla and me. When he turned to catch sight of Dov and Silas, he figured it out.

"You weren't going to tell me?" he yelped.

"We're about to go into battle, Justin. We don't need distractions," I chastised.

"Who said anything about distractions, Goldilocks? This is something to fight *for!*" He smiled as his eyes darted around to find his brother, ready to hold it over him that he knew first.

"Justin, now is not the time," I reminded him.

"You're not going to tell Talley and Devin?" he looked disappointed.

"I will…but *quietly*," I relented.

"Move out," Berwyn instructed loudly.

The last of the fires were put out as we turned to go. I couldn't help feeling like I was back with Lowell's people, moving from one campsite to the next. Sherman and Nikko's presence didn't help the feeling as they walked along next to Shadoe. Nikko carefully aligned himself closer to me.

We hurried toward the town, quickly leaving the trees behind. We sprinted down the streets, warning people as we went. They grumbled as we roused them from their beds, but quickly made arrangements for those that couldn't stay behind to fight, to go to the storehouses.

The half town emptied of people, leaving only our fighters to take their place. Moving into houses, we took on the look of residents. We prepared to go out into the towns and run the market as they would normally do, our goal to corral them in one central location only hours away.

"We're out of time," Ben shouted, running toward us from where he had gone to scout ahead. "Here we go!"

It was still dark, the sun behind the town line as we scrambled into empty houses. We would no longer be able to turn on them in the market. I bumped into Berwyn as we closed the door behind us, thirty people crammed into the tiny house.

"You'd better not do anything stupid out there, Auluria," he grumbled harshly into my ear.

"Not planning on it," I snapped, annoyed.

"Dov won't survive it if you die out there, especially now."

"What do you—" I cut off my words, realizing he knew Dov had proposed. He probably had to get Berwyn's permission anyway, so it shouldn't have surprised me.

My hand rested on the wooden door, waiting to push it open on Berwyn's signal. Dov peered out the window, watching for our opening. Berwyn kept his eyes focused on his brother, waiting for his mark.

Society soldiers marched through the streets, their footsteps falling so loud that we could hear them several streets away. In the dark of early morning, everything reverberated off the buildings much louder than in the brightness of day.

Each approaching step brought me closer and closer to the day of my hanging. A tightness grew in my chest, and I had the overwhelming feeling that we wouldn't make it through this battle.

Faces flashed through my mind; my parents, my aunt, little Jasleen, even Lowell. I looked nervously around the room at the people who had become my family. Silas stood at Dov's side, ready to fight to the death for his people. Reyla waited by my side, Anetta watching me intently. My future brother and sister loomed near the door, tenseness holding their bodies captive. My former handler looked ready to murder. Nikko, Sherman, Ella, Locust and a few of his spies stood by his side. The Hersh siblings hovered by another window, watching from the other side. Necesta quietly waited by them, insisting on fighting with us. Gregory stood by Maylin and Carter, while Henry wrapped an arm around Katarina's waist, murmuring soft words into her ear. The room was filled with people I knew and cared about, while my love prepared to give the signal to attack.

I saw Dov tense up and knew they were drawing near. Terror washed over me. Not everyone would survive this. It might be a miracle if *any* of us did.

Focusing on the door, I calmed my thundering heart down as my cousin had taught me to do. I watched one spot on the wood, tracing the grain of the door with my eye just enough to form a repetitive pattern. Over and over, one circle after the next. Up, down, up down. Calm. Breathe...in, out.

Everything fell into an overwhelming hush despite the boots colliding with the street outside. My breathing filled my senses, in, out. It flooded my ears leaving only the sound of air and my heartbeats.

Cutting off the inner dialogue running through my head telling me what to do, I switched my focus, picking one sole breath out of the masses. Dov breathed in and out, short and quick. I focused on him, followed his moves, watching every tiny thing he did. I would fight for him.

His eyes latched on to Berwyn's, and he gave a slight nod, looking worried. Berwyn swallowed, turned, and dropped his hand. I collided with the door, pushing it open.

We spilled out into the street, the entire legion of Society soldiers turning in surprise. The house across the street opened as well, more of our men pouring into the open with loud yells.

The houses were immediately set on fire by the soldiers, but our people had more than enough time to exit and join the fight. The soldiers closest to us never had a chance. Shadoe ripped into them as fiercely as Berwyn did, using the claw he had once slashed Dov's brother with once again.

Raselin ran toward us from the other house, trying to identify the leaders of the Society soldiers, knife dripping blood as he yelled. Talley stayed by Necesta's side, attempting to protect her.

My knife came out bloody as the first soldier fell at my feet. Droplets covered the back of my hand and wrist. He squinted his eyes at me, dragging his knife across the top of my wrist, leaving a trail of my own blood to pool at my feet. The sharp sting brought me back to reality.

Turning, I threw my elbow at a soldier, crashing into his nose. It broke with a ferocious shattering noise. He screamed in pain, both hands flying to his face. Twisting my body, I used my other elbow to slam into his stomach. He doubled over, allowing me to deliver a clean hook to his face, sending him reeling backward.

Another soldier ran at me, giving me just enough time to flip him over my back. I brought my boot down on his face, praying I had only knocked him out and not snapped his neck.

One of the boys from the camp ran past me at full speed, colliding with a Society man. He grunted as they toppled to the ground. The boy got the upper hand and the fight grew louder around us. He didn't stop punching the man's face until he was unrecognizable, a bloody mass in the middle of the road.

The fire crackled from the homes the soldiers had lit up the moment they realized it was an ambush, giving a harsh orange glow to the area. Ashes fluttered in the sky like snow, or a million gray and black butterflies come to collect what was theirs; their life-pollen the blood spilled across the dirt and stone.

I whipped around, my hair trailing behind me in my signature move. It slapped into my side before falling to rest for the briefest moment before I started running.

The soldiers moved back, running around the houses to find a new angle to attack from. I wasn't about to let them escape or get the upper hand on us. Our only hope of survival was to take them out there—in that moment—as we took them by surprise.

The house we had vacated began to crumble as the man I was chasing suddenly fell. A wound in his temple opened up, draining red into the street, though I hadn't touched him and no one else was in sight.

"Go," a voice called from high above. A man from the town stood in the window, fire filling the room behind him. He lifted his slingshot again, taking aim at another man I likely would not catch.

The rock struck the soldier, silencing him, as the man in the window cried out in pain. He stood, hanging out of the window as the fire licked at him. He burned as he took down my opponents one at a time as I battled them on my own. His shrieks filled my head and he crumbled under the searing flames, sacrificing himself so that I could live to fight.

The remaining two soldiers turned to take me on, but they didn't expect me to be able to fight for myself. I shattered them, breaking bones and drawing blood. The man on the left fell first; the soldier on the right going down at nearly the same time as Dov pulled his knife from the man's back.

"Let's go," he said grimly. "More escaped that way."

A loud explosion sounded, rocking the area. I fell to my knees, pitching forward. I narrowly avoided slamming my face off of the ground. Dov scooped me up, forcing me to run. We rounded the structure to find more building pieces fluttering to the ground.

"Reyla!" I shrieked, alerting Silas to the impending danger. He turned, pushing Reyla behind him.

I gasped as Dov matched Silas' movements, pushing me around him. Devin ran at us, taking out the man Dov was trying to protect me from. They toppled onto the ground, wrestling for control of the situation. Dov jumped forward to help him as I sprinted toward Silas to lend my assistance.

I kicked the man, knocking him off balance enough for Silas to take him out. Reyla had turned, engaging another soldier. She pulled his feet out from under him as I slashed at his throat. I felt like my insides had crawled out of me when the nasty red line scratched across his skin.

"No!" Lydia screamed, forcing us to whip around to her. She was barreling at a soldier but never stood a chance of reaching him in time. Chester was on the ground before Lydia crashed into his murderer. She sprawled on the ground, tumbling over the Society man. She slammed into his shoulder with her knife, ripping the muscles so viciously I don't know how she didn't amputate his arm.

Chester lay on his back, facing the glowing sky, as ashes rained down on his face. The pieces covered his clothing. Reyla reached him first, slapping the embers that burned tiny holes into his wardrobe.

He gagged, fighting to speak as blood began to pool in his mouth.

"Tell Barone…I'm sorry I failed him…" he managed around the blood. It dripped from the corners of his mouth.

"You didn't," we both shook our heads violently as the life faded from him.

He choked, coughing weakly, sending tiny droplets of blood into the air. For a moment, he looked peaceful, then his eyes dulled.

I looked the length of him, discovering a gaping wound in his abdomen. It wouldn't have saved him even if we had held pressure on it. Reyla held his hand to her chest and I couldn't help but picture her hovering over Peter's body had she been there the day he had died to save me.

"We have to go," Lydia instructed, dragging herself over to us.

"Lydia, you're hurt," I felt my face drain of its color.

"It's mostly his," she nodded to the soldier she had maimed. "I'm okay. Just tie this around my arm."

I quickly reached for the strip of fabric and tied it securely over the hole in her arm. She nodded, watching for soldiers.

"We have to go," she repeated herself.

"Ladies, time to move," Fitch exclaimed, reaching around his wife to guide her away. He noticed her arm, giving her a concerned look.

"I'm fine," she assured him, offering a weak smile.

I grabbed Reyla's hand, running behind them, as Chester's shell continued to watch the ashy butterflies in the sky.

Dov paused, waiting for me to catch up to him. Berwyn and Eden were at my heels as we followed the youngest Baer around the corner, following the sounds of a large group of soldiers. Reinforcements were coming.

The clouds looked darker than the sky itself, a mix of purple with hints of orange sparkling through them as the fires sizzled. We slowed at the edge of the buildings, knowing we were about to meet a new group of Society men. Silas slinked forward, creeping around the corner of the building to check. He darted back quickly.

He leaned to look around us, realizing more of our people had joined our team. I glanced back, seeing a large following. Silas held up a hand and nodded. Quietly counting down, he gave us the signal to move.

We ambushed them, hitting them hard before they saw us coming. The inevitable battle cry went up, surrounding us in chaos once more. Fists slammed into flesh, making people cry out. Knives cut, etching the battle lines into our very beings.

"Babe," Dov said gently to let me know he was there, taking up a place beside me.

"Good timing," I yelped, ducking under a blade. I lifted my hands up as the man's hand passed over me, jerking his arm up. His knife skittered to the ground. Dov slammed his heel into it, bending it unnaturally, as I twisted the man's arm enough to flip him.

Another explosion rocked the earth where we had left the rest of the group. It sent tremors along the ground we stood on. The Society soldier groaned on the ground, his shoulder painfully out of place. I left him, knowing I was needed elsewhere. I was desperately trying to kill as few people as possible.

"You okay?" Reed asked, sidling up next to me. His hand crashed into a man who thought he could take us on.

"I'm fine," I tossed a grin at him. "You?"

"I'd rather climb over a wall any day," he grinned, thinking about helping his people across the Wall. "You realize that hair isn't doing you any favors, don't you?"

I raised my eyebrow at him, nearly crossing my arms in challenge during our reprieve from the fight as he knocked the man out.

"They're targeting you, Auluria. Might want to tuck that back."

"Isn't that the point?" I asked.

"The point is to get yourself killed?" he joked, rolling his eyes.

"My hair is still less likely to get me killed than Nian's." I protested.

"That is a very good point," he laughed.

A cloud of smoke from the explosions and burning buildings floated toward us, hovering over our fight. It reflected the orange glow from the distance, creating a strange look to the sky. I sneezed as the scent of the smoke hit my nose.

"Now!" a voice yelled. I turned to find Locust running down the street, Martin chasing behind him. Cupping his hand, Locust lifted Martin into the air. He crashed into a large board the soldiers had erected near one of the buildings, knocking it over.

Martin rolled as he hit the ground. The soldiers descended on him as Locust fought off two of them. Reed ran to help them, taking out soldiers along the way.

"Behind you," Nian said, nearly making me jump out of my skin. He flipped his hair and grinned. "You okay?"

"I'm fine, what are you doing?" I asked, arms up and ready to take on another attack.

"There!" he shouted, darting toward the building. He paused for a moment before squatting to the ground. He stuck his leg out just in time to trip a line of soldiers. The first man fell over him, the others tripping over the tangled heap of a man on the ground. They crashed hard on top of each other.

I screamed as Sherman appeared out of nowhere with an ax, eliminating the problem in a pile at his feet. Nian backed away as quickly as he could, retching as the men screamed for mercy.

I fixated on the pool of blood forming around the bodies, slowly leaking further away from its origin point. The smoke above us shifted, revealing the beginnings of a beautiful morning sky. A new orange color filled the sky beyond the clouds as the sun started to rise. Just as quickly, the smoke moved, covering it again.

I started to move to Nian to help him up when shouting broke out.

"No!" Locust screamed. It was the most terrifying noise I had ever heard come from a person, including the torture I had suffered at the hands of Canton's men.

I froze and followed his gaze to a set of nearby trees. Ropes had been strung over the branches. Four soldiers held onto two of our men as a swarm of Society men grabbed hold of the free ends of the ropes wrapped around Martin and Reed's necks.

Locust tried to free himself, desperate to reach them in time. I screamed louder than I had when Canton's man had burned me, tears clouding my eyes. The soldiers threw themselves to the ground, jerking the ropes up, snapping Martin and Reed's necks.

"Reed!" I fought, but it was too late.

They were gone.

Sobbing, I felt Nian scoot over to me. He was trembling as he realized what had happened. We sat, shaking with tears and hatred until Dov launched himself at the man coming for us. They tumbled in front of us, snapping us awake.

When I looked up, Justin and Devin were taking on the men who had hung our friend. Dov wrestled the solider in front of us, slamming the man's skull into the ground.

"Go," he grunted.

I grabbed Nian's hand, pulling him to his feet. Once moving, he ran faster than me, reaching the fray long before I did. We dove into the middle of it, lashing out at anyone we could find.

I ran into a soldier, knocking him to the ground. I had no remorse when I beat him, still reeling from Reed's gruesome death. This man had murdered him—not to defend himself, but to prove a simple point: that he could.

"Auluria," Eden finally pulled me off of the man as he lay unconscious beneath my pounding fists.

I pointed to the bodies still hanging from the tree and watched the rage slip on like a mask. She turned, taking on a solider with a vicious cry. Somehow, Eden managed to get her hands on a set of the spiked claws that Shadoe had used on Berwyn. My blood ran cold thinking about what that might mean.

"Do you even know how to use that?" I shrieked at her, landing a punch to a Society man. He reared back in pain.

"Don't look at me like that, Auluria," she snarled. "I wasn't a complete idiot when I hung around Lowell. I picked a few things up."

The metal piece left angry lines down the side of the man's face and I prayed it wasn't laced with poison.

"Where did you get that?" I begged for information.

"Never you mind, Goldilocks. Pay attention to your own fight." She kicked at the man, sending him into a tree. For a moment, I was jealous I didn't have one as well. I wouldn't have minded marking up the soldiers who had hung my friend.

My throat burned, though whether it was from the smoke or a not-so-distant reminder of my own almost-hanging, I couldn't be sure. I felt as if the rope was wrapped around my neck, tightening, squeezing out all the air, leaving me dark.

By the time it was over, the soldiers lay in a messy heap on the ground. Silas, Dov, and Berwyn had finished off the men who hadn't been a part of the hanging.

Justin and Devin quietly worked to take Reed down out of the tree. Nian and I helped guide his feet to the ground, silently laying him out. Nian stayed with Reed and the Hersh brothers and I untangled Martin's body from the rope. Tears burned against my eyes.

"We can't stay," Dov whispered as we all surrounded Reed's body.

Reyla cried into Silas' shoulder as he held her. I sat on the ground with Justin and Devin. Dov stood beside me, holding my hand in the air for so long that it started to tingle. Nikko stood over Martin, mourning the loss of his friend silently as he brooded.

I leaned forward, kissing Reed on the cheek. He was one of the first people to welcome when I started training people over the Wall.

"We have to go," I whispered to him and the others. "We have to go."

I sniffed, gathering myself and forcing my tears in check. I pulled on Dov's hand, using him to lift myself. I was grateful for his constant balance when I didn't topple him and myself.

"We're not done yet," I said as another outburst from a street over filled the air.

Chapter 12

Using my sleeve, I wiped the tears and soot off my face, clearing my sight. We slowed as we approached the source of the sound. Someone cried so strongly it turned into a wail.

Soldiers and men lay in agony in the middle of the street, begging for mercy; begging for an ending. We branched off, helping our people when we could.

I saw her before the others did. Her leg was missing, torn off in the explosion. Bits of paper littered her brown hair. Her lip quivered as I knelt down.

She cringed when I brushed her hair back out of her eyes.

"Go away," Ella murmured, trying to turn her head from me.

"Take my hand, Ella," I tried to comfort her.

"Where is Shadoe?" she asked, her voice sounding like a child whining.

"I don't know," I apologized quietly.

"Ella?" Nikko's shock hit us before he made it to her side. He threw himself on the ground, taking her hand from me. "Ella."

"Where is Shadoe?" she insisted. Her leg bled more fiercely than the other wounds on her body.

"Get Shadoe," Nikko begged.

I nodded, running. A street over, I found him, clawing at his enemy. When I screamed his name, he plunged the claw into the man, raking it through his body.

"It's Ella," I informed him. "Come quickly."

He stared at me, not moving.

"Shadoe, you can't just stand here; Ella's been hurt. She's dying, Shadoe, and she's asking for you." Hysteria rose in my voice, making Shadoe shrink back. "Don't you dare do this. She needs you, now come on."

I pulled him down the street and around the corner, instructing him on how to behave. He knelt down next to her, taking her hand. I swallowed, giving him one final glare to force him into taking care of the girl before I sprinted off, knowing she didn't want me there. We hadn't been friends, but I never wanted to see her die like this.

I watched carefully, looking for signs of life among the corpses in the street. None appeared to be clinging to life, but I checked anyway.

Arin raced past me, several of our men following him. I spun, watching them run, but didn't join them. Instead, I looked for Dov, Silas, Reyla, Justin…anyone I loved.

"Auluria," he called to me. Dov waved me forward.

I ran down the street, only to be followed by Shadoe, Sherman, and a very distraught Nikko. The buildings loomed over us, starting to sparkle in the early morning sun as it worked its way through the smoke. It glinted and glared, making it a horrific sight as we tried to avoid it while running.

We passed a large building surrounded by patterned rocks. A small garden sat out front, and, though dead, it sparked something in me.

I knew this place.

The further we ran, the more I recognized. It had changed since I was last there, long before I ever met the Baers, but I would know it anywhere. I was home.

A group of soldiers appeared, looking like they hadn't seen any of our battle. Their uniforms looked crisp and clean, no blood in sight. They spotted us and took off in our direction.

"Dov, go left," I instructed. I bolted to reach him as the others followed behind me.

"We'll hold them off," Shadoe said, realizing my plan.

"No, Shadoe—" I protested.

"Just go; we'll be right behind you." He spun, taking Sherman with him. Nikko stayed by my side. I wondered if Shadoe was trying to earn his way back into our favor.

I sprinted as fast as I could, guiding the large group down the road. Justin and Devin aligned themselves with me as we ran, only giving enough space for Dov to run at my side. Silas kept a watchful arm around Reyla and Maylin, while Henry guarded Katarina. Ben ran with Sharone and Gloria, sheltering Sharone as they ran.

Berwyn called to me, asking me what I was doing.

"Going home, Berwyn," I shouted back.

"It can't be," Eden yelped when she too recognized the neighborhood. "It's her aunt's house."

"We're going to *Lowell's* house?" Berwyn sounded shocked.

"It's the best place for us right now, Berwyn," I yelled over my shoulder. "Trust me."

I crashed through the yard, up the walk to the house. We fought to open the door, but quickly enough, we were inside.

"Here," I shouted, rushing to the trap door Lowell had hidden in the house. When I threw the door open, I was hit with the familiar damp scent.

"Go," I yelped, pointing down.

"What is it?" Justin grimaced.

"It's safety, now move," I lectured. "There's a door to escape. You can escape and reach the other side."

"We're not just going to leave you," Justin argued.

"I don't expect you to," I said, knowing he'd never leave without us. "But you have to go down there. Once you're sure the others are safe, this will give you a way to take the soldiers by surprise. Once you're down there, they can't get to you, but you can get back to us up here."

He nodded, understanding my plan.

"Hurry," I willed them to move faster as everyone quickly jumped down into the hidden room under the house.

"What's the plan for us, Auluria?" Dov asked.

I handed off responsibility of the door to Silas as he forced Reyla to climb down. Racing through the house, I checked as many of Lowell's hiding places as possible in case he had added any weapons since the last time I was in the house. Dov watched me in amazement as I flew through the steps to access the secret recesses.

To my dismay, Lowell hadn't hidden anything, though my first hint should have been the intense layer of dust and cobwebs scattered over the modest home. My knife, however, was just where I had left it the last time I had been there, long before I met the Baers.

"Lowell sure liked his secrets, didn't he?" Dov asked.

"This one is mine," I said in a flat voice, making him nod once. "Are you ready for this?"

He took a deep breath, "I am. But first, before we mess up this nice house, do you want to show me around your home?"

He smirked, but I knew he was serious. This was my only link to my past, and he wanted to be let into it before it was gone.

"Quickly," Berwyn instructed as he and Eden took up positions at the windows.

I grabbed Dov's hand and quickly showed him my aunt's house, pointing out important things I wanted him to take notice of for the stories I would tell him later. His eyes raked over every inch, committing it to memory.

When we were out of sight of everyone, he pushed me against the wall, into the shadows.

"I'm sorry this is about to happen," he said sadly, kissing me. "I promise I'll give you a home even better than this one when this is all over. If there's anything you want from here, now is the time to get it."

"I took all I wanted before I left the first time, Dov. I'll be sad to see it go, but I'll be okay," I promised him.

"They're here," Eden's voice sounded calm. Silas tapped on the floor, letting Justin know.

Dov and I walked into the main room, ready to face the Society once and for all...or at least until we had to handle the other magistrates. Everyone tucked themselves away where it would be harder to find us.

Silence filled the room. It stretched on so long I thought they might have gone, ignoring the tiny, dark house. The door cracking against the heel of a man's boot sent my heart into overdrive. Dov squeezed my hand.

Four men entered the house, dressed in Society uniforms, weapons ready. They crept in slowly, investigating the scene. Seeing nothing, they relaxed. Moments ticked by, slowly dragging out before us.

One man gasped as he came face-to-face with Berwyn Baer, son of the great Griz Baer. Berwyn stepped menacingly from the shadows, covered in darkness. It dripped off of him as he stepped into the light; a truly terrifying sight.

Berwyn towered over the short soldier. The Society man quivered as Berwyn took another silent step toward him. The man's eyes grew so wide, I thought it might break his face. Berwyn lifted his arm, taking care of it for him as he backhanded him so hard, the man collapsed on the ground and didn't get back up.

The other three turned as the man hit the floor. We moved, ripping ourselves away from our hiding places in the dark corners of the house. Lowell had known what he was doing when he added in places to watch and hide, changing the existing structure of his mother's home.

When the soldiers didn't return outside, they sent in reinforcements. One by one, we took them out, silencing them before they could scream a warning. It wasn't until we heard the commotion out in my aunt's yard that we knew Shadoe had arrived.

Soldiers poured into the house, weapons ready, as their counterparts clashed with Shadoe and his men outside. Vicious growls mixed with dying whimpers as people from both sides suffered in agony.

"This is like old times," Eden said sarcastically, backing up to me. "Seems like we were just here, doesn't it?" She nodded to the window and my gaze fell on the yard where I had seen her for the first time when I was much younger, long before I knew who she or any of the Baers were or would become.

"Did you see me back then?" I grunted as a soldier kicked me, attempting to pull my leg out from under me.

"No," she responded. "I would have remembered the hair and put it all together."

Her point was not lost on me. The best-laid plans could unravel if even one thing slipped out of place.

Berwyn slammed a soldier against the wall, choking him until he passed out. The man slid to the floor with a thud. Dov elbowed a man, reaching behind him and bringing him over his shoulder in a calculated throw.

I was attacked from the side. My body spun away from the safety of Eden's back. The soldier picked me up from behind, lifting my feet off the ground.

My hair slammed into my face as I struggled to free myself. I gathered all of my strength, lifted my feet in the air, and brought them down, slamming into the man's knees. He dropped me, and I crashed into the floor, a sharp pain radiating through my wrist.

Acting on its own, my body twisted around so that I was on my side. I kicked at the man who had dropped me. His bone cracked as he fell to the floor. I tried not to smile. The kick Berwyn sent to the man's head stopped the screaming. I looked up at him in horror.

"You okay?" he asked, reaching down his hand to me. I set my uninjured hand in his and allowed him to pull me to my feet.

He pulled me to his chest, wrapping me in his arms as a soldier lashed out at me. I could feel the raised scars beneath his shirt. He had far less than Dov did, but they were still there.

Berwyn grimaced, using his arm to push the man away before releasing me. "To the right," he said, alerting me to turn.

The noise outside the window caught the soldier's attention. I used the opportunity to push him through the glass. He toppled out, face first. I pushed his feet for good measure, making sure he couldn't catch himself.

Beyond the yard, I saw our people, fighting against the Society men. They had gone around through the secret door and doubled back to aid our fight. Reyla, Katarina, and Henry stood just beyond my aunt's laundry line where we used to hang sheets and quilts out to dry in the warmer months.

"They're outside, we have to go," I yelled to the Baers.

"Auluria," Justin yelled, opening up the secret door.

I whipped around to face him, not realizing he was still there.

"I have an idea," he added, climbing into the room. "I had them block off the entrance before coming back. If we can get them in here, we can trap them."

"How do you plan on doing that?" Berwyn asked, join the conversation now that the soldiers were all incapacitated inside the house.

"Lure them in," Justin said. "It doesn't matter how. Stand in the doorway and wave for all I care. Just get them in here. If we can get them close to the trap door, we can open it up, push them all inside, and move the furniture in the house over the door. No getting in or out."

"Not bad," Eden mused. "Berwyn?"

"It could work." He turned to his brother. "Handle this. Eden and I will help everyone outside."

Dov nodded as his brother and sister-in-law bolted out the door toward the fight. He watched them for a moment before turning back to us.

"How are we going to do this?"

I stood outside of the house, creeping around the corner. Dov waited just inside the front door, listening for me, while Justin hid down inside the secret hiding space under the house. When the soldiers chased me, I would know enough to jump over the trapdoor as Justin flung it open, but the soldiers wouldn't have enough time to process what was happening. Justin could easily swing around the ladder and climb up before the Society men had enough time to pick themselves up off the floor once they tumbled in.

Knowing I had to engage at least one of the men, I steeled myself to pull away from the safety of the building. The noise rushed around me, intensifying as I jogged into the yard, quickly drawing attention to myself.

The wind blew, sending an icy chill down my spine as my hair wrapped around in front of me. Swallowing, I shook my hair, demanding attention.

"It's her," one man shouted, pointing. "The girl the magistrates are looking for!"

I bit back my smile, turning to run toward the front of the house where Dov waited behind the door. They followed as I charged into the house. I felt my fiancé's presence behind me, quietly hiding.

Justin timed it perfectly, throwing the door open just before I darted to the side. The soldiers fell in, cursing as they toppled at awkward angles. They piled on top of each other as Justin lurched around the steps, climbing them as quickly as he could. The top soldier was just starting to climb off the others when I slammed the door, missing Justin's ankle by a mere breath.

"Cutting it a little close there, aren't we?" He looked at me with wide eyes.

"A little on the slow side today, aren't we, Justin?" I mimicked his expression.

"I didn't have to lift a finger," Dov mused with a shrug, looking at his hand. "This is my kind of mission."

I jerked upward as the men tried to open the door beneath me. Justin and Dov paled before rushing to move the couch. Once situated, we piled as much loose furniture as possible over the couch and door, trapping the men below. They pounded against it, wailing to be set free. We didn't relent.

"Devin," Justin dodged around us, launching himself toward the door. My mind flashed to Reed hanging in the tree, feet dangling in the air. We followed Justin, leaving the accusatory voices behind.

Only a few soldiers remained upright when we appraised the scene before us. Shadoe's men—*my* men—had been vicious, brutally attacking the Society men.

I slide down along the house, watching the end of the battle play out. Justin moved quickly to his brother's side as Dov hovered between me and the fight, eyeing me cautiously.

"I'm fine," I waved him off. Hesitantly, he went to help finish the fight.

I rested my head in my hands, pulling my knees close. My skirt had ripped at some point. If I angled the hole right, I could see one of the scars I had endured on Canton's torture table. My skin tingled at the sight of it. I would have traded more of my blood to have seen less of others' blood.

Dov had been right. One spark *could* light the entire universe on fire —it was playing out before me. My choices, my actions, my words all lead to this moment. Dov's had too…and Justin's, Silas', Reyla's, Berwyn's and Eden's. Each and every one of us made choices that led to this.

"It's time to find the magistrates," I whispered to myself.

It took a full minute before I stood up, brushing off my skirt. I walked slowly, intentionally, straight toward the man Dov had cornered. The soldier looked over Dov's shoulder, wary of my approach. His expression made Dov pause.

I made a noise so Dov would know it was me before I reached over his shoulder, pushing the soldier back.

"Where are the magistrates?" I asked in an even, controlled voice.

"What?" he stumbled.

"Where are the magistrates?" I asked, slower and more deliberately. "Do you know where they are?"

I began pushing him faster, nearly tripping him as I backed him up at knifepoint.

"I…I…" he stammered.

"You know; I can see it in your eyes." I held the knife up to his eye. "Take us."

He was one of their leaders.

I smiled sweetly, meaning it to scare him. I made my point. He nodded fiercely.

"Take him over there. Have the boys round up the rest. We need to go see the magistrates." I told Dov, exerting my leadership in front of the scared soldier.

Dov nodded, grabbing the man's collar. He shoved him toward the crowd.

"This is your chance, gentlemen, to surrender," he yelled loudly, using the man as an example. "Work with us now, and you can have a life after we take down the magistrates."

Several men surrendered, making Shadoe sneer. Dov accepted their abdications of their posts as they knelt on the ground. We rounded them up, sequestering them where they couldn't do any more damage.

We left Shadoe and Nikko in charge as we looked for survivors from our team on the other streets. The fighting had died down, leaving fires raging and blue skies peering through the smoke and clouds hovering above us.

"We need to find Talley." Justin sounded nervous. His eyes darted back and forth, sweeping the area for his sister.

"We'll find her," Devin sounded grim, his voice tight as he spoke.

The pressure in my chest grew the further we walked from my aunt's house. It was taking too long to find people. Silas and Dov stopped each time they saw one of our team, checking for signs of life. We moved on when they found none.

She sat against the crumbled remains of a stand in the former market. Ashes still floated in the air as the orange glow of the fire died down. Tears streamed down her face.

Talley looked up at us. When she saw us, she began sobbing uncontrollably, jerking the woman lying in her lap. Necesta's hair lolled over her vacant face with the violent movements.

Justin and Devin looked sick as they lowered themselves next to their sister. I froze, staring at the scene. One heartbeat, two heartbeats.

"Reed," Devin whispered to Talley, making her shake even more fiercely.

Dov and Silas wrapped their arms around me, catching me before I even had the impulse to fall to my knees. I let them support me, giving into gravity.

Necesta looked so quiet. Her hand rested over her chest casually. I waited for her to take her next breath, but it never came. My fingers found their way to the necklace she had given me. It wouldn't help her now.

I wasn't sure if I wanted to touch her or not. I wanted to say goodbye—to hold her hand one last time—but I didn't know if I could bear to say goodbye to anyone else. Certainly not to Necesta.

Raselin stumbled over, appearing out of nowhere. He sank down next to Devin and watched Talley cry. Eventually, he ran his fingers through a strand of her hair before wiping his silent tears.

"You were a good woman, Necesta," he choked out. "You were

brave and strong and smarter than any of us. If it weren't for you, we never would have made it this far. Thank you."

He lifted her hand to his lips, quietly kissing the back of her wrist. Raselin set his friend's hand back down on her chest, pulling away.

"We'll honor her sacrifice," he announced, standing.

"We will," Dov echoed, gently pushing me forward. It was my turn.

"I'm sorry," I croaked into her ear, knowing she wasn't there to hear me. I felt as if I were losing my aunt all over again. Sorrow ripped at my insides, eating me alive.

I don't know how long I sat there, but when I finally ripped myself away, I threw my tired body into Dov's arms. I apologized for the way I was acting as he brushed my hair back with his hand.

"I'm here to love you in your hardest times, Auluria."

His words echoed in my head as we trudged away, leaving the wreckage of our hearts on the streets of my aunt's town as we started toward the remaining magistrates.

Chapter 13

"YOU'RE SURE THEY ARE THERE?" I ASKED SHADOE AS HE STALKED around the corner.

"Are you actually questioning my work?" He glared at me.

"I just want to be sure," I snapped at him, losing patience.

"Auluria," Dov said softly, reminding me to be gentle with Shadoe. We couldn't afford to lose my influence over him; not now. We still needed him.

"How do we get in?" I asked, tempering my voice.

"We've already taken down most of their men. They'll have left a contingency to protect themselves, but they're hiding in a safe house. There can't be that many men there." Shadoe's footsteps fell heavy as he picked up the pace.

I worried that Shadoe may turn on us now that he had lost his rank. When the fight was over, he would no longer oversee our people. He would be allowed to train our fighters, but he would never plan another battle again. I wasn't sure if that would be enough for him, especially if he tried to live up to Lowell's standards for him.

When I had told him that we had lost Necesta, he flinched. Shadoe didn't even flinch when we talked about Lowell's death. He had been leery of her when we first met, but she had grown on him, especially when she stood up for him. He was probably worried no one would stand for him now, but I always would. Despite everything he had done.

I was also willing to let him do whatever needed to be done to end this war. I followed him around the building.

"There," he said, pointing. "That's where they said it would be. Nikko and Sherman watched it all day. They're definitely there."

"What do you suggest?" Dov asked authoritatively.

"I think it's not my job anymore, Baer." Shadoe straightened his shoulders.

Fitch shifted behind me, trying to get a better view.

"I think we should do a blitz attack. We should move in at once," he eyed the innocuous door. "I think we need to surround it and let a smaller group breach. When they try to run, there will be nowhere to go. We'll have a few teams waiting by the tunnels we found, so even if they make it to the escape, they'll walk right to us."

"That could work," Dov mused, turning to Silas. "We'll go."

Silas nodded. "We can take the guys."

"Why is it *always* the same ones that go into every fight?" I asked, annoyed.

"I'll go too," Fitch jumped in. "Shadoe, you can bring Canton along. I imagine we'll be able to use him against the other magistrates."

"We're putting on a show now?" Shadoe scoffed.

"You *like* shows," I reminded him. "Bring the trainer from the camp, too."

"So, what do you want me to do, Lur, rough Canton up?" Shadoe glared at me.

It wasn't a bad idea. It would add an extra layer of fear when the magistrates saw us. Shadoe's intimidation tactics were far from my liking, but a few bruises and cuts wouldn't hurt.

"Why don't you let me handle that," I said, hoping he'd let me. We didn't need a repeat of what happened to Justice Kenton.

"We don't want him looking like Kenton," Fitch added, echoing my thoughts.

"So I'll leave his fingers in place," Shadoe shrugged, ready to take some of his aggression out on the man who had destroyed our lives for so many years.

"Shadoe," I scolded, trying to keep my eyes from growing large enough to take up my entire face.

He narrowed his eyes at me.

"What are you going to do, seduce him?"

"When have I ever needed to resort to that?" I shot back.

He nodded at Dov, raising an eyebrow in challenge.

"She didn't need to seduce me, Shadoe," Dov corrected him. "She had me from the moment I met her. Unlike you."

Shadoe's next step fell heavy, lurching him forward just enough to know the comment hurt. Dov kept his face even, never flinching. A lesser man would have gloated.

"I'll handle Canton," Silas suggested, turning to lead us back. "We should get moving. We know they're here. They're not going anywhere. Leave your scouts, Shadoe, and let's go get Canton."

The walk back was filled with details for our plan. Dov, Silas, Shadoe, and Sherman would take the front entrance. Ben, Gregory, Henry, and Carter would take the back entrance. Fitch and a few of his men would be the second wave, entering through the front entrance after Dov's team entered. The rest of us would surround the building with a few fringe teams further out to cover the escape routes we had located.

I would work with Nikko, Locust, Justin, and Talley near one of the escapes that we found during our intelligence-gathering mission. We had located two others and placed Arin and Berwyn, and Raselin and Devin's teams near those posts.

When we arrived back to the main group, I was greeted by the girls from the camp we had liberated. They stood, quietly waiting for me, looking annoyed.

"Ladies," I approached them cautiously while Silas slipped away to handle Canton, Dov at his heels.

"We want to do more than hang out in the background," one of them said.

"You've been fighting alongside everyone else," I reminded them.

"Give us a job," she insisted. "We need to do something more than this."

In the distance, Eden walked by, stomping through the dying grass, still wet from where the frost had melted in the sun. She ignored us.

"Eden!" I waved her over. She begrudgingly walked over to us.

"Eden, you've met the girls from the camp," I grinned, knowing Eden was about to temporarily hate me. She'd forgive me in time though. "They're a little bored just fighting with the rest of us. They want something else to do."

"And?" Eden shook her head, her voice flat.

"And," I paused before rushing on. "You're in charge. Good luck."

I raced away as Eden shouted at me. We both knew she needed a job and training these girls after the takeover was finished would give her something more productive to do than sulk and plan her revenge on the men that had kidnapped her and tried to sell her on the underground market.

Her screeching followed me all the way until I reached Berwyn.

"What did you do?" he asked, eyes wide.

"I gave her a job," I met his gaze, refusing to flinch. "She needs something productive to do so I told her to train the girls. She'll hate it for a while, but give it a few months and see how good she becomes."

He watched me, thinking over my words.

"Do you honestly think she won't have the most effective team of spies this group has ever seen when she's done? Match her up with Brittella and the two of them will be unstoppable." I planted the idea in his head.

"What about me?" Brittella asked, looking up from where she was packing her bag.

"Eden is about to train the girls to be spies. I thought you could help," I said before Berwyn could speak.

She would need a new friend after losing Necesta so quickly. Eden and Brittella wouldn't ordinarily mix, but if they worked together, I imagined they'd learn to like each other.

"I—" Berwyn started.

"Brilliant idea, Auluria. I'll do it." She smiled and sauntered over to Eden who was still furious. Her hands waved in the air as Brittella approached her and told her that they'd be working together.

Eden swerved around to look at me where I stood with Berwyn. I raised my hand to wave, plastering a smile on my face.

"Now or never, Berwyn. Give her a job or watch her slowly lose herself every single day from this point on." I paused. "Give her a reason to keep going once we take the Society down."

Berwyn grunted next to me but nodded to his wife who turned a brilliant shade of red. I smiled bigger, angering her even more.

"You'll pay for that," Berwyn smirked, sounding like his brother.

"Yeah, but only for a few months and it will be worth it in the end," I replied, walking away.

"You're more like him than you know," Berwyn called. I paused, turning to look back, wondering what he meant. "You're selfless. Like Dov."

I blinked at him, processing his words.

"Good luck dealing with her wrath." He smiled sarcastically. "You know how she gets…"

He sauntered off, leaving me to think through all of the vicious torment Eden Baer would put me through, assuming I survived the attack on the magistrates. Maybe I should switch places with Shadoe and go in head-first to the danger. Death couldn't be that bad.

The girls hovered around Eden as we spread out to take our places for the siege. She looked like a mother duck with her goslings. Every step she took, they also took, backing up whenever she turned around.

The closer we came to the attack, the more focused Eden became and the less she cared about the younger girls following her. Brittella watched from a distance, giving me a smug look each time she made eye contact with me.

Nikko branched off as we entered the edge of the woods, just far enough out of sight to make a decently-covered escape. Justin stayed by my side, Talley following right behind us.

"Over here," Shadoe grumbled.

We waited by the covered entrance Shadoe had found the day before. The sun cast dark shadows through the tree branches. I angled myself with my back to the sun, attempting to stand in the bits of light between the branches. It warmed my legs and back where it kissed my clothing. I was grateful for the dark colors I was wearing, absorbing more of the warmth.

A crow flew overhead, landing in the tree above me. It's shadow left a cold streak across my neck for a moment, making me shudder when the sun left my skin. It sat silently in the tree, watching us curiously. It flinched as the wind kicked up.

Locust leaned against a tree, the lowest branches higher than his head. Crossing his arms, he surveyed the scene. A few times, he glanced at me with a questioning look. I hadn't told Shadoe what he had done, but it didn't matter. Shadoe would no longer be making the decisions after he went behind our backs. Locust's fate rested in my hands now.

Talley sighed quietly, trying not to distract us. I leaned toward her as the wind gusted again.

"You okay?" she mumbled under her breath.

"Yeah, you?" I replied, running my hands over my arms to warm them up as I turned to put my left side in the sun.

"It's far too cold out to be doing this," she muttered. I agreed.

"They're here," Nikko said quietly as he stood from where he had been kneeling near the hidden entrance, listening.

We straightened, preparing to stop their flight. The group moved so that the men wouldn't see us immediately when they exited the tunnel in hopes that we could easily surround them.

Two guards burst through the door. Shadoe and Sherman grabbed hold of them, pulling them away, out of sight.

When the others didn't immediately follow, I stepped in front of the entrance.

"Gentlemen," I glanced inside, seeing two men in red robes surrounded by four other soldiers. "I suggest you do not make us come in there to get you. If we have to come into that tunnel, you won't make it out. But if you come out now, you'll see the other side of this battle."

"We give you our word," Justin added. "But you have to decide now."

The magistrate was the first to concede, pushing a soldier in front of him. The man exited, blinking in the brightness of day.

"Magistrate Markel," Shadoe sounded impressed. "I suppose I shouldn't be surprised *you* survived."

"Do I know you?" Markel glared at Shadoe, blinking in the light even though his hand blocked his eyes from the sun.

"Not yet," Shadoe sneered, voice dark and dangerous. Markel swallowed hard. Shadoe turned to face the second man in red. "Justice Hollis, you've made it too. *You* and *I* have a bit of a connection."

Hollis looked up at him, trying not to cower. I watched Shadoe stare him down, trying to figure out the connection.

"You worked for my boss, Lowell," Shadoe grinned deviously.

Of course he did. Lowell had connections everywhere. I wondered if Hollis was the reason Lowell was able to get an audience with me in Canton's cells before our hanging took place.

Justin, Sherman, Talley, and Nikko bound the soldiers, leaving the magistrate and justice to face us alone.

"Lowell is dead," Hollis said cautiously.

"Oh, we know," Shadoe glowered. "This is his cousin, you remember her..."

He motioned to me as the men in red turned toward me. I threw my shoulders back, trying to look striking and intimidating. At just the right moment, my hair blew in front of me in a glorious curtain of gold, making me grin.

"Oh, so I have *you* to thank for that," I said, trying to show as much detest for Hollis as possible. The color in his eyes dulled as they grew wide.

"Him?" Talley asked, walking over, finger pointing. She decided to get in on the fun. "This man?"

"Apparently," I crooned, playing along.

"Tsk, tsk," Talley sighed, walking closer as she pushed her charge closer. "You should have played nicer, justice."

Magistrate Markel looked horrified as we closed in on the man. One of the soldiers took it as an opportunity to save his magistrate and attacked, throwing himself back toward Locust.

He fell to the ground, bringing Locust with him. They grappled, but the young soldier knew what he was doing. He slipped his feet through his hands where they were bound, bringing them in front of him.

Talley and I launched ourselves at Hollis and Markel, wrestling them to the ground as Justin and Shadoe tried to keep order among the other soldiers. Nikko threw his charge to the ground—kicking him hard enough to knock him out—before rushing to help Locust.

Hollis fought against me as I tried to subdue him. He pushed me, nearly knocking me off of him. I clawed at his face, hoping each line I left would remind him of the price of working for my cousin.

I should have known a surrender could never be that easy.

Talley held Markel down. He wasn't a small man, but she was tall enough to win in a battle of wills against him.

Hollis batted at me. I kneed his hip, making him shudder. He doubled over on himself as I flipped him over and restrained him. He calmed, knowing he couldn't get away. Once he stopped struggling, I tuned back into the scene around me.

Two of the soldiers were dead, Shadoe and Nikko stood over the remaining soldiers, wiping the blood off their knives. The soldiers huddled on the ground, making it very clear that they surrendered.

Sherman knelt next to Locust as he struggled for breath. A nasty line ripped through his stomach. I clenched my teeth, preparing to lose another teammate.

"Oh dear," Talley said when she realized what was happening. "This never gets easier."

"No, it doesn't." I sighed, tightening my grip on Justice Hollis. I would hold him accountable for Locust's death in the trials we would hold after we controlled the Society.

I rushed to Locust's side, fiddling with the necklace, hoping for a solution. Its answers failed me. I couldn't save him. His eyes fixated on the sky, watching the branches sway back and forth.

"Auluria," Shadoe called to me. I moved back, following orders.

Nikko stayed with Locust until he has passed, allowing the rest of us to take our prisoners back to where the team waited. I prayed the other groups hadn't lost men.

When we arrived back at the main entrance to the hiding place, Dov and Silas waited for us, surrounded by what was left of our people. They held the other justices and magistrates captive. The men looked terrified.

When we had upset their plans, the remaining magistrates and justices had fled to the one place they felt they could survive—the safe house. They hadn't anticipated that Canton had survived, nor that he had told us about the existence of the safe house.

Several of our people guarded the trainer from the camp off to the side. We wouldn't need him for the surrender.

Shadoe dragged Canton out in front of the group, covered in enough cuts and bruises to worry his contemporaries. He didn't resist as Shadoe propelled him forward.

"We are here to initiate a conversation on the terms of your surrender," Berwyn led the conversation. He crossed in front of the men.

Raselin met him halfway, taking up the discussion as if they had planned it.

"We will offer you leniency if you cooperate," he said gently, but firmly. "Surrender now, and you will stand trial. Don't surrender and we'll do this the hard way."

"We want to make this transition easy for the people," Berwyn continued. "We want everyone to be aligned with this transition of power."

Dov pushed me forward. "You're up."

Now that Shadoe had been removed from power, I was left in

charge of Lowell's people. Anetta hovered by me, ready to back me up.

"If you step down now and allow us to take over your places without a fight, we won't need to have a conversation with your families...your people," I crossed my arms as I walked toward them. "I know you gentlemen are rather self-centered, but there have to be people you care about...people you don't want to die on your behalf because they assume you don't support this and try to fight against us."

"But more than that," Dov stepped in, "if *any* of your people die on *your* behalf, we will hold you accountable for that as well."

Gregory smirked from where he stood behind Magistrate Markel. Carter elbowed Henry; Dov had to force himself not to grin at the looks on the magistrate's faces.

"You will all be held accountable for your actions and will sit through trials, but those of you who cooperate will be given a certain amount of grace when the time comes to face your charges." Berwyn paced in front of them.

"All we ask is that you step down, take responsibility for your actions, and turn the rest of your soldiers over to us," I added. "In exchange for a little leniency. I suppose we don't need all of you to agree though."

I planted the idea that whoever cooperated first, would benefit the most, hoping it would spur them into agreeing.

"Now, who would like to talk about peaceful terms for your surrender?" Raselin asked in a certain voice.

Hollis—knowing he had aligned himself with too many people—looked around nervously. The magistrates would turn on him when they found out how many people had been bribing him. If he worked with Lowell, I assumed there had to be more. Markel glared at him, fully prepared to hand Hollis over to save himself. All of the magistrates looked ready to make deals and betray the others.

A few of the men nodded, prepared to throw themselves on our temporary mercy. A sudden movement caught my attention as Hollis jumped out of his seat, throwing himself backward, trying to escape —or at least make his death less drawn out.

"You will not turn on me," he shrieked, holding something to Ben's throat. Ben attempted to bring his hands up to defend himself, but Hollis pinned them against his sides with his free hand. I instantly regretted giving them the respect of removing their bindings for this meeting. "Don't move."

He looked around nervously.

"Back," he hissed in Ben's ear. Hollis dragged him back, trying to escape as the magistrates turned on him, shouting out every transgression he had committed. Markel jumped to his feet, but Silas slammed him down so hard that the entire group froze.

"They did this," Hollis shouted, jutting his chin out at the magistrates and justices. "They're responsible for the atrocities you suffered."

The men argued back.

"Everyone will be held accountable for what they have done. No one will take the entire blame," Raselin tried to reason with him.

"I won't go down for this!" He tripped as he stepped back, nicking Ben's throat. A small drip of blood spilled from his neck, forming a red path to his collarbone.

"Justice Hollis, please, no one is going to put all the blame on you," I tried to calm him.

"Lowell warned me about you," his voice rose. "He told me you couldn't be trusted, that you'd try to pin everything on other people, including him. You got him killed, and you're going to do the same to me because I worked with him."

Fear sparked in his eyes as his nostrils flared. He breathed deeply, his jolts of breath forcing Ben's hair to move back and forth.

"Lowell said you're the ultimate manipulator," he glared at me, "but I won't go down for this."

Dov had carefully worked his way out of Hollis' line of sight as he had been shouting to us. Dov lunged at the man, knocking into him in an effort to stop him and free Ben. Hollis panicked when he realized what was happening.

The justice dragged his hand across Ben, slitting his throat.

Chapter 14

Air filled my lungs as I swung my legs out of the bed. Red still filled the room, but not as much as it had the last time I was inside the mansion.

"Babe, are you ready?" Dov knocked at my door.

"Almost," I scrambled to get dressed. Reyla bolted out of the bed we were temporarily sharing and rushed for her things.

"We shouldn't have stayed up so late," she grumbled.

Outside the door, Silas asked Dov what was taking so long. I picked up a pillow and threw it at the door. They jump on the other side as Reyla snickered.

When I swung the door open, both men were standing in white shirts and dark pants, looking far better rested than they had since we returned to the mansion a week ago. With the Society men cleaned out of the magistrate buildings and the remaining leadership in custody, we were all breathing easier.

Canton had played his part beautifully, orchestrating a surrender on behalf of the other magistrates, with Shadoe acting as his oversight. The magistrates and justices had given us everything we asked from them. When we paraded them in front of the towns, they gave full power over to us.

"Time to go," Dov offered his arm to me. I slipped my hand through his elbow and let him lead me down the hall.

"Looks like it's you and me, my lady," Silas said behind us.

"Why thank you, good sir," Reyla replied, playing along.

"Don't they look so adorable together?" Silas asked. I could hear him grinning at us.

"Indeed, they do. They should get married or something," Reyla laughed.

"Working on it," Dov called over his shoulder without looking at me. He kept his eyes straight ahead, grinning smugly.

"We have other matters to attend to first," I said loudly, shaking my head.

The room was larger without the moveable walls creating cells on the side of the room. This time, Magistrate Canton sat in modest clothing on a simple chair. His colorful robes were gone, stripping him of his power. He waited for his sentencing.

He caught my eye when I walked into the room, silently begging me to stand for him against the masses. His eyes accused me when I shook my head, but I hadn't tried to save his soldiers from everything, only from death. I wanted him—and all of his men—to take responsibility for their actions, but I never believed they should die at the hands of an angry man bent on revenge. With our leadership presiding over the trials, they would receive a fair hearing and would atone for their sins.

We had time before the foreign nations figured out that the men under their power we no longer in leadership of the Society.

Mornings were spent sorting through the trials and gathering information from the former leadership during their hearings. Afternoons were spent working on a plan to truly liberate our society.

Canton—having caused the most trouble—would be sentenced first. We stood, taking turns questioning him. Raselin opened the floor, followed by Berwyn. Canton didn't have much new information for us—Shadoe had already found out everything we needed before we went after the other magistrates—but he answered our questions for the rest of our people to hear.

Dov, Berwyn, Eden, Raselin, Fitch, Talley, Silas, Anetta, and I were overseeing the trials until the towns could select representatives. We would remain on as leadership, representing our groups in the new Society and work alongside the new representatives.

"This is getting old, really fast," Silas leaned over to me from the long table we sat behind.

"Find something nice to look at," Brittella leaned forward, whispering. "Focus on that and it will make it easier."

I nudged him under the table, prompting a curious look from him.

I tapped the flower tucked away in my hair, mostly hidden by my long mane, and batted my eyelashes. His face dropped.

"You know?" Silas hissed.

"I had to find out at some point." I grinned at him.

"You'll pay for this, Baer," he leaned in front of me, pretending to glare at my fiancé.

"I'm doing you a favor, buddy, now pay attention—Canton is saying something about being the wealthiest man in the Society or something equally as pretentious," Dov smirked.

"I knew he was working with him," Canton confirmed. "I allowed Hollis to take bribes from him, knowing I'd be able to use the information he fed me."

My stomach dropped.

"Wait, who is he talking about?"

Talley leaned around Silas. "They're talking about your cousin."

Canton knew what Lowell was doing all along. He had always known.

"Lowell surpassed his usefulness to us. He didn't know we were watching him as closely as we did, but he was always so willing to believe that he could bribe whomever he wanted and be given complete allegiance."

"Lowell was a fool," Eden muttered loud enough for everyone at the table to hear her. Canton wasn't phased.

"He had no idea we were watching him," Canton continued, puffing up his chest.

"Don't be absurd," Brittella whispered behind me. "Lowell knew exactly what Canton was doing. He played him. Your cousin told me all about Hollis running off to Canton. He manipulated the situation for a very long time."

"Which would explain how he was able to frame us," Dov mumbled with a sigh. "I wonder if he had all these connections when he framed my father."

"I doubt we'll ever know," I said sadly. "Lowell wasn't one to confide in people. I doubt even Shadoe's father knew the extent of Lowell's plans back then. Shadoe certainly didn't when he took over."

One of the girls Eden was training walked into the room. Still new to what Eden and Brittella were teaching her, she was more obvious than she tried to be. She bent down, whispering in Eden's ear.

Eden nodded, sending the girl off before she circled something on a map and pushed it down the table. When it reached us, I realized it was the site of another small pocket of soldiers. They worked for the richer men in the society—the men who didn't want the power structure to change. They were attempting to save their own power when they withheld the soldiers that worked for them.

Berwyn held his hand up as he stood, silencing Canton in the middle of his unending speech. He waved Nian over, quietly giving him instructions to send a group of our people to handle the situation. Nian brushed his hair back before taking care of his assignment, having jostled his locks when he nodded.

After a few hours, we ended the hearing for the day. Shadoe returned Canton to his cell while Berwyn and Raselin called our spies in for a meeting about what they had learned.

"There are more people outside," Nikko informed me as I exited the room. He followed behind me.

"Are we really going to let him follow us around all the time?" Anetta asked in desperation.

"Would you rather *not* know where he is?" I countered.

"Couldn't we send him down to the cells to deal with Marty and Jake? I'm sure there are still body parts we could cut off?" she scoffed.

"There will be no more body parts removed," I reminded her, exasperated. "Not even for Marjorie. Speaking of, have you been down there yet?"

"No and I don't intend to." She shook her head.

"Hello, ladies," Lydia said, walking past us. Her arm was healing nicely. "Have you seen my husband?"

"He's in the meeting with the spies," I replied. "We're on our way outside to see the new group of people if you want to join us."

"Sure." Lydia changed course, stepping in line with the group walking outside.

The doors opened, letting the bright sun spill across the floor of the foyer. It sparkled off the tapestries we had yet to remove. It was cold outside, making me wish I had dressed warmer. Dov shuffled closer to me, keeping me warm.

"What do we have today, Louis?" I asked the red-haired boy as he stood at his post.

"I have a feeling it will be more appealing to the Baer's group than Lowell's," he commented, nodding toward the crowd.

Young faces flooded the courtyard.

"Eli," I was surprised to see him. "How did you get here so fast?"

"We heard you had control. We moved everyone that we could."

"Reyla!" a voice shouted from the crowd. Hannah sat in a cart, cradling her new baby.

"Get Sharone," I ordered loudly, hoping someone would listen.

We rushed forward to help Hannah up. She handed her baby to me, wrapped in so many blankets, you could hardly see her face. Dov and Silas pulled her up. Reyla wrapped her in an embrace as soon as she was standing. We fussed over the baby until Sharone arrived.

"What is going on?" Sharone grumbled.

"Just come on," Henry said, Katarina trailing behind him. The two girls gasped as they saw Hannah.

Sharone ran to her sister, throwing her arms around her as she sobbed. The second Hannah pulled back, I shoved the baby into Sharone's arms and let Hannah introduce her sister to her new niece.

"That's so sweet," Lydia said, tears in her eyes.

"A mother's love," Brittella crooned behind me. She latched on to Lydia's gaze.

"Oh, do you have to know *everything* before_everyone, Brittella?" Lydia growled.

"Necesta told me," Brittella snipped. "She also wanted you to have this."

She slipped her hand into her pocket and pulled something out. She dropped it into Lydia's hand before sauntering away. "For the little one."

All eyes turned on Lydia.

"We were going to tell you later," she sighed. She shouted as we jostled her in a group hug, "Careful!"

We laughed together at her good news, enjoying the moment.

"I have no idea how Necesta knew; I didn't even know." Lydia smiled. She ran a finger over her gift from Necesta.

"I'd like to talk about my position here," Eli interrupted.

"The others are in a meeting now, Eli, but come sit with us for dinner and we'll talk about what might suit you," I promised. "Thank you for bringing the girls home."

"All right, let's get these people inside," Dov raised his voice to be heard. "It's freezing out here."

Everyone shuffled inside. They would stay with us in the mansion for a few days until we were able to return them to their families or find places for them to stay. The children happily ran around, playing between their mothers as they walked inside.

"Well, hello there, Goldilocks," a gentle voice said behind me.

I turned back around to find myself staring into the eyes of Barone.

"You made it," I grinned, hugging him.

"This young lady made sure of it." Maylin stepped out from behind him.

"I knew you wouldn't want me to leave without him. He's been… interesting company," she teased. "I left the doctors with a few of the girls who couldn't travel. They'll be along when they can. I thought I could be of more use to you here."

"I'm glad you're back Maylin. I didn't think you'd keep your promise so soon, but I'm glad you did. Come inside, you must be dying for a warm place to sit by now." I wrapped my arm around her and led her inside.

"Look who's back!" I cheered as Katarina rushed to us. I left the two to catch up.

Barone limped behind them, nodding when he saw Dov slow his steps. I would have to tell him about Chester later. The look on his face told me he already knew of his cousin's fate.

Dov wrapped his arm around my shoulder as we walked away.

"We're finally free," he said softly.

"We're finally free," I repeated, leaning my head on his shoulder.

"The last of Wallace's men have been rounded up," Justin said, nearly colliding with us as we rounded the corner. "Marty is still downstairs demanding to speak with you. I told him I'd give him a hand, but only if he twisted my arm."

"Callous," I said in a deadpan voice. I managed to hold the sincerity of it only a second longer than it took for my face to morph into a laugh.

"We should probably handle this," Dov sighed. "Want to come along?"

Justin fell into step behind us. We waved Reyla, Silas, and Eden over when we saw them along the way. Together, we took the steps down to the cells.

Miraculously, it was warmer in the cells than it had been in the foyer. We moved into the wing where Marty was being held. Dov nodded to Sherman, explaining that we would speak with Marty.

We waited inside an interrogation room. Dov was seated at the table, while the rest of us leaned against the back wall. It was dark, but not nearly as terrifying as when Canton's men had put me in one of the interrogation rooms with Lowell.

One of Sherman's men brought Marty in, pointing him toward a chair. With only one hand left to restrain, he remained with his hand free. He watched us warily.

"What is it, Marty?" Dov asked diplomatically.

"You take my hand and that's how you treat me?" He sounded unimpressed. If he still had both hands, I imagine he would have been picking at his fingernails in distaste.

"I had nothing to do with that, and you know it." Dov countered, resting his wrists on the table.

I raised my eyebrow, daring him to continue to waste our time.

"You're the one who started all of this, golden boy," Marty sneered. "Whether it was Shadoe or it was you, it's because you stole the golden girl."

"You and Jake never could let go of a grudge," Dov mused.

Marty set his stump on the table, tugging off the bandage. A tangled mess of skin where his hand used to be looked back at us as he set the bandage a few inches away. He examined his amputation.

"Yeah, well, I can't hold on to much these days," he held up his hand, moving his fingers as if he were about to clutch something, "so it looks like grudges are all I've got. Heard Marjorie had it out with you."

He sneered at Dov. I wanted to smack the look off of his face. He looked up and smiled at me.

"I hear they've been calling you *Goldilocks*. Looks like I was right after all." His eyes traced the length of me. "Too bad Jake had to handle Marjorie's meltdown and couldn't take care of you, golden girl."

"Too bad," I murmured. "I would have liked to have put him through a wall…or a tree. You've had decent experiences with trees, right? I'm sure he wouldn't volunteer for that though.

"Speaking of, since you missed us so much, would you like me to go get Shadoe? He's upstairs somewhere and I'm sure he'd love to catch up."

"Well, if he's not here, it's probably a good time to remind you—" Marty grinned, leaning forward to move the bandage. His grin morphed into something dark and evil as he dropped his voice. "—the golden boy doesn't always win."

Marty used his wrist to hold the bandage down while his remaining hand pulled out a small-but-fierce looking weapon. He lunged across the table at Dov who immediately shot back, the chair tipping over behind him.

Marty skillfully leaped around the table, still going after Dov. I reached him first, stepping between them as Silas shouted and tried to pull Marty away.

Eden screamed, kicking at Marty to fend him off as Reyla

screamed, reaching out to steady Dov before he could fall over the toppled chair.

The room was chaotic as I crashed to the ground.

My name was yelled, over and over. Silas threw Marty across the room, slamming him into the wall.

"Get Maylin," Reyla shrieked.

I blinked.

"Auluria?" Dov's voice called to me, forcing my eyes open. "Auluria, open your eyes. Open them. Come on now."

He cradled my head in his fingers, using them to keep me up off the floor.

"That's my girl, open those eyes," he said kindly, persistently keeping me awake.

"Keep her awake Dov," Reyla cautioned in the distance. "Eden, try to stop the bleeding."

A burning sensation crept through my chest.

Then everything went black.

Chapter **15**

The first thing I smelled was sweet spices. A wave of warmth washed over me, coaxing me out of my sleep.

Someone was breathing on me.

When I opened my eyes, all I saw was blue. Blue so deep and so intense I had to blink to bring it into focus. Dark fringe fell over the blue color as it sparked and flashed, awakening me fully. Those were eyes. The most brilliant blue eyes I'd ever seen.

Then it hit me...and I relaxed.

"What happened?" I asked Dov.

"Marty attacked me and you jumped in the way," he smirked. "You hit your head when you fell. You've been in and out all afternoon."

My hand floated to my shoulder where I found bandages. I tried to catch my face before it fell into a frown, but wasn't fast enough.

"He cut you," Dov's lips turned down. "I'm sorry, babe. It will heal though."

"Oh great," I tried to laugh. "Now we'll have matching scars."

He erupted in laughter.

"Mine are on my back, but if you want us to match, I can handle one more."

"Don't you dare," I lectured him. "No more scars, Mr. Baer."

"You don't like them?" he asked, adjusting his collar. "I think they're rather becoming."

He grinned down at me.

"And here I thought you'd find them attractive. If I had known, I would have avoided all of those beatings. There's just no pleasing you, is there?"

"None whatsoever," I agreed. I reached out my hand, running it over the muscles on his arm. "At least this time I didn't fall off the bed when you woke me."

"I didn't make you fall off the bed the first time either," he teased. "You did that all on your own, Goldilocks."

"Yeah, yeah." I brushed him off as he leaned toward me. "Do we have a plan figured out yet?"

"You mean after the meeting this afternoon?" he questioned.

"Yes," I settled back against the pillow and waited.

"We do, but we should have you checked out first." Dov insisted, standing to walk to the door.

Just as he opened it, Berwyn stepped inside.

"Still haven't gotten rid of her, I see," he joked. "So close this time."

He took a seat at the table, leaning back in the chair.

"It's my fault. I never should have told you to let her stay that first morning," Eden said, slipping into the other chair at the small round table. "Here I thought it would be nice to have another girl around…"

She rolled her eyes but smiled at me.

"Are you okay?" she asked.

"Eden basically destroyed Marty for you, so you don't need to worry about him again," Dov informed me.

"You always pull the scary strength out when you're saving one of us, Eden. I'm pretty sure if we had just handed Berwyn over to Canton in the first place, this would have been over within the first hour."

She glared at me but softened at the idea that she could hold such strength.

"You have a point."

"I noticed you're warming up to the girls from the camp," I hinted, making her scowled at me.

"She's up," Silas grinned, walking into the room. "About time. Come on in, guys."

Justin and Devin pushed each other, both trying to enter at the same time. They tripped into the room, barely righting themselves before hitting the floor.

"That's right, children, keep pushing and see how that works for you," Talley mock scolded them. She turned to me

as she flopped onto the bed next to me. "Hey, little one."

"Hey, that's my spot," Reyla pouted, taking up a post at the end of the bed. Katarina and Sharone hurried around the bed, sitting at Dov's feet near me. Maylin started her examination of me quietly.

"Goldilocks!" Gregory shouted, noticing all of the activity in the room. "And here we thought you were gone forever!"

He dramatically took a seat by the girls on the floor. Henry kept a watchful eye on Ben as he lowered himself to the ground, the bandage still wrapped around his throat. Ben waved to me, honoring his promise to keep the talking to a minimum until his wound had healed.

"They're in there," Nikki said from the hallway. "They're *all* in there.

Raselin and Nian rounded the corner.

"Holding the meeting in here, are we?" Raselin winked at me, his step lighter than it had been since I agreed to train his people to fight. "We handled Marty—or what was left of him, anyway. Fitch and Lydia should be here momentarily."

As if on cue, Fitch guided Lydia into the room. They both asked how I was doing before Fitch leaned against the wall and Lydia found a spot next to Talley on the bed.

"All of the towns are choosing their representatives within the week," Silas started. "Carter just checked in an hour ago. He's getting some rest now, but all of our people are in place to help assist the towns with the transition."

"We opened the markets back up, so trade will continue as before," Berwyn added.

It had been a productive afternoon while I was unconscious.

"Speaking of the markets," Eden interrupted. "Do we have confirmation on the underground markets yet?"

"Yes, Eden. They're all closed down. We rescued fifty women. I just found out in the meeting and forgot to tell you when Auluria decided to get herself killed...again." He tossed me a look. I bit my tongue to keep from sticking it out. "They're on their way to Markel's mansion. There are a few doctors there that will look over them and then we'll get them reunited with their families."

"We caught a number of the traders as well," Raselin added. "They'll be going through their own trials soon enough.

Eden looked satisfied, though I wasn't sure how long that would last. I assumed only until the sentencing when she decided their punishments weren't strong enough.

"Oh," Silas interrupted. "We found the camp trainer's family and reunited them. He still has a trial to get through, but I think he will cooperate now that he has his family back."

I was glad we had located them. At least something had gone as planned.

"Have you heard anything from home, Raselin?" I asked, hoping our spies had brought word of the country we had abandoned to cross back into the Society.

He took a deep breath. It was like the life was sucked out of the room.

"Things are getting worse there, just like we knew they would. It's becoming dangerously close to what it was like here, even on the outskirts. I think we're going to have trouble getting back in."

Maylin finished looking me over and sat down with her friends.

"We won't let that stop us," I promised. "I'm sure we'll find a way."

"Our priority needs to be here first," Raselin said diplomatically. "We have to stabilize the Society first. Once we have everyone settled here and the country back in working order, we can figure out a plan to stop the Northwestern countries and free the rest of them to the east and south."

"What are our plans for fixing things here?" Reyla asked. "I mean, aside from waiting for the towns to send representatives?"

"Better yet, how long do we have to stay here?" Maylin asked, finding a sudden spring of bravery. "I'd like to go home."

"We'd all like to go home, Maylin," Eden said kindly. It was a little unnerving to hear the lack of harshness in her voice. "Once we get through this, we can go home."

"Who is going to stay here if we all go home? Katarina piped in.

"I'll be staying," Raselin said, surveying the group. "I don't have a place in the Society anymore, so I'm not losing anything by staying here. Anyone who would like to stay is welcome, but none of you are required to stay."

He looked at the Hersh siblings. Talley leaned toward me. They would be coming back to the forest with us when the time came. I took her hand in mine, letting her know I was excited not to lose her.

"I would say by this time next year, we'll all be home," Berwyn announced. "Assuming there *is* a home."

"You haven't heard yet?" I asked, astonished that we would have information about foreign countries but not the Baers' house.

"The storehouses are fine. We've checked on everyone there and have already started moving them back to their homes and into the towns," Berwyn corrected himself. "We just didn't take the time to prioritize looking into things like the cabin."

"What does it matter to you, anyway, Auluria? It's not like you'll be living there." Eden scoffed. My heart started beating out of my chest. "As soon as you're married, you two will need your own place."

Everyone turned to me, wild grins plastered across their faces.

"We might need a little help building a house," Dov informed them. Something told me he had the perfect spot in mind.

"Do you have plans for the wedding yet?" Katarina asked, grinning wickedly.

"When would we have had time to discuss that?" I snapped, grinning to let her know I was teasing.

"I don't know, somewhere between you almost dying and him almost dying." She shrugged casually. She leaned back against Henry who looked like he was in heaven just being in her presence. "You'll have to work it in between all these near-death experiences somewhere since you two love those so much."

"Thank you, Katarina, that was helpful," I rolled my eyes playfully.

She looked up at me and batted her eyelashes. "That's what I'm here for." She stroked Henry's arm making him blush.

I rubbed my finger over Dov's hand as it rested on the bed. I wanted to lean against him too, but he was too far away in the chair. He gave me a knowing look.

"Once we get everything settled here," Berwyn continued, getting us back on track, "and we move back home, we'll be having meetings every week or so. Long term, we're hoping to have the Society back on track within a year or two and then we can start working on helping the people over the Wall after that.

"That doesn't mean we won't do what we can to help them now, but we can't orchestrate a rebellion with their people until we're stable here first."

"They're going to need all the help they can get," Silas added. "It's best to make sure we're prepared before we take that on. We barely survived *this* war."

"This time, we'll have more of a chance to plan our attack out," I smirked, squeezing Dov's hand.

I looked around the room at my new family. I would die for these people if that's what it came to and I knew they'd do the same for me. We had all been willing to die to make the world a better place for our friends and family. Not everyone had made it, some made the ultimate sacrifice, but it took each and every one of us to get to this point.

"Canton is still being helpful, as are the others. We'll know everything we need to know about outside the Wall soon enough," Dov assured us.

Anetta darted into the room.

"You're up," her voice was flat. She turned to Berwyn. "Shadoe would like a word. He said he has new information about the Wall."

Berwyn stood, pulled Eden to her feet.

"You'd better all come. No need to repeat this." They all slowly followed.

I started to get up, but Dov pushed me back down. "Not you, Goldilocks."

"I'm fine," I insisted. "We need to see what Shadoe found out."

With the room cleared of people, it suddenly felt cool and densely silent.

"You and I have been through the worst of this war, Auluria. Taking a few minutes to rest won't stop anything from happening. I promise the world will go on."

He stroked my hair. I tolerated it for a moment before kicking my legs over the side of the bed.

"Auluria," he begged.

"We're just going downstairs, darling, it will be fine." I smiled sweetly. "You didn't even make this big of a fuss the first time I hit my head."

"You hadn't been tortured and thrown off a cliff at that point," he protested with a smile.

"Really? You're going to bring *that* up again?"

"Someone obviously has to." He waited as I slipped on my boots. I pushed my skirt aside, trying to avoid tangling it inside of my footwear.

When I stood up, he was watching me quietly.

"What?" I asked.

"Nothing." He grinned devilishly. He shrugged as I waited for more.

"Dov Baer!" I demanded an answer.

"You're beautiful. And somehow your hair is even longer than the last time I pointed out how long it was."

"Yes, well, time will do that. Grow things, that is."

"Like us," he said it so casually I almost missed it. "It took a little time, but look at us now. Seems like just yesterday we were dancing in my living room."

"Pretty soon we'll have our own living room to dance in, from what I hear." I took his hand.

He pulled his fingers out of mine, slipping it underneath my palm so he could raise it to his chest. I stepped forward with him, lingering in his presence. Dov smiled.

"Yes, Auluria, we will. But first, we go downstairs and find out what this big break is."

He stepped to the side, holding out his hand, gesturing that I should go first. Dov wrapped an arm around my shoulder, holding my other hand in his. We walked together, neither one of us in the lead or following behind, just as we had done and would continue to do for as long as we knew each other.

Dov squeezed my hand.

"I love you, Auluria."

"I love you, Dov." My heart sang so many extra words, but I didn't need to say them out loud.

I let go of his hand, wrapping my arms around his waist, clinging to his body as we walked.

"Is this okay?" I asked, realizing it was a little hard to walk without tripping.

"It's all right," Dov responded with a little laugh.

"*Just* all right?" I looked up into his glittering deep blue eyes.

"It's *just right*, my darling," he said loudly as we stepped into the hallway. "It's absolutely perfect."

Epilogue

"Uncle Dov!" a voice cheered, shaking the entire bed.

"How are you up so early?" Dov grinned, grabbing his nephew by the waist and turning him upside down.

"Mommy told me to go see you!" he grinned devilishly.

"*Of course* she did." Dov messed up his hair. "Remind me to thank her for that later. Now go play."

Dov sent the boy off before turning back to me. I sighed, snuggling closer to him under the sheets.

"Good morning, wife," he smiled down at me.

"Good morning, my love." I inhaled his scent, drifting back to the first time I had met him all those years ago.

I kicked my legs out from under the sheets, wrapping them around him. His fingers traced over my legs.

"I still think these are beautiful," he murmured, brushing over my burn scars. I grimaced.

His scars were beautiful and etched across his body just for me. Mine were a constant reminder that I had listened to people like a fool and nearly gotten everyone killed.

"They are, Auluria," he buried his face in my hair as he lay back down next to me. "You took each one of these for me so that I didn't have to suffer. They're beautiful."

My hands automatically went to his arms, even stronger than they were the day he caught me in the woods and carried me to his home. He let me trace the marks on his arms and back before winking at me.

"Come on; we should handle them," Dov finally said. He tossed the covers back and stepped out of bed.

In the kitchen, we settled down to make breakfast. Dov started cooking while I stepped outside for fresh berries from our bushes. The pond glittered and I considered inviting Dov for an early morning swim when a little blonde girl raced past me.

"Now, you two get back inside," I pretended to lecture. "You're parents would be furious to know you were running around out here."

"Aunt Auluria," the little girl put her hands on her hips, "Mommy lets me go outside all the time."

"Yes, but that's when she's awake," I grinned, knowing I shouldn't. "Maybe you should go wake her up."

The two raced into the house to wake up Berwyn and Eden in the guest room where they had spent the evening in preparation for the meeting today. I hoped the fresh berries would make up for the rude wake up call.

"Did you really just do that?" Dov gave me a look when I walked inside.

I shrugged flirtatiously as I set the bowl down. "Maybe."

"What's the worst they can do?" Reyla asked, walking in the door. "They can't do anything to upset the baby, now can they?"

She bent down to talk to my stomach, gently brushing over the bump I carried. She gasped, grabbing her husband's hand.

"I felt her kick!" Reyla exclaimed as she pushed Silas' remaining fingers against my stomach. My heart broke every time I saw the place where his fingers had been just a year ago. He grinned up at me, hand tucked neatly under Reyla's.

"It's still a bit early for that, Rey." I teased.

"Well, it's not my fault you two had to beat us." She joked back, daring me to take her joy away.

"We're only a little behind," Silas beamed.

"What?" Dov said, nearly dropping the pan he was cooking with. He set it down and raced to his friend to congratulate him. When Reyla nodded, confirming her announcement, I threw myself into her arms.

"What is all of this noise?" Eden asked groggily, rubbing her eyes.

"Have you never heard of quiet?" Berwyn snapped.

"Not when there's a baby around," I realized too late that I sounded like a bird chirping first thing in the morning. "And I'm not talking about mine."

Eden's jaw dropped. Her children circled her, running around her feet.

"Kids, sit," she ordered, pointing them to the couch. They hurriedly sat, knowing how to obey their parents the first time they spoke. The two were more obedient than Eden's spies.

Berwyn clapped Silas on the back, the scars on his hand showing under his sleeve. We had all gained more scars than I cared to think about over the years, but each had been well earned and well worth it.

After a few moments, we sat to eat. The sun glittered off the pond, reflecting all the way to the house. After we ate, we would meet with Raselin and his team to discuss the next mission over the Wall. I felt confident that we would soon find our foothold into the nation to the northeast of the Society, though Talley still insisted we should free one of the southern countries because it would be easier. A promise was a promise though, and I wanted to honor our word to Necesta.

Tomorrow we would meet with Shadoe to see how the training was going for our new volunteers. He had quickly transformed our fighters into an army with skills unmatched by any of the surrounding countries. While he was no longer allowed to make tactical decisions, he seemed to be satisfied training the men and women who worked with us.

We looked up when a knock sounded on the door. Devin slipped inside.

"Morning," he waved, inviting himself to join us. He popped a berry into his mouth.

"Did you find anything?" Dov asked, standing to get Devin a plate.

"We did," Devin confirmed. "I have to make it quick though, Maylin needs help with some doctor stuff today."

"What does she have you doing today?" I questioned, reaching for more berries.

"Collecting supplies or something. Can you believe she's *still* going through Necesta's notes after all these years?"

"Who knew she brought so much which her when we crossed the Wall!" I laughed. "She was a tricky one, that's for sure."

Devin laughed at the nostalgia. He quickly filled us in on what he had learned in his brief time over the Wall to the South.

"Hey!" Justin said, slamming into the room. He glared at his brother. "I saw you come in. You didn't even have the decency to tell me you were back?"

He reached over and took food from my plate. I slapped him with my fork. "You would dare take food from your niece or nephew?"

"She won't mind sharing with Uncle Justin," he grinned.

"You don't know it's a girl," I insisted.

"It's a girl," Dov said. Eden and Berwyn echoed his response, making me shake my head.

Reyla tucked her hair behind her ear, highlighting the flower she wore. Just like every morning that she and Silas joined us for breakfast, she wore the flower that Silas gave her—a symbol of the flowers that had mysteriously shown up in the storehouse after she and I had been hurt and were recovering.

Dov reached over, pulling one from the small pot he had sitting on the window ledge. He tucked it in my hair—a reminder of his love for me. His hand floated to my lap where I placed mine in his. He picked my hand up and kissed it.

"It's a girl," he whispered, making me roll my eyes.

"At the rate we're going, we won't free the Northeast country until your kids are halfway grown," Justin said between a mouthful of food.

"That's not a bad thing," Reyla interjected. "Auluria and I can't exactly fight in our conditions, now can we?"

Justin and Devin's eyes grew wide as they realized her announcement. They laughed, congratulating the happy couple.

"Relax," Eden called us back to attention. "We'll just have Jasleen or Hannah's girl watch the kids while we're out playing Goldilocks and the three Baers again."

My breath still hitched anytime someone used that silly story name. Necesta really had known what she was doing when she started that because the entire country had seemingly forgotten I had a name that wasn't attached to my hair color.

"We really need to find a new name," I quipped.

"Why? I like being able to say I know you four," Justin protested. He grinned. "It really helped me impress that girl last week."

"Oh yeah, how is she?" I asked. "Do we like her?"

"I didn't get a say in Dov, you don't get a say in this," he reminded me, threatening to throw a forkful of food at me.

"Hey!" Dov chuckled.

"Shut up, Baer, this is between me and the girl," Justin teased.

"*My* girl," Dov reminded him.

"*Girls.*" I hissed the plural form of the word, realizing what I had said after it was too late.

"She admits it!" Berwyn cheered.

"I told you it was going to be a girl," Eden threw me a satisfied smirk.

"We still don't know," I argued.

"Ask Maylin, she knows everything," Devin added, leaning forward on his elbow.

"Aunt Goldilocks, are you having a girl?" my nephew asked in surprise.

"Oh!" Justin nearly choked on his laughter, tossing the boy a wink. "Nice one, little man."

It was chaos. It was madness. It was mine.

I had lost my only remaining relative to the Baers and the Society, but it had freed me to live my life as fearlessly as Dov Baer lived his. He fought for his people and taught me to do the same, even when it hurt, even when it meant I would lose.

This freedom gave me my new family, and they gave me the hope to keep going, to keep pushing forward, to keep living and helping others live.

Tomorrow would be a new day that would bring us one step closer to freeing our enemies. Tomorrow we would push forward and change lives. But today, we had each other and that was more than enough.

"Love you, Goldilocks," Dov winked at me, turning my chin toward him for a kiss.

"Love you too, Baby," I smiled.

Our daughter really did move this time.

ACKNOWLEDGMENTS

My incredible readers, thank you so much for going on this journey
with me. Since the time I started The Golden Trilogy, we've been
through so much together—including Golden becoming a bestseller.
I couldn't be more thrilled!

I hope that you've enjoyed Dov and Auluria's story as much as I
have. If you're like me, you're probably devastated that it has come to
an end…or has it? All I'm saying is that you should keep a close eye
out for something in the future. Mostly because I'm not ready to say
goodbye yet and there's still so much story to tell! Anyone want to
learn more about this Duluria baby? Who do you think she might be?
I'm not giving out any hints…yet.

Special thanks to Sissy and Jess for all of your hard work proofing
this book and your incredibly loyal support!

Thank you to my lovely editor, Jody Desroches for all of your
hard work!

Alexis, I'm so grateful to have you in my life! Your artwork on the chapter headers for The Golden Trilogy has been so incredible! The fans all love finding the hidden pictures!

To Auluria and Dov, thank you for letting me tell your story. You two have been in my head since I was a little girl, and while it took a long time to figure you out, I'm so glad I did! Forever and always, my babies, I love you!

Special thanks to all of you fabulous fans. I could not have gone on this journey without you. Thank you for your unending support, love, and the fabulous emails and DMs you send. You make this all worth it!

Remember, you have the ability to change people's lives, so live in a way that is meaningful, do the right thing, even when it's hard, and be a light in the darkness. You're a spark that will change the world, baby. Believe it. Live it.

FORGED

A GOLDEN TRILOGY PREQUEL NOVELLA

*To those who have found themselves in situations that were less than ideal,
and handled them with grace and courage anyway.*

The story of Goldilocks hits a few of the main parts of my tale, but my story started long before I met the Baers.

When people neglect to tell the part about me being sent on a mission to destroy the Baer family, they also forget to mention my training, my manipulative cousin, my overbearing mentor, and that I was a vicious fighter.

My name is Auluria, but once upon a time, I was a young girl known as Lur. This is the story of how that deceptive girl known as Goldilocks came to be.

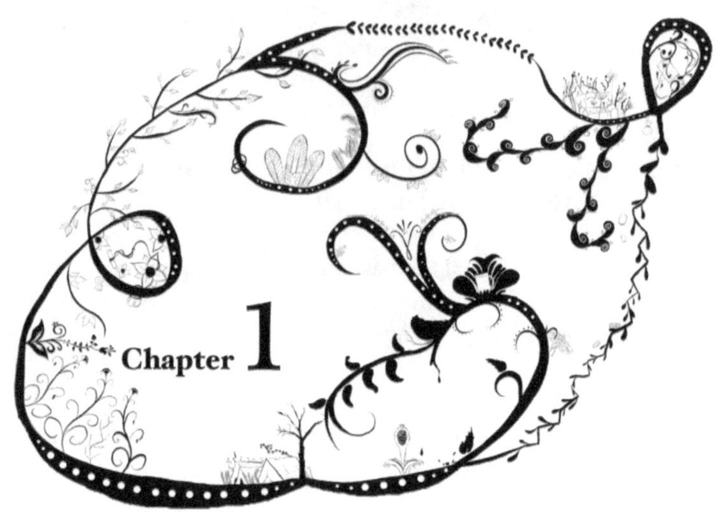

Chapter 1

WHAP!

I fell hard on my backside.

"Get up," his voice commanded.

I tried to sit up, but pain shot through my back.

"Get up, we have work to do," he demanded again.

"I'm trying," I said through gritted teeth.

Shadoe was quite possibly my least favorite person. It had only been a week since my aunt had died and my cousin, Lowell, had brought me into his group of fighters where he was working to end the corrupt Society we lived in. I was lucky I had a cousin to care for me at all. I had lost my parents and my aunt; Lowell was the only family I had left.

Shadoe reached down to me and pulled me to my feet. Stepping back, he paused as I took a breath of air. Before I could even gasp, he launched himself at me yet again, pummeling me to the ground.

I shrieked as I hit the dirt, brown dusty particles covering my forearms and hands. Lowell stood several yards away raising his eyebrow at me. *I was weak* and he didn't like it.

"*Lur,*" Shadoe said, using the name I so despised.

"That is *not* my name," I growled.

"Get it right." He scowled.

I hated him.

But Lowell would not save me.

He paired me with Shadoe; a man who had been born to work with Lowell. His father before him worked with my cousin, until his death a few years before, and now Shadoe was his right-hand man.

I rose to my feet, determined not to fall again. Raising a hand in front of me, I protected my face like Shadoe had shown me. He threw a punch and I blocked it with one hand, then swept my foot around the back of his leg and pulled his knee out.

He faltered and I slammed the heel of my hand into his jaw, forcing him back.

I knew Lowell was watching, so I continued my attack. Punching him in the stomach, Shadoe fell to his knees. I took the opportunity to bring my knee up, connecting it with his face. As I did, he gripped my leg; I once again landed on the ground. I struggled for air as he wrapped his hands around my throat. It hurt, but he didn't cut off my air supply.

"Better," he said, releasing me.

"You're improving, Auluria," Lowell commented as he walked over to us. He motioned for me to follow him. I was grateful for the reprieve.

"I know this has not been an easy transition for you, Auluria, but I appreciate that you are making the effort. I know Shadoe is training you hard, but it's only because I want you to survive. This fight that we are in is not easy. I won't send you out there unprepared."

"I'm trying," I said weakly.

"I know you are." He nodded. "You just have to *keep* trying. You did better today. But now that you are doing better, he's going to push you harder. It won't seem like it's getting any easier, even though you are improving each day. Don't get discouraged."

We walked along through the field toward the trees.

I wished Lowell would spend more time with me. We were never close, but at least when I was a child, he'd spend time playing with me. Now he only spoke to me when necessary. He let Shadoe oversee everything I did.

"Auluria, you know what we're doing is the right thing, don't you?" Lowell asked, his words drawn out.

"I do," I said with measured breath.

We continued forward to his temporary shelter. Lowell's group had a transient nature to it. They were always moving from place to place. They never stayed still for long. All of the housing was short term. We lived in the woods, in fields, and, on occasion, we spent a few nights in an actual home.

I never did understand why Lowell chose this over his parents' home. It sat abandoned in town since Lowell had taken me in. I missed the walls and the protection the small house offered. I missed the privacy.

"The government needs to be destroyed and reestablished," Lowell continued, sitting down in front of a fire. "You are smart, Auluria; once you finish your training, I know you will be a great asset to our campaign. I can see you rising in the ranks quickly. Even as a child, you were very good at problem-solving."

His lips tugged up just a touch as he remembered our childhood games. My own followed suit as I stretched a hand out toward the fire. The evenings were cool, and as we sat in the twilight I could feel the sweat on my skin take a frosty turn. I shifted closer to the fire.

"I'll do my best, Lowell," I assured him.

I hated the idea of fighting. I didn't like that I needed to be trained. But I also wanted to be prepared. I knew what happened to girls like me if the Society caught us alone.

We lived in a place that was haunted by threats from foreign nations. Our government gave them our food and resources to secure safety and protection, but it wasn't enough. They demanded more, and the more they demanded, the more the Society took from its people. A wall was constructed around the nation to protect it, keeping invaders at bay. The people were left with barely enough to survive. Like the fire in front of me, the nations only grew, demanding everything in their paths. The government wanted an army to defeat our enemies. The boys were sent to training camps to learn to fight while the girls that were captured were sent to breeding camps to further populate the country. Orphans were taken first, then young people, then anyone the soldiers found alone that could be easily overtaken.

I knew learning to fight would give me the power to protect myself, so I tolerated my lessons with Shadoe. I also knew Lowell was protecting me and I needed to help him. I wanted to stop the government too; the government that had destroyed us all.

"Auluria, Shadoe is doing a good job training you. I know it isn't easy right now, but trust me, it's for the best."

"I know Lowell, I trust you."

I saw his eyes brighten, the skin on his face tightening as he suppressed a grin. "Good."

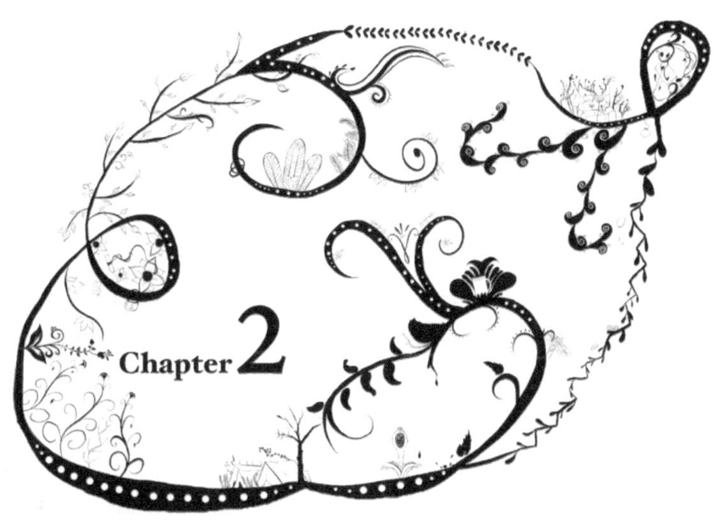

Chapter 2

"You have to be faster than that," Shadoe shouted as I dangled from a tree. "You can't take your time climbing. You have to be sure of yourself. If you need to evade your enemy, you must be quick."

"*And silent, and cunning. I know,*" I said sarcastically. "I have the words down, Shadoe; it's the putting into practice part that's the problem."

"Get down," he demanded.

The last thing I wanted was to be too slow again, so I released my hands and dropped. I shouldn't have from the height I was at, but the shooting pain in my ankle subsided quickly enough.

"I've had enough of tree climbing for today, follow me," Shadoe said gruffly after demonstrating a flawless climb once again.

We walked through the forest and into a marshy area. The grass was tall, wild and unruly. Frogs jumped away as we approached.

"Take your clothes off and get in," he said.

I looked at him, horrified.

"Well, go on, we don't have all day."

"But—" I started.

"Move it!" he insisted.

I pulled my dress over my head once he turned his back to me, leaving my under clothes in place. The nights had been cool and the water felt too cold against my skin. I held my gasp in so Shadoe couldn't criticize me.

"Swim," he ordered once he heard me enter the water.

He watched as I swam laps back and forth from one end of the pond to the other. After what seemed an eternity I saw him slip into the water behind me. I swam away as he stepped in.

When I turned back around, he was watching me. I swam in his direction, waiting for instructions. Instead of him speaking to me, the water told me what to do next: fight for my life.

Shadoe held me under the water. He stood over me and forced me into a shallow, watery grave. I planted my feet against the bottom and pushed upward as hard as I could. My skull slammed into his jaw, but he propelled me back down. I sputtered in my seconds above the water, trying to inhale as much air as possible.

His strong arms held me down, burying my feet in the mud below. I reached up and scratched at his hands, but it didn't seem to faze him. Turning my head to the side, I bit down hard on his knuckles. I could hear his angry words under the water.

When even that didn't work, I held still. I let my body go limp and forced the panic from my thoughts. Waiting, I let the air bubble from my lips, only retaining a bit in my lungs. They burned as I forced myself not to move. I thought I would die.

I held still long enough to scare Shadoe. He pulled me from the water, but I remained motionless. I resisted the urge to gasp for air, though I desperately needed it. Shadoe shook me, still holding my shoulders. I could feel the terrified look creep over his face, even though I couldn't see with my eyes closed. The muscles tensed in his hands around me.

When he threw me over his shoulder, I gasped for air, taking a deep gulp. The crashing water prevented him from hearing my breath. Holding still again I let him rush me toward the shore.

"Shadoe!" I heard Lowell shout in the distance. His rapidly approaching footsteps told me he was running toward us and he was nervous I was hurt.

My instructor set me down on the ground far too hard. He leaned down to me and felt for breath. I stilled my lungs, satisfied that I would worry him.

"Auluria?" He sounded scared. He tapped my face as Lowell drew closer.

"*Auluria?*" Shadoe repeated. Panic set in.

As he leaned back down to check for a pulse, I kicked my leg up over him, knocking him off balance. My hand caught his face, sending his head backward. As he recoiled, I pulled my knee toward my body and forced it out, kicking him as hard as I could in the face. The noise that came from him was terrifying and I suddenly felt terrible for tricking him like that.

He fell back into the pond, unconscious. I left him there for Lowell to fish out of the water. I knew I should stay and apologize, but in that moment, he was the man who tried to drown me, and I hated him.

I stomped back to the camp.

"That was cruel," Lowell said later that night.

"He tried to drown me," I objected.

"He was training you."

"By killing me?" My rage had only grown since I left the marsh.

"Yes," Lowell's answer surprised me. "If you knew everything he was going to do before he did it, you'd always be prepared. The enemy isn't going to warn you before they strike. You need to be prepared to handle those situations."

It made sense, in a twisted kind of way.

"But, *Missy*," now he was angry, "No more knocking him out. Teach him a lesson, *show off* if you want; take him down a peg or two for all I care, but I need him *conscious* and functioning. Do you understand?"

"I understand."

"Shadoe is a good teacher," he softened "And a good man. You'll learn to trust him in time."

"I should apologize," I relented.

"Yes, you should," Lowell said, a little too quickly. I didn't like that he sided with Shadoe over his own cousin.

I wandered through the field we were camping in. We were far out in the wastelands by the edge of the woods where the Society wouldn't bother us. I wove my way around the rest of Lowell's flock until I found Shadoe sitting by a fire, a mug in his hand.

Sitting down beside him, I decided not speak. Shadoe made no effort to talk either. The silence surrounded us and I listened to the fire snap.

"Water?" he asked after fifteen minutes had passed. He held his mug out to me.

I shook my head.

"I'm sorry I knocked you out today," I said unhappily.

He didn't respond.

"I know you're trying to help," I added.

"You need to be able to protect yourself. I'm only trying to help you do that," he said.

"I know," I patronized.

"You're a good fighter," Shadoe added as the fire sparked and hissed at us. "Just… inexperienced. Once you've done this for a bit, you could be as good as any of the men here. You're a fighter, Lur."

"Why do you keep calling me that?"

"Because I know you hate it," he shrugged. "It motivates you to prove me wrong. And Auluria is so *feminine* sounding—*Lur* is stronger. Not to mention it's shorter." He actually grinned at the last comment. It was the first time I'd ever seen him do anything but scowl.

I smiled. "I still hate it."

"And you still hate *me*. I get it," he concluded. "But at least you're getting better."

He held his mug out to me again, insisting I drink. I started to reach for it, but stopped.

"You're not going to attack me again, are you?" I asked, pulling back my hand.

"No." He half grinned. "We're taking the night off, Lur. Take it," he nodded to the mug.

True to his word, I was not attacked.

The water felt good on my throat. The fire cast an orange glow on us as its flames danced. We sat in silence for a while longer before I finally rose.

"I should get back," I said, handing him the mug.

He nodded, turning back to the fire as I left. He never watched me walk away. A gentleman would have made sure I arrived at home—or *temporary home*—safely. Shadoe didn't care.

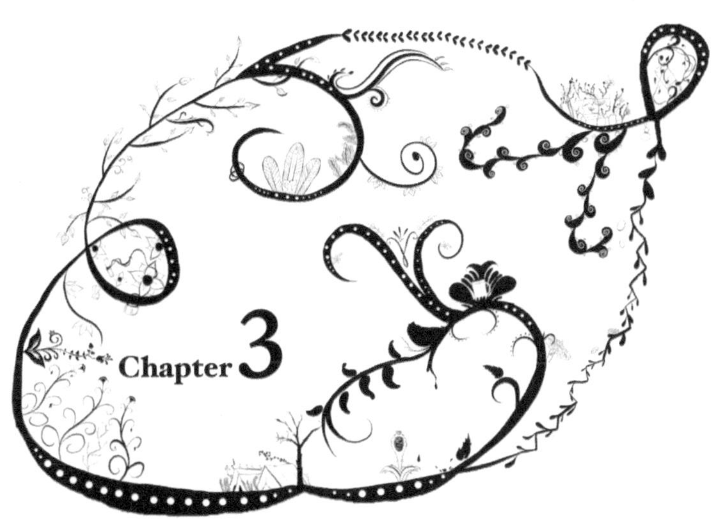

Chapter 3

"WHAT AM I SUPPOSED TO DO WITH THIS?" I ASKED, A TREMBLE IN MY voice.

I held a cold, metal knife in my hands. I prayed I wouldn't have to use it on some poor, unassuming animal.

"Throw it," Shadoe said. "Like this."

He raised his hands in the air, one for balance and one for aim. The knife sailed through the air and buried itself deep into a tree trunk.

"Now you." He motioned to the knife I held.

I mimicked his pose, spacing myself out just as he had. I balanced myself with my left hand, holding the knife tightly in my right. I watched my stationary target; a nearby tree. Stepping forward, I raised the knife and propelled it toward the trunk. It landed in the bark with a satisfying thud. I turned to look at Shadoe triumphantly.

"And you even breathed correctly when you released it." He almost sounded impressed.

"I watched you," I said, indicating I noted his exact movements as he demonstrated.

"Well, Lur, it looks like you are finally learning," he nodded appreciatively. I was finally starting to make some headway with the stoic man.

"Do it again. This time, hit *here*."

He made a mark on the tree, a target for me to focus on.

I raised my arms and released my weapon. It found its mark several inches below Shadoe's indentation.

"At least it hit the tree," he said. The anger of the first few weeks of training could no longer be found in his voice.

Over the last few weeks since the incident in the water, we found our stride. He no longer yelled at me and I no longer despised him as much. He talked to me and I talked back. Shadoe explained calmly and rationally; I understood and put it into practice. We were cool to each other, but no longer harsh.

Raising my hands, I threw the knife again. This time it landed closer to my target. My fourth try hit with the wrong side and bounced off, sending me skittering backward to avoid being hit. Shadoe made me practice for two hours. My arms were sore, but I pushed forward, the knife feeling more and more like an extension of myself with each attempt.

Shadoe released me from practice, but I tackled him from behind. Taken by surprise, he tried to flip me over his shoulder, but I clung on. Unsuccessfully, he tried again. Finally, my handler crashed into a tree, pinning me between the bark and his body.

He whipped around to face me, my back still pressed against the tree. A flash of anger rippled through his face before he slowly grinned at me. He actually held appreciation in his eyes.

"Better."

I smiled back, but before he could grab me and pummel me, I added, "I want you to teach me how to get through the woods unnoticed."

He gave me a questioning look.

"You're training me how to defend myself and fight, but it's not going to do me much good if I can't sneak up on someone or get away without them tracking me," I announced. "I want you to focus on that too. Not that we can't do the physical training, but I want *stealth* to become a main component of my daily training, too."

While the statement was true enough, I also wanted an excuse to not be constantly beat up the entirety of each training day.

"All right," he said thoughtfully. "I wasn't going to do that until later, but I suppose you're right. Let's go."

Slipping into the woods, we trekked up a small incline. I listened as every branch snapped under my feet, seeming unusually loud. Shadoe, however, was practically unnoticeable.

"Walk on the outsides of your feet," he said, "like this."

I mimicked him and the sound muffled. I must have looked amused because he snickered.

"What else?" I redirected.

"Look for softer earth to step on. If you step on leaves and branches, it's going to make a louder sound."

"You want me to avoid the leaves?" I mocked. "The leaves that cover literally every inch of the earth here? *Those* leaves?"

With that, Shadoe took off ahead of me, silent as a deer. I let out an annoyed huff and followed, trying to catch up. He disappeared from my sight and despite my efforts, I couldn't find him.

"Shadoe?" I asked. *Nothing.*

"Shadoe?" I said again, hoping he would appear and guide us back to camp.

When he didn't reply I gave up. "Fine, I'll figure it out myself."

I swung up into a tree and skittered to the top. I considered looking for him, but decided I didn't care enough. We hadn't gone that far and I could find my way back when I wanted to later; I had come to enjoy my time in the trees, sometimes it was the only peace I had.

I settled myself onto a high branch and watched the world fold out before me. Birds sang as they darted from tree to tree. The leaves tickled my skin as the wind brushed them against me. I could see the smoke from the fires at Lowell's camp.

Closing my eyes, I thought back to my younger years. I could barely remember my parents. I had a few memories to hold on to, but most were fading away. My mother used to take me to a lake and play with me in the shallow water. I remember my father being tall. He had handsome features. I had always seen him as a protector. He would hate to see the vicious way I was learning to fight.

I reached down to arrange my skirt around my knees, only to

remember I was in pants that day. Lowell had the women in his group train in both their dresses and pants so that they were prepared to fight either way. The women in his fold were tough. While I preferred the feminine dresses, the pants were easier to train in, especially when I wanted to remain modest while kicking Shadoe in the throat.

"Lur?" I heard a voice say quietly below.

I looked down and saw Shadoe walking toward the tree, having returned to find me, head sweeping from side to side. He didn't know where I was.

"Lur?" he asked again.

I let him walk past me without answering. It was nice to ignore him.

I let him get far enough out of sight before I climbed down. I followed after him, hiding whenever he turned around. As far as I could tell he didn't know I was trailing him. I wished I had thought far enough ahead that I had run back toward the camp and tackled him as he exited the tree line. Of course, I hadn't thought things through.

My mind raced ahead of us, picturing the layout we had traversed earlier. I fought to find a way to gain an advantage. If I took the long way around I could race ahead and catch him. I doubted I would make it.

Staying behind him, I slowly inched closer—step by step—keeping as silent as I could. As Shadoe stepped out of the trees and started toward the camp, I ran as fast as I could. He turned just as my feet left the ground. I collided into his chest and sent us both tumbling to the dirt. The men standing a few yards away burst into laughter as we collapsed.

Shadoe flipped me over onto my back and hovered over me, his eyes wild. He looked as if he wanted to say something; his lips kept twitching, but no words came out. Finally, he let go of my arms and stood up. He walked away without looking back. I couldn't tell if I had won the victory or not.

"...as if he'd never heard her. Isn't that right, Marjorie?" Lowell howled at his own story.

Marjorie sat on his right, giggling at the tale. Annetta, the blonde image of perfection, sat to my right, opposite Lowell. She joined in, encouraging him to continue. Marjorie flipped her short, curly red hair and leaned into Lowell's arm.

My cousin's groupies had joined us for dinner. Every night Lowell had a different parade of women eating with us. I rarely saw him alone. The women cared nothing about me and I had nothing in common with them, so I had become accustomed to dropping my head and staring at my food intently during the course of the meal.

"Auluria," Lowell said jovially, snapping me to attention, "how was training today?"

"It was fine," I said, keeping my words brief, "we worked on knife throwing and stealth training today."

"Good. That's good," he said, almost smiling. I worried about what was in his cup. "Annetta, you're good at being stealthy, aren't you?"

"Yes, Lowell, of course." She giggled back. I saw her reach out with her foot to brush his leg under the makeshift table. She laughed again and Marjorie looked annoyed. "I'm *very* stealthy."

I hated these dinners. I always felt so unwanted. I sighed quietly as I picked at my food.

"Lur," Shadoe said from outside the large tent door. He waved me forward and I looked to Lowell for permission. He nodded and waved me off, so I stood and walked to the door.

I waited for him to give me directions.

"Looked like you needed an excuse to get out of there," Shadoe commented as he turned and walked away.

"Oh," I said, slightly confused. "Thanks."

Unsure of what to do, I followed him. He glanced back, a bit surprised to see me.

"Did you eat?" he asked.

"Not really," I answered.

"Hard with the fans, huh?" Shadoe said knowingly.

"Yeah, they aren't exactly good for the appetite."

"Makes you want to gag, doesn't it?" He almost chuckled.

"Yeah, it kind of does," I agreed. It was nice of him to rescue me.

He led us to a fire on the far side of the camp. Like the day with the water mug, we sat and stared at the fire. I forced some food down, only because I knew I would need my strength for whatever training Shadoe had planned for when we were done. I knew there was no way I'd escape without having to practice, even that late at night.

"Locust!" Shadoe summoned the man over.

"Yeah?" he yelled from across the fire.

Locust, whose real name was not Locust, was slightly older than Shadoe. His brown, floppy hair swept into his face in an interesting way. I had heard he was called Locust because he ate everything in sight.

"I need your help. Come here."

He muttered something unkind and walked over to join us.

"I'm training Lur and I need your help," Shadoe motioned to me still sitting by the fire.

"Well, now that's a different story." His eyebrows shot up and he grinned at me.

"Shut up, Locust. I'm teaching her to pick pocket and I need a dummy," Shadoe said curtly.

"Even better," his grin stretched wider.

Shadoe stooped and picked up a stone from the ground. He handed it to Locust, who showed it to me before putting it in his coat pocket.

"The goal, Lur, is to get the rock out of the pocket without him knowing it."

"What's the point in that?" I interrupted. "We're not thieves."

"No, we're not, but we're not doing it to steal things *just to steal them*. We're doing it in case we ever need to retrieve information from the Society. They write things down and send them with the soldiers all the time. If we can lift that information from them, we have the advantage," Shadoe informed me.

"It's especially important for the pretty girls to know how to do it, because you can usually get so much closer to them without being questioned. In fact, they encourage beautiful women to be near them," Locust said. "Which is, in fact, why I'm not horribly upset to stand here and endure this. Once you get the basics down, you'll be working on the…more *complicated* version." he winked at me.

I frowned. I wasn't sure what he meant.

"Stop it, Locust," Shadoe warned.

"I'm just saying… *You can't do it* because you know what she's doing. You have to be able to watch and correct her form…and *I'm* volunteering to be the test subject again." He elbowed Shadoe happily.

"What are you talking about?" I asked, my voice terse.

"You don't have to do it tonight, and I won't ever make you do it with him," Shadoe assured me.

"Do what, Shadoe?"

He sighed. "The soldiers like pretty girls; they like to be near them.

The best way to get close to them is to flirt with them, and usually that leads to kissing them. There's a lot you can accomplish while kissing someone because they are usually so distracted." I knew I looked horrified and Shadoe looked almost as embarrassed as I felt.

"But we're not doing that tonight, so don't worry about it now," he assured me.

It *did* worry me. I didn't want to kiss Locust or anyone in Lowell's fold for that matter. I saw no reason to be kissing at my age. Other girls my age were seeing different boys, but I had never felt the need to while I was so young. I had plenty of time for that.

Shadoe showed me how to use two fingers to reach into the pocket so I was less likely to be noticed. We practiced well into the night, the fire crackling and the stars sparkling. Locust wasn't a bad guy when you got to know him, though I knew I wouldn't be able to put up with him for long periods of time.

By the end of our training session, I had a good grasp on the concept. I was excited to show Lowell the next day.

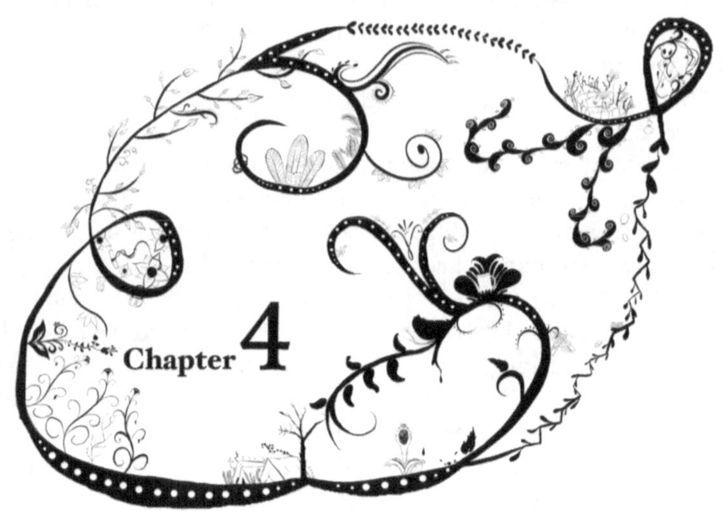

Chapter 4

"LOWELL!" I SAID, GRINNING WHEN MY COUSIN WALKED PAST ME THE next morning. "I have something to show you!"

He looked a little upset that I had delayed him from wherever he was going, but he turned around and walked back to me.

I held out my hand, a paper clutched between two fingers. I grinned, waiting for him to catch on.

His eyebrows furrowed, trying to understand. Leaning closer, he realized what the paper was. His hand flew to his pocket and came up empty. He sputtered.

"How?"

I grinned in return, handing him back the paper.

"Huh." He grinned, for the first time looking impressed with me.

"I learned last night."

"Impressive," he confirmed. "I want to see you and Shadoe this morning. Come find me in an hour or so."

I nodded as he walked away.

Walking around the camp, I set out to find Shadoe. Lowell hadn't said it, but I knew it was my job to find him and get him to the meeting on time.

"Well, if it isn't the pickpocket thief that stole my heart," Locust crowed when he saw me approaching.

"Clearly, I took your *rationality* and *sense of self-preservation* as well, Locust," I said as I turned and walked away.

I decided then that I didn't want to be friends with Locust.

It took me twenty minutes, but I finally tracked Shadoe down on the far side of the camp, opposite where he would usually set up his tent. He was smashing his fist into a younger boy's nose. It cracked loudly as I approached. I barely winced, having become familiar with his no-holds method of teaching.

"And that, boys, is how we handle annoyances." A red-haired boy said as I approached. He looked to be about my age; one of Shadoe's former recruits. He laughed as he waved the boys off and took the bleeder to get medical attention.

"Lur," Shadoe addressed me.

"Lowell wants to see us," I said. When he raised his eyebrows in question, I clarified. "I don't know why. I did, however, pick his pocket this morning. He actually seemed impressed."

I grinned. I wanted him to know I had done something right, something *impressive.*

"Good for you," he said just over a mumble. "Come on."

"You wanted to see us?" Shadoe asked as we walked up to Lowell.

We had found him in a meeting with two other men at the far end of the camp. Shadoe waited until the men stepped away before advancing, expecting me to follow behind him.

"Yes. Shadoe, good job with Auluria's training. I can see she's really improving. You two make a very good team," Lowell said as he motioned for us to follow.

We wove a path around the remaining tents and out into the spacious field we found ourselves camping near.

"I think Auluria is ready for her first mission." He threw a glance at Shadoe. "With your oversight, of course. We'll keep it simple at first, but we'll work her up to your level more quickly than the others. I think she can handle it."

I jumped over a small dip in the ground, careful not to twist an ankle before my first mission for Lowell. The tall grass tickled my arms as we walked through it.

"I have decided I like the two of you as a team. You work well together. I think in time, once she is on your level, you will balance each other out," my cousin said, slowing his steps. He stopped and turned to us.

"Shadoe, I want you to look out for Auluria. Yes, you are to train her, but you are also to protect her. There is no one I trust more than the two of you. I know you will work well as a team and you'll be happy together. You make a fine pair, and one day—soon—you both will be my right-hand men. I want you—*together*—to be my second in command."

Lowell kept talking, but I could no longer hear him. *What had he just said? Did he.... Did he really just.... commit me to Shadoe? Did he commit me to Shadoe as more than just a partner... Because it certainly sounded like I was just given to him as the ultimate partner: a bride.*

"You'd like that, wouldn't you, Cousin?" His voice invaded my thoughts again.

"I...what?"

"*Missy*, you will start listening to me when I speak to you, do I make myself clear?" he was annoyed.

"I'm sorry, Lowell, I got a little lost. Did you say you're partnering us together?"

"Of course!" he was restraining himself from shouting. "Haven't you been listening at all?" he rolled his eyes. "Go. Shadoe, go get her ready for the mission. *Honestly*, Auluria, maybe you aren't ready," he spat his words like venom.

I wanted desperately to impress him; to be the leader he wanted me to be. But before I could say anything, Shadoe swept me away, back to the camp to prepare for our mission.

"I'm sorry, Shadoe, that whole partner thing just threw me," I tried to explain.

"It doesn't matter, Lur, how much did you hear?"

"None of the mission details," I admitted sheepishly.

"We're moving; setting up camp elsewhere. Once we arrive and set up, you and I are going on a scouting mission. Nothing too danger-ous, but it will be good practice for you," he said. "Go get packed up and we'll talk it over once we arrive."

I sighed and split away from him, walking back to my tent.

I hated having to move. Lowell said it was for the best, but I still didn't like it. It was so much unnecessary work. Most of Lowell's people lived in the towns to avoid suspicion. Some of us moved from site to site to avoid detection. We made regular appearances in the towns, but we never lived in one place for very long.

I gathered my things together, putting my clothing in my bags. We were responsible for our own belongings, so we could take whatever we could carry. I brought several dresses and a few sets of pants and shirts. I had a hairbrush that belonged to my mother with me, and letters from my father. There were a few small trinkets from my childhood I brought along, but I didn't have much to start with.

The tents were taken down and the entire world Lowell created collapsed into bags. We settled into a steady pace, moving to our new temporary home. Shadoe found his way next to me and we walked in silence.

His arm brushed against mine several times on our journey, but I ignored it. I didn't like Lowell telling me what to do, and I imagine Shadoe didn't either, but we'd both do as he said. We were committed to Lowell, and therefore, committed to each other.

I heard him coming before I heard his voice. "Hey, *beautiful*," Locust called to me from several yards away. Before he could finish, Shadoe's strong, clear voice cut him off.

"Back off, Locust," he said so low and quiet I almost missed it.

Shadoe's arm slid around my waist under my pack, his hand gripping my arm. I unintentionally stiffened at his touch. Not meaning to, I turned my head to him just in time to see Locust in my peripheral vision. He eyes became incredibly wide and his face flushed white, followed by deep crimson. Locust would no longer be a problem of mine.

Shadoe held his arm around me for a few more yards before he released me, ensuring that people had taken notice. I was claimed. I was Shadoe's. Lowell had proclaimed it so and now Shadoe took ownership of the fact that we were together. I had no choice but to accept it.

When we arrived, Shadoe set his tent up next to mine. The proximity of my trainer was unnerving. I was only starting to get used to him as a mentor, now I had to get used to him as my partner and the man I was committed to. I needed some distance.

"Let's go, Lur," he said as soon as we were both set up.

I wanted to rest; to sit and listen to the crickets, close my eyes and let my mind take me somewhere far away. Instead, I stood and joined him.

He walked closer to me than usual through the camp. Word had already made its way through most of the group just during our journey to the new campsite. Eyes followed us as we walked. Once we were out of eyesight, Shadoe moved away from me, giving me the distance I craved.

"We're going into town." He broke the silence. "One of our spies is there and he needs to pass a message to us. You will be in charge of finding him and procuring the missive. I am there as back up only."

I nodded. My first mission and I was already on my own.

"You know our man; you've seen him before. I will not tell you who he is. You will point him out to me. Then it will be your job to get to him and get the message without anyone noticing. You will run your idea past me first, you may use whatever you need to in order to accomplish the mission. Questions?"

"No, I understand." I started walking faster toward the town and Shadoe kept pace.

"Good. It's busy; it's the middle of the day. That should help with your cover. But don't get caught," he warned.

I wished I knew the layout of the town. If I knew in advance what I was working with, I could have formulated a plan while we walked. Instead, I had wait until we approached to finalize my thoughts.

I searched the crowd for our mark. We were perched up on a hill, lying in the grass, looking down at the market. Business was being held on the outskirts of the town, clearly a good place for our kind of people to gather. It had the advantage of easy exits; a person could run to the woods, through the town, or hide in a nearby house or store if needed. There was a clear sightline to the main roads both *in* the town and *entering* the town. If the Society showed up, they would know and be able to escape.

Men wandered everywhere. Women hastened children along. I could hear the hum of conversation even from on the hill. My eyes swept the crowd again, looking for anything familiar.

I pointed to a man in dark clothing. His beard hid most of his face, and what wasn't hidden was covered by a low-pulled hat. When Shadoe nodded my heart jumped. *I can do this.*

Now I needed a plan. I glanced around, calculating my next move. Merchants were selling goods. Men were trying to haggle for better prices. A fight broke out and we could hear the shouting.

I stood to run, seeing my opportunity. Shadoe pulled me back. "I have to go, now!" I hissed.

He pressed something cold and metallic into my hand. A knife. I took it and slipped it into my boot, not telling him I already had knives safely tucked away in both my boot and belt.

I slipped over the grass and looped around the back of the group. No one noticed me come up behind them. Most were turned to make sure they stayed out of the range of the fight.

Walking up to a merchant who was selling bags and pouches, I leaned against his makeshift stand, admiring his creations. I ran my fingers across the smooth fabrics and leathers of the bags.

"You like?" he asked.

I gave him a small smile, "Yes, they're very nice."

I ran my fingers across them again, examining each one. I saw my contact approach the stand next to the one I was at, only a few feet away.

"I'm looking for something I can attach to my belt at the hip," I said, "This one isn't very effective." I pointed to the small bag I was carrying.

When Shadoe had handed me the knife, I balanced myself on his arm as I slipped it into my boot. I forced myself to stumble into him as I righted myself, and I stole his money pouch. I kept it hidden in front of me as I ran.

I picked up a bag and let it dangle in my fingers. Holding it to my hip, I tried it on for size. Amazingly, it fit perfectly, especially since I hadn't planned it.

"This one, I think." I held it up to the light once more, admiring the detail work.

He named a price; too high. I bartered; he bartered back. Once we finally reached an agreement, I set the bag on the very edge of the stand, next to my contact.

Opening Shadoe's pouch, I intentionally spilled part of the contents.

"Oh," I gasped and reached forward to scoop it up. The man reached forward to help me; I saw my contact slip the letter into the bag I had just set down. I picked it up as the bag-maker scooped up the last of my coins, counting them out for me. With pouch clutched firmly in my hand, I pulled a few extra coins out to make up the difference of what the merchant had in his hand.

I felt the thick paper in the pouch, but was careful not to crinkle it. I thanked the man and turned to walk away. My contact stayed at his table, still waiting for his turn to be served. I was grateful it had been a busy booth, selling food to the men and women of the town.

I weaved my way around merchants and people. Attaching my new pouch to my belt, I felt strangely exhilarated. I stopped at several stands, examining the goods I had no intention of buying. I didn't want to make myself noticed by appearing at one stand and then disappearing.

A hand reached around me and snaked its way to the pouch on my belt. I had my knife against his wrist before I realized it was Shadoe testing me. I removed it, but not before lightly scraping it across his skin, causing blood to bubble up. I smiled to myself.

"Let's go," he said, wiping the blood away and moving fully to my side. In his hand, he clutched a few supplies he must have attained while watching me.

"How did you get those?" I asked, realizing I had taken his money.

"I carry money in more than one place, Lur, I didn't steal these." He sounded offended.

"Well, how was I to know?" I shot back.

"I see you brought your own knife," he commented.

"Two, actually," I corrected.

"You're learning," We started back up the hill. "Let me have the letter." He reached out his hand, waiting for me to hand it to him, a wise choice, considering I would have sliced his hand again if he had tried to take it.

"No, I think I'll carry it back to Lowell," I said, "It is my first mission, after all, and I want to see it through."

"This is going to be a fun partnership, isn't it?" he sounded annoyed again.

"Apparently," I agreed.

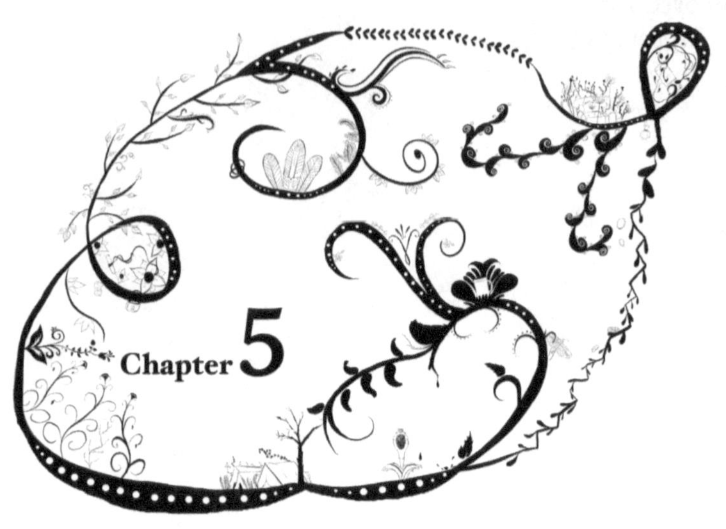

Chapter 5

LOWELL KICKED ME OUT IMMEDIATELY, OPTING TO TALK ONLY TO Shadoe. When I was finally allowed back in, two more of Lowell's groupies were sitting at the table, fawning over him. It made me sick the way his women threw themselves at him. At least I'd never have to do that with Shadoe.

"You're going back out," Lowell said jovially as the women laughed. "Eat quickly, then go."

"No, we'll eat on the way," Shadoe said, grabbing my arm and spinning me out of the room.

"You don't want to stay there," he whispered as we walked away from Lowell's large tent.

The truth was, I never liked being around Lowell when he had women around. If Shadoe spared me another wasted night with my cousin sitting in silence with my head hanging down, then I was grateful to him.

Weaving our way around the tents, we picked up food from his friends as we moved past them. We ate as we walked and I let him guide me to our next mission.

"Where are we going, Shadoe?"

"There has been some unrest near the town. We need to go see what's been happening," he said.

584

I hesitated once we reached the woods. Shadoe had said we were going to gather information on the unrest near the town, he had never said we were going into the woods.

It wasn't that I feared the woods. I liked the woods, especially when everything was so calm and peaceful. But something immediately didn't feel right as we stepped through the tree line.

A branch cracked to my left and I stopped. Shadoe kept walking, but I knew he had to have heard it. Suddenly they were everywhere. Screams filled the night as footsteps raced toward me.

I saw Shadoe fall to the ground in front of me, a boy collapsed on top of him. Arms wrap around me in a collision of great speed. I flipped him over me, knowing it was coming before he even touched me. More noise clouded the air.

"Shadoe!" I screamed, hoping for an answer.

"I'm here Lur," he yelled back. I could see him grappling with someone on the ground.

I could hear flesh striking flesh as I struggled against the attack. Someone grunted but I couldn't tell if it was Shadoe or one of the other men. My face snapped back as a fist hit me, sending searing pain throughout my jaw.

I turned and lashed out at my attacker. He yelped in pain as I connected. I guessed there were five or six men who had ambushed us. Someone grabbed me around the waist from behind and lifted me into the air.

"Settle down," he commanded as I kicked in the air.

The voice. I recognized it. It was one of Shadoe's men. It wasn't an ambush…*it was a test.*

I wrapped my foot around the back of his ankle and kicked it out, sending us both toppling to the ground. I pushed him off of me, spinning on my knee. I regretted it instantly as twigs drove their way into my kneecap. Swinging my other leg over him, I pinned him to the ground and I started in on his face.

Another man pulled me away several punches later. I jerked my head back, crashing into his jaw causing him to stumble and release me. I slammed the heel of my hand into his nose and heard it crack. He cursed as I shoved his shoulders, sending him to the ground.

The man reached for my ankle and I fell. A foot embedded itself in my side. Groaning, I pulled myself upright. I lashed my hand out at the man, clawing his face.

I ran toward the man pinning Shadoe down. Now that I knew that he wasn't actually being attacked, I considered letting him stay there.

I hoped the man had time to get a few good punches in before I tackled him. On the ground, I kicked the man in the stomach and he doubled over. I took the opportunity to bring my boot up and kick him in the groin, ensuring he would stay on the ground.

Shadoe had "taken out" the other two men, so I turned my fury on Shadoe. He was just standing up as I pushed him backwards. I shoved him again, and then one more time for good measure. My hand reeled back, winding up to slap him when he reached out and grabbed my hand to stop me.

"Lur!" he warned.

I took the opportunity to turn away from him, twisting out of his grasp, as I brought my boot down hard on his foot.

"Ow! *Lur!*"

"What is the *matter* with you?" I yelled. "You had your men attack me? What was the point in that?" I shouted.

"If you wanted me to train against them, all you had to do was pair me with them! You didn't need to drag me out to the woods in the dark of night and have them attack me!" My voice grew louder. "I *hope* they got some good punches in, because if *they* didn't mess up your face, *I will!*"

I was enraged. My face throbbed. My side hurt where I had been kicked and I knew there would be a massive bruise in the morning. I felt like I had been shattered.

"*Auluria, stop!*" he commanded, the spark in his eyes dulling.

I froze and retracted my hand. I couldn't steady my breathing though. Then I realized the piece I had been missing.

"Lowell knew," I said quietly. "He sent me out here for this."

"Yes," Shadoe said quietly, stepping toward me. "He knew." He turned and dismissed the others, leaving us alone.

"It's a rite of passage, Lur. Everyone involved in missions goes through a jumping. We have to make sure you can handle yourself if something goes sideways on a mission. We need to know you could take care of yourself if something happens to your partner."

"*Well I think we've established I can,*" I said spitefully, cradling my dominant hand, covered in fresh blood.

He reached for my shoulder but I pulled away. I started walking back to the camp, Shadoe trailing behind me. I refused to listen to him so he finally gave up trying to explain. We settled into our cold, common, silence.

I crashed into Lowell's tent, the two girls still hanging on him.

"You knew!" I screeched. I didn't care. "You knew and you sent me anyway! You didn't even warn me."

"You weren't supposed to know, Auluria," he slurred. "That's the whole point."

I wanted to slap him. I wanted to knock him to the ground and spit at him. Instead I stood, seething, before him. My chest rose and fell so deeply I could feel my entire body move with it.

Lowell's demeanor shifted and the girls backed away. Slipping out of the tent behind Lowell, they left us to our conversation.

"You listen to me, *Missy*," he said between gritted teeth. "This is the way things are here. You *will* comply."

He was angry even in his inebriated state.

"We had to make sure you could handle yourself and you proved you could… At least, I assume you did. " He looked me up and down before continuing. "And you did it a heck of a lot faster than most people do it. That's why I'm trusting you to be my second in command and to be with Shadoe."

He seemed to calm a bit. "*You*, Cousin, are the key to our success. You know that. Just do as I say and the time will come for you to take your rightful place as my Second with Shadoe soon."

He looked ready to pass out. Suddenly my anger dimmed, though it didn't extinguish. I caught his hand and guided him to a seat. My side was pierced with pain and my breath caught as I lowered him.

"And what if I just want a normal life, Lowell?" I asked quietly, knowing he'd never remember in the morning.

"Oh, but dear Cousin, you were meant for so much more." He gave me a half smile, as his eyes rolled back and closed.

"You were meant to champion the fight and help bring us to glory…" His voice trailed off.

I left him hanging out of the chair.

Stepping into my tent, I sunk onto my mattress. I pulled the blankets around me, not bothering to change. Everything hurt. My head ached. I just wanted peace.

"Lur?"

"Go away, Shadoe," I said angrily.

"Can I come in?" he asked.

I threw a pillow at the entrance. Without turning to see my aim, I heard it hit before sliding to the ground. Shadoe stepped in anyway.

"Get out!" I shouted.

"I have to make sure you're okay first," he responded, walking to my side.

I thought about hitting him, but it required too much energy. I just wanted to stop for the day.

"Let me see," he insisted.

"Leave me alone, Shadoe. I don't need you and I certainly don't want you," I said, viciousness lacing my voice.

It was hard to see in the small tent, but in the moonlight filtering through the fabric of the tent, I was positive I saw him pull back slightly.

"Martin said he kicked you. Just let me check it." He reached for me and I didn't stop him. "You know it wasn't my choice, right?" he muttered softly while he examined my side.

"Of course it was," I snapped back, louder than I meant to. "You always have a choice, Shadoe. Always."

"Lowell said–"

"I don't care what Lowell said. *You* are my mentor. You're *supposed* to be my partner, and from what I can tell, *my fiancé. You're* supposed to look out for me. I should come first, before Lowell or any of his stupid mandates. You knew I was ready, so there was no need for that," I huffed. "I can't believe I was actually worried for you. When they attacked, I genuinely thought they had hurt you and I was terrified you were going to get hurt worse."

I heard him breathe in sharply, though whether it was directed at my words or my injuries, I didn't know.

"One thing is for sure, I'll never worry about you again," I spat. "You're on your own, I don't care what Lowell says. If I have to see you every day for the rest of our lives, so be it, but I won't lose any sleep over you getting hurt."

"Lur, stop talking," he said quietly. "I need to see this."

He wanted me to stop and I didn't care. This place, these people... They had destroyed any softness I once had long ago, when I first came to this group. All that was left was a fighter. They had trained me and molded me and I was exactly what they wanted: a soldier devoid of free will—or maybe the will to care.

He finished checking my injuries and left. The dark was welcoming. I watched the moonlight cast shadows through my tent. I wanted to crawl out and see the stars, but I hurt too much to move. I finally drifted off to sleep.

Chapter 6

A month later, I had finally given up on despising Shadoe. I had long since forgiven Lowell, my only remaining family. Shadoe and I worked together; each day I became a little less cold toward him.

Eventually, we returned to our comfortable silence. We carried out our assignments, learned to read each other's signals, and we fell into a comfortable working partnership.

"Go around," he whispered to me as we walked into the town.

I nodded and split off. I slipped around to the backside of the group, Shadoe wandering in from the front.

The mission was simple enough: retrieve weapons from a Society stockpile. We would be breaking into a makeshift building and taking as much as we could. *Our* job was to break in and open it up to the other team members who would follow.

The sun had set and people were wandering back to their homes for the evening. Soon our team would be cloaked in darkness and could easily sneak in.

I wandered toward the building, avoiding the people walking toward me. I kept my eyes down, refusing to make eye contact. My hand brushed over the pouch on my hip, my knife resting under it, hidden from sight.

Shadoe approached the building first and slipped into the

shadows along its side. The streets quieted as I joined him. We sunk into the depths of the darkness and waited. Once it was silent, Shadoe checked to make sure we really were alone.

He blocked me from view as I broke the lock on the makeshift building. If we were caught, it would be easier for *him* to explain away why he was out so late. It would not be nearly as easy for me, a woman, to explain why I was out alone so late at night.

Within moments I had the door open and we slipped in together. It would be a bit before the rest of the team arrived. We examined the boxes and bags sitting in the room.

"Here," Shadoe said, handing me something. "Eat, there's time."

I bit into the apple, grateful for the sweet taste. It had been a long time since I had been able to enjoy my food. Usually I was rushing to eat so I could get to my training or a mission. It tasted like relief.

"They'll be here soon," he stated after a few minutes.

"We should decide what we need," I added.

We rifled through the contents of the makeshift building. Shadoe and I started shifting knives and weapons under our clothing. Within minutes the team arrived and started doing the same.

Shadoe and I positioned ourselves outside the building and acted as lookouts, having already taken on our loads to transport. My eyes adjusted to the dark outside that was only slightly brighter than the inside of the building because of the stars and uninhibited moon.

I crept around to the back of the building and waited. The crickets chirped lazily nearby as I settled into my watch post. Everything seemed so still. I tried to keep my mind from wandering, focusing intently on the landscape before me.

It wasn't until I heard the crickets drop off one by one that I started to worry. I could sense danger coming. Taking a deep breath, I edged my way back to the front of the makeshift building.

Shadoe saw me clinging to the side of the building as I entered into the space he was monitoring. He turned and signaled into the building. The team started moving quickly toward us, having nearly reached the door at the same time as I did.

"Halt!" The voice nearly made me jump.

Shadoe and I froze. The man stood closest to me, his men behind him. I slowly turned and straightened. Facing him, I caught sight of his government uniform: Society.

"What are you doing?" He addressed me.

I waited for Shadoe's signal but it never came. I moved so quickly the man never expected it. The blow to his face sent him careening backward into two of his men. They all stumbled, one falling to the ground entirely.

I didn't wait. I launched myself at another man and Shadoe followed suit. The people poured out from the building, some helping us in the brawl, others keeping the stolen supplies safe by running.

Pain radiated through my shoulder as a soldier pulled my arm behind me. "Don't move," he ordered.

I heard a snap and the pressure released. The man lay on the ground behind me, Shadoe standing over him; he snapped the soldier's neck.

"You okay?" he asked. I nodded and he turned to hold back another man's punch, crushing a bone in his wrist.

I started to help one of the team members when a pair of arms wrapped tightly around my waist.

"Look here boys, we have a girl!" the soldier shouted.

"Hang on to her—they'll want her at the camps," another replied.

The thought of the camps terrified me. If a young person was caught alone, they tended to disappear. Boys were sent to training camps to learn to fight against the foreign countries that wanted to invade. Girls were sent to breeding camps to boost the population count. I didn't know which was worse. Orphans were always the first to be taken, but if they found you isolated, they'd take you too. I'd even heard rumors about them taking older women when they could. The government would do anything to avoid attack.

As he mentioned the camps I could feel myself panic. Everything in me stiffened. I knew I had to get out of his grasp. I clawed at his hands and arms, but he only laughed.

"This one's a fighter."

"Strong willed, huh?" his friend retorted.

He moved over next to us and ran his hands through my hair, brushing it away from my face. "Pretty, too. I bet we could get a pretty penny for this one—"

Before he could finish, I bit him. It was so hard I drew blood. He scowled and backed away.

The first man wrenched me away from the soldier I just bit. Kneeing the back of my legs, he sent me sprawling to the ground. He collapsed on top of me so I could not escape. His legs straddled either side of me, pinning me to the ground in a kneeling position.

Throwing my head back, I collided with his nose and jaw and the man let out a shriek of pain.

"Get away from me!" I yelped, trying to get free.

His hand clawed at my shoulder, trying desperately to hold me in place. I was grateful to be wearing pants during the mission; had I been in a dress, I would have tangled myself up in it trying to free myself of his hold. I threw my elbow back at him, hitting him in the face again. This time he let go.

I felt Shadoe's hand grab mine and pull me the rest of the way to my feet.

"Go," he ordered and I obeyed. I heard the man take his last breath as Shadoe finished him off. A moment later my partner was at my side.

We rallied in the woods. We had escaped with only a few minor injuries, most of the damage being done to the Society soldiers.

"You okay?" Shadoe asked, glancing at me for only a moment to make sure I had no life-threatening injuries.

"I'm fine," I brushed the dirt off of myself as we waited for the last of our team to trickle in. "You?"

"Fine," he said.

"Lowell's not going to be happy we got caught tonight," I commented.

"No, but at least we all got away."

"And we got most of what we went for," I added with a shrug.

The camp was quiet when we entered. Shadoe and I found Lowell in his tent, going over some papers in his hands.

"Well?" he asked without looking up.

"We ran into some trouble with some soldiers, but we all made it back."

Lowell's gaze shot up for a moment, burning into Shadoe. Then he relaxed and turned back to his papers. "And you got everything?"

"Yes," Shadoe confirmed.

"Good," he nodded. "Tomorrow you and Auluria need to go to town. One of our men will be delivering a message to us."

"And you can't send someone less over qualified?" I mutter.

His head whipped up when he heard me and I immediately backed down.

"I would like for you and Shadoe to handle this, *Missy*."

"Of course, Lowell. Whatever you need," I said softly.

He dismissed us and we made our way back to our tents.

"Well, that turned out well," I muttered and Shadoe shot me a withering look. It didn't matter how Lowell spoke to us, Shadoe would always take his side.

Without commenting further, I slipped into my tent.

The town was crowded the next morning. We were on high alert because there was a good chance the soldiers were looking for us after the events of the previous night.

I was operating on minimal sleep, but the bright sun was enough to keep me focused as it blinded me from above. Shadoe and I split apart and made our way down into the throngs of people.

I tried to blend in as I wove my way around the streets. Our spy would be meeting with Shadoe, I was merely there for distraction or back up if necessary. I watched as he moved ahead of me, making his way to our contact.

I stopped to examine some food that different vendors were selling in the streets, turning my attention completely away from my partner. My ears were sharply focused in for the sound of his voice, even if I wasn't watching him with my eyes.

"Looks good, doesn't it, miss?" A man's voice caught my attention.

I met his gaze and found him holding something out to me to examine.

"Yes, it looks wonderful," I said. "I'm not sure what I want though."

"We have a wonderful assortment of breads. Would you like to try one?" he tempted me, holding out a small piece he ripped off of a loaf.

I reached out to take it, savoring the crispness of it.

I heard a commotion over my shoulder and turned to look. Shadoe was slowly backing away from his contact, trying to blend with the crowd. His contact was standing in the middle of a large group, yelling.

Another man, he looked to be a vendor, was shouting at him, accusing him of something. Shadoe stared at me until he could tell I had turned my gaze on him and he motioned for us to get out.

I thanked the man, but declined his offer. Turning I tried to slip away, only to find myself confronted by a wall of people. They gathered around to watch the fight, blocking my escape. I ducked back the way I had come and tried to make my way around the vendors to a side street.

When I caught sight of Shadoe again, he was making his escape hastily away from the crowd. He never saw the man step toward him, readying his knife.

Before I could call out, a second man joined the first. As I began to panic, I saw the second man carefully stick out his leg, catching the first man's foot, causing him to stumble, as if it were all an accident.

The second man bent down, catching the first man's arm before he hit the ground. Apologizing profusely, he helped dust the man off, pocketing the knife he had dropped during the fall. The first man swatted at him and cursed. He looked around for his knife as the second man slipped into the crowd and hid from view.

The man who saved Shadoe glanced up just in time to catch my gaze. He shot me a brilliant grin that lit up his blue eyes. His eyebrows moved up in a yeah-I-just-saved-that-guy way, tousling his dark hair. Before I could move, he was gone again, slipping through the crowd.

He had no idea who Shadoe was or what he was doing, but he saved him anyway, even knowing it could have caused his own stabbing. I was surprised by his actions, but didn't have time to question it.

The first man came back into my view, and I realized he was wearing a Society uniform. He must have seen the exchange, or at least suspected. He was off duty, so his uniform was minimal, but could still be identified as one of them.

I ran to meet Shadoe, concerned that the first man might come back to look for him. When I caught up to him, he confirmed he had the message we had been there to transfer, but had no idea how the man had spotted him. It didn't matter though; we needed to move.

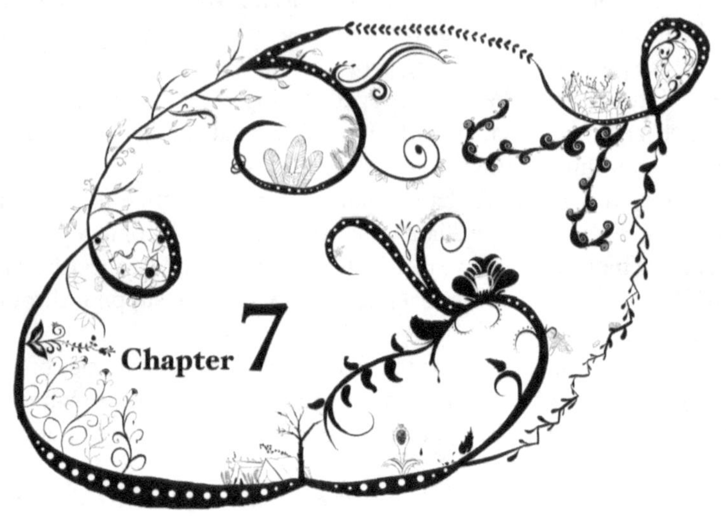

Chapter 7

"This is good," Lowell says, studying the papers. He looked up at us and added, "You both did very well. This is information regarding the master plan. It was incredibly important we got this information. Well done."

Shadoe nodded, but I could tell he was proud to have accomplished something so important for Lowell. I was still worried about almost being caught.

"You both need to start taking on more responsibility," Lowell continued. "Auluria, I think this is the perfect time for you to plan our next mission. What do you think, Shadoe?"

"I think she'll do fine, Lowell." He nodded, hands behind his back like the perfect soldier.

"Good, good. We're moving in three days. Once we get to the new town, we'll need to do some scouting. Have Auluria prepare a team; let's see how she does."

I spent the next two days putting together a team and formulating a plan. I decided everything from the rendezvous point to what time we would leave on the mission. Shadoe oversaw and only offered a few changes to my plan.

I took a small team for the mission. It went smoothly and we were not noticed. I was proud of myself as I delivered the information to Lowell. He was almost as proud.

"You haven't been with us long, Auluria, but already you have proven yourself to be one of our greatest achievements. I no longer see the need to oversee you. Your training is complete. Now you can take your place in the ranks," my cousin said as we walked.

"Shadoe will still be your partner, but no longer your mentor. You'll work together as a team."

"I understand," I confirm, lifting my skirt as I stepped over a fallen tree branch.

"The pieces are falling together, Auluria. For now, focus on the missions I give you, but know: your day is coming. When it draws near, we'll give you some more specific training you will need for the mission, but that won't be until you are a bit older."

Time passed quickly and slowly all at once. A year later Shadoe and I quickly became regarded as Lowell's right-hand man and his highly esteemed, *female*, cousin.

More time passed and the people started looking to Shadoe for leadership almost as much as they did to Lowell. Lowell stepped further and further back, letting Shadoe take on more responsibility. He was training Shadoe to take over for him, if the time ever came.

Later, when I was seventeen, Lowell came to find me one late afternoon with something on his mind, ready to move forward with his plan.

"Auluria, I think it's time we add a few new skills to your training," Lowell said as we walked around the camp.

"All right," I said cautiously.

"I'd like you to spend some time with a woman I know from town."

My heart dropped to my stomach. I never liked the women Lowell knew, and I imagined this one would be no exception.

"Tomorrow morning, you'll go to her and spend a few days with her. She'll have a bed waiting for you there."

My heart jumped at the thought of a real bed to sleep in. It had been so long since the days when I lived in my aunt's house. The bed was small and lumpy, but it was better than sleeping on the ground.

"I'll take you there myself in the morning. I want to check in on her anyway. Shadoe will pick you up before we move on."

I thought about pressing for more information, but I knew that would just result in a lecture, so I kept quiet.

"I need you to do whatever she tells you to do, Auluria. She knows what she is talking about."

I nodded to let him know I was listening, though my mind was already spinning off in different directions, trying to figure out what lessons she would be teaching me.

The next day I found Shadoe waiting outside my tent.

"You're leaving?" he asked.

"Lowell didn't tell you?"

"No." He shook his head as my cousin approached us.

"Where is she going, Lowell?" Shadoe confronted him gently.

"I'm sending her to training. I figured it was better coming from Brittella than from you." He smirked, making me uneasy.

The look in Shadoe's eyes did nothing to alleviate that fear.

"She's going to see Brittella?"

"Would you rather we let Locust teach her?"

"No," Shadoe said far too quickly.

"What exactly does this Brittella teach?" I interjected.

"Come along and you'll find out," Lowell said as he started to walk away.

I try catching Shadoe's eye but he refused to look at me.

"I'll come get you in a few days, Lur," Shadoe said before turning and sauntering off.

I rushed after Lowell to catch up, my bag over my shoulder. A gentleman might have offered to carry my pack, but Lowell was a leader and did no such thing.

Toward the edge of town, Lowell walked up to a door and knocked. After a moment, the door swung open and I found a woman fifteen years older than Lowell staring back at us.

"Lowell, come in," she greeted us warmly, her voice low and soothing.

Her dark hair was swept back, leaving part of it cascading over her back; the other half was woven in intricate patterns on her head.

Her dress was slightly fancier than mine, enough to show she was of higher standing, but not enough to draw attention from the soldiers.

"Who have you brought me?" she asks, slipping her arm into Lowell's.

She was unlike the girls that followed Lowell around. Rather than hang on him, she allowed him to fuss over *her*, using her touch to illicit responses from him. She guided him to the kitchen, leaving me in the doorway. I waited as they talked for a few moments before Lowell stood up from his seat at her table.

"Listen to her, Auluria, and don't give her any trouble," he pointed at me.

He walked to the door, but was stopped by the sound of Brittella clearing her throat. She stood in the entryway and waited as he made his way back to her, quickly moving her against the wall. He fell into her arms faster than I had ever seen him move with any of the girls that followed him around.

Her movements demanded that she be kissed, and he obeyed submissively. She pushed him back and sent him on his way. I could tell he hadn't had his fill of time with her, but she was clear in her motions and sent him away.

When she turned back to me, I realized why I was there. She was to teach me the art of manipulating a man.

My eyes must have grown fiercely wide, because she grinned at me.

"Don't worry, child. You won't have to do anything you aren't comfortable with," she assured me. "You must be hungry. Come, let's get to know each other."

She led me back to the table where Lowell had just been seated at. Setting food before me, we stared at each other.

"So, Auluria, Lowell tells me you are engaged to a young man. You must be excited."

"It was Lowell's idea," I muttered.

She laughed in response.

"Well, perhaps we'll get you a little more excited about the idea of marrying him by the time we're through. Is he a good lover?"

"I...I..." I was shocked.

"You've never kissed him then, I take it."

"No." I shook my head quickly.

"Well, my dear, at some point you will have to, and it's best to learn the right way to do so. I'll tell you all about that. But more than that, you will be learning how to manipulate and coerce men into doing what you want them to do. Even more than that, you can use these methods to manipulate anyone into doing anything for you." She grinned. "How do you think I got Lowell, a man fifteen years younger than me and constantly surrounded by beautiful women, to think so fondly of me?"

I swallowed.

"I promise, it's not as scary as it sounds." She sat back and gazed kindly at me.

We spent the next three days running over techniques of flirtation and manipulation. I learned to sway when I walked. She showed me how to touch a person's arms to get them to relax and trust me. Brittella taught me how to be unassuming, gentle and graceful so that no one would suspect I was manipulating them. I learned how to captivate attention simply from the way I walked, moved my hair, batted my eyelashes or spoke.

I learned all the right words to say. She brought in people to test me and made me comfortable with being around people. By the time Shadoe arrived to pick me up before the fold left, she decided I was ready.

"So, this is your young man coming to pick you up then?" she asked as we sat on her couch.

"It should be Shadoe, yes."

"You should practice on him," she said, her eyes glittering. "I don't have to watch if you don't like."

My worry had faded away over the three days and I became comfortable with her presence, but what she was suggesting disturbed me. I had no intention of kissing Shadoe to prove a point, much less trying any of the other skills she had begged me to learn despite my refusal.

"I will do no such thing."

"All right, all right. At least try touching his arm a bit. See how he responds. It doesn't have to be here, but perhaps later today or tomorrow. When he's not expecting it. It might just get you both to warm up to each other." She laughed again, the idea of young love filling her manipulative mind.

"Brittella, I really don't see that happening," I said, to which she only rolled her eyes.

"At least I've taught you," the woman said. "What you do now is up to you. You are ready for whatever Lowell's plan is. Even the parts you wouldn't try, you've been given enough information to figure it out as you go if you need to."

She smiled again. "You'll do splendidly, Auluria. I know you will."

The knock on the door cut her off and she rose and swayed her way over to her door. Opening it, Shadoe stepped into view, appearing more nervous than usual.

"I'm here for Auluria," he said.

"Yes, I know." Brittella appraised him, looking him up and down. "Come in," she added seductively and I saw Shadoe swallow.

"Time to go," he said, locking eyes with me.

I picked up my bag and followed him out to the street. I turned to thank Brittella but she was already gone, having beckoned a handsome man into her door.

We didn't talk at first. I could sense we were both embarrassed by the situation.

"Did I miss anything while I was at training?" I asked, wanting to break the silence.

"Not really," Shadoe replied. "The rest of them already left, so we're catching up with them now. We should meet up with them soon."

"That's good," I said, searching for something else to say. When I found nothing, we fell back into silence.

"How did your training go?" Lowell asked when he saw we had joined the group.

"Britella was… *informative*," I supplied, unsure of what to say.

I saw Locust look in my direction when he realized we were talking. Word must have made its way around that I was being trained by Brittella. I tore my gaze away from the hungry look in his eyes. I still didn't like the man.

"Good," Lowell replied. "Tomorrow we're going to put that to the test."

Before I could speak, Lowell cut me off. "We need you to distract a man tomorrow. You can do it however you see fit. Shadoe is going to be stealing something from his store and you need to assist him."

I couldn't object so I simply nodded.

I thought Shadoe might say something to me, but he didn't. He remained as cool toward me as always. I suppose I was glad he hadn't changed over this.

Chapter 8

I LEANED IN TOWARD THE MAN, GENTLY PLACING MY HAND ON HIS ARM as I gazed down at the tray he was holding. He inclined his head, studying me as I looked at the metal pieces on the tray.

Taking my hand off of his arm, I moved the tip of my shoulder to his arm, and brushed my fingertips over the contents of the tray while I murmured questions to him.

He answered every one, never taking his eyes off of me. I could sense Shadoe slip behind us and into a back room. Moments later, he returned and walked to the door. Once he was outside, I began to pout that the pieces were too much for me.

The man tried to negotiate, but I continued to pout. He couldn't part with the pieces without selling them, but he offered bits of scraps that he had turned into a necklace for me. I pocketed it and slipped out the door. His eyes didn't leave me until I was out of sight.

"Did you get it?" I asked, dropping the act the moment I had rounded the corner.

Shadoe held up several items for me to inspect.

"What is it?" I asked.

"Here, look," he said, handing me several of the pieces, but keeping one in his hand. He slipped his fingers through it and the piece sat on his knuckles, a harsh and merciless weapon.

"It's like claws," I gasped.

"It's more than that, Lur," he grinned at me but refused to further elaborate.

"What's it for?" I asked.

"Certain missions. Don't worry about it," he said, depositing them in his pack as we walked back to camp.

"Shadoe, do we know what Lowell's big plan is yet? He hasn't told me, but has he talked to you about it?"

"Yes, Lur. I know some of the details, but it's up to Lowell to tell you himself."

"Am I really that important to this plan?" I asked, annoyed.

"Yes, Lur, you really are."

I couldn't imagine how that could be possible if I hadn't even been given any details yet.

"What happens after we finish the plan? How are we going to change the Society? Does Lowell have a plan for that too?" I questioned.

"Yes, Lur. He has a plan. Haven't you realized by now that your cousin has *everything* figured out?"

"I suppose. I just wish he wouldn't leave me in the dark."

"Then talk to him about it."

His insistence on always deferring to Lowell was starting to bother me. It was as if we couldn't even have a conversation as partners without him referring to our leader.

"I should have stayed at Britella's" I muttered under my breath. "At least she talked to me like a person."

"What?" Shadoe asked, knowing I was complaining about something.

"Nothing. Let's get back."

Each week brought more missions, always with Shadoe by my side. We refrained from talking most of the time, but we worked well together. We had learned each other's moves and knew what the other would do. We made an exceptional team that could anticipate everything before it happened.

Early one afternoon, Shadoe and I walked back to camp after planting a communication in one of the towns. I tripped in a covered hole and twisted my ankle. Shadoe bent down to check it, placing me against a tree for balance.

When he stood back up, he assured me it would be fine. Without warning, he stepped closer to me. He placed his hand on my hip and leaned in toward me, brushing his lips against mine. I was so surprised I couldn't move.

He pulled back to look at me. Without a word, he leaned in once more, kissing my lips again. I stood frozen against the tree as he walked off.

I should have known it had to come eventually, but I had always thought my first kiss would be…more.

There was nothing I could do, so I followed after him. Neither of us spoke about it.

Two weeks later, we were swimming in a pond, working to keep our stamina up to training standards, when I found myself face to face with Shadoe again.

His arm found its way around my waist and he held me to him as he kissed me. This kiss was longer, but shared the same lack of passion. I kissed him back, trying to please him, knowing he was the only man I'd ever be with and I should make the effort to make it work. He pulled back and swam away.

My heart sank. I was bound to Shadoe. I'd be married to him one day. This was the man I would be with. He wasn't what I had imagined for myself, but I accepted it.

At least he made the effort. In public, he showed little care for me, in private he barely showed more. But this was a start. Perhaps one day we could grow to care for each other. I had no choice, so, I, at least, would try. If he wanted to kiss, I would kiss him. It was the best effort I could make.

Our next kiss was a few weeks later. We found ourselves in a fight with an opposing group out in the woods. Shadoe and I were attacked first and I suffered a few serious injuries.

Once we fought off our attackers, Shadoe brought me back to my tent and laid me down. He inspected my injuries and for the first time I saw genuine worry on his face.

Without telling me what was wrong, he leaned over me and buried his lips against mine. His hand grazed my hip and I recoiled in pain. His lips didn't leave mine as he kissed me again. He pulled back a moment later, his hand flitting over my hair.

"I'm sorry," he whispered and rushed out of my tent.

I looked down to examine my own injuries. A few days later, I was walking around camp as if nothing too tragic had happened, my injuries having quickly started to heal.

"How are you feeling?" Lowell asked a few days later.

"I'm fine, Lowell. Do you need me for something?"

"Yes, actually." He waved me over. "Take a look here. I need you to familiarize yourself with this, can you do that?"

I looked over the paper in front of him and nodded.

"What are these?" I asked, "Is this… information on people?"

"Yes, Cousin, that's exactly what it is. This is for your next mission. I want to make sure you can learn about these people and then use the information to handle a mission. This is our last big step before the master plan is put into play."

"You have a few hours to look these over. Be back here this afternoon."

Walking away, I looked over the writing. My target appeared to be a man and a woman from the town near where we were camping. I followed along with the words that were written on the pages, committing each notation to memory. When I felt prepared, I found Lowell early.

"I'm ready," I announced.

"Good, let's go."

He walked me toward the town. Silence stretched between us.

"Do well with this, Auluria," he finally said "and we will be ready to move forward; it won't be long now."

"What exactly am I supposed to do once I find these people?"

"Get into their home. You can find your way in. Once you are there, gain their trust, then find a way to be alone and locate the lock that fits this key and retrieve whatever is inside."

I reached out and took the key from him, slipping it into my boot alongside my knife. He pointed out a small home in the middle of the town and sent me on my way.

Walking by myself was a relief. It had been such a long time since I was alone with my thoughts, perhaps even years. I had time alone in my tent every night, but being surrounded by Lowell's people did nothing to give me the solitude I craved.

Shifting my knife and the key away from my boot and into my

belt, I watched the house for a few minutes. When I was sure the woman could see me, I loudly walked by her house, throwing myself to the ground with a sharp cry.

I allowed the tears to spring to my eyes, though my deceitful injury caused me no real pain. The bruising I sustained from the attack days before was enough to make the woman cringe. She forced her husband to carry me into their home.

She rushed about her house, gathering supplies to wrap my ankle before the swelling set in. She was kind and I nearly felt bad about tricking her.

The husband watched me closely, looking for any signs that I was dangerous. I let a few more tears glide down my cheeks and it seemed to alleviate any fears he had.

The wife sat with me, ordering her husband to fetch me some water. He reluctantly turned and walked toward their kitchen. She shifted closer to me and stroked my hair to comfort me, asking me questions about myself.

I gave her a false name and told her my parents were gone. Making her believe I was working day-to-day to earn money for food was easy. She believed every word I said as I teared up on her couch.

I leaned back against the arm of the couch and settled in, as if grateful to be somewhere warm and clean for the time being. When she asked me to spend the night, I declined.

She insisted I let her feed me before I made any decisions. They allowed me to eat their food and made sure I was comfortable. The couple moved to the kitchen to speak to one another and I stood from my resting place and pathetically tried to escape without them noticing, not wanting to be an imposition. I intentionally let them catch me hobbling away and they forced me back inside where I would spend the night.

It was glorious to sleep on a couch again. The last time I had spent the night in a home was when I trained with Brittella. I sank into an easy sleep, certain I had nothing to fear from the couple. I had played on their every trigger. The list that Lowell gave me had helped immensely to know which tricks to use.

The couple had never had children of their own, but the wife had a soft spot for them, and her husband had a soft spot for her. When *she* decided to take me in, he did as she wanted.

Morning came and I found myself awake before either of them rose. I stayed nestled on the couch, peeking out from under my nearly-closed lashes. My eyes searched the room until I found several places I wanted to check for the lock.

I ate when they offered me breakfast, the warm food tasting like Heaven. I nearly felt bad for deceiving them, but then I remembered what Lowell had told me they had done. They were aiding our enemy and damaging Lowell's plans. I couldn't understand how any group would work against people that were working to bring down our corrupt government, but still, they were.

Later, when the husband left for work, the wife let me rest awhile on my own as she attended to her laundry outside. I immediately sprang in to action, checking the areas I had isolated as possible lock locations. I focused on the window, watching her every move as I raced around the room.

On the fourth try, I found what I was looking for. Hidden behind a false wall, there was a lock. I inserted the key and it clicked open. Reaching inside, I pulled out the contents and shoved them into my hidden pouch on the inside of my dress skirt.

I settled myself back down, then pretended to struggle to get back up almost immediately as the wife walked into the room.

"Are you leaving, dear?"

"Yes, I have to work, but thank you so much for your graciousness. I would have been lost without you."

I allowed her to fawn and fret over me for a few moments before she insisted I take a meal with me. She watched as I hobbled away, never knowing what I had done. I was certain I saw tears in her eyes as I rounded the final corner out of her sight.

For a woman who had known me for less than a day, I had certainly managed to attach myself to her. Perhaps I really *was* ready for whatever Lowell had planned for me.

Chapter 9

Once I made it to the woods, I left my fake limp behind and picked up my pace back to the temporary campsite. When I heard the snap off to my right I froze.

"Hello, little girl," a voice said. I knew I was in trouble. "Where are you off to this fine day?"

Without looking back, I broke into a run. I heard several sets of footsteps following me. I was grateful I had several yards on them but they started to gain speed.

I searched for a tree to climb. If I could reach the top, I could move from tree to tree faster than they could follow me. Unfortunately, I found no such option, the trees being too far spaced out in those woods.

One man caught up with me, and I dove at a tree branch. As he moved to wrap his arms around my waist, I flung myself upward, lifting my feet so he hit nothing but empty space. He crashed to the ground and I landed on top of him, intentionally digging my heels into his back as I pushed off of him.

With his knife in my hand, I turned and whirled it at the oncoming men. It found its mark and sank into the lead man's shoulder. He skidded to a stop, hindering the other men as he thrashed to remove it from his flesh.

The mercenaries advanced on me, intent on gaining their prize. If caught, I would be sold to the soldiers to be sent to the camps. The reward was enough to make the men vicious and relentless.

Knowing I could no longer outrun them, I turned to face them. They weren't expecting me to stop, and the surprised moment gave me just enough time to knock out the man closest to me.

A second man tackled me, pinning me to the ground.

"This one is a fighter," he grinned at his only remaining companion.

"Get her up, let's go," the second man commanded.

They struggled to get me to my feet as I ferociously fought against them. My hand found a branch and I brought it to the first man's head, a painful crack echoing in the forest.

I swung the branch toward the second man, connecting with such force that it shattered the branch. I ran. I dared one glance back, but the men were not following me. Rather, they were staggering to their feet, trying to get their bearings.

I had never run so fast in my life. I threw myself into the camp and screamed that the men may be following me. A wall of our men formed, ready for the mercenaries to approach. When they did, their fate was sealed.

My heartbeat pounded in my ears and all I could feel were the jarring effects of my feet crashing against the ground and my heart beating against my chest as I ran further into the camp.

I slammed against Shadoe as he stepped into my path, ready to catch me.

"Where's Lowell?" I shouted, struggling to get by him.

"Slow down, Lur." He tried to calm me, but I pushed forward out of his grasp.

"Where is he?" I whipped around, running backward so I could face him.

"Over there." He pointed.

I turned and ran, feet still flying.

I knew I was safe, I was back with the fold and there was no reason to fear those men any longer. I wasn't afraid, but the adrenaline from the chase still coursed through my body and I needed to work it out.

In my bag, I held the final piece, the last part of the plan before Lowell would tell me everything. It had been years waiting for this moment; years of training, years of waiting, and now finally, *finally*, I would know why I had to do it all.

Lowell's eye darted to me as I crashed into view. I didn't bother to hide my footfall; I wanted him to know I was approaching. He immediately sent away the men he was talking to and waited for me to draw near enough that he didn't have to shout.

"Did you…?" he began.

"It's here," I gasped, cutting him off. "It's here."

His face radiated with what I could only conclude was absolute joy as he stretched out his hand to me.

Opening the pouch on my hip, I carefully took out the papers I had worked so hard to protect, even through the fight. I knew I was smiling, and tried to suppress my grin.

He appraised me for a moment before taking the papers from my hand. The glint in his eyes told me he thought I was ready to take on the mission he had been grooming me for.

I waited as he opened the papers, eyes glancing over them. He thumbed through the small stack of pages. The way his eyes darted suggested he was looking for something specific, but they lingered just long enough to confirm he wanted to read every word scribbled in his hands.

I felt Shadoe step up behind me, his presence having become so well known to me, that I was certain I would always be able to tell when he was near. He hovered just behind my shoulder, not near enough to touch me, but enough for his heat to warm my arm.

He let out a short, tiny breath just forceful enough to send my below waist length hair dancing. For a moment, I wanted to close my eyes and tilt my head up to feel the slight breeze linger in the air as it caressed my face and moved my golden locks, but I remained still, terrified that if I moved, I might break the trance Lowell was in as he digested the information on the papers I had acquired.

Lowell looked up and nodded to Shadoe. As Shadoe stepped forward, everything in me sank. Once again, I was to be left out.

Stepping forward, I opened my mouth to speak, but Shadoe silenced me with a barely noticeable shake of the head. I was commanded to wait.

They walked away, leaving me alone. Perhaps I would never be as important as Lowell said I would be; Shadoe certainly was though.

Chapter 10

ONE WEEK PASSED WITHOUT A WORD FROM LOWELL. SHADOE REFUSED to speak about their meeting.

A second week and I put aside any hopes of knowing.

A third week and stories started to surface about the people we would be fighting against. I even heard drunken tales of them really being wild animals, ravaging the people working against the Society from the safety of the woods. I didn't put much faith in these tales, nor would I believe anything until it came from Lowell himself.

I worked my hair back into a long braid that traveled the length of my back. It was warm, and I wanted it out of my way as I trained. Venturing into the woods, I carried a few extra knives with me, wrapped tightly in a carrier slung across my back.

Finding a tree deep in the heart of the woods and far from prying eyes, I released them one after the other. They found their marks almost every time. When they all rested in the trunk of the trees, I slipped low to the ground, resting against a large rock.

Sitting, I waited for clarity.

I knew Lowell's mission was important: we needed to stop the Society. What I couldn't understand was how long we had to wait to make any advancements on Lowell's plan. I had been with Lowell's fold for so long that, I couldn't even remember what it was like to live in my aunt's house. I had known about Lowell's master plan since my arrival, and still, I knew no details. My training was complete, my entire life had been planned, and still I sat in the middle of the forest, alone and waiting.

"Must you lurk, Shadoe?" I asked, finally.

"You're getting better at this, Lur."

"I've been good at this for a long time now, Shadoe," I corrected as he took a seat near me.

"He's going to tell you soon, you know."

"I'm sure he will," I replied absentmindedly.

"It's happening soon, Lur. Very soon—" He glanced at me long enough to make eye contact before looking back to the knives in the bark across from us.

"You're vital to this. If you fail, we all fail."

"How reassuring," I sniped.

"Pull it together, Lur," he suddenly shouted, whipping toward me. "We need a fighter, not some little girl. You're better than this, so stop sulking and pull it together."

"Well, excuse me for wanting to spend some time as weak little *Auluria* and not trained fighter *Lur!*" I spit back at him, feeling my anger rising.

"You *are* a fighter, *Auluria*. You haven't been a weak little girl in *years* and you know it. Don't go soft on us now. *Pull it together*. Prove to Lowell, and to me, that you can do this."

He was on his feet and walking toward the knives in the trees. Knowing what was coming, I ducked behind the rock I had been leaning against and pulled my last remaining knife out of my boot.

He turned and flung a knife at me, just as I released mine. It caught his sleeve and pinned his arm to the tree. I heard the fabric rip as he pulled away, muttering unkind words.

His knife had been sent off course when mine collided with his sleeve and it clattered against the rock. I scooped it up in case he tried again. He didn't.

He glared at me for a moment before walking over to me and transferred the knives into my arms. Slowly, I put them back into the carrier I laid out on top of the rock.

Shadoe walked away without another word. I nearly followed him, but decided against it. I would be attached to Shadoe for the rest of my life; there was no need to spend all of my time following his leadership.

After a few moments, I started back toward the camp. All of

nature seemed to guide my steps as I slowly made my way back. By the time I reached the fold, my anger had dissipated.

I put the weapons away in my tent before wandering to the edge of the camp.

"Well, if it isn't the pickpocket," an eager voice shouted.

"Leave me alone, Locust," I said, brushing past him.

"What's the matter, having a lover's quarrel?" He grinned. "Because I can help with that."

The girl sitting near him frowned. She looked ready to slit his throat, and I'm sure if she thought Lowell would let it slide, she would have.

I turned and walked away from where they were sitting. I had never taken the time to be social with most of Lowell's people and I wasn't about to start at that point. I made it half way around the perimeter before I heard people starting to pack.

"What's going on?" I asked a red haired young man.

"We're leaving. Second to last stop before we enact the plan." His voice radiated excitement.

I nodded and started off to my own tent. The center of camp was crowded as young people darted back and forth getting in the way.

I made it back to my tent and gathered my belongings. Within minutes I was packed and had my tent down and ready to be moved.

Shadoe kept his distance as we walked. I knew he was keeping an eye on me, but he was far enough behind me that I didn't have to see or think about him.

I watched as perfect, blonde Anetta attached herself to Lowell's side, forcing the other girls away. They huffed as they slipped away. Anetta giggled as Lowell talked to her. I was surprised she was still hanging on to him after all this time.

Walking gave me time to think—but I had no desire to think. Instead, I tried to focus on my surroundings. I memorized every tree, every cloud, every star that eventually forced its way into the darkening sky.

A cool wind swept back my hair and made me shudder. The walk took an exceptionally long time. It was the next afternoon before we finally settled in a hidden field far from the town.

I slowed my pace near the end of the trip, falling to the back of the group, not wanting to be surrounded by the fold. Once they were distracted by setting up their tents, I slipped away into the trees.

When I neared the town, something inside of me sparked. Recognition.

I had grown up in that town, many lifetimes ago. My aunt's house was nestled in the far end of the town, still close enough to the center to have access to food, but far enough away that prying eyes weren't a terrible plague.

I had to see it. The house.

When I arrived, I waited down the street, watching for signs of new owners. When I was satisfied that I was alone, I crept toward the building. The windows were dirty, but I could tell the house was not being used.

I assumed Lowell had kept it under his control, so I pried the door open and stepped inside. It was almost as I had left it on the day Lowell came for me.

The couch still sat against the same wall. The table in the kitchen had been moved in what I assumed must have been an effort to facilitate the meetings I knew Lowell must have occasionally held there in the infrequent times he had visited the home since I left.

My room was tiny, barely a closet, but the bed still sat, waiting for the little girl to come back to it. I wanted desperately to throw myself into its painfully comforting holds and stay there until I was a child again.

I breathed in the dust-saturated air and stifled a cough. Despite its latent appearance, that place was the last time I felt cared for. I was grateful to Lowell for taking me in and training me, but at least with my aunt I felt... Like I had some real human contact.

Going back to the couch, I removed a sheet and settled myself onto the bare cushions. Throwing my hands over the armrest on one side, I relaxed my head down until I was cradling my face in my arms.

Sleep came quickly, deeply, and desperately.

The next morning, I expected to find myself being dragged back to the camp by one of Lowell's men, but no one came for me. I was sure Lowell must have known where I was; Lowell was aware of everything it seemed.

Making my way to the back of the house, I found the trap door that led down into the earth. Lowell had insisted we have such a hiding place when his mother was still alive. He installed it long before I lived with my aunt, but only toward the end of my stay with her did I know of its existence.

Crawling down the steps into the ground, I felt the temperature change immediately. The cool earth gave off a damp smell and made me wrinkle my nose.

I had hoped to find Lowell had kept the secret place stocked with food, but when I swept my head from side to side, I discovered it to be empty. Climbing back out, I closed the door and hid it once more.

Outside, people had begun to trade and sell their goods. I watched as two of Lowell's men slipped through the crowd and met a third man: one of our spies. I kept out of sight, hoping they wouldn't report back to Lowell.

I wasn't worried about being recognized in the town; it had been so long since any of them had seen me. Most never knew who I was to begin with; my aunt tried to keep us as far from the public eye as possible knowing the dangers, especially for a young girl.

I recognized a few faces as I worked my way through the crowd, but no one that stood out. Finding food, I paid for it, and started back toward my aunt's home.

I ate as I walked, ducking my head low so as not to draw attention. When I heard the scream, I was so shocked I nearly dropped my last bite of bread.

I looked up just in time to see a young girl being pulled down the street. Several men surrounded her. They clamped their hands around her mouth to muffle her cries. The Society guards dragged her away as she fought against them.

I lurched forward, willing myself to run to her aid. Before I could move, they dropped her dead body to the ground. She had struggled too much and her movements caused them to restrain her to the point of snapping her neck. Her lifeless body toppled to the ground with a heart-wrenching thud.

As they looked up, I darted behind a corner. All I could think of was that despite the fact that she was dead, at least she wasn't taken to those horrible camps. She was free now.

Once inside my aunt's house, I closed the door and took a post at the window. Watching, I waited for the men to come for me. When I felt it was safe, I made my way further into the house.

If Lowell created the secure room, he probably hid other things in the house too.

Moving methodically from one room to the next, I forced

thoughts of the dead girl out of my head. I searched each room, finding several hiding places, all of which were empty.

The Society did that to her. They caused her death. They need to be destroyed.

My hands brushed along the walls, looking for anything irregular about them. The floors were an obvious place to search. Inside of cabinets and within doors, I found deceptive recesses that Lowell must have once used to conceal items.

I will do whatever it takes to stop the Society. For that girl... For all of us.

Lowell proved to be very good at hiding things. I found twenty-three unique hiding places in my aunt's house.

If only we could hide from the Society so easily.

I covered up the hidden places once more, leaving them to rest in the peace my presence had disturbed. I hid one knife in the hardest of the places to find, deep in the heart of the house. Should I ever need to return, it would be there, waiting for me.

Sleep eluded me that night. The moon glistened off the floor, bouncing through the window and cascading around the walls. It illuminated my thoughts and brought clarity to the muddled confusion.

By morning, I knew I would have to return to Lowell's camp. I would do as he asked, knowing how important it was to free the people from the Society's rule.

Once Lowell had completed his master plan, he would set the Society straight, and we could fight off the villains on the other side of the wall that had been terrorizing us. Lowell would make things right, and Shadoe and I would help him succeed.

I slipped into town that afternoon, hoping to gather intelligence for Lowell before my return. I was certain he'd be upset over my absence and I needed to make up for it.

I followed a set of Society soldiers as they made their way through the town, taking what they wanted and forcing people out of their way. I thought once to send a knife into the back of their heads, but I had never been able to handle such disregard for life.

Following them, I watched them enter a tavern late that evening. I had hoped to find where they went, but I knew they would offer no further information to me beyond those walls.

I slept soundly on the pathetic couch in my aunt's house, waking early and making my way back to the tavern in time to see the same two men stumble out. Several others cast them disgusted looks, knowing soldiers weren't supposed to behave like that.

By the end of the day, I had spoken to several men from the town, learning more about the soldier's schedules. I tested their knowledge and returned to my aunt's home with several stolen Society weapons to prove the point.

Knowing it would be my last night with a real couch, I slept early. The crickets sang as I slipped into a fitful sleep. Thoughts of Lowell's master plan and what it might entail invaded my dreams. Early in the morning I sank into a comfortable rest.

"Auluria?" Lowell said, appearing in front of me. "I think we should talk."

I sat up, staring at the only remaining family I had left. Of course he had known where I had been.

"Things are progressing and we're ready to start activating our plan. Are you ready for that?"

"Yes," I answered truthfully. I'd been waiting for this day for a long time.

"Good." He motioned for me to get up and follow him to the kitchen table.

"I'm ready to do whatever you need me to do, Lowell," I informed him as he walked away, giving me enough time to focus myself.

"I have information on the Society soldier's schedules in the town here," I added, making sure he knew I had helpful information for him.

"Good," he called. "We can use that."

When I rounded the corner, I found him already sitting in one of the chairs, papers spread out in front of him.

"It's time we talk about your targets, Auluria," he said, motioning me to sit. "These people are incredibly bad; they're the reason the Society continues to exist. Those papers you procured for us from the house with the lock, gave us their current location."

I met his eyes and saw hatred in them. I steeled myself for the next words out of his mouth as he handed me papers, much like the information I had learned about the couple with the lock I had broken into.

I took the papers without looking at them, focusing on Lowell's bitterly angry words. They came out like venom, laced with vindication.

"It's time we talk about Berwyn Baer and his kid brother."

ACKNOWLEDGMENTS

Thank you all so much for joining me on this trip into Auluria's past. And, yes, that *was* a little glimpse of you-know-who tucked away in there! I figured we'd *all* appreciate that!

Special thanks to my amazing Robins-you all are incredible and I couldn't be more grateful to you all for your willingness to help and support me as my Street Team.

Extra special thanks to Yentl, Jess, Danna, Sissy, and Alexis for going above and beyond as my Elites. You all are the best! I can't even tell you how cool you ladies are! You're the most fabulous support system a lady could ask for! *high five* and *confetti*

So much love to Awnna for being so wonderful through this process and Elissa for always stepping up and going above and beyond! Thank you, thank you, thank you.

And to you, dearest reader of mine, I thank you for sticking with me. If you're here, that means you've been through Golden and have fallen for this charming little tale of mine and I could not be more thrilled that you're continuing this journey with me. I adore you-I hope you know that!

That being said—reach out. Contact me on social media, send me an email, or chat with me during a live broadcast. I want to be friends! My social media door is always open to you and I'd love to chat and get to know you better! Please don't ever hesitate to reach out!

I can't wait for you to read the sequel to Golden where we see some of these people make new appearances in the Golden tale, and see how some of Auluria's past ends up playing a role in her future. It's going to be magnificent!

Until then,

Stay inspired,

-K.M.

TEMPERED

A GOLDEN TRILOGY PREQUEL NOVELLA

To those who have been through the worst in this life and decided to be a light in the darkness anyway.

The story of Goldilocks touches on what the Baers went through when she disrupted our lives, but my story started long before she woke up in my house.

What they forget to talk about during her story is what led up to the Baers' demise. They skip over everything we went through before she came crashing into our lives. They never mention what I had to go through to be turned into the man she met that day in the woods.

My name is Dov Baer, but once upon a time, I wasn't the leader of my people. I was a young boy, thrown into power at an early age, fighting to protect my family and myself. This is the story of what caused me to become part of Goldilocks' legend.

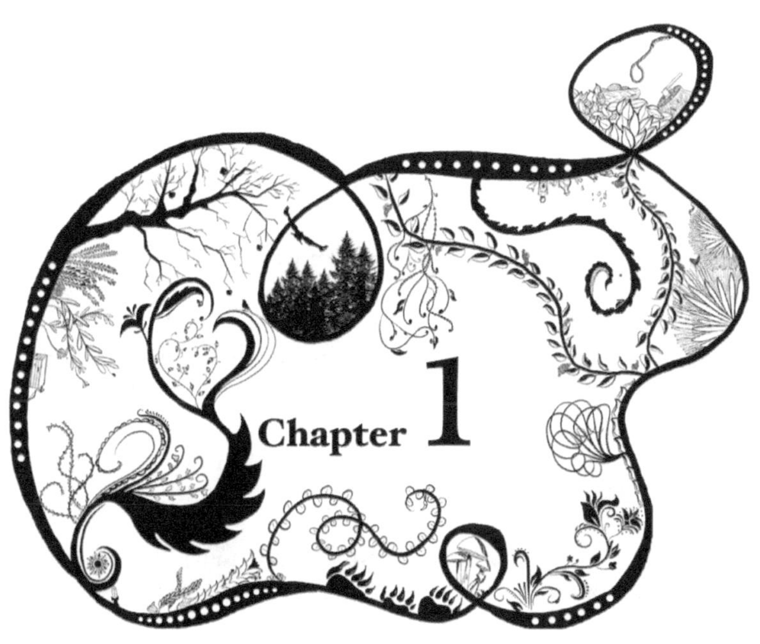

Chapter 1

"Get up," Berwyn sounded angry.

"I'm up," I mumbled, rolling over on the cot. I untangled myself from the sheets, setting my feet on the cold floor.

"We have places to be, baby brother, now let's move," Berwyn chides.

"How are you up before me?" I run my fingers through my hair, working out a couple of knots. "You're never up this early."

"Only when we have a mission."

"We're going on a mission?" I asked, now fully awake.

"Dad has somewhere for us to be today—now, let's go."

"Okay, I'm up, I'm up." I scrambled to get dressed and pull my boots on. "What's the mission?"

"We're going to town," Berwyn said, grabbing a few berries from the bowl on the table. "We have a contact to meet."

"Is Dad coming too?" I hurried to the table to grab something to eat before we left.

"Yes, he wants to introduce us to the contact so that we can run messages for him."

"Ready, boys?" Dad asked, strolling into the room with an easy smile.

We nodded and followed him outside. I grabbed a few berries to take along the way.

The trees were bathed in yellow light. I ducked under the low branches next to my dad as I walked beside him—I was quickly approaching his height. To be fair, neither Berwyn nor I would ever be as tall as Griz Baer was, but I was happy with catching up.

"Apple?" he asked, pulling one down from a branch as we passed.

Berwyn reached up, plucking his own from the tree. I bit into the one my father tossed to me, the flavor making my jaw tingle into my ears—it was *perfect*.

"Where are we headed?" I asked, crunching on another bite of the apple.

"I need to take you two to meet someone today," Dad says, glancing over at Berwyn. "He used to be one of Lowell's contacts, but now that he's taking a step back, I need you two to step up and fill the void."

He put Lowell's probation in a softer light than he should have.

"Have you talked to him recently?" Berwyn asked, looking at our father out of the corner of his eye.

"Yes, we've talked," Dad nodded. "He understands that he needs to stay on course if he wishes to continue working with us to bring down the Society and restore a more peaceful nation. He's been doing well accommodating his restrictions."

Berwyn ducked under a tree branch as we stepped out of the woods. The dirt road was packed down so hard that the dust didn't even kick up as we walk into the town.

People bustled by, trading goods and having conversations. I waved to a guy my age sitting in his father's shop as he worked. Peter and his father secretly worked with our family, acting as our lookouts in the town—one of many.

We wove our way around carts and tables, only stopping once or twice to pick a few supplies up. Berwyn kept a watchful eye on me as if I might wander off, but my father's wink softened the oversight.

"This is Lionel," Dad nodded ahead, waving his hand slightly. "He's your new contact."

Lionel greeted my father warmly as we approached.

"Griz," he said, smiling. "Glad you made it. Lowell still on probation?"

"He is," my father answered. "He's coming around though. I think he just needed to get it out of his system. For now, you're going to be working with my boys. You remember Berwyn and Dov, right?"

"I do. Hello, boys." He smiled politely at us. "It's been quite a while since I've seen either of you. You were both pretty young the last time I was out your way. It's nice to officially meet you again."

"Nice to meet you, Lionel," Berwyn greeted him.

"Let's take a little walk," Lionel said as he turned. "I'll show you our locations for meetings."

He guided us around the town to several places, telling us what signals to watch for at each location so we would know when it was safe to approach. It was nice that he included me as part of the team— usually Berwyn did most of the work because he was older and respected more.

"Dov," my dad pulled me back as Lionel showed Berwyn around. "I know you've been looking to take on more authority in the group. I'd like to expand some of your responsibilities, starting with this. You've been handling quite a bit of the lower-level work with our contacts, but now I want you to start taking on more of our crucial work. I've already started Berwyn, but now it's your turn."

"I'd like that," I answered.

"You've been doing a great job, son," he replied. "I think you have a real talent for this. Silas too. I'd like to give him more responsibility as well. I've already spoken to his father about it. You two make a great team, and I'd like to pair you together for a few missions."

Silas was like a brother to Berwyn and me. The only thing that truly separated us was having different parents. Silas had been with us for as long as I could remember—our mothers were good friends when they were younger.

"That would be great, Dad."

"I need you to pay close attention to this. Lionel will be your brother's contact, but you'll need to meet with him on occasion too. You and Silas are going to be doing more intelligence gathering for me rather than this type of work, but you'll still need to be familiar with it. Think you can handle that?"

"Absolutely," I confirmed. I was beginning to like this trip.

"Good. Pay attention—I'm sending you back here later," he warned me.

I watched everywhere we went, trying to commit it all to memory. *I'd be back soon.*

"Lionel," I greeted him quietly, slipping up next to the man at a stand. He looked at a pile of apples, examining each one before setting them back down.

"Dov, Silas," he responded without looking at us. "Do you have it?"

I took the bag off my shoulder, letting it rest in my hand. Lionel casually reached down and took it from me, shifting it onto his own shoulder after a minute.

"That one, please," he said, pointing to a small basket of apples. "Thanks."

He handed the man money for his purchase and turned to me.

"Well, it's been a few weeks, how do you boys think it's going?" he asked.

"I feel like I've learned a lot," Silas responded. "Griz has been sending us on a lot of missions—I think we've done well."

"I agree," I added. "I feel like I have a much better grasp on doing reconnaissance work. Yesterday, we helped Arin out with a mission."

"That's good," Lionel responded. "Have you seen Peter yet today?"

"We stopped there first. He's actually coming back with us for a few days."

"Dov!" We heard him before we saw him in the crowd.

"Speaking of..." Silas mumbled quietly.

"Dov," Peter was out of breath when he approached me. He breathed heavily as he rested a hand on my shoulder, bent over to try to regulate his oxygen intake. "There's a problem."

"What's wrong?" Lionel asked, taking over.

"Something happened in the next town over," Peter gasped. "I don't know what it is, but my father sent me to find you. They're blaming your father for something. You need to go warn him."

Silas' face matched my own. Lionel gripped my shoulder, turning me to face him.

"Now, listen, Dov. You go find your father, and then send Arin to meet me by the edge of town. I'm going to do some digging today to find out what happened." He turned to Peter. "I want you to go with them and make sure everyone is in a safe location until we know what is going on. I'll send your father after you—don't go back to him."

We nodded.

"Go quickly and don't come back until we know what's happened. Avoid the Society men at all costs," he added. Lionel pushed us down the street, away from the town. "Hurry and don't get caught."

We rushed through the streets as quickly as we could without running. Once we reached the woods, we took off, racing as fast as possible up hills and under low tree branches.

"How bad is this?" I asked when we were far enough away that we wouldn't be overheard.

"Bad," Peter shook his head. "I don't know what happened, but, Dov, they're coming for your dad. I don't think its safe."

I took a deep breath, forcing myself not to stop running to process his words. We'd figure something out—we always did.

"What do you think Griz is going to do?" Silas wondered, darting around a tangled mass of roots sticking out of the ground.

"I don't know, but I think it's a smart idea to get him where the Society can't find him," I replied, using my hand to lift a branch as I fly under it. It snapped back behind me when I let it go.

"That's probably a good idea," Silas commented.

"Where will he go?" Peter asked, trying to keep up with us. He spent most of his life in the town, leaving him without our strict training and physical conditioning. He had done some of it with us, just not to the extent we had been trained.

"We have a few safe houses that we keep for this reason. We've also got the storehouses if we need somewhere else to stay," I informed him. "We have options—Dad has always been prepared."

"I have a feeling you'll be staying with us for a while, Peter," Silas mused as he pulled forward just enough to make Peter work harder to keep up. We were trying to do our best to wait for him, but we needed to get back to the group.

"Can't say it would be the worst thing in the world," Peter tried to grin. "Almost there."

He lowered his head as he pushed forward, trying to make the last bit of the sprint to the storehouse where we would find my father. We burst through doors, causing everyone within a twenty-foot radius to turn to us.

I scanned the crowd, searching for my father and Berwyn. The great Griz Baer leans around Arin to look at me. When he saw the look on my face, he marched over to me, Arin and my brother close behind.

"Peter and his father sent word that there was an incident in the next town over," I reported. "We don't know what is it yet—Lionel was going to look into it—but the Society is blaming you. We were sent to tell you."

My father's face paled.

"We had a mission there today." His voice was low and gravelly, a sign that he was worried. "We need to check on our men."

He moved toward the door, but Silas and I blocked him.

"You can't," I protested. "They're looking for you."

"I'll go," Berwyn volunteered.

I shook my head.

"Lionel said to send Arin," I responded, turning to the tall man. "You need to meet him by the edge of town for a report."

Arin turned to look at my father. After a long pause, Dad released him to go investigate.

"We think you need to stay in a safe house," I proposed. "We can't have the Society catch you before we even know what is going on."

"Dov, I know your heart is in the right place, but I'm not just going to leave our men out there to face the Society on their own." He stooped down to place his hand on my shoulder and looked me in the eyes. "I'll be okay. You wait here with your brother and I'll be back soon."

"I think you need to stay," Berwyn objected. "*I just….*you need to stay."

Berwyn didn't often have trouble with words, so it got my father's attention.

"You really think so?"

"I do," Berwyn nodded emphatically.

"Sometimes our bodies know things our brains don't, boys. *Sometimes*, you need to listen to that intuition." He took a step back. "We'll wait for Arin to report back."

Relief flooded over me. I watched as he wandered over to a group of people to start informing them of what was going on. I knew he wouldn't take this sitting down—he'd start making a plan immediately.

"At least we got him to stay," Silas murmured next to me.

"*Berwyn* got him to stay," I corrected him, running my hand through my hair.

"Yeah, let's remember that trick next time," Silas smirked.

"Good call," I grin. "Hey, where did Peter go?"

"He's over there talking to the girls," Silas waved in their general direction.

"Oh," I replied, looking down. I shouldn't have been surprised

Peter would be taking advantage of spending time with the girls while he was here—he doesn't get to see them often. "Maybe you should go and talk to them too."

He shrugged as if it didn't matter, but it did. I knew Silas had a fondness for one of the girls but hadn't said anything to her yet.

"Maybe *you* should, buddy. *You're* the one they all dote over."

"Yeah," I rolled my eyes. "That's only because I'm Berwyn's brother and Dad's son."

"Probably," he agreed. His face lit up mischievously. If we weren't inside, I would have pummeled him. Too bad he was aware of that too and played into it. "But we've got to find you a girl *somehow*, my friend. *Take what you can get.*"

"Did I just hear you say that you're available, Dov?" a soft voice interrupted the conversation.

"Hi, Kat," Silas greeted Katarina, swinging around. "Long time, no see."

"Hello, Silas," she purred, sidling up next to him. She waved her hand around at the various meetings happening in the room. "You want to tell me what's going on or do I have to flirt with Dov to get it out of you two?"

Silas grinned, having much more fun with the conversation than I was—he wiped the look off his face before answering.

"It looks like one of our missions went sideways, and the Society figured out we were involved. We're waiting to see what happens."

Katarina pulls an apple out of her bag.

"When was the last time you boys ate?" she asked, twisting the apple in her hand. "You two should eat something now, in case you don't have time later."

"What's going on?" Reyla demanded playfully as she approached.

"Something is up and the boys need to eat before they go running off to handle it," Katarina announced. Silas grew quiet.

"We'll be okay," I supplied, "but thank you, Katarina."

"Fine, be that way." She sashayed away. "But don't say I didn't warn you."

"Okay," I called after her, turning back to Silas. Reyla followed after her friend. "You know, she was probably right."

"So, we'll go find food. It's probably a wise choice for your father to eat too. Let's go grab something for him."

We spend the next hour foraging for food and information.

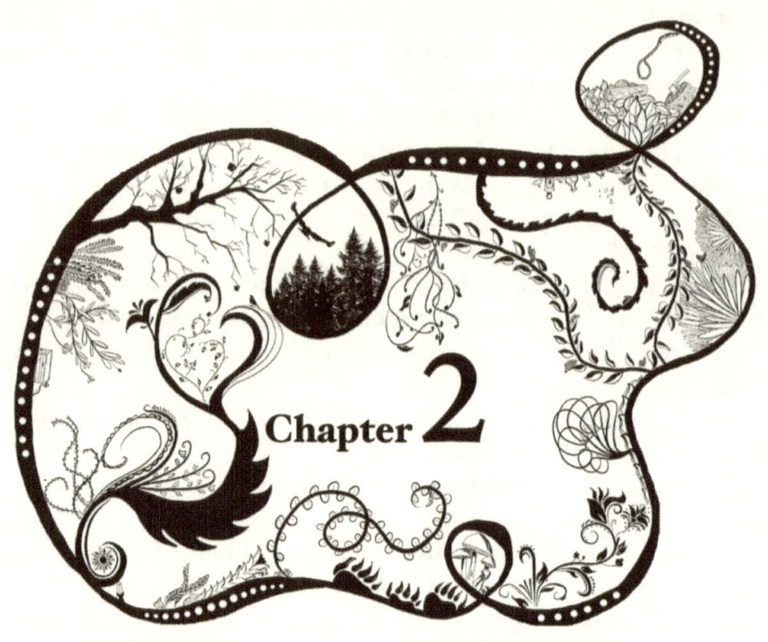

Chapter 2

BERWYN BARRELED IN THE DOOR AHEAD OF ARIN, YELLING. ARIN STAYED close on his heels, running straight toward my father. Dad slowed them down with hands in the air.

"What happened?" Dad asked.

"They're coming for us," Berwyn announced, glancing at me—I've never seen him so worried in my life.

"Sir, the Society is calling for your execution."

Everything inside of me dropped to my feet. I felt as though I had been punched, but hadn't doubled over yet. I couldn't breathe, couldn't move, couldn't think.

Once the Society called for an enemy's execution, they wouldn't stop until they found them and hanged them. There was very little hope of escaping—and hiding could only last for so long.

When the walls finished caving in on me, I looked to my father for his reaction.

"We need to get everyone underground," he said, thinking of our people first. "The Society is after me, and they'll use any and all of you to find me."

He turned, spinning to address the group.

"The Society is coming after us. They are specifically looking for me. Whatever happened today during the mission in town, it has led the Society to search for us. Go to your homes, get your families, and get them to the safe houses and storehouses. We'll be sending representatives to each location—get to your assigned place and wait for directions. Don't leave anyone behind! Make sure everyone gets out!"

The crowd broke away from each other, rushing toward the exits. The place quickly emptied.

"Lionel and his wife volunteered to stay. They weren't compromised," Arin informed us as we turned to face him. "He's going to tell the others to join us, but if anyone wants to stay and is sure they aren't compromised, they're going to stay put."

"I don't like that," Dad growled.

"It doesn't matter—it's done," Berwyn snapped at him. "You need to get to a safe house and let the rest of us handle working with the contacts."

"*You're* not going anywhere, Berwyn. You and Dov are banned from leaving this storehouse, and if you can't abide by that, I'll lock the two of you in one of those tiny safe houses with me until this is over," Dad threatened him. "You're my sons and if they catch you, they will do unspeakable things to you to get to me—you are not leaving my sight."

Berywn looked ready to argue, but he refrained. I trusted my father's judgment, but I didn't like the idea of not being able to help.

"How long are we here for?" I asked.

"Until it's safe, Dov. I don't know how long that will be." He sounded helpless. "Arin, you should go check on our people. The boys and I will start to set this place up for people to move in."

Arin nodded and took off out the door, leaving Berwyn, Silas, and me to stand in silence with my father.

"Boys," my dad turned to us, "this is going to get complicated very fast. We have a lot of people about to move into this storehouse. It's going to get cramped and people are going to start to frustrate other people. Our job is to keep the peace and keep morale up. Do you understand?"

We all nodded silently.

"Good, now, we need to move these tables and clear out space for people to sleep on the floor. We'll need areas for families with younger children, areas for older children, and space for the adults without children." He pointed around the room, guiding us. "Get all of the food and supplies moved to that side and put anything extra in the rooms back there.

"We don't have long, so let's hurry."

Together, we rushed around the large room, moving supplies from one place to another to clear off the long tables we had built inside to hold food and goods that our people would need. We repositioned tables and transferred everything we could to areas that would better accommodate a shared living space.

The first few families started to arrive as we were finishing and helped us move the tables and goods. I was exhausted by the time a steady stream of people arrived.

They all claimed spaces on the floor, setting up the few possessions they brought with them—mostly clothing and blankets. We directed them where to go as they walked through the doors to help ensure everyone found enough space.

"Dad," Silas called as his father walked in. The man waved us over as he walked to my father. We hurried over.

"Gabriel," my father regarded his friend.

"Griz," Silas' father said seriously. "The mission didn't go sideways *accidentally*—"

"What?" my father cut him off.

"It wasn't an accident. Our mission was sabotaged. It turned violent and people died," he paused. "The Society's people died, Griz. They're coming after us for this."

"Who sabotaged us?" Berwyn interjected. *I* already knew.

Gabriel turned to Berwyn and took a deep breath.

"It was Lowell," my father responded, his voice nearly as sad as when we learned my mother had died—Lowell had broken his heart.

Lowell was like another son to my father. He had taken him in after his own father had died and trained him to be a leader. When Lowell acted out, my father had reprimanded him. We all thought he was under control, but apparently not.

"What happened?" His voice came out in a whisper as he dragged his eyes away from Berwyn.

"From what we can tell, Lowell wanted revenge—on the Society and on you for holding him back—so he hijacked our mission and turned it violent. Then he made sure they knew it was your men." He shook his head. "He disappeared, Griz. He's gone."

"He'll be back," my father growled. "He's not going far—he has a point to make."

"It looks like he has some followers too," Gabriel added. "We're missing a few people."

"I know exactly who they are." His misery was written all over his face. Dad's shoulders slumped, and he looked ready to pass out. Dad had never done well with betrayal.

"We'll be okay, Dad," Berwyn told him. He looked as concerned as I felt.

"I know we will," Dad whispered.

"We'll find him," I promised. "We'll find him, and we'll stop him from hurting more people."

"I hope that's true, Dov." He wrapped his arm around my shoulder. "For now, we just need to take care of these people."

Days passed and we settled into life in the storehouse. People began to find their footing inside the space that still felt way too small for me. Berwyn, however, looked ready to break down the door.

"I can't believe he would do this," he muttered, pacing in the corner.

"*I* can't believe we haven't found him," I murmured back.

"Of course we haven't found him, Dov," Berwyn spit at me. "We trained him. He knows how to hide from the Society—it's no different to hide from us."

"He makes a good point," Silas said under his breath. He picked up his head and looked to Berwyn. "Arin hasn't found anything yet?"

"Nothing."

"Do we know anything else about the Society?" I questioned.

We hadn't been let out of the storehouse since everyone moved in. Berwyn and I had been kept out of the loop for a few days, but Dad finally started letting us in on the meetings. Thankfully, Berwyn had convinced him to let us sit in so we could learn how to handle that type of situation.

"Just that they're hunting us. Whatever Lowell did, he made sure the Society wouldn't rest until they've found us." Berwyn shook his head. He released his arms from where they were crossed over his chest and slipped a hand behind his neck to rub it.

"How are we going to protect him?" I asked.

"We can't, baby brother," Berwyn said spitefully. "If he wants to go out, he's going to go out. You can't expect him to sit by and not try to fix the situation."

"I don't expect him to let others do the work while he stays safe in here," I replied, annoyed. "But we're in here and he isn't."

"He'll be back soon," Silas offered. "And my dad is with him. They'll both be safe."

"We need to do something," Berwyn began pacing again, clasping his hands behind his back. "I can't sit in here any longer."

"Maybe we could go collect some food or something," I suggested. "We wouldn't have to go far, but it would get us out of here for a little while."

Berwyn rolled his eyes at me.

"They're back." Silas stood up as our fathers walked in the door.

"Well?" Berwyn beat us all to our father. "What happened?"

"It's bad out there, boys. They found a few of our spies. We're trying to free them now."

"Arin and the guys will get them back," Gabriel tried to convince us. "Silas, a word."

Gabriel waved his son over, pulling him off to the side to talk.

"We need to talk too," my father motions us toward the door—freedom. "Come on."

The fresh air was unimaginably crisp as we walked outside. It hit my lungs, almost burning into them—it was perfect.

The sun filtered through the trees as the late afternoon breeze picked up, rustling the branches. Birds flew from tree to tree, whistling as if all was right with the world.

It's a shame it wasn't.

Dad led us a few yards away from the storehouse entrance—still close enough to see the door, but not close enough to be overheard.

"I'm not going to lie to you boys," he said once we took a seat on a fallen tree trunk. "We're in a bad situation. Lowell stirred up the Society and I don't think this is going away. I think we'll always be looking over our shoulders."

I couldn't help but think that he looked tired. His arms rested on his knees as he leaned forward to talk to us, and his eyes looked heavier than usual. Dad's breathing was deeper than normal, moving his shoulder just a touch more than usual. I felt the weight of what he was carrying—the loss of our mother, the hardships of caring for our people, and the challenges of escaping the Society while trying to bring about the change that would set us free of the oppression that we constantly lived under.

He made eye contact with me and it was like looking in a mirror. Dad, Berwyn, and I shared the same eyes and nose, though Berwyn and I had inherited our mother's smile and thick manes. I realized I was mimicking how he was sitting, leaning forward.

"Boys, we need to talk." I've never liked when he grew serious. I much preferred the happy, carefree version of my father that I knew as a child when he hid the harsh realities of the world from Berwyn and me, and he came home and taught us how to fish and hunt and scout. "I'm not sure there's a way out of this one. If anything happens to me—"

"Nothing is going to happen to you, Dad," Berwyn cut him off. "Don't even talk like that."

"Now, son, I know it's not easy to think about, but if something happens, I need you boys to be prepared." He held up his hand, silencing Berwyn. "Don't cut me off, son."

Berwyn bit his tongue, ducking his head as an indication that he would cooperate.

"Now, if something happens to me, there are a few things you need to know," he continued. "You already know all of the safe houses and storehouses. You know all of our contacts and whom you can trust both in the group and in the towns. We have informants everywhere—if something happens, you need to stay in contact with them.

"Use your resources here—Arin, Gabriel, even Silas at this point. We have a leadership structure set up for a reason. Berwyn, you're going to take over and Dov is going to help you—no excuses. You will both step up and lead these people. Do whatever you need to in order to protect them.

"And boys, take care of each other too. Don't forget to take care of your brother." He looked between us. "Can you do that?"

We both agreed.

"I know it wasn't easy moving on after your mother," he continued, nearly bringing us all to tears. Losing our mother had nearly destroyed us.

A bird flew overhead, chattering. Mom would have loved it, but even thinking of her love for things like that crushed my soul. My father's eyes darkened as he glanced up at the winged creature too.

"I know it won't be easy if anything happens to me, but I need you two to rely on each other." He nodded as if telling us that he believed in us. "Don't get lost in the madness of this world. Our people still need you—they need someone who is going to guide them and help protect them. Don't be like Lowell, as tempting as it may be, boys. Don't drown in that darkness."

"Berwyn, I know you can be a great leader. You've got all the skills to make the necessary choices to protect them and put the group's good above your own wants and desires. When it comes down to it, you'll make the decisions you need to in order to protect all of those people in there and in the other storehouses. I know you will."

Berwyn swallowed hard, nodding as he tried to keep his tears in check.

"Dov," Dad turned to me, "You are filled with so much light and so much goodness. I know you'll keep your brother on the right track. You need to support him and be there for him—he will have some of the toughest choices to make of anyone either of *us* will ever know.

"Leading can be lonely. Don't let him retreat into his position, Dov. Keep him in the world with you, and support him however he needs you to."

"I will." I smiled, reaching out to take his hand. He grinned back, pride radiating across his face.

"Your mother gave me this," he reached inside his collar and pulled out his medallion, "before you boys were born. It was a wedding present, actually."

He handed it to Berwyn to examine. Berwyn's fingers trace over the silver paw print—Mom's symbol to my father.

Dad reached out and took it from him, transferring it to my hands. My fingers traced along the black cord it dangles from. The metal of the bear claw feels cool in my hand despite the fact that it had just been warmed by my brother.

"She gave this to me to symbolize our family. It's a play on words, of course, but this has long been a symbol of the Baers.

"Your mother used to tell me the different parts of the paw represented different things, but you know your mother—always changing her mind." He chuckled. "One day it represented valor and honor and then next it was strength and courage. Whatever I needed to hear that day, she spun it into a fantastic story with sound logic to back it up.

"She used to run her fingers over it as she talked and then tuck it back inside my shirt when she was done, sending me off on my way to take care of whoever needed saving that day." He smiled, fondly remembering her. "She was an incredible woman. I hope the same for you boys one day."

He stretched to the side, digging in his pocket.

"Speaking of which," he said, as he pulled something out and handed it to Berwyn. "This will be yours one day."

Berwyn opened his hand to find our mother's ring. I felt like I was gut-punched.

"And this will be yours, Dov." He lifted the cord in my hand—I would have his medallion one day. "Something from your mother and me for each of you."

He smiled mischievously, holding out both hands. We placed the ring and medallion in his palms.

"Of course, I'll hold on to them for now." He winked making me grin. He was always so good at making us smile.

We spent the next hour talking about Mom and her impact on our lives—she was a brave woman who fought unendingly for us. When we finally slipped back inside, it was beginning to get dark.

Our confinement had only *just* begun.

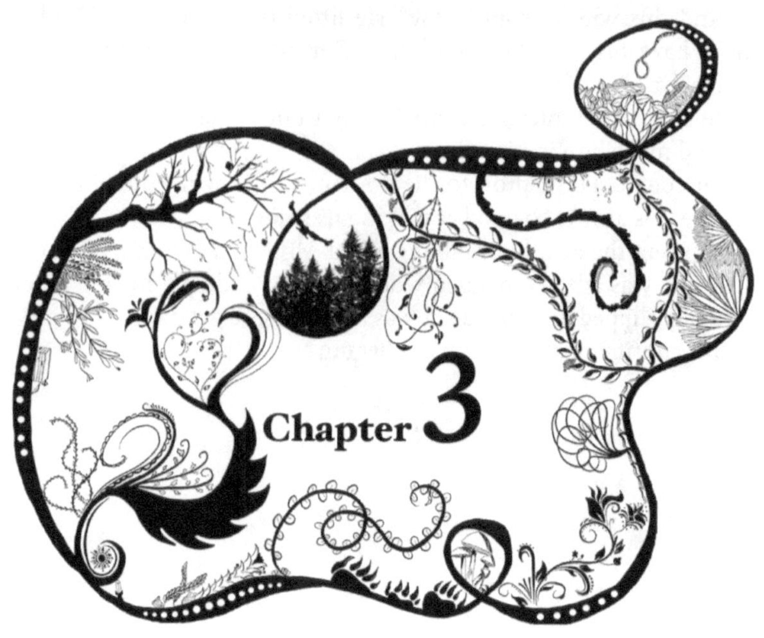

Chapter 3

I CRINGED WHEN HE HIT THE FLOOR. HE STIRRED, GROANING AS HE picked himself up off the ground.

"Next time, you have to block me," I told Peter, motioning for him to lift his hands. "You're improving, but you need to be faster than that."

Six months of hiding inside the storehouse had done nothing for our morale, so we took to training inside the buildings in the afternoons when it got too hot to be outside working. In the underground storehouse, everything felt much cooler.

"Gregory, focus," Silas demanded as Gregory's attention drifted to one of the girls in the corner.

"I'm focused," he joked back, tearing his gaze from Maylin and Reyla as they watched us train.

I ducked as Peter swung at me, nearly connecting when I was distracted by my friends. I lashed out with my foot and he managed to side step my kick.

"Better," I encouraged him.

"You know, this might be more fun if the girls joined us," Peter suggested, lifting his hands to strike. I blocked his punch, sweeping my foot behind his knee. I pulled it out and sent him toppling to the ground.

"You really want them to see *that*, buddy?" Silas smirked.

"Oh, they *definitely* saw that." I reached down to help him up as the girls giggled in the corner. I muttered quietly to Silas, "You know, that *could* be more fun."

"Don't," Silas cautioned. "They have their own training time."

"*Okay,*" I replied dramatically. Despite having feelings toward one of the girls, but he always insisted on keeping a respectful distance—something my father and I agreed with at our young age. There would be plenty of time for dating later. "You're going to need to start being more assertive soon, Silas, or you're going to miss out."

"Yes, because I see *you* being so assertive right now," he quipped, pummeling Gregory.

"Hey!" Gregory yelled as he hit the floor. "You two better watch it or I'll take care of this myself."

"Then the next time, you won't get up off the floor, Gregory," Silas said coolly. After a moment, he grinned, making us both laugh.

"Well, *I'm* happy to go talk to them, if you guys won't," Peter replied, pulling away from us. "I think that's enough for today anyway."

We stared as he walked over to the girls. He would get a girlfriend before any of us ever did.

"You know what," Gregory mumbled. "There's a lot I can learn from you two—*and you'd think with the way the women follow you boys around, I'd be able to learn this too*—but I think this is one thing I'm going to need to learn from Peter. Bye."

Gregory peeled away, following in Peter's footsteps.

"Don't tell me *Gregory* is going to get a date before we are," Silas groaned.

"Probably, at the rate we're going." I shrugged. "We have more important things to do anyway. Careful though, it looks like Peter is moving in on your woman."

We watched for a moment as Peter focused on Silas' crush. Before we could say anything else, we were interrupted.

Arin ran into the room, gathering a group of men.

"*Stay here,*" my father growled a warning when he saw us approach. He pointed his finger at us as he ran out the door.

"Explain," Berwyn snarled, grabbing Gabriel's arm as he rushed past us.

"We're being attacked. They found some of our spies. We're going to rescue them before the Society can execute them."

He pushed away from us, leaving us standing in the doorway.

"Dad just—"

"I know," Berwyn cut me off.

"But he—" I tried to object.

"Walked straight into the Society's hands. I know," Berwyn spoke over me again.

"Berwyn, we can't let him do that," I protested.

"We're not," he said, starting toward the door. "Come on."

"You're not leaving, are you?" Silas put his hand on my shoulder. "They said to stay here."

"Cover for us, Silas," I begged him. "We have to make sure he's okay. We'll be fine."

He looked like he wanted to argue but he bit his tongue.

"Be careful."

"We will. Hold down everything here. We'll be back soon." I nod to him before rushing after Berwyn.

"What's the plan?" I asked, catching up to him.

"Follow them," Berwyn answered. "We'll stay back out of the way and if they don't need us, fine, but if they need help, we'll be there to step in."

"Dad's going to kill us for this when he finds out," I remarked, knowing neither of us cared.

We raced behind the men, ensuring that we stayed far enough behind them that we could easily hide if we needed to. The leaves crunched beneath our feet, snapping like every last nerve in my body as my head pounded with worry.

Berwyn slowed me with a hand to my shoulder when we eventually near the town. The group ahead had stopped, still far enough away that the streets could not be seen.

We crept ahead, carefully gaining ground on the group as they hid in trees and bushes, watching something.

"Come out," a loud voice commanded. "We know you're there. We want Griz Baer."

The Society had found us.

"Your spies will be released if you turn yourself over," they tried to force my father into the clearing ahead.

"Don't do it," Berwyn whispered, begging our father not to give himself up.

"We've got your men here. Come out or they will suffer *for* you," the voice called again.

"I can't see," I whispered to my brother, trying to find a sightline around the trees.

"Come on," Berwyn motions me to move as we inch forward. When we could finally see the clearing, Berwyn stopped us, tucking us behind a grove of trees that had grown tightly together, nearly forming a wall of trunks.

"Fine, have it your way," the Society man yelled. He dropped his arm, signaling one of the others to act.

I blinked, coming out of the fog I was in after an eternity. A shudder ran through my back at the same time Berwyn snapped out of it.

A bloody ax rested on the ground, the red color so vibrant that I could see it dripping off the blade into the grass. Our spy's head had rolled a few feet away, sitting at an awkward angle.

"Enough," my father's voice rumbled so deeply that the birds flew out of the trees, terrified for their lives.

The remaining spies bit their lips, furious that my father had given himself up to save their lives. Their captors held them in place as they fought to free themselves and help my father.

Berwyn's hand scrapped along the bark of the wall of trees. Without thinking, I grabbed his shirt, holding him back.

"No," I hissed at him. "Let Gabriel rescue him. If he can't, Dad is going to need us to get our people together to rescue him. They won't kill him without a trial."

"But they'll kill everyone else," Berwyn seethed.

"If you run over there, Berwyn, that only leaves *me* to lead our people. Do you really think I'm ready to take that on?" I thought about slapping him to calm him down, but I decided against it—he'd probably punch me and run off.

A war erupted in the clearing. Several of our spies were slaughtered on the spot. Berwyn clung to the tree while he watched as if his life depended on it.

I looked away at one point, not wanting to see the carnage.

My father, Gabriel, Arin, and the others fought against the Society men, but were far outnumbered. They dragged my father away, leaving the rest of their men to fight against our people. An even mix of our people and theirs lay dead at the end of the battle.

When the fighting quieted, Berwyn and I slipped forward, rushing to our friends' aid. Gabriel forced us back. Silas' father had been like a second father to me and all I wanted was for him to put an arm around my shoulder and tell me what to do.

"Over there," he pointed before returning to check on our wounded. Berwyn and I followed where he motioned us.

After an intense search, we found where my father had thrown his medallion into the bushes—a signal to those of us who would find the scene that the Society had him. On it, the ring rested around the chain. His gifts to his sons were safe.

"It's time to go back, boys," Gabriel said quietly. "We need to tell the others."

"We have to go after him," Berwyn nearly choked on his words.

I slipped both the medallion and ring around my neck to keep them safe.

"We will, Berwyn. We need a plan first. If we go running into the Society blindly, we'll all die and no one will be able to rescue your father or the men that they took. I promise we aren't leaving him," Gabriel insisted. "We were prepared for something like this—your father knew it was coming. I just need you to trust us."

I nodded miserably. Berwyn looked ready to murder everyone, every muscle in his body tensing as it sparked with electric energy.

Gabriel guided us back to the storehouse, informing everyone of what had happened.

Two weeks passed without any word on the fate of Griz Baer. None of our spies could locate him. He hadn't been released, nor had he been publicly executed.

"Dov, you've got to eat," Silas finally said. "I know you're worried, but you have to stop moving long enough to eat something."

"Dov, you won't be any good to your father if you've wasted away to nothing," Reyla adds, joining us.

I sat down next to her, picking up the food she offered me.

"I don't understand why we can't find him," I mumbled between bites.

"Dad is working on it," Silas reminded me. "Arin's working on it too. They'll figure it out. As soon as we know, we can plan an attack."

"Berwyn isn't doing well," I replied, glancing up.

"Dad's watching him."

"And your job is to watch me?" I tried to joke.

"Did you expect anything less?" He offered me a sad smile.

"We'll find him, Dov," Reyla rested her hand on my shoulder. "Just stay focused on his rescue—the rest doesn't matter."

"Guys, Arin is back," Katarina rushed up to the group. We flew to our feet.

"We located him," Arin barked, searching for Berwyn.

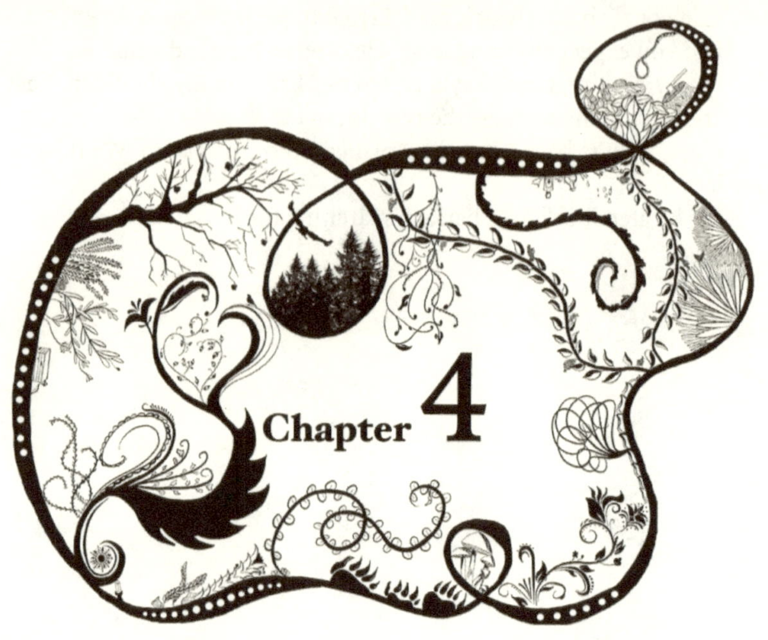

Chapter 4

WE STOOD IN THE MAGISTRATE'S COURTYARD, SURROUNDED BY OUR team. Berwyn tried to contain himself next to me as he bounced in his toes. Neither of us was handling watching our father's sentencing well.

Teams of our people were scattered throughout the courtyard. We were under strict orders not to get involved. Gabriel had posted enough men around us that if either of us tried to pull something, they could easily and instantly stop us.

We huddled toward the back of the masses, watching from a distance. If the rescue operation went sideways, we would be forced away as quickly as possible back to the storehouse.

I stood between Silas and Berwyn, waiting for them to bring my father out into the crisp afternoon air, convinced that waiting any longer might actually kill me.

Silas watched me from the corner of his eye. For as much devotion as he had toward my father, he had more toward me. He would be the first to force me to safety—something I would try not to hold against him if it happened.

The entire crowd stretched up when the Society men burst through the mansion doors, dragging my father behind them. His eyes rapidly searched the crowd, finding man after man from our group looking back at him, waiting to spring into action. He never hesitated when he saw Arin, Gabriel, and the others—he was too busy searching for his children.

My first instinct was to wave to him, letting him know where we were, but I held my arms still at my sides. The Society man yelled, listing charges against my father—none of which were true, most of which were *completely* made up.

His face was bruised, covered in cuts that had been scabbed over and broken open again. His temple was swollen, as was his lip. He held his arm gently against his side, cradling it to protect it from taking any more abuse.

My father's jaw tightened when he noticed us. Panic sparked in his expression. For a moment, it looked like he would strain against his captors, but he held back, biding his time.

Berwyn's arms shook as he fought against himself to stay in place. I ground my teeth together to stay focused—*follow the plan.*

My father only looked away when he realized he was being too obvious about watching us. To protect us, he forced himself to tear his gaze away—it hurt worse than anything else in my life, aside from losing my mother.

When they finished listing the charges, the Society men dragged the great Griz Baer back toward a small stand underneath a noose. He struggled against them, knowing what was coming. One of our men stood alongside him, being forced to his own death. The stage erupted with shouting as the two men tried to force themselves away from the ropes.

Our team launched into action, attacking the front of the stage. A hand grabbed at my arm, forcing me into place. The men rush the stage, but the Society was ready for them.

The fighting quickly swelled, sending the onlookers into a frenzy as they tried to escape the violence. People turned, pushing us back as they tried to run. I nearly stumbled over the person behind me as a hand slammed into my chest to move me out of the way.

"We have to go," Silas yelled, pulling on me.

More hands clamped down on my arms, dragging me away from the scene as I fought to reach my father. Berwyn struggled against our team members, clawing at their hands as they restrained him.

"You don't have a choice," one of our men shouted.

It took the entire group of people watching us to drag my brother and me away. Silas begged for me to cooperate as we left both of our fathers behind to the madness of the rescue mission.

"We can't leave them," Berwyn shouted once we're several streets away.

"They'll meet us," Gregory's father yells back. "You don't get to call the shots yet, Berwyn, now move!"

Once we reached the trees and made it far enough into the woods that we would not be seen, the men finally released us. My shoulders heaved up and down with the weight of every breath.

We watched for our people, hiding behind trees and bushes. They straggle back a few at a time, some injured. They took up vigil next to us, hiding in the protection of the forest.

"Are you okay?" Berwyn asked, finally acknowledging my presence.

"Yeah. Are you? You didn't get hurt, did you?" I glanced at him, checking for the injuries I hadn't thought to look for until that moment.

"If I *ever* see Lowell again, I will end him," Berwyn threatened.

I couldn't help but feel the same way.

Half an hour went by before my father arrived—the most agonizing thirty minutes of my life. He limped toward us, running as fast as he could.

Berwyn gasped beside me, overwhelmed that he had made it back alive. My smile only lasted for a moment, however.

My brother and I stayed in place—finally breathing—as a few of our people ran out to assist my father. Gabriel walked with my father —also nursing his injuries—as our people slipped under their arms to lend their support.

They froze as a knife sailed by them, landing on the ground ahead. It bounced, rolling in the dirt.

"Don't move," A society man demanded. A line of soldiers appeared from over the horizon, looking as though they had morphed out of the trees.

The second knife hit Gabriel in the back of the leg, pitching him forward. Silas gasped next to me. I dig my nails into his wrist, forcing him to hold still.

"Don't," I warned.

He looked at me, panic in his eyes. He fought against himself, deciding what to do. After a tense moment, he nodded and forced himself into place.

We watched as our fathers turned to face the Society men, a handful of our friends at their sides.

Blood dripped down the back of Gabriel's leg, but the injury was to the side, avoiding any serious damage.

"It will be okay," I whispered to my friend. "It's a flesh wound."

He nodded again, fingers tightening around the trunk of the tree we were hiding behind.

"We just need Baer," one of the Society men shouted. "We'll let the rest of you go."

"No, you won't," my father challenged him. "You're here for all of our blood. My death won't change that."

"You're right," the Society man sneered. "It won't."

The soldiers charged at the small group of men, easily overtaking them. The rest of our group poured out of the trees, save for a select group in the back tasked with protecting my brother and me—once again, we were forced to watch as people attempted to murder our father.

The woods filled with the noises of an intense battle, but it only lasted momentarily as the soldier in charge dragged Gabriel back from the crowd.

"You or your friend, Baer!" he shouted.

The group froze, watching and listening to the man making threats. He held a knife to Silas' father's throat.

"Don't, Griz," Gabriel warned.

The knife pressed into his throat, drawing blood.

Silas shook beside me, partially out of fear and partially out of anger. Berwyn raged on my other side, watching the scene unfold.

"Stop," my father yelled back, reaching out his hand. I had watched him many times before as he calmed a crowd. His practicality and rationality could bring even the most enraged souls to a quiet state, but the Society men wouldn't be swayed.

They pressed the blade against Gabriel again, making him blanch.

"I'm fine," he squeaked out.

"I'll trade," my father replied.

"What?" the soldier demanded.

"I'll trade. Me for him," my father motioned between them. "We'll meet half way. You send one of your men out with him and I'll come over alone. He will let my friend go and turn his blade on me. This is how we will make the trade."

"No," the Society man tried to negotiate.

"You aren't listening," my father replied. "This is the only way this will work. One man brings him out and takes me back. Otherwise, there's too many ways you can slaughter my people or my friend and I can escape. This is the only way it works for both of us. It's in your best interest to do as I say."

"You're the only thing holding your people back right now, Baer," the man sneers. "The second we trade, you'll have them attack."

"They won't, on my orders," my father responds, taking one terrifying step toward the men. "But even if they did, you outnumber us. It would only serve to have more people die from both sides.

"This gets you what you want and limits the death toll. Now, make your choice."

Our father stood defiantly, staring down the man in charge of the ambush.

The world around us was so tense that even the wind silenced itself in reverence. No one moved until the Society man made his decision.

"Fine," he said, pushing Gabriel forward.

"No," Silas, Berwyn, and I whispered harshly at the same time.

Gabriel stumbled forward, yelling for my father to stay put. He pleaded with him to let him take the fall, but my father would not have it—he always believed in putting his people before himself.

Nervous hands came down on our shoulders, forcing us into place once more. Someone kneed my back, pushing me against the tree. Pinned in place, I couldn't escape. Berwyn quickly hit the tree after I did, his movements restricted. Even Silas was held against his will.

We couldn't struggle—we couldn't do anything but watch.

The distance between the men closed as my father took Gabriel's place. The two men exchanged words quickly before the knife was transferred to my father's throat. The Society man kicked Gabriel's back, forcing him to the ground.

"Take care of each other," my father shouted loud enough for the entire group to hear.

The Society man pushed him, rushing him toward the line of Society men waiting to restrain him.

"We know your game," the soldier turns around, calling to us as soon as his men grabbed my father. "Griz Baer has worked against the Society for long enough! This is your only chance to change your ways—leave now and stop working against us, and you will be allowed to live. But if we *ever* catch you again, you will suffer the same fate."

He threw his arm backward, pointing to a nearby tree where

someone had managed to string up a noose. They shoved my father at it.

"No!" Berwyn shouted, no longer caring. We all struggled against our teammates.

"Test us again, and you'll die like your pathetic leader!"

The man drops his arm as his people threw themselves to the ground, snapping the neck of the great Griz Baer. I sagged against the tree, unable to move as my father dangled lifelessly from the branches of a tree in the middle of the woods, alone.

Our men attacked, but the Society held them off, rushing away before any real damage could be done.

Berwyn and I had to be forced back to the safe house.

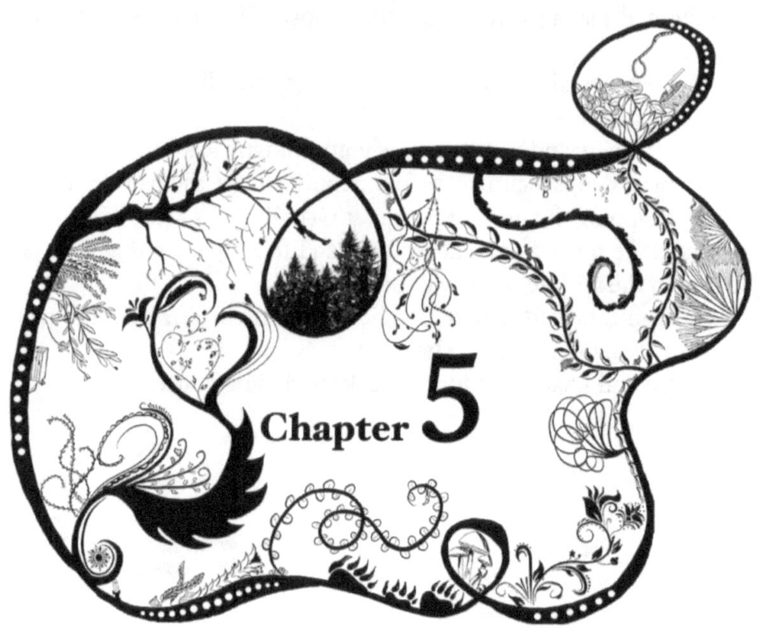

Chapter 5

GABRIEL SET HIS HAND ON MY SHOULDER. BERWYN AND I HAD LOCKED ourselves in one of the side rooms in the storehouse, mourning the loss of our father.

Berwyn had finally fallen asleep.

"Can I get you anything?" Gabriel asked. Silas hovered near the door.

"You should be resting, Gabriel," I commented. "Is your leg okay?"

"I'll be fine, Dov. Tell me what I can do for *you*?"

"There's nothing you can do, Gabriel," I replied sadly, hand still resting on my brother's shoulder as he slept beside me, the anger having drained him completely.

Gabriel looked around at the room, supplies thrown everywhere. Berwyn had been intentional about his rage, trying not to frighten the people outside the room, but he had managed to cause enough destruction to calm himself slightly.

"Can I help with that?" he asked, nodding to the mess.

"I think it needs to be us," I said quietly. "I think it just needs to be us for a while."

"I understand," Gabriel replied, moving back toward the door.

"When you boys are ready, your father said something before we were separated. I'll tell you both together."

I wanted to shake Berwyn awake, but he had only just settled. I knew he would need the rest now that he was in charge of so many people. My job wouldn't be nearly as hard, so I could wait and give my brother the rest he needed.

"You're good boys, Dov," he smiled sadly. "I know it doesn't seem like it now, but you're going to make it through this."

I swallowed as he shut the door, blinking back tears.

Gabriel nodded as Berwyn opened the meeting. Several weeks had gone by and Berwyn was stepping up to fill my father's position in the group.

Everyone had gone underground, heeding the Society's warning at Berwyn's insistence. Pointing out that we would be just like Lowell if we attacked the Society had certainly helped to make his decision.

I stood next to my brother, watching Gabriel as he oversaw the meeting. He kept the focus firmly on Berwyn, ensuring the group would look to him rather than some of the older, more experienced leaders.

Everyone helped to support the sons of Griz Baer. We initiated stronger training tactics, forcing everyone to participate so they could defend themselves should the need arise. While we didn't expect everyone on the battle lines when the time came, it would be far too easy for the fighting to come to our people, and we wanted everyone to have the training that would help them survive.

"We believe it is safe for us to leave the storehouses," Berwyn informed the people. "We've monitored the situation for months and it seems like the Society has finally moved on."

"You're sure?" Reyla's mother asked, holding her daughter around the waist.

"Yes," Arin added, confirming that he felt safe releasing our people.

"We're going to move deeper into the woods, and no one will be going back to the towns for the time being," Berwyn continued. "We're increasing our training time for everyone and we'll be having weekly meetings, daily for some people."

"Our goal now is to avoid the Society and help the people we can help," I added when Berwyn elbowed me. "The camps are still running, the underground markets are still happening—people are being taken every day for both."

"We want to stop as much of the Society's work as possible, but our priority right now is making sure our people are safe," Berwyn concluded.

"We'll be giving out assignments later today," Arin added. "We'll start the process of shifting people out of the storehouse tomorrow."

"It will take a few days, so please do not despair if you are not part of the first group to leave—your time is coming soon. We just want to be cautious about this." Gabriel dismissed the group with a final nod before turning back to us. "Well done."

"I'm worried about the move," Berwyn confided in him.

"You're wise to take it slow, Berwyn. It's what Griz would have done." Gabriel put his hand on my brother's shoulder, guiding him across the room

"I still can't believe we aren't going after them for this," Arin mumbled, following along next to Berwyn.

"We have to be strategic, Arin," Gabriel patiently instructed the younger man. "Our time will come, but we have priorities now. Besides, they're still watching over their shoulder for us—we need to give it time to lull them into a false sense of security."

"If we can't attack the Society directly, I want to disrupt as much of their work as possible," Berwyn grumbled. "We'll go after the camps and underground markets."

"Markets first, Berwyn. The camps are a lofty undertaking." Gabriel gave me a pointed look, reminding me to back him when it was just my brother and me later on.

"What do we know about the camps?" Berwyn asked, taking a seat at a table.

Gabriel and three of the other men spent the rest of the afternoon teaching us everything they knew about the underground markets before we split up to give out moving assignments to the people.

"It's entirely too quiet," Berwyn grumbled, crossing his arms as he sulked at the table.

"It was *always* quiet here after we lost Mom," I reminded him.

"It's worse now."

It *was*, but I wasn't about to encourage that line of thought.

"We're fine. Just bang around a little more," I retort.

"I don't like this," Berwyn protested.

"It's been two weeks, Berwyn, give it a chance," I tried to convince him to settle down.

"I need to do something. I'm going crazy in this house." He stood, pacing around the room.

"Like what?"

"I'm going to start going on missions again," Berwyn announced, turning to face me.

"What?" The shock in my voice surprised me. I set down the apple I was holding. "You can't get involved so soon. What if something happens?"

"It will be fine," Berwyn ignored my plea.

"Berwyn Baer, don't be ridiculous." My hand smacked against the table, startling my brother. "You're not going out into the field."

Testing my limits probably wasn't my best choice.

"I do not need *your* permission to do *anything*, Dov," he shouted at me.

"Someone has to tell you when you're making bad decisions, Berwyn," I yelled back, standing behind the table.

Silas barely waited for us to register his knock before walking into my family's house. He paused dramatically as he stepped inside, foot hanging in the air.

"I picked the wrong time, didn't I?" he asked, eyes wide.

"Yes—" I started to say.

"What is it, Silas," Berwyn demanded, cutting me off.

"We found one of the markets," Silas replied. "And by that, I mean that Arin and Dad found it."

"Good," Berwyn stormed toward the door. "You two are in charge. I'm going to talk to Arin and Gabriel."

He slammed the door behind him.

"What was that all about?" Silas asked, taking a seat at the table. He picked through our food.

"*That* was Berwyn going stir crazy," I replied, taking a seat again.

"Not a fan of being home, huh?" He bit into an apple.

"Not without Dad," I sighed.

"You know he's going to get involved in the underground market operations whether we like it or not," Silas gave me a look.

"I'm aware," I rolled my eyes, taking another bite of my apple. "And before you suggest it, Berwyn won't let us be involved. I already checked."

"Great," Silas grimaced.

"We don't look old enough to be there anyway," I mumbled, turning away.

"Also a valid point," Silas smirks. "That's fine. Let Berwyn run off and play the white knight. You and I will start our own venture here."

"I hate to ask." I pretended to shudder. We both grinned.

"Again," I instructed, holding my hands up to take the hit.

Katarina launched herself at me, trying to knock me off balance.

"Good, now go for the knees," I commanded.

She kicked out, trying to sweep my leg out from under me. I side-stepped, throwing her off balance.

"Dov," Gregory called, approaching from the trees. He dropped his voice when he saw that Katarina was standing next to me. "Hey, Kat."

He grinned wildly at her as she rolled her eyes.

"Arin sent me to find you," Gregory informed me. "He said Lionel needs to see you."

"Any idea why?" I blocked Katarina as she tried to take advantage of the situation. She huffed when she missed me.

"Nope. Arin said he's in town."

I perked up at his last words—freedom.

"Thanks," I replied, stepping back. "You can take over if you'd like."

I motion toward Katarina who still had her hands up in a defensive position."

"I'm good," she quickly replied, stepping back and dropping her arms. I smirked and Gregory feigned being hurt.

I took off quickly toward the town, making my way through the trees. Once I reached the road, I intentionally slowed down to keep from drawing attention.

An hour passed before I finally found Lionel milling about near the vendors. He purchased a loaf of bread, slipping it into his bag before casually walking to another booth.

When he spotted me, he gave me a signal to meet him on one of the side streets. After a few moments, I made a quick purchase to avoid suspicion and wandered over to the meeting place.

"Dov," he regarded me.

"What happened?" I asked, skipping the pleasantries.

"I heard we're taking on the underground markets now," he mused.

I blinked, waiting for him to continue.

Lionel glanced around, making sure no one was near us. He leaned in toward me.

"I heard there is a meeting tonight. They're selling brides. It's rumored that Magistrate Canton and his men will be there."

He ducked his head, waiting for me to respond, assuming I would know what to say.

"And you want us to stop it?"

"I want you to keep your brother away from it. I know he's been getting involved in the rescue missions. If Canton is there, he will recognize Berwyn. You and your brother look far too much like your father to put yourselves in situations where the Society might recognize you," he warned me. "Send the others, but keep Berwyn out of it."

"You know if he finds out Canton is there, he'll want to go."

"Which is why I asked for you and not your brother," he snapped. "Handle it, Dov."

Lionel quickly slipped a map into my hands detailing the location of the meeting.

"Be careful," he warned. "I have to go—my wife is waiting for me."

"Thanks," I called quietly after him.

Deterring Berwyn would not be an easy task.

I spend the walk back to our house coming up with ideas to persuade him to stay put. Before I could put any of them into action, I ran into Gabriel.

Volunteering to do the work for me, he gave Berwyn another mission to focus on while our people handled the underground market. Gabriel had to avoid them too since several Society men had learned his face the day my father was killed.

That evening, we crept down to the road just outside of the town. The air was cold as we waited in the tall grass. A shipment of supplies was supposed to be passing through and our goal was to relieve the Society men of the provisions they were moving.

The Society men paused at a building to unload the crates they had brought with them. We watched as the soldiers unloaded box after box into the temporary shelter.

"Now," Gabriel said once the men were gone.

We quietly slipped into the shadows of night and made our way to the building the soldiers had constructed specifically to house and temporarily store supplies. Breaking in was easier than we expected.

The moon offered us the only visibility we had both inside and outside of the building. The light bounced through the door, partially illuminating the boxes.

"Take that one," Berwyn instructed, moving toward a second box. Gabriel and Silas made their way to different crates, as did the other people in our small group.

"We're sure we aren't going to get caught?" I asked quietly, snapping the seal on the crate.

Inside, I discovered the box was filled with food.

"Food," I informed them.

"Same here," Silas replied, holding up something that I couldn't see in the dark.

"Put as much as you can in your bags," Berwyn announced. "Next time, we'll have to be better prepared."

"We're fine, Berwyn. This is just a test run. We'll be reallocating things for a long time to come now that we know how the Society moves their goods." I could hear the grin in Gabriel's voice as he spoke.

My fingers ran over loaves of bread—this would save us a lot of trouble later. I stuffed as many as I could into my pack.

"I have grain," Berwyn informed us. "When you're done, everyone come over and fill up the spaces between your supplies with the grain."

"Good idea," Gabriel affirmed. "No sense wasting space."

We work quickly in the dark, filling our bags. The grain added weight to the packs, but it was worth it to take the extra home with us.

"Remember, we don't want them getting suspicious," Berwyn reminded us. "Make it look like it wasn't broken open. Even out the layers of supplies in the crates, lock it back up, and make it look untouched.

"If they catch on to us, they'll start watching us."

I flattened the layer of bread in my crate before closing it up. We worked diligently to remove pieces from different boxes to avoid depleting any one container in a noticeable way.

When we finally left the building, the moon had shifted positions.

Our shadows were long and dangerous as we snuck back to the tall grass.

We reconvened at our house to count what supplies we had found on our first reallocation mission.

Chapter 6

WE TIMED OUR MISSIONS TO BE SEVERAL WEEKS APART TO AVOID THE Society taking notice. Other groups started to pop up, causing damage and frustrating the Society while we laid low—we used their appearances to our advantage.

Lowell stayed out of our way, never crossing our paths. We were grateful he had never been to our home in the woods—we had kept our people far from that area until after Lowell betrayed us. My father had moved our group further into the woods, taking us back to our childhood home. We watched for Lowell, but never saw him or his people.

My brother continued his missions into the towns to find and stop the underground markets. Every so often, he would bring new members back to the group. Having learned from the debacle with Lowell, we interrogated each new member first, making sure they weren't there to cause us harm.

Arin and a few of the men became quite good at extracting information from people. Berwyn allowed me to watch a few times, but I didn't have the stomach for enduring it on a regular basis. Still, I learned a few of their techniques to use should the need arise.

I spent most of my time teaching our people how to survive—

everything from finding food, to building shelters, to defending themselves, to spy work. I quickly rose in admiration as one of the most trusted spies in the group, alongside Silas.

"You're sure of the location?" I asked.

"Positive," Gloria responded. "I saw them move it there."

"Okay, lead the way," I replied, motioning for her to walk.

Silas gave me a look, questioning my decision to let Gloria participate in the raid. She had trained harder than any of the other girls had and I felt comfortable letting her go on her first mission into the Society that involved anything other than intelligent gathering.

She threw a sarcastic look at Silas as she guided us toward the streets of the town. We hid in the tall grass until dusk had fallen and the street cleared out.

I gave the signal, moving our team forward.

Inside the temporary building, we found crates—just like always.

These crates were different, however. They contained weapons.

"This is bad," Silas hissed. "What are we supposed to do?"

Until this point, we hadn't found weapons in any of the boxes—it had always been food and supplies.

"Should we take it all?" I asked him.

"I have no idea," Silas breathed. "If we do, they'll definitely notice. If we don't, we're letting the Society have weapons to use against us."

"We should take them," Gloria jumped in.

"We can't," I protested. "We can't let them know what we're doing, and we certainly can't move all of this without help. We need to go back and talk to Berwyn about this."

"We'll leave someone to watch it, but I doubt these boxes are going anywhere tonight. If the group decides to move them, we'll all come back before sunrise," Silas added.

Footsteps fell heavily outside, traipsing down the road—Society men on patrol.

We all froze. One of our men by the door leaped to shut it.

"No," I hissed, knowing that a moving door would cause more trouble than an open one. "Hide."

We dove behind crates as quietly as possible, waiting to be discovered. Each heartbeat hammered in my ears, pulsing just enough to let me know that everyone within a mile could likely hear my heart race.

The soldiers discovered the door ajar. They peered inside but saw nothing. After several tense moments, they finally locked us inside, backing away from the building. When we were positive they had continued on their route, we crept out of hiding.

"That was close," Silas remarked.

"From now on, we need to start leaving watchmen outside," Gloria huffed, annoyed that her mission had nearly been ruined.

"We need to get out of this building," I directed everyone. "More importantly, we need to get to Berwyn."

The door was impossible to open from the inside. Finally, we broke part of the wall, forcing Gloria to climb through and release us —thank goodness she was tiny.

Once we were sure it was clear, we darted into the night, leaving the weapons behind. We ran the entire way back to my house. I slammed the door open, shouting for my brother.

"What?" he demanded, nearly slipping on the floor as he rounded the corner at full speed.

"We found weapons," I explained.

"What?"

"Weapons," I repeated myself. Berwyn wasn't a good listener when he was tired. "Gloria found the location of a new delivery and we went to raid it. Instead of food and supplies, we found weapons, Berwyn."

"Did you take them?" he demanded, running his hands through his hair.

"No. The Society soldiers nearly found us," I said as my brother's face fell. "We hid and they inadvertently locked us inside, but we broke out and came straight here. We left Thaddeus to watch everything."

Berwyn's jaw ticked. Taking a deep breath, he confirmed that we needed to go back. Pulling his boots on, he sent the others to find Gabriel, Arin, and a few of our strongest men—if we were moving weapons, we'd need strength on our side.

Silas and I guided Berwyn back to the location of the building that housed the crates full of weapons. Instead of finding everything as we left it, we discovered Thaddeus was missing.

We spread out to look for him, searching the tall grass, the buildings, and even the surrounding streets.

"Here," Berwyn called. Silas and I quickly ran, knowing if Berwyn was being careless about his volume, there was a reason.

Berwyn faced off with two men holding Thaddeus captive. They each strung an arm through his, pinning them behind his back.

"I'm sorry," Thaddeus yelped as they lifted up on his arms, making his shoulders pop out at a painful angle. His eyes widened in fear.

"Let him go," Berwyn commanded, stepping toward the two men.

"No," they protested. "Whatever he is here for, we want to know about it."

"He was spying for us, that's all," Berwyn insisted, refusing to tell the people about the weapons stashed a street and a half away—it was a miracle they didn't find it in the first place.

"Who are you?" one of the men demanded.

"It doesn't matter," Berwyn answered, refusing to give up ground.

"It does to us," the man challenged him. He pulled a knife and walked toward Berwyn, giving control of Thaddeus up to his friend.

"You first," Berwyn snapped. "If we matter, then so do you."

"We work for Wallace," the second man replied. His friend turned to glare at him for his lack of awareness.

"Your turn," the first man sneered.

"Let my friend go and I'll tell you," Berwyn offered, sounding as diplomatic as our father had. "I sincerely doubt your boss is going to be happy if he finds out you didn't get my name. What was it...Wallace?"

The man paled slightly, his movements stiffening just enough to become awkward. He took a heavy step toward us, knife still pointed toward Berwyn. My hand migrated toward my own weapon slowly enough that he didn't notice it.

"Who are you?" he asked again.

"Let him go," Berwyn reminded him.

The man grimaced, finally relenting. He motioned to his partner to release Thaddeus. Our friend rushed toward us as Silas and I stepped forward to shield him from the men.

"Name," the first man demanded.

"Baer," Berwyn replied proudly. "Now, go home."

The two men took off, knowing they couldn't take on all four of us.

"We'll be watching for you, Baer."

Berwyn turned, his bravado fading into fury.

We left the weapons. Going back could have easily led Wallace's men to discover what we were doing. Thaddeus' capture had forced our hand—we gave the weapons up to be used by the Society.

"What happened?" Berwyn shouted, fists balled up at his sides.

"I'm sorry, sir," Thaddeus cowered. "They got the drop on me. I didn't see them coming."

He looked ready to vomit.

Berwyn glared at me.

"How did this happen?"

"I don't know," I replied, shocked that he would yell at me so viciously. "I was with you."

"You trained him—wasn't he prepared for this?" Berwyn turned to Thaddeus, dismissing him. "Get out."

Thaddeus scampered out of the house, running through the dark woods.

"So you thought scaring him would be wise?" I questioned my brother's choices.

"We lost all of those weapons to the Society tonight, Dov. All of those things can now be used to hurt our people. You think I'm just supposed to let that go?" Berwyn roared.

"They'll understand," I assured him.

"You remember that when one of our spies comes back in pieces, Dov." His eyes snap fiercely.

"What do you expect us to do?" I fired back.

"We have to take responsibility for this, Dov. Someone has to pay for letting this happen."

"You're going to blame this on Thaddeus? He was in the wrong place at the wrong time—you can't blame him for this."

"If he had been better trained, he wouldn't have been caught off guard like that," Berwyn charged.

"Blame me if you like, but it wasn't his fault," I shouted back. Every muscle in my body was tense as we fought.

"You can't take the fall for this—they'll never trust you again," Berwyn protested.

"Fine, then they don't trust me," I countered. "But it's not his fault. If this really happened because he wasn't trained properly, then it's my fault, Berwyn. Let them take it out on me. I'll state my case and try to change their minds, but I'd rather take the blame for this than to let you throw Thaddeus to the wolves for something that wasn't his fault."

"We need to find out who this Wallace guy is," Berwyn changed the subject.

"So that's it? We're done with this conversation?" I stomped my foot, making a point.

"You wanted to take the blame—take the blame. I don't care. We'll inform the group tomorrow at the meeting," Berwyn waved his hand around dramatically. "More importantly, we need to know who we're dealing with now. If these people are going to be harassing us, we need to know what we're up against."

"Maybe it was just those two that stepped out of line," I offered, not even believing my own suggestion.

"That's like assuming Lowell is going to see the light," Berwyn scowled. "Tomorrow, we'll tell the group what happened, and then I'll send Gabriel out to get more information on these people. We need to know who they are and where they are."

I quietly accepted my fate—to be the scapegoat for the group—and sat down to help my brother plan the mission to find Wallace's men as the darkness gently slipped into daylight.

The punishment was more severe than I had realized it would be. For a month, I wasn't allowed to go on any missions. I had to do all of the grunt work for the group, taking on the hardest labor jobs meant for men much stronger than I was. I didn't get to speak at any of the meetings, though Berwyn did allow me to help plan them when we weren't in front of the group.

My isolation afforded me extra time near our people, which I used to my advantage...*as did they*.

"Hi, Dov," Sharone smiled as she approached me. "Do you think you could show me that defensive move you taught us last week one more time?"

"You mean the one I wasn't supposed to teach you last week?" I teased back.

"Yes, that one," her eyes sparkled as she tried to get my attention.

"I think it went something like this," Katarina stepped in front of me, wrapping my arms around her. She paused for a moment before slowly pretending to break free from me.

"Yes, something like that," I joked back. "It seems you ladies already have that one figured out though."

"You really have to stop demanding the attention of every girl in this group, Baer," Peter taunted as soon as Sharone and Katarina had gone back to work. "It's not fair."

"I'm pretty sure you already worked your magic, Peter," I grinned. "You don't need any of the other girls."

"Yeah, well, she's not mine yet," he mumbled.

"Peter aside," Ben remarked, joining us, "It would be nice if the rest of us had a chance without you and your perfect hair swooping in every single time you're near the girls."

"I'm not doing it intentionally," I promised, picking up the tree branches I had split before I was interrupted.

"Your flirting isn't intentional?" Peter looked at me skeptically, helping to pick up the pieces of firewood.

"He does it to everyone," Gloria interrupted, sneaking up on us. "It's just how he speaks now. Don't get so uppity about it—at least *one of* the guys talks to us without acting like a moron."

She waltzed away, carrying a basket of apples so heavy it looked like her arms might break.

"I don't think there's another girl like her in existence," Peter mumbled.

"She's unique," I responded, watching her go.

"You should keep her in mind, Dov—she'd be perfect for you. Not one of those soft, flowery girls, but a leader for a leader," Ben muttered. "And she clearly has a thing for you."

"She's tiny, but she packs a punch," Peter smirked. "She might be a better leader than you *or* your brother. I think we've found your new wife, buddy."

"Helpful," I rolled my eyes, stooping to pick up more split tree branches to add to the pile in my arms.

"Yeah, keep taunting him, Peter—he's going to swoop in and steal all the girls' attention just to make a point now," Ben complained jokingly.

It wasn't a bad idea.

"I think you're right though—Gloria is good at this. Maybe we should give her a little more room to take on some leadership roles," I mused.

"Replacing me already?" Silas commented, dropping his ax on the ground as he joined us. "What are you just standing around for, gentlmen? I'm ready to go."

He nodded to the pile of logs in his arm.

"All right, all right," we laughed. "Let's go."

"I know you're on probation right now—"

"Which is ridiculous," Ben cut Silas off.

"It is," Peter added.

"I know you're on probation right now," Silas tried again, "but I can't say this is the worst work in the world. At least we're not being chased down by the Society."

"You're only saying that because they nearly spotted you yesterday," I chastised him. "And let's just remember, *I'm* the only one on restriction here. *You* are still out there running missions."

"When does your brother intend on ending this punishment?" Ben asked.

"I don't know—probably when we find out where Wallace's camp is," I ventured a guess.

"He does realize that we'd find that a lot faster if he just let you do your job, right? You're better at locating people than any of us are," Peter proclaimed, ducking under a tree branch. "Careful."

The branch snapped back, nearly colliding with Ben's face.

"A little more warning next time," he shouted, recovering from the near miss.

"I've had enough of this. I think we need to talk to Berwyn," Silas announced.

"I think your father would have better luck," I replied, leaning forward to balance myself as I walked up an incline.

"I already asked. He said we have to handle this one," Silas frowned. "Between the two of us, I'm sure we can convince him."

"If you say so," I mumbled.

Miraculously, once we arrived back at the house, Berwyn agreed with our request, lifting the ban.

"I need you to handle something anyway," Berwyn turned to face me. "You too, Silas."

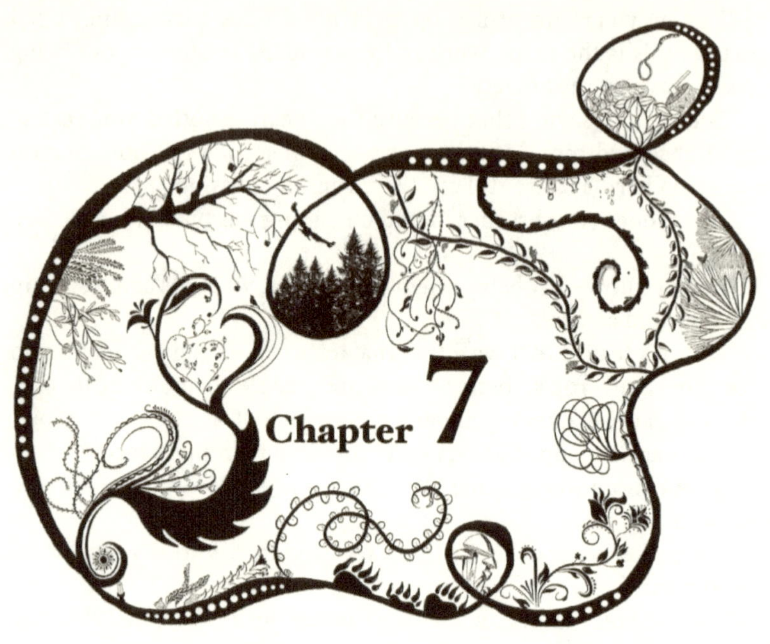

Chapter 7

Over the next year, we ran several big missions to gather intelligence and hinder the Society's plans without the blame falling on our group. Silas and I continued training our people, all while spying on the Society.

Berwyn focused his efforts on the underground markets, eventually planning to make our way to the camps. Slowly, our people started moving back toward the towns, placing our people in strategic locations.

We survived the year without having to go back into hiding at the storehouses, though we lost a few of our spies along the way. In the midst of our work, we found new members, rescued from the towns, taken from the soldiers, and saved from the underground markets. We took turns housing new members until we could find them a permanent place to live.

"He's catching on quickly," I remarked.

"He's learned really fast. I'm impressed," Silas replied, crossing his arms as we watched Carter run drills with Gregory, Peter, and Ben. "He did well with the reallocation mission last week too."

"Is it quiet now that he and his family are out of your house?"

"I'm not going to deny it, I'm glad to have the space again. I was starting to feel like we were back in the storehouse."

I laughed—I couldn't blame him there. Having extra people in your space was never something anyone wanted to do for very long.

"I think we'll bring him along this afternoon," I added.

"Berwyn isn't coming with us, right?" Silas confirmed.

"No, he and your father are handling the market today. Lionel said this one is supposed to be pretty big."

"One more time," Silas shouted to the guys, making me flinch. The boys ran the drill again. "Hopefully they can stop as much if it as possible."

"It's getting harder and harder to rescue people from those things —the price is going up so high."

"We're just going to have to work harder and bring in extra money," Silas sighed. "Maybe we could do a little of that this afternoon while we're acting as distractions."

"Leave that to me—you handle running the mission and I'll do the side work."

"Should I ask what that means?" he teased, trying to hold off a grin.

"Probably not," I bit back my own smile.

When they finished running the drill, we called them over, explaining what we would be doing in town to keep the focus off of Berwyn's trip to the underground market. We gave them assignments and I left Silas in charge.

Once we reached the town, I slipped away, looking for a little easy work. Berwyn didn't like when I took extra jobs, but if we were going to continue to rescue woman from the underground markets, we needed extra income.

I spent two hours running trades, delivering goods, trading information, and monitoring the crowded marketplace. Vendors shouted to people walking by, trying to force their goods on them.

I heard the shouting before I saw it. A crowd of men gathered around a booth, the vendor shouting wildly. The scene began to get out of hand.

A knife glistened in the sunlight as it peeked between the clouds. A guy I did not recognize stepped toward a blond man, knife ready to strike as he took advantage of the chaos the fight had created. Without thinking, I stepped up to him, trying to protect the blond man.

I carefully tipped my leg into his way at the last moment, causing him to tumble forward. It was only after he started pitching forward that I realized he could have fallen on his knife. For a moment, terror washed over me, but I quickly reached out, catching his arm in my hand.

"I'm so sorry," I apologized as if it had been an accident as his knife bounced toward me on the ground.

I made a show of helping to dust him off, batting at his clothing to distract him while I pocketed his knife. The man lashed out at me, smacking my hands away, cursing loudly.

Darting into the crowd, I tried to blend in with the people in case the man took my actions too personally. I looked around, checking to make sure he didn't follow me.

Instead, I was confronted with a softer face. She watched me from a distance, shock creasing her features. I grinned at her flirtatiously—it wouldn't hurt since I'd never see her again. It wasn't like I was flirting with Maylin—something that would result in many unwanted conversations.

She sucked in a breath as I quirked my eyebrows up at her, letting her know that I saw her watching me. Before she could react, I turned and slipped back into the crowd, keeping my head down.

I kept a watchful eye out for her the rest of the time I was working to earn more money for my brother's plan to save the world, but I never saw her again. My day was far less exciting after that.

"Where did you get this?" Berwyn asked when I set the money on the table, arriving home much later than he did.

"Don't worry about it," I smiled, walking toward the kitchen to make us something to eat. "I know we need to start building up our available money if we're going to continue helping at the under-ground markets, so I took a few extra jobs today."

"When you were supposed to running a mission?" Berwyn looked at me skeptically. I could tell he wanted to count the coins, but he held his fingers in place as they drummed on the table.

"Silas had that mission covered and you know it. I just made a side trip, that's all," I argued. "Now you can go to the next sale and save someone. Just say thank you, big brother."

He grumbled under his breath.

"When is the next one, anyway?" I asked, warming the food.

"Next month," Berwyn replied, annoyance clearly overriding his ability to speak softly.

"Great, go buy yourself a wife."

When he turned around to face me, I offered him my biggest smile to let him know I was joking—he was not amused.

Gloria gasped beside me as we watched the Society men close in on the young boy. On the outskirts of town, the streets were quiet. We lurked in the shadows of a building, watching the scene unfold.

The boy turned, noticing he was being followed. Instead of running, he froze.

"No," Gloria whispered.

"Come on, kid," I mumbled. *"Make an effort.* Help us to help you."

The boy dropped his bag off his shoulder. It rested on the ground at his feet, the strap still dangling from his fingers.

"What's the plan?" Gloria turned to me, determined to save the child. "I can distract them, maybe get them to chase me, and you can get the kid."

"What happens if you can't outrun them?" I questioned sarcastically.

"I'll outrun them," she replied, looking like she wanted to hit me. The sharp pain in my shoulder begs for me to avoid being hit again.

"You're injured, Dov. Let me handle this one," she insisted.

"Okay," I gave in, having no other choice—we were out of time.

"Ready?" Gloria asked, waiting for my signal. I nodded, releasing her to run into the open.

She jogged into the street, making it look like she was distracted and in a rush. Turning just enough to make it believable that she hadn't noticed the men right away, she rummaged through her bag.

Looking up, she pretended to notice them, feigned panic washing over her face. The men looked to each other, deciding what to do— keep the child who wouldn't be of any service to the Society for a number of years, or go after the girl they could sell in the underground markets.

The choice was easy for them.

They released the boy, kicking him hard enough to send him to the ground wailing, just in case they could come back and retrieve him as well. Gloria took off, running in the opposite direction to lure the soldiers away from the child.

The moment they were beyond me, I slipped out of the shadows and raced to the child. He looked up at me, frightened.

"It's okay," I said quietly, trying to calm him. "I'm here to help.

I scooped him up in my arms, moving his bag to my shoulder. He sobbed against me.

"Where are your parents?"

The boy was heavier than he looked—I might have misjudged his age. His light brown hair tumbled into his eyes as he tried to rub the tears away.

"I need to take you home," I tried to gently convince him to guide me back to his family. "Tell me where to go."

He quieted, staring at me with tear-filled eyes.

"Do you have a family?" I asked.

He shook his head.

"What happened to them?" I questioned, moving toward the cover of the building.

"The soldiers killed my father and took my mother."

I nodded—it was a familiar story.

"I have a big family. Would you like to come stay with us? There are people that will protect you," I offered.

He studied me carefully before nodding.

I considered setting him down, but that might have slowed us down. Instead, I shifted him around to my back, letting him cling to my neck and waist.

"Hold tight," I instructed him, pain coursing through my injured shoulder.

I navigated through the town, avoiding the streets with large numbers of people. The boy clung tighter with every street, nearly cutting off my ability to breathe.

Eventually, Gloria joined me.

"He's coming with us," I informed her. "Did you have any trouble?"

"Nothing I couldn't handle," she replied smugly. "We should get back."

Behind us, a voice boomed.

"I know you."

Gloria turned first, hand on my elbow in case I needed to run with the child.

"Who are you?" she demanded.

"Your boyfriend knows," the man retorted.

Gloria prepared herself in case she needed to catch the child if I needed to defend us against the man and had to drop him quickly.

When I faced the man, some semblance of recognition sparks in my mind, but placing him is difficult.

"We met last year. You're a Baer," he remarked, tipping his head with a nasty sneer.

"You work for Wallace," I said specifically so that Gloria would know whom we were dealing with at the moment. Her lip curled. "You've been causing all sorts of chaos lately, haven't you?"

"At least one of us is doing something about the Society, Baer," he spits back.

"I'd say it's less about the Society for you and more about causing destruction and having fun." The child's wrists bit into my throat as his nervousness came flooding back.

"Fine, you caught us. We don't care about the Society—we just want to live our lives. What's the harm in that?" He took a dangerous step toward us.

"You get more people killed with your antics than actually make it out, so I hear," I confronted him.

"Our numbers are none of your business, Baer," he sneered.

Sensing the impending fight, Gloria reached up and took the boy from me. Despite my shoulder injury, I prepared myself to engage in a fistfight.

"Go," I instructed my partner. Gloria hurried the boy away from the scene, taking him back to the safety of the woods.

The man circled around me, assessing my skills. I gave him no hint of my talent, holding my hands at my side. I spun as he walked around me.

The fight was brutal—my shoulder screamed in pain by the time I slammed him to the ground, threatening him to stay down. He listened but not before leaving me with a final threat—apparently, Wallace's men would not make it easy on me from this point forward.

I doubted they cared enough to go after me over the bruised ego of one of their men—they barely saw past the evening, much less started war for a long-term grudge.

I wandered through the town, ensuring the man couldn't follow me. When I was positive that it was clear, I left the safety of the bustling people and made my way to the woods.

Gloria hovered in the dense trees halfway back, the child pushed down into a bush. When she confirmed I was alone, she allowed him to stand.

"You know the girls are going to adore him," I quipped, knowing Gloria wasn't a fan of working with children.

"I'm aware," Gloria grumbled back.

"Hi," I got down on my knees to talk to the boy. "I'm Dov. What's your name?"

"Reuben," he murmured, looking at the ground.

"Well, Reuben, there are some people who are going to be very excited to meet you. Are you ready to go?"

Gloria sidled up next to me as we walked back.

"You know, I think Wallace's people are going to be a bigger problem than we think."

"They're more of a nuisance than anything else at this point."

"Well, this is interesting," Silas interrupted, walking toward us.

"This is Reuben, actually," I swung my head forward to face him. "He's coming to stay with us."

"Great, have Gloria take him back—you and I have somewhere to be."

I passed Rueben's hand off to Gloria, giving her a look meant to instruct her to be nice to the kid. She rolled her eyes and guided him away.

"Where are we going?"

"Berwyn and Dad are back and apparently it's not going so well. Gregory saw them walking in and came to find us."

"What's happening?" I picked up the pace, following behind my friend.

"Apparently one of the girls is on the angry side."

"Angry?"

We break into a run toward the house where the new girls will be staying until we can interrogate them and decide if we're going to allow them to join the group.

"She's not happy to have been rescued I guess," he shrugged.

"That's a first." I blinked back my surprise.

When we arrived, Gabriel was standing far enough away from the scene that we couldn't really hear what was happening.

"Gabriel?"

"Don't ask me, I have no idea what's going on," he motioned toward the scene. "I found them like this."

"Dov rescued a kid," Silas informed his father as we watched the scene unfold. For a moment, I was worried the woman was going to attack my brother.

"Did he now?" Gabriel replied, absentmindedly.

Berwyn took a step back as a woman slapped his arm away. Her face sparked with rage as she glared at him. Even from so far away, I could see that she wanted to say something, but she held back.

The woman stomped her foot, forcing herself not to yell at my brother. Berwyn looked overwhelmed with her reaction—few people took him on and even less matched his angry emotions.

This woman wasn't hiding anything.

I watched as the blonde marched across the field, storming off toward the cabin.

"Who is *that?*" I asked with a laugh as Berwyn joined us.

"I don't know yet—she won't tell us her name," Berwyn grimaced.

"Looks like she's going to be a lot of fun," Silas added, matching my crossed arms as he leaned back against a tree trunk.

"That one's got a chip on her shoulder." Gabriel blinked, watching the girl walk away.

"I see the rescue operation went well," I smirked.

Berwyn watched her walk away in silence.

"I think *this one* is a game-changer, gentlemen," I added.

"I have a feeling she's going to take down the Society single-handedly," Berwyn murmured, rubbing his chin with his hand. "Speaking of which, we found new intelligence on Wallace's men."

"Actually, so did I."

Silas raised an eyebrow at me, silently asking why I hadn't informed him on the run over.

The girl screamed inside the house, throwing something against the wall as we started to walk away.

"Yeah, she's a great addition to the group," I quipped.

"Maybe she's exactly what we need," Berwyn said under his breath.

"On the topic of things we need, any word on Lowell?" Gabriel asked.

"Not yet, but I'm positive we haven't seen the last of him," Berwyn said louder. "Come on, we have to do some scouting tonight to see if any of this information pans out. We have a meeting in an hour to make a plan."

We picked up the pace, eventually jogging toward the storehouse to figure out our next move.

ACKNOWLEDGMENTS

I feel like I've learned a few things about the Baer family through this novella, don't you? In fact, I feel like I've learned *a lot* that I didn't know before…and I love it!

Dov has always been a favorite of mine, as have Eden and Berwyn (and Silas, Reyla, and the crew!) so to be able to explore their story before Auluria…well, that's just really cool for me!

I hope you enjoyed this look at the circumstances that turned Dov into…well, the swoony guy we've all fallen for.

Special thanks to Elissa and Jess for all of your help with this—you ladies continue to astound me!

Thanks to Yentl for all of the encouragement and for listening to me talk about Dov's story while writing without actually telling you anything about it. You're a rockstar, girl!

Huge shout out to Alexis for another stunning Golden header! I appreciate all your hard work!

To my fabulous fans and readers, thank you for sticking with me through this entire series—you have turned Golden into what it is today and I couldn't be more thrilled! You're the absolute best!

As always, to those of you out there changing the world and making a difference even when it's hard, thank you for who you are!

Stay inspired!

BONUS SCENES

Want to read bonus scenes from Golden? We're giving out exclusive bonus scenes over on the K.M. Robinson Facebook page where you can read scenes from Dov and Reyla's perspectives.

Get them by sending the page a direct message
facebook.com/kmrobinsonbooks

We're constantly giving out additional bonus scenes for preorder swag, giveaways, and more, so watch the social media pages carefully for the next scene giveaway.

You can also get bonus scenes through my newsletter!

Join newsletter.kmrobinsonbooks.com for behind the scenes,
bonuses, games, and more!

WORLD PORTALS

Ready to learn exclusive facts about The Golden Trilogy and other K.M. Robinson Series?

World Portals are now available on www.kmrobinsonbooks.com

Learn behind the scenes facts, watch videos, play games, check out our book filters, find out where to get bonus scenes, view fan art, and get access to other secrets we've hidden away inside the World Portals on the website.

The World Portals are constantly changing and information is being taken away and added all the time, so check back frequently for new content!

GOLDEN MISSION GAME

AULURIA IS BEING SENT ON ONE LAST MISSION BEFORE LOWELL AND Shadoe send her to destroy Dov and Berwyn Baer and she needs your help.

Are you ready to assist Goldilocks and locate the Baers?

This interactive, choose-your-own-adventure game is played

through Facebook messenger so you never miss a mission. Played over the course of one-two days, Auluria will send several missions which you can then go back into the story to see how your choices affected Auluria and Dov's journey.

goldenmission.kmrobinsonbooks.com

BONUS FACEBOOK FILTERS

WANT TO GET YOUR HANDS ON SOME INCREDIBLE FACEBOOK FILTERS for Golden? Now you have the ability to get filters for the story, characters, etc right inside your phone.

You can use these on your photos, profile pictures, videos, and live broadcasts. All you have to do is like my author page and they will automatically show up in your filters!

I've even taken these clips and put them on Instagram Stories by saving them to my phone and uploading them to Instagram.

Visit www.facebook.com/kmrobinsonbooks to grab these filters for your photos, videos, and broadcasts! Bonus points for tagging me

@kmrobinsonbooks so I can see how you're supporting The Golden Trilogy.

ABOUT THE AUTHOR

K.M. Robinson is a storyteller who creates new worlds both in her writing and in her fine arts conceptual photography. She is a marketing, branding and social media strategy educator who is recognized at first sight by her very long hair. She is a creative who focuses on photography, videography, couture dress making, and writing to express the stories she needs to tell. She almost always has a camera within reach. Visit her at her website: www.kmrobinsonbooks.com

CONNECT ON SOCIAL MEDIA

facebook.com/kmrobinsonbooks

instagram.com/kmrobinsonbooks

twitter.com/kmrobinsonbooks

Get free excerpts of other K.M. Robinson books at excerpt.
kmrobinsonbooks.com

ALSO BY K.M. ROBINSON

The Golden Trilogy
Golden
Forged: A Golden Novella
Locked
Edge
Tempered: A Golden Novella

The Jaded Duology
Jaded
Risen

The Legends Chronicles
Along Came A Spider: A Prequel Novelette
And They'll Come Home: A Prequel Novelette

Virtually Sleeping Beauty: A Novella Retelling

The Siren Wars Saga

The Siren Wars (Coming May 2018)
Darker Depths (Coming June 2018)
Beyond The Shores (Coming July 2018)

JADED: BOOK ONE OF THE JADED DUOLOGY

Her father failed in his mission to take control from the Commander, a defeat that has cost Jade her life. She will die as punishment. Now she belongs to the Commander's son—as his wife. Knowing his intent is to quietly kill her in revenge, Jade's every move is calculated to survive—until she learns her death ensures the safety of her father and her entire town.

Roan doesn't want to kill Jade, but once his family isolates her from her father and community, his only choice is to go through with the plan. Jade doesn't make it easy as she tries to sway him into falling for her. Each misstep makes him question his cause. Each moment makes every decision harder, but the Commander won't allow him to fail.

One chooses life. One chooses death. In the midst of the chaos, only one will succeed.

Now available at jadedinfo.kmrobinsonbooks.com

ALONG CAME A SPIDER: THE FIRST PREQUEL NOVELETTE TO THE LEGENDS CHRONICLES

Little Hacker Muffet
sat on her tuffet
destroying her cords and Way.
Along came a hacker named Spider,
who sat down beside her
and frightened his opponent away.

WHEN FET, ONE OF THE MOST SKILLED HACKERS IN THE LEGENDS, discovers her best friend and leader of her group has been abducted and held for ransom, she must escape unnoticed and find Peep before it's too late.

When Spider, a new recruit training to join her hacker ring, slips out with her and claims to have a plan to save her friend, Fet is forced to bring him along. As she discovers he's not who he claims to be, she faces grave danger and learns just how deadly a spider bite can be.

Now available at acasinfo.kmrobinsonbooks.com

VIRTUALLY SLEEPING BEAUTY

She may be doing battle in the virtual world, but in the real world, they can't wake her up...

All Rora wants is to help people as class president, give her time to local charities, and quietly earn her way to the top level of the virtual reality system that the entire country uses without anyone noticing she's the second best player in the game.

All Royce wants to do is level up as a knight inside the gaming system, slay dragons, and eventually play his way to controlling the palace as he takes the crown away from the reigning queen.

When his Aunt Perry calls him, hysterically screaming that her goddaughter, Rora, has been inside for more than the four hours the game allows, Royce rushes over to help.

Entering the game, Royce soon discovers that Rora is trapped inside the system after an encounter with an evil magician who can change forms inside the game and control the virtual world. If he and his friend can't help her beat the game, she might not be able to wake up in the real world at all.

. . .

When virtual knights and princesses meet to slay dragons and defeat evil rulers, there's nothing stopping them from suffering real-world consequences too.

To wake her up, he must enter the game and help her beat it.

Now available at vsbinfo.kmrobinsonbooks.com

THE SIREN WARS: BOOK ONE OF THE SIREN WARS SAGA

War has hovered around the kingdom of Scylla for generations ever since the original sirens left the mer collection generations ago after nearly drowning the human prince. Over the years, select mermaids from the royal bloodline have been trained as spies to work for the reigning kings and queens, keeping the collection safe from sirens and humans.

Celena and her partner, Merrick, work covertly for the royals—not even her twin brother knows. When they discover the sirens have broken through the barriers the mer set up to keep the sirens out, Celena and her friends must race to the old kingdom of Metten to stop them from starting a war within their borders.

When she's dragged to the surface, Celena realizes that the war above the waters is as deadly as the one below the waves—and sacrificing herself may be the only way to protect her family.

The Siren Wars have only just begun.

Now available at sirenwarsinfo.kmrobinsonbooks.com